THREE
ADVENTURE NOVELS

of

H. RIDER HAGGARD

SHE
KING SOLOMON'S MINES
ALLAN QUATERMAIN

Each Complete and Unabridged

DOVER PUBLICATIONS, INC.
NEW YORK

This Dover edition contains the complete unabridged texts of *She, King Solomon's Mines* and *Allan Quatermain.*

International Standard Book Number: 0-486-20643-2
Library of Congress Catalog Card Number: 60-20211

Manufactured in the United States of America
Dover Publications, Inc.
180 Varick Street
New York, N.Y. 10014

CONTENTS

SHE

INTRODUCTION

In giving to the world the record of what, considered as an adventure only, is, I suppose one of the most wonderful and mysterious experiences ever undergone by mortal men, I feel it incumbent on me to explain my exact connection with it So I will say at once that I am not the narrator but only the editor of this extraordinary history, and then go on to tell how it found its way into my hands.

Some years ago I, the editor, was stopping with a friend, *'vir doctissimus et amicus meus,'* at a certain University, which for the purposes of this history we will call Cambridge, and one day was impressed with the appearance of two persons whom I saw walking arm-in-arm down the street. One of these gentlemen was, I think without exception, the handsomest young fellow I have ever seen. He was very tall, very broad, and had a look of power and a grace of bearing that seemed as native to him as to a wild stag. In addition his face was almost without flaw—a good face as well as a beautiful one, and when he lifted his hat, which he did just then to a passing lady, I saw that his head was covered with little golden curls growing close to the scalp.

"Do you see that man?" I said to my friend, with whom I was walking; "why, he looks like a statue of Apollo come to life. What a splendid fellow he is!"

"Yes," he answered, "he is the handsomest man in the University, and one of the nicest too. They call him 'the Greek god.' But look at the other one; he is Vincey's (that's the god's name) guardian, and supposed to be full of every kind of information. They call him 'Charon,' either because of his forbidding appearance or because he has ferried his ward across the deep waters of examination—I don't know which."

I looked, and found the older man quite as interesting in his way as the glorified specimen of humanity at his side. He appeared to be about forty years of age, and I think was as ugly as his companion was handsome. To begin with, he was short, rather bow-legged, very deep chested, and with unusually long arms. He had dark hair and small eyes, and the hair grew down on his forehead, and his whiskers grew quite up to his hair, so that there was uncommonly little of his countenance to be seen. Altogether he reminded me forcibly of a gorilla, and yet there was something very pleasing and genial about the man's eye. I remember saying that I should like to know him.

"All right," answered my friend, "nothing easier. I know Vincey; I'll introduce you," and he did, and for some minutes we stood chatting—about the Zulu people, I think, for I had just returned from the Cape at the time. Presently, however, a stout lady, whose name I do not remember, came along the pavement, accompanied by a pretty fair-haired girl, and Mr. Vincey, who clearly knew them well, at once joined these two, walking off in their company. I remember being rather amused by the change in the expression of the elder man, whose name I discovered was Holly, when he saw the ladies advancing. Suddenly he stopped short in his talk, cast a reproachful look at his companion, and, with an abrupt nod to myself, turned and marched off alone across the street. I heard afterwards that he was popularly supposed to be as much afraid of a woman as most people are of a mad dog, which accounted for his precipitate retreat. I cannot say, however, that young Vincey showed much aversion to feminine society on this occasion. Indeed I remember laughing, and remarking to my friend at the time that he was not the sort of man whom it would be desirable to introduce to the lady one was going to marry, since it was exceedingly probable that the acquaintance would end in a transfer of her affections. He was altogether too good-looking, and, what is more, he had none of that self-consciousness and conceit about him which usually afflicts handsome men, and makes them deservedly disliked by their fellows.

That same evening my visit came to an end, and this was the last I saw or heard of 'Charon' and 'the Greek god' for many a long day. Indeed, I have never seen either of them from that hour to this, and do not think it probable that I shall. But a month ago I received a letter and two packets, one of manuscript, and on opening the former found that it was signed by 'Horace Holly,' a name which at the moment was not familiar to me. It ran as follows:—

"—College, Cambridge, May 1, 18—

"My Dear Sir,—You will be surprised, considering the very slight nature of our acquaintance, to get a letter from me. Indeed, I think I had better begin by reminding you that we once met, now several years ago, when I and my ward Leo Vincey were introduced to you in the street at Cambridge. To be brief and come to my business. I have recently read with much interest a book of yours describing a Central African adventure. I take it that this book is partly true, and partly an effort of the imagination. However this may be, it has given me an idea. It happens, how you will see in the accompanying manuscript (which together with the Scarab, the 'Royal Son of the Sun,' and the original sherd, I am sending to you by hand), that my ward, or rather my adopted son Leo Vincey, and myself have recently passed through a real African adventure, of a nature so much more mavellous than the one which you describe, that to tell the truth I am almost ashamed to submit it to you lest you should disbelieve my tale. You will see it stated in this manuscript that I, or rather we, had made up our minds not to make this history public during our joint lives. Nor should we alter our determination were it not for a circumstance which has recently arisen. For reasons that, after perusing this manuscript, you may be able to guess, we are going away again, this time to Central Asia, where, if anywhere upon this earth wisdom is to be found, and we anticipate that our sojourn there will be a long one. Possibly we shall not return. Under these altered conditions it has become a question whether we are justified in withholding from the world an account of a phenomenon which we believe to be of unparalleled interest, merely because our private life is involved, or because we are afraid of ridicule and doubt being cast upon our statements. I hold one view about this matter, and Leo holds another, and finally, after much discussion, we have come to a compromise, namely, to send the history to you, giving you full leave to publish it if you think fit, the only stipulation being that you shall disguise our real names, and as much concerning our personal indentity as is consistent with the maintenance of the *bona fides* of the narrative.

"And now what am I to say further? I really do not know, beyond once more repeating that everything is described in the accompanying manuscript exactly as it happened. As regards *She* herself, I have nothing to add. Day by day we have greater occasion to regret that we did not better avail ourselves of our opportunities to obtain more information from that marvellous woman. Who was she? How did she first come to the Caves of Kôr, and what was her real religion? We never ascertained, and now, alas! we never shall, at least not yet. These and many other questions arise in my mind, but what is the good of asking them now?

"Will you undertake the task? We give you complete freedom, and as a reward you will, we believe, have the credit of presenting to the world the most wonderful history, as distinguished from romance, that its records can show. Read the manuscript (which I have copied out fairly for your benefit), and let me know.

"Believe me, very truly yours,

"L. Horace Holly.[1]

"P. S.—Of course, if any profit results from the sale of the writing, should you care to undertake its publication, you can do what you like with it; but if there is a loss I will leave instructions with my lawyers, Messrs. Geoffrey and Jordan, to meet it. We entrust the sherd, the scarab, and the parchments to your keeping, till such time as we demand them back again.—L. H. H."

This letter, as may be imagined, astonished me considerably; but when I came to look at the MS., which the pressure of other work prevented me from doing for a fortnight, I was still more astonished, as I think the reader will be also, and at once made up my mind to press on with the matter. I wrote to this effect to Mr. Holly, but a week afterwards I received a letter from that gentleman's lawyers, returning my own, with the information that their client and Mr. Leo Vincey had already left this country for Thibet, and they did not at present know their address.

Well, that is all I have to say. Of the history itself the reader must judge. I give it to him, with the exception of a very few alterations, made with the object of concealing the identity of the actors from the general public, exactly as it has come to me. Personally I have made up my mind to refrain from comments. At first I was inclined to believe that this history of a woman, clothed in the majesty of her almost endless years, on whom the shadow of Eternity itself lay like the dark wing of Night, was some gigantic allegory of which I could not catch the meaning. Then I thought that it might be a bold attempt to portray the possible results of practical immortality, informing the substance of a mortal who yet drew her strength from Earth, and in whose human bosom passions yet rose and fell and beat as in the un-

---

[1] This name is varied here and throughout in accordance with the writer's request.—Editor.

dying world around her the winds and the tides rise and fall and beat unceasingly. But as I read on I abandoned that idea also. To me the story seems to bear the stamp of truth upon its face. Its explanation I must leave to others. With this slight preface, which circumstances make necessary, I introduce the world to Ayesha and the Caves of Kôr.—THE EDITOR.

P. S.—On consideration there is one thing which, after a reperusal of this history, struck me with so much force that I cannot resist calling the attention of the reader to it. He will observe that, so far as we are made acquainted with him, there appears to be nothing in the character of Leo Vincey which in the opinion of most people would have been likely to attract an intellect so powerful as that of Ayesha. He is not even, at any rate to my view, particularly interesting. Indeed, we might imagine that Mr. Holly under ordinary circumstances would have easily outstripped him in the favour of *She*. Can it be that extremes meet, and that the very excess and splendour of her mind led her by means of some strange physical reaction to worship at the shrine of matter? Was the ancient Kallikrates nothing but a splendid animal beloved for his hereditary Greek beauty? Or is the true explanation what I believe it to be—namely, that Ayesha, seeing further than we can, perceived the germ and smouldering spark of greatness which lay hid within her lover's soul, and well knew that under the influence of her gift of life, watered by her wisdom, and shone upon with the sunshine of her presence, it would bloom like a flower and flash out like a star, filling the world with light and fragrance?

Here also I am unable to answer, but perforce must leave the reader to form his own judgment on the facts before him, as they are detailed by Mr. Holly in the following pages.

CHAPTER I

THERE are some events of which each circumstance and surrounding detail seem to be graven on the memory in such fashion that we cannot forget them. So it is with the scene that I am about to describe; it rises as clearly before my mind at this moment as though it happened yesterday.

It was in this very month something over twenty years ago that I, Ludwig Horace Holly, sat one night in my rooms at Cambridge, grinding away at some mathematical work, I forget what. I was to go up for my fellowship within a week, and was expected by my tutor and my college generally to distinguish myself. At last, wearied out, I flung my book down, and, walking to the mantelpiece, took up a pipe and filled it. There was a candle burning on this mantelpiece, and a long, narrow glass at the back of it; and as I was in the act of lighting the pipe I caught sight of my own countenance in the glass, and paused to reflect. The lighted match burnt away till it scorched my fingers, forcing me to drop it; but still I stood and stared at myself in the glass, and reflected.

"Well," I said aloud, at last, "it is to be hoped that I shall be able to do something with the inside of my head, for I shall certainly never to do anything by the help of the outside."

This remark will doubtless strike anybody who reads it as being slightly obscure, but in fact I was alluding to my physical deficiencies. Most men of twenty-two are endowed with some share, at any rate, of the comeliness of youth, but to me even this was denied. Short, thick-set, and deep-chested almost to deformity, with long sinewy arms, heavy features, hollow grey eyes, a low brow half overgrown with a mop of thick black hair, like a deserted clearing on which the forest had once more begun to

7

encroach; such was my appearance nearly a quarter of a century ago, and such, with modification, is it to this day. Like Cain, I was branded—branded by Nature with the stamp of abnormal ugliness, as I was gifted by Nature with iron and abnormal strength and considerable intellectual powers. So ugly was I that the spruce young men of my College, though they were proud enough of my feats of endurance and physical prowess, did not care even to be seen walking with me. Was it wonderful that I was misanthropic and sullen? Was it wonderful that I brooded and worked alone, and had no friends—at least, only one? I was set apart by Nature to live alone, and draw comfort from her breast, and hers only. Women hated the sight of me. Only a week before I had heard one call me a 'monster' when she thought I was out of hearing, and say that I had converted her to the monkey theory. Once, indeed, a woman pretended to care for me, and I lavished all the pent-up affection of my nature upon her. Then money that was to have come to me went elsewhere, and she discarded me. I pleaded with her as I have never pleaded with any living creature before or since, for I was caught by her sweet face, and loved her; and in the end by way of answer she took me to the glass, and stood side by side with me, and looked into it.

"Now," she said, "if I am Beauty, who are you?"

That was when I was only twenty.

And so I stood and stared, and felt a sort of grim satisfaction in the sense of my own loneliness—for I had neither father, nor mother, nor brother; and as I stared there came a knock at my door.

I listened before I went to answer it, for it was nearly twelve o'clock at night, and I was in no mood to admit any stranger. I had but one friend in the College, or, indeed, in the world—perhaps it was he.

Just then the person outside the door coughed, and I hastened to open it, for I knew the cough.

A tall man of about thirty, with the remains of singular personal beauty, hurried in, staggering beneath the weight of a massive iron box, which he carried by a handle with his right hand. He placed the box upon the table, and then fell into an awful fit of coughing. He coughed and coughed till his face became quite purple, and at last he sank into a chair and began to spit up blood. I poured out some whiskey into a tumbler, and gave it to him. He drank it, and seemed better; although his better was very bad indeed.

"Why did you keep me standing there in the cold?" he asked pettishly. "You know the draughts are death to me."

"I did not know who it was," I answered. "You are a late visitor."

"Yes; and verily I believe it is my last visit," he answered, with a ghastly attempt at a smile. "I am done for, Holly I am done for. I do not believe that I shall see to-morrow!"

"Nonsense!" I said. "Let me go for a doctor."

He waved me back imperiously with his hand. "It is sober sense; but I want no doctors. I have studied medicine and I know all about it. No doctors can help me. My last hour has come! For a year past I have only lived by a miracle. Now listen to me as you never listened to anybody before; for you will not have the opportunity of getting me to repeat my words. We have been friends for two years; tell me how much do you know about me?"

"I know that you are rich, and have had the fancy to come to College long after the age when most men leave it. I know that you have been married, and that your wife died; and that you have been the best, indeed almost the only, friend I ever made."

"Did you know that I have a son?"

"No."

"I have. He is five years old. He cost me his mother's life, and I have never been able to bear to look upon his face in consequence. Holly, if you will accept the trust, I am going to leave you as that boy's sole guardian."

I sprang almost out of my chair. *"Me!"* I said.

"Yes, you. I have not studied you for two years for nothing. I have known for sometime that I could not last, and since I faced the fact I have been searching for someone to whom I could confide the boy and this," and he tapped the iron box. "You are the man, Holly; for, like a rugged tree, you are hard and sound at core.

"Listen; this boy will be the only representative of one of the most ancient families in the world, that is, so far as families can be traced. You will laugh at me when I say it, but one day it will be proved to you beyond a doubt that my sixty-fifth or sixty-sixth lineal ancestor was an Egyptian priest of Isis, though he was himself of Grecian extraction, and was called Kallikrates.[1] His father was one of the Greek mercenaries raised by Hak-Hor, a Mendesian Pharaoh of the twenty-ninth dynasty, and his grandfather or great-grandfather, I believe, was that very Kallikrates mentioned by Herodotus.[2] In or about the year 339 before Christ,

[1] The strong and Beautiful, or more accurately, the Beautiful in strength.
[2] The Kallikrates here referred to by my friend was a Spartan, spoken of by

just at the time of the final fall of the Pharaohs, this Kallikrates (the priest) broke his vows of celibacy and fled from Egypt with a Princess of royal blood who had fallen in love with him. His ship was wrecked upon the coast of Africa, somewhere, as I believe, in the neighbourhood of where Delagoa Bay now is, or rather to the north of it, he and his wife being saved, and all the remainder of their company destroyed in one way or another. Here they endured great hardships, but were at last entertained by the powerful Queen of a savage people, a white woman, of peculiar loveliness, who, under circumstances which I cannot enter into, but which you will one day learn, if you live, from the contents of the box, finally murdered my ancestor Kallikrates. His wife, however, escaped, how, I know not, to Athens, bearing a child with her, whom she named Tisisthenes or the Mighty Avenger.

"Five hundred years or more afterwards the family migrated to Rome under circumstances of which no trace remains, and here, probably with the idea of preserving the idea of vengeance which we find set out in the name of Tisisthenes, they appear with some regularity to have assumed the cognomen of Vindex, or Avenger. Here, too, they remained for another five centuries or more, till about 770 A.D., when Charlemagne invaded Lombardy, where they were then settled, whereon the head of the family seems to have attached himself to the great Emperor, to have returned with him across the Alps, and finally to have settled in Brittany. Eight generations later his lineal representative crossed to England in the reign of Edward the Confessor, and in the time of William the Conqueror was advanced to great honour and power. From that time to the present day I can trace my descent without a break. Not that the Vinceys—for that was the final corruption of the name after its bearers took root in English soil—have been particularly distinguished—they never came much to the fore. Sometimes they were soldiers, sometimes merchants, but on the whole they have preserved a dead level of respectability, and a

---

Herodotus (Herod. ix. 72) as being remarkable for his beauty. He fell at the glorious battle of Platæa (September 22, B.C. 479), when the Lacedæmonians and Athenians under Pausanias routed the Persians, putting nearly 300,000 of them to the sword. The following is a translation of the passage: "For Kallikrates died out of the battle, he came to the army the most beautiful man of the Greeks of that day—not only of the Lacedæmonians themselves, but of the other Greeks also. He, when Pausanias was sacrificing, was wounded in the side by an arrow; and then they fought, but on being carried off he regretted his death, and said to Arimnestus, a Platæan, that he did not grieve at dying for Greece, but at not having struck a blow, or, although he desired so to do, performed any deed worthy of himself." This Kallikrates, who appears to have been as brave as he was beautiful, is subsequently mentioned by Herodotus as having been buried among the ἱρέες (young commanders), apart from the other Spartans and the Helots.—L. H. H.

still deader level of mediocrity. From the time of Charles II. till the beginning of the present century they were merchants. About 1790 my grandfather made a considerable fortune out of brewing, and retired. In 1821 he died, and my father succeeded him, and dissipated most of the money. Ten years ago he died also, leaving me a net income of about two thousand a year. Then it was that I undertook an expedition in connection with *that*," and he pointed to the iron chest, "which ended disastrously enough. On my way back I travelled in the South of Europe, and finally reached Athens. There I met my beloved wife, who might well also have been called the 'Beautiful,' like my old Greek ancestor. There I married her, and there, a year afterwards, when my boy was born, she died."

He paused a while, his head sunk upon his hand, and then continued:

"My marriage had diverted me from a project which I cannot enter into now. I have no time, Holly—I have no time! One day, if you accept my trust, you will learn all about it. After my wife's death I turned my mind to it again. But first it was necessary, or, at least I conceived that it was necessary, that I should attain to a perfect knowledge of Eastern dialects, especially Arabic. It was to facilitate my studies that I came here. Very soon, however, my disease developed itself, and now there is an end of me." And as though to emphasize his words he burst into another terrible fit of coughing.

I gave him some more whisky, and after resting he went on:

"I have never seen my boy, Leo, since he was a tiny baby. I could never bear to see him, but they tell me that he is a quick and handsome child. In this envelope," and he produced a letter from his pocket addressed to myself, "I have jotted down the course I wish followed in the boy's education. It is a somewhat peculiar one. At any rate, I could not entrust it to a stranger. Once more, will you undertake it?"

"I must first know that I am to undertake," I answered.

"You are to undertake to have the boy, Leo, to live with you till he is twenty-five years of age—not to send him to school remember. On his twenty-fifth birthday your guardianship will end, and you will then, with the keys that I give you now" (and he placed them on the table), "open the iron box, and let him see and read the contents, and say whether or no he is willing to undertake the quest. There is no obligation on him to do so. Now, as regards terms. My present income is two thousand two hundred a year. Half of that income I have secured to you by will for life, contingently on your undertaking the guardianship—that is, one thousand a year remuneration to yourself, for you will have to give up your life to it, and one hundred a year to pay for the board of the boy. The rest is to accumulate till Leo is twenty-five, so that there may be a sum in hand should he wish to undertake the quest of which I spoke."

"And suppose I were to die?" I asked.

"Then the boy must become a ward of Chancery and take his chance. Only, be careful that the iron chest is passed on to him by your will. Listen, Holly; don't refuse me. Believe me, this is to your advantage. You are not fit to mix with the world—it would only embitter you. In a few weeks you will become a Fellow of your College, and the income which you will derive from it combined with what I have left you will enable you to live a life of learned leisure, alternated with the sport of which you are so fond, such as will exactly suit you."

He paused and looked at me anxiously, but I still hesitated. The charge seemed so very strange.

"For my sake, Holly. We have been good friends, and I have no time to make other arrangements."

"Very well," I said, "I will do it, provided there is nothing in this paper to make me change my mind," and I touched the envelope he had put upon the table by the keys.

"Thank you, Holly, thank you. There is nothing at all. Swear to me by God that you will be a father to the boy, and follow my directions to the letter."

"I swear it," I answered solemnly.

"Very well; remember that perhaps one day I shall ask for the account of your oath, for though I am dead and forgotten, yet shall I live. There is no such thing as death, Holly, only a change, and, as you may perhaps learn in time to come, I believe that even here that change could under certain circumstances be indefinitely postponed," and again he broke into one of his dreadful fits of coughing.

"There," he said, "I must go; you have the chest, and my will can be found among my papers, under the authority of which the child will be handed over to you. You will be well paid, Holly, and I know that you are honest; but if you betray my trust, by Heaven, I will haunt you."

I said nothing, being, indeed, too bewildered to speak.

He held up the candle, and looked at his own face in the glass. It had been a beautiful face, but disease had wrecked it. "Food for the worms," he said. "Curious to think that in a few hours I shall be stiff and cold—the journey done, the little game played out. Ah me, Holly! life is not worth the trouble of life, except when one is in love—at least, mine has not been; but the boy Leo's may be if he has the courage and the faith. Good-bye, my friend!" and with a sudden access of tenderness he flung his arm about me and kissed me on the forehead, and then turned to go.

"Look here, Vincey," I said; "if you are ill as you think, you had better let me fetch a doctor."

"No, no," he said earnestly. "Promise me that you won't. I am going to die, and, like a poisoned rat, I wish to die alone."

"I don't believe that you are going to do anything of the sort," I answered. He smiled, and, with the word "Remember" on his lips, was gone. As for myself, I sat down and rubbed my eyes, wondering if I had been asleep. As this idea would not bear investigation I gave it up, and began to think that Vincey must have been drinking. I knew that he was, and had been, very ill, but still it seemed impossible that he could be in such a pass as to be able to know for certain that he would not outlive the night. Had he been so near dissolution surely he would scarcely have been able to walk, and to carry a heavy iron box with him. The story, on reflection, seemed to me utterly incredible, for I was then not old enough to be aware how many things happen in this world that the commonsense of the average man would set down as so improbable as to be absolutely impossible. This is a fact that I have only recently mastered. Was it likely that a man would have a son five years of age whom he had never seen since he was a tiny infant? No. Was it likely that ne could foretell his own death so accurately? No. Was it likely that he could trace his pedigree for more than three centuries before Christ, or that he would suddenly confide the absolute guardianship of his child, and leave half his fortune, to a college friend? Most certainly not. Clearly Vincey was either drunk or mad. That being so, what did it mean? And what was in the sealed iron chest?

The position baffled and puzzled me to such an extent that at last I could bear the thought of it no longer, and determined to sleep over it. So having put away the keys and the letter that Vincey had left into my despatch-box, and hidden the iron chest in a large portmanteau, I went to bed, and was soon fast asleep.

As it seemed to me, I had only been asleep for a few minutes when I was awakened by somebody calling me. I sat up and rubbed my eyes; it was broad daylight—eight o'clock, in fact.

"Why, what is the matter with you, John?" I asked of the gyp who waited on Vincey and myself. "You look as though you had seen a ghost!"

"Yes, sir, and so I have," he answered, "leastways I've seen a corpse, which is worse. I've been in to call Mr. Vincey, as usual, and there he lies stark and dead!"

CHAPTER II

THE YEARS ROLL BY

As might be expected, poor Vincey's sudden death created a great stir in the College; but, as he was known to be very ill, and a satisfactory doctor's certificate was forthcoming, no inquest was held. They were not so particular about inquests in those days as we are now; indeed, they were generally disliked, because of the attendant scandal. Under these circumstances, being asked no questions, I did not feel it necessary to volunteer information about our interview on the night of Vincey's decease, beyond saying that, as was not unusual with him, he had come into my rooms. On the day of the funeral a lawyer came down from London and followed my poor friend's remains to the grave, and then returned with his papers and effects, except, of course, the iron chest which had been left in my keeping. For a week after this I heard no more of the matter; and, indeed, my attention was amply occupied in other ways, for I was up for my Fellowship, a fact that had prevented me from attending the funeral or seeing the lawyer. At last, however, the examination was over, and I came back to my rooms and sank into an easy chair with a happy consciousness that I had got through it very fairly.

Soon, however, my thoughts, relieved of the pressure that had crushed them into a single groove during the last few days, turned to the events of the night of poor Vincey's death, and again I asked myself what it all meant, and wondered if I should hear anything more of the matter, and if I did not, what it would be my duty to do with the curious iron chest. I sat there and thought and thought till I began to grow seriously disturbed over the occurrence: the mysterious midnight visit, the prophecy of death so shortly to be fulfilled, the solemn oath that I had taken, and which Vincey had called on me to answer to in another world than this. Had the man committed suicide? It looked like it. And what was the quest of which he spoke? The circumstances were uncanny, so much so that, though I am by no means nervous, or apt to be alarmed at anything which may seem to cross the bounds of the natural, I grew afraid, and began to wish I had nothing to do with them. How much more do I wish it now, over twenty years afterwards!

As I sat and thought, there came a knock at the door, and a letter, in a big blue envelope, was brought to me. I saw at once that it must be a lawyer's letter, and an instinct told me that it was connected with my trust. The letter which I still have, runs thus:—

"SIR,—Our client, the late M. L. Vincey, Esq., who died on the 9th instant in — College, Cambridge, has left behind him a Will of which we are the executors, whereof you will please find copy enclosed. Under this Will you will perceive that you take a life-interest in about half of the late Mr. Vincey's property, now invested in Consols, subject to your acceptance of the guardianship of his only son, Leo Vincey, an infant, aged five. Had we not ourselves drawn up the document in question in obedience to Mr. Vincey's clear and precise instructions, both personal and written, and had he not then assured us that he had very good reasons for what he was doing, we ought to tell you that its provisions seem to us of so unusual a nature, that we should have felt bound to call the attention of the Court of Chancery to them, in order that such steps might be taken as seemed desirable to it, either by contesting the capacity of the testator or otherwise, to safeguard the interests of the infant. As it is, knowing that Mr. Vincey was a gentleman of the highest intelligence and acumen, and that he has absolutely no relations living to whom he could have confided the guardianship of the child, we do not feel justified in taking this course.

"Awaiting such instructions as you may please to send us as regards the delivery of the infant and the payment of the proportion of the dividends due to you,

"We remain, Sir, faithfully yours,

"Horace L. Holly, Esq."   "GEOFFREY AND JORDAN.

I put down the letter, and ran my eye through the Will, which appeared, from its utter unintelligibility, to have been drawn on the strictest legal principles. So far as I could discover, however, it exactly bore out what my friend Vincey had told me on the night of his death. Then it was true after all. I must take the boy. Suddenly I remembered the letter which Vincey had left with the box. I fetched and opened it. It contained only such directions as he had already given to me as to opening the chest on Leo's twenty-fifth birthday, and laid down the outlines of the boy's education, which was to include Greek, the higher Mathematics, and

Arabic. At the end there was a postscript to the effect that if the child died under the age of twenty-five, which, however, the writer did not believe would occur, I was to open the chest, and act on the information therein contained if I saw fit. If I did not see fit, I was to destroy all the contents. On no account was I to pass them on to a stranger.

As this letter added nothing material to my knowledge, and certainly raised no further objection in my mind to entering on the task I had promised my dead friend to undertake, there was only one course open to me—namely, to write to Messrs. Geoffrey and Jordan, and express my acceptance of the trust, stating that I should be willing to commence my guardianship of Leo in ten days' time. This done I went to the authorities of my College, and having told them as much of the story as I considered desirable, which was not very much, after some difficulty I succeeded in persuading them to stretch a point, and, in the event of my having obtained a Fellowship, which I was almost certain was the case, to allow me to take the child to live with me. Their consent, however, was only granted on the condition that I vacated my rooms in College and took lodgings. This I did, and after an active search I obtained very good apartments quite close to the College gates. The next thing was to find a nurse. Now on this point I came to a decision. I would have no woman to lord it over me about the child, and steal his affections from me. The boy was old enough to do without female assistance, so I set to work to find a suitable male attendant. After some difficulty I was fortunate in hiring a most respectable round-faced young man, who had been a helper in a hunting-stable, but who said that he was one of a family of seventeen and well-accustomed to the ways of children, and professed himself quite willing to undertake the charge of Master Leo when he arrived. Then, having carried the iron box to town, and with my own hands deposited it at my banker's, I bought some books upon the health and management of infants, and read them, first to myself, then aloud to Job—that was the young man's name—and waited.

At length the child arrived in the charge of an elderly person, who wept bitterly at parting with him; and a beautiful boy he was. Indeed, I do not think that I ever saw such a perfect child before or since. His eyes were grey, his forehead was broad, and his face, even at that early age, clean cut as a cameo, without being pinched or thin. But perhaps his most attractive point was his hair, which was pure gold in colour and tightly curled over his shapely head. He cried a little when at last his nurse tore herself away and left him with us. Never shall I forget the scene. There he stood, with the sunlight from the window playing upon his golden curls, his fist screwed over one eye, while he took us in with the other. I was seated in a chair, and stretched out my hand to him to induce him to come to me, while Job, in the corner, made a sort of clucking noise, which, arguing from his previous experience, or from the analogy of the hen, he judged would have a soothing effect, and inspire confidence in the youthful mind, and ran a wooden horse of peculiar hideousness backwards and forwards in a way that was little short of inane. This went on for some minutes, and then all of a sudden the lad stretched out both his little arms and ran to me.

"I like you," he said: "you is ugly, but you is good."

Ten minutes afterwards he was eating large slices of bread-and-butter, with every sign of satisfaction; Job wanted to put jam on to them, but I sternly reminded him of the excellent works that we had read, and forbade it.

In a very little while (for, as I expected, I gained my Fellowship) the boy became the favourite of the whole College—where, orders and regulations to the contrary notwithstanding, he was continually in and out—a sort of infant libertine, in whose favour all rules were relaxed. The offerings made at his shrine were without number, and thereon I had a serious difference of opinion with one old resident Fellow, now long dead, who was supposed to be the crustiest man in the University, and to abhor the sight of a child. And yet I discovered, when a frequently recurring fit of sickness had forced Job to keep a strict look-out, that this unprincipled old man was in the habit of enticing the boy to his rooms and there feeding him upon unlimited quantities of 'brandy-balls' and of making him promise to say nothing about it. Job told him that he ought to be ashamed of himself, "at his age, too, when he might have been a grandfather if he had done what was right," by which Job understood had married. Thence arose the quarrel.

But I have no space to dwell upon those delightful years, around which happy memories still linger. One by one they went by, and as they passed we two grew dearer and yet more dear to each other. Few sons have been loved as I love Leo, and few fathers know the deep and continuous affection that Leo bears to me.

The child grew into the boy, and the boy into the young man, while one by one the remorseless years flew by, and as he grew and increased so did his beauty and the beauty of his mind grow with him. When he was about fifteen they christened him Beauty about the College, and me they nicknamed the Beast. Beauty and

the Beast was what they called us when we went out walking together, as we were wont to do every day. Once Leo attacked a
strapping butcher's man, twice his size, because he sang it out
after us, and thrashed him, too—thrashed him fairly. I walked on
and pretended not to see, till the combat grew too exciting, when I
turned round and cheered him on to victory. It was the chaff of
the College at the time, but I could not help it. Then, when he
was a little older the undergraduates found fresh names for us.
They styled me Charon, and Leo the Greek god! I will pass over
my own appellation with the humble remark that I was never
handsome, and did not grow more so as I aged. As for his title,
there was no doubt about its fitness. Leo at twenty-one might
have stood for a statue of the youthful Apollo. I never saw anybody to equal him in looks, nor anybody so absolutely unconscious of them. As for his mind, he was brilliant and keen-witted,
but no scholar. He had not the dulness necessary to that result.
We followed out his father's instructions as to his education
strictly enough, and on the whole the results, especially with
regard to Greek and Arabic, were satisfactory. I learnt the latter
language in order to help to teach it to him, but after five years of
it he knew it as well as I did—almost as well as the professor who
instructed us both. I was always a great sportsman—it is my one
passion—and every autumn we went away shooting or fishing,
sometimes to Scotland, sometimes to Norway, once indeed to
Russia. I am a good shot, but even in this he learnt to excel me.

When Leo was eighteen I moved back into my rooms, and entered him at my own College, and at twenty-one he took his degree—a respectable degree, but not a very high one. Then it was
that, for the first time, I told him something of his own story, and
of the mystery which loomed ahead. Naturally he was very curious about it, and of course I explained to him that his curiosity
could not be gratified at present. After this, to pass the time
away, I suggested that he should read for the Bar; and this he
did, studying at Cambridge, and going to London to eat his din-
ners.

I had only one trouble about Leo, and it was that every young
woman whom he met, or, if not every one, most of them, insisted
on falling in love with him. Hence arose difficulties into which
I need not enter here, though they were troublesome enough at
the time. On the whole he behaved fairly well; I cannot say more
than that.

And so the years went by till at last Leo reached his twenty-
fifth birthday, at which date this strange and, in some ways,
awful history really begins.

CHAPTER III

THE SHERD OF AMENARTAS

On the day preceding Leo's twenty-fifth birthday we both journeyed to London, and extracted the mysterious chest from the bank where I had deposited it twenty years before. It was, I recollect, brought up by the same clerk who had taken it down. He perfectly remembered having hidden away the box. Had he not done so, he said, he should have had difficulty in finding it, it was so covered up with cobwebs.

In the evening we returned with our precious burden to Cambridge, and I think that we might both of us have given away all the sleep we won that night and not have been much the poorer. At daybreak Leo arrived at my room in a dressing-gown, and suggested that we should at once proceed to business, an idea which I scouted as showing an unworthy curiosity. The chest had waited twenty years, I said, so it could very well continue to wait until after breakfast. Accordingly at nine—an unusually sharp nine—we breakfasted; and so occupied was I with my own thoughts that I regret to state that I put a piece of bacon in Leo's tea in mistake for a lump of sugar. Job, too, to whom the contagion of excitement had, of course, spread, managed to break the handle off my Sevres china teacup, the identical one, I believe, that Marat had used just before he was stabbed in his bath.

At last, however, breakfast was cleared away, and Job, at my request, fetched the chest, and placed it upon the table in a somewhat gingerly fashion, as though he mistrusted it. Then he prepared to leave the room.

"Stop a moment, Job," I said. "If Mr. Leo has no objection, I should prefer to have an independent witness to this business, who can be relied upon to hold his tongue unless he is asked to speak."

"Certainly, Uncle Horace," answered Leo; for I had brought him up to call me uncle—though he varied the appellation somewhat disrespectfully by styling me "old fellow," or even "my avuncular relative."

Job touched his head, not having a hat on.

"Lock the door, Job," I said, "and bring me my despatch-box."

He obeyed, and from the box I took the keys that poor Vincey, Leo's father, had given me on the night of his death. There were three of them: the largest a comparatively modern key, the second an exceedingly ancient one, and the third entirely unlike anything of the sort that we had ever seen before, being fashioned apparently from a strip of solid silver, with a bar placed across it to serve as a handle, and having some nicks cut in the edge of the bar. It was more like a clumsy railway key than anything I can think of.

"Now are you both ready?" I said, as people do when they are about to fire a mine. There was no answer, so I took the big key, rubbed some salad oil into the wards, and after one or two mistakes, for my hands were shaking, managed to fit it, and shoot the lock. Leo bent over and caught the massive lid in both his hands, and with an effort, for the hinges had rusted, he forced it back, revealing another case covered with dust. This we extracted from the iron chest without any difficulty, and removed the accumulated filth of years from it with a clothes-brush.

It was, or appeared to be, of ebony, or some such close-grained black wood, and was bound in every direction with flat bands of iron. Its antiquity must have been extreme, for in parts the dense heavy wood was commencing to crumble from age.

"Now for it," I said, inserting the second key.

Job and Leo bent forward in breathless expectancy. The key turned, I flung back the lid and uttered an exclamation; and no wonder, for inside the ebony case was a magificent silver casket, about twelve inches square by eight high. It was doubtless of Egyptian workmanship, for the four legs were formed of Sphinxes, and the dome-shaped cover was also surmounted by a Sphinx. The casket was of course much tarnished and dinted with age, but otherwise in very sound condition.

I drew it out and set it on the table, and then, in the midst of the most perfect silence, I inserted the strange-looking silver key, and pressed this way and that until at last the lock yielded, and the casket stood open before us. It was filled to the brim with some brown shredded material, more like vegetable fibre than paper, the nature of which I have never been able to discover. This I carefully removed to the depth of some three inches, when I came to a letter enclosed in an ordinary modern-looking envelope, and addressed, in the handwriting of my dead friend Vincey:

"To my son Leo, should he live to open this casket."

I handed the letter to Leo, who glanced at the envelope, and then put it down upon the table, making a motion to me to continue the investigation of the casket.

The next thing that I found was a parchment carefully rolled up. I unrolled it, and seeing that it was also in Vincey's handwriting, and headed, 'Translation of the Uncial Greek writing on the Potsherd,' I put it down by the letter. Then followed another ancient roll of parchment, that had become yellow and crinkled with the passage of years. This I also unrolled. It was likewise a translation of the same Greek original, but into black-letter Latin, which at the first glance from the style and character appeared to me to date from about the beginning of the sixteenth century.

Immediately beneath this roll was something hard and heavy, wrapped up in yellow linen, and reposing upon another layer of the fibrous material. Slowly and carefully we unrolled the linen, exposing to view a very large but undoubtedly ancient potsherd of a dirty yellow colour! This potsherd, in my judgment, had once been a part of an ordinary amphora of medium size. For the rest, it measured ten and a half inches in length by seven in width, was about a quarter of an inch thick, and densely covered on the convex side that lay towards the bottom of the box with writing in the later uncial Greek character, faded here and there, but for the most part perfectly legible, the inscription having evidently been executed with the greatest care, and by means of a reed pen, such as the ancients often used. I must not forget to mention that in some remote age this wonderful fragment had been broken in two, and rejoined with cement and eight long rivets. Also there were numerous inscriptions on the inner side, but these were of the most erratic character, and clearly had been made by different hands and in many different ages. Of them, together with the writings on the parchments, I shall have to speak presently.

"Is there anything more?" asked Leo, in an excited whisper.

I groped about, and produced something hard, done up in a little linen bag. Out of the bag we took first a very beautiful miniature painted upon ivory, and, secondly, a small chocolate-coloured composition *scarabæus*, marked thus:—

symbols which, we have since ascertained, mean "Suten se Ra," that is, being translated, the "Royal Son of Ra or the Sun." The miniature was the picture of Leo's Greek mother—a lovely, dark-eyed creature. On the back of it was written, in poor Vincey's handwriting, "My beloved wife."

"That is all," I said.

"Very well," answered Leo, putting down the miniature, at which he had been gazing affectionately; "and now let us read the letter," and without further ado he broke the seal, and read aloud as follows:—

"MY SON LEO,—When you open this, if you ever live to do so, you will have attained to manhood, and I shall have been long enough dead to be absolutely forgotten by nearly all who knew me. Yet in reading remember that I have been, and for anything you know may still be, and that herein, through this link of pen and paper, I stretch out my hand to you across the gulf of death, and my voice speaks to you from the silence of the grave. Though I am dead, and no memory of me remains in your mind, yet am I with you in this hour as you read. Since your birth to this day I have scarcely seen your face. Forgive me this. Your life supplanted the life of one whom I loved better than women are often loved, and the bitterness of it endureth yet. Had I lived I should in time have conquered this foolish feeling, but I am not destined to live. My sufferings, physical and mental, are more than I can bear, and when such small arrangements as I have to make for your future well-being are completed it is my intention to put a period to them. May God forgive me if I do wrong. At the best I could not live more than another year."

"So he killed himself," I exclaimed. "I thought so."

"And now," Leo went on, without replying, "enough of myself. What has to be said belongs to you who live, not to me, who am dead, and almost as much forgotten as though I had never been. Holly, my friend (to whom, if he will accept the trust, it is my intention to confide you), will have told you something of the extraordinary antiquity of your race. In the contents of this casket you will find sufficient to prove it. The strange legend that you will see inscribed by your remote ancestress upon the potsherd was communicated to me by my father on his death-bed, and took strong hold in my imagination. When I was only nineteen years of age I determined, as, to his misfortune, did one of our ancestors about the time of Elizabeth, to investigate its truth. Into all that befell me I cannot enter now. But this I saw with my own eyes. On the coast of Africa, in a hitherto unexplored region, some distance to the north of where the Zambesi falls into the sea, there is a headland, at the extremity of which a peak towers up, shaped like the head of a negro, similar to that whereof the writing speaks. I landed there, and learnt from a wandering native, who had been cast out by his people because of some crime which he had committed, that far inland are great mountains shaped like cups, and caves surrounded by measureless swamps. I learnt also that the people there speak a dialect of Arabic, and are ruled over by a *beautiful white woman* who is seldom seen by them, but who is reported to have power over all things living and dead. Two days after I had ascertained this the man died of fever contracted in crossing the swamps, and I was forced by want of provisions and by symptoms of an illness which afterwards prostrated me to take to my dhow again.

"Of the adventures that befell me after this I need not now speak. I was wrecked upon the coast of Madagascar, and rescued some months afterwards by an English ship that brought me to Aden, whence I started for England, intending to prosecute my search as soon as I had made sufficient preparations. On my way I stopped in Greece, and there, for *Omnia vincit amor,* I met your beloved mother, and married her, and there you were born and she died. Then it was that my last illness seized me, and I returned hither to die. But still I hoped against hope, and set myself to work to learn Arabic, with the intention, should I ever get better, of returning to the coast of Africa, and solving the mystery of which the tradition has lived so many centuries in our family. But I have not got better, and so far as I am concerned, the story is at an end.

"For you, however, my son, it is not at an end, and to you I hand on these the results of my labour, together with the hereditary proofs of its origin. It is my purpose to provide that they shall not be put into your hands until you have reached an age when you will be able to judge for yourself whether or no you will choose to investigate what, if it is true, must be the greatest mystery in the world, or to put it by as an idle fable, originating in the first place in a woman's disordered brain.

"I do not believe that it is a fable; I believe that if it can only be re-discovered, there is a spot where the vital forces of the world visibly exist. Life exists; why therefore should not the means of preserving it indefinitely exist also? But I have no wish to prejudice your mind about the matter. Read and judge for yourself. If you are inclined to undertake the search, I have so provided that you will not lack for means. If, on the other hand, you are satisfied that the legend is a chimera, then I adjure you, destroy the potsherd and the writings, and let a cause of troubling be removed from our race for ever. Perhaps that will be wisest. The unknown is generally taken to be terrible, not as the proverb would infer, from the inherent superstition of man, but because it so often *is* terrible. He who would tamper with the vast and secret forces that animate the world may well fall a victim to them. And if the end were attained, if at last you emerged from the trial ever beautiful and ever young, defying time and evil, and lifted above the natural decay of flesh and intellect, who shall say that the awesome change would bring you happiness? Choose, my son, and may the Power who rules all things, and who says 'thus far shalt thou go, and thus much shalt thou learn,' direct the choice to your own welfare and the welfare of the world, which, in the event of your success, you would one day certainly rule by the pure force of accumulated experience.— Farewell!"

Thus the letter, which was unsigned and undated, abruptly ended.

"What do you make of that, Uncle Holly?" said Leo, with a gasp, as he replaced the paper on the table. "We have been looking for a mystery, and certainly we seem to have found one."

"What do I make of it? Why, that your poor dear father was off his head, of course," I answered, testily. "I guessed as much that night, twenty years ago, when he came into my room. You see he evidently hurried his own end, poor man. It is absolute balderdash."

"That's it, sir!" said Job, solemnly. Job was a most matter-of-fact specimen of a matter-of-fact class.

"Well, let's see what the potsherd has to say, at any rate," said Leo, taking up the translation in his father's writing, and commencing to read:—

"I, Amenartas, of the Royal House of the Pharaohs of Egypt, wife of Kallikrates (the Beautiful in Strength), *a Priest of Isis whom the gods cherish and the demons obey, being about to die, to my little son Tisisthenes* (the Mighty Avenger). *I fled with thy father from Egypt in the days of Nectanebes,*[1] *causing him through love to break the vows that he had vowed. We fled southward, across the waters, and we wandered for twice twelve moons on the coast of Libya* (Africa) *that looks toward the rising sun, where by a river is a great rock cavern like the head of an Ethiopian. Four days on the water from the mouth of a mighty river were we cast away, and some were drowned and some died of sickness. But us wild men took through wastes and marshes, where the sea fowl hid the sky, bearing us ten days' journey till we came to a hollow mountain, where a great city had been and fallen, and where there are caves of which no man hath seen the*

---

[1]Nekht-nebf, or Nectanebo H., the last native Pharaoh of Egypt, fled from Ochus to Ethiopia, B.C. 339.—EDITOR.

*end and they brought us to the Queen of the people who place
pots upon the heads of strangers, who is a magician having a
knowledge of all things, and life and loveliness that does not die.
And she cast eyes of love upon thy father, Kallikrates, and would
have slain me, and taken him to husband, but he loved me and
feared her, and would not. Then did she take us, and lead us by
terrible ways, by means of dark magic, to where the great pit is,
in the mouth of which the old philosopher lay dead, and showed
to us the rolling Pillar of Life that dies not, whereof the voice is
as the voice of thunder; and she did stand in the flames, and come
forth unharmed, and yet more beautiful. Then did she swear to
make thy father undying even as she is, if he would but slay me,
and give himself to her, for me she could not slay because of the
magic of my own people that I have, and that prevailed thus
far against her. And he held his hand before his eyes to hide her
beauty, and would not. Then in her rage did she smite him by
her magic, and he died, but she wept over him, and bore him
thence with lamentations; and being afraid, me she sent to the
mouth of the great river where the ships come, and I was carried
far away on the ships where I gave thee birth, and hither to
Athens I came at last after many wanderings. Now I say to thee,
my son, Tisisthenes, seek out the woman, and learn the secret of
Life, and if thou mayest find a way slay her, because of thy
father Kallikrates, and if thou dost fear or fail, this I say to all
of thy seed who come after thee, till at last a brave man be
found among them who shall bathe in the fire and sit in the
place of the Pharaohs. I speak of those things, that though they
be past belief, yet I have known, and I lie not."*

"May the Lord forgive her for that," groaned Job, who had
been listening to this marvellous composition with his mouth
open.

As for myself, I said nothing: my first idea being that my
poor friend, when demented, had composed the whole tale, though
it scarcely seemed likely that such a story could have been
invented by anybody. It was too original. To solve my doubts
I took up the potsherd and began to read the close uncial Greek
writing on it; and very good Greek of the period it is, considering
that it came from the pen of an Egyptian born. Here is an exact
transcript of it:—

ΑΜΕΝΑΡΤΑΣΤΟΥΒΑΣΙΛΙΚΟΥΓΕΝΟΥΣΤΟΥΑ
ΙΓΥΓΤΙΟΥΗΤΟΥΚΑΛΛΙΚΡΑΤΟΥΣΙΣΙΔΟΣΙΕΡ
ΕΩΣΗΝΟΙΜΕΝΘΕΟΙΤΡΕΦΟΥΣΙΤΑΔΕΔΑΙΜΟ
ΝΙΑΥΓΟΤΑΣΣΕΤΑΙΗΔΗΤΕΛΕΥΤΩΣΑΤΙΣΙΣ

ΘΕΝΕΙΤΩΓΑΙΔΙΕΓΙΣΤΕΛΛΕΙΤΑΔΕΣΥΝΕΦΥΓΟ
ΝΓΑΡΓΟΤΕΕΚΤΗΣΑΙΓΥΓΤΙΑΣΕΓΙΝΕΚΤΑΝΕΒ
ΟΥΜΕΤΑΤΟΥΣΟΥΓΑΤΡΟΣΔΙΑΤΟΝΕΡΩΤΑΤΟ
ΝΕΜΟΝΕΓΙΟΡΚΗΣΑΝΤΟΣΦΥΓΟΝΤΕΣΔΕΓΡΟ
ΣΝΟΤΟΝΔΙΑΓΟΝΤΙΟΙΚΑΙΚΔΜΗΝΑΣΚΑΤΑΤΑ
ΓΑΡΑΘΑΛΑΣΣΙΑΤΗΣΛΙΒΥΗΣΤΑΓΡΟΣΗΛΙΟΥ
ΑΝΑΤΟΛΑΣΓΛΑΝΗΘΕΝΤΕΣΕΝΘΑΓΕΡΓΕΤΡΑ
ΤΙΣΜΕΓΑΛΗΓΛΥΓΤΟΝΟΜΟΙΩΜΑΑΙΘΙΟΓΟΣ
ΚΕΦΑΛΗΣΕΙΤΑΗΜΕΡΑΣΔΑΓΟΣΤΟΜΑΤΟΣΓΟ
ΤΑΜΟΥΜΕΓΑΛΟΥΕΚΓΕΣΟΝΤΕΣΟΙΜΕΝΚΑΤΕ
ΓΟΝΤΙΣΘΗΜΕΝΟΙΔΕΝΟΣΩΙΑΓΕΘΑΝΟΜΕΝΤ
ΕΛΟΣΔΕΥΓΑΓΡΙΩΝΑΝΘΡΩΓΩΝΕΦΕΡΟΜΕΘΑ
ΔΙΑΕΛΕΩΝΤΕΚΑΙΤΕΝΑΓΕΩΝΕΝΘΑΓΕΡΓΤΗΝ
ΩΝΓΛΗΘΟΣΑΓΟΚΡΥΓΤΕΙΤΟΝΟΥΡΑΝΟΝΗΜ
ΕΡΑΣΙΕΩΣΗΛΘΟΜΕΝΕΙΣΚΟΙΛΟΝΤΙΟΡΟΣΕΝ
ΘΑΓΟΤΕΜΕΓΑΛΗΜΕΝΓΟΛΙΣΗΝΑΝΤΡΑΔΕΑΓ
ΕΙΡΟΝΑΗΓΑΓΟΝΔΕΩΣΒΑΣΙΛΕΙΑΝΤΗΝΤΩΝΞ
ΕΝΟΥΣΧΥΤΡΑΙΣΣΤΕΦΑΝΟΥΝΤΩΝΗΤΙΣΜΑΓΕ
ΙΑΜΕΝΕΧΡΗΤΟΕΓΙΣΤΗΜΗΔΕΓΑΝΤΩΝΚΑΙΔ
ΗΚΑΙΚΑΛΛΟΣΚΑΙΡΩΜΗΝΑΓΗΡΩΣΗΝΗΔΕΚΑ
ΛΛΙΚΡΑΤΟΥΣΤΟΥΣΟΥΓΑΤΡΟΣΕΡΑΣΘΕΙΣΑΤ
ΟΜΕΝΓΡΩΤΟΝΣΥΝΟΙΚΕΙΝΕΒΟΥΛΕΤΟΕΜΕΔ
ΕΑΝΕΛΕΙΝΕΓΕΙΤΑΩΣΟΥΚΑΝΕΓΕΙΘΕΝΕΜΕΓΑ
ΡΥΓΕΡΕΦΙΛΕΙΚΑΙΤΗΝΞΕΝΗΝΕΦΟΒΕΙΤΟΑΓΗ
ΓΑΓΕΝΗΜΑΣΥΓΟΜΑΓΕΙΑΣΚΑΘΟΔΟΥΣΣΦΑΛ
ΕΡΑΣΕΝΘΑΤΟΒΑΡΑΘΡΟΝΤΟΜΕΓΑΟΥΚΑΤΑΣ
ΤΟΜΑΕΚΕΙΤΟΟΓΕΡΩΝΟΦΙΛΟΣΟΦΟΣΤΕΘΝΕ
ΩΣΑΦΙΚΟΜΕΝΟΙΣΔΕΔΕΙΞΕΦΩΣΤΟΥΒΙΟΥΕΥ
ΘΥΟΙΟΝΚΙΟΝΑΕΛΙΣΣΟΜΕΝΟΝΦΩΝΗΝΙΕΝΤ
ΑΚΑΘΑΓΕΡΒΡΟΝΤΗΣΕΙΤΑΔΙΑΓΥΡΟΣΒΕΒΗΚ
ΥΙΑΑΒΛΑΒΗΣΚΑΙΕΤΙΚΑΛΛΙΩΝΑΥΤΗΕΑΥΤΗΣ
ΕΞΕΦΑΝΗΕΚΔΕΤΟΥΤΩΝΩΜΟΣΕΚΑΙΤΟΝΣΟ
ΝΓΑΤΕΡΑΑΘΑΝΑΤΟΝΑΓΟΔΕΙΞΕΙΝΕΙΣΥΝΟΙΚ
ΕΙΝΟΙΒΟΥΛΟΙΤΟΕΜΕΔΕΑΝΕΛΕΙΝΟΥΓΑΡΟΥ
ΝΑΥΤΗΑΝΕΛΕΙΝΙΣΧΥΕΝΥΓΟΤΩΝΗΜΕΔΑΓΩ
ΝΗΝΚΑΙΑΥΤΗΕΧΩΜΑΓΕΙΑΣΟΔΟΥΔΕΝΤΙΜΑ
ΛΛΟΝΗΘΕΛΕΤΩΧΕΙΡΕΤΩΝΟΜΜΑΤΩΝΓΡΟΙ
ΣΧΩΝΙΝΑΔΗΤΟΤΗΣΓΥΝΑΙΚΟΣΚΑΛΛΟΣΜΗ
ΟΡΩΗΓΕΙΤΑΟΡΓΙΣΘΕΙΣΑΚΑΤΕΓΟΗΤΕΥΣΕΜ
ΕΝΑΥΤΟΝΑΓΟΛΟΜΕΝΟΝΜΕΝΤΟΙΚΛΑΟΥΣΑ
ΚΑΙΟΔΥΡΟΜΕΝΗΕΚΕΙΘΕΝΑΓΗΝΕΓΚΕΝΕΜΕΔ
ΕΦΟΒΩΙΑΦΗΚΕΝΕΙΣΣΤΟΜΑΤΟΥΜΕΓΑΛΟΥΓ
ΟΤΑΜΟΥΤΟΥΝΑΥΣΙΓΟΡΟΥΓΟΡΡΩΔΕΝΑΥΣΙ
ΝΕΦΩΝΓΕΡΓΛΕΟΥΣΑΕΤΕΚΟΝΣΕΑΓΟΓΛΕΥΣ
ΑΣΑΜΟΛΙΣΓΟΤΕΔΕΥΡΟΑΘΗΝΑΖΕΚΑΤΗΓΑΓ
ΟΜΗΝΣΥΔΕΩΤΙΣΙΣΘΕΝΕΣΩΝΕΓΙΣΤΕΛΛΩΜ
ΗΟΛΙΓΩΡΕΙΔΕΙΓΑΡΤΗΝΓΥΝΑΙΚΑΑΝΑΖΗΤΕΙ
ΝΗΝΓΩΣΤΟΤΟΥΒΙΟΥΜΥΣΤΗΡΙΟΝΑΝΕΥΡΗ
ΣΚΑΙΑΝΑΙΡΕΙΝΗΝΓΟΥΓΑΡΑΣΧΗΔΙΑΤΟΝΣΟ
ΝΓΑΤΕΡΑΚΑΛΛΙΚΡΑΤΗΝΕΙΔΕΦΟΒΟΥΜΕΝΟ
ΣΗΔΙΑΑΛΛΟΤΙΑΥΤΟΣΛΕΙΓΕΙΤΟΥΕΡΓΟΥΓΑ

ΣΙΤΟΙΣΥΣΤΕΡΟΝΑΥΤΟΤΟΥΤΟΕΓΙΣΤΕΛΛΩΕ
ΩΣΓΟΤΕΑΓΑΘΟΣΤΙΣΓΕΝΟΜΕΝΟΣΤΩΓΥΡΙΛ
ΟΥΣΑΣΘΑΙΤΟΛΜΗΣΕΙΚΑΙΤΑΑΡΙΣΤΕΙΑΕΧΩΝ
ΒΑΣΙΛΕΥΣΑΙΤΩΝΑΝΘΡΩΓΩΝΑΓΙΣΤΑΜΕΝΔ
ΗΤΑΤΟΙΑΥΤΑΛΕΓΩΟΜΩΣΔΕΑΑΥΤΗΕΓΝΩΚ
ΑΟΥΚΕΨΕΥΣΑΜΗΝ

For general convenience in reading, I have here accurately
transcribed this inscription into the cursive character.

Ἀμενάρτας, τοῦ βασιλικοῦ γένους τοῦ Αἰγυπτίου, ἡ
τοῦ Καλλικράτους Ἴσιδος ἱερέως, ἣν οἱ μὲν θεοὶ τρέφουσι
τὰ δὲ δαιμόνια ὑποτάσσεται, ἤδη τελευτῶσα Τισισθένει
τῷ παιδὶ ἐπιστέλλει τάδε· συνέφυγον γάρ ποτε ἐκ τῆς
Αἰγυπτίας ἐπὶ Νεκτανέβου μετὰ τοῦ σοῦ πατρός, διὰ τὸν
ἔρωτα τὸν ἐμὸν ἐπιορκήσαντος. φυγόντες δὲ πρὸς νότου
διαπόντιοι καὶ κ'δ' μῆνας κατὰ τὰ παραθαλάσσια τῆς
Λιβύης τὰ πρός ἡλίου ἀνατολὰς πλανηθέντες, ἔνθαπερ
πέτρα τις μεγάλη, γλυπτὸν ὁμοίωμα Αἰθίοπος κεφαλῆς,
εἶτα ἡμέρας δ' ἀπὸ στόματος ποταμοῦ μεγάλου ἐκπεσόντες,
οἱ μέν κατεποντίσθημεν, οἱ δὲ νόσῳ ἀπεθάνομεν· τέλος
δὲ ὑπ' ἀγρίων ἀνθρώπων ἐφερόμεθα διὰ ἑλέων τε καὶ τενα-
γέων ἔνθαπερ πτηνῶν πλῆθος ἀποκρύπτει τὸν οὐρανὸν,
ἡμέρας ί, ἕως ἤλθομεν εἰς κοῖλόν τι ὄρος, ἔνθα ποτὲ μεγάλη
μὲν πόλις ἦν, ἄντρα δὲ ἀπείρονα· ἤγαγον δὲ ὡς βασίλειαν
τὴν τῶν ξένους χύτραις στεφανούντων, ἥτις μαγείᾳ μὲν
ἐχρῆτο ἐπιστήμῃ δὲ πάντων καὶ δὴ καὶ κάλλος καὶ ῥώμην
ἀγήρως ἦν· ἡ δὲ Καλλικράτους τοῦ σοῦ πατρὸς ἐρασθεῖσα
τὸ μὲν πρῶτον συνοικεῖν ἐβούλετο ἐμὲ δὲ ἀνελεῖν· ἔπειτα,
ὡς οὐκ ἀνέπειθεν, ἐμὲ γὰρ ὑπερεφίλει καὶ τὴν ξένην ἐφο-
βεῖτο, ἀπήγαγεν ἡμᾶς ὑπὸ μαγείας καθ' ὁδοὺς σφαλερὰς
ἔνθα τὸ βάραθρον τὸ μέγα, οὗ κατὰ στόμα ἔκειτο ὁ γέρων
ὁ φιλόσοφος τεθνεώς, ἀφικομένοις δ' ἔδειξε φῶς τοῦ βίου
εὐθύ, οἷον κίονα ἑλισσόμενον φωνὴν ἱέντα καθάπερ βροντῆς,
εἶτα διὰ πυρὸς βεβηκυῖα ἀβλαβὴς καὶ ἔτι καλλίων αὐτὴ
ἑαυτῆς ἐξεφάνη. ἐκ δὲ τούτων ὤμοσε καὶ τὸν σὸν πατέρα
ἀθάνατον ἀποδείξειν, εἰ συνοικεῖν οἱ βούλοιτο ἐμὲ δε ἀνελεῖν, οὐ γὰρ οὖν αὐτὴ ἀνελεῖν ἴσχυεν ὑπὸ τῶν ἡμεδαπῶν
ἦν καὶ αὐτὴ ἔχω μαγείας. ὁ δ' οὐδέν τι μᾶλλον ἤθελε,
τὼ χεῖρε τῶν ὀμμάτων προΐσχων ἵνα δὴ τὸ τῆς γυναικὸς
κάλλος μὴ ὁρῴη· ἔπειτα ὀργισθεῖσα κατεγοήτευσε μὲν
αὐτόν, ἀπολόμενον μέντοι κλάουσα καὶ ὀδυρομένη ἐκεῖθεν
ἀπήνεγκεν, ἐμὲ δὲ φόβῳ ἀφῆκεν εἰς στόμα τοῦ μεγάλου
ποταμοῦ τοῦ ναυσιπόρου, πόρρω δὲ ναυσίν, ἐφ' ὧνπερ
πλέουσα ἔτεκόν σε, ἀποπλεύσασα μόλις ποτὲ δεῦρο Ἀθή-
ναζε κατηγαγόμην. σὺ δέ, ὦ Τισίσθενες, ὧν ἐπιστέλλω
μὴ ὀλιγώρει· δεῖ γὰρ τὴν γυναῖκα ἀναζητεῖν ἤν πως τὸ τοῦ

λούσασθαι τολμήσει καὶ τὰ ἀριστεῖα ἔχων βασιλεῦσαι τῶν ἀνθρώπων· ἄπιστα μὲν δὴ τὰ τοιαῦτα λέγω, ὅμως δὲ ἃ αὐτὴ ἔγνωκα οὐκ ἐψευσάμην.

The English translation is, as I discovered on further investigation, and as the reader may easily see for himself by comparison, both accurate and elegant.

Besides the uncial writing on the convex side of the sherd, at the top, painted in dull red on what had once been the lip of the amphora, was the cartouche already mentioned as appearing on the *scarabœus,* which we had found in the casket. The hieroglyphics or symbols, however, were reversed, just as though they had been pressed on wax. Whether this was the cartouche of the original Kallikrates,[1] or of some Prince or Pharaoh from whom his wife Amenartas was descended, I am not sure, nor can I tell if it was drawn upon the sherd at the same time that the uncial Greek was inscribed, or copied more recently from the Scarab by some other member of the family. Nor was this all. At the foot of the writing, painted in the same dull red, appeared the outline of a somewhat rude drawing of the head and shoulders of a Sphinx wearing two feathers, symbols of majesty, which, though common enough upon the effigies of sacred bulls and gods, I have never before met with on a Sphinx.

Also on the right-hand side of this surface of the sherd, written obliquely in red on the space not covered by the uncial characters, and signed in blue paint, was the following quaint inscription:—

> IN EARTH AND SKIE AND SEA
> STRANGE THYNGES THER BE.
> HOC FECIT
> DOROTHEA VINCEY.

Perfectly bewildered, I turned the relic over. It was covered from top to bottom with notes and signatures in Greek, Latin, and English. The first in uncial Greek was by Tisisthenes, the son to whom the writing was addressed. It was, "I could not go. Tisisthenes to his son, Kallikrates." Here it is in fac-simile with its cursive equivalent:—

ΟΥΚΑΝΔΥΝΑΙΜΗΝΓΟΡΕΥΕϹΘΑΙΤΙϹΙϹΘΕΝΗ
ϹΚΑΛΛΙΚΡΑΤΕΙΤΩΙΓΑΙΔΙ

---

[1]The cartouche, if it be a true cartouche, cannot have been that of Kallikrates, as Mr. Holly suggests. Kallikrates was a priest and not entitled to a cartouche, which was the prerogative of Egyptian royalty, though he might have inscribed his name or title upon an *oval.*—EDITOR.

οὐκ ἂν δυναίμην πορεύεσθαι.
Τισισθένης Καλλικράτει τῷ παιδί.

This Kallikrates (probably in the Greek fashion, so named after his grandfather) evidently made some attempt to start on the quest, for his entry written in very faint and almost illegible uncial is, 'I ceased from my going, the gods being against me. Kallikrates to his son.' Here it is also:—

**ΤΩΝΘΕΩΝΑΝΤΙΣΤΑΝΤΩΝΕΓΑΥΣΑΜΗΝΤΗΣ
ΓΟΡΕΙΑΣΚΑΛΛΙΚΡΑΤΗΣΤΩΓΑΙΔΙ**

τῶν θεῶν ἀντιστάντων ἐπαυσάμην τῆς πορείας.
Καλλικράτης τῷ παιδί.

Between these two ancient writings, the second of which was inscribed upside down, and was so faint and worn that had it not been for the transcript of it executed by Vincey I should scarcely have been able to read it, since, owing to its having been written on that portion of the tile which, in the course of ages, had undergone most of the handling, it was nearly rubbed out, was the bold, modern-looking signature of one Lionel Vincey, 'Ætate sua 17,' inscribed thereon, as I think, by Leo's grandfather. To the right of this were the initials 'J. B. V.,' and below came a variety of Greek signatures, in uncial and cursive character, and what appeared to be some carelessly executed repetitions of the sentence (to my son), showing that the relic was passed on religiously from generation to generation.

The next thing legible after the Greek signatures was the word 'ROMAE, A.U.C.,' indicating that the family had now migrated to Rome. Unfortunately, however, with the exception of its termination (cvi) the date of their settlement there is for ever lost, for just where it had been placed a piece of the potsherd is broken away.

Then followed twelve Latin signatures, jotted about here and there, wherever there was a space upon the tile suitable to their inscription. These signatures, with three exceptions only, ended with the name 'Vindex' or 'the Avenger,' which seems to have been adopted by the family after its migration to Rome as a kind of equivalent to the Grecian 'Tisisthenes,' which also means an avenger. Ultimately, as might be expected, this Latin cognomen of Vindex was transformed first into De Vincey, and then into the plain, modern Vincey. It is curious to observe how this hereditary duty of revenge, bequeathed by an Egyptian who lived before the time of Christ, is thus, as it were, embalmed in an English family name.

A few of the Roman names inscribed upon the sherd I have since found mentioned in history and other records. They are, if I remember right,

> MVSSIVS. VINDEX
> SEX. VARIVS. MARVLLVS
> C. FVFIDIVS. C. F. VINDEX

and

> LABERIA POMPEIANA. CONIVX. MACRINI. VINDICIS

the last being, of course, the name of a Roman lady.

The following list, however, comprises all the Latin names upon the sherd:—

> C. CAECILIVS VINDEX
> M. AIMILIVS VINDEX
> SEX. VARIVS. MARVLLVS
> Q. SOSIVS PRISCVS SENECIO VINDEX
> L. VALERIVS COMINIVS VINDEX
> SEX. OTACILIVS. M. F.
> L. ATTIVS. VINDEX
> MVSSIVS VINDEX
> C. CAECILIVS VINDEX
> LICINIVS FAVSTVS
> LABERIA POMPEIANA CONIVX MACRINI VINDICIS
> MANILIA LVCILLA CONIVX MARVLLI VINDICIS

After the series of Roman names there is a gap of very many centuries. Nobody will ever know now what was the history of the relic during those dark ages, or how it came to be preserved in the family. My poor friend Vincey, it will be remembered, had told me that his Roman ancestors finally settled in Lombardy, and when Charlemagne invaded it, returned with him across the Alps, and made their home in Brittany, whence they crossed to England in the reign of Edward the Confessor. How he knew this I am not aware, for there is no reference to Lombardy or Charlemagne upon the tile, though, as will be seen presently, there is a reference to Brittany. To continue: the next entries on the sherd, if I may except a long splash either of blood or red colouring matter of some sort, consist of two crosses drawn in red pigment, probably representing Crusaders' swords, and a rather neat monogram ('D. V.') in scarlet and blue, perhaps executed by that same Dorothea Vincey who wrote, or rather painted, the doggerel couplet. To the left of this, inscribed in faint blue, are the initials A. V., and after them a date, 1800.

Then came what was perhaps as curious an item as anything upon this extraordinary relic of the past. It is executed in black letter, written over the crosses or Crusaders' swords, and dated fourteen hundred and forty-five. As the best plan will be to allow it to speak for itself, I here give the black-letter fac-simile, together with the original Latin without the contractions, from which it will be seen that the writer was a fair mediaeval Latinist. Further we discovered what is still more curious, an English version of the black-letter Latin. This, also written in black letter, we found inscribed on a second parchment that was in the coffer, apparently somewhat older in date than that on which was written the mediaeval Latin translation of the uncial Greek of which I shall speak presently. This I also give in full.

Fac-simile of Black-Letter Inscription on the Sherd of Amenartas.

Ista reliquia est valde misticum et myrificum opus quod maiores mei ex Armorica ſſ Brittania miore secu cōvehebāt et quidm scs clericus super pri meo in manu ferebat quod peitus illud destrueret affirmās quod esset ab ipso sathana cōflatū prestigiosa et dyabolica arte qre pter mevs cōfregit illud i dvas ptes qs quidm ego Johs de Uiceto salvas servavi et adaptavi sicut apparet die lūe. px poſt foſt heate Marie virͣa anni gre mccccxlv.

Expanded Version of the above Black-Letter Inscription.

'ISTA reliquia est valde misticum et myrificum opus, quod majores mei ex Armorica, scilicet Britannia Minore, secum convehebant; et quidam sanctus clericus semper patri meo in manu ferebat quod penitus illud destrueret, affirmans quod esset ab ipso Sathana conflatum prestigiosa et dyabolica arte, quare pater meus confregit illud in duas partes, quas quidem ego Johannes de Vinceto salvas servavi et adaptavi sicut apparet die lune proximo post festum beate Marie Virginis anni gratie MCCCCXLV.'

Fac-simile of the Old English Black-Letter Translation of the above Latin Inscription from the Sherd of Amenartas found inscribed upon a parchment.

Thys rellike ys a ryghte mistycall worke &
a marveylous ye whyche myne aunceteres
afore tyme dyd conveighe hider wt ym ffrom
Armoryke whe ys to seien Britayne ye lesse & a
certayne holye clerke shoulde allweyes beare my
ffadir on honde yt he owghte vttirly ffor to
ffrusshe ye same affirmynge yt yt was ffourmyd &
confflatyd off sathanas hym selffe by arte magike
& dyvellysshe wherefore my ffadir dyd take ye
same & to brast yt yn twepne but I John de
Uincey dyd save whool ye twepe ptes therof &
topeecyd ym togydder agayne soe as yee se on ys
deye mondaye next ffolowynge after ye ffeeste of
seynte Marye ye blessed vyrgyne yn ye yeere of
salvacioun ffowertene hundreth & ffyve & ffowrti.

*Modernised Version of the above Black-Letter
Translation.*

'THYS rellike ys a ryghte mistycall worke and a marvaylous,
ye whyche myne aunceteres aforetyme dyd conveigh hider with
them from Armoryke which ys to seien Britaine ye Lesse and a
certayne holye clerke should allweyes beare my fadir on honde
that he owghte uttirly for to frusshe ye same, affyrmynge that yt
was fourmed and conflatyd of Sathanas hym selfe by arte magike
and dyvellysshe wherefore my fadir dyd take ye same and tobrast
yt yn tweyne, but I, John de Vincey, dyd save whool ye tweye
partes therof and topeecyd them togydder agayne soe as yee se,
on this daye mondaye next followynge after ye feeste of Seynte
Marye ye Blessed Vyrgyne yn ye yeere of Salvacioun fowertene
hundreth and fyve and fowerti.'

The next and, save one, last entry was Elizabethan, and dated
1564: 'A most strange historie, and one that did cost my father
his life; for in seekynge for the place upon the east coast of
Africa, his pinnance was sunk by a Portuguese galleon off Lor-
enzo Marquez, and he himself perished.—JOHN VINCEY.'

Then came the last entry, which, to judge by the style of writing, had been made by some representative of the family in the
middle of the eighteenth century. It was a misquotation of the
well-known lines in 'Hamlet,' and ran thus: 'There are more

things in Heaven and earth than are dreamt of in your philosophy, Horatio.'[1]

And now there remained but one more document to be examined—namely, the ancient black-letter translation into mediæval Latin of the uncial inscription on the sherd. As will be seen, this translation was executed and subscribed in the year 1495, by a certain 'learned man,' Edmundus de Prato (Edmund Pratt) by name, licentiate in Canon Law, of Exeter College, Oxford, who had actually been a pupil of Grocyn, the first scholar who taught Greek in England.[2] No doubt, on the fame of this new learning reaching his ears, the Vincey of the day, perhaps that same John de Vincey who years before had saved the relic from destruction and made the black-letter entry on the sherd in 1445, hurried to Oxford to discover if perchance it might avail to solve the secret of the mysterious inscription. Nor was he disappointed, for the learned Edmundus was equal to the task. Indeed his rendering is so excellent an example of mediæval scholarship and Latinity that, even at the risk of sating the learned reader with too many antiquities, I have made up my mind to give it in facsimile, together with an expanded version for the benefit of those who find the contractions troublesome. The translation has several peculiarities, whereon this is not the place to dwell, but I would in passing call the attention of scholars to the passage 'duxerunt autem nos ad reginam *advenaslasaniscoronantium,*' which strikes me as a delightful rendering of the original,

Mediæval Black-Letter Latin Translation of the Uncial Inscription on the Sherd of Amenartas, executed by Edmundus de Prato in 1495.

Amenartas e gen. reg. Egyptii vxor Callicratis
  sacerdot Isidis quā dei fovēt demonia at=
tedūt filiol' suo Tisictheni iā moribūda ita mādat:
Effugi quodā ex Egypto regnāte Nectanebo cū
patre tuo, ppter mei amorē pejerato. Fugiētes

[1] Another thing that makes me fix the date of this entry at the middle of the eighteenth century is that, curiously enough, I have an acting copy of "Hamlet," written about 1740, in which these two lines are misquoted almost exactly in the same way, and I have little doubt but that the Vincey who wrote them on the potsherd heard them so misquoted at that date. Of course, the true reading of the lines is:—

There are more things in heaven and earth, Horatio,
Than are dreamt of in your philosophy.—L. H. H.

[2] Grocyn, the instructor of Erasmus, studied Greek under Chalcondylas the Byzantine at Florence, and first lectured in the Hall of Exeter College, Oxford, in 1491.—EDITOR.

autē v'sus Notū traus mare et xxiiij mēses p'r
litora Libye v'sus Oriētē erranī vbi est petra
quedā m̄gna scvlpta instar Ethioꝑ capis, deinde
dies iiij ab ost sium̄ m̄gni eiecti p'tim submersi
sumus p'tim morbo mortui sum̄ : in sine autē a
serꝟ hōībs portabamur ꝕr palvd et vada. vbi aviū
m'titvdo celū obūbrat dies x. donec advenim̄ ad
cabū quēdā montē, ubi olim m̄gna vrbs erat,
cauerne quoꝗ im̄ēse : dvxerūt autē nos ad reginā
Aduenassasamiscoronātiū que magicꝟ vtebasr et
peritia omniū reꝟ et saltē pvlcriſ et vigore īsēescī
bil' erat. Hec m̄gno patrꝟ tui amore ꝓcvlsa p'mū
q'dē ei coñubiū michi mortē parabat. postea v'ro
recvsāte Callicrate amore' mei et timore regine
affecto nos ꝓr magicā abduxit p'r vias horribil'
vbi est puteus ille ꝓsūdus, cuius iuxta aditū
iacebat senioꝟ philosophi cadauer, et advēiētib
mōstrabit ssam̄ā Uite erectā, īstar columne volu꞊
tātis, voces emittētē ꝗsi tonitrvs : tūc ꝓr ignē
īpetu nociuo expers trāsiit et iā ipsa sese formosior
visa est.

Quib sacꝟ iurabit se patrē tuū quoꝗ im̄ortalē
ostēsurā esse, si mé prius occisa regine cōtvberniū.
mallet ; neꝗ enī ipsa me occidere valuit, ꝓpter nos꞊
tratū m̄gicā cuius egomet ꝓtem habeo. Ille vero
nichil huius geñ maluit, manib ante ocuꝟ passis
ne mulierꝟ formositatē adspiceret : postea eū m̄gica
ꝓcussit arte, at mortuū esserebat īde cū ssetib et
vagitib, me ꝓr timorē expulit ad ostiū m̄gni
ssumiñ veliuoli porro in nave in qua te peperi,
uix post dies hvc Athenas invecta sū. At tu,
O Tisistheñ, ne q'd quorū mādo nauci sac : necesse
enī est mulierē 'exqvirere si qva Uite mysteriū
īpetres et vidicare, quātū in te est, patrē tuū
Callicraꝟ in regine morte. Sin timore seu aliꝗ
cavsa rē relīquis īsectā, hoc ipsū oīb posterꝟ mādo

dū bonꝰ ꝗꝫ inueniatur qꝫi ignis lauacrū nō
prħorreſcet et ꝑtentia digñ dōlabiꝼ ħōīū.
Talia dico incredibilia ꝗdē at mñe ꬃcta de reꝫ
micħi cognitis.

Hec Grece ſcripta Latine reddidit ꝫir doctus
Edīīdꝫ de Prato, in Decretis Licenciatus e Coll.
pupillis, Jꝰ. Apr. Aº. Dūi. MCCCCLXXXXº.

*Expanded Version of the above Mediæval Latin
Translation.*

AMENARTAS, e genere regio Egyptii, uxor Callicratis, sacerdotis
Isidis, quam dei fovent demonia attendunt, filiolo suo Tisistheni
jam moribunda ita mandat: Effugi quondam ex Egypto, regnante
Nectanebo, cum patre tuo, propter mei amorem pejerato. Fugi-
entes autem versus Notum trans mare, et viginti quatuor menses
per litora Libye versus Orientem errantes, ubi est petra quedam
magna sculpta instar Ethiopis capitis, deinde dies quatuor ab
ostio fluminis magni ejecti partim submersi sumus partim morbo
mortui sumus: in fine autem a feris hominibus portabamur per
paludes et vada, ubi avium multitudo celum obumbrat, dies
decem, donec advenimus ad cavum quendam montem, ubi olim
magna urbs erat, caverne quoque immense; duxerunt autem nos
ad reginam Advenaslasaniscoronantium, que magica utebatur et
peritia omnium rerum, et saltem pulcritudine et vigore insenes-
cibilis erat. Hec magno patris tui amore perculsa, primum
quidem ei connubium michi mortem parabat; postea vero, recu-
sante Callicrate, amore mei et timore regine affecto, nos per
magicam abduxit per vias horribiles ubi est puteus ille profundus,
cujus juxta aditum jacebat senioris philosophi cadaver, et ad-
venientibus monstravit flammam Vite erectam, instar columne
volutantis, voces emittentem quasi tonitrus: tunc per ignem im-
petu nocivo expers transiit et jam ipsa sese formosior visa est.

Quibus factis juravit se patrem tuum quoque immortalem
ostensuram esse, si me prius occisa regine contubernium mallet;
neque enim ipsa me occidere valuit, propter nostratum magicam
cujus egomet partem habeo. Ille vero nichil hujus generis male-
bat, manibus ante oculos passis, ne mulieris formositatem
adspiceret: postea illum magica percussit arte, at mortuum ef-
ferebat inde cum fletibus et vagitibus, et me per timorem expulit
ad ostium magni fluminis, velivoli, porro in nave, in qua te peperi,
vix post dies huc Athenas vecta sum. At tu, O Tisisthenes, ne

quid quorum mando nauci fac: necesse enim est mulierem ex-
quirere si qua Vite mysterium impetres et vindicare, quantam
in te est, patrem tuum Callicratem in regine morte. Sin timore
seu aliqua causa rem relinquis infectam, hoc ipsum omnibus
posteris mando, dum bonus quis inveniatur qui ignis lavacrum
non perhorrescet, et potentia dignus dominabitur hominum.

Talia dico incredibilia quidem at minime ficta de rebus michi
cognitis.

Hec Grece scripta Latine reddidit vir doctus Edmundus de
Prato, in Decretis Licenciatus, e Collegio Exoniensi Oxoniensi
doctissimi Grocyni quondam e pupillis, Idibus Aprilis Anno
Domini MCCCCLXXXXV°.

"Well," I said, when at length I had read out and carefully
examined these writings and paragraphs, at least those of them
that were still easily legible, "that is the conclusion of the whole
matter, Leo, and now you can form your own opinion on it. I
have already formed mine."

"And what is it?" he asked, in his quick way.

"It is this. I believe the potsherd to be perfectly genuine,
and that, wonderful as it may seem, it has come down in your
family from since the fourth century before Christ. The entries
absolutely prove it, therefore, however improbable it may seem,
the fact must be accepted. But there I stop. That your remote
ancestress, the Egyptian princess, or some scribe under her direction, wrote that which we see on the sherd I have no doubt, nor
have I the slightest doubt but that her sufferings and the loss
of her husband had turned her head and that she was not of
sound mind when she did write it."

"How do you account for what my father saw and heard
there?" asked Leo.

"Coincidence. No doubt there are bluffs on the coast of
Africa that look something like a man's head, and plenty of
people who speak bastard Arabic. Also, I believe that there
are lots of swamps. Another thing is, Leo, though I am sorry
to say it, I do not think that your poor father was quite sane
when he wrote that letter. He had met with a great trouble,
also he had allowed this story to prey on his imagination, and
he was a very imaginative man. Anyway, I believe that the
legend as it reaches us is rubbish. I know that there are curious
forces in nature which we rarely meet with, and that, when we
do meet them, we cannot understand. But until I see it with
my own eyes, which I am not likely to do, I never will believe
that there exist means of avoiding death, even for a time, or

that there is or was a white sorceress living in the heart of an African swamp. It is bosh, my boy, all bosh!—What do you say, Job?"

"I say, sir, that it is a lie, and, if it is true, I hope Mr. Leo won't meddle with no such things, for no good can't come of it."

"Perhaps you are both right," said Leo, very quietly. "I express no opinion. But I say this. I intend to set the matter at rest once and for all, and if you won't come with me I will go by myself."

I looked at the young man, and saw that he meant what he said. When Leo means what he says one may always know it by a curious expression about the mouth, which has been a trick of his from a child. Now, as a matter of fact, I had no intention of allowing Leo to go anywhere by himself, for my own sake, if not for his. I was far too much attached to him for that. I am not a man of many ties or affections. Circumstances have been against me in this respect, and men and women shrink from me, or at least I fancy that they do, which comes to the same thing, thinking, perhaps, that my somewhat forbidding exterior is a key to my character. Rather than be thus shunned I have, to a great extent, retired from society, and cut myself off from those opportunities which with most men result in the formation of ties more or less intimate. Therefore Leo was all the world to me—brother, child, and friend—and until he wearied of me, where he went there I should go too. But, of course, it would not do to let him see how great a hold he had over me; so I cast about for some means whereby I might surrender with a good grace.

"Yes, I shall go, Uncle," he repeated; "and if I don't find the 'rolling Pillar of Life,' at any rate I shall get some first-class shooting."

Here was my opportunity, and I took it.

"Shooting?" I said. "Ah! yes; I never thought of that. It must be a very wild stretch of country, and full of big game. I have always wanted to kill a buffalo before I die. Do you know, my boy, I don't believe in the quest, but I do believe in big game, and really on the whole, if, after thinking it over, you make up your mind to start, I will take a holiday, and come with you."

"Ah," said Leo, "I thought that you would not lose such a chance. But how about money? We shall want a good lot."

"You need not trouble about that," I answered. "There is all your income which has been accumulating for years, and besides that I have saved two-thirds of what your father left to me, as I consider, in trust for you. There is plenty of cash."

"Very well, then, we may as well stow these things away and go up to town to see about our guns. By the way, Job, are you coming too? It's time you began to see the world."

"Well, sir," answered Job, stolidly, "I don't hold much with foreign parts, but if both you gentlemen are going you will want somebody to look after you, and I am not the man to stop behind after serving you for twenty years."

"That's right, Job," said I. "You won't find out anything wonderful, but you will get some good shooting. And now look here, both of you. I won't have a word said to a living soul about this nonsense," and I pointed to the potsherd. "If it were known, and anything happened to me, my next of kin would dispute my will on the ground of insanity, and I should become the laughing-stock of Cambridge."

That day three months we were on the ocean, bound for Zanzibar.

CHAPTER IV

THE SQUALL

How different is the scene whereof I have now to tell from that which has just been told! Gone are the quiet College rooms, gone the wind-swayed English elms, the cawing rooks, and the familiar volumes on the shelves, and in their place there rises a vision of the great calm ocean gleaming in shaded silver lights beneath the beams of a full African moon. A gentle breeze fills the huge sail of our dhow, and draws us through the water that ripples musically against her sides. Most of the men are sleeping forward, for it is near midnight, but a stout, swarthy Arab, Mahomed by name, stands at the tiller, lazily steering by the stars. Three miles or more to our starboard is a low, dim line. It is the Eastern shore of Central Africa. We are running to the southward, before the north-east monsoon, between the mainland and the reef that for hundreds of miles fringes this perilous coast. The night is quiet, so quiet that a whisper can be heard fore and aft the dhow; so quiet that a faint booming sound rolls across the water to us from the distant land.

The Arab at the tiller holds up his hand, and says one word:— "*Simba* (lion)!"

We all sit up and listen. Then it comes again, a slow majestic sound that thrills us to the marrow.

"To-morrow by ten o'clock," I say, "we ought, if the captain is not out in his reckoning, which I think very probable, to make this mysterious rock with a man's head, and begin our shooting."

"And begin our search for the ruined city and the Fire of Life," corrected Leo, taking his pipe from his mouth, and laughing a little.

"Nonsense!" I answered. "You were airing your Arabic with that man at the tiller this afternoon. What did he tell you? He has been trading (slave-trading probably) up and down these latitudes for half of his iniquitous life, and once landed on this very 'man' rock. Did he ever hear anything of the ruined city or the caves?"

"No," answered Leo. "He says that the country is all swamp behind, and full of snakes, especially pythons, and game, and that no man lives there. But then there is a belt of swamp all along the East African coast, so that does not go for much."

"Yes," I said, "it does—it goes for malaria. You see what sort of an opinion these gentry have of the country. Not one of them will come with us. They think that we are mad, and upon my word I believe that they are right. If ever we see old England again I shall be astonished. However, it does not greatly matter to me at my age, but I am anxious for you, Leo, and for Job. It's a Tom Fool's business, my boy."

"All right, Uncle Horace. So far as I am concerned, I am willing to take my chance. Look! What is that cloud?" and he pointed to a dark blotch upon the starry sky some miles astern of us.

"Go and ask the man at the tiller," I said.

He rose, stretched his arms, and went. Presently he returned.

"He says it is a squall, but that it will pass far on one side of us."

Just then Job came up, looking very stout and English is his shooting-suit of brown flannel, and with a sort of perplexed appearance upon his honest round face that had been very common with him since he sailed into these strange waters.

"Please, sir," he said, touching his sun hat, which was stuck on to the back of his head in a somewhat ludicrous fashion, "as we have got all those guns and things in the whale-boat astern, to say nothing of the provisions in the lockers, I think it would be best if I slipped down and slept in her. I don't like the looks" (here he dropped his voice to a portentous whisper) "of these black gentry; they have such a wonderful thievish way about them. Supposing now that some of them were to sneak into the boat at night and cut the cable, and make off with her? That would be a pretty go, that would."

The whale-boat, I may explain, was one specially built for us at Dundee, in Scotland. We had brought it with us as we knew that this coast is a network of creeks, and that we might require something in which to navigate them. She was a beautiful boat, thirty feet in length, with a centre-board for sailing, copper-bottomed to keep the worm out of her, and full of water-tight compartments. The captain of the dhow had told us that when we reached the rock, which he knew, and that appeared to be identical with the one described upon the sherd and by Leo's father he would probably not be able to run up to it on account of the shallows and breakers. Therefore we had employed three hours that very morning, whilst we were totally becalmed, the wind having dropped at sunrise, in transferring most of our goods and chattles to the whale-boat, and placing the guns, ammunition, and preserved provisions in the water-tight lockers specially prepared for them, so that when we did sight the fabled rock we should have nothing to do but get into the boat, and run her ashore. Another reason that induced us to take this precautionary step was that Arab captains are apt to run past the point which they are making, either from carelessness or owing to a mistake in its identity. Now, as sailors know, it is quite impossible for a dhow that is only rigged to run before the monsoon to beat back against it. Therefore we made our boat ready to row for the rock at any moment.

"Yes, Job," I said, "perhaps it would be as well. There are plenty of blankets there, only be careful to keep out of the moon, as it may turn your head or blind you."

"Lord, sir! I don't think it would much matter of it did, it is that turned already with the sight of these blackamoors and their filthy, thieving ways. They are only fit for muck, they are; and they smell bad enough for it already."

Job, it will be perceived, was no admirer of the manners and customs of our dark-skinned brothers.

Accordingly we hauled up the boat by the tow-rope till it was right under the stern of the dhow, and Job bundled into her with all the grace of a falling sack of potatoes. Then we returned and sat down on the deck again, and smoked and talked in little gusts and jerks. The night was so lovely, and our brains were so full of suppressed excitement of one sort and another, that we did not feel inclined to turn in. For nearly an hour we sat thus, and then, I think, we both dozed off. At least I have a faint recollection of Leo sleepily explaining that the head was not a bad place to hit a buffalo, if you could catch him exactly between the horns, or send your bullet down his throat, or some nonsense of the sort.

I remember no more; till quite suddenly—a frightful roar of

wind, a shriek of terror from the awakening crew, and a whip-like sting of water in our faces. Some of the men ran to let go the halyards and lower the sail, but the parrel jammed and the yard would not come down. I sprang to my feet and hung on to a rope. The sky aft was dark as pitch, but the moon still shone brightly ahead of us and lit up the blackness. Beneath its sheen a huge white-topped breaker twenty feet high or more, was rushing on to us. It was on the break—the moon shone on its crest and tipped its foam with light. On it rushed beneath the inky sky, driven by the awful squall behind it. Suddenly, in the twinkling of an eye, I saw the black shape of the whale-boat cast high into the air on the crown of the breaking wave. Then—a shock of water, a wild rush of boiling foam, and I was clinging for my life to the shroud, ay, swept straight out from it like a flag in a gale.

We were pooped.

The wave passed. It seemed to me that I was under water for minutes—really it was seconds. I looked forward. The blast had torn out the great sail, and high in the air it was fluttering away to leeward like a huge wounded bird. Now for a moment there was comparative calm, and in it I heard Job's voice yelling wildly, "Come here to the boat!"

Bewildered and half drowned as I was, I had the sense to rush aft. I felt the dhow sinking beneath me—she was full of water. Under her counter the whale-boat was tossing furiously, and I saw the Arab Mahomed, who had been steering, leap into her. I gave one desperate pull at the taut tow-rope to bring her along-side. Wildly I sprang also, Job caught me by one arm, and I rolled into the bottom of the boat. Down went the dhow bodily, and as she sank Mahomed drew his curved knife and severed the fibre rope by which we were fast to her, and in another second we were driving before the storm over the place where the dhow had been.

"Great Heaven!" I shrieked, "where is Leo? *Leo! Leo!*"

"He's gone, sir, God help him!" roared Job into my ear; and such was the fury of the squall that his voice sounded like a whisper.

I wrung my hands in agony. Leo was drowned, and I was left alive to mourn him.

"Look out," yelled Job; "here comes another."

I turned; a second huge wave was overtaking us, which I half hoped would drown me. With a curious fascination I watched its awful advent. The moon was nearly hidden now by the wreaths of the rushing storm, but a little light still caught the crest of the devouring breaker. There was something dark on it—a piece of wreckage. It was on us now, and the boat was nearly full of water. But she was built in air-tight compartments—Heaven bless the man who invented them!—and lifted up through it like a swan. Amidst the foam and turmoil I saw the black thing on the wave hurrying right at me. I put out my right arm to ward it from me, and my hand closed on another arm, the wrist of which my fingers gripped like a vice. I am a very strong man, and had something to hold to, but my shoulder was nearly torn from its socket by the strain and weight of the floating body. Had the rush lasted another two seconds I must either have let go or gone with it. But it passed, leaving us up to our knees in water.

"Bail out! bail out!" shouted Job, suiting the action to the word.

But I could not bail just then, for as the moon went out and left us in total darkness, one faint, flying ray of light lit upon the face of the man I had gripped, who was now half lying, half floating in the bottom of the boat.

It was *Leo.* Leo brought back by the wave—back, dead or alive, from the very jaws of Death.

"Bail out! bail out!" yelled Job, "or we shall founder."

I seized a large tin bowl with a handle to it, which was fixed under one of the seats, and the three of us bailed away for dear life. The furious tempest drove over and round us, flinging the boat this way and that, the wind and the storm wreaths and the sheets of stinging spray blinded and bewildered us, but through it all we worked like demons with the wild exhilaration of despair, for even despair can exhilarate. One minute! three minutes! six minutes! The boat began to lighten, and no fresh wave swamped us. Five minutes more, and she was almost clear. Then, suddenly, above the awful shriekings of the hurricane came a duller, deeper roar. Great Heavens! It was the voice of breakers!

At that instant the moon began to shine forth again—this time behind the path of the squall. Out far across the torn bosom of the ocean shot the ragged arrows of her light, and there, half a mile ahead of us, ran a white line of foam, then a little space of open-mouthed blackness, and beyond another streak of white. It was the breakers, and their roar sounded clearer and yet more clear as we sped down upon them like a swallow. There they were, boiling up in snowy spouts of spray, smiting and gnashing their crests together like the gleaming teeth of hell.

"Take the tiller, Mahomed!" I roared in Arabic. "We must try and shoot them." At the same moment I seized an oar, and got it out, motioning to Job to do likewise.

Mahomed clambered aft, and took hold of the tiller, and with some difficulty Job, who had at times pulled a tub upon the homely Cam, shipped his oar. In another minute the boat's head was straight on to the ever-nearing foam, towards which she plunged and tore with the speed of a racehorse. Just in front of us the first line of breakers seemed a little thinner than to the right or left, for here was a gap of rather deeper water. I turned and pointed to it.

"Steer for your life, Mahomed!" I yelled. He was a skilful steersman, and well acquainted with the dangers of this most perilous coast, and I saw him grip the tiller, bend his heavy frame forward, and stare at the foaming terror till his big round eyes looked as though they would start out of his head. The send of the sea was driving that boat's head round to starboard. If we struck the line of breakers fifty yards to starboard of the gap we must sink, for there was a great field of twisting, spouting waves. Mahomed planted his foot against the seat before him, and glancing at him, I saw his brown toes spread out like a hand beneath the weight he put upon them as he took the strain of the tiller. She came round a bit, but not enough. I roared to Job to back water, whilst I dragged and laboured at my oar. She answered now, and not too soon.

Heavens, we were in them! And then followed a couple of minutes of heart-breaking excitement such as I cannot hope to describe. All that I remember is a shrieking sea of foam, out of which the billows rose here, there, and everywhere like avenging ghosts from their ocean grave. Once we were whirled right round, but either by chance, or through Mahomed's skilful steering, the boat's head came straight again before a breaker filled us. One more—a monster. We were through it or over it—more through than over—and then, with a wild yell of exultation from the Arab, we shot out between the teeth-like lines of gnashing waves into the comparatively smooth water of the mouth of sea.

But we were nearly full of water again, and not more than half a mile ahead raved the second line of breakers. Again we set to and bailed furiously. Fortunately the storm had now quite gone by, and the moon shone brightly, revealing a rocky headland running half mile or more out into the sea, of which point these breakers appeared to be a continuation. At any rate, they boiled around its foot. Probably the ridge that formed the headland pushed out into the ocean, only at a lower level, and made the reef also. This bluff terminated in a curious peak that seemed to be not more than a mile away from us. Just as we bailed the boat clear for the second time, Leo, to my immense relief, opened his eyes, remarking that the clothes had tumbled off his bed, and that he supposed it was time to get up for chapel. I told him to shut his eyes and keep quiet, which he did without in the slightest degree realising the position. As for myself, his reference to chapel made me reflect, with a sort of sick longing, on my comfortable rooms at Cambridge. Why had I been such a fool as to leave them? This is a reflection that has often recurred to me since that night, and with an ever-increasing force.

But now again we were drifting down on the breakers, though with lessened speed, for the wind had fallen, and only the current or the tide (it afterwards proved to be the tide) was driving us.

Another minute, and with a dismal howl to Allah from the Arab, a pious ejaculation from myself, and something that was not pious from Job, we were in them. Thereon the performance, down to our final escape, repeated itself, only not quite so violently. Mahomed's skilful steering and the air-tight compartments saved our lives. In five minutes we were through, and drifting—for we were too exhausted to do anything to help ourselves except keep the boat's head straight—with the most startling rapidity round the headland which I have described.

Round we went with the tide, until we got well under the lee of the point, when suddenly the speed slackened, we ceased to make way, and finally appeared to be in dead water. The storm had passed, leaving a calm, clean-washed sky behind it; the headland intercepted the heavy sea that was occasioned by the squall, and the tide, which had been running so fiercely up the river (for we were now in the mouth of a river), was sluggish as it turned, so we floated at peace, and before the moon went down managed to bail out the boat thoroughly and get her a little ship-shape. Leo was sleeping profoundly, and on the whole I judged it wise not to wake him. It was true he was lying in wet clothes, but the night was now so warm that I thought (and so did Job) that this was not likely to injure a man of his unusually vigorous constitution. Besides, we had no dry change at hand.

Presently the moon went down, and we were left floating on the waters, now only heaving like some troubled woman's breast, with leisure to reflect upon all that we had gone through and all that we had escaped. Job stationed himself at the bow, Mahomed kept his post at the tiller, and I sat on a seat in the middle of the boat close to where Leo was lying.

The moon went slowly down in loveliness; she departed into the depth of the horizon, and long veil-like shadows crept up the sky through which the stars appeared. Soon, however, they too began to pale before a splendour in the east, and the advent of the dawn declared itself in the newborn blue of heaven. Quieter and yet more quiet grew the sea, quiet as the soft mist that brooded on her bosom, and covered up her troubling, as in our tempestuous life the transitory wreaths of sleep brood upon a pain-racked soul, causing it to forget its sorrow. From the east to the west sped those angels of the Dawn, from sea to sea, from mountain-top to mountain-top, scattering light from breast and wing. On they sped out of the darkness, perfect, glorious; on, over the quiet sea, over the low coast-line, and the swamps beyond, and the mountains above them; over those who slept in peace and those who woke in sorrow; over the evil and the good; over the living and the dead; over the wide world and all that breathes or has breathed thereon.

It was a beautiful sight, and yet a sad one, perhaps because of its excess of beauty. The arising sun the setting sun! There we have the symbol and the type of humanity, and of all things with which humanity has to do. On that morning this came home to me with a peculiar force. The sun that rose to-day for us had set last night for eighteen of our fellow-voyagers!—had set everlastingly for eighteen whom we knew!

The dhow had gone down with them; they were tossing among the rocks and seaweed, so much human drift on the great ocean of Death! And we four were saved!

CHAPTER V

THE HEAD OF THE ETHIOPIAN

At length the heralds and forerunners of the royal sun had done their work, and, searching out the shadows, caused them to flee away. Then up he came in glory from his ocean bed, and flooded the earth with warmth and light. I sat there in the boat listening to the gentle lapping of the water and watched him rise, till presently the slight drift of the boat brought the odd-shaped rock, or peak, at the end of the promontory which we had weathered with so much peril, between me and the majestic sight, blotting it from my view, I still continued, however, to stare at the rock, absently enough, till presently it became edged with the fire of the growing light behind it. Then I started, as well I might, for I perceived that the top of the peak, which was about eighty feet high by one hundred and fifty thick at its base, was shaped like a negro's head and face, whereon was stamped a most fiendish and terrifying expression. There was no doubt about it; before me were the thick lips, fat cheeks, and squat nose standing out with startling clearness against that flaming background. There, too, was the round skull, washed into shape perhaps by thousands of years of wind and weather, and, to complete the resemblance, there was a scrubby growth of weeds or lichen upon it, which against the sun looked for all the world like the wool on a colossal negro's head. Certainly it was very odd; so odd that now I believe this is not a mere freak of nature but a gigantic monument fashioned, like the well-known Egyptian Sphinx, by a forgotten people out of a pile of rock that lent itself to their design, perhaps as an emblem of warning and defiance to any enemies who approached the harbour. Unfortunately, we were never able to ascertain whether or not this was the case, inasmuch as the rock is difficult of access both from the land and the waterside, and we had other things to attend to. To-day, considering the matter in the light of what we saw afterwards, I believe that it was fashioned by man; but however this may be, there the effigy stands, and stares from age to age across the changing ocean—there it stood two thousand years and more ago, when Amenartas, the Egyptian princess, and the wife of Leo's remote ancestor Kallikrates, gazed upon its devilish face—and there I have no doubt it will stand when as many centuries as are numbered between her day and our own are added to the year which bore us to oblivion.

"What do you think of that, Job?" I asked of our retainer, who was seated on the edge of the boat, trying to absorb as much sunshine as possible, and generally looking very wretched, and I pointed to the fiery and demoniacal head.

"Oh Lord, sir!" answered Job, who now perceived the object for the first time, "I think that the Old Gentleman must have been sitting for his portrait on them rocks."

I laughed, and the laugh woke up Leo.

"Hullo!" he said, "what's the matter with me? I am all stiff. Where is the dhow? Give me some brandy, please."

"You may be thankful that you are not stiffer, my boy," I answered. "The dhow is sunk, everybody on board of her is drowned with the exception of us four, and your own life was only saved by a miracle." Then whilst Job, now that it was light enough, searched about in a locker for the brandy for which Leo asked, I told him the history of our night's adventure.

"Great Heavens!" he said faintly! "and to think that we should have been chosen to live through it!"

By this time the brandy was forthcoming, and we all took a good pull, and thankful enough we were for it. Also the sun

was beginning to gain strength, and warm our chilled bones, for
we had been wet through for five hours or more.

"Why," said Leo, with a gasp, as he put down the brandy
bottle, "there is the head the writing talks of, the 'rock carven like
the head of an Ethiopian.'"

"Yes," I said, "there it is."

"Well, then," he answered, "the whole thing is true."

"I don't at all see that it follows," I answered. "We knew
this head was here; your father saw it. Very likely it is not the
same head of which the writing tells; or if it is, it proves nothing."

Leo smiled at me in a superior way. "You are an unbelieving
Jew, Uncle Horace," he said. "Those who live will see."

"Exactly so," I answered; "and now perhaps you will observe
that we are drifting across a sandbank into the mouth of the
river. Get hold of your oar, Job, and we will row in and see if
we can find a place to land."

The river mouth which we are entering did not appear to be
a very wide one, though as yet the long banks of steaming mist
that clung about its shores had not lifted sufficiently to enable
us to see its exact measure. As is the case with nearly every
East African river, there was a considerable bar at the mouth,
which when the wind was on shore and the tide running out,
no doubt was absolutely impassable even for a boat drawing
only a few inches. But as things were it proved manageable
enough, and we did not ship a cupful of water. In twenty minutes we were well across, with but slight assistance from ourselves, and being carried by a strong though somewhat variable
breeze straight up the harbour. By this time the mist had
vanished beneath the sun, which was growing uncomfortably
hot, and we saw that the mouth of the little estuary was here
about half a mile across, and that the banks were very marshy,
and crowded with crocodiles lying on the mud like logs. A mile
or so ahead of us, however, lay what appeared to be a strip of
firm land, and for this we steered. In another quarter of an hour
we were there, and making the boat fast to a beautiful tree with
broad shining leaves, and flowers of the magnolia species, only
they were rose-coloured and not white,[1] which hung over the
water, we disembarked. This done we undressed, washed ourselves, and spread our clothes in the sun to dry, together with
the contents of the boat, which they did very quickly. Then, taking shelter from the heat under some trees, we made a hearty
breakfast off an excellent potted tongue, of which we had brought

[1]There is a known species of magnolia with pink flowers. It is indigenous
in Sikkim, and known as *Magnolia Campbellii.*—EDITOR.

a quantity with us, congratulating ourselves the while on our good fortune in having loaded and provisioned the boat on the previous day before the hurricane destroyed the dhow. By the time that we had finished our meal our clothes were quite dry, and we hastened to put them on, feeling not a little refreshed. Indeed, with the exception of weariness and a few bruises, none of us was the worse for the terrifying adventure which had been fatal to all companions. Leo, it is true, had been half drowned, but that is no great matter to a vigorous young athlete of five-and-twenty.

After breakfast we started to look round us. We were on a strip of dry land about two hundred yards broad by five hundred long, bordered on one side by the river, and on the other three by endless desolate swamps, that stretched far as the eye could reach. This strip of land was raised about twenty-five feet above the plain of the surrounding morasses and the river-level: indeed it had every appearance of having been made by the hand of man.

"This place has been a wharf," said Leo, dogmatically.

"Nonsense," I answered. "Who would be stupid enough to build a wharf in the middle of these dreadful marshes in a country inhabited by savages—that is, if it is inhabited at all?"

"Perhaps it was not always marsh, and perhaps the people were not always savage," he said drily, looking down the steep bank, for we were standing by the river. "See there," he went on, pointing to a spot where the hurricane of the previous night had torn up by its roots one of the magnolia trees which had grown on the extreme edge of the bank just where it sloped down to the water, and lifted a large cake of earth with them. "Is not that stonework? If not, it is very like it."

"Nonsense," I said again; but we clambered down to the spot, and stood between the upturned roots and the bank.

"Well?" he said.

But this time I did not answer. I only whistled. For there, bared by the removal of the earth, was an undoubted facing of solid stone laid in large blocks, bound together with brown cement so hard that I could make no impression on it with the file in my shooting-knife. Nor was this all; seeing something projecting through the soil at the bottom of the bared patch of walling, I removed the loose earth with my hands, and revealed a huge stone ring, a foot or more in diameter, and about three inches thick. This discovery absolutely silenced me.

"Looks rather like a wharf where good-sized vessels have been moored, does it not Uncle Horace?" said Leo, with an excited grin.

I tried to say "Nonsense" again, but the word stuck in my throat—the worn ring spoke for itself. In some past age vessels *had* been moored there, and this stone wall was undoubtedly the remnant of a solidly constructed wharf. Probably the city to which it had belonged lay buried beneath the swamp behind it.

"Begins to look as though there were something in the story after all, Uncle Horace," said the exultant Leo; and reflecting on the mysterious negro's head and the equally mysterious stone-work, I made no direct reply.

"A country like Africa," I said, "is sure to be full of the relics of long dead and forgotten civilisations. Nobody knows the age of the Egyptian civilisations, and very likely it had offshoots. Then there were the Babylonians and the Phœnicians, and the Persians, and other peoples, all of them more or less civilised, to say nothing of the Jews whom everybody 'wants' nowadays. It is possible that they, or any one of them, may have had colonies or trading stations about here. Remember those buried Persian cities that the Consul showed us at Kilwa."[1]

"Quite so," said Leo, "but that is not what you said before."

"Well, what is to be done now?" I asked, turning the conversation.

As no answer was forthcoming we walked to the edge of the swamp and looked over it. Apparently it was boundless, and vast flocks of every sort of waterfowl flew from its recesses, till it was sometimes difficult to see the sky. Also, now that the sun was heightening it drew sickly looking clouds of poisonous vapour from the surface of the marsh and from the scummy pools of stagnant water.

"Two things are clear to me," I said, addressing my three companions, who stared at this spectacle in dismay: "first, that we can't go across there" (I pointed to the swamp), "and, secondly, that if we stop here we shall certainly die of fever."

"That's as plain as a haystack, sir," said Job.

"Very well, then; there are two alternatives before us. One

[1]Near Kilwa, on the East Coast of Africa, about 400 miles south of Zanzibar, is a cliff which has been recently washed by the waves. On the top of this cliff are Persian tombs known to be at least seven centuries old by the dates still legible upon them. Beneath these tombs is a layer of *débris* representing a city. Farther down the cliff is a second layer representing an older city, and farther down still a third layer, the remains of yet another city of vast and unknown antiquity. Beneath the bottom city were recently found some specimens of glazed earthenware, such as are occasionally to be met with on that coast to this day. I believe that they are now in the possession of Sir John Kirk.—EDITOR.

is to 'bout ship, and try to run for some port in the whale-boat, which would be a sufficiently risky proceeding, and the other to sail or row on up the river, and see where we come to."

"I don't know what you are going to do," said Leo, setting his mouth, "but I am going up that river."

Job turned up the whites of his eyes and groaned, and the Arab murmured "Allah," and groaned also. For my part, I remarked sweetly that as we seemed to be between the devil and the deep sea, it did not much matter where we went. But in reality I was as anxious to proceed as Leo. The colossal negro's head and the stone wharf had excited my curiosity to an extent of which I was secretly ashamed, and I was prepared to gratify it at any cost. Accordingly, having carefully fitted the mast, restowed the boat, and got out our rifles, we embarked. Fortunately the wind was blowing on shore from the ocean, so we were able to hoist the sail. Indeed, we afterwards discovered that as a general rule the wind set on shore from daybreak for some hours, and off shore again at sunset. The explanation that I offer of this fact is, that when the earth is cooled by the dew and the night the hot air rises, and the draught rushes in from the sea till the sun has once more heated it through. At least that appears to be the rule in this latitude.

Taking advantage of this favouring wind, we sailed merrily up the river for three or four hours. Once we came across a school of hippopotami, which rose, and bellowed dreadfully at us within ten or a dozen fathoms of the boat, much to Job's alarm, and, I will confess, to my own. These were the first hippopotami that we had ever seen, and, to judge by their insatiable curiosity, I should say that we were the first white men whom they had ever seen. Upon my word, I thought once or twice that they were coming into the boat to gratify it. Leo wanted to fire at them, but I dissuaded him, fearing the consequences. Also, we saw hundreds of crocodiles basking on the muddy banks, and thousands upon thousands of water-fowl. Some of these birds we shot, among them a wild goose, which, in addition to the sharp-curved spurs on its wings, had a third spur, three-quarters of an inch long, growing from its skull just between the eyes. We never shot another like it, so I do not know if it was a 'sport' or a distinct species. In the latter case this incident may interest naturalists. Job named it the Unicorn Goose.

About midday the sun grew intensely hot, and the stench drawn up by it from the marshes which the river drains was something too awful, and caused us instantly to swallow precautionary doses of quinine. Shortly afterwards the breeze died away altogether, and as rowing our heavy boat against stream in the heat was out of the question, we were thankful to clamber under the shade of a group of trees—a species of willow —that grew by the edge of the river, and lie there and gasp till at length the approach of sunset put a period to our miseries. Seeing what appeared to be an open space of water straight ahead of us, we determined to row thither before settling what to do for the night. Just as we were about to loosen the boat, however, a beautiful waterbuck, with great horns curving forward, and a white stripe across the rump, came down to the river to drink, without perceiving us hidden away within fifty yards under the willows. Leo was the first to catch sight of it, and, being an ardent sportsman, thirsting for the blood of big game, about which he had been dreaming for months, instantly he stiffened all over, and pointed like a setter dog. Seeing what was the matter, I handed him his Express rifle, at the same time taking my own.

"Now then," I said, "mind you don't miss."

"Miss!" he whispered contemptuously; "I could not miss it if I tried."

He lifted the rifle, and the roan-coloured buck, having drunk his fill, raised his head and looked across the river. He was standing out against the sunset sky on a little eminence, or ridge of ground, which ran through the swamp, evidently a favourite path for game, and there was something very beautiful about him. Indeed, I do not think if I live to a hundred that I shall ever forget this desolate and yet most fascinating scene; it is stamped upon my memory. To the right and left were wide stretches of lonely death-breeding swamp, unbroken and unrelieved so far as the eye could reach except here and there by ponds of black and peaty water that, mirror-like, flashed up the red rays of the setting sun. Behind and before us stretched a vista of the sluggish river, ending in glimpses of a reed-fringed lagoon, on whose surface the long lights of the evening played as the faint breeze stirred the shadows. To the west loomed the huge red ball of the sinking sun, now vanishing into the vapoury horizon, and filling the great heaven, high across whose arch the cranes and wildfowl streamed in line, square, and triangle, with flashes of flying gold and the lurid stain of blood. And then ourselves—three modern Englishmen in a modern English boat —seeming to jar upon and be out of tone with that measureless desolation; and in front of us the noble buck limned upon a background of ruddy sky.

Bang! Away he goes with a mighty bound. Leo has missed him. *Bang!* right under him again. Now for a shot. I must have one, though he is flying like an arrow, and a hundred yards away and more. By jove! over and over and over! "Well, I think I've wiped your eye there, Master Leo," I say, struggling against the ungenerous exultation that in such a supreme moment of existence will rise in the best-mannered sportsman's breast.

"Confound you! yes," growled Leo; and added, with the quick smile that is one of his charms lighting up his handsome face like a ray of light, "I beg your pardon, old fellow. I congratulate you; it was a lovely shot, and mine were vile."

We leapt from the boat and ran to the buck, which was shot through the spine and stone-dead. It took us a quarter of an hour or more to clean it and cut off as much of the best meat as we could carry, so that, having packed this away, we had barely enough light to row to the lagoon-like space, into which, there being a hollow in the swamp, the river here expanded. Just as the darkness fell we cast anchor about thirty fathoms from the edge of this lake. We did not dare to go ashore, not knowing if we should find dry ground to camp on, and greatly fearing the poisonous exhalations from the marsh, of which we thought we should be freer on the water. So we lighted a lantern, and made our evening meal off another potted tongue in the best fashion that we could, and then prepared to go to sleep, only, however, to find that sleep was impossible. For, whether they were attracted by the lantern, or by the unaccustomed smell of a white man that they had awaited for the last thousand years or so, I know not; but certainly we were attacked presently by tens of thousands of the most bloodthirsty, pertinacious, and huge mosquitoes that I ever read of or saw. In clouds they came, and pinged and buzzed and bit till we were nearly mad. Tobacco-smoke only seemed to stir them into a merrier and more active life, till at length we were driven to covering ourselves with blankets, heads and all, and sitting to stew slowly and scratch and swear continually beneath them. And as we sat, suddenly rolling out like thunder through the silence rose the deep roar of a lion, and then of a second lion, moving among the reeds within sixty yards of us.

"I say," said Leo, poking out his head from under the blanket, "lucky we ain't on the bank, eh, Avuncular?" (Leo sometimes addressed me in this disrespectful way.) "Curse it! a mosquito has bitten me on the nose" and the head vanished again.

Shortly after this the moon came up, and nothwithstanding every variety of roar that echoed over the water to us from the lions on the banks, thinking ourselves perfectly secure, we began to doze.

I do not quite know what it was that caused me to lift my head from the friendly shelter of the blanket, perhaps because I found that the mosquitoes were biting through it. Anyhow, as I did so I heard Job whisper, in a frightened voice—

"Oh, my stars, look there!"

Instantly we all of us looked, and this was what we saw in the moonlight. Near the shore were two wide and everwidening circles of concentric rings rippling away across the surface of the water, and in the heart and centre of these circles appeared two dark moving objects.

"What is it?" asked I.

"It is those damned lions, sir," answered Job, in a tone which suggested an odd mixture of a sense of personal injury, habitual respect, and acknowledged fear, "and they are swimming here to *heat* us," he added nervously, picking up an "h" in his agitation.

I looked again: there was no doubt about it; I could catch the glare of their ferocious eyes. Attracted either by the smell of the newly killed waterbuck meat or of ourselves, the hungry beasts were storming our position.

Leo already had a rifle in his hand. I called to him to wait till they were nearer, and meanwhile found my own. Some fifteen feet from us the water shallowed on a bank to the depth of about fifteen inches, and presently the first of them—it was the lioness—waded to it, shook herself, and roared. At that moment Leo fired; the bullet traveled down her open mouth and out at the back of her neck, and down she dropped, with a splash, dead. The other lion—a full-grown male—was some two paces behind her. At this second he set his forepaws on the bank, when something happened. There was a rush and disturbance of the water, such as one sees in a pond in England when a pike takes a little fish, only a thousand times fiercer and larger, then suddenly the lion uttered a terrific snarling roar and sprang forward on to the bank, dragging something black with him.

"Allah!" shouted Mahomed, "a crocodile has got him by the leg!" and sure enough he had. We could see the long snout with its gleaming lines of teeth and the reptile body behind it.

Then followed a most extraordinary scene. The lion managed to struggle on to the bank, the crocodile half standing and half swimming, still nipping his hind leg. He roared till the air quivered with the sound; then, with a savage, shrieking snarl, he turned and clawed hold of the crocodile's head. The reptile shifted his grip, having, as we discovered afterwards, had one of his eyes torn out, and advanced slightly; whereon the lion took him by the throat and held it, and over and over they rolled upon the bank, struggling hideously. It was impossible to follow their movements, but when next we had a clear view the tables were turned, for the crocodile, whose head seemed to be a mass of gore, held the lion's body in his iron jaws just above the hips, and was squeezing him, shaking him to and fro. For his part, the tortured brute, roaring in agony, clawed and bit madly at his enemy's scaly head, and fixing his great hind claws in the softer skin of the crocodile's throat, ripped it open as one would rip a glove.

Then, of a sudden, the end came. The lion's head fell forward on the reptile's back, and with an awful groan he died, and the crocodile, after standing for a minute motionless, slowly rolled over to his side, his jaws still fixed across the carcase of the lion, which, as we found, he had bitten almost in halves.

This duel to the death was a wonderful and a shocking sight, and one that I suppose few men have seen. And thus it ended.

When it was all over, leaving Mahomed to keep a look out, we spent the rest of the night in such comparative peace as the mosquitoes would allow.

CHAPTER VI

AN EARLY CHRISTIAN CEREMONY

NEXT morning, at the earliest light of dawn, we rose, performed such ablutions as circumstances would allow, and made ourselves ready to start. I am bound to say that when there was sufficient light to enable us to see each other's faces I, for one, was moved to laughter, for Job's fat and comfortable countenance had swollen to nearly twice its natural size from mosquito bites, and Leo's condition was not much better. Indeed, of the three I had come off the best probably owing to the toughness of my dark skin, and to the fact that a good deal of it was covered by hair, for since we sailed from England I had allowed my naturally luxuriant beard to grow at its own will. But the other two were comparatively clean shaved, which of course afforded the enemy a larger extent of open country to explore, although in Mahomed's case the mosquitoes, recognizing the taste of a true believer, would not touch him at any price. How often, I wonder, during the next week or so did we wish that we were flavoured like an Arab!

By the time that we had done laughing as heartily as our swollen lips would allow it was daylight, and the morning breeze, drawing up from the sea, cut lanes through the dense marsh mists, here and there rolling them before it in great balls of fleecy vapour. So we set our sail, and having carefully examined the two dead lions and the alligator, which we were of course unable to skin, being destitute of means of curing the pelts, we started, and, sailing through the lagoon, followed the course of the river on its further side. At midday, when the breeze dropped, we were fortunate enough to find a convenient spot of dry land on which to camp and light a fire, and here we cooked two wild-ducks and some of the waterbuck's flesh—not in a very appetising way, it is true, but still sufficiently. The rest of the buck's flesh we cut into strips and hung in the sun to dry into 'biltong,' as, I believe, the South African Dutch call flesh thus prepared. On this welcome patch of dry land we stayed till the following dawn, as before, spending the night in warfare with the mosquitoes, but without other troubles. The next day or two passed in similar fashion, and without noticeable adventures, except that we shot a specimen of a peculiarly graceful hornless buck, and saw many varieties of water-lilies in full bloom, some of them blue and of exquisite beauty, though few of the flowers were perfect, owing to the presence of a white water-maggot with a green head that fed upon them.

It was on the fifth day of our journey, when we had travelled, so far as we could reckon, about one hundred and thirty-five to a hundred and forty miles westwards from the coast, that the first event of any real importance occurred. On that morning the usual wind failed us about eleven o'clock, and after pulling a little way we were forced to halt, more or less exhausted, at what appeared to be the junction of our stream with another of a uniform width of about fifty feet. Some trees grew near at hand—the only trees in all this country were along the banks of the river—and under these we rested; then, the land being fairly dry just here, we walked a little way along the edge of the river to prospect, and shoot a few waterfowl for food. Before we had gone fifty yards we perceived that all hopes of pushing further up the stream in the whale-boat were at an end, for not two hundred yards above where we had landed we found a succession of shallows and mudbanks, with not six inches of water over them. It was a watery *cul de sac*.

Turning back, we walked some way along the banks of the other river, and soon came to the conclusion, from various indications, that it was not a river at all, but an ancient canal, like the one which is to be seen above Mombasa, on the Zanzibar coast, connecting the Tana River with the Ozy, in such a way as to enable the shipping coming down the Tana to cross to the Ozy, and reach the sea by it, and thus avoid the very dangerous bar that blocks the mouth of the Tana. The canal before us evidently had been dug out by man at some remote period of the world's history, and the results of his digging still remained in the shape of the raised banks that had no doubt once formed towing-paths. Except here and there, where they had been hollowed out by the water or fallen in, these banks of stiff binding clay were at a uniform distance from each other, and the depth of the stream also appeared to be uniform. Current there was little or none, and, as a consequence, the surface of the canal was choked with vegetable growth, intersected by little paths of clear water, made, I suppose, by the constant passage of waterfowl, iguanas, and other vermin. Now, as it was evident that we could not proceed up the river, it became equally evident that we must either try the canal or else return to the sea. We could not stop where we were, to be baked by the sun and eaten up by the mosquitoes, till we died of fever in that dreary marsh.

"Well, I suppose that we must try it," I said; and the others assented in their various ways—Leo, as though it were the best joke in the world; Job, in respectful disgust; and Mahomed, with an invocation to the Prophet, and a comprehensive curse upon all unbelievers and their ways of thought and travel.

Accordingly, so soon as the sun sank low, having little or nothing more to hope for from our friendly wind, we started. For the first hour or so we managed to row the boat, though with great labour; but after that the weeds became too thick to allow of it, and we were obliged to resort to the primitive and most exhausting resource of towing her. For two hours we laboured, Mahomed, Job, and I, who was supposed to be strong enough to pull against the two of them, on the bank, while Leo sat in the bow of the boat, and brushed away the weeds which collected round the cutwater with Mahomed's sword. At dark we halted for some hours to rest and enjoy the mosquitoes, but about midnight we went on again, taking advantage of the comparative cool of the night. At dawn we rested for three hours, then started once more, and laboured on till about ten o'clock, when a thunderstorm, accompanied by a deluge of rain, overtook us, and we spent the next six hours practically under water.

I do not know that there is any necessity for me to describe the next four days of our voyage in detail, further than to say that they were, on the whole, the most miserable that I ever spent in my life, forming one monotonous record of heavy labour, heat, misery, and mosquitoes. All that dreary way we passed through a region of almost endless swamp, and I can only attribute our escape from fever and death to the constant doses of quinine and purgatives that we swallowed, and the unceasing toil which we were forced to undergo. On the third day of our journey up the canal we had sighted a round hill that loomed dimly through the vapours of the marsh, and on the evening of the fourth night, when we camped, this hill seemed to be within five-and-twenty or thirty miles of us.

By now we were utterly exhausted, and felt as though our blistered hands could not pull the boat a yard farther, and that the best thing which we could do would be to lie down to die in that dreadful wilderness of swamp. It was an awful position, and one in which I trust no other white men will often be placed; and as I threw myself down in the boat to sleep the sleep of utter exhaustion, bitterly I cursed my folly in having become a party to such a mad undertaking, which could, I saw, only end in our deaths in this ghastly land. I thought, I remember, as I slowly sank into a doze, of what the appearance of the boat and her unhappy crew would be in two or three months' time from that night. There she would lie, with gaping seams and half-filled with fœtid water, which, when the mist-laden wind stirred her, would wash backwards and forwards through our mouldering bones, and that must be the end of her, and of those in her who would follow after myths and seek out the secrets of Nature.

Already I seemed to hear the water rippling against the desiccated bones, and rattling them together, rolling my skull against Mahomed's, and his against mine, till at last the Arab's stood straight upon its vertebræ, and, glaring at me through its empty eyeholes, cursed me with its grinning jaws because I, a dog of a Christian, disturbed the last sleep of a true believer. I opened my eyes, shuddering at the horrid dream, then shuddered again at something that was not a dream, for two great eyes were gazing at me through the misty darkness. I struggled to my feet, and in my terror and confusion shrieked, and shrieked again, so that the others sprang up too, reeling, and drunken with sleep and fear. Then all of a sudden there was a flash of cold steel, and a broad spear was held against my throat, and behind it other spears gleamed cruelly.

"Peace," said a voice, speaking in Arabic, or rather in some dialect into which Arabic entered very largely; "who are you that come hither swimming on the water? Speak, or ye die," and the steel pressed sharply against my throat, sending a cold chill through me.

"We are travellers, and have come hither by chance," I answered in my best Arabic, which appeared to be understood, for the man turned his head, and, addressing a tall form that was visible in the background, said, "Father, shall we slay?"

"What is the colour of the men?" asked a deep voice in answer.

"White is their colour."

"Slay not," was the reply. "Four suns since was the word brought to me from 'She-who-must-be-obeyed,' 'White men come; if white men come, kill them not.' Let them be brought to the house of 'She-who-must-be-obeyed.' Bring forth the men, and let that which they have with them be brought forth also."

"Come!" said the man, half leading and half dragging me from the boat, and as he did so I perceived others doing the same kind office to my companions.

On the bank were gathered a company of some fifty men. In that light all I could discover was that they were armed with huge spears, were very tall, and strongly built, comparatively light in colour, and naked, save for a leopard skin tied tightly round the middle.

Presently Leo and Job were thrust forward and placed beside me.

"What on earth is the matter?" asked Leo, rubbing his eyes.

"Oh, Lord! sir, here's a rum go," ejaculated Job; and just at that moment a disturbance ensued, and Mahomed tumbled between us, followed by a shadowy form with an uplifted spear.

"Allah! Allah!" howled Mahomed, feeling that he had little hope from man, "protect me! protect me!"

"Father, it is a black one," said a voice. "What was the word of 'She-who-must-be-obeyed' about the black one?"

"She said no word of him; but slay him not. Come hither, my son."

The man advanced, and the tall shadowy form bent forward and whispered something.

"Yes, yes," answered the other, and chuckled in a rather blood-curdling tone.

"Are the three white men there?" asked the form.

"Yes, they are there."

"Then bring up that which is made ready for them, and take with you all that can be brought from the thing which floats."

Hardly had he spoken when men advanced, carrying on their shoulders several covered palanquins, each borne by four bearers and two spare men, into which it was indicated that we were expected to mount.

"Well!" said Leo, "it is a blessing to find anybody to carry us after having to carry ourselves so long."

Leo always takes a cheerful view of things.

As there was no help for it, after seeing the others into theirs I climbed into my own litter, and very comfortable I found it. It appeared to be manufactured of cloth woven from grass-fibre, which stretched and yielded to every motion of the body, and, being bound top and bottom to the bearing-pole, gave a grateful support to the head and neck.

Scarcely had I settled myself when, accompanying their steps with a monotonous song, the bearers started at a swinging trot. For half an hour or so I lay still, reflecting on the very remarkable experiences that we were going through, and wondering whether any of my eminently respectable fossil friends at Cambridge would believe me if I were miraculously to be set at the familiar dinner-table for the purpose of relating them. I do not wish to convey any imputation or slight when I call those good and learned men fossils, but my experience is that people are apt to petrify, even at a University, if they follow the same paths too persistently. I was becoming fossilised myself but of late my stock of ideas has been very much enlarged. Well, I lay and reflected, and wondered what on earth would be the end of it all, till at last I ceased to wonder, and went to sleep.

I suppose I must have slept for seven or eight hours, taking the first real rest that I had won since the night before the loss of the dhow, for when I woke the sun was high in the heavens. We were still journeying on at a pace of about four miles an hour. Peeping out through the thin curtains of the litter, which were fixed ingeniously to the bearing-pole, I perceived, to my infinite relief, that we had passed out of the region of eternal swamp, and were now travelling over swelling grassy plains towards a cup-shaped hill. Whether or not it was the same hill that we had seen from the canal I do not know, and have never since been able to discover, for, as we learned afterwards, these people will give little information upon such points. Next I glanced at the men who were bearing me. They were of a magnificent build, few of them being under six feet in height, and yellowish in colour. Generally their appearance had a good deal in common with that of the East African Somali, only their hair was not frizzed up, but hung in thick black locks upon their shoulders. Their features were aquiline, and in many cases exceedingly handsome, the teeth being especially regular and beautiful. But notwithstanding their beauty, it struck me that, on the whole, I had never seen more evil faces. There was an aspect of cold and sullen cruelty stamped upon them that revolted me, which, indeed, in some cases was almost uncanny in its intensity.

Another thing which I noticed about them was that they never seemed to smile. Sometimes they sang the monotonous song whereof I have spoken, but when they were not singing they remained almost perfectly silent, and the light of a laugh never came to brighten their sombre and wicked countenances. Of what race could these people be? Their language was a bastard Arabic, and yet they were not Arabs; I was quite sure of that. For one thing they were too dark, or rather yellow. I could not say why, but I know that their appearance filled me with a sick fear of which I felt ashamed. While I was still wondering another litter ranged alongside of mine. In it—for the curtains were drawn— sat an old man, clothed in a whitish robe, made apparently, from coarse linen, that hung loosely about him, who, as I at once concluded, was the shadowy figure that had stood on the bank and been addressed as 'Father.' He was a wonderful-looking old man. with a snowy beard, so long that the ends of it hung over the sides of the litter, and he had a hooked nose, above which flashed a pair of eyes as keen as a snake's, while his whole countenance was instinct with a look of wise and sardonic humour impossible to describe on paper.

"Art thou awake, stranger?" he said in a deep and low voice.

"Surely, my father," I answered courteously, feeling certain that I should do well to conciliate this ancient Mammon of Unrighteousness.

He stroked his beautiful white beard, and smiled faintly.

"From whatever country thou wanderest," he said, "and by the way it must be from one where somewhat of our language is known, they teach their children courtesy there, my stranger son. And now, wherefore comest thou unto this land, which scarce an alien foot has pressed from the time that man knoweth? Art thou and are those with thee weary of life?"

"We came to find new things," I answered boldly. "We are tired of the old things; we have risen up out of the sea to know that which is unknown. We are of a brave race who fear not death, my very much respected father—that is, if we can win a little fresh information before we die."

"Humph!" said the old gentleman, "that may be true; it is rash to contradict, otherwise I should declare that thou wast lying, my son. However, I dare to say that *'She-who-must-be-obeyed'* will meet thy wishes in the matter."

"Who is 'She-who-must-be-obeyed'?" I asked curiously.

The old man glanced at the bearers, and then answered, with a little smile that somehow sent my blood to my heart—

"Surely, my stranger son, thou wilt learn soon enough, if it be her pleasure to see thee at all in the flesh."

"In the flesh?" I answered. "What may my father wish to convey?"

But the old man only laughed a dreadful laugh, and made no reply.

"What is the name of my father's people?" I asked.

"The name of my people is Amahagger, the People of the Rocks."

"And if a son might ask, what is the name of my father?"

"My name is Billali."

"And whither go we, my father?"

"That shalt thou see," and at a sign from him his bearers started forward at a run till they reached the litter in which Job was reposing (with one leg hanging over the side). Apparently, however, he could not make much out of Job, for presently I saw his bearers trot forward to Leo's litter.

After this, as nothing fresh occurred, I yielded to the pleasant swaying motion of the litter, and went to sleep again. I was dreadfully tired. When I woke I found that we were passing through a rocky defile of a lava formation with precipitous sides, in which grew many beautiful trees and flowering shrubs.

Presently this defile took a turn, and a lovely sight unfolded itself to my eyes. Before us was a vast cup of earth from four to six miles in extent, and moulded to the shape of a Roman amphitheatre. The sides of this great cup were rocky, and clothed with bush, but its centre was of the richest meadow land, studded with single trees of magnificent growth, and watered by meandering brooks. On this rich plain grazed herds of goats and cattle, but I saw no sheep. At first I could not imagine what this strange spot might be, but presently it flashed upon me that it must represent the crater of some long-extinct volcano which afterwards had been a lake, and ultimately was drained in some unexplained fashion. And here I may state that from my subsequent experience of this and a much larger, but otherwise similar, place, which I shall have occasion to describe by-and-by, I have every reason to believe that this conclusion was correct. What puzzled me, however, was, that although there were people moving about herding the goats and cattle, I saw no signs of any human habitation. Where did they all live? I wondered. My curiosity was soon destined to be gratified. Turning to the left the string of litters followed the cliffy sides of the crater for a distance of about half a mile, or perhaps a little less, and then halted. Seeing my adopted 'father,' Billali, emerge from his litter, I followed his example, and so did Leo and Job. The first thing I noticed was our wretched Arab companion, Mahomed, lying exhausted on the ground. It appeared that he was not provided with a litter, but had been forced to run the entire distance, and, as he was already quite worn out when we started, his condition now seemed one of great prostration.

On looking round us we saw that the place where we had halted was a platform in front of the mouth of a great cave, and that piled upon this plaform were the contents of the whale-boat, even to the oars and sails. Round the cave stood groups of the men who had escorted us, and other men like to them. They were all tall and all handsome, though they varied in their degree of darkness of skin, some being as black as Mahomed, and some as yellow as a Chinese. They were naked, except for the leopard skin round the waist, and each of them carried a huge spear.

There were also some women among them, who, instead of the leopard skin, wore a tanned hide of a small red buck, something like that of the oribé, only rather darker in colour. These women were, as a class, exceedingly good-looking, with large, dark eyes, well-cut features, and a thick bush of curling hair—not crisp like a negro's—ranging from black to chestnut in hue with all shades of intermediate colour. Some, but very few of them, wore a yellowish linen garment, such as I have described as worn by Billali; but this, as we afterwards discovered, was a mark of rank, rather than an attempt at clothing. For the rest, their appearance was not quite so terrifying as that of the men, and they smiled sometimes, though rarely. As soon as we had alighted they gathered round us and examined us with curiosity, but without excitement. Leo's tall, athletic form and clear-cut Grecian face, however, evidently excited their attention, and when he politely lifted his hat to them, and showed his curling yellow hair, there was a slight murmur of admiration. Nor did it stop there; for after regarding him critically from head to foot, the handsomest of the young women—one wearing a robe, and with hair of a shade between brown and chestnut—deliberately advanced to him, and, in a way that would have been winning had it not been so determined, quietly put her arm round his neck, bent forward, and kissed him on the lips.

I gasped aloud, expecting to see Leo instantly speared; and Job ejaculated, "The hussy!—well, I never!" As for Leo, he looked slightly astonished; and then, remarking that clearly we had reached a country where they followed the customs of the early Christians, he deliberately returned the embrace.

Again I gasped, thinking that something would happen; but, to my surprise, though some of the young women showed traces of vexation, the older ones and the men only smiled faintly. When we came to understand the customs of this extraordinary people the mystery was explained. It then appeared that, in direct opposition to the habits of almost every other savage race in the world, women among the Amahagger live upon conditions of perfect equality with the men, and are not held to them by any binding ties. Descent is traced only through the line of the mother, and while individuals are as proud of a long and superior female ancestry as we are of our families in Europe, they never pay attention to, or even acknowledge, any man as their father, even when their male parentage is perfectly well known. There is but one titular male parent of each tribe, or, as they call it, 'Household,' and he is its elected and immediate ruler, with the title of 'Father.' For instance, the man Billali was the father of this 'Household,' which consisted of about seven thousand individuals all told, and no other man was ever called by that name. When a woman chanced to favour a man she signfied her preference by advancing and embracing him publicly, in the same way that this handsome and exceedingly prompt young lady, who was called Ustane, had embraced Leo. If he kissed her back it was a token that he accepted her, and the arrangement continued till one of them wearied of it. I am bound, however, to add that the change of husbands was not nearly so frequent as might have been expected. Nor did quarrels arise out of it, at least among the men, who, when their wives deserted them in favour of a rival, accepted the matter much as we accept the income tax or our marriage laws, as something not to be disputed, and as tending to the good of the community, however disagreeable they may prove to the individual in particular instances.

It is very curious to observe how the customs of mankind on this question vary in different countries, making morality an affair of latitude and religion, and what is right in one place wrong and improper in another. It must, however, be understood that, since all civilised nations appear to accept it as an axiom that ceremony is the touchstone of morals, there is, even according to our canons, nothing immoral about this Amahagger custom, since the public interchange of an embrace answers to our ceremony of marriage which, as we know, justifies most things.

CHAPTER VII

USTANE SINGS

WHEN the kissing *coram populo* was done—by the way, none of the young ladies offered to pet me in this fashion, though I saw one hovering round Job, to that respectable individual's evident alarm—the old man Billali advanced, and graciously waved us into the cave, whither we went, followed by Ustane, who did not seem inclined to take the hints I gave her that we liked privacy.

Before we had gone five paces it struck me that the cave which we were entering was none of Nature's handiwork, but, on the contrary, had been hollowed by the labour of man. So far as we could judge it appeared to be about one hundred feet in length by fifty wide, and very lofty, resembling a cathedral aisle more than anything else. From this main aisle opened passages at a distance of every twelve or fifteen feet, leading, I supposed, to smaller chambers. About fifty feet from the entrance of the cave, just where the light began to fade, a fire was burning, which threw huge shadows upon the gloomy walls around. Here Billali halted, and asked us to be seated, saying that the people would bring us food, and accordingly we sat ourselves down upon the rugs of skins which were spread for us, and waited. Presently the food, consisting of goat's flesh boiled, fresh milk in an earthenware pot, and roasted cobs of Indian corn, was brought by young girls. We were almost starving, and I do not think that in my life I ever before ate with such satisfaction. Indeed, before we finished we had devoured everything that was set before us.

When we had eaten, our somewhat saturnine host, Billali, who was watching us in absolute silence, rose and addressed us. He said that it was a wonderful thing which had happened. No man had ever known or heard of white strangers arriving in the country of the People of the Rocks. Sometimes, though rarely, black men had come here, and from them they had heard of the existence of men much whiter than themselves, who sailed on the sea in ships, but for the arrival of such there was no precedent. We had, however, been seen dragging the boat up the canal, and he told us frankly that he at once gave orders for our destruction, since it was unlawful for any stranger to enter here, when a message arrived from '*She-who-must-be-obeyed,*' saying that our lives must be spared, and that we were to be brought hither.

"Pardon me, my father," I interrupted at this point; "but if, as I understand, '*She-who-must-be-obeyed*' lives yet farther off, how could she have known of our approach?"

Billali turned, and seeing that we were alone—for the young lady, Ustane, had withdrawn when he began to speak—said, with a curious little laugh—

"Are there none in your land who can see without eyes and hear without ears? Ask no questions; *She* knew."

I shrugged my shoulders at this, and he went on to say that no further instructions had been received on the subject of our disposal, and this being so he was about to start to interview '*She-who-must-be-obeyed*,' generally spoken of, for the sake of brevity, as 'Hiya' or *She* simply, who, he gave us to understand, was the Queen of the Amahagger, and learn her wishes.

I asked him how long he proposed to be absent, and he said that by travelling hard he might be back on the fifth day, but there were many miles of marsh to cross before he came to where *She* was. He then said that every arrangement would be made for our comfort during his absence, and that, as personally he had taken a fancy to us, he trusted sincerely that the answer he should bring from *She* would be one favourable to the continuation of our existence. At the same time he did not wish to conceal from us that he thought this doubtful, as every stranger who had ever come into the country during his grandmother's life, his mother's life, and his own life, had been put to death without mercy, and in a way which he would not harrow our feelings by describing. This had been done by the order of *She* herself, at least he supposed that it was by her order. At any rate, she never interfered to save them.

"Why," I said, "but how can that be? You are an old man, and the time you talk of must reach back three men's lives. How, therefore, could *She* have ordered the death of anybody at the beginning of the life of your grandmother, seeing that herself she would not have been born?"

Again Billali smiled—that same peculiar smile—and with a deep bow departed, without making any answer; nor did we see him again for five days.

When he had gone we discussed the situation which filled me with alarm. I did not at all like the accounts of this mysterious Queen, '*She-who-must-be-obeyed*,' or more shortly, *She,* who apparently ordered the execution of any unfortunate stranger in a fashion so unmerciful. Leo, too, was depressed about it, but consoled himself triumphantly pointing out that this *She* was undoubtedly the person referred to in the writing on the potsherd and in his father's letter, in proof of which he advanced Billali's allusions to her age and power. I was by this time so overwhelmed with the course of events that I had not the heart left even to dispute a proposition so absurd, therefore I suggested that we should try to go out to take a bath, of which all of us stood sadly in need.

Accordingly, indicating our wish to a middle-aged individual of an unusually saturnine cast of countenance, even among this saturnine people, who appeared to be deputed to look after us now that the Father of the hamlet had departed, we started in a body—having first lit our pipes. Outside the cave we found quite a crowd of people evidently watching for our appearance, but, when they saw us emerge smoking they vanished this way and that, calling out that we were mighty magicians. Indeed, nothing about us created so great a sensation as our tobacco-smoke—not even our firearms.[1] After this we succeeded in reaching a stream that had its source in a strong ground spring, and taking our bath in peace, though some of the women, not excepting Ustane, showed a decided inclination to follow us even there.

By the time that we had finished this most refreshing bathe the sun was setting; indeed, when we came back to the big cavern it had already set. The cave itself was full of people gathered round fires—for several had now been lighted—who were eating their evening meal by the lurid glare, and by the light of lamps which were set about or hung upon the walls. These lamps were of a rude manufacture of baked earthenware, and of all shapes, some of them graceful enough. The larger ones were formed of big, red earthenware pots, filled with clarified melted fat, and having a reed wick let through a wooden disk which fitted the top of the pot. This sort of lamp required the most constant care to prevent its extinction whenever the wick burnt down, as there was no means of turning it up. The smaller hand lamps, however, which were also made of baked clay, were furnished with wicks manufactured from the pith of a palm-tree, or sometimes from the stem of a very handsome variety of fern. This kind of wick was passed through a round hole at the end of the lamp, to which a sharp piece of hard wood was attached wherewith to pierce and draw it up whenever it showed signs of burning low.

For a while we sat down and watched this grim people eating their evening meal in a silence grim as themselves, till at length, growing tired of contemplating them and the dark moving shad-

---

[1] We found tobacco growing in this country as it does in every other part of Africa, and, although they are so absolutely ignorant of its other blessed qualities, the Amahagger use it habitually in the form of snuff and also for medicinal purposes.—L. H. H.

ows on the rocky walls, I suggested to our new keeper that we should like to go to bed.

Without a word he rose, and, taking me politely by the hand, advanced with a lamp to one of the small passages that I had noticed opening out of the central cave. This we followed for about five paces, when suddenly it widened into a small chamber, about eight feet square, and hewn from the living rock. On one side of this chamber was a stone slab, raised three feet above the ground, and running its entire length like a bunk in a cabin, whereon my guide intimated that I was to sleep. There was no window or air-hole to the chamber, and no furniture; and, on looking at it more closely, I came to the disturbing conclusion —in which, as I afterwards discovered, I was quite right—that it had served originally as a sepulchre for the dead rather than a sleeping-place for the living, the slab being designed to receive the corpse of the departed. This thought made me shudder in spite of myself; but, seeing that I must sleep somewhere, I stifled my feelings as best I might, and returned to the cavern to fetch my blanket, which had been brought from the boat with the other thing. There I met Job, who, having been inducted to a similar apartment, had declined flatly to stop in it, saying that the look of the place "gave him the horrors," and that he might as well be dead and buried in his grandfather's brick grave at once. Now he expressed his determination of sleeping with me if I would allow him. This, of course, I was only too glad to do.

The night passed very comfortably on the whole. I say on the whole, for personally I experienced a horrible nightmare, wherein I was buried alive, induced, no doubt, by the sepulchral nature of my surroundings. At dawn we were aroused by a loud trumpeting sound, produced, as we discovered afterwards, by a young Amahagger blowing through a hole bored in its side into a hollowed elephant tusk, which was kept for the purpose.

Taking the hint, we rose and went down to the stream to wash, after which the morning meal was served. At breakfast one of the women, no longer quite young, advanced and publicly kissed Job. Putting its impropriety aside for a moment, I think it was in its way the most delightful thing that I ever saw. Never shall I forget the respectable Job's abject terror and disgust. Job, like myself, is something of a misogynist—owing I fancy to the fact of his having been born one of a family of seventeen—and the feelings expressed upon his countenance when he realised that he was not only being embraced publicly, and without authorisation on his own part, but also in the presence of his

masters, were too mixed and painful to admit of accurate description. He sprang to his feet, and pushed the woman, a buxom
person of about thirty, from him.

"Well, I never!" he gasped, whereupon probably thinking that
he was only coy, she embraced him again.

"Be off with you! Get away, you minx!" he shouted, waving
the wooden spoon, with which he was eating his breakfast, up and
down before the lady's face. "Beg your pardon, gentlemen, I
am sure I haven't encouraged her. Oh, Lord! she's coming for me
again. Hold her, Mr. Holly! please hold her! I can't stand it; I
can't indeed. This has never happened to me before, gentlemen,
never. There's nothing against my character." Here he broke
off, and ran as hard as he could down the cave, and for once I
saw the Amahagger laugh. As for the woman, however, she did
not laugh. On the contrary, she seemed to bristle with fury,
which the mockery of the other women about her only served to
intensify. She stood there literally snarling and shaking with
indignation, and, seeing her, I wished Job's scruples had been
at Jericho, for I could guess that his admirable behaviour had
endangered our throats. Nor, as the sequel shows, was I wrong.

The lady having retreated, Job returned in a state of great
nervousness, and looking with an anxious eye upon every woman
who came near him. I took an opportunity to explain to our
hosts that Job was a married man, who had met with unhappy
experiences in his domestic relations, which accounted for his
presence here and his terror at the sight of women. My remarks,
however, were received in silence, it being evident that our
retainer's behaviour was considered as a slight to the 'Household' at large, although the women, after the manner of some of
their more civilised sisters, made merry at the rebuff of their
companion.

After breakfast we took a walk and inspected the Amahagger
herds, also their cultivated lands. They have two breeds of
cattle, one large and angular, with no horns, but yielding beautiful milk; and the other, a red strain, very small and fat, excellent
for meat, but of no value for milking purposes. This last breed
closely resembles the Norfolk redpoll stock, only it has horns
which generally curve forward over the head, sometimes to such
an extent that they must be sawn to prevent them from growing
into the bones of the skull. The goats are long-haired, and are
used for eating only, at least I never saw them milked. As for
the Amahagger cultivation, it is primitive in the extreme, their
only implement being a spade made of iron, for these people

smelt and work iron. This spade is shaped more like a big spearhead than anything else, and has no shoulder to it on which the foot can be set. As a consequence, the labour of digging is very great. It is however, all done by the men, the women, contrary to the habits of most savage races, being entirely exempt from manual toil. But then, as I think I have said elsewhere, among the Amahagger the weaker sex has established its rights.

At first we were much puzzled as to the origin and laws of this most extraordinary race, points upon which they were singularly uncommunicative. As time went on, however—for the next four days passed without any striking event—we learnt something from Leo's lady friend, Ustane, who, by the way, clung to that young gentleman like his own shadow. As to origin, they had none, at least so far as she was aware. There were, however, she informed us, mounds of masonry and many pillars, called Kôr, near to the place where *She* lived, which the wise said had once been houses wherein men dwelt, and it was suggested that the Amahagger were descended from these men. No one, however, dared to go near these great ruins, because they were haunted: they only looked on them from a distance. Other similar ruins were to be seen, she had heard, in various parts of the country, that is, wherever one of the mountains rose above the level of the swamp. Also the caves in which they abode had been hollowed out of the rocks by men, perhaps the same who built the cities. They themselves had no written laws, only custom, which was, however, quite as binding as law. If any man offended against the custom, he was put to death by order of the Father of the 'Household.' I asked how he was put to death, but she only smiled in answer, and said that I might see one day soon.

They had a Queen, however. *She* was their Queen, but she appeared very rarely, perhaps once in two or three years, when she came forth to pass sentence on some offenders, and when seen she was muffled up in a big cloak, so that nobody could look upon her face. Those who waited upon her were deaf and dumb, and therefore could tell no tales, but it was reported that she was lovely as no other woman was lovely, or ever had been. It was rumoured also that she was immortal, and had power over all things, but she, Ustane, knew nothing about this. What she believed was that the Queen chose a husband from time to time, and so soon as a female child was born, this husband, who was never seen again, was put to death. Then the female child grew up and took the place of the Queen when its mother died, and had been buried in the great caves. But of these matters none could speak with certainty. Only *She* was obeyed throughout the length and breadth of the land, and to question her command was instant death. She kept a guard, but had no regular army, and to disobey her was to die.

I asked what size the land was, and how many people lived in it. She answered that there were ten 'Households,' like this that she knew of, including the big 'Household,' where the Queen was; that all the 'Households' lived in caves, in places resembling this stretch of raised country, dotted about in the vast extent of swamp, which could only be threaded by secret paths. Often the 'Households' made war on each other until *She* sent word that it was to stop, when they instantly obeyed her. Wars and the fever which they caught in crossing the swamps prevented their numbers from increasing too much. They had no connection with any other race, indeed none lived near them; also the swamps could not be crossed by foes. Once an army from the direction of the great river (presumably the Zambesi) had attempted to attack them, but lost themselves in the marshes, and at night, seeing the great balls of fire that move about there, tried to come to them, thinking that they marked the enemy's camp, and half of them were drowned. As for the rest, they soon died of fever and starvation, not a blow being struck at them. The marshes, she repeated, were absolutely impassable except to those who knew the paths, adding, what I could well believe, that we should never have reached this place where we now were had we not been brought thither.

These and many other things we learned from Ustane, during the four days' pause before our real adventures began, and, as may be imagined, they gave us considerable cause for thought. The whole story was exceedingly remarkable, almost incredibly so, indeed, and the oddest part of it was that so far it did more or less correspond to the ancient writing on the sherd. And now it appeared that there was a mysterious Queen clothed by rumour with dread and wonderful attributes, and commonly known by the impersonal, but, to my mind, rather awesome title of *She*. Altogether, I could not understand it, nor could Leo, though of course he was triumphant exceedingly over me because I had persistently mocked at the legend. As for Job he had long since abandoned any attempt to call his reason his own, and left it to drift upon the sea of circumstance. Mahomed, the Arab, who, by the way, was treated civilly indeed, but with chilling contempt, by the Amahagger was, I discovered, in a great fright, though I could not quite make out what it was that frightened him. He would sit crouched in a corner of the cave all day long, calling upon Allah and the Prophet for protection. When I pressed him about it, he said that he was afraid because these people were not men and women at all, but devils, and that this was an enchanted land; and, upon my word, once or twice since then I have been inclined to agree with him. And so the time went on, till the night of the fourth day after Billali had left, when something happened.

We three and Ustane were sitting round a fire in the cave just before bedtime, when suddenly the woman, who had been brooding in silence, rose, and laid her hand upon Leo's golden curls, and addressed him. Even now, when I shut my eyes, I can see her proud, shapely form, clothed alternately in dense shadow and the red flickering light of the fire, as she stood, the wild centre of as wild a scene as I ever witnessed, and delivered herself of the burden of her thoughts and forebodings in a rhythmical speech that ran something as follows:—

Thou art my chosen—I have waited for thee from the beginning!

Thou art very beautiful. Who hath hair like unto thee, or skin so white?

Who hath so strong an arm, who is so much a man?

Thine eyes are the sky, and the light in them is the stars.

Thou art perfect and of a happy face, and my heart turned itself towards thee.

Ay, when mine eyes fell upon thee I did desire thee,—

Then did I take thee to me—O thou Beloved,

And hold thee fast, lest harm should come unto thee.

Ay, I did cover thine head with mine hair, lest the sun should strike it;

And altogether was I thine, and thou wast altogether mine.

And so it went for a little space, till Time was in labour with an evil Day;

And then, what befell on that day? Alas! my Beloved, I know not!

But I, I saw thee no more—I, I was lost in the blackness.

And she who is stronger did take thee; ay, she who is fairer than Ustane.

Yet didst thou turn and call upon me, and let thine eyes search in the darkness.

But, nevertheless, she prevailed by Beauty, and led thee down horrible places,

And then, ah! then my Beloved——

Here this extraordinary woman broke off her speech, or chant, which was so much musical gibberish to us who could not understand of what she was talking, and seemed to fix her flashing eyes upon the deep shadow before her. Then in a moment they acquired a vacant, terrified stare, as though they were striving to picture some half-seen horror. She lifted her hand from Leo's head, and pointed into the darkness. We all looked, and could see nothing; but she saw something, or thought she did, and something evidently that effected even her iron nerves, for, without another sound, down she fell senseless between us.

Leo, who had grown really attached to this remarkable young person, became greatly alarmed and distressed, and, to be perfectly candid, my own condition was not far removed from that of superstitious fear. The scene and circumstances were so very uncanny.

Presently, however, she recovered, and sat up with a convulsive shudder.

"What didst thou mean, Ustane?" asked Leo, who, thanks to years of tuition, spoke Arabic very prettily.

"Nay, my chosen," she answered, with a little forced laugh, "I did but sing unto thee after the fashion of my people. Surely, I meant nothing. How could I speak of that which is not yet?"

"And what didst thou see, Ustane?" I asked, looking her sharply in the face.

"Nay," she answered again, "I saw naught. Ask me not what I saw. Why should I affright you?" Then, turning to Leo with a look of the most utter tenderness that I ever saw upon the face of a woman, civilised or savage, she took his head between her hands, and kissed him on the forehead as a mother might.

"When I am gone from thee, my chosen," she said; "when at night thou stretchest out thine hand and canst not find me, then shouldst thou think at times of me, for of a truth I love thee well, though I be not fit to wash thy feet. And now let us love and take that which is given us, and be happy; for in the grave there is no love and no warmth, nor any touching of the lips. Nothing perchance, or perchance but bitter memories of what might have been. To-night the hours are our own; how know we to whom they shall belong to-morrow?"

CHAPTER VIII

THE FEAST, AND AFTER!

ON the day following this remarkable scene—a scene calculated to make a deep impression upon anybody who beheld it, more because of what it suggested and seemed to foreshadow than of what it revealed—it was announced to us that a feast would be held that evening in our honour. I did my best to decline it, saying that we were modest people, who cared little for feasts, but as my remarks were received with the silence of displeasure, I thought it wisest to make no further objections.

Accordingly, just before sundown, I was informed that everything was ready, and, accompanied by Job, went into the cave, where I met Leo, who as usual was followed by Ustane. These two had been out walking somewhere, and knew nothing of the projected festivity till that moment. When Ustane heard of it I saw an expression of horror start upon her handsome features. Turning, she caught a man who was passing up the cave by the arm, and asked him something in an imperious tone. His answer seemed to reassure her a little, for she looked relieved, though far from satisfied. Next she appeared to attempt some remonstrance with the man, who was a person in authority, but he spoke angrily to her, and shook her off. Then, changing his mind, he took her by the arm, and sat her down between himself and another man in the circle round the fire, and I perceived that for some reason of her own she thought it best to submit.

The fire in the cave was unusually large that night and in a wide circle round it were gathered about thirty-five men and two women—Ustane and the woman to avoid whom Job had played the *rôle* of another Scriptural character. The men were sitting in perfect silence, as was their custom, each with his great spear upright behind him, in a socket cut in the rock for that purpose. Only one or two wore the yellowish linen garment of which I have spoken, the rest had nothing on except the leopard skin about the middle.

"What's up now, sir?" said Job, doubtfully. "Bless us and save us, there's that woman again. Now, surely, she can't be after me, seeing that I have given her no encouragement. They give me the creeps, the whole lot of them, and that's a fact. Why, look, they have asked Mahomed to dine, too. There, that lady of mine is talking to him in as nice and civil a way as possible. Well, I'm glad it isn't me, that's all!"

We looked, and surely enough the woman in question had risen, and was escorting the wretched Mahomed from his corner, where, overcome by some acute prescience of horror, he had been seated, shivering, and calling on Allah. He appeared unwilling enough to comply, if for no other reason perhaps because it was an unaccustomed honour, for hitherto his food had been given to him apart. Anyway, I could see that he was in a state of great terror, for his tottering legs would scarcely support his stout, bulky form, and I think it was rather owing to the resources of barbarism behind him, in the shape of a huge Amahagger with a proportionately huge spear, than to the seductions of the lady who led him by the hand, that he consented to come at all.

"Well," I said to the others, "I don't at all like the look of things, but I suppose we must face it out. Have you fellows got your revolvers on? because, if so, you had better see that they are loaded."

"I have, sir," said Job, tapping his Colt, "but Mr. Leo has only got his hunting-knife, though that is big enough, surely."

Feeling that it would not do to wait while the missing weapon was fetched, we advanced boldly, and seated ourselves in a line, with our backs against the side of the cave.

So soon as we were seated an earthenware jar was passed round containing a fermented fluid of by no means unpleasant taste, though apt to turn the stomach, made from crushed grain—not Indian corn, but a small brown grain that grows upon its stem in clusters, not unlike that which in the southern part of Africa is known by the name of Kafir corn. The vase which contained this liquor was very curious, and as it more or less resembled many hundreds of others in use among the Amahagger I may as well describe it. These vases are of a very ancient manufacture, and of all sizes. None such can have been made in the country for hundreds, or rather thousands, of years. They are found in the rock tombs, of which I shall give a description in their proper place, and my own belief is that they were used to receive the viscera of the dead, after the fashion of the Egyptians, with whom the former inhabitants of this country may have had some connection. Leo, however, is of opinion that, as in the case of Etruscan amphorae, they were placed there for the spiritual use of the deceased. They are mostly two-handled, and of all sizes, some measuring nearly three feet, and running from that height down to as many inches. In shape they vary, but are all exceedingly beautiful and graceful, being made of a very fine black ware, not lustrous, but slightly rough. On this groundwork are inlaid figures much more graceful and lifelike than any others that I have seen on antique vases. Some of these inlaid pictures represent love-scenes with a child-like simplicity and freedom of manner which would not commend itself to the taste of the present day. Others again give pictures of maidens dancing, and yet others of hunting-scenes. For instance, the very vase from which we were then drinking had on one side a most spirited drawing of men, apparently white in colour, attacking a bull-elephant with spears, while on the reverse was a picture, not quite so well done, of a hunter shooting an arrow at a running antelope, I should say from the look of it either an eland or a koodoo.

This is a digression at a critical moment, but it is not too long for the occasion, for the occasion itself was very long. With the exception of the periodical passing of the vase, and the movement necessary to throw fuel on to the fire, nothing happened for the best part of a whole hour. Nobody spoke a word. There we all sat in perfect silence, staring at the glare and glow of the large fire, and at the shadows thrown by the flickering earthenware lamps—which, by the way, were not ancient. On the open space between us and the fire lay a large wooden tray, with four short handles to it, exactly like a butcher's tray, only not hollowed out. By the side of the tray was a great pair of long-handled iron pincers, and on the other side of the fire was a similar pair. Somehow I did not at all like the appearance of this tray and of the accompanying pincers. There I sat contemplating them and the silent circle of the fierce moody faces of the men, reflecting that it was all very awful, and that we were absolutely in the power of this fearsome people, who, to me at any rate, were all the more formidable because their true character was still very much of a mystery to us. They might be better than I thought them, or they might be worse. I feared that they were worse, and I was not wrong. It was a curious sort of a feast, I reflected, in appearance indeed an entertainment of the Barmecide stamp, for there was absolutely nothing to eat.

At last, just as I had begun to feel as though I were being mesmerised, a move was made. Without the slightest warning, a man from the other side of the circle called out in a loud voice—

"Where is the flesh that we shall eat?"

Thereon everybody in the circle answered in a deep measured tone, and stretching out the right arm towards the fire as he spoke—

"The flesh will come."

"Is it a goat?" said the same man.

"It is a goat without horns, and more than a goat, and we shall slay it," they answered with one voice, and turning half round one and all they grasped the handles of their spears with the right hand, and then simultaneously released them.

"Is it an ox?" said the man again.

"It is an ox without horns, and more than an ox, and we shall slay it," was the answer, and again the spears were grasped, and again released.

Then came a pause, and I noticed, with horror and a rising of the hair, that the woman next to Mahomed began to fondle him, patting his cheeks, and calling him by names of endearment while her fierce eyes played up and down his trembling form. I do not know why the sight frightened me, but it did frighten us all dreadfully, especially Leo. The caressing was so snake-like, and so evidently a part of some ghastly formula that had to be gone through.[1] I saw Mahomed turn white under his brown skin, sickly white with fear.

"Is the meat ready to be cooked?" asked the voice, more rapidly.

"It is ready; it is ready."

"Is the pot hot to cook it?" it continued, in a sort of scream that echoed painfully down the great recesses of the cave.

"It is hot; it is hot."

"Great heavens!" shouted Leo, "remember the writing, *'The people who place pots upon the heads of strangers.'"*

As he said the words, before we could stir, or even take the matter in, two great ruffians sprang up, and, grasping the long pincers, plunged them into the heart of the fire, while the woman who had been caressing Mahomed suddenly produced a fibre noose from under her girdle or moocha, and, slipping it over his shoulders, ran it tight, the men next him seizing him by the legs. These two men with the pincers heaved simultaneously, and, scattering the fire this way and that upon the rocky floor, lifted from it a large earthenware pot, heated to a white glow. In an instant, almost with a single movement, they had reached the spot where Mahomed was struggling. He fought like a fiend, shrieking in the abandonment of his despair, and notwithstanding the noose round him, and the efforts of the men who held his legs, the advancing wretches were for the moment unable

---

[1] We afterwards learnt that its motive was to pretend to the victim that he was the object of love and admiration, and so to soothe his injured feelings, and cause him to expire in a happy and contented frame of mind. —L. H. H.

to accomplish their purpose, which, horrid and incredible as it seems, was *to put the red-hot pot upon his head.*

I sprang to my feet with a yell of horror, and drawing my revolver I fired it by instinct straight at the diabolical woman who had been caressing Mahomed, and who was now gripping him in her arms. The bullet struck her in the back and killed her, and to this day I am glad of it, for, as it transpired afterwards, she had availed herself of the anthropophagous customs of the Amahagger to organise this sacrifice in revenge of the slight put upon her by Job. She sank down dead, and as she dropped, to my terror and dismay, Mahomed, by a superhuman effort, burst from his tormentors, and, springing high into the air, fell dying upon her corpse. The heavy bullet from my pistol had driven through the bodies of both, at once striking down the murderess and saving her victim from a death a hundred times more dreadful. It was an awful and yet a most merciful accident.

For a moment there was a silence of astonishment. The Amahagger had never heard the report of a firearm before, and its effects dismayed them. The next instant a man close to us recovered himself, and seized his spear preparatory to making a lunge with it at Leo, who was the nearest to him.

"Run for it!" I shouted, setting the example by starting up the cave as hard as my legs would carry me. I would have headed for the open if it had been possible, but there were men in the way, besides I had caught sight of the forms of a crowd of people standing out clearly against the skyline beyond the entrance to the cave. Up the cave I went, and after me came the others, and after them thundered the whole crowd of cannibals, mad with fury at the death of the woman. With a bound I cleared the prostrate form of Mahomed. As I flew over him I felt the heat from the red-hot pot, which was lying close by, strike upon my legs, and by its glow saw his hands—for he was not quite dead—still feebly moving. At the top of the cave was a little platform of rock three feet or so high by about eight deep, on which two large lamps were placed at night. Whether this platform had been left as a seat, or as a raised point afterwards to be cut away when it had served its purpose as a standing-place from which to carry on the excavations, I do not know—at least, I did not then. At least we reached it, all three of us, and, jumping on to it, prepared to sell our lives as dearly as we could. For a few seconds the crowd that was pressing on our heels hung back when they saw us face round upon them. Job was on one side of the rock to the left, Leo in the centre, and I to the right. Behind us were the lamps. Leo bent forward, and looked down the long lane of shadows, terminating in the fire and lighted lamps, through which the quiet forms of our would-be murderers flitted to and fro with the faint light glinting on their spears, for even their fury was silent as a bulldog's. The only other thing visible was the red-hot pot still glowing angrily in the gloom. There was a curious gleam in Leo's eyes, and his handsome face was set like a stone. In his right hand was his heavy hunting-knife. He shifted its thong a little up his wrist, then he put his arm round me and embraced me.

"Good-bye, old fellow," he said, "my dear friend—my more than father. We have no chance against those scoundrels they will finish us in a few minutes, and eat us afterwards, I suppose. Good-bye. I led you into this. I hope you will forgive me. Good-bye, Job."

"God's will be done," I said, setting my teeth, as I prepared for the end. At that moment, with an exclamation, Job lifted his revolver, fired, and hit a man—not the man he had aimed at, by the way: anything that Job shot *at* was perfectly safe.

On they came with a rush, and I fired too as fast as I could, and checked them—between us, Job and I, besides the woman, killed or mortally wounded five men with our pistols before they were emptied. But we had no time to reload, and still they came on in a way which was almost splendid in its recklessness, since they did not know but that we could continue shooting for ever.

A great fellow bounded upon the platform, and Leo struck him dead with one blow of his powerful arm, sending the knife right through him. I did the same by another, but Job missed his stroke, and I saw a brawny Amahagger grip him by the middle and whirl him off the rock. The knife not being secured by a thong fell from Job's hand at that moment, and, by a most happy accident for him, lit upon its handle on the rock, just as the body of the Amahagger, who was undermost, struck upon its point and was transfixed thereon. What happened to Job after that I am sure I do not know, but my own impression is that he lay still upon the corpse of his deceased assailant, 'playing 'possum,' as the Americans say. As for myself, soon I was involved in a desperate encounter with two ruffians, who, luckily for me, had left their spears behind them; and for the first time in my life the great physical power with which Nature has endowed me stood me in good stead. I had hacked at the head of one man with my hunting-knife, which was almost as big and heavy as a short sword, with such vigour that the sharp steel split his skull down to the eyes, and was held so fast by it that

as he suddenly fell from me sideways the knife was twisted out
of my hand.

Then it was that the two others sprang upon me. I saw them
coming, and wound an arm round the waist of each, and down we
all fell upon the floor of the cave together, rolling over and over.
They were strong men, but I was mad with rage, and that awful
lust of battle which will creep into the hearts of the most civilised
of us when blows are flying, and life and death tremble on the
turn. My arms were about the two swarthy demons, and I hugged
them till I heard their ribs crack and crunch up beneath my gripe.
They twisted and writhed like snakes, and clawed and battered
at me with their fists, but I held on. Lying on my back there, so
that their bodies might protect me from spear thrusts from above,
I slowly crushed the life out of them, and as I did so, strange as
it may seem, I thought of what the amiable Head of my College
at Cambridge (who is a member of the Peace Society) and my
brother Fellows would say if by clairvoyance they could see me,
of all men, playing such a bloody game. Soon my assailants grew
faint, and almost ceased to struggle; their breath had failed them,
and they were dying, but still I dared not leave them, for they
died very slowly. I knew that if I relaxed my gripe they would
revive. The other savages probably thought—for the three of
us were lying in the shadow of the ledge—that we were all dead
together, at any rate they did not interfere with our little tragedy.

I turned my head, and as I lay gasping in the throes of that
awful struggle I could see that Leo was off the rock now, for the
lamplight fell full upon him. He was still on his feet, but in the
centre of a surging mass of struggling men, who were striving to
pull him down as wolves pull down a stag. Up above them
towered his beautiful pale face crowned with its bright curls as
he swayed to and fro, and I saw that he was fighting with a
desperate abandonment and an energy that was at once splendid
and hideous to behold. He drove his knife through one man—
they were so close to and mixed up with him that they could not
come at him to kill him with their big spears, and they had no
knives or sticks. The man fell, and then somehow the knife was
wrenched from Leo's hand, leaving him defenceless, and I thought
that the end had come. But no; with a desperate effort he broke
loose from them, seized the body of the man he had just slain,
and lifting it high in the air hurled it right at the mob of his assailants, so that the shock and weight of it swept some five or six
of them to the earth. But in a minute they were up again, all except one, whose skull was smashed, and had once more fastened

upon him. And now slowly, and with infinite labour and strug-gling, the wolves bore the lion down. Once even then he recovered himself, and felled an Amahagger with his fist, but it was more than any man could do to hold his own for long against so many, and at last he came crashing down upon the rock floor, falling as an oak falls, and bearing with him to the earth all those who clung about him. They gripped him by his arms and legs, and then cleared off his body.

"A spear," cried a voice—"a spear to cut his throat, and a ves-sel to catch his blood."

I shut my eyes, for I saw a man run up with the spear, and myself, I could not stir to Leo's help, for I was growing weak: the two men on me were not yet dead, and a deadly sickness overcame me.

Then suddenly there was a disturbance, and involuntarily I opened my eyes again, and looked towards the scene of murder. The girl Ustane had thrown herself on Leo's prostrate form, covering his body with her body, and fastening her arms about his neck. They tried to drag her from him, but she twisted her legs round his, and hung on like a bulldog, or rather like a creeper to a tree, and they could not. Then they tried to stab him in the side without hurting her, but somehow she shielded him, and he was only wounded.

At last they lost patience.

"Drive the spear through the man and the woman together," said a voice, the same voice which had asked the questions at that ghastly feast, "so of a verity shall they be wed."

Then I saw the man with the weapon straighten himself for the effort. I saw the cold steel gleam on high, and once more I shut my eyes.

Even as I did so I heard the voice of a man thunder out, in tones that rang and echoed down the rocky ways—

"Cease!"

Then I fainted, and as I sank away it flashed through my darkening mind that I was passing down into the last oblivion of death.

CHAPTER IX

A LITTLE FOOT

WHEN I opened my eyes again I found myself lying on a skin mat not far from the fire round which we had been gathered for that dreadful feast. Near to me lay Leo, still lost in a swoon, and over him bent the tall form of the girl Ustane, who was washing a deep spear wound in his side with cold water before binding it up with linen. Leaning against the wall of the cave behind her stood Job, apparently uninjured, but bruised and trembling. On the other side of the fire, tossed about this way and that, as though they had thrown themselves down to sleep in some moment of absolute exhaustion, were the bodies of those whom we had killed in our frightful struggle for life. I counted them: there were twelve besides the woman, and the corpse of poor Mahomed, who had died by my hand, which, the fire-stained pot at its side, was placed at the end of the irregular line. To the left a number of men were engaged in binding behind them the arms of the survivors of the cannibals, and in fastening them two and two. These villains were submitting to their fate with an air of sulky indifference which accorded ill with the baffled fury that gleamed in their sombre eyes. In front of the prisoners, directing the operations, stood no other than our friend Billali, looking rather tired, but particularly patriarchal with his flowing beard, and as cool and unconcerned as though he were superintending the cutting up of an ox.

Presently he turned, and perceiving that I was sitting up advanced to me, and with the utmost courtesy said that he trusted that I felt better. I answered that at present I scarcely knew how I felt, except that I ached all over.

Then he bent down and examined Leo's wound.

"It is an evil cut," he said, "but the spear has not pierced the entrails. He will recover."

"Thanks to thy arrival, my father," I answered. "In another minute we should all have been beyond the reach of recovery, for those devils of thine sought to slay us as they would have slain our servant," and I pointed towards Mahomed.

The old man ground his teeth, and I saw an extraordinary expression of malignity flare in his eyes.

"Fear not, my son," he answered. "Vengeance shall be taken on them such as would make the flesh twist upon the bones merely to hear of it. To *She* shall they go, and her revenge shall be worthy of her greatness. That man," pointing to Mahomed,

"I tell thee that man would have died a merciful death to the death these hyæna-men shall die. Tell me, I pray of thee, how it came about."

In a few words I sketched what had happened.

"Ah, so!" he answered. "Thou seest, my son, here there is a custom that if a stranger comes into this country, he may be slain by 'the pot,' and eaten."

"That is hospitality turned upside down," I answered feebly. "In our country we entertain a stranger, and give him food to eat. Here you eat him, and are entertained."

"It is a custom," he answered, with a shrug. "Myself, I think it an evil one; but then," he added by an afterthought, " I do not like the taste of strangers, especially after they have wandered through the swamps and lived on wildfowl. When '*She-who-must-be-obeyed*' sent orders that you were to be saved alive she said naught of the black man, therefore, being hyænas, these men lusted after his flesh, and it was the woman, whom thou didst rightly slay, who put it into their evil hearts to 'hotpot' him. Well, they will have their reward. Better for them would it be if they had never seen the light than that they should stand before *She* in her terrible anger. Happy are those of them who died by your hands."

"Ah," he went on, "it was a gallant fight that you fought. Knowest thou, long-armed old baboon that thou art, that thou hast crushed in the ribs of those two who are laid out there as though they were but the shell on an egg? And the young one, the lion, it was a beautiful stand that he made—one against so many; three did he slay outright, and that one there"—and he pointed to a body which was still moving a little—"will die anon, for his head is cracked across, and others of those who are bound are hurt. It was a gallant fight, and thou and he have made a friend of me by it, for I love to see a well-fought fray. But tell me, my son, the Baboon—and now I think of it thy face, too, is hairy, and altogether like a baboon's—how was it that you slew those with a hole in them?—You made a noise, they say, and slew them—they fell down on their faces at the noise?"

I explained to him as well as I could, but very shortly—for I felt terribly wearied, and was only persuaded to talk through fear of offending one so powerful if I refused to do so—what were the properties of gunpowder, whereupon he suggested that I should illustrate my words by operating on the person of one of the prisoners. One, he said, never would be counted, and the experiment would not only interest him, but would give me an immediate opportunity of revenge. He was greatly astounded when I told him that it was not our custom to wreak our wrongs in cold blood, and that we left vengeance to the law and a higher Power, of which he knew nothing. I added, however, that when I recovered I would take him out shooting with us, and that he should kill an animal for himself. With this prospect he was as pleased as is a child at the promise of a new toy.

Just then Leo opened his eyes beneath the stimulus of some brandy, of which we still had a little, that Job had poured down his throat, and our conversation came to an end.

After this we managed to carry Leo, who was in a very poor way indeed, and only half conscious, safely to bed, supported by Job and that brave girl Ustane, whom, had I not been afraid that she might resent it, I would certainly have kissed in acknowledgment of her courage in saving my boy's life at the risk of her own. But Ustane was a young person with whom I felt that it would be unadvisable to take liberties unless certain that they might not be misunderstood, so I repressed my inclinations. Then, bruised and battered, but with a sense of safety in my breast to which I had for some days been a stranger, I crept off to my own little sepulchre, not forgetting before I laid down in it to thank Providence from the bottom of my heart that it was not a sepulchre indeed, as, save for a merciful combination of events that I can only attribute to its protection, it would certainly have been for me this night. Few men have been nearer their end and yet escaped it than we were on that dreadful day.

I am a bad sleeper at the best of times, and my dreams that night when at last I sank to rest were not of the pleasantest. The awful sight of poor Mahomed struggling to escape the red-hot pot would haunt them. Then in the background of the vision a draped form hovered continually, which, from time to time, seemed to draw the coverings from its body, revealing now the perfect shape of a lovely blooming woman, and again the white bones of a grinning skeleton, which, as it veiled and unveiled, uttered the mysterious and apparently meaningless sentence:—

"That which is alive hath known death, and that which is dead yet can never die, for in the Circle of the Spirit life is naught and death is naught. Yea, all things live for ever, though at times they sleep and are forgotten."

The morning dawned at last, but when it came I found that I was too stiff and sore to rise. About seven Job arrived, limping terribly, his round face the colour of a rotten apple, and told me that Leo had slept fairly, but was very weak. Two hours afterwards Billali (Job called him 'Billy-goat,' to which animal his white beard gave him some resemblance, or more familiarly

'Billy') came too, bearing a lamp in his hand, his towering form reaching nearly to the roof of the little chamber. I pretended to be asleep, and through the cracks of my eyelids I watched his sardonic but handsome old face. He fixed his hawk-like eyes upon me, and stroked his glorious white beard, which, by the way, would have been worth a hundred a year to any London barber as an advertisement.

"Ah!" I heard him mutter (Billali had a habit of muttering to himself), "he is ugly—ugly as the other is beautiful—a very Baboon; it was a good name. But I like the man. Strange now, at my age, that I should like a man. What says the proverb —'Mistrust all men, and slay him whom thou mistrustest over-much; and as for women, flee from them, for they are evil, and in the end will destroy thee.' It is a good proverb, especially the last part of it: I think that it must have come down from the ancients. Nevertheless I like this Baboon, and I wonder where they taught him his tricks, and I trust that *She* will not bewitch him. Poor Baboon! he must be wearied after that fight. I will go lest I should awake him."

I waited till he had turned and was nearly through the entrance, walking softly on tiptoe, then I called after him.

"My father," I said, "is it thou?"

"Yes, my son, it is I; but let me not disturb thee. I did but come to see how thou didst fare, and to tell thee that those who would have slain thee, my Baboon, are by now far on their road to *She*. *She* said that you also were to come at once, but I fear you cannot yet."

"Nay," I said, "not till we have recovered a little; but have me borne out into the daylight, I pray thee, my father. I love not this place."

"Ah, no," he answered, "it hath a sad air. I remember when I was a boy I found the body of a fair woman lying where thou liest now—yes, on that very bench. She was so beautiful that I was wont to creep in hither with a lamp and gaze upon her. Had it not been for her cold hands, almost could I think that she slept and would one day awake, so fair and peaceful was she in her robes of white. White was she, too, and her hair was yellow, and fell down her almost to the feet. There are many such still in the tombs at the place where *She* is, for those who set them there had a way I know naught of whereby to save their beloved from the crumbling hand of Decay, even when Death had slain them. Ay, day by day I came hither, and gazed on her, till at last—laugh not at me, stranger, for I was but a silly lad—I learned to love that dead form, the shell which once had held a life that no more is. I would creep up to her and kiss her cold face, and wonder how many men had lived and died since she was, and who had loved her and embraced her in the days that long have passed away. And, my Baboon, I think I learned wisdom from that dead one, for of a truth it taught me of the littleness of Life, and the length of Death, and how all things that are under the sun go down one path, and are for ever forgotten. And so I mused, and it seemed to me that knowledge flowed into me from the dead, till one day my mother, a watchful woman, but hasty-minded, seeing I was changed, followed me, and saw the beautiful white one, and feared that I was bewitched, as, indeed I was. So, half in dread and half in anger, she took the lamp, and standing the dead woman up against the wall yonder, set fire to her hair, and she burnt fiercely, even down to the feet, for those who are thus kept burn excellently well.

"See, my son, the smoke of her burning still hangs upon the roof."

I looked up doubtfully, and there, sure enough, on the rock of the sepulchre, was spread an unctuous and sooty mark, three feet or more across. Doubtless in the course of years it had been rubbed off the sides of the little cave, but on the roof it remained, and there was no mistaking its appearance.

"She burned," he went on in a meditative voice, "even to the feet, but the feet I came back and saved, cutting the charred bone from them, and I hid them under the stone bench yonder, wrapped in a piece of linen. Surely, I remember it as though it were but yesterday. Perchance they are there, if none have found them, even to this hour. Of a truth I have not entered the chamber from that time to this very day. Stay, I will look," and, kneeling down, Billali groped with his long arm in the recess under the stone bench. Presently his face brightened, and with an exclamation he drew something forth which was caked in dust that he shook on to the floor. It was covered with the remains of a rotting rag, which he undid, and revealed to my astonished gaze a beautiful shaped and almost white woman's foot, looking as fresh and firm as though it had been placed there yesterday.

"Thou seest, my son the Baboon," he said, in a sad voice, "I spake the truth to thee, for here is yet one foot remaining. Take it, my son, and gaze upon it."

I took this cold fragment of mortality in my hand, and looked at in the light of the lamp with feelings which I cannot describe, so compounded were they of astonishment, fear, and fascination. It was light, much lighter I should say than it had been in the living state, and the flesh to all appearance was still flesh, though about it there clung a faintly aromatic odour. For the rest it was not shrunk or shrivelled, or even black and unsightly, like the flesh of Egyptian mummies, but plump and fair, and, except where it had been slightly scorched, perfect as on the day of death—a very triumph of embalming.

Poor little foot! I set it down upon the stone bench where it had lain for so many thousand years, and wondered whose was the beauty that it had upborne through the pomp and pageantry of a forgotten civilisation—first as a merry child's, then as a blushing maid's, and lastly as that of a perfect woman. Through what halls of Life had its step echoed, and in the end, with that courage had it trodden down the dusty ways of Death! To whose side had it stolen in the hush of night when the black slave slept upon the marble floor, and who had listened for its coming? Shapely little foot! Well might it have been set upon the proud neck of a conqueror bent at last to woman's beauty, and well might the lips of nobles and of kings have been pressed upon its jewelled whiteness.

I wrapped this relic of the past in the remnants of the old linen rag which, I believe, had been a portion of its owner's grave-clothes, for it was partially burnt, and hid it away in my travelling-bag—a strange resting-place, I thought. Then with Billali's help I staggered out to see Leo. I found him dreadfully bruised, worse even than myself, perhaps owing to the excessive whiteness of his skin, and faint and weak with the loss of blood from the flesh wound in his side, but for that very cheerful, and asking for some breakfast. Job and Ustane lifted him on to the bottom, or rather the sacking, of a litter, which was taken from its pole for that purpose, and with the aid of old Billali carried him out into the shade at the mouth of the cave, from which, by the way, every trace of the slaughter of the previous night had now been removed. There we all breakfasted, and indeed spent that day, and most of the two which followed.

On the third morning Job and myself were practically recovered. Leo also was so much better that I yielded to Billali's often expressed entreaty, and agreed to set out at once upon our journey to Kôr, which we were told was the name of the place where the mysterious *She* lived, though I still feared for its effect upon Leo, and especially lest the motion should cause his wound, which was scarcely skinned over, to break open again. Indeed, had it not been for Billali's evident anxiety to start, which led us to suspect that some difficulty or danger might threaten us if we did not comply with it, I would not have consented to go so soon.

CHAPTER X

SPECULATIONS

WITHIN an hour of our final decision to start five litters were brought up to the door of the cave, each accompanied by four bearers and two spare hands, and with them a band of fifty armed Amahagger, who were to form the escort and carry the baggage. Three of these litters, of course, were for us, and one for Billali, who, I was immensely relieved to hear, proposed to accompany us, while the fifth I presumed was for the use of Ustane.

"Does the lady go with us, my father?" I asked of Billali, as he stood superintending things in general.

He shrugged his shoulders as he answered—

"If she wills. In this country the women do what they please. We worship them, and give them their way, because without them the world could not go on; they are the source of life."

"Ah!" I said, the matter never having struck me quite in that light before.

"We worship them," he continued, "up to a point, till at last they grow unbearable, which," he added, "happens about every second generation."

"And then what do you do?" I asked with curiosity.

"Then," he answered, with a faint smile, "we rise, and kill the old ones as an example to the young ones, and to show them that we are the strongest. My poor wife was killed in that way three years ago. It was very sad, but to tell thee the truth, my son, life has been happier since, for my age protects me from the maidens."

"In short," I replied, quoting the saying of a politician whose wisdom has not yet lightened the darkness of the Amahagger, "thou hast found thy position one of greater freedom and less responsibility."

This phrase puzzled him a little at first from its vagueness, though I think my translation hit off the sense very well, but at last he understood, and appreciated it.

"Yes, yes, my Baboon," he said, "I see it now, but all the 'responsibilities' are killed, at least some of them are, and that is why there are so few old women about just now. Well, they brought it on themselves. As for this girl," he went on, in a graver tone, "I know not what to say. She is a brave girl, and she loves the Lion; thou sawest how she clung to him, and saved his life. Also, according to our custom, she is wed to him, and has a right to go where he goes, unless," he added significantly, "*She* would say her no, for her word overrides all rights."

"And if *She* bade her leave him, and the girl refused? What then?"

"If," he said, with a shrug, "the hurricane bids the tree to bend, and it will not, what happens?"

Then without waiting for an answer, he turned and walked to his litter, and in ten minutes from that time we were all well under way.

It took us an hour and more to cross the cup of the volcanic plain, and another half-hour or so to climb the edge on the farther side. Once there, however, the view was a very fine one. Before us lay a long steep slope of grassy plain, broken here and there by clumps of trees, mostly of the thorn tribe. At the bottom of this gentle slope, some nine or ten miles away, we could discern a dim sea of marsh, over which the foul vapours hung like smoke about a city. It was easy work for the bearers down the slopes, and by midday we had reached the borders of the dismal swamp. Here we halted to eat our midday meal, then, following a winding and devious track, we plunged into the morass. Presently the path, at any rate to our unaccustomed eyes, grew so faint as to be almost indistinguishable from those made by the aquatic beasts and birds, and it is to this day a mystery to me how our bearers found their way across the marshes. Ahead of the cavalcade marched two men with long poles, which they now and again plunged into the ground before them, the reason of this being that the nature of the soil frequently changed from causes with which I am not acquainted, so that places which might be safe enough to cross one month would certainly swallow the wayfarer the next. Never did I see a more dreary and depressing scene. Miles on miles of quagmire, varied only by bright green strips of comparatively solid ground, and by deep and sullen pools fringed with tall rushes, in which the bitterns boomed and the frogs croaked incessantly: miles upon miles of it without a break, unless the fever fog can be called a break. The only life in this great morass was that of the aquatic birds, and the animals that fed on them, of both of which there were vast numbers. Geese, cranes, ducks, teal, coot, snipe, and plover swarmed all around us, many being of varieties which were quite new to me, and all so tame that one could almost have knocked them over with a stick. Among these birds I noticed especially a very beautiful variety of painted snipe, almost the size of a woodcock, and with a flight more resembling that bird's than an English snipe's. In the pools, too, lived a species of small alligator or enormous iguana, I do not know which, that fed, Billali told me, upon the waterfowl, also large quantities of a hideous black water-snake, of which the

bite is dangerous, though not, I gathered, so deadly as that of
a cobra or a puff adder. The bullfrogs were also very large, with
voices proportionate to their size; and as for the mosquitoes
—the 'musquiteers,' as Job called them—they were, if possible,
even worse than they had been on the river, and tormented us
greatly. Undoubtedly, however, the worst feature of the swamp
was the awful smell of rotting vegetation that hung about it,
which at times was positively overpowering, and the malarious
exhalations that accompained it, which we were of course obliged
to breathe.

On we went through it all, till at last the sun sank in sullen
splendour just as we reached a spot of rising ground about two
acres in extent—an oasis of dry land in the midst of the miry
wilderness—where Billali announced that we were to camp. The
camping, however, turned out to be a very simple process, and
consisted, in fact, in sitting down on the ground round a scanty
fire built of sere reeds and some wood that had been brought with
us. However, we made the best we could of it, and smoked and
ate with such appetite as the smell of damp, stifling heat would
allow, for it was very hot on this low land, and yet, oddly enough,
chilly at times. But, however hot it was, we were glad enough
to keep near the fire, because we found that the mosquitoes did
not like the smoke. Presently we rolled ourselves up in our blankets and tried to go to sleep, but so far as I was concerned the
bullfrogs, and the extraordinary roaring and alarming sound
produced by hundreds of snipe hovering high in the air, made
sleep an impossibility, to say nothing of our other discomforts.
I turned and looked at Leo, who was next me; he was dozing,
but his face had a flushed appearance that I did not like, and by
the flickering firelight I saw Ustane, who was lying on the other
side of him, raise herself from time to time upon her elbow, and
glance at him anxiously enough.

However, I could do nothing to help him, for we had already
taken a good dose of quinine, the only preventive we possessed;
so I lay and watched the stars come out by thousands, till all the
immense arch of heaven was strewn with glittering points, and
every point a world! Here was a glorious sight by which man
might well measure his own insignificance! Soon I gave up thinking about it, for the mind wearies easily when it strives to grap-
ple with the Infinite, and to trace the footsteps of the Almighty
as He strides from sphere to sphere, or deduce His purpose from
His works. Such things are not for us to know. Knowledge is to
the strong, and we are weak. Too much wisdom perchance would
blind our imperfect sight, and too much strength would make us

drunk, and over-weight our feeble reason till it fell and we were drowned in the depths of our own vanity. For what is the first result of man's increased knowledge interpreted from Nature's book by the persistent effort of his purblind observation? Is it not but too often to make him question the existence of his Maker, or, indeed, of any intelligent purpose beyond his own? Truth is veiled, because we could no more look upon her glory than we can upon the sun. It would destroy us. Full knowledge is not for man as man is here, for his capacities, which he is apt to think so great, are indeed but small. The vessel is soon filled, and were one-thousandth part of the unutterable and silent Wisdom that directs the rolling of those shining spheres, and the Force which makes them roll, pressed into it, it would be shattered into fragments. Perhaps in some other place and time it may be otherwise. Who can tell? Here the lot of man born of the flesh is but to endure midst toil and tribulation; to catch at the bubbles blown by Fate, which he calls pleasures, thankful if before they burst they rest a moment in his hand, and when the tragedy is played out, and his hour comes to perish, to pass humbly whither he knows not.

Above me as I lay shone the eternal stars, and there at my feet the impish marsh-born balls of fire rolled this way and that, vapour-tossed and earth-desiring, and I thought that in the two I saw a type and image of what man is, and of what man may perchance become, if the living Power who ordained him and them should so ordain this also.

Many such speculations passed through my mind that night. They come to torment us all at times. I say to torment, for, alas! thinking can only serve to measure out the helplessness of thought. What is the purpose of our feeble crying in the silences of space? Can our dim intelligence read the secrets of that star-strewn sky? Does any answer come out of it? Never any at all —nothing but echoes and fantastic vision! And yet we believe that beyond the horizon of the grave there is an answer, and that Faith supplies it. Without Faith we should suffer moral death, and by the help of Faith we yet may climb to Heaven.

Wearied, but still sleepless, I fell to considering our undertaking, and how wild it was. Yet how strangely the story seemed to fit in with what had been written centuries ago upon the sherd! Who was this extraordinary woman, Queen over a people apparently as extraordinary as herself, and reigning amidst the vestiges of a lost civilisation? And what was the meaning of this story of the Fire which gave unending life? Could it be possible that any fluid or essence should exist which might so fortify these

fleshy walls that they could from age to age resist the mines and
batterings of decay? It was possible, though not probable. The
indefinite continuation of life would not, as poor Vincey said, be
so marvellous a thing as the production of life and its temporary
endurance. And if it were true, what then? The person who
found it might no doubt rule the world. He could accumulate
all the wealth in the world, and the power, and all the wisdom
that is power. He might give a lifetime to study of each art or
science. Well, if that were so, and if this *She* were practically
immortal, which I did not for one moment believe, how was it
that, with all these things at her feet, she preferred to remain
in a cave amongst a society of cannibals? Surely this settled
the question. The story was monstrous, and only worthy of the
superstitious days in which it was written. At any rate, I was
very certain that *I* would not attempt to attain unending life.
I had known far too many worries and disappointments and
secret bitternesses during my forty odd years of existence to
wish that this state of affairs should be continued indefinitely.
And yet I suppose that, comparatively speaking, my life has
been a happy one.

And then, reflecting that at the present moment there was
far more likelihood of our earthly careers being cut exceedingly
short than of their being unduly prolonged, at last I managed to
fall asleep, a fact for which anybody who reads this narrative,
if anybody ever does, may very probably be thankful.

When I woke again it was just dawning, and the guards and
bearers were moving about like ghosts through the dense morning mists making ready for our start. The fire had died quite
down, and I rose and stretched myself, shivering in every limb
with the damp cold of the dawn. Then I looked at Leo. He
was sitting up, holding his hands to his head, and I saw that his
face was flushed and his eyes bright, and yet yellow round the
pupils.

"Well, Leo," I said, "how do you feel?"

"I feel as though I were going to die," he answered hoarsely.
"My head is splitting, my body is trembling, and I am deathly
sick."

I whistled, or if I did not whistle I felt inclined to, for Leo
had a sharp attack of fever. I went to Job, and asked him for
the quinine, of which, fortunately, we had still a good supply,
only to find that Job himself was not much better. He complained
of pains across the back, and dizziness, and was almost incapable of helping himself. Then I did the only thing it was possible
to do under the circumstances—gave them both about ten grains

of quinine, and took a slightly smaller dose myself as a matter of precaution. After that I found Billali, and explained to him how matters stood, asking at the same time what he thought had best be done. He came with me, and looked at Leo and Job, whom, by the way, he had named the Pig on account of his fatness, round face, and small eyes.

"Ah!" he said, when we were out of earshot, "the fever! I thought so. The Lion has it badly, but he is young, and he may live. As for the Pig, his attack is not so bad; it is the 'little fever' which he has; that always begins with pains across the back; it will spend itself upon his fat."

"Can they go on, my father?" I asked.

"Nay, my son, they must go on. If they stop here they will certainly die; also, they will be better in the litters than on the ground. By to-night, if all goes well, we shall be across the marsh and in good air. Come, let us lift them into the litters and start, for it is very bad to stand still in this morning fog. We can eat our meal as we go."

This we did accordingly, and with a heavy heart I set out once more upon our strange journey. For the first three hours all went as well as could be expected, and then an accident happened that nearly lost us the pleasure of the company of our venerable friend Billali, whose litter was leading the procession. We were wading through a particularly dangerous stretch of quagmire, in which the bearers sometimes sank up to their knees. Indeed it was a mystery to me how they contrived to carry the heavy litters at all over such ground as that which we were traversing, though the two spare men, as well as the four bearers, had of course to put their shoulders to the pole.

Presently, as we blundered and floundered along, there was a sharp cry, then a storm of exclamations, and last of all, a most tremendous splash, and the whole caravan halted.

I jumped out of my litter and ran forward. About twenty yards ahead was the lip of one of those sullen peaty pools of which I have spoken, the path we were following running along the top of its bank, that, as it happened, was a steep one. Looking towards this pool, to my horror I saw that Billali's litter was floating on it, while as for Billali himself, he was nowhere to be seen. To make matters clear I may as well explain at once what had happened. One of Billali's bearers had unfortunately trodden on a basking snake, which bit him in the ankle, whereon not unnaturally he had to let go of the pole, and then, finding that he was tumbling down the bank, grasped at the litter to save himself. The result was exactly what might have been expected. The litter was pulled over the edge of the bank, the bearers let go, and together with Billali and the man who had been bitten rolled into the slimy pool. When I reached the edge of the water neither of them was to be seen; indeed, the unfortunate bearer never was seen again. Either he struck his head against something, or was wedged in the mud, or possibly the snake-bite paralysed him. At any rate he vanished. But though Billali had disappeared, his whereabouts was clear enough from the agitation of the floating litter, in the bearing cloth and curtains of which he lay entangled.

"He is there! Our father is there!" said one of the men, but he did not stir a finger to help him, nor did any of the others. They simply stood and stared at the water.

"Out of the way, you brutes!" I shouted in English, and, throwing off my hat, I took a run and sprang well out into the horrid slimy-looking pool. A couple of strokes took me to where Billali was struggling beneath the cloth.

Somehow, I do not quite know how, I managed to push it free of him, and his venerable head all covered with green slime, like that of a yellowish Bacchus with ivy leaves, emerged upon the surface of the water. The rest was easy, for Billali was an eminently practical individual, and had the common sense not to grasp hold of me as drowning people often do. So I caught him by the arm, and towed him to the bank, through the mud of which we were dragged with difficulty. Such a filthy spectacle as we presented I have never seen before or since, and it will perhaps give some idea of the almost superhuman dignity of Billali's appearance when I saw that, coughing, half drowned, and covered with mud and green slime as he was, with his beautiful beard drawn to a dripping point, like a Chinaman's freshly oiled pigtail, he still looked venerable and imposing.

"You dogs!" he said, addressing the bearers, so soon as he had recovered sufficiently to speak, "you left me, your father, to drown. Had it not been for this stranger, my son the Baboon, assuredly I should have drowned. Well, I will remember it," and he fixed them with his gleaming though slightly watery eye, in a way I saw that they did not like, although they tried to appear sulkily indifferent.

"As for thee, my son," the old man went on, turning towards me and grasping my hand, "rest assured that I am thy friend through good and evil. Thou hast saved my life: perchance a day may come when I shall save thine."

After that we cleaned ourselves as best we could, rescued the litter, and went on, *minus* the man who had been drowned. I do not know if it was because he chanced to be unpopular, or from native indifference and selfishness of temperament, but I am bound to say that nobody seemed to grieve much over his sudden and final disappearance, except the men who had to do his share of the work.

CHAPTER XI

THE PLAIN OF KÔR

ABOUT an hour before sundown, at last, to my unbounded gratitude, we emerged from the great belt of marsh on to land that swelled upwards in a succession of rolling waves. Just on the hither side of the crest of the first wave we halted for the night. My first care was to examine Leo's condition. It was, if anything, worse than in the morning, and a new and very distressing feature, vomiting, set in, and continued till dawn. Not one hour of sleep did I get that night, for I passed it in assisting Ustane, who was one of the most gentle and indefatigable nurses I ever saw, to wait upon Leo and Job. However, the air here was warm and genial without being too hot, and there were not many mosquitoes. Also we were above the level of the marsh mist, which lay stretched beneath us like the dim smokepall over a city, lit up here and there by the wandering globes of fen fire. Thus it will be seen that we were, speaking comparatively, very well off.

By dawn on the following morning Leo was quite light-headed, and fancied that he was divided into halves. I was dreadfully distressed, and began to wonder with a sort of sick fear what the end of his attack would be. Alas! I had heard but too much of how these fevers generally terminate. As I was wondering Billali came up and said that we must be moving on, more especially as, in his opinion, if Leo did not reach some spot where he could be quiet, and have proper nursing, within the next twelve hours, his death would be only a matter of a day or two. I could not but agree with him, so we placed Leo in the litter, and started, Ustane walking by his side to keep the flies off him, and watch that he did not throw himself out on to the ground.

Within half an hour of sunrise we had reached the top of the rise of which I have spoken, and a most beautiful view broke upon our gaze. Beneath us was a rich stretch of country, verdant with grass and lovely with foliage and flowers. In the background, at a distance, so far as I could judge, of some eighteen miles from where we then stood, a huge and extraordinary moun-

tain rose abruptly from the plain. The base of the great mountain appeared to consist of a grassy slope, but rising upon this,
I should say, from subsequent observation, at an altitude of
about five hundred feet above the level of the plain, was a
tremendous and absolutely precipitous wall of bare rock, quite
twelve or fifteen hundred feet in height. The shape of the mountain, which was undoubtedly of volcanic origin, seemed to be
round, but, as only a segment of its circle was visible, it proved
difficult to estimate its exact size, which was enormous. Afterwards I discovered that it could not cover less than fifty square
miles of ground. Anything more grand and imposing than the
sight presented by this great natural castle, starting in solitary
grandeur from the level of the plain, I never saw, and I suppose
I never shall. Its very solitude added to its majesty, and its
towering cliffs seemed to kiss the sky. Indeed for the most part
they were clothed in clouds that lay in fleecy masses upon their
broad and even battlements.

I sat up in my hammock and gazed across the plain at this
thrilling and majestic prospect, and I suppose that Billali noticed
me, for he brought his litter alongside.

"Behold the House of *'She-who-must-be-obeyed'*!" he said.
"Had ever a queen such a throne before?"

"It is wonderful, my father," I answered. "But how do we
enter? Those cliffs look hard to climb."

"Thou shalt see, my Baboon. Look now at the path below
us. What thinkest thou that it is? Thou art a wise man. Come,
tell me."

I looked, and saw what appeared to be a line of roadway
running straight towards the base of the mountain, though
it was covered with turf. There were high banks on each side
of it, broken here and there, but fairly continuous on the whole,
the meaning of which I did not understand. It seemed so very
odd that anybody should embank a roadway.

"Well, my father," I answered, "I suppose that it is a road,
otherwise I should have been inclined to say that it was the
bed of a river, or rather," I added, observing the extraordinary
directness of the cutting, "of a canal."

Billali—who, by the way, was none the worse for his immer-
sion of the day before—nodded his head sagely as he replied—

"Thou art right, my son. It is a channel cut out by those who
were before us in this place to carry away water. Of this I am
sure: within the rocky circle of the mountain whither we journey
was once a great lake till those who lived before us, by wonderful arts of which I know nothing, hewed a path for the water

through the solid rock of the mountain, piercing even to the bed of the lake. But first they cut the channel that thou seest across the plain. Then, when at last the water burst out, it rushed down the channel that had been made to receive it, and crossed this plain till it reached the low land behind the rise, and there, perchance, it made the swamp through which we have come. Then, when the lake was drained dry, the people of whom I speak built a mighty city on its bed, whereof naught but ruins and the name of Kôr yet remaineth, and from age to age hewed out the caves and passages that thou wilt see."

"It may be," I answered; "but if so, how is it that the lake does not fill up again with the rains and the water of the springs?"

"Nay, my son, the people were a wise people, and they left a drain to keep it clear. Seest thou that river to the right?" and he pointed to a fair-sized stream which wound away across the plain, some four miles from us. "That is the drain, and it comes out through the mountain wall where this cutting goes in. At first, perhaps, the water ran down this canal, but afterwards the people turned it, and used the cutting for a road."

"And is there, then, no other place where one may enter into the great mountain," I asked, "except through the drain?"

"There is a place," he answered, "where cattle and men on foot may cross with much labour, but it is a secret. A month mightest thou search and never find it. It is only used once a year, when the herds of cattle that have been fatting on the slopes of the mountain, and on this plain, are driven into the space within."

"And does *She* live there always?" I asked, "or does she come at times without the mountain?"

"Nay, my son, where she is, there she is."

By now we were well on to the great plain, and I was examining with delight the varied beauty of its semi-tropical flowers and trees, the latter of which grew singly, or at most in clumps of three or four, much of the timber being of large size, and belonging apparently to a variety of evergreen oak. There were also many palms, some of them more than one hundred feet high, and the largest and most beautiful tree ferns that I ever saw, about which hung clouds of jewelled honeysuckers and great-winged butterflies. Wandering there among the trees or crouching in the long and feathered grass were all varieties of game, from rhinoceroses to hares. I saw a rhinoceros, buffalo in large herds, eland, quagga, and sable antelope, the most beautiful of all the bucks, not to mention many smaller varieties of game, and three ostriches, which scudded away at our approach like white drift before a gale. So plentiful was the game that at last I could refrain no longer. With me in the litter I had a single-barrel sporting Martini, the 'Express' being too cumbersome, and espying a beautiful fat eland rubbing himself under one of the oak-like trees, I jumped out, and proceeded to creep as near to him as I could. He allowed me to come within some eighty yards, then turned his head and stared at me, preparatory to running away. I lifted the rifle, and taking him about midway down the shoulder, for he was side on to me, fired. I never made a cleaner shot or a better kill in all my small experience, for the great buck sprang right up into the air and fell dead. The bearers, who had halted to see what happened, gave a murmur of surprise, an unwonted compliment from these sullen people, who never appear to be surprised at anything, and a party of the guard at once ran off to cut up the animal. As for myself, though I was longing to inspect him, I sauntered back to my litter as though I had been in the habit of killing eland all my life, feeling that I had risen several degrees in the estimation of the Amahagger, who looked on the performance as a very high-class manifestation of witchcraft. As a matter of fact, however, I had never seen an eland in a wild state before. Billali received me with enthusiasm.

"It is wonderful, my son the Baboon," he cried; "wonderful! Thou art a very great man, though so ugly. Had I not seen, surely I would never have believed. And thou sayest that thou wilt teach me to slay in this fashion?"

"Certainly, my father," I said airily; "it is nothing."

But all the same I firmly made up my mind that when 'my father' Billali began to fire I would without fail lie down or take refuge behind a tree.

After this little incident nothing happened of any note till about an hour and a half before sundown, when we arrived beneath the shadow of the towering volcanic mass whereof I have already written. It is quite impossible for me to describe its grim grandeur as it appeared to me while my patient bearers toiled along the bed of the ancient watercourse towards the spot where the rich brownhued cliff shot up from precipice to precipice till its crown lost itself in cloud. All I can say is that it almost awed me by the intensity of its lonesome and most solemn greatness. On we went up the bright and sunny slope, till at last the creeping shadows from above swallowed its brightness, and presently we began to pass through a cutting hewn in the living rock. Deeper and deeper grew this marvellous work, which must, I should say, have employed thousands of

men for many years. Indeed, how it was ever executed at all
without the aid of blasting-powder or dynamite I cannot to
this day imagine. That is and must remain one of the mysteries
of this wild land. I can only suppose that these cuttings and
the vast caves that have been hollowed out of the rocks they
pierced were the State undertakings of the people of Kôr, who
lived here in the dim lost ages of the world, and that, as in the
case of the Egyptian monuments, they were executed by the
labour of tens of thousands of captives, carried on through an
indefinite number of centuries. But who were the people?

At last we reached the face of the precipice itself, and found
ourselves looking into the mouth of a dark tunnel that reminded
me forcibly of those undertaken by our nineteenth-century
engineers in the construction of railway lines. Out of this tunnel
flowed a considerable stream of water. Indeed, though I do not
think that I have mentioned it, from the spot where the cutting in
the solid rock commenced we had followed this stream, which
ultimately developed into the river I have already described as
winding away to the right. Half of this cutting formed a channel
for the stream, and half, which was placed on a slightly higher
level—eight feet, perhaps—was devoted to the purpose of a roadway. At the termination of the cutting, however, the stream
turned off across the plain and followed a bed of its own. At the
mouth of the cave the cavalcade was halted, and, while the men
employed themselves in lighting some earthenware lamps which
they had brought with them, Billali, descending from his litter, informed me politely but firmly that the orders of *She* were that we
must now be blindfolded, so that we should not learn the secret of
the paths through the bowels of the mountains. To this of course
I assented cheerfully enough, but Job, who was very much better,
notwithstanding the journey, did not like it at all, believing, I
think, that it was but a preliminary step to being hot-potted. He
was, however, a little consoled when I pointed out to him that
there was no hot pots at hand, and, so far as I knew, no fire to
heat them in. As for poor Leo, after turning restlessly for
hours, to my deep thankfulness, at last he had dropped off into a
sleep or stupor, I do not know which, so that there was no need
to blindfold him. This blindfolding was performed by binding
tightly round the eyes a piece of the yellowish linen whereof
those of the Amahagger made their dresses who condescended
to wear anything in particular. This linen I discovered afterwards was taken from the tombs, and was not, as I had at
first supposed, of native manufacture. The bandage was then
fastened at the back of the head, and the ends knotted under

the chin to prevent slipping.

Ustane, by the way, was also blindfold, I do not know why, unless it was from fear lest she should impart the secrets of the route to us.

This operation performed we started on once more, and soon, by the echoing sound of the footsteps of the bearers and the increased noise of the water caused by reverberation in a confined space, I knew that we were entering into the bowels of the great mountain. It was an eerie sensation, that of being borne into the dead heart of the rock we knew not whither, but I was growing accustomed to such experiences by this time, and not to be surprised at anything. So I lay still, and listened to the *tramp, tramp* of the bearers and the rushing of the water, and tried to believe that I was enjoying myself. Presently the men set up the melancholy little chant that I had heard on the evening when we were captured in the whale-boat, and the effect produced by their voices was very curious; indeed quite indescribable. After a while the stagnant air became exceedingly thick and heavy, so much so, indeed, that I felt as though I were about to choke, till at length the litter turned a corner, then another and another, and the sound of the running water ceased. After this the air grew fresher again, but the turns were continuous, and to me, blindfolded as I was, most bewildering. I tried to keep a map of them in my mind in case it might ever be necessary for us to try to escape by this route, but, needless to say, I failed utterly. Another half-hour or so went by, when suddenly I became aware that we had passed into the open air. I could see the light through my bandage and feel its freshness on my face. A few more minutes and the litters halted, and I heard Billali order Ustane to remove her bandage and undo ours. Without waiting for her attentions I loosed the knot of mine, and looked out.

As I anticipated, we had journeyed through the precipice, and were now on the farther side, and immediately beneath its beetling face. The first thing I noticed was that the cliff is not nearly so high here, not so high I should say by five hundred feet, which proved that the bed of the lake, or rather of the vast ancient crater in which we stood, was much above the level of the surrounding plain. For the rest, we found ourselves in a huge, rock-surrounded cup, not unlike that of the first place where we had sojourned, only ten times its size. Indeed, I could but just discern the frowning line of the opposite cliffs. A great portion of the plain thus enclosed by Nature was cultivated, and fenced in with walls of stone, placed there to prevent the cattle and goats, of which there were large herds, from breaking into the gardens.

Dotted about this plain rose grass mounds, and some miles away towards its centre I thought that I could see the outline of colossal ruins. I had no time to observe anything more at the moment, for we were instantly surrounded by crowds of Amahagger, similar in every particular to those with whom we were already familiar, who, though they spoke little, pressed round us so closely as to obscure the view to a person lying in a hammock. Then of a sudden a number of armed men arranged in companies appeared, running swiftly towards us, marshalled by officers who held ivory wands in their hands, having, so far as I could discover, emerged from the face of the precipice like ants from their burrows. These men as well as their officers were all robed in addition to the usual leopard skin and, as I gathered, they formed the bodyguard of *She* herself.

Their leader advanced to Billali, saluted him by placing his ivory wand transversely across his forehead, and then asked some question which I could not catch. Billali having answered him briefly, the regiment turned and marched along the side of the cliff, our cavalcade of litters following in their track. After journeying thus for half a mile we halted once more in front of the mouth of a tremendous cave measuring about sixty feet in height by eighty wide. Here Billali descended from his litter, requesting Job and myself to follow him, Leo, of course, being too ill to do anything of the sort. I obeyed, and we entered the great cave, into which the beams of the setting sun penetrated for some distance, while beyond the reach of the daylight it was faintly illuminated with lamps which seemed to me to stretch away for an almost immeasurable distance, like the gaslights of an empty London street.

The first thing I noticed was that the walls were covered with sculptures in bas-relief, for the most part of a sort similar to those upon the vases that I have described:—love-scenes principally, then hunting pieces, pictures of executions, and of the torture of criminals by the placing of a pot upon the head, presumably red-hot, thus showing whence our hosts had derived this pleasant practice. There were very few battle-scenes, though many of duels, and of men running and wrestling, and from this fact I am led to believe that this people were not much subject to attack by exterior foes, either on account of the isolation of their position or because of their great strength. Between the pictures were columns of stone characters of a nature absolutely new to me; at any rate they were neither Greek, nor

Egyptian, nor Hebrew, nor Assyrian—this I am sure of. They looked more like Chinese writings than any other that I am acquainted with. Near to the entrance of the cave both pictures and writings were worn away, but further on in many cases they were absolutely fresh and perfect as the day on which the sculptor had ceased to work upon them.

The regiment of guards did not come further than the entrance to the cave, where they formed up to let us pass through. On entering the place itself, however, we were met by a man robed in white, who bowed humbly, but said nothing, which was not very wonderful, as afterwards it appeared that he was a deaf mute.

Running at right angles to the great cave, at a distance of some twenty feet from its entrance, lay a smaller cave or wide gallery, that was pierced into the rock both to the right and to the left of the main cavern. In front of the gallery to our left stood two guards, from which circumstance I argued that it might be the entrance to the apartments of *She* herself. The mouth of the right-hand gallery was unguarded, and the mute indicated that we were to pass along it. Walking a few yards down this passage, which was lighted with lamps, we came to the entrance of a chamber having a curtain made of some grass material hung over the doorway, not unlike a Zanzibar mat in appearance. This the mute drew back with another profound obeisance, and led the way into a good-sized apartment, hewn, as usual, out of the solid rock, but to my great relief lighted by means of a shaft pierced in the face of the precipice. In this room were a stone bedstead, pots full of water for washing, and leopard skins beautifully tanned to serve as blankets.

Here we left Leo, who was still sleeping heavily, and Ustane stayed with him. I noticed that the deaf mute gave her a very sharp look, as much as to say, "Who are you, and by whose orders do you come here?" Next he conducted us to a very similar room, which Job took possession of, and then to two more that were occupied respectively by Billali and myself.

CHAPTER XII

"SHE"

THE first care of Job and myself, after attending to Leo, was to wash ourselves and put on clean clothing, for what we were wearing had not been changed since the loss of the dhow. Fortunately, as I think that I have said, by far the greater part of our personal baggage had been packed into the whale-boat, and therefore was saved, and brought hither by the bearers, although the stores laid in by us for barter and presents to the natives were lost. Nearly all our clothing was made of a well-shrunk and very strong grey flannel, and excellent I found it for travelling in these places. Though a Norfolk jacket, shirt, and a pair of trousers of this material only weighed about four pounds, a consideration in tropical countries, where every extra ounce tells on the wearer, it was warm, and offered a good resistance to the rays of the sun, and best of all to chills, which are so apt to result from sudden changes of temperature.

Never shall I forget the comfort of that 'wash and brush-up, and of those clean flannels. The only thing that was wanting to complete my joy was a cake of soap, of which we had none.

Afterwards I discovered that the Amahagger, who do not reckon dirt among their many disagreeable qualities, use a kind of burnt earth for washing purposes, which, though unpleasant to the touch till one is accustomed to it, forms a very fair substitute for soap.

By the time that I was dressed, and had combed and trimmed my black beard, the previous condition of which was certainly sufficiently unkempt to give weight to Billali's appellation for me of 'Baboon,' I began to feel most uncommonly hungry. Therefore I was by no means sorry when, without the slightest preparatory sound or warning, the curtain over the entrance to my cave was flung aside, and another mute, a young girl this time, announced to me by signs that I could not misunderstand— namely, by opening her mouth and pointing down it—that there was something ready to eat. Accordingly I followed her into the next chamber, which we had not yet entered, where I found Job, who, to his great embarrassment, had also been conducted thither by a fair mute. Job never forgot the advances the 'hot-pot' lady had made towards him, and suspected every girl who came near to him of similar designs.

"These young parties have a way of looking at one, sir," he would say apologetically, "which I don't call respectable."

This chamber was twice the size of the sleeping caves, and I saw at once that originally it had served as a refectory, and also, probably, as an embalming-room for the Priests of the Dead; for I may as well explain here that these hollowed-out caves were nothing more nor less than vast catacombs, in which for tens of ages the mortal remains of the great extinct race whose monuments surrounded us had been first preserved, with an art and a completeness that have never since been equalled, and then hidden away for all time. On each side of this particular rock-

chamber ran a long and solid stone table, about three feet wide
by three feet six in height, hewn out of the living rock, of which
it had formed part, and was still attached to at the base. These
tables were slightly hollowed out or curved inward, to give room
for the knees of anyone sitting on the stone ledge that had been
cut as a bench along the side of the cave at a distance of about
two feet from them. Each of them, also, was so arranged that it
ended just under a shaft pierced in the rock for the admission of
light and air. On examining them carefully, however, I saw that
there was a difference between them which had escaped my attention at first; namely, that one of the tables, that to the left as
we entered the cave, had evidently been used, not to eat upon,
but for the purposes of embalming. That this was beyond all
question the case was clear from five shallow depressions in the
stone of the table, all shaped like a human form, with a separate
place for the head to lie in, and a little bridge to support the neck,
each depression being of a different size, to accommodate bodies
varying in stature from a full-grown man's to that of a child, and
having holes bored in it at intervals to carry off fluid. Indeed,
if any further confirmation were required, we had but to look at
the wall of the cave above to find it. For there, sculptured round
the apartment, looking nearly as fresh as on the day of completion,
was the pictorial representation of the death, embalming, and
burial of an old man with a long beard, probably an ancient king
or grandee of this country.

The first picture represented his death. He was lying upon a
couch supported by four curved corner-posts fashioned to a knob
at the end, and in appearance resembling written notes of music.
Evidently he was in the very act of expiring, for gathered round
the couch were women and children weeping, the former with
their hair hanging down their backs. The next scene represented
the embalmment of the body, which lay stark upon a table with
depressions in it, similar to the one before us; probably, indeed,
it was a picture of the same table. Three men were employed at
the work—one superintending; one supporting a funnel shaped
exactly like a port-wine strainer, of which the narrow end was
fixed in an incision in the breast, no doubt in the great pectoral
artery; while the third, who was depicted as standing straddle-
legged over the corpse, held a very large jug high in his hand, and
poured from it some steaming fluid which fell accurately into the
funnel. The most curious part of this sculpture is that both the
man with the funnel and the man who pours the fluid are depicted
as holding their noses, either I suppose because of the stench
arising from the body, or more probably to keep out the aromatic

fumes of the hot fluid which was being forced into the dead man's veins. Another curious thing which I am unable to explain is that all three men are represented with a band of linen tied round the face having holes in it for the eyes.

The third sculpture was a picture of the burial of the deceased. There he lay, stiff and cold, clothed in a linen robe, and reposing on a stone slab such as I had slept upon at our first sojourning-place. At his head and feet burnt lamps, and by his side were placed several of the beautiful painted vases that I have described, which were perhaps supposed to be full of provisions. The little chamber was crowded with mourners, and with musicians playing on instruments resembling a lyre, while near the foot of the corpse stood a man holding a sheet, with which he was about to cover it from view.

These sculptures, looked at merely as works of art, were so remarkable that I make no apology for describing them rather fully. I consider them also of surpassing interest as representing, probably with studious accuracy, the rites of the dead as practised among an utterly lost people, and even then I thought how envious some antiquarian friends of my own at Cambridge would be if ever I found an opportunity of describing these wonderful remains to them. Probably they would say that I was exaggerating, notwithstanding that every page of this history must bear so much internal evidence of its truth that obviously it would have been quite impossible for me to have invented it.

To return. So soon as I had hastily examined these sculptures, which I think I omitted to mention are executed in relief, we sat down to a very excellent meal of boiled goat's-flesh, fresh milk, and cakes made of meal, the whole being served upon clean wooden platters.

When we had eaten we returned to see how poor Leo went on, Billali saying that he must now wait upon *She,* and hear her commands. On reaching Leo's room we found him exceedingly ill. He had awakened from his torpor altogether off his head, and was inclined to be violent, babbling incessantly about some boat-race on the Cam. Indeed, when we entered the room Ustane was holding him down. I spoke to him, and my voice seemed to soothe him; at any rate he grew much quieter, and was persuaded to swallow a dose of quinine.

I had been sitting with him for an hour, perhaps—at least I remember it was becoming so dark that I could only just see his head lying like a gleam of gold upon the pillow which we extemporised out of a bag covered with a blanket—when suddenly Billali arrived with an air of great importance, and informed me that *She* herself had deigned to express a wish to see me—an honour, he added, accorded to but very few. I think that he was a little horrified at my cool way of taking the honour, but the truth is that I did not feel overwhelmed with gratitude at the prospect of meeting some savage, dusky queen, however absolute and mysterious she might be, more especially as my mind was full of dear Leo, for whose life I began to have great fears. However, I rose to follow him, and as I went I caught sight of something bright lying on the floor, which I picked up. Perhaps the reader will remember that with the potsherd in the casket was a 'composition' scarabæus marked with a round O, a goose, and another curious hieroglyphic, the meaning of which signs is 'Suten se Ra,' or 'Royal Son of the Sun.' This scarab, which is a very small one, Leo had insisted upon having set in a massive gold ring, such as is generally used for signets, and it was this very ring that I now found. He had pulled it off in the paroxysm of his fever, at least I suppose so, and flung it down upon the rock-floor. Thinking that if I left it about it might be lost, I slipped it on to my own little finger, and then followed Billali, leaving Job and Ustane with Leo.

We passed down the passage, crossed the great aisle-like cave, and came to the corresponding passage on the other side, at the mouth of which the guards stood like two statues. As we came they bowed their heads in salutation, and then, lifting their long spears, placed them transversely across their foreheads, as the leader of the soldiers that met us had done with his ivory wand. We stepped between them, and found ourselves in a gallery exactly similar to that which led to our own apartments, only this passage, by comparison, was brilliantly lighted. A few paces down it we were met by four mutes—two men and two women— who bowed low and then disposed themselves, the women in front and the men behind us, and in this order we continued our procession past several doorways hung with curtains resembling those in our own quarters, which I afterwards discovered opened into chambers occupied by mutes who attended on *She*. A few paces more and we came to another doorway facing us, and not to our left like the others, which seemed to mark the termination of the passage. Here two more white-, or rather yellow-robed guards were standing, who also bowed, saluted, and let us pass through heavy curtains into a great antechamber, quite forty feet long by as many wide, in which some eight or ten yellow-haired women, most of them young and handsome, sat on cushions, working with ivory needles at what had the appearance of being embroidery-frames. These women were also deaf and dumb. At the farther end of this great lamp-lit apartment was a second opening, closed in with heavy Oriental-looking tapestries, quite unlike those that hung before the doors of our own rooms, where stood two particularly handsome girl mutes, their heads bowed upon their bosoms and their hands crossed in an attitude of the humblest submission. As we advanced they each stretched out an arm and drew back the curtains. Thereupon Billali did a curious thing. Down he went, that venerable-looking old gentleman—for Billali is a gentleman at the bottom—down on to his hands and knees, and in this undignified position, with his long white beard trailing on the ground, he began to creep into the apartment beyond. I followed him, standing on my feet in the usual fashion. Looking over his shoulder he perceived it.

"Down, my son; down, my Baboon; down on to thy hands and knees. We enter the presence of *She,* and, if thou art not humble, of a surety she will blast thee where thou standest."

I halted, and felt frightened. Indeed, my knees began to give way of their own mere motion; but reflection came to my aid. I am an Englishman, and why, I asked myself, should I creep into the presence of some savage woman as though I were a monkey in fact as well as in name? I would not and could not do it, that is, unless I was absolutely sure that my life or comfort depended thereon. If once I began to creep upon my knees I should always have to creep, which would be a patent acknowledgment of inferiority. So, fortified by an insular prejudice against 'kootooing' that, like most of our so-called prejudices, has a good deal of common sense to recommend it, I marched in boldly. Presently I found myself in another apartment, considerably smaller than the anteroom, of which the walls were hung about with rich-looking curtains of the same make as those over the door, the work, I discovered subsequently, of the mutes who sat in the antechamber and wove them in strips, that were afterwards sewn together. Also, here and there about the room stood settees of a beautiful black wood of the ebony species, inlaid with ivory, and spread upon the floor were other tapestries, or rather rugs. At the top end of this apartment was what appeared to be a recess, also draped with curtains, through which shone rays of light. For the rest the place was empty and untenanted.

Painfully and slowly old Billali crept up the length of the cave, and with the most dignified stride which I could command I followed after him. But I felt that it was more or less of a failure. To begin with, it is not possible to appear dignified when you are following in the wake of an old man writhing along on his stom-

ach like a snake. Thus, in order to walk sufficiently slowly, either
I had to wave my leg for some seconds in the air at every step,
or else to advance with a full stop between each stride, like Mary,
Queen of Scots, going to execution in a play. Billali was not expert at crawling—I suppose his years stood in the way—and our
progress up that apartment was a very long affair. I was immediately behind him, and on several occasions was sorely
tempted to help him forward with a kick. It seemed absurd to
advance into the presence of savage royalty after the fashion of
an Irishman driving a pig to market. That is what we looked
like, and the idea nearly made me laugh aloud. Indeed. I was
obliged to work off the tendency to unseemly merriment by blowing my nose, a proceeding which filled old Billali with horror,
for he looked over his shoulder and, making a ghastly face at me,
murmured, "Oh, my poor Baboon!"

At last we reached the curtains, where Billali collapsed flat on
to his breast, with his hands stretched out before him as though
he were dead, and I, not knowing what to do, began to stare about
the chamber. Presently I became aware that somebody was looking at me from behind the curtains. I could not see the person,
but I could distinctly feel his or her gaze, and, what is more, it
produced a very odd effect upon my nerves. I was frightened,
I do not know why. The place was a strange one, it is true, and
looked lonely, notwithstanding its rich hangings and the soft glow
of the lamps—indeed, these accessories added to, rather than
detracted from, its loneliness, just as an empty lighted street
at night has always a more solitary appearance than one that is
dark. It was so silent, and there lay Billali like a corpse before the
heavy curtains, through which the odour of perfumes seemed to
float up towards the gloom of the arched roof above. Minute
grew into minute, and still there was no sign of life, nor did the
hangings move; but I felt the gaze of a watching being sink
through and through me, filling me with a nameless terror, till
the perspiration stood in beads upon my brow.

At length the curtain began to stir. Who could be behind it?
—some naked savage queen, a languishing Oriental beauty, or a
nineteenth-century young lady, drinking afternoon tea? I had
not the slightest idea, and should not have been astonished at
seeing any of the three. Indeed, I was beyond astonishment.
Presently the hanging agitated itself, then from between its folds
there appeared a most beautiful white hand, white as snow, and
with long tapering fingers, ending in the pinkest nails. This hand
grasped the curtain, drawing it aside, and a voice spoke, I think
the softest and yet most silvery voice that I ever heard. It re-

minded me of the murmur of a brook.

"Stranger," said the voice in Arabic, but much purer and more classical Arabic than the Amahagger talk—"stranger, wherefore art thou so much afraid?"

Now I flattered myself that, in spite of my inward terrors, I had kept a complete command of my countenance, and was therefore a little astonished at this question. Before I had made up my mind how to answer it, however, the curtain was drawn, and a tall figure stood before us. I say a figure, for not only the body, but also the face, was wrapped with a soft white and gauzy material in such a way as at first sight to remind me most forcibly of a corpse in its grave-clothes. And yet I do not know why it should have given me this idea, seeing that the wrappings were so thin that I could distinctly see the gleam of the pink flesh beneath them. I suppose it was owing to the way in which they were arranged, either accidentally, or more probably by design. Anyhow, I felt more frightened than ever at this ghost-like apparition, and the hair began to rise upon my head as a certainty crept over me that I was in the presence of something that was not canny. I could clearly distinguish, however, that the swathed mummy-like form before me was that of a tall and lovely woman, instinct with beauty in every part, and also with a certain snake-like grace which heretofore I had never seen anything to equal. When she moved a hand or foot her entire frame seemed to undulate, and the neck did not bend, it curved.

"Why art thou so frightened, stranger?" asked the sweet voice again—a voice which, like the strains of softest music, seemed to draw the heart out of me. "Is there that about me which should affright a man? Then surely are men changed from what they used to be!" And with a little coquettish movement she turned herself, holding up one arm, so as to reveal all its loveliness and the rich hair of raven blackness that streamed in soft ripples down the snowy robes, almost to her sandalled feet.

"It is thy beauty that makes me fear, O Queen," I answered humbly, scarcely knowing what to say, and I thought that as I spoke I heard old Billali, who was still lying prostrate on the floor, mutter, "Good, my Baboon, good!"

"I see that men still know how to beguile us women with false words," she answered, with a laugh which sounded like distant silver bells. "Ah, stranger, thou wast afraid because mine eyes were searching out thine heart; therefore wast thou afraid. Yet, being but a woman, I will forgive thee the lie, for it was courteously said. And now tell me how came ye hither to this land of the dwellers among caves—a land of swamps and evil things and dead old shadows of the dead? What came ye for to see? How is it that ye hold your lives so cheap as to place them in the hollow of the hand of *Hiya,* into the hand of *'She-who-must-be-obeyed'* Tell me also how comest thou to know the tongue I talk. It is an ancient tongue, that sweet child of the old Syriac. Liveth it yet in the world? Thou seest that I dwell among caves and the dead, and naught know I of the affairs of men, nor have I cared to know. I have lived, O stranger, with my memories, and my memories are in a grave which mine hands hollowed, for it hath been truly said that the child of man maketh his own path evil;" and her beautiful voice quivered, and broke in a note as soft as any woodbird's. Suddenly her eyes fell upon the sprawling frame of Billali, and she seemed to recollect herself.

"Ah! thou art there, old man. Tell me how it is that things have gone wrong in thine household. Forsooth, it seems that these my guests were set upon. Ay, and one was nigh to being slain by the 'hot-pot,' to be eaten of those brutes, thy children, and had not the others fought gallantly they too had been slain, and not even I could have called back the life which once was loosed from the body. What means it, old man? What hast thou to say that I should not give thee over to those who execute my vengeance?"

The woman's voice had risen in her anger till it rang clear and cold against the rocky walls and I thought that I could see her eyes flash through the gauze which hid them. Poor Billali, whom I had believed to be a very fearless person, positively quivered with terror at her words.

"O 'Hiya!' O *She!*" he said, without lifting his white head from the floor. "O *She,* as thou art great, be merciful, for I am now as ever thy servant to obey. It was no plan or fault of mine, O *She;* it was those wicked ones who are called my children. Led on by a woman whom thy guest the Pig had scorned, they would have followed the ancient custom of the land, and eaten the fat black stranger who came hither with these thy guests the Baboon and the Lion who is sick, thinking that no word had come from thee about the Black One. But when the Baboon and the Lion saw what they would do, they slew the woman, and slew also their servant to save him from the horror of the pot. Then those evil ones, ay, those children of the Wicked One who lives in the Pit, they went mad with the lust of blood, and flew at the throats of the Lion and the Baboon and the Pig. But gallantly they fought. O *Hiya!* they fought like very men, and killed many, and held their own, and then I came and saved them, and the evildoers have I sent on hither to Kôr to be judged of thy greatness, O

She! and here they are."

"Ay, old man, I know it, and to-morrow I will sit in the great hall and do justice upon them, fear not. And for thee, I forgive thee, though hardly. See that thou dost keep thine household better. Go!"

Billali rose upon his knees with astonishing alacrity, bowed his head thrice, and his white beard sweeping the ground, crawled down the apartment as he had crawled up it, till finally he vanished through the curtains, leaving me, not a little to my alarm, alone with this terrible but most fascinating woman.

CHAPTER XIII

AYESHA UNVEILS

"There," said *She*, "he has gone, the white-bearded old fool! Ah! how little knowledge does a man acquire in his life. He gathers it up like water, but like water it runs between his fingers, and yet, if his hands be but wet as though with dew, behold a generation of fools call out, 'See, he is a wise man!' Is it not so? But how call they thee? 'Baboon,' he says," and she laughed; "but that is the way of these savages, who lack imagination, and fly to the beasts they are kin to for a name. How do they call thee in thine own country, stranger?"

"They call me Holly, O Queen," I answered.

"Holly," she said, speaking the word with difficulty and yet with a most charming accent; "and what is 'Holly'?"

" 'Holly' is a prickly tree," I replied.

"So. Well, thou hast a prickly and yet a tree-like look. Strong art thou, and ugly, but, if my wisdom be not at fault, honest at the core, and a staff to lean on; also one who thinks. But stay, thou Holly, stand not there; enter with me and be seated by me. I would not see thee crawl before me like those slaves. I am aweary of their worship and their terror; sometimes when they vex me I could blast them for very sport, and to see the rest turn white, even to the heart." And she held the curtain aside with her ivory hand that I might pass in.

I entered, shuddering. This woman was very terrible. Within the curtains was a recess measuring about twelve feet by ten, and in it a couch, and a table on which were fruit and sparkling water. By it, at its end, stood a vessel like a font cut in carved stone, also full of pure water. The place was softly lit with lamps formed out of the beautiful vessels of which I have spoken, and the air and curtains were laden with a subtle perfume. Perfume too seemed to emanate from the glorious hair and white clinging vestments of *She* herself. I entered the little room, and stood there uncertain.

"Sit," said *She,* pointing to the couch. "As yet thou hast no cause to fear me. If thou hast cause, thou shalt not fear for long, for I shall slay thee. Therefore let thy heart be light."

I sat down on the foot of the couch near to the font-like basin of water, and *She* sank down slowly on to its other end.

"Now, Holly," she said, "how comest thou to speak Arabic? It is my own dear tongue, for Arabian am I by my birth, even 'al Arab al Ariba,' an Arab of the Arabs, and of the race of our father Yárab, the son of Kâhtan, for in that fair and ancient city Ozal I was born, in the province of Yaman the Happy. Yet thou dost not speak it as we used to speak. Thy talk lacks the music of the sweet tongue of the tribes of Hamyar which I was wont to hear. Some of the words, too, seemed changed, even as among these Amahagger, who have debased and defiled its purity, so that I must speak with them in what is to me another tongue."[1]

"I have studied it," I answered, "for many years. Also the language is spoken in Egypt and elsewhere."

"So it is still spoken, and there is yet an Egypt? And what Pharaoh sits upon the throne? Still one of the spawn of the Persian Ochus, or are the Achæmenians gone, for it is far to the days of Ochus?"

"The Persians have been gone from Egypt for nigh two thousand years, and since then the Ptolemies, the Romans, and many others have flourished and held sway upon the Nile, to fall when their time was ripe," I said, aghast. "What canst thou know of the Persian Artaxerxes?"

She laughed, making no answer, and again a cold chill went through me. "And Greece," she said; "is there still a Greece? Ah, I loved the Greeks. They were beautiful as the day, and

---

[1] Yárab, the son of Kâhtan, who lived some centuries before the time of Abraham, was the father of the ancient Arabs, and gave its name Araba to the country. In speaking of herself as 'al Arab al Ariba,' *She* no doubt meant to convey that she was of the true Arab blood as distinguished from the naturalised Arabs, the descendants of Ishmael, the son of Abraham and Hagar, who were known as 'al Arab al mostáreba.' The dialect of the Koreish was usually called the clear or 'perspicuous' Arabic, but the Hamaritic dialect approached nearer to the purity of the mother Syriac.— L. H. H.

clever, but fierce at heart and fickle, notwithstanding."

"Yes," I said, "there is a Greece; and, just now, it is once more a people. Yet the Greeks of to-day are not what the Greeks of the old time were, and Greece herself is but a mockery of the Greece that was."

"So! The Hebrews, are they yet at Jerusalem? And does the Temple stand that the Wise King built, and if so, what God do they worship there? Is that Messiah come, of whom they preached so much and prophesied so loudly, and doth He rule the earth?"

"The Jews are broken and gone; the fragments of their people strew the world, and Jerusalem is no more. As for the temple that Herod built—"

"Herod!" she said. "I know not Herod. But tell on."

"The Romans burnt it, and the Roman eagles flew across its ruins and now Judæa is a desert."

"So, so! They were a great people, those Romans, and went straight to their end—ay, they sped to it like Fate, or like their own eagles on the prey!—and left peace behind them."

"Solitudinem faciunt, pacem appellant," I suggested.

"Ah, thou canst speak the Latin tongue, too!" she said, in surprise. "It has a strange ring in my ears after all these days, and I doubt me that thy accent does not fall as the Romans put it. Who was it wrote that? I know not the saying, but it is a true one of this great people. It seems that I have found a learned man—one whose hands have held the water of the world's knowledge. Knowest thou Greek also?"

"Yes, O Queen, and something of Hebrew, but not to speak them well. They are all dead languages now."

She clapped her hands in childish glee. "Of a truth, ugly tree that thou art, thou growest the fruits of wisdom, O Holly," she said; "but of those Jews whom I hated, for they called me 'Gentile' and 'heathen' when I would have taught them my philosophy—did their Messiah come, and doth He rule the world?"

"Their Messiah came," I answered with reverence; "but He came poor and lowly, and they would have none of Him. They scourged Him, and crucified Him upon a tree, but yet His words and His works live on, for He was the Son of God, and now of a truth He doth rule half the world, but not with an empire of the world."

"Ah, the fierce-hearted wolves," she said, "the followers of Sense and many gods—greedy of gain and faction-torn. I can see their dark faces yet. So they crucified their Messiah? Well can I believe it. That He was a Son of the Living Spirit would be naught to them, if indeed He was so, and of that we will talk afterwards. They would care little for any God if He came not with pomp and power. They, a chosen people, a vessel of Him they call Jehovah, ay, and a vessel of Baal, and a vessel of Astoreth, and a vessel of the gods of the Egyptians—a high-stomached people, eager of aught that brought them wealth and power. So they crucified their Messiah because He came in lowly guise —and now they are scattered about the earth? Why if I remember, so said one of their prophets that it should be. Well, let them go—they broke my heart, those Jews, and made me look with evil eyes across the world, ay, and drove me to this wilderness—this place of a nation that was before them. When I would have taught them wisdom in Jerusalem they stoned me, yes, at the Gate of the Temple those white-bearded hypocrites and Rabbis hounded the people on to stone me! See, here is the mark of it to this day!" and with a sudden movement she rolled back the gauzy wrapping on her rounded arm, and pointed to a little scar that showed red against its milky beauty.

I shrank back horrified.

"Pardon me, O Queen," I said, "but I am bewildered. Nigh upon two thousand years have rolled across the earth since the Jewish Messiah hung upon His cross at Golgotha. How, then, canst thou have taught thy philosophy to the Jews before He was? Thou art a woman, and no spirit. How can a woman live two thousand years? Why does thou befool me, O Queen?"

She leaned back on the couch, and once more I felt her hidden eyes playing upon me and searching out my heart.

"O man!" she said at last, speaking very slowly and deliberately, "it seems that there remain secrets upon the earth of which thou knowest little. Dost thou still believe that all creations die, even as those very Jews believed? I tell thee that naught dies. There is no such thing as Death, although there be a thing called Change. See," and she pointed to some sculptures on the rocky wall "Three times two thousand years have passed since the last of the great race that hewed those pictures fell before the breath of the pestilence which destroyed them, yet they are not dead. Even now they live; perchance their spirits are drawn toward us at this very hour," and she glanced round. "Of a surety it sometimes seems to me that my eyes can see them."

"Yes, but to this world they are dead."

"Ay, for a time; but even to the world they are born again and yet again. I, yes I, Ayesha[1]—for that, stranger, is my name —I say to thee that I wait now for one I loved to be born anew, and I tarry here till he finds me, knowing of a surety that hither

[1] Pronounced Assha.—L. H. H.

he will come, and that here, and here only, he shall greet me. Why dost thou believe that I, who am all-powerful, I, whose loveliness is more than the loveliness of that Grecian Helen of whom poets used to sing, and whose wisdom is wider, ay, far more wide and deep than the wisdom of Solomon the Wise,—I, who know the secrets of the earth and its riches, and can turn all things to my uses,—I, who have even for a while overcome Change, that ye call Death,—why, I say, O stranger, dost thou think that I herd here with barbarians lower than beasts?"

"I cannot tell," I said humbly.

"Because I wait for him I love. My life has perchance been evil—I know not, for who can say what is evil and what good? Therefore I fear to die to go to find him where he is, even if I could die, which I may not until mine hour comes; for between us there might rise a wall I could not climb; at the least, I dread it. Surely it would be easy also to lose the way in seeking him through those great spaces wherein the planets wander on forever. But the day must come, it may be when five thousand more years have passed, and are lost and melted into the vault of Time, even as the little clouds melt into the gloom of night, or it may be to-morrow, when he, my love, shall be born again, and then, following the law that is stronger than any human plan he shall find me *here*, where once we kissed, and of a surety his heart will soften towards me, although I sinned against him. Ay, even if he knew me not again, yet must he love me, if only for my beauty's sake!"

For a moment I was dumfounded, and could not answer. The matter was so overpowering for my intellect to grasp.

"But even thus, O Queen," I said at last, "even if we men be born again and again, that is not so with thee, if thou speakest truly." Here she looked up sharply and once more I caught the ash of those hidden eyes; "thou," I went on hurriedly, "who hast never died?"

"That is so," she said; "and it is because, half by chance and half by learning, I have solved one of the great secrets of the world. Tell me, stranger: life is—why, therefore, should not life be lengthened for a while? What are ten or twenty or fifty thousand years in the history of life? Why, in ten thousand years scarce will the rain and storms lessen a mountain-top by a span in thickness. In two thousand years these caves have not changed, nothing has changed but the beasts, and man, who is as the beasts. There is naught that is wonderful about the matter, couldst thou but understand. Life is wonderful, ay, but that it should be lengthened is not wonderful. Nature hath her animating spirit as well as man who is Nature's child, and he who can find that spirit, and let it breathe upon him, shall live with her life. He shall not live eternally, for Nature is not eternal, and she herself must die, even as the nature of the moon hath died. She herself must die, I say, or rather change, and sleep till it be time for her to live again. But when shall she die? Not yet, I ween, and while she lives, so shall he who hath all her secret live with her. All I have not, yet I have some, more perchance than any who were before me. Now, to thee I doubt not that this thing is a great mystery, therefore I will not overcome thee with it now. Another time I will tell thee more if the mood be on me though perchance I shall never speak thereof again. Dost thou wonder how I knew that ye were coming to this land, and so saved your head from the burning?"

"Ay, O Queen," I answered feebly.

"Then gaze upon that water," and, pointing to the font-like vessel, she bent forward and held her hand over it.

I rose and gazed, and instantly the water darkened. Then it cleared, and I saw as distinctly as I ever saw anything in my life— I saw, I say, our boat upon that horrible canal. There was Leo lying at the bottom asleep in it, with a coat thrown over him to keep off the mosquitoes, in such a fashion as to hide his face, and there were myself, Job, and Mahomed towing on the bank.

I started back aghast, and cried out that it was magic, for I recognised every detail of the pictured scene—it was one which had actually occurred.

"Nay, nay; O Holly," she answered, "it is no magic—that is a dream of ignorance. There is no such thing as magic, though there is such a thing as knowledge of the hidden ways of Nature. This water is my glass; in it I see what passes when at times it is my will to summon it before me. Therein I can show thee what thou wilt of the past, if it be anything that has to do with this country and with what I have known, or anything that thou, the gazer, hast known. Think of a face if thou wilt, and it shall be reflected from thy mind upon the water. I know not all the secret yet—I can read nothing in the future. But it is an old secret; I did not find it. In Arabia and in Egypt the sorcerers found it centuries ago. Thus one day I chanced to bethink me of that old canal—some twenty ages since I sailed upon it, and I was minded to look thereon again. So I looked, and there I saw the boat, and three men walking, and one, whose face I could not see, but a youth of noble form, sleeping in the boat, and so I sent and saved you. And now farewell. But stay, tell me of this youth—the Lion, as the old man calls him. I would look

upon him, but he is sick, thou sayest—sick with the fever, and
also wounded in the fray."

"He is very sick," I answered sadly; "canst thou do nothing
for him, O Queen! who knowest so much?"

"Of a surety I can; I can cure him. But why speakest thou
so sadly? Dost thou love the youth? Is he perchance thy son?"

"He is my adopted son, O Queen! Shall he be brought in
before thee?"

"Nay. How long hath the fever taken him?"

"This is the third day."

"Good; let him lie another day. Then he will perchance throw
it off by his own strength, and that is better than that I should cure
him, for my medicine is of a sort to shake the life in its very
citadel. If, however, by tomorrow night, at that hour when the
fever first took him, he doth not begin to mend, then I will come
to him and cure him. Stay; who nurses him?"

"Our white servant, he whom Billali names the Pig; also," and
here I spoke with some little hesitation, "a women called Ustane,
a very handsome woman of this country, who came and embraced him when first she saw him, and hath stayed by him ever
since, as I understand is the fashion of thy people, O Queen."

"My people! Speak not to me of my people," she answered
hastily; "these slaves are no people of mine, they are but dogs to
do my bidding till the day of my deliverance comes; and as for
their customs, I have naught to do with them. Also, call me not
Queen—I am weary of flattery and titles—call me Ayesha; the
name hath a sweet sound in mine ears, it is an echo from the past.
As for this Ustane, I know not. I wonder if it be she against whom
I was warned, and whom I in turn did warn? Hath she—stay, I
will see;" and, bending forward, she passed her hand over the
font of water and gazed intently into it. "See," she said quietly,
"is that the woman?"

I looked into the water, and there, mirrored upon its placid
surface, was the silhouette of Ustane's stately face. She was
bending forward, a look of infinite tenderness upon her features,
watching something beneath her, and with her chestnut locks
falling on to her right shoulder.

"It is she," I said, in a low voice, for once more I felt much
disturbed at this most uncommon sight. "She watches Leo
asleep."

"Leo!" said Ayesha, in an absent voice; "why, that is 'lion'
in the Latin tongue. The old man has named happily for once.
It is strange," she went on, speaking to herself, "most strange.
So like—but it is not possible!" With an impatient gesture she

passed her hand over the water once more. It darkened, and the image vanished silently and mysteriously as it had risen, and once more the lamplight, and the lamplight only, shone on the placid surface of that limpid, living mirror.

"Hast thou aught to ask me before thou goest, O Holly?" she said, after a few moments of reflection. "It is but a rude life that thou must live here, for these people are savages, and know not the ways of cultivated man. Not that I am troubled thereby, for behold my food," and she pointed to the fruit upon the little table. "Naught but fruit doth ever pass my lips—fruit and cakes of flour, and a little water. I have bidden my girls to wait upon thee. They are mutes, thou knowest, deaf are they and dumb, and therefore the safest of servants, save to those who can read their faces and their signs. I bred them so—the task has needed many centuries and much trouble; but at last I triumphed. Once I succeeded before, but the breed was too ugly, so I let it die away; but now, as thou seest, they are otherwise. Once, too, I reared a race of giants, but after a while Nature sickened of it, and it withered away. Hast thou aught to ask of me?"

"Ay, one thing, O Ayesha," I said boldly, but feeling by no means so bold as I trust I looked. "I would gaze upon thy face."

She laughed out in her bell-like notes. "Bethink thee, Holly," she answered; "bethink thee. It seems that thou knowest the old myths of the gods of Greece. Was there not one Actæon who perished miserably because he looked on too much beauty? If I show thee my face, perchance thou wouldst perish miserably also; perchance thou wouldst eat out thy life in impotent desire; for know I am not for thee—I am for no man, save one, who hath been, but is not yet."

"As thou wilt, Ayesha," I said. "I fear not thy beauty. I have turned my heart away from such vanity as woman's loveliness, that passes like a flower."

"Nay, thou errest," she said; "that does *not* pass. My loveliness endures even as I endure; still, if thou wilt, O rash man, have thy will; but blame not me if passions mount thy reason, as the Egyptian breakers used to mount a colt, and guide it whither thou wilt not. Never may the man to whom my beauty is once unveiled put it from his mind, and therefore even among these savages I go hidden, lest they vex me, and I should slay them. Say, wilt thou see?"

"I will," I answered, my curiosity overpowering me.

She lifted her white and rounded arms—never had I seen such arms before—and slowly, very slowly, she withdrew some fastening beneath her hair. Then of a sudden the long, corpse-like wrappings fell from her to the ground, and my eyes travelled up her form, now robed only in a garb of clinging white that did but serve to show its rich and imperial shape, instinct with a life that was more than life, and with a certain serpent-like grace which was more than human. On her little feet were sandals, fastened with studs of gold. Then came ankles more perfect than ever sculptor dreamed of. About the waist her white kirtle was fastened by a double-headed snake of solid gold, above which her gracious form swelled up in lines as pure as they were lovely, till the kirtle ended at the snowy argent of her breast, whereon her arms were folded. I gazed above them at her face, and—I do not romance—shrank back blinded and amazed. I have heard of the beauty of celestial beings, now I saw it; only this beauty, with all its awful loveliness and purity, was *evil*—or rather, at the time, it impressed me as evil. How am I to describe it? I cannot—simply I cannot! The man does not live whose pen could convey a sense of what I saw. I might talk of the great changing eyes of deepest, softest black, of the tinted face, of the broad and noble brow, on which the hair grew low, and delicate, straight features. But, beautiful, surpassingly beautiful as were all these, her loveliness did not lie in them. It lay rather, if it can be said to have had any abiding home, in a visible majesty, in an imperial grace, in a godlike stamp of softened power, which shone upon that radiant countenance like a living halo. Never before had I guessed what beauty made sublime could be—and yet, the sublimity was a dark one—the glory was not all of heaven —but none the less was it glorious. Though the face before me was that of a young woman of certainly not more than thirty years, in perfect health and the first flush of ripened beauty, yet it bore stamped upon it a seal of unutterable experience, and of deep acquaintance with grief and passion. Not even the slow smile that crept about the dimples of her mouth could hide this shadow of sin and sorrow. It shone even in the light of those glorious eyes, it was present in the air of majesty, and it seemed to say: "Behold me, lovely as no woman was or is, undying and half-divine; memory haunts me from age to age, and passion leads me by the hand—evil have I done, and with sorrow have I made acquaintance from age to age, and from age to age evil I shall do, and sorrow shall I know till my redemption comes."

Drawn by some magnetic force which I could not resist, I let my eyes rest upon her shining orbs, and felt a current pass from them to me that bewildered and half blinded me.

She laughed—ah, how musically!—and nodded her little head

at me with an air of sublime coquetry that would have been worthy of the Venus Victrix.

"Rash man!" she said; "like Actæon, thou hast had thy will; be careful lest, like Actæon, thou too dost perish miserably, torn to pieces by the ban-hounds of thine own passions. I too, O Holly, am a virgin goddess, not to be moved of any man, save one, and it is not thou. Say, hast thou seen enough?"

"I have looked on beauty, and I am blinded," I said hoarsely, lifting my hand to cover up my eyes.

"So! what did I tell thee? Beauty is like the lightning: it is lovely, but it destroys—especially trees, O Holly!" and again she nodded and laughed.

Ayesha paused, and through my fingers I saw an awful change come upon her countenance. The great eyes suddenly fixed themselves into an expression in which horror seemed to struggle with some tremendous hope arising through the depths of her dark soul. The lovely face grew rigid, and the gracious willowy form seemed to erect itself.

"Man!" she half whispered, half hissed, throwing back her head like a snake about to strike—"Man! whence hadst thou that scarab on thy hand? Speak, or by the Spirit of Life I will blast thee where thou standest!" and she took one light step towards me, while from her eyes there shone such an awful light—to me it seemed almost like a flame—that I fell, then and there, to the ground before her, babbling confusedly in my terror.

"Peace!" she said, with a sudden charge of manner, and speaking in her former soft voice, "I did affright thee. Forgive me! But at times, O Holly, the almost infinite mind grows impatient of the slowness of the very finite, and I am tempted to use my power out of vexation. Very nearly wast thou dead, but I remembered——. But the scarab—about the scarabæus?"

"I found it," I stammered feebly, as I gained my feet once more, and it is a solemn fact that my mind was so disturbed that at the moment I could remember nothing else about the ring except the finding of it in Leo's cave.

"It is very strange," she said with a sudden access of woman-like trembling and agitation which seemed out of place in this awful woman—"but once I knew a scarab fashioned thus. It—hung round the neck—of one I loved," and she gave a little sob, and I saw that after all she was only a woman, although she might be a very old one.

"So," she went on, "it must be one like to it, and yet never did I see its fellow, for thereto hung a history, and he who wore it prized it much.[1] But the scarab that I knew was not set thus in the bezel of a ring. Go now, Holly, go, and if thou canst, try to forget that of thy folly thou hast looked on Ayesha's beauty," and, turning from me, she threw herself upon her couch, and buried her face in the cushions.

As for me, I stumbled from her presence, and how I reached my own cave I do not remember.

CHAPTER XIV

A SOUL IN HELL

It was nearly ten o'clock at night when I cast myself down upon my bed, and I began to gather my scattered wits, and to reflect upon what I had seen and heard. But the more I reflected the less I could understand it. Was I mad, or drunk, or dreaming, or was I merely the victim of a gigantic and most elaborate hoax? How was it credible that I, a rational man, not unacquainted with the leading scientific facts of our history, and hitherto an absolute and utter disbeliever in all the hocus-pocus which in Europe goes by the name of the supernatural, could believe that within the last few minutes I had been engaged in conservation with a woman two thousand and odd years old? The thing was quite adverse to the experience of humanity, and absolutely and utterly impossible. It must be a hoax, and yet, if it were a hoax, what was I to make of it? What, too, could be said of the figures in the water, of the woman's extraordinary acquaintance with the remote past, and her ignorance, or apparent ignorance, of any subsequent history? What, too, of her wonderful and awful loveliness? This, at any rate, was a patent fact, and beyond the experience of the world. No merely mortal woman could shine with such a supernatural radiance. As to that, at least, she had been in the right—it was not safe for any man to look upon such beauty. I was a hardened vessel in such matters, with the exception of one painful experience of my green and tender youth, having thrust the softer sex (I sometimes think that this is a misnomer) almost entirely out of my thoughts. But now, to my intense horror, I *knew* that I could never put away the vision of those glorious eyes; and

[1] I am informed by a renowned and most learned Egyptologist, to whom I have submitted this very interesting and beautifully finished scarab, 'Suten se Rā,' that he has never seen one resembling it. Although it bears a title frequently given to Egyptian royalty, he is of opinion that it is not necessarily the cartouche of a Pharaoh, on which either the throne or personal name of the monarch is generally inscribed. What the history of this particular scarab may have been we can now, unfortunately, never know, though

alas; the very *diablerie* of the woman, whilst it horrified and
repelled, attracted in an even greater degree. A person with the
experience of two thousand years behind her, with the command
of such tremendous powers, and the knowledge of a mystery that
could hold off death, was certainly worth falling in love with,
if ever woman was. But, alas! it was not a question of whether
or no she were worth it, for so far as I could judge, not being
versed in such matters, I, a Fellow of my college, noted for what
my acquaintances are pleased to call my misogyny, and a respectable man now well on in middle life, had succumbed absolutely and hopelessly before this white sorceress. Nonsense; it
must be nonsense! She had warned me fairly, and I had refused
to take the warning. Curses on the fatal curiosity that is ever
prompting man to draw the veil from woman, and curses on the
natural impulse which begets it! It is the cause of half—ay, and
more than half—of our misfortunes. Why cannot man rest content to live alone and be happy, and let the women live alone
and be happy also? But perhaps they would not be happy, and
I am not sure that we should either. Here was a nice state of
affairs—I, at my age, to fall a victim to this modern Circe!
But then she was not modern, at least she said not. She was
almost as ancient as the original Circe.

I tore my hair, and jumped up from my couch, feeling that
if I did not do something I should go quite mad. What did she
mean about the scarabæus, too? It was Leo's scarabæus, and had
come out of the old coffer that Vincey had left in my rooms
nearly one-and-twenty years before. Could it be, after all, that
the story was true, and that the writing on the sherd was *not* a
forgery, or the invention of some crack-brained, long-forgotten
individual? And if so, could it be that *Leo* was the man whom
She awaited—the dead man who was to be born again! Impossible! The supposition was insane! Who ever heard of a man
being reborn?

But if it were possible that a woman could exist for two thousand years, this might be possible also—anything might be
possible. For aught I knew I myself might be a reincarnation of
some other forgotten self, or perhaps the last of a long line of
ancestral selves. Well, *vive la guerre!* why not? Only, unfortunately, I had no recollection of these previous conditions. The
idea was so absurd to me that I burst out laughing, and,
addressing the sculptured picture of a grim-looking warrior on

I have little doubt but that it played some part in the tragic story of the
Princess Amenartas and her lover Kallikrates, the forsworn priest of
Isis.—EDITOR.

the cave wall, called out to him aloud, "Who knows, old fellow?—perhaps I was your contemporary. By Jove! perhaps I was you and you are I," and then I laughed again at my own folly, and the sound of my laughter rang dismally along the vaulted roof, as though the ghost of the warrior had echoed the ghost of a laugh.

Next I bethought me that I had not been to see how Leo fared, so, taking one of the lamps which were burning at my bedside, I slipped off my shoes and crept down the passage to the entrance of his sleeping-cave. The draught of the night air was lifting his curtain to and fro gently, as though spirit hands were drawing and redrawing it. I slid into the vault-like apartment, and looked round. There was a light by which I could see that Leo was lying on the couch, tossing restlessly in his fever, but asleep. At his side, half prostrate on the floor, half leaning against the stone couch, was Ustane. She held his hand in one of hers, but she too dozed, and the two made a pretty, or rather a pathetic, picture. Poor Leo! his cheek was burning red, there were dark shadows beneath his eyes, and his breath came heavily. He was very, very ill; and again the horrible fear seized me that he might die, and I be left alone in the world. And yet if he lived he would perhaps be my rival with Ayesha; even if he were not the man, what chance should I, middle-aged and hideous, have against his bright youth and beauty? Well, thank Heaven! my sense of right was not dead. *She* had not killed that yet; and, as I stood there, I prayed to Heaven in my heart that my boy, my more than son, might live—ay, even if he proved to be the man.

Then I went back as softly as I had come, but still I could not sleep; the sight and thought of Leo lying so ill yonder had but added fuel to the fire of my unrest. My wearied body and overstrained mind awakened all my imagination into preternatural activity. Ideas, visions, almost inspirations, floated before it with startling vividness. Most of them were grotesque enough, some were ghastly, some recalled thoughts and sensations that for years had been buried in the *debris* of my past life. But behind and above them all hovered the shape of that awful woman, and through them gleamed the memory of her entrancing loveliness. Up and down the cave I strode—up and down.

Suddenly I observed, what I had not noticed before, that there was a narrow aperture in the rocky wall. I took up the lamp and examined it; the aperture led to a passage. Now I was still sufficiently sensible to remember that it is not pleasant, in such a situation as was ours, to find passages running into your bed-chamber from no one knows where. If there are passages, people can come along them; they can come when one is asleep. Partly to see where it went to, and partly from a restless desire to be doing something, I followed this passage. It led to a stone stair, which I descended; the stair ended in another passage, or rather tunnel, also hewn out of the bed-rock, and running, so far as I could judge, exactly beneath the gallery that led to the entrance of our rooms, and across the great central cave. I went down it: it was silent as the grave, but still, drawn by some sensation or attraction that I cannot define, I followed on, my stockinged feet falling without noise on the smooth and rocky floor. When I had traversed some fifty yards of space, I came to a third passage running at right angles, and here an awful thing happened to me: the sharp draught caught my lamp and extinguished it, leaving me in utter darkness in the bowels of that mysterious place. I took a couple of strides forward so as to clear the bisecting tunnel, being terribly afraid lest I should turn up it in the dark if once I grew confused as to the direction. Then I paused to think. What was I to do? I had no match; it seemed awful to attempt that long journey back through the utter gloom, and yet I could not stand there all night, and, if I did, probably it could not help me much, for in the bowels of the rock it would be as dark at midday as at midnight. I looked back over my shoulder—not a sight or a sound. I peered forward down the darkness: surely, far away, I saw something like the faint glow of fire. Perhaps it was a cave where I could find a light— at any rate, it was worth investigating. Slowly and painfully I crept along the tunnel, keeping my hand against its wall, and feeling at every step with my foot before I set it down, fearing lest I should fall into some pit. Thirty paces—there was a light, a broad light that came and went, shining through curtains! Fifty paces—it was at hand! Sixty—oh, great heaven!

I was at the curtains, and they did not hang close, so I could see clearly into the little cavern beyond them. This had the appearance of a tomb, and was lit up by a fire that burnt in its centre with a whitish flame and without smoke. Indeed, there, to the left, was a stone shelf with a little ledge to it three inches or so high, and on the shelf lay what I imagined to be a corpse; at any rate, it looked like one, with something white thrown over it. To the right was a similar shelf, on which broidered coverings were strewn. Over the fire bent the figure of a woman who seemed to be staring at the flickering flame; she knelt sideways to me, facing the corpse, and was wrapped in a dark mantle that hid her like a nun's cloak. Suddenly, as I was trying to make up my mind what to do, with a convulsive movement that suggested an impulse of despairing energy, the woman rose to her feet and cast the dark cloak from her.

It was *She* herself!

She was clothed, as I had seen her when she unveiled, in the kirtle of clinging white, cut low upon her bosom, and bound in at the waist with the barbaric double-headed snake, and her rippling black hair fell in heavy masses almost to her feet. But it was her face that caught my eye, and held me as in a vice, not this time by the force of its beauty, but with the power of fascinated terror. The beauty was still there, indeed, but the agony, the blind passion, and the awful vindictiveness displayed upon those quivering features, and in the tortured look of the upturned eyes, were such as surpass my powers of description.

For a moment she stood still, her hands raised high above her head, and as she stood the white robe slipped from her down to her golden girdle, baring the blinding loveliness of her form. She stood there, her fingers clenched, while the awful look of malevolence gathered and deepened on her face.

Suddenly I thought of what would happen if she discovered me, and the reflection turned me sick and faint. But, even if I had known that I must die if I stayed, I do not believe that I could have moved, for I was absolutely fascinated. Still I knew my danger. Supposing that she should hear me, or see me through the curtain, supposing I even sneezed, or that her magic told her that she was being watched—swift indeed would be my doom.

Down came the clenched hands to her sides, then up they rose above her head, and, as I am a living and honourable man, the white flame of the fire leapt after them, almost to the roof, throwing a fierce and ghastly glare upon *She* herself, upon the white figure beneath the covering, and every scroll and detail of the rockwork.

Down came the ivory arms again, and as they fell she spoke, or rather hissed, in Arabic, in a note that curdled my blood, and for a second stopped my heart.

"Curse her, may she be everlastingly accursed."

The arms sank and the flame sank. Up they went again, and the broad tongue of fire shot after them; and then again they fell.

"Curse her memory—accursed be the memory of the Egyptian."

Up again, and again down.

"Curse her, the daughter of the Nile, because of her beauty.

"Curse her, because her magic hath prevailed against me.

"Curse her, because she held my beloved from me."

And again the flame dwindled and shrank.

She placed her hands before her eyes, and, abandoning the hissing tone, she cried aloud:—

"Where is the use of cursing?—she prevailed, and she is gone."

Then she recommenced with an even more frightful energy:—

"Curse her where she is. Let my curses reach her where she is and disturb her rest.

"Curse her through the starry spaces. Let her shadow be accursed.

"Let my power find her even there.

"Let her hear me even there. Let her hide herself in the blackness.

"Let her go down into the pit of despair, because I shall one day find her."

Again the flame fell, and again she covered her eyes with her hands.

"It is folly," she wailed; "who can reach those who sleep beneath the wings of Power? Not even I can reach them."

Then once more she began her unholy rites.

"Curse her when she shall be born again. Let her be born accursed.

"Let her be utterly accursed from the hour of her new birth until sleep finds her.

"Yea then, let her be accursed; for then shall I overtake her with my vengeance, and utterly destroy her."

And so on. The flame rose and fell, reflecting itself in Ayesha's agonised eyes; the hissing sound of her terrible maledictions, and no words of mine can convey how terrible they were, ran round the walls and died away in little echoes, and the fierce light and deep gloom alternated themselves on the white and dreadful form stretched upon that bier of stone.

But at length she seemed to wear herself out and ceased. She sat herself down upon the rocky floor, shaking the dense cloud of beautiful hair over her face and breast, and began to sob terribly in the torture of a heartrending despair.

"Two thousand years," she moaned—"two thousand years have I waited and endured; but though century doth still creep on to century, and time give place to time, the sting of memory hath not lessened, the light of hope doth not shine more bright. Oh, to have lived two thousand years, with all my passion eating at my heart, and with my sin ever before me! Oh, that for me life cannot bring forgetfulness! Oh, for the weary ages that have been and are yet to come, and evermore to come, endless and without end!

"My love! my love! my love! Why did that stranger bring thee back to me after this sort? For five long centuries I have not suffered thus. Oh, if I sinned against thee, have I not wiped away the sin? When wilt thou come back to me who have all, and yet without thee have naught? What is there that I can do? What? What? What? And perchance she—perchance that Egyptian doth abide with thee where thou art, and mock my memory. Oh, why could I not die with thee, I who slew thee? Alas, that I cannot die! Alas! Alas!" and she flung herself prone upon the ground, and sobbed and wept till I thought that her heart must burst.

Suddenly she ceased, raised herself to her feet, rearranged her robe, and, tossing back her long locks impatiently, swept across to where the body lay upon the bench.

"O Kallikrates!" she cried, and I trembled at the name, "I must look upon thy face again, though it be agony. It is a generation since I looked upon thee whom I slew—slew with mine own hand," and with trembling fingers she seized the corner of the sheet-like wrapping that covered the form upon the stone bier, and paused. When she spoke again, it was in an awed whisper, as though her thought were terrible even to herself.

"Shall I raise thee," she said, apparently addressing the corpse, "so that thou standest there before me, as of old? I *can* raise thee," and she held out her hands over the sheeted dead, while her frame became rigid and terrible to see, and her eyes grew fixed and dull. I shrank in horror behind the curtain, my hair stood up upon my head, and, whether it was my imagination or a fact I am unable to say, but I thought that the quiet form beneath the coverings began to quiver, and the winding sheet to lift as though it lay on the breast of one who slept. Suddenly Ayesha withdrew her hands, and the motion of the corpse seemed to me to cease.

"To what purpose?" she said heavily. "Of what service is it to recall the semblance of life when I cannot recall the spirit? Even if thou stoodest before me thou wouldst not know me, and couldst do but what I bid thee. The life in thee would be *my* life, and not *thy* life, Kallikrates!"

For a moment she remained thus, brooding; then she cast herself down on her knees beside the form, and began to press her lips against the sheet, and to weep. There was something so horrible about the sight of this awe-inspiring woman letting loose her passion on the dead—so much more horrible even than anything which had gone before—that I could no longer bear to look at it, and, turning, began to creep, shaking as I was in every limb, slowly along the pitch-dark passage, feeling in my trembling heart that I had seen a vision of a Soul in Hell.

On I stumbled, I scarcely know how. Twice I fell, once I turned up the bisecting passage, but fortunately found out my mistake in time. For twenty minutes or more I crept along, till at last it occurred to me that I must have passed the little stair by which I had descended. So, utterly exhausted, and nearly frightened to death, I lay down there on the stone flooring, and sank into oblivion.

When I came to myself I noticed a ray of light in the passage behind me. I crept to it, and found that the weak dawn was stealing down to the little stair. Passing up it, I gained my chamber in safety, and, flinging myself on the couch, was soon lost in sleep, or rather in stupor.

CHAPTER XV

AYESHA GIVES JUDGMENT

THE next thing that I remember was opening my eyes and perceiving the form of Job, who had now almost recovered from his attack of fever. He was standing in a beam of light that pierced into the cave from the outer air, shaking out my clothes as a makeshift for brushing them, which he could not do because there was no brush, then folding them up neatly and laying them on the foot of the stone couch. This done, he took my leather dressing-case out of the travelling bag, and opened it ready for my use. First he stood it on the foot of the couch also, then, being afraid, I suppose, that I should kick it off, he placed it upon a leopard skin on the floor, and stepped back a pace or two to observe the effect. It was not satisfactory, so he shut up the bag, turned it on end, and, having stood it against the end of the couch, rested the dressing-case on it. Next he looked at the pots full of water, which constituted our washing apparatus. "Ah!" I heard him murmur, "no hot water in this beastly place. I suppose these poor creatures only use it to boil each other in," and he sighed deeply.

"What is the matter, Job?" I said.

"Beg pardon, sir," he said, touching his hair. "I thought you were asleep, sir: and I am sure you seem as though you want it. One might think from the look of you that you had been having a night of it."

I only groaned by way of answer. I had, indeed, been "having a night of it," such as I hope never to have again.

"How is Mr. Leo, Job?"

"Much the same, sir. If he don't soon mend, he'll end, sir; and that's all about it; though I must say that that there savage, Ustane, do do her best for him, almost like a baptised Christian. She is always hanging round and looking after him, and if I ventures to interfere it's awful to see her; her hair seems to stand on end, and she curses and swears away in her heathen talk—at least I fancy she must be cursing, from the look of her."

"And what do you do then?"

"I make her a perlite bow, and I say, 'Young woman, your position is one that I don't quite understand, and can't recognise. Let me tell you that I has a duty to perform to my master as is incapacitated by illness, and that I am going to perform it until I am incapacitated too,' but she don't take no heed, not she—only curses and swears away worse than ever. Last night she put her hand under that sort of nightshirt she wears, and whips out a knife with a kind of a curl in the blade; so I whips out my revolver, and we walks round and round each other till at last she bursts out laughing. It isn't nice treatment for a Christian man to have to put up with from a savage, however handsome she may be, but it is what people must expect as is *fools* enough" (Job laid great emphasis on the 'fools') "to come to such a place to look for things no man is meant to find. It's a judgment on us, sir—that's my view; and I, for one, is of opinion that the judgment isn't half done yet, and when it is done we shall be done too, and just stop in these beastly caves with the ghosts and the corpses for once and all. And now, sir, I must be seeing about Mr. Leo's broth, if that wild cat will let me; and perhaps you would like to get up, sir, because it's past nine o'clock."

Job's remarks were not exactly of a cheering order to a man who had just passed through such a night; and, what is more, they had the weight of truth. Taking one thing with another, it appeared to me to be an utter impossibility that we should escape from this place where we were. Supposing that Leo recovered, and supposing that *She* would let us go, which was exceedingly doubtful, and that she did not 'blast' us in some moment of vexation, and that we were not 'hot-potted' by the Amahagger, it would be quite impracticable for us to find our way across the network of marshes which, stretching for scores and scores of miles, formed a stronger and more impassable fortification round the various Amahagger 'Households' than any that could be built or designed by man. No, there was but one thing to do—face it out; and, speaking for my own part, I was so intensely interested in the whole weird story that, notwithstanding the shattered state of my nerves, I asked nothing better, even if my life paid forfeit to my curiosity. What man for whom physiology has charms could forbear to study such a character as that of this wonderful Ayesha when the opportunity presented itself? The very terror of the pursuit added to its fascination; moreover, as I was forced to own to myself even now in the sober light of day, the woman had attractions that I could not forget. Not even the dreadful sight which I had witnessed during the night could drive that folly from my mind; and, alas that I should have to admit it! it has not been driven thence to this hour.

After I had dressed myself I passed into the eating, or rather embalming chamber, and took some food, which as before was brought to me by the girl mutes. When I had finished I went to see poor Leo, who was quite light-headed, and did not even know me. I asked Ustane how she thought he did; but she only shook her head and began to cry a little. Evidently her hopes were small; and then and there I made up my mind that, if it were possible, I would persuade *She* to come to see him. Surely she would cure him if she had the power—at any rate she said so. While I was in the room, Billali entered, and also shook his head.

"He will die at nightfall," he said.

"God forbid, my father," I answered, and turned away with a heavy heart.

"*She-who-must-be-obeyed* commands thy presence, my Baboon," said the old man so soon as we passed the curtain; "but, oh, my dear son, be more careful. Yesterday I made sure in my heart that *She* would blast thee when thou didst not crawl upon thy stomach before her. She will sit in the great hall presently to do justice upon those who would have smitten thee and the Lion. Come, my son; come swiftly."

I turned, and followed him down the passage, and when we reached the central cave I saw that many Amahagger, some robed, and some clad only in the sweet simplicity of a leopard skin, were hurrying along it. We mingled with the throng, and walked up the enormous and, indeed, almost interminable cavern. All its walls were most elaborately sculptured, and every twenty paces or so passages opened out of it at right angles, leading, Billali told me, to tombs, hollowed in the rock by 'the people who were before.' Nobody visited those tombs now, he said; and I admit that my heart rejoiced when I thought of the opportunities of antiquarian research which lay open to me.

At last we came to the head of the cave, where there was a rock daïs almost exactly similar to the one on which we had been so furiously attacked, a fact that proved to me that these daïs must have been used as altars, probably for the celebration of religious ceremonies, and more especially of rites connected with the interment of the dead. On either side of this platform were passages leading, Billali informed me, to other caves full of dead bodies. "Indeed," he added, "the whole mountain is peopled with dead, and nearly all of them perfect."

In front of the daïs were gathered a great number of people of both sexes, who stood staring about in their peculiar gloomy fashion, which would have reduced Mark Tapley himself to misery within five minutes. On the platform was a rude chair of black wood inlaid with ivory, having a seat made of grass fibre, and a footstool formed of a wooden slab attached to the framework of the chair.

Suddenly there rose a cry of "Hiya! Hiya!" (*"She! She!"*), whereupon the entire crowd of spectators instantly precipitated themselves to the ground, and lay still as though they were individually and collectively stricken dead, leaving me standing like some solitary survivor of a massacre. At that moment, too, a string of guards began to defile from a passage to the left, and ranged themselves on either side of the daïs. Then came about a score of male mutes, followed by as many women mutes bearing lamps, and lastly a tall white figure, swathed from head to foot, in whom I recognised *She* herself. She mounted the platform, and, sitting down upon the chair, spoke to me in *Greek,* I suppose because she did not wish those present to understand what she said.

"Come hither, O Holly," she said, "and sit thou at my feet, and see me do justice on those who would have slain thee. Forgive me if my Greek doth halt like a lame man; it is so long since I have heard the sound of it that my tongue is stiff, and will not bend rightly to the words."

I bowed, and, mounting the daïs, sat down at her feet.

"How hast thou slept, my Holly?" she asked.

"I slept not well, O Ayesha!" I answered with perfect truth, and with an inward fear that perhaps she knew how I had passed the heart of the night.

"So," she said, with a little laugh; "I, too, have not slept well. Last night I had dreams, and methinks that thou didst call them to me, my Holly."

"Of what didst thou dream, Ayesha?" I asked indifferently.

"I dreamed," she answered quickly, "of one I hate and one I love," and then, as though to turn the conversation, she addressed the captain of her guard in Arabic, saying: "Let the men be brought before me."

The captain bowed low, for the guard and her attendants did not prostrate themselves, but remained standing, and departed with his underlings down a passage to the right.

Then came a silence. *She* leaned her swathed head upon her hand and appeared to be lost in thought, while the multitude before her continued to grovel upon their stomachs, only twisting their heads round a little so as to have a view of us with one eye. It seemed that their Queen so rarely appeared in public that they were willing to undergo this inconvenience, and even graver risks, to gain the opportunity of looking on her, or rather on her garments, for no living man there except myself had ever seen her face. At last we caught sight of the waving of lights, and heard the tramp of men advancing down the passage. Then in filed the guard, and with them the survivors of our would-be murderers, to the number of twenty or more, on whose countenances a natural expression of sullenness struggled with the terror that evidently filled their savage hearts. They were ranged in front of the daïs, and would have cast themselves upon the floor of the cave like the spectators, but *She* stopped them.

"Nay," she said in her softest voice, "stand; I pray you stand. Perchance the time will soon come when ye shall grow weary of being stretched out," and she laughed melodiously.

I saw a cringe of terror run along the rank of the doomed wretches, and, wicked villains as they were, I felt sorry for them. Some minutes, perhaps two or three, passed before anything fresh occurred, during which *She* appeared from the movement of her head—for, of course, we could not see her eyes—to slowly and carefully examine each delinquent. At last she spoke, addressing herself to me in a quiet and deliberate tone.

"Dost thou, O my guest, recognise these men?"

"Ay, O Queen, nearly all of them," I said, and I saw them glower at me as I said it.

"Then tell to me, and this great company, the tale whereof I have heard."

Thus adjured, in as few words as I could I related the history of the cannibal feast, and of the attempted torture of our poor servant. The narrative was received in perfect silence, both by the accused and by the audience, and also by *She* herself. When I had done, Ayesha called upon Billali by name, and, lifting his head from the ground, but without rising, the old man confirmed my story. No further evidence was taken.

"Ye have heard," said *She* at length, in a cold, clear voice, very different from her usual tones—indeed, it was one of the most remarkable things about this extraordinary creature that her voice had the power of suiting itself in a wonderful manner to the mood of the moment. "What have you to say, ye rebellious children, why vengeance should not be done upon you?"

For some time there was no answer, but at last one of the men, a fine, broad-chested fellow, well on in the middle life, with deep-graven features and an eye like a hawk's, spoke. He said that the orders which they had received were not to harm the white men; none were given as to their black servant, so, egged on thereto by a woman who was now dead, they proceeded to try to 'hot-pot' him after the ancient and honourable custom of their country, with the view of eating him in due course. As for their attack upon ourselves, it was made in an access of sudden fury, and they deeply regretted it. He ended by humbly praying that mercy might be extended to them; or, at least, that they might be banished into the swamps, to live or die as it might chance; but I saw it written on his face that he had very little hope of mercy.

Then came a pause, and the most intense silence reigned over the dim place, which, faintly illuminated by the flicker of the lamps striking out broad patterns of light and shadow upon the rocky walls, seemed strange as any I ever saw, even in that unholy land. Upon the ground before the daïs were stretched scores of the corpselike forms of the spectators, till at last the long lines of them were lost in the gloomy background. Before this prostrate audience were the knots of evil-doers, trying to cover up their natural terrors with a brave appearance of unconcern. On the right and left stood the silent guards, robed in white and armed with great spears and daggers, and men and women mutes watching with hard, curious eyes. Then, seated in her barbaric chair above them all, with myself at her feet, was the veiled white woman, whose loveliness and awesome power seemed to shine visibly about her like a halo, or rather like the glow from some unseen light. Never have I seen her veiled shape look more terrible than it did at that time while she gathered herself up for vengeance.

At last it came.

"Dogs and serpents," *She* began in a low voice that gradually gathered power as she went on, till the place rang with it— "Eaters of human flesh, two things have ye done. First, ye have attacked these strangers, being white men, and would have slain their servant, and for that alone death is your reward. But this is not all. Ye have dared to disobey me. Did I not send my word unto you by Billali, my servant, and the father of your household? Did I not bid you to hospitably entertain these strangers,

whom now ye have striven to slay, and whom, had not they been
brave and strong beyond the strength of men, ye would cruelly
have murdered? Hath it not been taught to you from childhood
that the law of *Hiya* is an ever-fixed law, and that he who break-
eth it by so much as one jot or tittle shall perish? And is not my
lightest word a law? Have not your fathers taught you this, I
say, whilst as yet ye were but children? Do ye not know that as
well might ye bid these great caves to fall upon you, or the sun to
cease its journeyings, as to hope to turn me from courses, or make
my word light or heavy, according to your minds? Well do ye
know it, ye Wicked Ones. But ye are all evil—evil to the core—the
wickedness bubbles up in you like a fountain in the springtime.
Were it not for me, generations since ye had ceased to be, for of
your own evil way ye had destroyed each other. And now, because ye have done this thing, because ye have striven to put
these men, my guests, to death, and yet more because ye have
dared to disobey my word, this is the doom whereto I doom you:
That ye be taken to the cave of torture,[1] and given over to the
tormentors, and that on the going down of to-morrow's sun those
of you who yet remain alive be slain, even as ye would have slain
the servant of this my guest."

She ceased, and a faint murmur of horror ran round the cave.
As for the victims, as soon as they knew the full hideousness of
their doom their stoicism forsook them, and they flung themselves down upon the ground and wept, imploring for mercy in a
way that was dreadful to behold. I, too, turned to Ayesha, and
begged her to spare them, or at least to mete out their fate in
some less awful way. But she proved hard as adamant.

"My Holly," she said, again speaking in Greek which, to tell
the truth, although I have always been considered a better
scholar of that language than most men, I found it rather difficult to follow, chiefly because of the change in the fall of the
accent.[2] "My Holly, it cannot be. Were I to show mercy to those
wolves, your lives would not be safe among this people for a

[1]"The cave of torture."—I afterwards saw this dreadful place, also a
legacy from the prehistoric people who lived in Kôr. The only objects in
the cave itself were slabs of rock arranged in various positions to facilitate
the operations of the torturers. Many of these slabs, which were of a
porous stone, were stained quite dark with the blood of ancient victims
that had soaked into them. Also in the centre of the room was a place for
a furnace, with a cavity wherein to heat the historic pot. But the most
dreadful thing about the cave was that over each slab was a sculptured
illustration of the appropriate torment being applied. These sculptures were
so awful that I will not harrow the reader by attempting a description of
them.—L. H. H.

[2]Ayesha, of course, talked with the accent of her contemporaries, whereas

day. Thou knowest them not. They are tigers to lap blood, and even now they hunger for your lives. How thinkest thou that I rule this people? I have but a regiment of guards to do my bidding, therefore it is not by force. It is by terror. My empire is of the imagination. Once in a lifetime mayhap I do as I have done but now, and slay a score by torture. Believe not that I would be cruel, or take vengeance on anything so low. What can it profit me to be avenged on such as these? Those who live long, my Holly, have no passions, save where they have interests. Though I may seem to slay in wrath, or because my mood is crossed, it is not so. Thou hast seen how in the heavens the little clouds blow this way and that without a cause, yet behind them is the great wind sweeping on its path whither it listeth. So is it with me, O Holly. My moods and changes are the little clouds, and fitfully these seem to turn; but behind them the great wind of my purpose blows ever. Nay, the men must die; and die as I have said." Then, suddenly turning to the captain of the guard, she added:

"As my word is, so be it!"

CHAPTER XVI

THE TOMBS OF KÔR

AFTER the prisoners had been removed Ayesha waved her hand, and the spectators, turning round, began to crawl away down the cave like a scattered flock of sheep. When they were at some distance from the daïs, however, they rose and walked, leaving their Queen and myself alone, with the exception of the mutes and a few guards, for the most of these had departed with the doomed men. Thinking this a good opportunity, I asked *She* to come to visit Leo, telling her of his serious condition; but she would not, saying that he certainly would not die before the evening, as people never died of that fever except at nightfall or the dawn. Also she said it would be better that the sickness should spend its course as much as possible before she cured it. Accordingly, I was rising to leave, when she bade me follow her, as she would talk with me, and show me the wonders of the caves.

I was too much involved in the web of her fascinations to say her no, even had I wished it, so I bowed in assent; whereon she rose from her chair, and, making some signs to the mutes, descended from the daïs. As she came four of the girls took lamps,

we have only tradition and the modern tongue to guide us as to the exact pronunciation.—L. H. H.

and ranged themselves two in front of and two behind us, but the others went away, as also did the guards.

"Now," she said, "wouldst thou see some of the wonders of this place, O Holly? Look upon this great cave. Sawest thou ever its like? Yet was it, and many others, hollowed out by the hands of the dead race that once lived here in the city on the plain. A great and a wonderful people they must have been, those men of Kôr, but, like the Egyptians, they thought more of the dead than of the living. How many men, thinkest thou, working for how many years, did it need to the hewing of this cave and all its endless galleries?"

"Tens of thousands," I answered.

"So, O Holly. This people was an old people before the Egyptians were. A little can I read of their inscriptions, having found the key to them—and, see thou here, this was one of the last of the caves that they fashioned," and, turning to the rock beside her, she motioned the mutes to hold up the lamps. Carven over the daïs was the figure of an old man seated in a chair, with an ivory rod in his hand, and it struck me that his features were exceedingly similar to those of the man whose embalmment was represented in the chamber where we took our meals. Beneath the chair, that, by the way was shaped exactly like the one in which Ayesha had sat to give judgment, was a short inscription in the extraordinary characters whereof I have already spoken, but which I do not remember sufficiently to reproduce. It looked more like Chinese writing than any other that I am acquainted with. This inscription, with some difficulty and hesitation, Ayesha proceeded to read aloud and to translate. It ran as follows:—

"In the year four thousand two hundred and fifty-nine from the founding of the City of imperial Kôr was this cave (or burial place) completed by Tisno, King of Kôr, the people thereof and their slaves having laboured thereat for three generations, to be a tomb for their citizens of rank who shall come after. May the blessing of the heaven above the heaven rest upon their work, and make the sleep of Tisno, the mighty monarch, the likeness of whose features is graven above, a sound and happy sleep till the day of awakening,[1] and also the sleep of his servants, and of those of his race who, rising up after him, shall yet lay their heads as low."

"Thou seest, O Holly," she said, "this people founded the city, of which the ruins yet cumber the plain yonder, four thousand years before this cave was finished. Yet, when first mine eyes

---

[1] This phrase is remarkable, as seeming to indicate a belief in a future state.—EDITOR.

beheld it two thousand years ago, it was even as it is now. Judge, therefore, how old must that city have been! And now, follow thou me, and I will show thee after what fashion this great people fell when the time was come for it to fall." Then she led the way to the centre of the cave, stopping at a spot where a round rock had been let into a kind of large manhole in the flooring, accurately filling it just as iron plates fill the holes in the London pavements down which the coals are thrown. "Thou seest," she said. "Tell me, what is it?"

"Nay, I know not," I answered; whereon she crossed to the left-hand side of the cave (looking towards the entrance) and signed to the mutes to hold up the lamps. On the wall was something painted with a red pigment in similar characters to those hewn beneath the sculpture of Tisno, King of Kôr. This long inscription Ayesha translated to me, the pigment still being quite fresh enough to show the form of the letters. It ran as follows:—

"I, Junis, a priest of the Great Temple of Kôr, write this upon the rock of the burying-place in the year four thousand eight hundred and three from the founding of Kôr. Kôr is fallen! No more shall the mighty feast in her halls, no more shall she rule the world, and her navies go out to commerce with the world. Kôr is fallen! and her mighty works, and all the cities of Kôr, and all the harbours that she built and the canals that she made, are for the wolf and the owl and the wild swan, and the barbarian who comes after. Twenty and five moons ago did a cloud settle upon Kôr, and the hundred cities of Kôr, and out of the cloud came a pestilence that slew her people, old and young, one with another, and spared not. One with another they turned black and died—the young and the old, the rich and the poor, the man and the woman, the prince and the slave. The pestilence slew and slew, and ceased not by day or night, and those escaped from the pestilence were slain of the famine. No longer could the bodies of the children of Kôr be preserved according to the ancient rites, because of the number of the dead, therefore were they hurled into the great pit beneath this cave, through the hole in the floor of the cave. Then, at last, a remnant of this great people, the light of the whole world, went down to the coast and took ship and sailed northwards; and now am I, the Priest Junis, who write, the last man left alive of this great city of men, but whether there be any left in the other cities I know not. This do I write in misery of heart before I die, because Kôr the Imperial is no more, and because there are none to worship in her temple, and all her palaces are empty, and her

*princes and her captains and her traders and her fair women
have passed off the face of the earth for ever."*

I sighed in astonishment—the utter desolation depicted in
that rude scrawl was overpowering. It was terrible to think
of this solitary survivor of a mighty people recording its fate
before he too went down into darkness. What must the old man
have felt as, in ghastly terrifying solitude, by the light of one
lamp feebly illumining a little space of gloom, in a few brief
lines he daubed the history of his nation's death upon the cavern
wall? What a subject for the moralist, or the painter, or indeed
for any one who can reflect!

"Dost thou not think, O Holly," said Ayesha, laying her hand
upon my shoulder, "that those men who sailed north may have
been the fathers of the first Egyptians?"

"Nay, I know not," I answered; "it seems that the world is
very old."

"Old? Yes, it is old indeed. Time after time have nations, ay,
and rich and strong nations, learned in the arts, been, and passed
away to be forgotten, so that no memory of them remains. This is
but one of several; for Time eats up the works of man, unless,
indeed, he digs in caves like the people of Kôr, and then mayhap
the sea swallows them, or the earthquakes shakes them in. Who
knows what hath been on the earth, or what shall be? There is
no new thing under the sun, as the wise Hebrew wrote long ago.
Yet these people were not utterly destroyed, as I think. Some
few remained in the other cities, for their cities were many.
But the barbarians from the south, or perchance my people, the
Arabs, came down upon them, and took their women to wife,
and the race of the Amahagger that is now is a bastard brood of
the mighty sons of Kôr, and behold it dwelleth in the tombs
with its father's bones.[1] But I know not: who can know? My
arts cannot pierce so far into the blackness of Time's night.
They were a great people. They conquered till none were left
to conquer, and then they dwelt at ease within their rocky
mountain walls, with their manservants and their maidservants,
their minstrels, their sculptors, and their concubines, and traded
and quarrelled, and ate and hunted and slept and made merry
till their time came. But come, I will show thee that great pit
beneath the cavern whereof the writing speaks. Never shall
thine eyes witness such another sight."

[1]The name of the tribe, 'Ama-hagger,' would seem to indicate a curious
mingling of races such as might easily have occurred in the neighbourhood
of the Zambesi. The prefix 'Ama' is common to the Zulu and kindred
races, and signifies 'people,' while 'hagger' is an Arabic word meaning a
stone.—EDITOR.

Accordingly I followed her to a side passage opening out of the main cave, then down a great number of steps, and along an underground shaft which cannot have been less than sixty feet beneath the surface of the rock, and was ventilated by curious borings that ran upward, I do not know where. Suddenly the passage ended, and Ayesha halted, bidding the mutes hold up the lamps, and, as she had prophesied, I saw a scene such as I am not likely to behold again. We were standing in an enormous pit, or rather on the brink of it, for it went down deeper—I do not know how much—than the level on which we stood, and was edged in with a low wall of rock. So far as I could judge, this pit was about the size of the space beneath the dome of St. Paul's in London, and when the lamps were held up I saw that it was nothing but one vast charnel-house, being literally full of thousands of human skeletons, which lay piled up in an enormous gleaming pyramid, formed by the slipping down of the bodies at the apex as others were dropped in from above. Anything more appalling than this jumbled mass of the remains of a departed race I cannot imagine, and what made it even more dreadful was that in this dry air a considerable number of the bodies had become desiccated with the skin still on them, and now, fixed in every conceivable position, stared at us out of the mountain of white bones, grotesquely horrible caricatures of humanity. In my astonishment I uttered an ejaculation, and the echoes of my voice, ringing in that vaulted space, disturbed a skull which had been accurately balanced for many thousands of years near the apex of the pile. Down it came with a run, bounding along merrily towards us, and of course bringing an avalanche of other bones after it, till at last the whole pit rattled with their movement, even as though the skeletons were rising up to greet us.

"Come," I said, "let us go hence. These are the bodies of those who died of the great sickness—is it not so?" I added, as we turned away.

"Yea. The children of Kôr ever embalmed their dead, as did the Egyptians, but their art was greater than the art of the Egyptians, for, whereas the Egyptians disembowelled and drew the brain, the people of Kôr injected fluid into the veins, and thus reached every part. But stay, thou shalt see," and she halted at haphazard by one of the little doorways opening out of the passage along which we were walking, and motioned to the mutes to light us in. We entered a small chamber similar to that in which I had slept at our first stopping-place, only instead of one there were two stone benches or beds in it. On

the benches lay figures covered with yellow linen,[1] on which a
fine and impalpable dust had gathered in the course of ages,
but to nothing like the extent that might have been anticipated,
for in these deep-hewn caves there is no material to turn to dust.
About the bodies on the stone shelves and floor of the tomb
were many painted vases, but I saw very few ornaments or
weapons in any of the vaults.

"Withdraw the cloths, O Holly," said Ayesha, but when I
put out my hand to obey I drew it back again. It seemed a
sacrilege, and, to speak the truth, I was awed by the dread
solemnity of the place, and of the presences before us. Then,
with a laugh at my fears, she removed them herself, only to
discover other and yet finer wrappings lying over the forms
upon the stone bench. These also she withdrew, and for the
first time for thousands upon thousands of years did living eyes
look upon the face of that chilly dead. It was a woman; she
might have been thirty-five years of age, or perhaps a little less,
and certainly had been beautiful. Even now her calm clear-cut
features, marked out with delicate eyebrows and long eye-
lashes which threw upon the ivory face little lines of shadow in
the lamplight, were wonderfully beautiful. There, robed in
white, down which her blue-black hair was streaming, she slept
her last long sleep, and on her arm, its face pressed against
her breast, there lay a little babe. So sweet was the sight,
although so awful, that—I confess it without shame—I could
scarcely withhold my tears. It took me back across the dim gulf
of the ages to some happy home in dead Imperial Kôr, where
this winsome lady girt about with beauty had lived and died,
and dying had taken her last-born with her to the tomb. There
they slept before us, mother and child, the white memories of
a forgotten human history speaking more eloquently to the heart
than could any written record of their lives. Reverently I replaced
the grave-clothes, and, with a sigh that in the purpose of the
Everlasting flowers so fair should have bloomed only to be
gathered to the grave, I turned to the body on the opposite shelf,
and gently unveiled it. It was that of a man in advanced life,
with a long grizzled beard, also robed in white, and probably the
husband of the lady, who, after surviving her many years, came
at the last to sleep once more for good and all beside her.

We left the place and entered others. It would be too long to
describe the many things I saw in them. Each one had its

[1] All the linen that the Amahagger wore was taken from the tombs, which
accounted for its yellow hue. If it was well washed, however, and properly
rebleached, it acquired its former snowy whiteness, and was the softest and
best linen I ever saw.—L. H. H.

occupants—for evidently the five hundred and odd years that had elasped between the completion of the cave and the destruction of the race had sufficed to fill these catacombs, numberless as they were—and all appeared to have been undisturbed since the day when they were placed there. I could fill a book with the description of them, but to do so would only repeat what I have said, with variations.

Nearly all the bodies, so masterly was the art with which they had been treated, were as perfect as on the day of death thousands of years before. Nothing came to injure them in the deep silence of the living rock; they were beyond the reach of heat and cold and damp, and the aromatic drugs with which they had been saturated were, it seems, practically everlasting in their effect. Here and there, however, we saw an exception, and in these cases, although the flesh looked sound enough externally, if touched it fell in, and revealed the fact that the figure was but a pile of dust. This arose, Ayesha told me, from these particular bodies, either owing to haste in the burial or other causes, having been soaked in the preservative,[1] instead of its being injected into the substance of the flesh.

About the last tomb we visited I must, however, say a word for its contents spoke even more eloquently to the human sympathies than those of the first. It had but two occupants, and they lay together on a single shelf. I withdrew the grave-clothes, and there, clasped heart to heart, were a young man and a blooming girl. Her head rested on his arm, and his lips were pressed against her brow. I opened the man's linen robe, and found over his heart a dagger-wound, while beneath the girl's fair breast was a like cruel stab, through which her life had ebbed away. On the rock above was an inscription in three words. Ayesha translated it. It read, *'Wedded in Death.'*

What was the life-history of these two, who, of a truth, were beautiful in their lives, and in their death were not divided?

I closed my eyes, and imagination, taking up the thread of

[1]Ayesha afterwards showed me the tree from the leaves of which this ancient preservative was manufactured. It is a low bush-like tree, that to this day grows in wonderful plenty upon the sides of the mountains, or rather upon the slopes leading up to its rocky walls. The leaves are long and narrow, a vivid green in colour, but turning a bright red in the autumn, and not unlike those of a laurel in general appearance. They have little smell when green, but if boiled the aromatic odour from them is so strong that one can hardly bear it. The best mixture, however, was made from the roots, and among the people of Kôr there was a law, alluded to on some of the inscriptions which Ayesha showed me, to the effect that on pain of heavy penalties no one under a certain rank was to be embalmed with the drugs prepared from these roots. The object and effect of this law was, of course, to preserve the trees from extermination. The sale of the leaves and

thought, shot its swift shuttle back across the ages, weaving a picture on their blackness so real and vivid in its detail that I could almost for a moment think that I had triumphed over Time, and that my vision had pierced the mystery of the Past.

I seemed to see this fair girl's form—the yellow hair streaming down her, glittering against her garments snowy white, and the bosom that was whiter than her robes, even dimming with its lustre the ornaments of burnished gold. I seemed to see the great cave filled with warriors, bearded and clad in mail, and, on the lighted daïs whence Ayesha had given judgment, a man standing, robed, and surrounded by the symbols of his priestly office. Now up the cave there came one clad in purple, and before and behind him marched minstrels and fair maidens, chanting a wedding song. White stood the maid against the altar, fairer than the fairest there—purer than a lily, and more cold than the dew that glistens in its heart. But as the man drew near she shuddered. Then out of the press and throng there sprang a dark-haired youth, and put his arm about this long-forgotten girl, and kissed her pale face, in which the blood shot up like lights of the red dawn across the silent sky. Next there was turmoil and uproar, and flashing of swords, and they tore the youth from her arms, and stabbed him, but with a cry she snatched the dagger from his belt, and drove it into her snowy breast, home to the heart, and down she fell. Then, with cries and wailing, and every sound of lamentation, the pageant rolled away from the arena of my vision, and once more the Past shut its book.

Let him who reads forgive the intrusion of a dream into a history of fact. But it came so home to me—I saw it all so clearly in a moment, as it were; moreover, who shall say what proportion of fact, past, present, or to come, may lie in the imagination? What is imagination? Perhaps it is a shadow of the intangible truth, perhaps it is the soul's thought!

In an instant the picture had passed through my brain, and *She* was addressing me.

"Behold the lot of man!" said the veiled Ayesha, as she drew the winding-sheets back over the dead lovers, speaking in a solemn, thrilling voice, which accorded well with the dream that I dreamed: "to the tomb, and to the forgetfulness that hides the tomb, must we all come at last! Ay, even I who live so long. Even for me, O Holly, thousands upon thousands of years hence; thousands of years after thou hast gone through

---

roots was a Government monopoly, and from it the Kings of Kôr derived a large proportion of their private revenue.—L. H. H.

the gate and been lost in the mists, a day will dawn whereon I shall die, and be even as thou art and these are. And then what will it avail that I have lived a little longer, holding off death by the knowledge I have wrung from Nature, since at last I too must die? What is a span of ten thousand years, or ten times ten thousand years, in the history of time? It is as naught—it is as the mists that roll up in the sunlight; it fleeth away like an hour of sleep or the melting winter snows. Behold the lot of man! Certainly it shall overtake us, and we shall sleep. Certainly, too, we shall awake and live again, and again shall sleep, and so on and on, through periods, spaces, and times, from æon unto æon, till the world is dead, and the worlds beyond the world are dead, and naught liveth save the Spirit that is Life. But for us twain and for these dead ones shall the end of ends be Life, or shall it be Death? As yet Death is but Life's Night, but out of the Night is the Morrow born anew, and doth again beget the Night. Only, when Day and Night, and Life and Death, are ended and swallowed up in that from which they came, what shall be our fate, O Holly? Who can see so far? Not even I!"

Then she added, with a sudden change of tone and manner—

"Hast thou seen enough, my stranger guest, or shall I show thee more of the wonders of these tombs that are my palace halls? If thou wilt, I can lead thee to where Tisno, the mightiest and most valorous King of Kôr, in whose day these caves were ended, lies in a pomp that seems to mock at nothingness, and bid the empty shadows of the past do homage to his sculptured vanity!"

"I have seen enough, O Queen," I answered, "for my heart is overwhelmed by the power of this present death. Mortality is weak and easily oppressed in the company of that dust which waits upon its end. Take me hence, O Ayesha!"

CHAPTER XVII

THE BALANCE TURNS

FOLLOWING the lamps of the deaf mutes, which, held out from their bodies as a bearer holds water in a vessel, had the appearance of floating along by themselves, we came presently to a stair which led us to *She's* anteroom, the same that Billali had travelled upon all fours on the previous day. Here I wished to bid the Queen adieu, but she would not suffer it.

"Nay," she said, "enter with me, O Holly, for of a truth thy talk pleases me. Think, Holly; for two thousand years I have found none to speak with save slaves and my own soul, and though of all this thinking hath much wisdom come, and many secrets been made plain, yet I am weary of my thoughts, and have come to loathe mine own society, for surely the food that memory gives to eat is bitter to the taste, and it is only with the teeth of hope that we can bear to chew it. Now, though thy brain is green and tender, as becometh a man so young, yet is it that of one who thinks. In truth thou dost bring back to my mind certain of those old philosophers with whom in days bygone I have disputed at Athens, and at Becca in Arabia for thou hast the same crabbed air and dusty look, as though thou hadst passed thy days in reading ill-writ Greek, and been stained dark with the grime of manuscripts. So draw the curtain, and sit here by my side, and we will eat fruit, and talk of pleasant things. See, I will again unveil to thee. Thou hast brought it on thyself, O Holly; I have warned thee straightly—and thou shalt call me beautiful as even those old philosophers were wont to do. Fie upon them, for-getting their philosophy!"

And without more ado she stood up and shook the white wrappings from her, and came forth shining and splendid like some glittering snake when it has cast is slough; ay, and fixed her wonderful eyes upon me—more deadly than any Basi-lisk's—and pierced me through and through with their beauty, and sent her light laugh ringing down the air like chimes of silver bells.

A new mood was on her, and the colour of her fathomless mind had changed beneath it. It was no longer torture-torn and hateful, as I had seen it when she was cursing her dead rival by the leaping flames, no longer icily terrible as in the judgment-hall; no longer rich, and sombre, and splendid, like to a Tyrian cloth, as in the dwellings of the dead. No, her mood now was that of Aphrodité triumphing. Life—radiant, ecstatic, wonderful—seemed to flow from her and around her. Softly she laughed and sighed, and swift her glances flew. She shook her heavy tresses, and their perfume filled the place; she struck her little sandalled foot upon the floor, and hummed a snatch of some old Greek epithalamium. All the majesty was gone, or it did but lurk and flicker faintly through her laughing eyes, like lightning seen through sunlight. She had cast off her terror of the leaping flame, the cold power of judg-ment that even now was being done, and the wise sadness of the tombs—cast them off and put them behind her, like the white shroud she wore, and now she stood out an incarnation of lovely tempting womanhood, made more perfect—and in a way more spiritual—than ever woman was before her.

"So, my Holly, sit there where thou canst see me. It is by thine own wish, remember—again I say, blame me not if thou doest wear away thy little span with such a sick pain at the heart that thou wouldst fain have died before ever thy curious eyes were set upon me. There, sit so, and tell me, for in truth now I desire praises—tell me, am I not beautiful? Nay, speak not so hastily; consider well the point; take me feature by feature, forgetting not my form, and my hands and feet, and my hair, and the whiteness of my skin, and then say truly, hast thou ever known a woman who in aught, ay, in one little portion of her beauty, in the curve of an eyelash even, or the modelling of a shell-like ear, is justified to hold a lamp before my loveliness? Now, my waist! Perchance thou thinkest it too large, but of a truth it is not so; it is this golden snake that is too large, and doth not bind it as it should. It is a wise snake, and knoweth that it is ill to tie in the waist. But see, give me thy hands—so—now press them round me: There, with but a little force, thy fingers almost touch, O Holly!"

I could bear it no longer. I am but a man, and she was more than a woman. Heaven knows what she was—I do not! But then and there I fell upon my knees before her, and told her in a sad mixture of languages—for such moments confuse the thoughts—that I worshipped her as never woman was worshipped, and that I would give my immortal soul to marry her, which at that time I certainly would have done, and so, indeed, would any other man, or all the race of men rolled into one. For a moment she looked a little surprised; then she began to laugh, and to clap her hands in glee.

"Oh, so soon, my Holly!" she said. "I wondered how many minutes it would need to bring thee to thy knees. I have not seen a man kneel before me for so many ages, and, believe me, to a woman's heart the sight is sweet—ay, wisdom and length of days take not from that dear pleasure which is our sex's only right.

"What wouldst thou?—what wouldst thou? Thou dost not know what thou doest. Have I not told thee that I am not for thee? I love but one, and thou art not the man. Ah Holly, for all thy wisdom—and in a way thou art wise—thou art but a fool running after folly. Thou wouldst look into mine eyes—thou wouldst kiss me! Well, if it pleaseth thee, *look!*" and

she bent herself towards me, and fixed her dark and thrilling
orbs upon my own; "ay, and *kiss* too if thou wilt, for, thanks
be given to the scheme of things, kisses leave no scars, except
upon the heart. But if thou dost kiss, I tell thee of a surety
thou wilt eat out thy breast with love of me, and die!" and
she bent yet further towards me till her soft hair brushed my
brow, and her fragrant breath played upon my face, and made
me faint and weak. Then of a sudden, even as I stretched out
my arms to clasp, she straightened herself, and a quick change
passed over her. Reaching out her hand, she held it over my
head, and it seemed to me that something flowed from it which
chilled me back to common sense, and a knowledge of pro-
priety and the domestic virtues.

"Enough of this wanton play," she said with a touch of stern-
ness. "Listen, Holly. Thou art a good and honest man, and
I fain would spare thee; but, oh! it is so hard for woman to be
merciful. I have said I am not for thee, therefore let thy
thoughts pass by me like an idle wind, and the dust of thy
imaginings sink again into the depths—well, of despair, if thou
wilt. Thou dost not know me, Holly. Hadst thou seen me but
ten hours past, when my passion seized me, thou hadst shrunk
from me in fear and trembling. I am of many moods, and,
like the water in that vessel, I reflect many things; but they pass,
my Holly; they pass, and are forgotten. Only the water is the
water still, and I still am I, and that which maketh the water
maketh it, and that which maketh me maketh me, nor can my
quality be altered. Therefore, pay no heed to what I seem,
seeing that thou canst not know what I am. If thou troublest
me again I will veil myself, and thou shalt behold my face no
more."

I rose, and sank on the cushioned couch beside her, yet quivering with emotion, though for a moment my mad passion had
left me, as the leaves of a tree quiver still, although the gust be
gone that stirred them. I did not dare to tell her that I *had* seen
her in that deep and hellish mood, muttering incantations to the
fire in the tomb.

"So," she went on, "eat of this fruit; believe me, it is the only
true food for man. Now tell me of the philosophy of that Hebrew
Messiah, who came after me, and who, thou sayest, to-day doth
rule Rome, and Greece, and Egypt and the barbarians beyond. It
must have been a strange philosophy that He taught for in my
time the peoples would have naught of our philosophies. Revel
and lust and drink, blood and cold steel, and the shock of men
gathered in battle—these were the canons of their creeds."

I had recovered myself a little by now, and, feeling bitterly ashamed of the weakness into which I had been betrayed, I did my best to expound to her the doctrines of Christianity, to which, however, with the single exception of our theory of Heaven and Hell, I found that she paid but faint attention, her interest being all directed towards the Man who taught them. Also I told her that among her own people, the Arabs, another prophet, one Mohammed, had arisen, preaching a new faith, to which many millions of mankind now adhered.

"Ah!" she said; "I understand—*two* new religions! I have known so many and doubtless there have been others since I knew aught beyond these caves of Kôr. Mankind asks ever of the skies to vision out what lies behind them. It is terror for the end, and but a subtler form of selfishness—this it is that breeds religions. Mark, my Holly, each religion claims the future for its followers; or, at the least, the good thereof. The evil is for those benighted ones who will have none of it; seeing that light which the true believers worship, as the fishes see the stars, but dimly. The religions come and the religions pass, and civilisations come and pass, and naught endures but the world and human nature. Ah! if man would but see that hope is from within, and not from without—that he himself must work out his own salvation! He is there, and within him is the breath of life and a knowledge of good and evil, as good and evil are to him. Thereon let him build and stand erect, and not cast himself before the image of some unknown God, modelled like his poor self, but with a larger brain to think the evil thing, and a longer arm to do it."

I thought to myself—which shows how old such reasoning is, being, indeed, one of the recurring quantities of theological discussion—that her argument sounded very like some that I have heard in the nineteenth century, and in other places than the caves of Kôr—with which, by the way, I totally disagree—but I did not care to try to discuss the question with her. To begin with, my mind was too weary with all the emotions through which I had passed, and, in the second place, I knew that I should get the worst of it. It is weary work enough to argue with an ordinary materialist, who hurls statistics and whole strata of geological facts at your head, whilst you can only buffet him with deductions and instincts and the snowflakes of faith, that are, alas! so apt to melt in the hot embers of our troubles. How little chance, then, should I have against one whose brain was supernaturally sharpened, and who had two thousand years of experience, besides all manner of knowledge of the secrets of

Nature at her command! Feeling that she would be more likely to convert me than I should to convert her, I thought it best to leave the matter alone and so sat silent. Many a time since then have I regretted bitterly that I did so, for thereby I lost the only opportunity I can remember of ascertaining what Ayesha *really* believed, and what was her 'philosophy.'

"Well, my Holly," she continued, "and so those people of mine have also found a prophet—a false prophet thou sayest, for he is not thine own, and, indeed, I doubt it not. Yet in my day it was otherwise, for then we Arabs had many gods. Allât there was, and Saba, the Host of Heaven; Al Uzza, and Manah the stony one, for whom the blood of victims flowed; and Wadd and Sawâ, and Yaghûth the Lion of the dwellers in Yaman; and Yäûk, the Horse of Morad; and Nasr the Eagle of Hamyar; ay, and many more. Oh, the folly of it all, the shame and the pitiful folly! Yet when I rose in wisdom and spoke thereof, surely they would have slain me in the name of their outraged gods. Well, so it hath ever been;—but, my Holly, art thou weary of me already, that thou dost sit so silent? Or dost thou fear lest I should teach thee my philosophy?—for know I have a philosophy! What would a teacher be without her own philosophy? And if thou dost vex me overmuch, beware! for I will have thee learn it, and thou shalt be my disciple, and we twain will found a faith that shall swallow up all the others. Inconstant man! But half an hour since thou wast upon thy knees—the posture does not become thee, Holly—swearing that thou didst love me. What shall we do?—Nay, I have it! I will come and see this youth, the Lion, as the old man Billali calls him, who came with thee, and who is sick. The fever must have run its course by now, and if he is about to die I will recover him. Fear not, my Holly; I shall use no magic. Have I not told thee that there is no such thing as magic, though there is such a thing as mastering and commanding the forces which are in Nature? Go, now, and presently, when I have made the drug ready, I will follow thee."[1]

Accordingly I went, only to find Job and Ustane in an excess of grief, declaring that Leo was in the throes of death, and that they had been searching for me everywhere. I rushed to the couch, and glanced at him: clearly he was dying. He was senseless and breathing heavily, but his lips were quivering, and every now and again a little shudder ran down his frame. I knew enough of doctoring to see that in another hour he would be beyond the reach of earthly help—perhaps in another five

---

[1] Ayesha was a great chemist; indeed, chemistry appears to have been her only amusement and occupation. One of the caves was fitted up as a

minutes. How I cursed my selfishness and the folly that had kept me lingering by Ayesha's side while my dear boy lay dying! Alas and alas! how easily the best of us are lighted down to evil by the gleam of a woman's eyes! What a wicked wretch was I! Actually, for the last half-hour I had scarcely thought of Leo— and this, be it remembered, of the man who for twenty years had been my dearest companion, and the chief interest of my existence. And now, perhaps, it was too late!

I wrung my hands, and glanced round. Ustane was sitting by the couch, and in her eyes burnt the dull light of despair. Job was blubbering—I am sorry I cannot name his distress by any more delicate word—audibly in the corner. Seeing my eye fixed upon him, he went outside to give way to his grief in the passage. Obviously the only hope lay in Ayesha. She, and she alone, could save him—unless, indeed, she was an impostor, which I did not believe. I would go and implore her to come. As I started on this errand, however, Job came flying into the room, his hair literally standing on end with terror.

"Oh, God help us, sir!" he ejaculated in a frightened whisper, "here's a corpse a-coming sliding down the passage!"

For a moment I was puzzled, but presently, of course, it struck me that he must have seen Ayesha, wrapped in her grave-like garment, and been deceived by the extraordinary undulating smoothness of her walk into a belief that she was a white ghost gliding towards him. Indeed, at that very moment the question was settled, for Ayesha herself appeared in the apartment, or rather cave. Job turned, and saw her sheeted form, then, with a convulsive howl of "Here it comes!" he sprang into a corner, and hid his head against the wall; while Ustane, guessing whose the dread presence must be, prostrated herself upon her face.

"Thou comest in a good time, Ayesha," I said, "for my boy lies at the point of death."

"So," she said softly; "if he be not dead, it is no matter, for I can bring him back to life, my Holly. Is that man there thy servant, and is that the fashion wherewith the servants greet strangers in thy country?"

"He is frightened of thy garb—it has a death-like air," I answered.

She laughed.

"And the girl? Ah, I see now. It is she of whom thou didst speak to me. Well, bid them both to leave us, and we will see to

laboratory, and, although her appliances were necessarily rude, the results that she attained, as will become clear in the course of this narrative, were sufficiently surprising.—L. H. H.

this sick Lion of thine. I love not that underlings should perceive my wisdom."

Thereon I told Ustane in Arabic and Job in English both to leave the room; an order which the latter obeyed readily enough, and was glad to obey, for he could not in any way subdue his fear. But it was otherwise with Ustane.

"What does *She* want?" she whispered, divided between her dread of the terrible Queen and her anxiety to remain near Leo. "It is surely the right of a wife to be with her husband when he dies. Nay, I will not go, my lord the Baboon."

"Why doth not that woman depart, my Holly?" asked Ayesha from the other end of the cave, where she was engaged in examining some of the sculptures on the wall.

"She is not willing to leave Leo," I answered, not knowing what to say. Ayesha wheeled round, and, pointing at the girl Ustane, said one word, and one only, but it was quite enough, for the tone in which she uttered it meant volumes.

"Go!"

Then Ustane crept past her on her hands and knees, and went.

"Thou seest, my Holly," said Ayesha, with a little laugh, "it was needful that I should give these people a lesson in obedience. That girl went nigh to disobeying me, but then, she did not learn this noon how I treat the disobedient. Well, she has gone; now let me see the youth," and she glided towards the couch on which Leo lay, with his face in the shadow and turned towards the wall.

"He has a noble shape," she said, as she bent over him to look upon his face.

The next second her tall and willowy form was staggering back across the room, as though she had been shot or stabbed, staggering back till at last she struck the cavern wall, and then there burst from her lips the most awful and unearthly scream that it has ever been my lot to hear.

"What is it, Ayesha?" I cried. "Is he dead?"

She turned and sprang towards me like a tigress.

"Thou dog!" she said, in her terrible whisper, which sounded like the hiss of a snake, "why didst thou hide this from me?" And she stretched out her arm, so that I thought she was about to slay me.

"What?" I ejaculated, in the most lively terror; "what?"

"Ah!" she said, "perchance thou didst not know. Learn, my Holly, learn: there—there lies my lost Kallikrates. Kallikrates, who has come back to me at last, as I knew he must, as I knew he must!" and she began to sob and laugh, and, indeed, to conduct herself like any other lady who is overcome, murmuring "Kallikrates, Kallikrates!"

"Nonsense," I though to myself, but I did not dare to say it; and, indeed, at the moment I was thinking of Leo's life, having forgotten everything else in that terrible anxiety. What I feared now was that he might die while Ayesha was unnerved by hysteria.

"Unless thou art able to help him, Ayesha," I suggested humbly, "thy Kallikrates will soon be far beyond thy calling. Surely he dies even now."

"True," she said, with a start. "Oh! why did I not come before? I am shaken—my hand trembles, even mine—and yet it is very easy. Here, thou Holly, take this phial," and she produced a tiny jar of pottery from the folds of her garment, "and pour the liquid in it down his throat. It will cure him if he be not dead. Swift, now! Swift! The man dies!"

I glanced towards him; it was true enough—Leo was in his death-struggle. I saw his poor face turning ashen, and heard the breath begin to rattle in his throat. The phial was stoppered with a little piece of wood. I drew it with my teeth, and a drop of the fluid within flew out upon my tongue. It had a sweet flavour, and for a second caused my head to swim and a mist to gather before my eyes, but happily the effect passed away as quickly as it had arisen.

When I reached Leo he was on the point of expiring—his golden head turned slowly from side to side, and his mouth was slightly open. I called to Ayesha to hold his head, and this she managed to do, although the woman was quivering from head to foot, like an aspen-leaf or a startled horse. Then, forcing the jaws a little further open, I poured the contents of the phial into his mouth. Instantly some vapours arose from it, as happens when one disturbs nitric acid, and this sight did not increase my hopes, already faint enough, of the efficacy of the treatment.

One thing, however, was certain, the death-throes ceased—at first I thought because he had gone beyond them, and crossed the awful river. His face turned to a livid pallor, and his heart-beats, which had been feeble enough before, seemed to die away altogether—only the eyelids still twitched a little. In my doubt I looked up at Ayesha, whose head-wrapping had slipped back in her excitement when she reeled across the room. She was still holding Leo's head, and, with a face as pale as his own, watched his countenance with such an expression of agonised anxiety as I had never seen before. Clearly she did not know if he would live or die. Five minutes passed slowly, and I saw that she was abandoning hope; her lovely oval face seemed to fall in and visibly grow thinner beneath the pressure of a mental agony whose pencil drew black lines about the hollows of her eyes. The coral faded even from her lips, till they were as white as Leo's face, and quivered pitifully. It was shocking to see her: even in my own grief I felt for hers.

"Is it too late?" I gasped.

She hid her face in her hands, and made no answer, and I also turned away. But as I turned I heard a deep-drawn breath, and looking down perceived a line of colour creeping up Leo's face, then another and another, and, wonder of wonders, the man whom we had thought dead rolled over on his side.

"Thou seest," I said in a whisper.

"I see," she answered hoarsely. "He is saved. I thought we were too late; another moment—one little moment more—and he had been gone!" and she burst into an awful flood of tears, sobbing as though her heart would break, and yet looking lovelier than ever as she wept. At last she ceased.

"Forgive me, my Holly—forgive me for my weakness," she said. "Thou seest after all I am a very woman. Think—now think of it! This morning thou didst speak of the place of torment appointed by this new religion of thine. Hell or Hades thou didst call it—a place where the vital essence lives and retains an individual memory, and where all the errors and faults of judgment, and unsatisfied passions, and the unsubstantial terrors of the mind wherewith it hath at any time had to do, come to mock and haunt and gibe and wring the heart for ever and for ever with the vision of its own hopelessness. Thus, even thus, have I lived for full two thousand years—for some six-and-sixty generations, as ye reckon time—in a Hell, as thou callest it— tormented by the memory of a crime, tortured day and night with an unfulfilled desire—without companionship, without comfort, without death, and led on only down my dreary road by the marshlights of Hope, which, though they flickered here and there, and now glowed strong, and now were not, yet, as my skill foretold, would one day lead me to my deliverer.

"And then—think of it still, O Holly, for never shalt thou hear such another tale, or see such another scene, nay, not even if I give thee ten thousand years of life—and thou shalt have them in payment if thou wilt—think: at last my deliverer came—he for whom I had watched and waited through the generations— at the appointed time he came to seek me, as I knew that he must come, for my wisdom could not err, though I knew not when or how. Yet see how ignorant I was! See how small my knowledge, and how faint my strength! For hours he lay here sick unto death, and, I felt it not—I who had waited for him for two thousand years—I knew it not! And then at last I see him, and behold! my chance is gone but for a hair's breadth even before I win it, for he is in the very jaws of death, whence no power of mine can draw him. And if he die, surely must the Hell be lived through once more—once more I must face the weary centuries, and wait and wait till time in its fulness shall bring my Beloved back to me. And then thou gavest him the medicine, and that five minutes passed before I knew whether he would live or die, and I tell thee that all the sixty generations that are gone were not so long as that five minutes. But they passed at length, and still he showed no sign, and I knew that if the drug worked not then, so far as I have had knowledge, it would not work at all. Then I thought that once more he was dead, and all the tortures of all the years gathered themselves into a single venomed spear, and pierced me through and through, because again I had lost Kallikrates! And then, when all was done, behold! he sighed, behold! he lived, and I was sure that he would live, for none die on whom the drug takes hold. Think of it now, my Holly—think of the wonder of it! He will sleep for twelve hours, and then the sickness will have left him—will have left him to life and me!"

She ceased, and laid her hand upon the golden head, then she bent down and kissed his brow with a chastened abandonment of tenderness that would have been beautiful to behold had not the sight cut me to the heart—for I was jealous.

CHAPTER XVIII

"GO, WOMAN!"

THEN followed a silence of a minute or so, during which, if one might judge from the almost angelic rapture of her face—for she looked angelic sometimes—*She* appeared to be plunged in a happy ecstasy. Suddenly, however, a new thought struck her, and her expression became the very reverse of angelic.

"Almost had I forgotten," she said; "that woman, Ustane. What is she to Kallikrates—his servant, or——" and she paused, and her voice trembled.

I shrugged my shoulders. "I understand that she is wed to him according to the custom of the Amahagger," I answered; "but I know not."

Her face grew dark as a thundercloud. Old as she was, Ayesha had not outlived jealousy.

"Then there is an end," she said; "she must die, even now!"

"For what crime?" I asked, horrified. "She is guilty of nothing that thou are not guilty of thyself, O Ayesha. She loves the man, and he has been pleased to accept her love; where, then, is her sin?"

"Truly, O Holly, thou art foolish," she answered, almost petulantly. "Where is her sin? Her sin is that she stands between me and my desire. I know well that I can take him from her—for dwells there a man upon this earth, O Holly, who could resist me if I put out my strength? Men are faithful for so long only as temptations pass them by. If the temptation be but strong enough, then will the man yield, for every man, like every rope, hath his breaking strain, and passion is to men what gold and power are to women—the weight upon their weakness. Believe me, ill will it go with mortal women in that heaven of which thou speakest if only the spirits be more fair, for their lords will never turn to look upon them, and their Heaven will become their Hell. For man can be bought with woman's beauty, if it be but beautiful enough; and woman's beauty can be ever bought with gold, if only there be gold enough. So was it in my day, and so it will be to the end of time. The world is a great mart, my Holly, where all things are for sale to him who bids the highest in the currency of our desires."

These remarks, which were as cynical as might have been expected from a woman of Ayesha's age and experience, jarred upon me, and I answered, testily, that in our heaven there was no marriage or giving in marriage.

"Else would it not be heaven, dost thou mean?" she put in. "Fie upon thee, Holly, to think so ill of us poor women! Is it, then, marriage that marks the line between thy Heaven and thy Hell? But enough of this. Now is no time for disputing and the challenge of our wits. Why dost thou always dispute? Art thou also a philosopher of these latter days? As for this woman, she must die; for, though I can take her lover from her, yet, while she lived, he might think tenderly of her, and that I cannot suffer. No other woman shall dwell in my lord's thoughts; my empire must be all my own. She has had her day, let her be content; for better is an hour with love than a century of loneliness—now night shall swallow her."

"Nay, nay," I cried, "it would be a wicked crime; and from a crime naught comes but what is evil. For thine own sake do not this deed."

"Is it, then, a crime, O foolish man, to put away that which stands between us and our ends? Then is our life one long crime,

my Holly; for day by day we destroy that we may live, since in
this world none save the strongest can endure. Those who are
weak must perish; the earth is to the strong, and the fruits thereof.
For every tree that grows a score shall wither, that the strong one
may take their share. We run to place and power over the dead
bodies of those who fail and fall; ay, we win the food we eat from
out the mouths of starving babes. It is the scheme of things.
Thou sayest, too, that a crime breeds evil, but therein thou dost
lack experience; for out of crimes come many good things, and
out of good grows much evil. The cruel rage of the tyrant may
prove the blessing of thousands who come after him, and the
sweetheartedness of a holy man may make a nation slaves. Man
doeth this and doeth that from the good or evil of his heart; but
he knows not to what end his sense doth prompt him; for when
he strikes he is blind to where the blow shall fall, nor can he
count the airy threads that weave the web of circumstance. Good
and evil, love and hate, night and day, sweet and bitter, man
and woman, heaven above and the earth beneath—all these
things are needful, one to the other, and who knows the end of
each? I tell thee that there is a Hand of Fate who twines them up
to bear the burden of his purpose, and all things are gathered in
that great rope to which all things are requisite. Therefore doth
it not become us to say this thing is evil and that good, or the
dark is hateful and the light lovely; for to other eyes than ours
the evil may be the good and the darkness more beautiful than the
day, or all alike be fair: Hearest thou, my Holly?"

I felt that it was hopeless to argue against casuistry of
this nature, which, if it were carried to its logical conclusion,
would absolutely destroy all morality, as we understand it. But
Ayesha's talk gave me a fresh thrill of fear, for what may not be
possible to a being who, unconstrained by human law, is also absolutely unshackled by a moral sense of right and wrong, which,
however partial and conventional it may be, is yet based, as our
conscience tells us, upon the great wall of individual responsibility that marks off mankind from the beasts?

Still I was most anxious to save Ustane, whom I liked and
respected, from the dire fate that overshadowed her at the hands
of her mighty rival. So I made one more appeal.

"Ayesha," I said, "thou are too subtle for me; but thou thyself hast told me that each man should be a law unto himself,
and follow the teaching of his heart. Has thy heart no mercy towards her whose place thou wouldst take? Bethink thee, as thou
sayest—though to me the thing is incredible—he whom thou
desirest has returned to thee after many ages, and but now thou

hast, as thou sayest also, wrung him from the jaws of death. Wilt thou celebrate his coming by the murder of one who loved him, and whom perchance he loved—one, at the least, who saved his life for thee when the spears of thy slaves would have made an end of it? Thou sayest also that in past days thou didst grievously wrong this man, that with thine own hand thou didst slay him because of the Egyptian Amenartas whom he loved."

"How knowest thou that, O stranger? How knowest thou that name? I spoke it not to thee," she broke in with a cry, catching at my arm.

"Perchance I dreamed it," I answered; "strange dreams do hover about these caves of Kôr. It seems that the dream was, indeed, a shadow of the truth. What came to thee of thy mad crime? Two thousand years of waiting, was it not? And now wouldst thou repeat this history? Say what thou wilt, I tell thee that evil will come of it; for to him who doeth, at the least, good breeds good and evil evil, even though in after days out of the evil cometh good. Offences must needs come; but woe to him by whom the offence cometh. So said that Messiah of whom I spoke to thee, and it was truly said. If thou slayest this innocent woman, I say unto thee that thou shalt be accursed, and pluck no fruit from thine ancient tree of love. Also what thinkest thou? How will this man take thee red-handed from the slaughter of her who loved and tended him?"

"As to that," she answered, "I have already answered thee. Had I slain thee as well as her, yet should he love me, Holly, because he could not save himself therefrom any more than thou couldst save thyself from dying, if by chance I slew thee, O Holly. And yet maybe there is truth in what thou dost say; for in some way it presses on my mind. If it may be, I will spare this woman; for have I not told thee that I am not cruel for the sake of cruelty? I love not to see suffering, or to cause it. Let her come before me—quick now, ere my mood changes," and she covered her face hastily with its gauzy wrapping.

Well pleased to have succeeded even to this extent, I passed out into the passage and called to Ustane, whose white garment I caught sight of some yards away, huddled up against one of the earthenware lamps that were placed at intervals along the tunnel. She rose, and ran towards me.

"Is my lord dead? Oh, say not he is dead!" she cried, lifting her noble-looking face up to me, all stained as it was with tears, with an air of infinite beseeching that went straight to my heart.

"Nay, he lives," I answered. "*She* hath saved him. Come."

She sighed deeply, entered, and fell upon her hands and knees, after the custom of the Amahagger people, in the presence of the dread *She*.

"Rise," said Ayesha, in her coldest voice, "and come hither."

Ustane obeyed, standing before her with bowed head.

Then came a pause, which Ayesha broke.

"Who is this man?" she said, pointing to the sleeping form of Leo.

"The man is my husband," she answered in a low voice.

"Who gave him to thee for a husband?"

"I took him, according to the custom of our country, O *She*."

"Thou hast done evil, woman, in taking this man, who is a stranger. He is not of thine own race, and the custom fails. Listen: perchance thou didst this thing through ignorance, therefore, woman, do I spare thee, otherwise hadst thou died. Listen again. Go hence back to thine own place, and never dare to speak with or to set thine eyes upon this man again. He is not for thee. Listen a third time. If thou breakest this my law, that moment thou diest. Go!"

But Ustane did not move.

"Go, woman!"

Then Ustane looked up, and I saw that her face was torn with passion.

"Nay, O *She*, I will not go," she answered in a choked voice: "the man is my husband, and I love him—I love him, and I will not leave him. What right hast thou to command me to leave my husband?"

I saw a quiver pass down Ayesha's frame, and shuddered myself, fearing the worst.

"Be pitiful," I said in Latin; "it is but Nature working."

"I am pitiful," she answered coldly in the same language; "had I not been pitiful she had been dead even now." Then, addressing Ustane: "Woman, I say to thee, go before I destroy thee where thou art?"

"I will not go! He is mine—mine!" she cried in anguish. "I took him, and I saved his life! Destroy me, then, if thou hast the power! I will not give thee my husband—never—never!"

Ayesha made a movement so swift that I could scarcely follow it, but it seemed to me that she struck the poor girl lightly upon the head with her hand. I looked at Ustane, and staggered back in horror, for there upon her hair, straight across her bronze-like tresses, appeared three fingermarks *white as snow*. As for the girl herself, she lifted her hands to her head like one who is dazed.

"Great heavens!" I said, aghast at this most dreadful manifestation of inhuman power; but *She* did but laugh a little.

"Thou thinkest, poor ignorant fool," she said to the bewildered woman, "that I have not power to slay. Look, there lies a mirror," and she pointed to Leo's round shaving-glass that had been arranged by Job with other things upon his baggage; "give it to this woman, my Holly, and let her learn that which lies across her hair, and whether or no I have power to slay."

I took the glass, and held it before Ustane's eyes. She gazed, felt at her hair, then gazed again, and presently sank upon the ground with a stifled sob.

"Now wilt thou go, or must I strike a second time?" asked Ayesha, in mockery. "See, I have set my seal upon thee, so that I may know thee till thy hair is all as white as it. If I behold thy face again, be sure, too, that thy bones shall soon be whiter than my stamp upon thy hair."

Utterly awed and broken down, the poor creature rose, and, marked with that awful mark, she crept from the room, sobbing bitterly.

"Look not so frightened, my Holly," said Ayesha, when she had gone. "I tell thee I deal not in magic—there is no magic. 'Tis only a force that thou dost not understand. I marked her to strike terror to her heart, else must I have slain her. And now I will bid my servants bear my lord Kallikrates to a chamber near my own, that I may watch over him, and be ready to greet him when he wakes; and thither, too, shalt thou come, my Holly, and the white man, thy servant. But one thing remember at thy peril. Naught shalt thou say to Kallikrates as to how this woman went, and as little as may be of me. Now, I have warned thee!" And she glided away to give her orders, leaving me more absolutely confounded than ever. Indeed, so bewildered was I, so racked and torn with such a succession of various emotions, that I began to think that I must be going mad. However, perhaps fortunately, I had but little time to reflect, for presently the mutes arrived to carry the sleeping Leo and our possessions across the central cave, so for a while all was bustle. Our new rooms were situated immediately behind what we named Ayesha's boudoir—that curtained space where I had first seen her. Where she herself slept I did not then know, but it was close at hand.

That night I passed in Leo's room, but he slumbered through it like the dead, never once stirring. I also slept well, as, indeed, I needed to do, but my sleep was full of dreams of all the horrors and wonders I had undergone. Chiefly, however, I was haunted by that frightful piece of *diablerie* by which Ayesha left her finger-marks upon her rival's hair. There was something so terrible about her swift, snake-like movement, and the instantaneous blanching of that threefold line, that, if the results to Ustane had been much more tremendous, I doubt if they would have impressed me so deeply. To this day I often dream of that awful scene, and see the weeping woman, bereaved, and marked like Cain, cast a last look at her lover, and creep from the presence of her dread Queen.

Another dream which troubled me originated in the huge pyramid of bones. I dreamed that they all arose and marched past me in thousands and tens of thousands—in squadrons, companies, and armies—with the sunlight shining through their hollow ribs. On they rushed across the plain to Kôr, their imperial home; I saw the drawbridges fall before them, and heard their skeletons clank beneath the brazen gates. On they went, up the splendid streets, on past fountains, palaces, and temples such as the eye of mortal never saw. But there was no man to greet them in the market-place, and no woman's face appeared at the windows—only a bodiless voice went before them, calling: *"Fallen is Imperial Kôr—fallen!—fallen!—fallen!"* On, through the city, marched these gleaming phalanxes, and the rattle of their bony tread echoed in the silent air as they pressed grimly forward. They passed through the city and clomb the wall, and strode along the great roadway that was made upon the wall, till at length once more they reached the drawbridge. Then, as the sun was sinking, they returned again towards their sepulchre, and his light shone luridly in the sockets of their empty eyes, throwing gigantic shadows of their bones, that stretched away, and crept and crept like huge spiders' legs as their armies wound across the plain. Now they came to the cave, and once more one by one they flung themselves in unending files through the hole in to the pit of death, and I awoke, shuddering, to see *She,* who had been standing between my couch and Leo's, glide like a shadow from the room.

After this I slept again, soundly this time, till morning, when I awoke much refreshed, and rose. At last the hour drew near when, according to Ayesha, Leo was to be awake, and with it came the veiled *She* herself.

"Thou shalt see, O Holly," she said: "presently he will awake in his right mind, the fever having left him."

Hardly were the words out of her mouth when Leo turned round and, stretching out his arms, yawned, opened his eyes, then, perceiving a female form bending over him, threw his arms about her and kissed her, in mistake, perhaps, for Ustane. At any rate, he said, in Arabic, "Hullo Ustane! why have you tied your head up like that? Have you got the toothache?" and then in English, "I say, I'm awfully hungry. Why, Job, you old son of a gun, where the deuce have we got to now—eh?"

"I am sure I wish I knew, Mr. Leo," said Job, suspiciously edging past Ayesha, whom he still regarded with the utmost disgust and horror, being by no means sure that she was not an animated corpse; "but you mustn't talk, Mr. Leo, you've been very ill, and given us a great deal of anxiety, and if this lady," looking at Ayesha, "would be so kind as to move, I'll bring you your soup."

This turned Leo's attention to the 'lady,' who was standing by in perfect silence. "Why!" he said, "that is not Ustane—where is Ustane?"

Then, for the first time, Ayesha spoke to him, and her first words were a lie. "She has gone from hence upon a visit," she said; "and, behold! I am here in her place as thine handmaiden."

Ayesha's silver notes seemed to puzzle Leo's half-awakened intellect as much as did her corpse-like wrappings. However, he said nothing in answer, but, drinking off his soup greedily, turned over and slept again till the evening. When he awoke for the second time he saw me, and began to question me as to what had happened, but I put him off as best I could till the morrow, when he awoke miraculously better. Then I told him something of his illness and of my doings, but as Ayesha was present I could not tell him much, except that she was the Queen of the country, and well disposed towards us, and that it was her pleasure to go veiled; for though of course I spoke in English, I was afraid that she might understand what we were saying from the expression on our faces; besides, I remembered her warning.

On the following morning Leo rose almost entirely recovered. The flesh wound in his side was healed, and his constitution, naturally a vigorous one, had shaken off the exhaustion consequent on his terrible fever with a rapidity that I can only attribute to the effects of the wonderful drug which Ayesha had given to him, and perhaps to the fact that his illness had been too short to reduce him very much. With his returning health came back full recollection of all his adventures up to the time when he had lost consciousness in the marsh, and of course of Ustane also, to whom I discovered he had grown considerably attached. Indeed, he overwhelmed me with questions about the poor girl, which I did not dare to answer, for after Leo's first awakening *She* had sent for me, and again warned me solemnly that I was to reveal nothing of the story to him, delicately hinting that if I did it would be the worse for me. Further, for the second time, she cautioned me not to tell Leo anything more than I was obliged about herself, saying that she would reveal all to him in her own hour.

Indeed, her whole manner changed. After all that I had learned I expected that she would take the earliest opportunity of claiming the man whom she believed to be her old-world lover, but this, for some reason of her own, which at the time was quite inscrutable to me, she did not do. All that she did do was to attend to his wants quietly, and with a humility which was in striking contrast to her former imperious bearing, addressing him always in a tone of something very like respect, and keeping him with her as much as possible. Of course his curiosity was as much excited about this mysterious woman as my own had been, and he was particularly anxious to see her face, which, without entering into particulars, I had told him was as lovely as her form and voice. This in itself was enough to raise the expectations of any young man to a dangerous pitch, and, had it not been that he was still suffering from the effects of his illness, and much troubled in mind about Ustane, of whose tenderness and brave devotion he spoke in touching terms, I have no doubt but that he would have entered into Ayesha's plans, and fallen in love with her by anticipation. As it chanced, however, he was merely curious, and also, like myself, somewhat awed, for, though no hint had been given to him by *She* of her extraordinary age, not unnaturally he came to identify her with the woman spoken of on the potsherd. At last, quite driven into a corner by his continual questions, which he showered on me while he was dressing on this third morning, I referred him to Ayesha, saying, with perfect truth, that I did not know where Ustane was. Accordingly, after Leo had eaten a hearty breakfast, we adjourned into *She's* presence, for her mutes had orders to admit us at all hours.

As usual, she was seated in what, for want of a better term, we called her boudoir, and on the curtains being drawn she rose from her couch and, stretching out both hands, came forward to greet us, or rather Leo; for, as may be imagined, I was now left quite in the cold. It was a pretty sight to see her veiled form gliding towards the sturdy young Englishman, dressed in his grey flannel suit; for, though he is half a Greek by blood, with the exception of his hair, Leo is one of the most English-looking men I ever saw. He has nothing of the supple form or slippery manner of the modern Greek about him, though I presume that he inherits his personal beauty from his foreign mother, whose portrait he resembles not a little. He is very tall and broad-chested, and yet not awkward, as so many big men are, and his head is set upon him in such a fashion as to give him a proud and vigorous air, which was well described by his Amahagger name of 'Lion.'

"Greeting to thee, my lord and guest," Ayesha said in her softest voice. "Right glad am I to see thee standing upon thy feet. Believe me, had I not saved thee at the last, never wouldst thou have stood upon those feet again. But the danger is done and it shall be my care"—she flung a world of meaning into these words—"that it returns no more."

Leo bowed; then, in his best Arabic, he thanked her for all her kindness and courtesy in tending an unknown stranger.

"Nay," she answered softly. "ill could the world spare such a man. Beauty is too rare upon it. Give me no thanks, who am made happy by thy coming."

"Humph! old fellow," said Leo aside to me in English, "the lady is very civil. We seem to have tumbled into the clover. I hope that you have made the most of your opportunities. By Jove! what a pair of arms!"

I signed to him to be quiet, for I had caught a suspicious gleam from Ayesha's veiled eyes, which were watching me curiously.

"I trust," she went on, "that my servants have attended thee well; if there can be comfort in this poor place, be sure it waits on thee. Is there aught else that thou desirest?"

"Yes, O *She*," answered Leo hastily. "I would learn whither the woman who was with me has vanished."

"Ah!" said Ayesha: "the girl—yes, I saw her. Nay, I know not; she said that she would go, I know not where. Perchance she will return, perchance not. It is wearisome waiting on the sick, and these savage women are fickle."

Leo looked both puzzled and distressed at this intelligence.

"It's very odd," he said to me in English; and then addressing *She,* he added: "I cannot understand; the young lady and I— well—we had regard for each other."

Ayesha laughed a little, very musically, and changed the subject.

CHAPTER XIX

"GIVE ME A BLACK GOAT!"

THE conversation after this was of so desultory an order that I do not quite recollect it. For some reason, perhaps from a desire to keep her identity and character in reserve, Ayesha did not talk freely, as was her custom. Presently, however, she informed Leo that she had arranged a dance that night for our amusement. I was astonished to hear this, imagining that the Amahagger were much too gloomy a folk to indulge in any such frivolity; but, as will presently appear more clearly, it proved that an Amahagger dance has little in common with these fantastic festivities in other countries, savage or civilised. Then, as we were about to withdraw, she suggested that Leo might like to see some of the wonders of the caves, and accordingly thither we departed, accompanied by Job and Billali.

To describe our visit would only be to repeat a great deal of what I have already said. The tombs we entered were different indeed, for the whole rock is a honeycomb of sepulchres,[1] but their contents varied but little. Afterwards we visited the pyramid of bones that had haunted my dreams on the previous night, and thence went down a long passage to one of the great vaults occupied by the remains of the poorer citizens of Imperial Kôr. These bodies were not nearly so well preserved as were those of the wealthier classes. Many of them had no linen covering on them; also, from five hundred to one thousand of them were buried in a single large vault, the corpses in some instances being piled thickly one upon another, like a heap of slain.

Of course Leo was intensely interested in this stupendous and unequalled sight, which, indeed, was enough to awaken in to the most active life all the imagination a man possessed. But to poor Job it did not prove attractive. As may be imagined, his nerves, already seriously shaken by what he had undergone since we had reached this terrible country, were yet further disturbed by the spectacle of these masses of departed humanity, whereof the forms still remained perfect before his eyes, though their voices were for ever lost in the eternal silence of the tomb. Nor was he comforted when old Billali, by way

---

[1] For a long while it puzzled me to know how the enormous quantities of rock that must have been dug out of these vast caves had been disposed of; but I discovered afterwards that it was, for the most part, built into the walls and palaces of Kôr. Also it was used to line the reservoirs and sewers.—L. H. H.

of soothing his evident agitation, informed him that he should
not be frightened of these dead men, as he would soon be like
them himself.

"That's a nice thing to say of a man, sir," he ejaculated,
when I translated this little remark; "but there, what can one
expect of an old cannibal savage? Not but what I dare say
he's right," and Job sighed.

When we had finished inspecting the caves we returned and
ate our meal, for it was now past four in the afternoon, and
we all needed food and rest—especially Leo. At six o'clock,
together with Job, we waited on Ayesha, who proceeded to
terrify our poor servant still more by showing him pictures of
the pool of water in the font-like vessel. She learnt from me
that he was one of seventeen children, and then bid him think
of all his brothers and sisters, or as many of them as he could,
gathered together in his father's cottage. Next she told him
to look into the water, and there, reflected on its stilly surface,
appeared that dead scene of many years gone by, as it was
recalled to our retainer's brain. Some of the faces were clear
enough, but some were mere blurs and blotches or had one feature grossly exaggerated; the fact being that, in these instances,
Job was unable to recall the exact appearances of the individuals, or recollected them only by a peculiarity of his tribe,
and the water could but reflect what he saw with his mind's eye.
It must be remembered, indeed, that *She's* power in this matter was strictly limited; since, except in very rare instances,
she could merely photograph upon the water what was in the
mind of someone present, and then only through his will. But
if she was personally acquainted with a locality, as in the case
of ourselves and the whale-boat, she could throw its reflection
upon the water, and also, it seems, the reflection of anything
extraneous that was passing there at the time. This power,
however, did not extend to the minds of others. For instance,
she could show me the interior of my college chapel, as I remembered it, but not as it was at the moment of vision; since,
where other people were concerned, her art was limited strictly
to the facts or memories present to *their* consciousness at the
moment. So much was this the case that when we tried, for
her amusement, to show her pictures of noted buildings, such
as St. Paul's or the Houses of Parliament, the result was most
imperfect; for, of course, though we had a general idea of their
appearance, we were unable to recall the architectural details,
and therefore the minutiæ necessary to a perfect reflection
were wanting. But Job could not be made to understand this,

and, so far from accepting a natural explanation of the matter, which, though strange enough in all conscience, was nothing more than an instance of glorified and perfected telepathy, he set the phenomenon down as a manifestation of the blackest magic. I shall never forget the howl of terror which he uttered when he saw the more or less perfect portraits of his long-scattered brethren staring at him from the quiet water, or the merry peal of laughter with which Ayesha greeted his consternation. Nor did Leo altogether like the performance, but ran his fingers through his yellow curls, and remarked that it gave him "the creeps."

After about an hour of this amusement, in the latter part of which Job did not participate, the mutes indicated by signs that Billali was waiting for an audience. Accordingly he was told to "crawl up," which he did as awkwardly as usual, and announced that the dance was ready to begin if *She* and the white strangers would be pleased to attend. Shortly afterwards we all rose, and, Ayesha having thrown a dark cloak over her white wrappings (the same by the way, that she had worn when I saw her cursing by the fire), we started. The dance was to be held in the open air, on the smooth rocky plateau in front of the great cave, and thither we made our way. About fifteen paces from the mouth of the cave we found three chairs placed, and here we sat and waited, for as yet no dancers were to be seen. The night was almost, but not quite, dark, the moon not having risen as yet, which made us wonder how we should be able to see the dancing.

"Thou wilt understand presently," said Ayesha, with a little laugh, when Leo questioned her.

Scarcely were the words out of her mouth when from every point we saw dark forms rushing along, each of them bearing what at first we took to be an enormous flaming torch. Whatever these were, they burned furiously, for the flames stood out a yard or more behind their bearers. On came the men, fifty or more of them, carrying their blazing burdens and looking like so many devils from hell. Leo was the first to discover what these burdens were.

"Great heavens!" he said, "they are corpses on fire!"

I stared and stared again. He was perfectly right—the torches that were to light our entertainment were human mummies from the caves!

On rushed the bearers of the flaming corpses, and, meeting at a spot about twenty paces in front of us, built their ghastly loads crossways into a huge bonfire. Heavens! how they roared and flared! No tar barrel could have burnt as did those mummies. Nor was this all. Suddenly I saw one great fellow seize a flaming human arm that had fallen from its parent frame, and rush off into the darkness. Presently he stopped, and a tall streak of fire shot up into the air, illuminating the gloom, and also the lamp from which it sprang. That lamp was the mummy of a woman tied to a stout stake let into the rock, and he had fired her hair. On he went a few paces and touched a second, then a third, and a fourth, till at last we were surrounded on all three sides by a great ring of bodies flaring furiously, the material with which they were preserved having rendered them so inflammable that literally the flames would spout out of the ears and mouth in tongues of fire a foot or more in length.

Nero illuminated his gardens with living Christians soaked in tar, and we were now treated to a similar spectacle, probably for the first time since his day, only happily our lamps were not alive.

But although, unfortunately, this element of horror was wanting to describe the awful and hideous grandeur of the spectacle thus presented to us is, I feel, so absolutely beyond my poor powers that I scarcely dare attempt it. To begin with, it appealed to the moral as well as to the physical susceptibilities. There was something very terrible, and yet most fascinating, about this employment of the remote dead to illumine the orgies of the living; in itself the thing was a satire, both on the living and the dead. Cæsar's dust—or is it Alexander's?—may stop a bunghole, but the office of these dead Cæsars of the past was to light a savage fetish dance. To such base uses may we come, of so little account may we be in the minds of the eager multitudes that we shall breed, many of whom, so far from revering our memory, will live to curse us for begetting them into such a world of woe.

Then there was the physical side of the spectacle, and a wild and splendid one it was. Those old citizens of Kôr burnt as, to judge from their sculptures and inscriptions, they had lived, very fast, and with the utmost liberality. What is more, there were plenty of them. So soon as a mummy was consumed to the ankles, which happened in about twenty minutes, the feet were kicked away, and another was put in its place. The bonfire was fed on the same generous scale, and its flames shot up, with a hiss and a crackle, twenty or thirty feet into the air, throwing great flashes of light far out into the gloom, through which the dark forms of the Amahagger flitted to and fro like devils replenishing the infernal fires. We all stood and stared aghast—shocked, and yet fascinated at so strange a spectacle, and half expecting to see the spirits those flaming forms had once enclosed come creeping from the shadows to work vengeance on their desecrators.

"I promised thee a strange sight, my Holly," laughed Ayesha, whose nerves alone did not seem to be affected; "and, behold! I have not failed thee. Also, it hath its lesson. Trust not to the future, for who knows what the future may bring! Therefore, live for the day, and endeavour not to escape the dust which seems to be man's end. What thinkest thou that those long-forgotten nobles and ladies would have felt had they known that in an age to be their delicate bodies should flare to light the dance of savages? But see, here come the mummers; a merry crew—are they not? The stage is lit—now for the play."

As she spoke we perceived advancing round the human bon-fire two lines of figures, one of males and the other of females, to the number of about a hundred, each arrayed only in the usual leopard and buck skins. They formed up, in perfect silence, facing each other between us and the fire, and then the dance—a sort of infernal and fiendish cancan—began. To describe it is quite impossible, but, though there was a good deal of tossing of legs and double-scuffling, it seemed to our untutored minds to be a play rather than a dance, and, as is usual among this dreadful people, whose character takes its colour from the caves wherein they live, and whose jokes and amusements are drawn from the inexhaustible stores of preserved mortality with which they share their homes, the subject was most ghastly.

In the first place it represented an attempted murder, then the burial alive of the victim and his struggling from the grave; each act of the abominable drama, which was carried on in perfect silence, being rounded off and finished with a furious and very revolting dance about the supposed victim, who writhed upon the ground in the red light of the bonfire.

Suddenly, however, this pleasing piece was interrupted. There was a slight commotion, and a large powerful woman, whom I had noted as one of the most vigorous of the dancers, made mad and drunken with unholy excitement, bounded and staggered towards us, shrieking out as she came:—

"I want a Black Goat, I must have a Black Goat, bring me a Black Goat!" and down she fell upon the rocky floor, foaming and writhing, and shrieking for a Black Goat, affording as hideous a spectacle as can be conceived.

Instantly most of the dancers assembled themselves round her, though some still continued their capers in the background.

"She has a Devil," called out one of them. "Run and get a black goat. There, Devil, keep quiet! keep quiet! You shall have the goat presently. They have gone to fetch it, Devil."

"I want a Black Goat, I must have a Black Goat!" shrieked the foaming rolling creature again.

"All right, Devil, the goat will be here presently; keep quiet, there's a good Devil!"

And so on till the goat, taken from a neighbouring kraal, arrived at last, being dragged bleating to the scene by its horns.

"Is it a Black One? is it a Black One?" shrieked the possessed.

"Yes, yes, Devil, as black as night;" then aside, "keep it behind thee, don't let the Devil see that it has got a white spot on its rump and another on its belly. In one minute, Devil. There, cut its throat quick. Where is the saucer?"

"The Goat! the Goat! the Goat! Give me the blood of my black goat! I must have it, don't you see I must have it? Oh! oh! oh! give me the blood of the goat."

At this moment a terrified *bah!* announced that the poor animal had been sacrificed, and presently a woman ran up with a saucer full of the blood. This the possessed creature, who was then raving and foaming her wildest, seized and *drank,* and was instantly recovered, and without a trace of hysteria, or fits, or possession, or whatever dreadful thing it was from which she suffered. She stretched out her arms, smiled faintly, and walked back to the dancers, who then withdrew in a double line as they had come, leaving the space between us and the bonfire deserted

I thought that the entertainment was now over, and, feeling sick, was about to ask *She* if we could rise, when suddenly what at first I took to be a baboon came hopping round the fire, to be met upon the other side by a lion, or rather by a human being dressed in a lion's skin. Then appeared a goat, then a man wrapped in an ox-hide, with the horns swinging ludicrously to and fro. After him followed a blesbok, then an impala, then a koodoo, then more goats, and many other animals, including a girl sewn up in the shining scaly skin of a boa-constrictor, several yards of which trailed along the ground behind her. When all the maskers had collected they began to dance about in a lumbering, unnatural fashion, and to imitate the sounds produced by the respective animals they represented, until the air was alive with roars and bleating and the hissing of snakes.

This went on for a long time, till, tiring of the pantomime, I asked Ayesha if Leo and myself could walk round to inspect the human torches, and, as she did not object, we started, turning to the left. After looking at one or two of the flaming bodies, we were about to return, thoroughly disgusted with the grotesque weirdness of the spectacle, when our attention was attracted by one of the dancers, a particularly active leopard, that had separated itself from its fellow-beasts, and was whisking about in our immediate neighbourhood, but gradually drawing towards a spot where the shadow was darkest, equidistant between two of the burning mummies. Led by curiosity, we followed it, when suddenly it darted past us into the gloom beyond, and as it went erected itself and whispered, "Come," in a voice which we both recognised as that of Ustane. Without waiting to consult me Leo turned and followed her into the outer darkness, and, filled with fear, I hurried after them. The leopard crawled on for about fifty paces—a sufficient distance to be quite beyond the light of the fire and torches—and then Leo overtook it, or rather Ustane.

"Oh, my lord," I heard her whisper, "at length I have found thee! Listen. I am in peril of my life from 'She-who-must-be-obeyed.' Surely the Baboon has told thee how she drove me from thee? I love thee, my lord, and thou art mine according to the custom of this country. I saved thy life; then canst thou cast me off, my love, my love!"

"Of course not," ejaculated Leo; "I have been seeking thee, Ustane. Let us go and explain to the Queen."

"Nay, nay, she would slay us. Thou knowest not her power—the Baboon there, he knoweth, for he saw. Hearken! There is but one way: if thou wilt cleave to me, thou must flee with me across the marshes this very hour, and then perchance we may escape."

"For Heaven's sake, Leo," I began, but she broke in—

"Nay, listen not to him. Swift—be swift—death is in the air we breathe. Even now, mayhap, *She* hears us," and without more ado she proceeded to enforce her arguments by throwing herself into his arms. As she did so the leopard's head slipped from her hair, and I saw the three white finger-marks upon it, gleaming faintly in the star-light. Terrified by the desperate nature of the position, once more I was about to interpose, for I knew that Leo is not too strong-minded where women are concerned, when I heard a little silvery laugh behind me. I turned round, and—oh horror!—there was *She* herself, and with her Billali and two male mutes. I gasped and nearly fell, for I was certain that such a situation must result in some dreadful tragedy, of which it seemed exceedingly probable that I should be the first victim.

As for Ustane, loosing her lover, she covered her eyes with her hands, while Leo, not knowing the full terror of the position, merely coloured, and looked foolish, as a man caught in such a trap would naturally do.

CHAPTER XX

TRIUMPH

THEN followed a moment of the most painful silence that I ever endured. It was broken by Ayesha, who addressed herself to Leo.

"Nay, now, my lord and guest," she said in her softest tones, which yet had the ring of steel about them, "look not so bashful. Surely the sight was a pretty one—the leopard and the lion!"

"Oh, bother!" said Leo in English.

"And thou, Ustane," she went on, "in truth I should have passed thee by, had not the light fallen on the stripes across thy hair," and she pointed to the bright edge of the rising moon which was now appearing above the horizon. "Well! well! the dance is done—see, the tapers have burnt down, and all things end in silence and in ashes. So thou thoughtest it a fit time for love, Ustane, my servant—and I, dreaming not that I could be disobeyed, deemed thee already far away."

"Play not with me," moaned the wretched woman; "kill me, and let there be an end."

"Nay, why? It is not well to go swift from the hot lips of love down to the cold mouth of the grave," and Ayesha motioned to the mutes, who instantly stepped up and caught the girl by either arm. With an oath Leo sprang upon the nearest, and hurled him to the ground, and then stood over him with his face set and his fist ready.

Again Ayesha laughed. "It was well thrown, my guest; thou hast a strong arm for one who so late was sick. But now of thy courtesy I pray thee let that man live and do my bidding. He shall not harm the girl; the night air grows chill, and I would welcome her in mine own place. Surely she whom thou dost favour shall be favoured of me also."

I took Leo by the arm, dragging him from the prostrate mute, and, half bewildered, he yielded and left the man. Then we set out for the cave across the plateau, whence the dancers had vanished, and where a pile of white human ashes was all that remained of the fire which had lit their dancing.

In due course we gained Ayesha's boudoir—all too soon it seemed to me, having a sad presage of what was to come lying heavy on my heart.

Ayesha seated herself upon her cushions, and, having dismissed Job and Billali, by signs she bade the mutes tend the lamps and retire—all save one girl, who was her favourite personal attendant. We three remained standing, the unfortunate Ustane a little to the left of the rest of us.

"Now, O Holly," Ayesha began, "how came it that thou who didst hear my words bidding this evil-doer"—and she pointed to Ustane—"to go hence—thou at whose prayer I weakly spared her life—how came it, I say, that thou hadst part in what I saw to-night? Answer, and for thine own sake, I say, speak all the truth, for I am not minded to hear lies upon this matter!"

"It was by accident, O Queen," I answered. "I knew nothing of it."

"I believe thee, Holly," she answered coldly, "and well it is for thee that I do. Then does the whole guilt rest upon her."

"I do not find any guilt herein," interrupted Leo. "She is no other man's wife, and it seems that she has married me according to the custom of this awful place, so who is harmed? Any way, madam, whatever she has done I have done, so if she is to be punished let me be punished also; and I tell thee," he went on, working himself up into a fury, "that if thou biddest one of those deaf and dumb villains to touch her again I will tear him to pieces!"

Ayesha listened in icy silence, and made no remark. When he had finished, however, she addressed Ustane.

"Hast thou aught to say, woman? Thou silly straw, thou feather, who didst think to float towards thy passion's petty ends, even against the great wind of my will! Tell me, for I fain would understand, why didst thou this thing?"

Then I think that I saw the most wonderful example of moral courage and intrepidity which it is possible to conceive. For this poor, doomed girl, knowing what she had to expect at the hands of her terrible Queen, knowing, too, from bitter experience, how great was her adversary's power, yet stood unshaken, and out of the very depths of her despair drew the strength to defy her.

"I did it, O *She*," she answered, drawing herself up to the full of her stately height, and throwing back the panther skin from her head, "because my love is deeper than the grave. I did it because my life without this man whom my heart chose would be but a living death. Therefore I risked my life, and now, when I know that it is forfeit to thine anger, still am I glad that I risked it, and must pay it away, in the risking, ay, because he embraced me once, and told me that he loved me yet."

Here Ayesha half rose from her couch, and then sank down again.

"I have no magic," went on Ustane, her rich voice ringing strong and full, "and I am not a Queen, nor do I live for ever: but a woman's heart is heavy to sink through waters, however deep, O Queen! and a woman's eyes are quick to see—even through thy veil, O Queen!

"Listen: I know it, thou dost love this man thyself, and therefore wouldst thou destroy me who stand across thy path. Ay, I die—I die, and go into the darkness, nor know I whither I go. But this I know. There is a light shining in my breast, and by that light, as by a lamp, I see the truth, and the future that I shall not share, unroll itself before me like a scroll. When first I knew my lord," and she pointed to Leo, "I knew also that death would be the bridal gift he gave me—it rushed upon me of a sudden, but I turned not back, being ready to pay the price, and, behold, death is here! And now, even as I knew this, so, standing on the steps of doom, do I know that thou shalt not reap the profit of thy crime. Mine he is, and, though thy beauty shine like a sun among the stars, mine he shall remain for thee. Never here in this life shall he look thee in the eyes and call thee spouse. Thou too art doomed, I see"—and her voice rose like the cry of an inspired prophetess; "ah, I see——"

Then there rang an answering cry of rage and terror. I turned my head. Ayesha had risen, and was standing with her outstretched hand pointing at Ustane, who had suddenly become silent. I gazed at the poor woman, and as I gazed there fell upon her face that same woful, fixed expression of terror which I had seen before when she broke into her wild chant. Her eyes grew large, her nostrils dilated, and her lips blanched.

Ayesha said nothing, she made no sound, she only drew herself up, stretched out her arm, and, her tall veiled frame quivering like an aspen-leaf, appeared to look fixedly at her victim. Even as she looked Ustane put her hands to her head, uttered one piercing scream, turned round twice, and then fell backwards with a thud—prone upon the floor. Both Leo and myself rushed to her. She was stone dead—blasted in to death by some mysterious electric agency or overwhelming will-force whereof the dread *She* had command.

For a moment Leo did not quite understand what had happened. But, when it came home to him, his face was awful to see. With a savage oath he rose from beside the corpse, and, turning, literally sprang at Ayesha. But she was watching, and, seeing him come, stretched out her hand again, and he went staggering back towards me, and would have fallen, had I not caught him. Afterwards he told me that he felt as though he had suddenly received a violent blow in the chest, and, what is more, utterly cowed, as if all the manhood had been taken out of him.

Then Ayesha spoke. "Forgive me, my guest," she said softly, addressing him, "if I have shocked thee with my justice."

"Forgive thee, thou fiend!" shouted poor Leo, wringing his hands in his rage and grief. "Forgive thee, thou murderess! By Heaven, I will kill thee if I can!"

"Nay, nay," she answered in the same soft voice, "thou dost not understand—the time has come for thee to learn. *Thou* art my love, my Kallikrates, my Beautiful, my Strong! For two thousand years, Kallikrates, I have waited for *thee,* and now at length thou hast come back to me; and as for this woman," pointing to the corpse, "she stood between me and thee, therefore have I laid her in the dust, Kallikrates."

"It is a lie!" said Leo. "My name is not Kallikrates! I am Leo Vincey; my ancestor was Kallikrates—at least, I believe he was."

"Ah, thou sayest it—thine ancestor was Kallikrates, and thou, even thou, art Kallikrates reborn, come back—and mine own dear lord!"

"I am not Kallikrates, and as for being thy lord, or having aught to do with thee, I had sooner be the lord of a fiend from hell, for she would be better than thou."

"Sayest thou so—sayest thou so, Kallikrates? Nay, but thou hast not seen me for so long a time that no memory remains. Yet am I very fair, Kallikrates!"

"I hate thee, murderess, and I have no wish to see thee. What is it to me how fair thou art? I hate thee, I say."

"Yet within a very little space shalt thou creep to my knee, and swear that thou dost love me," answered Ayesha, with a sweet, mocking laugh. "Come, there is no time like the present time. Here, before this dead girl who loved thee, let us put it to the proof.

"Look now on me, Kallikrates!" and with a sudden motion she shook her gauzy covering from her, and stood forth in her low kirtle and her snaky zone, in her glorious radiant beauty and her imperial grace, rising from her wrappings, as it were, like Venus from the wave, or Galatea from her marble, or a beatified spirit from the tomb. She stood forth, and fixed, her deep and glowing eyes upon Leo's eyes, and I saw his clenched fists unclasp, and his set and quivering features relax beneath her gaze. I saw his wonder and astonishment grow into admiration, then into longing, and the more he struggled the more I saw the power of her dread beauty fasten on him and take hold of his senses, drugging them, and drawing the heart out of him. Did I not know the process? Had not I, who was twice his age, gone through it myself? Was I not going through it afresh even then, although her sweet and passionate gaze was not for me? Yes, alas! I was. Alas! that I should have to confess that at this very moment I was rent by mad and furious jealousy. I could have flown at him, shame upon me! This woman had confounded and almost destroyed my moral sense, as indeed she must confound all who looked upon her superhuman loveliness. But—I do not know how —I mastered myself, and once more turned to see the climax of the awful tragedy.

"Oh, great Heaven!" gasped Leo, "art thou a woman?"

"A woman in truth—in very truth—and thine own spouse, Kallikrates!" she answered, stretching out her rounded ivory arms towards him, and smiling, ah, so sweetly!

He looked and looked, and slowly I perceived that he was drawing nearer to her. Suddenly his eye fell upon the corpse of poor Ustane, and he shuddered and stood still.

"How can I?" he said hoarsely. "Thou art a murderess; she loved me."

Observe, he was already forgetting that he had loved her.

"It is nothing," Ayesha murmured, and her voice sounded sweet as the night-wind passing through the trees. "It is naught at all. If I have sinned, let my beauty answer for my sin. If I have sinned, it is for love of thee: let my sin, therefore, be put away and forgotten;" and once more she stretched out her arms and whispered *"Come."* Then in a few seconds it was over.

I saw him struggle—I saw him even turn to fly; but her eyes drew him more strongly than iron bounds, and the magic of her beauty and concentrated will and passion entered into him and overpowered him—ay, even there, in the presence of the body of the woman who had loved him well enough to die for him. It sounds horrible and wicked indeed, but he should not be too greatly blamed, and be sure his sin has found him out. The temptress who drew him into evil was more than human, and her beauty was greater than the loveliness of the daughters of men.

I looked up again, and now her perfect form lay in his arms, and her lips were pressed against his own; and thus, with the corpse of his dead love for an altar, did Leo Vincey plight his troth to her red-handed murderess—plight it for ever and a day. For those who sell themselves into a like dominion, paying down the price of their own honour, and throwing their soul into the balance to sink the scale to the level of their lusts, must win deliverance hardly. As they have sown, so shall they reap and reap, even when the poppy flowers of passion have withered in their hands, and their harvest is but bitter tares, garnered in satiety.

Suddenly, with a snake-like motion she seemed to slip from his embrace, and again she broke out into her low laugh of triumphant mockery, and said, pointing to the dead Ustane:

"Did I not tell thee that within a little space thou wouldst creep to my knee, O Kallikrates? Surely the space has been no great one!"

Leo groaned in shame and misery; for though he was overcome and stricken down, he was not so lost as to be unaware of the depth of the degradation to which he had sunk. On the contrary, his better nature rose up in arms against his fallen self, as I was to learn that night.

Ayesha laughed a third time, then, veiling herself quickly, she made a sign to the mute, who had been watching the strange scene with curious, startled eyes. The girl left, and returned presently, followed by two male mutes, to whom the Queen made another sign. Thereon they all three seized the body of poor Ustane by the arms, dragging it heavily down the cavern and away through the curtains at the end. Leo watched it for a little while, then he covered his face with his hand. To my excited fancy, the glazing eyes of dead Ustane also seemed to watch us as they went.

"There passes the dead past," said Ayesha, solemnly, as the curtains shook and fell back into their places, when the ghastly procession had vanished behind them. Then, with one of those wild changes of mood of which I have already spoken, again she threw off her veil, and, after the ancient and poetic fashion of the dwellers in Arabia,[1] broke into a pæan of triumph, or epithalamium, that, rich and beautiful as it was, is most difficult to render into English; that ought, indeed, to be sung to music rather than written and read. It was divided into two parts—

[1] Among the ancient Arabians the power of poetic declamation, either in verse or prose, was held in the highest honour and esteem, and he who excelled in it was known as 'Khâteb,' or Orator. Every year a general assembly was held, at which the rival poets repeated their compositions, and, so soon as the knowledge of the art of writing became general, those poems which were judged to be the best were inscribed on silk in letters of gold, and publicly exhibited, being known as 'Al Modhahabât,' or 'golden verses.' In the chant given above by Mr. Holly, Ayesha evidently followed the traditional poetic manner of her people, which was to embody their thoughts in a series of somewhat disconnected sentences, each remarkable for its beauty and the grace of its expression.—EDITOR.

one descriptive, the other personal; and, as nearly as I can remember, it ran as follows:—

Love is like a flower in the desert.

It is like the aloe of Arabia, that blooms but once and dies; it blooms in the salt emptiness of Life, and the brightness of its beauty is set upon the waste as a star set upon a storm.

It hath the sun above that is the Spirit, and about it blows the air of its divinity.

At the echoing of a step Love blooms, I say; I say Love blooms, and bends her beauty down to him who passeth by.

He plucketh it, yea, he plucketh the red cup that is full of honey, and beareth it away; away across the desert, away till the flower be withered, away till the desert is done.

There is only one perfect flower in the wilderness of Life.

That flower is Love!

There is only one fixed light in the mists of our wandering.

That light is Love!

There is only one hope in our despairing night.

That hope is Love!

All else is false. All else is shadow moving upon water. All else is wind and vanity.

Who shall say what is the weight or the measure of Love?

It is born of the flesh, it dwelleth in the spirit. From each doth it draw its comfort.

For beauty it is as a star.

Many are its shapes, but all are beautiful, and none know whence that star rose, or the horizon where it shall set.

Then, turning to Leo, and laying her hand upon his shoulder Ayesha went on in a fuller and more triumphant tone, speaking in balanced sentences that gradually grew and swelled from romantic prose into pure and majestic verse—

Long have I loved thee, O my love; yet has my love not lessened.

Long have I waited for thee, and behold my reward is at hand —is here!

Far away I saw thee once, and thou wast taken from me.

Then in a grave sowed I the seed of patience, and shone upon it with the sun of hope, and watered it with tears of repentance, and breathed on it with the breath of my knowledge.

And now, lo! it hath sprung up, and borne fruit. Lo! out of the grave hath it sprung. Yea, from among the dry bones and ashes of the dead.

I have waited, and my reward is with me.

I have overcome Death, and Death has brought back to me him that was dead.

Therefore do I rejoice, for fair is the future.

Green are the paths that we shall tread across the everlasting meadows.

The hour is at hand. Night hath fled away into the valleys.

The dawn kisseth the mountain-tops.

Soft shall we live, my love, and easy shall we go.

Crowned shall we be with the diadem of Kings.

Worshipping and wonder-struck all people of the world,

Blinded, shall fall before our beauty and our might.

From time unto times shall our greatness thunder on,

Rolling like a chariot through the dust of endless days.

Laughing, shall we speed in our victory and pomp,

Laughing like the Daylight as he leaps along the hills.

Onward, still triumphant, to a triumph ever new!

Onward, in our power, to a power unattained!

Onward, never weary, clad with splendour for a robe!

Till accomplished be our fate, and the night is rushing down.

She paused in her strange and most thrilling allegorical chant, of which, unfortunately, I am only able to give the burden, I fear but feebly. Then she said:

"Perchance thou dost not believe my word, Kallikrates—perchance thou thinkest that I do delude thee, that I have not lived these many years, and that thou hast not been born again to me Nay, look not thus—put away that pale cast of doubt, for oh, be sure, herein can error find no foothold! Sooner shall the suns forget their course and the swallow miss her nest, than my soul shall swear a lie and be led astray from thee, Kallikrates. Blind me, take away mine eyes, and let the darkness utterly fence me in, and still mine ears would catch the sound of thine unforgotten voice, striking more loud against the portals of my sense than can the call of brazen-throated clarions:—Stop up mine hearing also, and let a thousand touch me on the brow, and I would name thee out of all:—Yea, rob me of every sense, and see me stand deaf, and blind, and dumb, and with nerves that cannot weigh the value of a touch, yet would my spirit leap within me like a quickening child and cry unto my heart: 'Behold, Kallikrates! Behold, thou watcher, the watches of thy night are ended! Behold, thou who seekest in the night season, thy morning Star ariseth.' "

She ceased awhile, and presently continued, "Stay; if thy heart is yet hardened against the mighty truth, and thou seekest some outward pledge of that which thou dost find too strange to under-

stand, even now it shall be given to thee, and to thee also, O my
Holly. Take a lamp each one of you, and follow after me whither
I shall lead you."

Without pausing to think—indeed, speaking for myself, I had
almost abandoned the attempt in circumstances which seemed to
render it futile, since thought fell hourly helpless against a black
wall of wonder—we took the lamps and followed her. Gliding
to the end of her chamber, Ayesha raised a curtain and revealed
a little stair of the sort that is so common in these dim caves of
Kôr. As we hurried down this stair I observed that the steps were
worn in the centre to such an extent that some of them had been
reduced from seven and a half inches, at which I guessed their
original height, to about three and a half inches. Now, the other
steps that I had seen in the caves were quite unworn, as might
be expected, since the only traffic which ever passed upon them
was that of those who bore a fresh burden to the tomb. Therefore this fact struck my notice with the curious force with which
little things do strike us when our minds are absolutely overwhelmed by a sudden rush of powerful sensations, beaten flat, as
it were, like a sea beneath the first burst of a hurricane, so that
each small object on its surface starts into an unnatural
prominence.

At the foot of the stairway I halted, and stared at the worn
steps, and Ayesha, turning, saw me.

"Dost thou wonder whose are the feet that have worn away
this rock, my Holly?" she asked. "They are mine—even my own
light feet! I can remember when yonder stairs were new and
level, but for two thousand years and more have I passed hither
day by day, and see, my sandals have eaten out the solid stone!"

I made no answer, but I do not think that anything which I had
heard or seen brought home to my limited understanding so clear
a sense of this being's overwhelming antiquity as the sight of this
hard granite hollowed out by her soft feet. How many hundreds
of thousands of times must she have glided up and down that stair
to bring about such a result?

The steps led to a tunnel, and a few paces from its mouth
opened a curtain-hung doorway, a glance at which told me that
it was the same whence I had witnessed that terrible scene by
the leaping flame. I recognised the pattern of the curtain, and
the sight of it brought that dread event vividly before my eyes,
and made me tremble even at its memory. Ayesha entered the
tomb, for it was a tomb, and we followed her—I, for one, rejoicing that the mystery of the place was about to be cleared up,
and yet afraid to face its solution.

CHAPTER XXI

THE DEAD AND LIVING MEET

"SEE now the place where I have slept for these two thousand years," said Ayesha, taking the lamp from Leo's hand and holding it above her head. Its rays fell upon a hollow in the floor, where I had seen the obedient leaping flame, but now the fire was out. They fell upon the white form stretched there beneath its wrappings upon a bed of stone, upon the fretted carving of the tomb, and upon another shelf of stone opposite to the one on which the body lay, and separated from it only by the breadth of the cave.

"Here," went on Ayesha, resting her hand upon the rock— "here have I slept night by night for all these generations, with but a cloak to cover me. It did not become me that I should lie soft when my spouse yonder," and she pointed to the rigid form, "lay stiff in death. Here night by night I have slept in his cold company—till, as thou seest, this thick slab, like the stairs down which we came, has worn thin with the tossing of my form—so faithful have I been to thee even in thy space of sleep, Kallikrates. And now, my lord, thou shalt see a wondrous thing—living, thou shalt behold thyself dead—for well have I tended thee during all these years, Kallikrates. Art thou prepared?"

We made no answer, but gazed at each other with frightened eyes, the scene was so awful and so solemn. Ayesha advanced, and laid her hand upon the corner of the shroud. Then once more she spoke.

"Be not affrighted," she said; "though the thing seem wonderful to thee—all we who live have thus lived before; nor are the very shapes that hold us strangers to the sun! Only we know it not, because memory writes no record, and earth hath gathered in the earth she lent us, for none have saved our glory from the grave. But I, by my arts and by the arts of those dead men of Kôr which I have learned, have held thee back, O Kallikrates, from the dust, that the waxen stamp of beauty on thy face should ever rest before mine eye. 'Twas a mask that memory might fill, serving to summon forth thy presence from the past, and give it strength to wander in the habitations of my thought, clad in a mummery of life that stayed my appetite with visions of dead days.

"Behold now, let the Dead and Living meet! Across the gulf of Time they still are one. Time has no power against Identity, though Sleep the merciful hath blotted out the tablets of our mind, and with oblivion sealed the sorrows that else would hound us down from life to life, stuffing the brain with gathered griefs till it burst in the madness of uttermost despair. Still are they one, for the wrappings of our rest shall roll away as thunderclouds before the wind; the frozen voices of the past shall melt in music like mountain snows beneath the sun; and the weeping and the laughter of the lost hours shall be heard once more sweetly echoing up the cliff of the inumerable years.

"Therefore have no fear, Kallikrates, when thou—living, and but lately born—shalt look upon thine own departed self, who breathed and died so long ago. I do but turn one page in thy Book of Being, and show thee what is writ thereon.

"Behold!"

With a sudden motion she drew the shroud from the cold form, and let the lamplight play upon it. I looked, and shrank back terrified; since, say what she might, the sight was an uncanny one—for her explanations were beyond the grasp of our finite minds, and when stripped from the mists of vague esoteric philosophy, and brought into conflict with cold and horrifying fact, they did not do much to break its force. For, stretched upon the stone bier before us, robed in white and perfectly preserved, was what appeared to be the body of Leo Vincey. I stared from Leo, standing *there* alive, to Leo lying *there* dead, and could see no difference between them; except, perhaps, that the body on the bier looked older. Feature for feature they were the same, yes, to the crop of little golden curls, which was Leo's most uncommon beauty. It even seemed to me, as I looked, that the expression on the dead man's face resembled that which I had sometimes seen upon Leo's when he was plunged in profound sleep. I can only sum up the closeness of the resemblance by saying that I never saw twins so exactly similar in appearance as were that dead and living pair.

I turned to see what effect was produced upon Leo by the sight of his dead self, and found it to be that of partial stupefaction. He stood for two or three minutes staring in silence, and when at last he spoke it was only to ejaculate—

"Cover it up, and take me away."

"Nay, wait Kallikrates," said Ayesha, who resembled an inspired Sibyl rather than a woman, as she stood, the lamp raised above her head flooding with its light her own rich beauty and the cold wonder of the death-clothed form upon the bier, and rolled out her majestic sentences with a grandeur and a freedom of utterance which, alas! I cannot render.

"Wait. I would show thee something, that no tittle of my crime may be hidden from thee. Do thou, O Holly, open the garment on the breast of the dead Kallikrates, for perchance my lord may fear to touch his perished self."

I obeyed with trembling fingers. It seemed a desecration and an unhallowed thing to handle that sleeping image of the living man at my side. Presently the cold breast was bare, and there upon it, over the heart, appeared a wound, evidently inflicted with a spear or dagger.

"Thou seest, Kallikrates," she said. "Know, then, that it was *I* who slew thee: in the place of Life *I* gave thee death. I slew thee because of the Egyptian Amenartas, whom thou didst love, for by her wiles she held thy heart, and her I could not smite as but now I smote yon woman, for she was too strong for me. In my haste and bitter anger I slew thee, and now for all these ages I have lamented thee, and waited for thy coming. And thou hast come, and naught can stand between thee and me, and of a truth now for death I will give thee life—not life eternal, for that none can give, but days and youth that shall endure for thousands upon thousands of years, and with them pomp, and power, and wealth, and all things that are good and beautiful, such as have been to no man before thee, nor shall be to any man who comes after. But one thing more, and thou shalt rest and make ready for the day of thy new birth. Thou seest this body, which was thine own. For all these centuries it hath been my cold comfort and my companion; now I need it no more, for I have thy living presence, and it can but serve to stir up memories of that which I would fain forget. Therefore let it go back to the dust whence I have held it.

"Behold! I have prepared against this happy hour!" Then, from the other shelf or stone ledge, which Ayesha said served her for a couch, she took a large vitrified double-handled vase, the mouth of which was covered with a bladder. This she loosed, and having first bent down and gently kissed the white forehead of the dead man, she undid the vase, and sprinkled its contents carefully over the corpse, taking, I observed, the greatest precautions against any drop of them touching us or herself; then poured out what remained of the liquid upon the chest and head. Instantly a dense vapour arose, and the cave was filled with choking fumes, which prevented us from seeing anything while the deadly acid did its work, for I presume it was some powerful preparation of the sort. From the spot where the body lay came a fierce fizzing and crackling sound, which ceased, however, before the fumes had cleared away. At last they were all gone, except a little cloud that still hung over the corpse. In two or three minutes more this had vanished also, and, wonderful as it may seem, it is a fact that on the stone bench which had supported the mortal remains of the ancient Kallikrates for so many centuries there was now nothing to be seen but a few handfuls of smoking white powder. The acid had utterly destroyed the body, and even in places eaten into the stone. Ayesha stooped down, and taking a handful of this powder, she threw it into the air, saying at the same time, in a voice of calm solemnity—

"Dust to dust!—the past to the past!—the lost to the lost!— Kallikrates is dead, and is born again!"

The ashes floated about us and fell to the rocky floor, while in awed silence we watched them fall, too overcome for words.

"Now leave me," she said, "and sleep if ye may. I must watch and think, for to-morrow night we go hence, and the time is long since I trod the path that we shall follow."

Accordingly we bowed, and left her.

As we passed to our own apartment I peeped into Job's sleeping-place, to see how he fared, for he had gone away, just before our interview with the murdered Ustane, quite prostrated by the terrors of the Amahagger festivity. He was sleeping soundly, good honest fellow that he was, and I rejoiced to think that his nerves, which, like those of most uneducated people, were far from strong, had been spared the closing scenes of this dreadful day. Then we entered our own chamber, and here at last poor Leo, who, ever since he had looked upon that frozen image of his living self, had been in a state not far removed from stupor, burst out into a torrent of grief. Now that he was no longer in the presence of the dread *She* his sense of the awfulness of all that had happened, and more especially of the wicked murder of Ustane, who was bound to him by ties so close, broke upon him like a storm, and lashed him into an agony of remorse and terror which was painful to witness. He cursed himself—he cursed the hour when we had first seen the writing on the sherd, which was being so mysteriously verified, and bitterly he cursed his own weakness. Ayesha he dared not curse—who would dare to speak evil of such a woman, whose spirit, for aught we knew, was watching us at the very moment?

"What am I to do, old fellow?" he groaned, resting his head against my shoulder in the extremity of his grief. "I let her be killed—not that I could help that, but within five minutes I was kissing her murderess over her body. I am a degraded brute, but I cannot resist this," and here his voice sank—"awful sorceress. I know I shall do the same to-morrow; I know that I am in her power for always; if I never saw her again I should think of no other woman during all my life; I must follow her as a needle follows a magnet; I would not go away if I might; I could not leave her, my legs would not carry me, but my mind is still clear enough, and in my mind I hate her—at least, I think so. It is all so horrible; and that—that dead man! What can I make of it? It was *I!* I am sold into bondage, old fellow, and she will take my soul as the price of herself!"

Then, for the first time, I told him that I was in but a very little better position; and I am bound to say that, notwithstanding his own infatuation, he had the decency to sympathise with me. Perhaps he did not think it worth while to be jealous, seeing that he had no cause so far as the lady was concerned. I went on to suggest that we should try to run away, but we soon rejected the project as futile, and, to be perfectly honest, I do not believe that either of us would really have left Ayesha, even if some superior power had suddenly offered to convey us from these gloomy caves and set us down in Cambridge. We could no more have left her than a moth can leave the light that destroys it. We were like confirmed opium-eaters: in our moments of reason we well knew the deadly nature of pursuit, but certainly we were not prepared to abandon its terrible delights.

No man who once had seen *She* unveiled, and heard the music of her voice, and drunk in the bitter wisdom of her words, would willingly give up that joy for a whole sea of placid pleasure. How much more, then, was this likely to be so when, as in Leo's case, to put myself out of the question, this extraodinary creature declared her utter and absolute devotion, and gave to him what appeared to be proofs of its endurance through some two thousand years?

No doubt she was a wicked person, and no doubt she had murdered Ustane when she stood in her path; but then, she was very faithful, and by a law of nature man is apt to think but lightly of a woman's crimes, especially if that woman be beautiful, and the crimes are committed for the love of himself.

For the rest, when had such a chance ever come to a man before as that which now lay in Leo's hand? True, in uniting himself to this dread woman he would place his life under the influence of a mysterious creature of evil tendencies,[1] but

[1] After some months of consideration of this statement I am bound to confess that I am not quite satisfied of its truth. It is perfectly true that

then, that would be likely enough to happen to him in any ordinary marriage. On the other hand, however, no ordinary marriage could bring him such awful beauty—for awful is the only word that can describe it—such divine devotion, such wisdom, and command over the secrets of nature, and the place and power which they must win, or, lastly, the royal crown of unending youth, if indeed she could give that. No, on the whole, it is not wonderful, though Leo was plunged in bitter shame and grief, such as any gentleman would have felt under the circumstances, that he was not ready to entertain the idea of running away from his extraordinary fortune.

My own opinion is that he would have been mad if he had done so. But then, I confess, my views on the matter must be accepted with qualifications. I am in love with Ayesha myself to this day, and I would rather have been the object of her affection for one short week than that of any other woman's in the world for a whole lifetime. And let me add that if anybody who doubts this statement, and thinks me foolish for making it, could have seen Ayesha draw her veil and flash out in beauty on his gaze, his view would exactly coincide with my own. Of course, I am speaking of any *man*. We never had the advantage of a lady's opinion of Ayesha, but I think it quite possible that she would have regarded the Queen with dislike; would have expressed

Ayesha committed a murder, but I suspect that, were we endowed with the same absolute power, and if we had the same tremendous interest at stake, we should be very apt to do likewise under parallel circumstances. Also, it must be remembered that she looked on it as an execution for disobedience under a system which made the slightest disobedience punishable by death. Putting aside this question of the murder, her evil-doing resolves itself into the expression of views and the acknowledgment of motives which are contrary to our preaching, if not to our practice. Now at first sight this might be fairly taken as a proof of an evil nature, but when we come to consider the great antiquity of the individual, it becomes doubtful if it was anything more than the natural cynicism which arises from age and bitter experience, and the possession of extraordinary powers of observation. It is a well-known fact that very often, putting the period of boyhood out of the argument, the older we grow the more cynical and hardened we become; indeed, many of us are only saved by timely death from moral petrifaction, if not from moral corruption. No one will deny that a young man is on the average better than an old one, for he is without that experience of the order of things which in certain thoughtful dispositions can hardly fail to produce cynicism ,and that disregard of acknowledged methods and established custom which we call evil. Now the oldest man upon the earth was but a babe compared to Ayesha, and the wisest man upon the earth was not one-third as wise. And the fruit of her wisdom was this, that there is but one thing worth living for, and that is Love in its highest sense, and to gain that good thing she was not prepared to stop at trifles. This is really the sum of her evil doings, and it must be remembered, on the other hand, that, whatever may be thought of them, she had some virtues developed to a degree very uncommon in either sex—constancy, for instance.—L. H. H.

her disapproval in some more or less pointed manner, and ultimately have been 'blasted.'

For two hours or more Leo and I sat with shaken nerves and
frightened eyes, and talked over the miraculous events through
which we were passing. It seemed like a dream or a fairy tale,
instead of solemn, sober fact. Who would have believed that
the writing on the potsherd was not only true, but that we
should live to verify it, and that we two seekers should find her
who was sought patiently awaiting our coming in the tombs of
Kôr? Who would have thought that in the person of Leo this
mysterious woman should, as she believed, discover the being
whom she awaited from century to century, and whose former earthly tenement she had till this very night preserved?
But so it was. In the face of all we had seen it was difficult
for us as ordinary reasoning men any longer to doubt its truth.
Therefore at last, with humble hearts and a deep sense of the
impotence of human knowledge, and the insolence of the assumption which denies the possibility of that whereof it has no
experience, we laid ourselves down to sleep, leaving our fates
in the hands of the watching Providence which had chosen thus
to allow us to draw the veil of human ignorance, and to reveal
to us for good or evil a glimpse of the potentialities of life.

CHAPTER XXII

JOB HAS A PRESENTIMENT

It was nine o'clock on the following morning when Job, who
still looked scared and tremulous, came in to call me, and at
the same time to breathe his gratitude at finding us alive in
our beds, which, it appeared, was more than he had expected.
When I told him of the awful end of poor Ustane he was even
more thankful for our survival, and much shocked; though,
indeed, Ustane had been no favourite of his, or he of hers. She
called him 'pig' in bastard Arabic, and he called her 'hussy' in
good English, but these amenities were forgotten in face of the
catastrophe that had overwhelmed her at the hands of her Queen.

"I don't want to say anything as mayn't be agreeable, sir,"
said Job, when he had finished exclaiming at my tale, "but it's
my opinion that that there *She* is Old Nick himself, or perhaps
his wife, if he has one, which I suppose he has, for he couldn't
be so wicked all alone. The Witch of Endor was a fool to her,
sir: bless you, she would make no more of raising every gentleman in the Bible out of these here musty tombs than I should
of growing cress on a bit of flannel! It's a country of devils,

this is, sir, and she's the master one of the lot; and if ever we get clear it will be more than I expect to do. I don't see no way out of it. That witch isn't likely to let a fine young man like Mr. Leo go."

"Come," I said, "at any rate she saved his life."

"Yes, and she'll take his soul to pay for it. She'll make him a witch, like herself. I say it's wicked to have anything to do with those sort of people. Last night, sir, I lay awake and read in my little Bible that my poor mother gave me about what is going to happen to sorceresses and them sort, till my hair stood on end. Lord, how the old lady would stare if she saw where her Job had got to!"

"Yes, it's a queer country, and a queer people, too, Job," I answered, with a sigh, for, though I am not superstitious like Job, I admit to a natural shrinking, which will not bear investigation, from the things that are above Nature.

"You are right, sir," he answered, "and if you won't think me very foolish, I should like to say something to you now that Mr. Leo is out of way"—(Leo had risen early and gone for a stroll)—"and that is, that I know it is the last country as ever I shall see in this world. I had a dream last night, and I dreamed that I saw my old father with a kind of night-shirt on him, something like these folk wear when they want to be in particular full-dress, and a bit of that feathery grass in his hand, which he may have gathered on the way, for I saw lots of it yesterday about three hundred yards from the mouth of this beastly cave.

" 'Job,' he said to me, solemn like, and yet with a kind of satisfaction shining through him, more like a Methody elder when he has sold a neighbour a marked horse for a sound one and cleared twenty pounds by the job than anything I can think on—'Job, time's up, Job; but I never did expect to come and hunt you out in this 'ere place, Job! Such ado as I have had to nose you up; it wasn't friendly to give your poor old father such a run, let alone that a wonderful lot of bad characters hail from this place Kôr.' "

"Regular cautions," I suggested.

"Yes, sir—of course, sir, that's just what he said they was— 'cautions, downright scorchers'—sir, and I'm sure I don't doubt it, seeing what I know of them and their hotpotting ways," went on Job, sadly. "Anyway, he was sure that time was up, and went away saying that we should see more than we cared for of each other soon, and I suppose he was a-thinking of the fact that father and I never could hit it off together for longer nor three days, and I daresay that things will be similar when we meet again."

"Surely," I said, "you don't think that you are going to die because you dreamed you saw your old father; if one dies because one dreams of one's father, what happens to a man who dreams of his mother-in-law?"

"Ah, sir, you're laughing at me," said Job; "but, you see, you didn't know my father. If it had been anybody else—my Aunt Mary, for instance, who never made much of a job—I should not have thought so much of it; but my father was that idle, which he shouldn't have been with seventeen children, that he would never have put himself out to come here just to see the place. No, sir; I know that he meant business. Well, sir, I can't help it; I suppose every man must go some time or other, though it is a hard thing to die in a hole like this, where Christian burial isn't to be had for its weight in gold. I've tried to be a good man, sir, and do my duty honest, and if it wasn't for the supercilus kind of way in which father carried on last night—a sort of sniffing at me as it were, as though he hadn't no opinion of my references and testimonials—I should feel easy enough in my mind. Anyway, sir, I've been a good servant to you and Mr. Leo, bless him!—why, it seems but the other day that I used to lead him about the streets with a penny whip;—and if ever you get out of this place—which, as father didn't allude to you, perhaps you may—I hope you will think kindly of my whitened bones, and never have anything more to do with Greek writing on flower-pots, sir, if I may make so bold as to say so."

"Come, come, Job," I said seriously, "this is all rubbish, you know. You mustn't be so silly as to get such ideas into your head. We've lived through some queer things and I hope that we may go on doing so."

"No, sir," answered Job, in a tone of conviction that jarred on me unpleasantly, "it isn't rubbish. I'm a doomed man, and I feel it, and a wonderful uncomfortable feeling it is, sir, for one can't help wondering how it's going to come about. If you are eating your dinner you think of poison, and it goes against your stomach, and if you are walking along these dark rabbit-burrows you think of knives, and Lord, don't you just shiver about the back! I ain't particular, sir, provided it's sharp, like that poor girl, who, now that she's gone, I am sorry to have spoke hard on, though I don't approve of her morals in getting married, which I consider too quick to be decent. Still, sir," and poor Job turned a shade paler as he said it, "I do hope it won't be that hot-pot game."

"Nonsense," I broke in angrily, "nonsense!"

"Very well, sir," said Job, "it isn't my place to differ from you, sir, but if you happen to be going anywhere, sir, I should be obliged if you could manage to take me with you, seeing that I shall be glad to have a friendly face to look at when the time comes, just to help one through, as it were. And now, sir, I'll be getting the breakfast," and he went leaving me in a very uncomfortable state of mind.

I was deeply attached to old Job, who was one of the best and honestest men I ever had to do with in any class of life, really more of a friend than a servant, and the mere idea of anything happening to him brought a lump in to my throat. Beneath all his ludicrous talk I could see that he himself was quite convinced that something was going to happen, and though in most cases these convictions turn out to be utter moonshine —and this particular one especially was to be amply accounted for by the gloomy and unaccustomed surroundings in which its victim was placed—still it did more or less carry a chill to my heart, as any dread that is obviously a genuine object of belief is apt to do, however absurd that belief may be.

Presently the breakfast arrived, and with it Leo, who had been taking a walk outside the cave—to clear his mind, he said; and very glad I was to see both, for they gave me a respite from my gloomy thoughts. After breakfast we went for another walk, and watched some of the Amahaggers sowing a plot of ground with the grain from which they made their beer. This they did in scriptural fashion—a man with a bag made of goat's hide fastened round his waist striding up and down the plot and scattering seed as he went. It was a positive relief to see one of these dreadful people do anything so homely and pleasant as sow a field, perhaps because it seemed to link them with the rest of humanity.

As we were returning Billali met us, and informed us that it was *She's* pleasure that we should wait upon her. Accordingly we entered her presence, not without trepidation, for Ayesha was certainly an exception to the accepted rule: familiarity with her might and did breed passion and wonder and horror, but it certainly did *not* breed contempt.

As usual we were shown in by the mutes, and after they had retired Ayesha unveiled, and once more bade Leo embrace her, which, his heart-searchings of the previous night notwithstanding, he did with more alacrity and fervour than in strictness courtesy required.

She laid her white hand upon his head, and looked him fondly in the eyes. "Dost thou wonder, my Kallikrates," she said, "when thou shalt call me all thine own, and when we shall of a truth be for one another and to one another? I will tell thee. First must thou be even as I am, not immortal indeed, for that I am not, but so cased and hardened against the attacks of Time that his arrows shall glance from the armour of thy vigorous life as the sunbeams glance from water. As yet I may not mate with thee, for thou and I are different, and the very brightness of my being would burn thee up, and perchance destroy thee. Thou couldst not even endure to look upon me for too long a time, lest thine eyes should ache and thy senses swim, therefore"—with a little nod—"shall I presently veil myself again." (This, by the way, she did not do.) "No: listen. Thou shalt not be tried beyond endurance, for this very evening, an hour before the sun goes down, we will start hence, and by tomorrow's dark, if all goes well, and the road is not lost to me, which I pray it may not be, we shall stand in the place of Life, and thou shalt bathe in the fire, and come forth glorified, as no man ever was before thee, and then, Kallikrates, thou mayest call me wife, and I will call thee husband."

Leo muttered something in answer to this astonishing statement, I do not know what, and she laughed a little at his confusion, and went on:

"And thou, too, O Holly; to thee also I will grant this boon, and then of a truth thou shalt be evergreen, and this I will do—well, because thou hast pleased me, Holly, for thou art not altogether a fool, like the most of the sons of men, and because, though thou hast a school of philosophy as full of nonsense as those of the old days, yet hast thou not forgotten how to turn a pretty phrase about a lady's eyes."

"Hulloa, uncle!" whispered Leo, with a return of his former cheerfulness, "have you been paying compliments? I should never have thought it of you!"

"I thank thee, Ayesha," I replied, with as much dignity as I could command; "but if there be such a place as thou dost describe, and if in this strange place there may be found a fiery virtue that can hold off Death when he comes to pluck us by the hand, yet I seek none of it. For me, O Ayesha, the world has not proved so soft a nest that I would lie in it for ever. A stony-hearted mother is our earth, and stones are the bread she gives her children for their daily food. Stones to eat and bitter water for their thirst, and stripes for tender nurture. Who would endure this for many lives? Who would so load up his back with memories of lost hours and loves, and of his neighbours' sorrows which he cannot lessen, and with wisdom that brings not consolation? It is hard to die, because our delicate flesh shrinks back from the worm it will not feel, and from that unknown which the winding-sheet curtains from our view. But harder still, to my thought, would it be to live on, green in the leaf and fair, but dead and rotten at the core, and to feel that other secret worm of memory gnawing ever at the heart."

"Bethink thee, Holly," she said; "yet do long life and strength and beauty beyond measure give power and all things that are dear to man."

"And what, O Queen," I answered, "are those things that are dear to man? Are they not bubbles? Is not ambition but an endless ladder by which no height is ever climbed till the last unreachable rung is mounted? For height leads on to height, and there is no resting-place upon them, and rung doth grow upon rung, and there is no limit to the number. Does not wealth satiate and become nauseous, and no longer serve to satisfy or pleasure, or to buy an hour's ease of mind? And is there any end to wisdom that we may hope to win it? Rather, the more we learn, shall we not thereby be able only to better compass out our ignorance? Did we live ten thousand years could we hope to solve the secrets of the suns, and of the space beyond the suns, and of the Hand that hung them in the heavens? Would not our wisdom be but as a gnawing hunger calling our consciousness day by day to a knowledge of the empty cravings of our souls? Would it not be but as a light in one of these great caverns, that, though bright it burn, and brighter yet, doth but the more serve to show the depths of the gloom around it? And what good thing is there beyond that we may gain by lengths of days?"

"Nay, my Holly, there is love—love, which makes all things beautiful, yes, and breathes divinity into the very dust we tread. With love shall life roll on gloriously from year to year, like the voice of some great music that has power to hold the hearer's heart poised on eagles' wings above the sordid shame and folly of the earth."

"It may be so," I answered; "but if the loved one prove a broken reed to pierce us, or if the love be loved in vain—what then? Shall a man grave his sorrows upon a stone when he has but need to write them on the water? Nay, O *She,* I will live my day and grow old with my generation, and die my appointed death, and be forgotten. For I do hope for an immortality to which the little span that perchance thou canst confer will be but as a finger's length laid against the measure of the great world;

and, mark this! the immortality to which I look, and which my faith dost promise to me, shall be free from the bonds that here must tie my spirit down. For, while the flesh endures, sorrow and evil and the scorpion whips of sin must endure also; but when the flesh has fallen from us, then shall the spirit shine forth clad in the brightness of eternal good, and for its common air shall breathe so rare an ether of most noble thoughts that the highest aspiration of our manhood, or the purest incense of a maiden's prayer, would prove too gross to float therein."

"Thou lookest high," answered Ayesha, with a little laugh, "and speakest clearly as a trumpet, and with no uncertain sound. And yet methinks that but now thou didst talk of 'that Unknown' from which the winding-sheet doth curtain us. Well, perchance thou seest with the eye of Faith, gazing on this brightness, that is to be, through the painted glass of thy imagination! Strange are the pictures of the future that mankind can thus draw with this brush of faith and these many-coloured pigments of the imagination! Strange, too, that no one of them tallies with another! I could tell thee—but there, to what end—why rob a fool of his bauble? Let it pass, and I pray, O Holly, that when thou shalt feel old age creeping slowly over thee, and the dull edge of eld working havoc in thy brain, thou mayst not bitterly regret that thou didst cast away the imperial boon I would have given thee. But so it has always been; man can never be content with that which his hand may pluck. If a lamp shines for him to light him through the darkness, straightway he casts it down because it is no star. Happiness dances ever a pace before his feet, like the marsh-fire in the swamps, and he must catch the fire, and he must win the star! Beauty is naught to him, because there are lips more honey-sweet; and wealth is poverty, because others can weigh him down with heavier shekels; and fame is emptiness, because there have been greater men than he. Thyself thou saidst it, and I turn thy word against thee. Well, thou dreamest that thou shalt clasp the star. I believe it not, and I name thee fool, my Holly, to throw away the lamp."

I made no answer, for, especially before Leo, I could not tell her that since I had seen her face I knew it must always be before my eyes, and that I had no wish to prolong an existence which must be ever haunted and tortured by her memory, and by the last bitterness of unsatisfied love. But so it was, and so, alas, is it to this hour!

"And now," went on *She,* changing her tone and the subject together, "tell me, my Kallikrates, for as yet I know it not, how came ye to seek me here? Yesternight thou didst say that

Kallikrates—him whom thou sawest dead—was thine ancestor. How was it? Tell me—thou dost not speak overmuch!"

Thus adjured, Leo told her the wonderful story of the casket and of the potsherd that, written on by his ancestress, the Egyptian Amenartas, had been the means of guiding us to her. Ayesha listened intently, and, when he had finished, spoke to me.

"Did I not tell thee once, while we talked of good and evil, O Holly—it was when my beloved lay so ill—that out of good came evil, and out of evil good—that they who sowed knew not what the crop should be, nor he who struck where the blow should fall? See, now: this Egyptian Amenartas, this royal child of the Nile, who hated me, and whom even now I hate, for in a measure she prevailed against me—see, I say, she herself hath been the guide to lead her lover to mine arms! For her sake I slew him, and now, behold, through her he has come back to me! She would have done me evil, and sowed her seeds that I might reap tares, and behold she hath given me more than all the world can give, and there is a strange square for thee to fit into thy circle of good and evil, O Holly!

"And so," she went on after a pause—"and so she bade her son destroy me if he might, because I slew his father. And thou, my Kallikrates, art the father, and in a sense thou art likewise the son; and wouldst thou avenge thy wrong, and the wrong of that far-off mother of thine, upon me, O Kallikrates? See," and she slid to her knees, and opened the white robe upon her ivory bosom—"see, here beats my heart, and there by thy side is a knife, heavy and long, and sharp, the very knife to slay an erring woman with. Take it now, and be avenged. Strike, and strike home!—so shalt thou be satisfied, Kallikrates, and go through life a happy man, because thou hast paid back the wrong, and obeyed the mandate of the past."

He looked at her; then he stretched out his hand and lifted her to her feet.

"Rise, Ayesha," he said sadly; "thou knowest well that I cannot harm thee, no, not even for the sake of her whom thou slewest but last night. I am in thy power, and a very slave to thee. How can I kill thee?—sooner should I slay myself."

"Almost dost thou begin to love me, Kallikrates," she answered, smiling. "And now tell me of thy country—'tis a great people, is it not? with an empire like that of Rome! Surely thou wilt return thither, and it is well, for I would not that thou shouldst dwell in these caves of Kôr. Nay, when once thou art even as I am we will go hence—fear not but that I shall find a path—and then will we journey to this England of thine, and live as it becometh us to live. Two thousand years have I waited for the day when I should see the last of these hateful caves and this gloomy-visaged folk, and now it is at hand, and my heart bounds up to meet it like a child's towards its holiday. For thou shalt rule this England——"

"But we have a queen already," interrupted Leo, hastily.

"It is naught, it is naught," said Ayesha; "she can be overthrown."

At this we both broke out into exclamations of dismay, and explained that we should as soon think of overthrowing ourselves.

"But here is a strange thing," said Ayesha, in astonishment—"a queen whom her people love! Surely the world must have changed since I dwelt in Kôr."

Again we explained that it was the character of monarchs that had changed, and that the sovereign under whom we lived was venerated and beloved by all right-thinking men in her vast realms. Also, we told her that real power in our country rested in the hands of the people; that, in fact, we were ruled by the votes of the lower and least educated classes of the community.

"Ah," she said, "a democracy—then surely there is a tyrant, for I have long since seen that democracies, having no clear will of their own, in the end set up a tyrant, and worship him."

"Yes," I said, "we have our tyrants."

"Well," she answered resignedly, "we can at any rate destroy these tyrants, and Kallikrates shall rule the land."

I instantly informed Ayesha that in England 'blasting' was not an amusement that could be indulged in with impunity, and that any such attempt would meet with the consideration of the law, and probably end upon a scaffold.

"The law!' she laughed with scorn—"the law! Canst thou not understand, O Holly, that I am above the law, and so shall Kallikrates be also? All human law will be to us as the north wind to a mountain. Does the wind bend the mountain, or the mountain the wind?

"And now leave me, I pray thee, and thou, too, my own Kallikrates, for I would make me ready against our journey, and so must ye both, and your servant also. But bring no great store of garments with thee, for I trust that we shall be but three days gone. Then must we return hither, and I will make a plan whereby we can bid farewell for ever to these sepulchres of Kôr. Yea, surely thou mayst kiss my hand!"

So I went, I, for one, meditating deeply on the awful nature of the problem that now opened out before us. Evidently the terrible *She* had determined to go to England, and it made me shudder to think what would be the result of her arrival there. What her powers were I knew, and I could not doubt but that she would exercise them to the full. It might be possible to control her for a while, but her proud, ambitious spirit would be certain to break loose and to avenge itself for the long centuries of its solitude. If necessary, and if the unaided power of her beauty did not prove sufficient for her purpose, she would blast her way to any end she set before her, and, as she could not die, and for aught I knew could not even be killed,[1] what was there to stay her? In the end, I had little doubt, she would assume absolute rule over the British dominions, and probably over the whole earth, and, though I was sure that she would speedily make ours the most glorious and prosperous empire that the world has ever seen, it must be at the cost of a terrible sacrifice of life.

The story sounded like a dream or some extraordinary invention of a speculative brain, and yet it was a fact—a wonderful fact—of which the universe would soon be called on to take notice. What was the meaning of it all? After much thinking I could only conclude that this marvellous creature, whose passion had kept her for so many centuries chained as it were, and comparatively harmless, was now about to be used by Providence as a means to change the order of the world, and possibly, by the building up of a power that could no more be rebelled against or questioned than the decrees of Fate, to change it materially for the better.

CHAPTER XXIII

THE TEMPLE OF TRUTH

Our preparations did not take us very long. We packed a change of clothing apiece and some spare boots into my handbag; also we took our revolvers and an Express rifle each, together with a good supply of ammunition, a precaution to which, under Providence, we subsequently owed our lives over and over again. The rest of our gear, together with our heavy rifles, we left behind us.

A few minutes before the appointed time we were summoned to Ayesha's 'boudoir,' and found her also ready, the dark cloak thrown over her corpselike wrappings.

[1] I regret to say that I was never able to ascertain if *She* was invulnerable against the accidents of life. Presumably this was so, else some misadventure would have been sure to put an end to her in the course of so many centuries. True, she suggested to Leo that he should kill her, but very probably this was only an experiment to try his temper and mental attitude towards herself. Ayesha never gave way to impulse without some valid object.—L. H. H.

"Are ye prepared for the great venture?" she said.

"We are," I answered, "though for my part, Ayesha, I have no faith in it."

"Of a truth, my Holly," she said, "thou art like those old Jews —of whom the memory vexes me so sorely—unbelieving, and slow to accept that which thou hast not known. But thou shalt see; for unless my mirror yonder lies," and she pointed to the font of crystal water, "the path is yet open as it was of old time. And now let us away, to begin the new life which shall end—who knoweth where?"

"Ah," I echoed, "who knows where?" and we passed down into the great central cave, and out into the light of day. At the mouth of the cave we found a single litter waiting, with six bearers, all of them mutes; and with these I was relieved to see our old friend Billali, for whom I had conceived a sort of affection. It appeared that, for reasons not necessary to explain at length, Ayesha had thought it best that, with the exception of herself, we should proceed on foot. This we were nothing loth to do after our long confinement in the caves, which however suitable they might be to serve as the last home of the dead, were depressing habitations for breathing mortals like ourselves. Either by accident or by the orders of *She,* the space in front of the cave where we had witnessed that awful dance was empty of spectators. Not a man could be seen, and consequently I do not believe that our departure was known to anyone, except, perhaps, to the mutes in attendance upon *She,* who were necessarily in the habit of keeping what they saw to themselves.

In a few minutes' time we were stepping out sharply across the great cultivated plain or lake bed, framed like a vast emerald in its setting of frowning cliff. Here we found fresh opportunity to wonder at the extraordinary nature of the site chosen by these old people of Kôr for their capital, and at the marvellous amount of labour, ingenuity, and engineering skill that must have been brought into requisition by the founders of the city to drain so huge a sheet of water, and to keep it free from subsequent accumulations. So far as my experience goes, it is, indeed, an unequalled instance of what man can do in the face of nature, for in my opinion such achievements as the Suez Canal, or even the Mont Cenis Tunnel, do not approach this ancient undertaking in magnitude and grandeur of conception.

When we had been walking for about half an hour, enjoying ourselves exceedingly in the delightful cool which at this time of the day always appeared to descend upon the great plain of Kôr, and that in some degree atoned for the want of any land or sea

breeze—for all wind was kept off by the rocky mountain wall—
we began to distinguish clearly the buildings which, as Billali
had informed us, were the ruins of the great city.

Even from that distance we could see how wonderful those
ruins were, a fact which became more evident at every step. The
town was not very large if compared to Babylon or Thebes, or
other cities of remote antiquity; perhaps its outer ditch contained
some twelve square miles of ground or a little more. Nor had the
walls, so far as we could judge when we reached them, been very
high, probably not more than forty feet, which was about their
present height where, through the sinking of the ground, or some
such cause, they had not fallen into ruin. The reason of this, no
doubt, was that the people of Kôr, being protected from outside
attack by far more tremendous ramparts than any that the hand
of man could rear, only required walls for show and to guard
against civil discord. But, on the other hand, they were as broad
as they were high, built entirely of dressed stone, hewn, probably,
from the vast caves, and surrounded by a great moat some sixty
feet in width, many reaches of which were still filled with water.
About ten minutes before the sun sank finally we reached this
moat, and passed down and through it, clambering across what
evidently were the piled-up fragments of a great bridge in order
to do so, and then with some little difficulty over the slope of the
wall to its summit. I wish that it lay within the power of my
pen to give an idea of the grandeur of the sight which met our
view. There, all bathed in the red glow of the sinking sun, were
miles upon miles of ruins—columns, temples, shrines and the
palaces of kings, varied with patches of green bush. Of course
the roofs of these buildings had long since fallen into decay and
vanished, but owing to the extreme massiveness of the masonry,
and to the hardness and durability of the rock employed, most
of the party walls and great columns still remained standing.[1]

Straight before us stretched away what evidently had been the
main thoroughfare of the city, for it was very wide and regular—
wider than the Thames Embankment. Being, as we afterwards
discovered, paved, or rather built throughout of blocks of dressed
stone, such as were employed in the walls, even now it was but

[1]In connection with the extraordinary state of preservation of these ruins
after so great a lapse of time—at least six thousand years—it must be
remembered that Kôr was not burnt or destroyed by an enemy or an
earthquake, but deserted, because of the ravages of a terrible plague. Consequently the houses were left unharmed; also the climate of the plain is
remarkably fine and dry, with very little rain or wind. As a result these
unique relics have only to contend against the unaided action of time, that
works but slowly upon such massive blocks of masonry.—L. H. H.

little overgrown with grass and shrubs, that could find no depth of soil to live in. What had been the parks and gardens, on the contrary, had become dense jungle. Indeed, it was easy even from a distance to trace the course of the various roads by the burnt-up appearance of the scanty herbage that grew upon them. On either side of this great thoroughfare were vast blocks of ruins, each block separated from its neighbour by a space of what had once, I suppose, been garden-ground, but was now thick and tangled bush. They were all built of the same coloured stone, and most of them had pillars, which was as much as we could see in the fading light as we passed swiftly up the main road, that, I believe I am right in saying, no human foot had pressed for thousands of years.[1]

Presently we came to an enormous pile, covering at least eight acres of ground, that we rightly took to be a temple, which was arranged in a series of courts, each one of them enclosing another of smaller size, on the principle of a Chinese nest of boxes, these courts being separated by rows of huge columns. While I think of it, I may as well describe the remarkable shape of these columns, which resembled none that I have ever seen or heard of, being fashioned to a narrow central waist, and swelling above and below it. At first we thought that this shape was meant roughly to symbolise or suggest the female form, after the common fashion of the ancient religious architects of many creeds. On the following day, however, as we climbed the slopes of the mountain, we discovered a large quantity of stately palms, whereof the trunks grew thus, and I have now no doubt but that the first designer of those columns drew his inspiration from the graceful bends of those very palms, or rather of their ancestors, that some eight or ten thousand years ago beautified the slopes of the mountain which formed the shores of the ancient volcanic lake.

At the *facade* of this huge temple, which, I should imagine, is almost as large as that of El-Karnac, at Thebes (some of the largest columns which I measured being between eighteen to twenty feet in diameter at the base, by about seventy feet in height) our little procession was halted, and Ayesha descended from her litter.

[1]Billali told me that the Amahagger believe that the site of the city is haunted, and could not be persuaded to enter it upon any consideration. Indeed, I could see that he himself did not at all like defying the custom, and was only consoled because he was under the direct protection of *She*. It struck Leo and myself as very curious that a people which has no objection to living amongst the dead, with whom their familiarity has perhaps bred contempt, and even to using their bodies as fuel, should be terrified at approaching the habitations that these very departed had occupied when alive. However, this is only a savage inconsistency.—L. H. H.

"There was a chamber here, Kallikrates," she said to Leo, who had gone to help her to alight, "where one might sleep. Two thousand years ago thou and I and that Egyptian asp rested therein, but since then I have not set foot here, and perchance it has fallen." Then, followed by the rest of us, she passed up a vast flight of broken steps into the outer court, and looked round into the gloom. Presently she seemed to recollect, and, walking a few paces along the wall to the left, she halted.

"It is here as of old," Ayesha said, beckoning to the two mutes, who were loaded with provisions and our few packages, to advance. One of them came forward, and producing a lamp, lit it from his brazier, for the Amahagger when on a journey always carried with them a little lighted brazier, from which to provide fire. The tinder of this brazier was made of broken fragments of mummy carefully dampened, and, if the admixture of moisture is properly managed, this unholy compound will smoulder for many hours.[1] So soon as the lamp was lit we entered the place before which Ayesha had halted. It proved to be a cell hollowed in the thickness of the wall, and, from the fact of its containing a massive stone table, I should imagine that it had served as a living-room, perhaps for one of the doorkeepers of the great temple.

Here we camped, and after cleaning the place out and making it as comfortable as circumstances and the darkness would permit, we ate some cold meat—at least Leo, Job, and I did, for Ayesha, as I think I have said elsewhere, never touched anything except cakes of flour, fruit and water. While we were still eating, the moon, which was at her full, rose above the mountain wall, and began to flood the place with silver rays.

"Know ye why I have brought you here to-night, my Holly?" said Ayesha, leaning her head upon her hand and watching the great orb as she rose, a very queen of heaven, above the solemn pillars of the temple. "I brought you—nay, it is strange, but knowest thou, Kallikrates, that thou liest at this moment upon that same spot where thy dead body lay when I bore thee back to those caves of Kôr so many years ago? The scene springs to my mind again. I can see it, and it is horrible to my sight!" and she shuddered.

Here Leo jumped up hastily and changed his seat. However the reminiscence might affect Ayesha, clearly it had few charms

---

[1] After all we are not much in advance of the Amahagger in these matters. 'Mummy,' *i.e.*, pounded ancient Egyptian, is, I believe, a pigment much used by artists, and especially by those of them who direct their talents to the reproduction of the works of the old masters.—EDITOR.

for him.

"*I* brought you," she went on presently, "that ye might look upon the most wonderful sight that ever the eye of man beheld—the full moon shining over ruined Kôr. When ye have done your eating—I would that I could teach thee to eat naught but fruit, Kallikrates, but that will come after thou hast washed in the fire; once I, too, ate flesh like a brute beast—when ye have done, I say, we will go out, and I will show you this great temple and the god whom men once worshipped there."

Of course we rose at once, and started. And here again my pen fails me. To give a string of measurements and details of the various courts of the temple would only be wearisome, supposing that I had them; yet I know not how I am to describe what we saw, magnificent as it was even in its ruin, almost beyond the power of realisation. Court upon dim court, row upon row of mighty pillars—some of them, especially at the gateways, sculptured from base to capital—space upon space of empty chambers that spoke more eloquently to the imagination than any crowded streets. And over all a dead silence of the dead, a sense of utter loneliness, and the brooding spirit of the Past! How beautiful it was, and yet how drear! We did not dare to speak aloud. Ayesha herself was awed in the presence of an antiquity compared to which even her length of days was but a little thing; we only whispered, and our whispers seemed to run from column to column, till they were lost in the quiet air. Bright fell the moonlight on pillar and court and shattered wall, hiding all their rents and imperfections in its silver garment, and clothing their hoar majesty with the peculiar glory of the night. It was a wonderful sight to see the full moon looking down on this ruined fane of Kôr. It was a wonderful thing to think for how many thousands of years the dead orb above and the dead city below had gazed thus upon each other, and in the utter solitude of space poured forth each to each the tale of their lost life and long-departed glory. The white light fell, and minute by minute the slow shadows crept across the grass-grown courts like the spirits of old priests haunting the habitations of their worship—the white light fell, and the long shadows grew, till the beauty and grandeur of the scene and the untamed majesty of its present death seemed to sink into our very souls, and to speak more loudly than the shouts of armies concerning the pomp and splendour that the grave had swallowed, and even memory had forgotten.

"Come," said Ayesha, after we had gazed and gazed, I know not for how long, "and I will show you the stony flower of Loveliness and Wonder's very crown, if yet it stands to mock time with its beauty and fill the heart of man with longing for that which is behind the veil," and, without waiting for an answer, she led us through two more pillared courts into the inner shrine of the ancient fane.

And there, in the midst of the inmost court, that might have been some fifty yards square, or a little more, we stood face to face with what is perhaps the grandest allegorical work of Art that the genius of her children has ever given to the world. For in the exact centre of the court, placed upon a thick square slab of rock, was a huge ball of dark-hued stone, about twenty feet in diameter, and standing on the ball was a colossal winged figure of a beauty so entrancing and divine that when first I gazed upon it, illuminated and shadowed as it was by the soft light of the moon, my breath stood still, and for an instant my heart ceased its beating.

This statue was hewn from marble so pure and white that even now, after all those ages, it shone as the moonbeams danced upon it; and its height, I should say, was over twenty feet. It represented the winged figure of a woman of such marvellous loveliness and delicacy of form that the size seemed rather to add to than to detract from its so human and yet more spiritual beauty. She stood bending forward and poising herself upon her half-spread wings as though to preserve her balance as she leant. Her arms were outstretched like those of some woman about to embrace one she dearly loved, while her whole attitude gave an impression of the tenderest beseeching. Her perfect and most gracious form was naked, save—and here is the extraordinary thing—the face which was thinly veiled, so that we could only distinguish the outline of her features. A gauzy veil was thrown round and about the head, and of its two ends one fell down across her left breast, which swelled beneath it, and one, now broken, streamed out upon the air behind her.

"Who is she?" I asked, so soon as I could take my eyes off the statue.

"Canst thou not guess, O Holly?" answered Ayesha. "Where, then, is thy imagination? It is Truth standing on the World, and calling to its children to unveil her face. See what is written upon the pedestal. Without doubt it is taken from the book of the Scriptures of these men of Kôr," and she led the way to the foot of the statue, where an inscription of the usual Chinese-looking hieroglyphics was so deeply graven as to be still quite legible, at least to Ayesha. According to her translation it ran thus:—

"Is there no man that will draw my veil and look upon my face, for it is very fair? Unto him who draws my veil shall I be,

and I will give him peace, and sweet children of knowledge and good works."

And a voice cried, "Though all those who seek after thee desire thee: Behold! Virgin art thou, and Virgin thou shalt go till Time be done. There is no man born of woman who may draw thy veil and live, nor shall be. By Death only can thy veil be drawn, O Truth!"

And Truth stretched out her arms and wept, because those who wooed her might not win her, nor look upon her face to face.

"Thou seest," said Ayesha, when she had finished translating, "Truth was the goddess of these people of old Kôr, and to her they built their shrines, and her they sought; knowing that they should never find, still they sought."

"And so," I added sadly, "do men seek to this very hour, but they find not; and, as this Scripture saith, nor shall they; for in Death only is Truth found."

Then, with one more look at this veiled and spiritualised loveliness—which was so perfect and so pure that almost we might fancy that the light of a living spirit shone through the marble prison to lead men on to high and ethereal thoughts—this poet's dream of beauty frozen into stone, which I never shall forget while I live—we turned and retraced our steps through the vast moonlit courts. I did not see the statue again, which I regret the more, because about the great ball of stone representing the World whereon the figure stood lines were drawn that, had there been light enough, probably we should have discovered to be a map of the Universe as it was known to the people of Kôr. It is at any rate suggestive of some scientific knowledge that these long-dead worshippers of Truth had recognised the fact that the globe is round.

CHAPTER XXIV

WALKING THE PLANK

Next day the mutes woke us before the dawn. By the time that we had rubbed the sleep out of our eyes, and refreshed ourselves by washing at a spring which still welled up into the remains of a marble basin in the centre of the north quadrangle of the vast outer court, we found *She* standing near the litter ready to start, while old Billali and the two bearer-mutes were busy collecting the baggage. As usual, Ayesha was veiled like the marble Truth, and it struck me then that she might have taken the idea of covering up her beauty from that statue. I noticed, how-

ever, that she seemed very depressed, and had none of that
proud and buoyant bearing which would have betrayed her
among a thousand women of the same stature, even if they had
been veiled like herself. She looked up as we came—for her
head was bowed—and greeted us. Leo asked her how she had
slept.

"Ill, my Kallikrates," she answered, "ill! This night strange
and hideous dreams have come creeping through my brain, and
I know not what they may portend. Almost do I feel as though
some evil overshadowed me; and yet, how can evil touch me?
I wonder," she went on with a sudden outbreak of womanly
tenderness, "I wonder, should aught happen to me, so that I
slept awhile and left thee waking, if thou wouldst think gently
of me? I wonder, my Kallikrates, if thou wouldst tarry till *I*
came again, as for so many centuries I have tarried for *thy*
coming?"

Then, without waiting for an answer, she went on: "Let
us be setting forth, for we have far to go, and before another
day is born in yonder blue we should stand in the place of Life."

In five minutes we were once more on our way through the
ruined city, which loomed on either side through the grey dawning in a fashion at once grand and oppressive. Just as the first
ray of the rising sun shot like a golden arrow athwart this storied
desolation we gained the further gateway of the outer wall.
Here, having given one more glance at the hoar and pillared
majesty through which we had journeyed, and—with the exception of Job, for whom ruins had no charms—breathed a sigh
of regret that we lacked time to explore it, we passed through
the encircling moat and on to the plain beyond.

As the sun rose so did Ayesha's spirits, till at length they
had regained their normal level, and she laughingly attributed
her sadness to the associations of the spot where she had slept.

"These barbarians swear that Kôr is haunted," she said,
"and of a truth I believe their saying, for never did I know so
ill a night save once. I remember it now. It was on that very
spot, when thou didst lie dead at my feet, Kallikrates. Never
will I visit it again; it is a place of evil omen."

After a very brief halt for breakfast we pressed on with such
good will that by two o'clock in the day we were at the foot
of the vast wall of rock forming the lip of the volcano, which
at this point towered up precipitously above us for fifteen hundred or two thousand feet. Here we halted, certainly not to my
astonishment, for I did not see how it was possible that we
should advance any farther.

"Now," said Ayesha, as she descended from her litter "our labours but commence, for here we part with these men, and henceforward must we bear ourselves." Then she added, addressing Billali, "do thou and these slaves remain here, and abide our return. By to-morrow at the miday we shall be with thee—if not, wait."

Billali bowed humbly, and said that her august bidding should be obeyed if they stopped there till they grew old.

"And this man, O Holly," said *She,* pointing to Job; "it is best that he should tarry also, for his heart be not high and his courage great, perchance some evil might overtake him. Also, the secrets of the place whither we go are not fit for common eyes."

I translated this to Job, who instantly and earnestly entreated me, almost with tears, not to leave him behind. He said he was sure that he could see nothing worse than he had already seen, and that he was terrified to death at the idea of being left alone with those 'dumb folk,' who, he thought, would probably take the opportunity to 'hotpot' him.

I translated what he said to Ayesha, who shrugged her shoulders, and answered, "Well, let him come, it is naught to me; on his own head be it. He will serve to bear the lamp and this," and she pointed to a narrow board, some sixteen feet in length, which had been bound above the long bearing-pole of her hammock, I had thought to give the curtains a wider spread, but, as it now appeared, for some unknown purpose connected with our extraordinary undertaking.

Accordingly the plank, which, though tough, was very light, was given to Job to carry, and also one of the lamps. I slung the other on to my back, together with a spare jar of oil, while Leo loaded himself with the provisions and some water in a kid's skin. When this was done *She* bade Billali and the six bearer-mutes to retreat behind a grove of flowering magnolias about a hundred yards away, and there to remain under pain of death till we had vanished. They bowed humbly, and went. As he departed, old Billali gave me a friendly shake of the hand, and whispered that he had rather that it were I than he who was going on this wonderful expedition with '*She-who-must be-obeyed,*' a view with which I felt inclined to agree. In another minute they were gone; then, having briefly asked us if we were ready, Ayesha turned and gazed at the towering cliff.

"Great heavens, Leo," I said, "surely we are not going to climb that precipice!"

Leo, who was in a state of half-fascinated, half-expectant mystification, shrugged his shoulders, and at that moment

Ayesha with a sudden spring began to scale the cliff, whither of course we must follow her. It was almost marvellous to see the ease and grace with which she sprang from rock to rock, and swung herself along the ledges. The ascent, however, was not so difficult as it seemed, although we passed one or two nasty places where it was unpleasant to look back; for here the rock still sloped, and was not absolutely precipitous, as it became above.

In this way, with no great toil—for the only troublesome thing to manage was Job's board—we mounted to the height of some fifty feet beyond our last standing-place, and in so doing drew sixty or seventy paces to the left of our starting-point, for we ascended as crabs walk, sideways. Presently we reached a ledge, narrow enough at first, but which widened as we followed it, and sloped inwards, moreover, like the petal of a flower, so that we sank gradually into a kind of rut or fold of rock that grew deeper and deeper, till at last it resembled a Devonshire lane in a stone, and hid us perfectly from the gaze of persons on the slope below, had anybody been there to gaze. This lane, which appeared to be a natural formation, continued for some thirty or forty yards, then suddenly ended in a cave, also natural, running at right angles to it. That it was not hollowed by the labour of man I am sure, because of its irregular, contorted shape and course, which gave it the appearance of having been blasted in the thickness of the mountain by some frightful eruption of gas following the line of the least resistance. All the caverns hollowed by the ancients of Kôr, on the other hand, were cut out with a symmetrical and perfect regularity.

At the mouth of this cave Ayesha halted, and bade us light the two lamps, which I did, giving one to her and keeping the other myself. Then, taking the lead, she advanced down the cavern, picking her way with great care, as indeed it was necessary to do, for the floor was most irregular—strewn with boulders like the bed of a stream, and in some places pitted with deep holes, in which it would have been easy to break a limb.

This cavern we pursued for twenty minutes or more. It was about a quarter of a mile long, so far as I could form a judgment, which, owing to its numerous twists and turns, was not an easy task.

At last, however, we halted at its farther end, and whilst I was still trying to accustom my eyes to the twilight without, a great gust of air came tearing down the cave, and extinguished both the lamps.

Ayesha called to us, and we crept up to her, for she was a little in front, to be rewarded with a view that was positively appalling in its gloom and grandeur. Before us was a mighty chasm in the black rock, jagged, torn, and splintered through it in a far past age by some awful convulsion of Nature, as though it had been cleft by stroke upon stroke of the lightning. This chasm, which was bounded by precipices, although at the moment we could not see that on the farther side, may have measured any width across, but from its darkness I do not think it can have been very broad. It was impossible to make out much of its outline, or how far it ran, for the simple reason that the point where we were standing was so far from the upper surface of the cliff, at least fifteen hundred or two thousand feet, that only a very dim light struggled down to us from above. The mouth of the cavern that we had been following gave on to a most curious and tremendous spur of rock, which jutted out through mid air into the gulf before us for a distance of some fifty yards, coming to a sharp point at its termination, and in shape resembling nothing that I can think of so much as the spur upon the leg of a cock. This huge spur was attached only to the parent precipice at its base, which was, of course, enormous, just as the cock's spur is attached to its leg. Otherwise it was utterly unsupported.

"Here must we pass," said Ayesha. "Be careful lest giddiness overcome you, or the wind sweep you into the gulf beneath, for of a truth it has no bottom;" and, without giving us further time to grow frightened, she began to walk along the spur, leaving us to follow her as best we might. I was next to her, then came Job, painfully dragging his plank, while Leo brought up the rear. It was a wonderful sight to see this intrepid woman gliding fearlessly along that dreadful place. For my part, when I had gone but a very few yards, what between the pressure of the air and the awful sense of the consequences that a slip would entail, I found it necessary to drop on to my hands and knees and crawl, and so did the others.

But Ayesha never condescended to this humble expedient. On she went, leaning her body against the gusts of wind, and not seeming to lose either her head or her balance.

In a few minutes we had crossed some twenty paces of this awful bridge, which grew narrower at every step, when of a sudden a great gust tore along the gorge. I saw Ayesha lean herself against it, but the strong draught forced itself beneath her dark cloak, wrenching it from her and away it went down the

wind flapping like a wounded bird. It was dreadful to see it
go, till it was lost in the blackness.

I clung to the saddle of the rock, and looked about me, while,
like a living thing, the great spur vibrated with a humming sound
beneath us. The sight was truly awesome. There we were poised
in the gloom between earth and heaven. Beneath us stretched
hundreds upon hundreds of feet of emptiness that gradually grew
darker, till at last it was absolutely black, and at what depth
it ended is more than I can guess. Above were measureless
spaces of giddy air, and far, far away a line of blue sky. And
down this vast gulf in which we were pinnacled the great draught
dashed and roared, driving clouds and misty wreaths of vapour
before it, till we were nearly blinded, and utterly confused.

Indeed the position was so tremendous and so absolutely unearthly, that I believe it actually lulled our sense of terror; but
to this hour I often see it in my dreams, and at its mere phantasy
wake up dripping with cold sweat.

"On! on!" cried the white form before us, for now that her
cloak had gone *She* was robed in white, and looked more like a
spirit riding down the gale than a woman; "On, or ye will fall
and be dashed to pieces. Fix your eyes upon the ground, and
cling closely to the rock."

We obeyed her, and crept painfully along the quivering path,
against which the wind shrieked and wailed as it shook it, causing it to murmur like some gigantic tuning-fork. On we went, I
do not know for how long, only gazing round now and again
when it was absolutely necessary, until at last we saw that we
had reached the very tip of the spur, a slab of rock, but little
larger than an ordinary table, that throbbed and jumped like
any over-engined steamer. There we lay, clinging to the stone,
and stared round us, while absolutely heedless of the hideous
depth that yawned beneath, Ayesha stood leaning out against
the wind, down which her long hair streamed, and pointed before
her. Then we saw why the narrow plank had been provided,
which Job and I had borne so painfully between us. In front
yawned an empty space, on the other side of which was something, as yet we could not see what, for here—either owing to
the shadow of the opposite cliff, or from some other cause—the
gloom was that of a cloudy night.

"We must wait awhile," called Ayesha; "soon there will be
light."

At the moment I could not imagine what she meant. How
could more light than there was ever come to this dreadful spot?
While I was still wondering, suddenly, like a great sword of

flame, a beam from the setting sun pierced the Stygian gloom, and smote upon the point of rock whereon we lay, illuminating Ayesha's lovely form with an unearthly splendour. I only wish I could describe the wild and marvellous beauty of that sword of fire, laid across the darkness and rushing mist-wreaths of the gulf. How it came there I do not to this moment know, but I presume that there was some cleft or hole in the opposing cliff, through which light flowed when the setting orb was in a direct line with it. All I can say is, the effect was the most wonderful that I ever saw. Right through the heart of the darkness that flaming sword was stabbed, and where it lay the light was surpassingly vivid, so vivid that even at a distance we could see the grain of the rock, while outside of it—yes, within a few inches of its keen edge—was naught but clustering shadows.

And now, by this vast sunbeam, for which *She* had been waiting, and timed our arrival to meet, knowing that at this season for thousands of years it had always struck thus at eve, we saw what was before us. Within eleven or twelve yards of the very tip of the tongue-like rock whereon we stood there arose, presumably from the far bottom of the gulf, a sugarloaf-shaped cone, of which the summit was exactly opposite to us. But had there been a summit only it would not have helped us much, for the nearest point of its circumference was some forty feet from where we were. On the lip of this summit, however, which was circular and hollow, rested a tremendous flat boulder, something like a glacier-stone—perhaps it was one, for all I know to the contrary—and the end of the boulder approached to within twelve feet of us. This huge mass was nothing more nor less than a gigantic rocking-stone, accurately balanced upon the edge of the cone or miniature crater, like a half-crown set on the rim of a wine-glass; for, in the fierce light that played upon it and us, we could see it oscillating in the gusts of wind.

"Quick!" said Ayesha; "the plank—we must cross while the light endures; presently it will be gone."

"Oh, Lord, sir! surely she don't mean us to walk across this here place on that there thing," groaned Job, as in obedience to my directions he thrust the long board towards me.

"That's it, Job," I holloaed in ghastly merriment, though the idea of walking the plank was no pleasanter to me than to him.

I passed the board to Ayesha, who ran it deftly across the gulf so that one end of it rested on the rocking-stone, the other remaining upon the extremity of the trembling spur. Then, placing her foot upon it to prevent it from being blown away, she turned to me.

"Since last I was here, O Holly," she called, "the support of the moving stone hath lessened somewhat, so that I am not sure whether it will bear our weight. Therefore I must cross the first, because no hurt will overtake me," and, without further ado, she trod lightly but firmly across the frail bridge, and in another second had gained the heaving stone.

"It is safe," she called. "See, hold thou the plank! I will stand on the farther side of the rock, so that it may not overbalance with your greater weights. Now come, O Holly, for presently the light will fail us."

I struggled to my knees, and if ever I felt terrified in my life it was then; indeed, I am not ashamed to say that I hesitated and hung back.

"Surely thou art not afraid," cried this strange creature, in a lull of the gale, from where she stood poised like a bird on the highest point of the rocking-stone. "Make way, then, for Kallikrates."

This decided me; it is better to fall down a precipice and die than be laughed at by such a woman! so I clenched my teeth, and in another instant I was on that narrow, bending plank, with bottomless space beneath and around me. I have always hated a great height, but never before did I appreciate the full horrors of which such a position is capable. Oh, the sickening sensation of that yielding board resting on the two moving supports. I grew dizzy, and thought that I must fall; my spine *crept*; it seemed to me that I was falling, and my delight at finding myself stretched upon the stone, which rose and fell beneath me like a boat in a swell, cannot be expressed in words. All I know is that briefly, but earnestly enough, I thanked Providence for preserving me thus far.

Then came Leo's turn, and, though he looked rather white, he ran across like a rope-dancer. Ayesha stretched out her hand to clasp his own, and I heard her say, "Bravely done, my love—bravely done! The old Greek spirit lives in thee yet!"

And now only poor Job remained on the farther side of the gulf. He crept up to the plank, and yelled out, "I can't do it, sir. I shall fall into that beastly place."

"You must," I remember answering with inappropriate facetiousness—"you must, Job, it's as easy as catching flies." I suppose that I must have said this to satisfy my conscience, because, although the expression conveys a wonderful idea of facility, as a matter of fact I know no more difficult operation in the whole world than catching flies—that is, in warm weather, unless, indeed, it is catching mosquitoes.

"I can't, sir—I can't indeed."

"Let the man come, or let him stay and perish there. See, the light is dying! In a moment it will be gone!" said Ayesha.

I looked. She was right. The sun was passing below the level of the hole or cleft in the precipice through which the ray reached us.

"If you stop there, Job, you will die alone," I called; "the light is going."

"Come, be a man, Job," shouted Leo; "it's quite easy."

Thus adjured, with a most awful yell, the miserable Job precipitated himself face downwards on the plank—he did not dare, small blame to him, to try to walk it—and commenced to draw himself across in little jerks, his poor legs hanging down on either side into the nothingness beneath.

His violent jerks at the frail board caused the great stone, which was only balanced on a few inches of rock, to oscillate in a most dreadful manner, and, to make matters worse, when he was halfway across the flying ray of lurid light suddenly went out, just as though a lamp had been extinguished in a curtained room, leaving the whole howling wilderness of air black with darkness.

"Come on, Job, for God's sake!" I shouted in an agony of fear, while the stone, gathering motion with every swing, rocked so violently that it was difficult to cling on to it. It was a truly awful position.

"Lord, have mercy on me!" cried poor Job from the darkness. "Oh, the plank's slipping!" and I heard a violent struggle, and thought that he was gone.

But at that moment his outstretched hand, clasping in agony at the air, met my own, and I tugged—ah! how I did tug, putting out all the strength that it has pleased Providence to give me in such abundance—till to my joy in another minute Job was gasping on the rock beside me. But the plank! I felt it slip, and heard it knock against a projecting knob of rock. Then it was gone.

"Great heavens!" I exclaimed. "How shall we get back?"

"I don't know," answered Leo out of the gloom. " 'Sufficient to the day is the evil thereof.' I am thankful enough to be here."

But Ayesha merely called to me to take her hand and follow her.

CHAPTER XXV

THE SPIRIT OF LIFE

I DID as I was bidden, and in fear and trembling felt myself guided over the edge of the stone. I thrust my legs out, but could touch nothing.

"I am going to fall!" I gasped.

"Fall then, and trust to me," answered Ayesha.

Now, if the position is considered, it will be easily understood that this was a heavier tax upon my confidence than was justified by my knowledge of Ayesha's character. For all I knew she might be in the very act of consigning me to a horrible doom. But in life we must sometimes lay our faith upon strange altars, and so it was now.

"Let thyself fall!" she cried again, and, having no choice, I did.

I felt myself slide a pace or two down the sloping surface of the rock, and then pass into the air, and the thought flashed through my brain that I was lost. But no! In another instant my feet struck against a rocky floor, and I knew that I was standing on something solid, out of reach of the wind, which I could hear singing overhead. As I stood there thanking Heaven for these small mercies, there was a slip and a scuffle, and down came Leo alongside of me.

"Hulloa, old fellow!" he exclaimed, "are you there? This is interesting, is it not?"

Just then, with a terrific howl, Job arrived right on the top of us, knocking us both down. By the time that we had struggled to our feet again Ayesha was standing among us, bidding us light the lamps, which fortunately remained uninjured, and with them the spare jar of oil.

I found my box of wax matches, and they struck as merrily there, in that awful place, as they could have done in a London drawing-room.

In another minute both lamps were alight, and they revealed a curious scene. We were huddled together in a rocky chamber, some ten feet square, and very scared we looked; that is, with the exception of Ayesha, who stood calmly, her arms folded, waiting for the lamps to burn up. This chamber appeared to be partly natural and partly hollowed out of the top of the crater. The roof of the natural part was formed by the swinging stone, and that over the back of the chamber, which sloped downwards, was hewn from the live rock. For the rest, the place was warm and dry—a perfect haven of rest compared to the giddy pinnacle above, and the quivering spur that shot out to meet it in mid air.

"So!" said *She,* "safely have we come, though once I feared that the rocking-stone would fall with you, and hurl you into the bottomless deeps beneath, for I do believe that yonder cleft goes down to the very womb of the world, and the rock whereon the boulder rests has crumbled beneath its swinging weight. But now that he," nodding towards Job, who was seated on the floor, feebly wiping his forehead with a red cotton pocket-handker-chief, "whom they rightly call the 'Pig,' for as a pig is he stupid, hath let fall the plank, it will not be easy to return across the gulf, and to that end I must make some plan. Rest you a while, and look upon this place. What think ye that it is?"

"We cannot say," I answered.

"Wouldst thou believe, O Holly, that once a man did choose this airy nest for a daily habitation, and here he dwelt for many years, leaving it but one day in every twelve to seek food and water and oil that the people brought, more than he could carry, and laid as an offering in the mouth of that tunnel through which we passed hither?"

I looked at her in question, and she continued—

"Yet so it was. There was a man—Noot, he named himself—who, though he lived in the latter days, had of the wisdom of the sons of Kôr. A hermit, and a philosopher, greatly skilled in the secrets of Nature, he it was who discovered the Fire that I shall show you, which is Nature's blood and life, and that the man who bathes therein and breathes thereof shall live while Nature lives. But like unto thee, O Holly, this Noot would not turn his knowledge to account. 'Ill,' he said, 'was it for man to live, for man is born to die.' Therefore he told his secret to none, and therefore did he abide here, where the seeker after Life must pass, and was revered of the Amahagger of that day as holy, and a hermit.

"Now, when first I came to this country—knowest thou how I came, Kallikrates? Another time I will tell thee; it is a strange tale—I heard of this philosopher, and waited for him when he sought his food yonder, and returned with him here, though I greatly feared to tread the gulf. Then did I beguile him with my beauty and my wit, and flatter him with my tongue, so that he led me down to the home of the Fire, and told me the secrets of the Fire; but he would not suffer me to step therein, and, fearing lest he should slay me, I refrained, knowing that the man was very old, and soon would die. So I returned, having learned from him all that he knew of the wonderful Spirit of the World, and that was much, for this man was wise and very ancient, and by purity and abstinence, and the contemplations of his innocent mind, had worn thin the evil between that which we see and those great invisible truths, the whisper of whose wings we hear at times as they sweep through the gross air of the world. Then—it was but a very few days after, I met thee, my Kallikrates, who hadst wandered hither with the beautiful Egyptian Amenartas, and I learned to love for the first and last time, once and for ever, so that it entered into my mind to come hither with thee, and receive the gift of Life for thee and me. Therefore came we, with that Egyptian who would not be left behind, and, behold! we found the old man Noot lying but newly dead. *There* he lay, and his white beard covered him like a garment," and she pointed to a spot near to which I was sitting; "but surely he has long since crumbled away, and the wind hath borne his ashes hence."

Here I put out my hand and felt in the dust, till presently my fingers touched something. It was a human tooth, very yellow, but sound. I held it up and showed it to Ayesha, who laughed.

"Yes," she said, "it is his without a doubt. Behold what remains of Noot and the wisdom of Noot—one little tooth! Yet that man had all life at his command, but for his conscience's sake he would have none of it. Well, he lay there newly dead, and we descended whither I shall lead you, and then, gathering up all my courage, and courting death that I might perchance win so glorious a crown of life, I stepped into the flames, and behold! Life such as ye can never know until ye feel it also flowed into me, and I came forth undying, and lovely beyond imagining. And I stretched out mine arms to thee, Kallikrates, bidding thee take thine own immortal bride, and behold! blinded by my naked beauty, thou didst turn from me, to hide thine eyes upon the breast of Amenartas. Then a great fury filled me, making me mad, and I seized the javelin that thou didst bear, and stabbed thee, so that, at my feet, in the very place of Life, thou didst groan and go down in to death. I knew not then that I had strength to slay with mine eyes and by the power of my will, therefore in my madness I slew with the javelin.[1]

[1] It will be observed that Ayesha's account of the death of Kallikrates differs materially from that written on the potsherd by Amenartas. The writing on the sherd says, 'Then in her rage did she smite him *by her magic*, and he died.' We never ascertained which was the correct version, but it will be remembered that the body of Kallikrates showed a spear-wound in the breast, which seems conclusive, unless, indeed, it was inflicted after

"And when thou wast dead, ah! I wept, because I was undying and thou wast dead. I wept there in the place of Life so that had I been mortal any more my heart had surely broken. And she, the swart Egyptian—she cursed me by her gods. By Osiris did she curse me and by Isis, by Nephthys and by Anubis, by Sekhet, the cat-headed, and by Set, calling down evil on me, evil and everlasting desolation. Ah! I can see her dark face now lowering o'er me like a storm, but she could not harm me, and I—I know not if I could harm her. I did not try; it was naught to me then; so together we bore thee hence. Afterwards I sent her—the Egyptian—away through the swamps, and it seems that she lived to bear a son and to write the tale that should lead thee, her husband, back to me, her rival and thy murderess.

"Such is the tale, my love, and now the hour is at hand that shall set a crown upon it. Like all things on the earth, it is compounded of evil and of good—more of evil than of good, perchance; and writ in a scroll of blood. It is the truth; I have hidden nothing from thee, Kallikrates. And now, one thing before the moment of thy trial. We go down into the presence of Death, for Life and Death are very near together, and—who knoweth—that might happen which shall separate us for another space of waiting? I am but a woman, and no prophetess, and I cannot read the future. But this I know—for I learned it from the lips of the wise man Noot—that my life is but prolonged and made more bright. It cannot endure for aye. Therefore, ere we go, tell me, O Kallikrates, that of a truth thou dost forgive me, and dost love me from thy heart. See, Kallikrates: much evil have I done—perchance it was evil but two nights since to strike that girl who loved thee cold in death, but she disobeyed me and angered me, prophesying misfortunes to me, and I smote. Be careful when power comes to thee also, lest thou too shouldst smite in thine anger or thy jealousy, for unconquerable strength is a sore weapon in the hands of erring man. Yea, I have sinned—out of the bitterness born of a great love have I sinned—yet do I know the good from the evil, nor is my heart altogether hardened. Thy love, Kallikrates, shall be the gate of my redemption, even as aforetime my passion was the path down which I ran to ill. For deep love unsatisfied is the hell of noble hearts and a portion for the accursed, but love

---

death. Another thing that we never ascertained was *how* the two women—*She* and the Egyptian Amenartas—were able to bear the corpse of the man they both loved across the dread gulf and down the shaking spur. What a spectacle the two distracted creatures must have presented in their grief and loveliness as they toiled along that awful place with the dead man between them! Probably, however, its passage was easier then.—L. H. H.

that is mirrored back more perfect from the soul of our desired
doth fashion wings to lift us above ourselves, and make us what
we might be. Therefore, Kallikrates, take me by the hand, and
lift my veil with no more fear than though I were some peasant
girl, and not the wisest and most beauteous woman in this wide
world, and look me in the eyes, and tell me that thou dost forgive me with all thine heart, and that with all thine heart thou
dost worship me."

She paused, and the infinite tenderness in her voice seemed
to hover round us like some memory of the dead. I know that
it moved me more even than her words, it was so very human—
so very womanly. Leo, too, was strangely touched. Hitherto
he had been fascinated against his better judgment, somewhat
as a bird is fascinated by a snake, but now I think that all this
passed away, and he knew that he really loved this strange and
glorious creature, as, alas! I loved her also. At any rate, I
saw his eyes fill with tears as, stepping swiftly to her, he undid
the gauzy veil, and taking her by the hand, gazed into her sweet
face, saying—

"Ayesha, I love thee with all my heart, and so far as forgiveness is possible I forgive thee the death of Ustane. For
the rest, it is between thee and thy Maker; I know nothing of
it. I know only that I love thee as I never loved before, and
that, be it near or far, I will cleave to thee to the end."

"Now," answered Ayesha, with proud humility—"now, when
my lord doth speak thus royally pardoning with so rich a
hand, it becomes me not to lag behind in gifts, and thus be
beggared of my generosity. Behold!" and she took his hand
and, placing it upon her shapely head, she bent herself slowly
down till one knee for an instant touched the ground—"Behold!
in token of submission do I bow me to my lord! Behold!" and
she kissed him on the lips, "in token of my wifely love do I
kiss my lord. Behold!" and she laid her hand upon his heart,
"by the sin I sinned, by my lonely centuries of waiting wherewith it was wiped out, by the great love with which I love,
and by the Spirit—the Eternal Thing that doth beget all life,
from Whom it ebbs, to Whom it must return again—I swear:—

"I swear, even in this first most holy hour of completed Womanhood, that I will cherish Good and abandon Evil. I swear
that I will be ever guided by thy voice in the straightest path
of duty. I swear that I will eschew Ambition, and through all
my length of endless days set Wisdom over me as a ruling star
to lead me unto Truth and a knowledge of the Right. I swear
also that I will honour and will cherish thee, Kallikrates, who

hast been swept by the wave of time back into my arms, ay, till my day of doom, come it soon or late. I swear—nay, I will swear no more, for what are words? Yet shalt thou learn that Ayesha hath no false tongue.

"So I have sworn, and thou, my Holly, art witness to the oath. Here, too, are we wed, my husband, with the gloom for bridal canopy—wed till the end of all things; here do we write our marriage vows upon the rushing winds, which shall bear them up to heaven, and round and continually round this rolling world.

"And for a bridal gift I crown thee with my beauty's starry crown, and enduring life, and wisdom without measure, and wealth that none can count. Behold! the great ones of the earth shall creep about thy feet, and its fair women shall cover up their eyes because of the shining glory of thy countenance, and its wise ones shall be abashed before thee. Thou shalt read the hearts of men as an open writing, and hither and thither shalt thou lead them as thy pleasure listeth. Like that old Sphinx of Egypt thou shalt sit aloft from age to age, and ever shall they cry to thee to solve the riddle of thy greatness, that doth not pass away, and ever shalt thou mock them with thy silence!

"Behold! once more I kiss thee, and with that kiss I give to thee dominion over sea and earth, over the peasant in his hovel, over the monarch in his palace halls, and cities crowned with towers, and all who breathe therein. Where'er the sun shakes out his spears, and the lonesome waters mirror up the moon, where'er storms roll, and Heaven's painted bows arch in the sky—from the pure North clad in snows, across the middle spaces of the world, to where the amorous South, lying like a bride upon her blue couch of seas, breathes in sighs made sweet with the odour of myrtles—there shall thy power pass and thy dominion find a home. Nor sickness, nor icy-fingered fear, nor sorrow, and pale waste of flesh and mind hovering ever o'er humanity, shall so much as shadow thee with the shadow of their wings. As a God shalt thou be, holding good and evil in the hollow of thy hand, and I, even I, humble myself before thee. Such is the power of Love, and such is the bridal gift I give unto thee, Kallikrates, my Lord and Lord of all.

"And now it is done; now for thee I loose my virgin zone; and come storm, come shine, come good, come ill, come life, come death, it never, never can be undone. For, of a truth, that, which is, is and being done, is done for aye, and cannot be changed. I have said—Let us hence, that all things may be accomplished in their order"; and, taking one of the lamps, she advanced towards the end of the chamber that was roofed in by the swaying stone, where she halted.

We followed her, and perceived that in the wall of the cone there was a stair, or, to be more accurate, that some projecting knobs of rock had been so shaped as to form a good imitation of a stair. Down these Ayesha began to climb, springing from step to step like a chamois, and after her we followed with less grace. When we had descended some fifteen or sixteen steps we found that they ended in a long rocky slope, shaped like an inverted cone or funnel.

This slope was very steep and often precipitous, but it was nowhere impassable, and by the light of the lamps we climbed down it with no great difficulty, though it was gloomy work enough travelling on thus, none of us knew whither, into the dead heart of a volcano. As we went, however, I took the precaution of noting our route as well as I could; and this was not so very difficult, owing to the extraordinary and most fantastic shapes of the rocks that were strewn about, many of which in that dim light looked more like the grim faces carven upon mediæval gargoyles than ordinary boulders.

For a considerable time we travelled on thus, half an hour I should say, till, after we had descended many hundreds of feet, I perceived that we had reached the point of the inverted cone, where, at the very apex of the funnel, we found a passage, so low and narrow that we were forced to stoop as we crept along it. After some fifty yards of this creeping the passage suddenly widened into a cave, so huge that we could see neither the roof nor the sides. Indeed, we only knew that it was a cave by the echo of our tread and the perfect quiet of the heavy air. On we went for many minutes in absolute awed silence, like lost souls in the depths of Hades, Ayesha's white and ghost-like form flitting in front of us, till once more the place ended in a passage which opened into a second cavern much smaller than the first. We could clearly distingish the arch and stony banks of this second cave, and, from their rent and jagged appearance, we judge that it had been torn in the bowels of the rock by the terrific force of some explosive gas, like that first long passage through the cliff down which we had passed before we reached the quivering spur. At length this cave ended in a third tunnel, where gleamed a faint glow of light.

I heard Ayesha utter a sigh of relief as this light dawned upon us, which flowed we knew not whence.

"It is well," she said; "prepare to enter the very womb of the Earth, wherein she doth conceive the Life that ye see brought forth in man and beast—ay, in every tree and flower. Prepare, O Men, for here ye shall be born anew!"

Swiftly she sped along, and after her we stumbled as best we might, our hearts filled like a cup with mingled dread and curiosity. What were we about to see? We passed down the tunnel; stronger and stronger grew the glow, reaching us now in great flashes like rays from a light house, as one by one they are thrown wide upon the darkness of the waters. Nor was this all, for with the flashes came a soul-shaking sound like that of thunder and crashing trees. Now we were through the passage, and—oh heavens!

We stood in a third cavern, some fifty feet in length by perhaps as great a height, and thirty wide. It was carpeted with fine white sand, and its walls had been worn smooth by the action of fire or water. This cavern was not dark like the others —it was filled with a soft glow of rose-coloured light, more beautiful to look on than anything that can be conceived. But at first we saw no flashes, and heard no more of the thunderous sound. Presently, however, as we stood in amaze, gazing at the marvellous sight and wondering whence the rosy radiance flowed, a dread and beautiful thing happened. Across the far end of the cavern, with a grinding and crashing noise—a noise so dreadful and awe-inspiring that we all trembled, and Job actually sank to his knees—there flamed out an awful cloud or pillar of fire, like a rainbow many-coloured, and like the lightning bright. For a space, perhaps forty seconds, it flamed and roared thus, turning slowly round and round; then by degrees the terrible noise ceased, and with the fire it passed away—I know not where—leaving behind it the same rosy glow that we had first seen.

"Draw near, draw near!" cried Ayesha, with a voice of thrilling exultation. "Behold the Fountain and the Heart of Life as it beats in the bosom of this great world. Behold the Substance from which all things draw their energy, the bright Spirit of this Globe, without which it cannot live, but must grow cold and dead as the dead moon. Draw near, and wash you in those living flames, and take their virtue into your poor bodies in all its virgin strength—not as now it feebly glows within your bosoms, filtered thereto through the fine strainers of a thousand intermediate lives, but as it is here in the very fount and source of earthly Being."

We followed her through the rosy glow up to the head of the cave, till we stood before the spot where the great pulse beat and the great flame passed. And as we went we became sensible of a wild and splendid exhilaration, of the glorious sense of such a fierce intensity of Life that beside it the most buoyant moments of our strength seemed flat and tame and feeble. It was the mere effluvium of the fire, the subtle ether that it cast off as it rolled, entering into us, and making us strong as giants and swift as eagles.

We reached the head of the cave, and gazed at each other in the glorious glow, laughing aloud in the lightness of our hearts and the divine intoxication of our brains—even Job laughed, who had not smiled for a week. I know that I felt as though the mantle of all the genius whereof the human intellect is capable had descended upon me. I could have spoken in blank verse of Shakesperian beauty; inspired visions flashed through my mind; it was as though the bonds of my flesh had been loosened, and had left the spirit free to soar to the empyrean of its unguessed powers. The sensations that poured in upon me are indescribable. I seemed to live more keenly, to reach to a higher joy, to sip the goblet of a subtler thought than ever it had been my lot to taste before. I was another and most glorified self, and all the avenues of the Possible were for a while laid open to my mortal footsteps.

Then, suddenly, whilst I rejoiced in this splendid vigour of a new-found self, from far away there came the dreadful muttering noise, that grew and grew to a crash and a roar, which combined in itself all that is terrible and yet splendid in the possibilities of sound. Nearer it came, and nearer yet, till it was close upon us, rolling down like all the thunder-wheels of heaven behind the horses of the lightning. On it travelled, and with it the glorious blinding cloud of many-coloured lights, and stood before us for a space, slowly revolving, as it seemed to us; then, acompanied by its attendant pomp of sound, it passed away I know not whither.

So astonishing was the wondrous sight that one and all of us, save *She,* who stood up and stretched her hands towards the fire, sank down before it, and hid our faces in the sand.

When it was gone Ayesha spoke.

"At length, Kallikrates," she said, "the moment is at hand. When the great flame comes again thou must bathe in it; but throw aside thy garments, for it will burn them, though thee it will not hurt. Thou must stand in the fire while thy senses will endure, and when it embraces thee suck the essence down into thy very heart, and let it leap and play around thy every limb, so that thou lose no moiety of its virtue. Hearest thou me, Kallikrates?"

"I hear thee, Ayesha," answered Leo, "but, of a truth—I am no coward—but I doubt me of that raging flame. How know I that it will not utterly destroy me, so that I lose myself and lose thee also? Nevertheless I will do it," he added.

Ayesha thought for a minute, and then said—

"It is not wonderful that thou shouldst doubt. Tell me, Kallikrates: if thou seest me stand in the flame and come forth unharmed, wilt thou enter also?"

"Yes," he answered, "I will enter even if it slay me. I have said that I will enter now."

"And that will I also," I cried.

"What, my Holly!" she laughed aloud; "methought that thou wouldst naught of length of days. Why, how is this?"

"Nay, I know not," I answered, "but there is that in my heart which calleth to me to taste of the flame and live."

"It is well," she said. "Thou art not altogether lost in folly. See now, I will for the second time bathe me in this living bath. Fain would I add to my beauty and to my length of days, if that be possible. If it be not possible, at the least it cannot harm me.

"Also," she continued, after a momentary pause, "there is another and a deeper cause why I would once again dip me in the fire. When first I tasted of its virtue my heart was full of passion and of hatred of that Egyptian Amenartas, and therefore, despite my strivings to be rid of them, passion and hatred have been stamped upon my soul from that sad hour to this. But now it is otherwise. Now is my mood a happy mood, and I am filled with the purest part of thought, and thus I would ever be. Therefore, Kallikrates, will I once more wash and make me pure and clean, and yet more meet for thee. Therefore also, when in turn thou dost stand in the fire, empty all thy heart of evil, and let contentment hold the balance of thy mind. Shake loose thy spirit's wings, muse upon thy mother's kiss, and turn thee toward the vision of the highest good that hath ever swept on silver wings across the silence of thy dreams. For from the seed of what thou art in that dread moment shall grow the fruit of what thou shalt be for all unreckoned time.

"Now, prepare thee, prepare! even as though thy last hour were at hand, and thou wast about to cross through Death to the Land of Shadow, and not by the Gates of Glory into the realm of Life made beautiful. Prepare, I say, Kallikrates!"

CHAPTER XXVI

WHAT WE SAW

THEN followed a few moments' pause, during which Ayesha seemed to be gathering up her strength for the fiery trial, while we clung to each other, and waited in utter silence.

At last, from far, far away, came the first murmur of sound, that grew and gathered till it began to crash and bellow in the distance. As she heard it Ayesha swiftly threw off her gauzy wrapping and loosened the golden snake from her kirtle. Then, shaking her lovely hair about her like a garment, beneath its cover she slipped off the white robe and replaced the snaky belt around her, outside the masses of her falling locks. There she stood before us as Eve might have stood before Adam, clad in nothing but her abundant hair, held round her by the golden band; and no words of mine can tell how sweet she looked—and how divine. Nearer and nearer drew the thunder wheels of fire, and as they came she pushed one ivory arm through the dark masses of her hair and wound it about Leo's neck.

"Oh, my love, my love!" she murmured, "wilt thou ever know how I have loved thee?" and she kissed him on the forehead, hesitated a little as though in doubt, then advanced and stood in the pathway of the flame of Life.

There was, I remember, something very touching to my mind about her words and that embrace upon Leo's forehead. It was like a mother's kiss, and seemed to carry a benediction with it.

On came the crashing, rolling noise, and the sound of it was as the sound of a forest being swept flat by a mighty wind, to be tossed up again like so much grass, and hurled in thunder down a mountain-side. Nearer and nearer it approached; now flashes of light, forerunners of the revolving pillar of flame, were passing like arrows through the rosy air; and now the edge of the pillar itself appeared. Ayesha turned towards it, and stretched out her arms to greet it. On it rolled very slowly and lapped her round with fire. I saw the essence run up her form. I saw her lift it with both hands as though it were water, and pour it over her head. I even saw her open her mouth and draw it down into her lungs, and it was a dread and wonderful sight.

Then she paused, and, stretching out her arms, she stood quite still, a heavenly smile upon her face, as though she were the very Spirit of the Flame.

The mysterious fire played up and down her dark and rolling locks, twining and twisting itself through and around them like threads of golden lace; it gleamed upon her ivory breast and shoulder, from which the hair had slipped aside; it slid along her pillared throat and delicate features, and seemed to find a home in the glorious eyes that shone and shone, more brightly even than the burning spiritual ether.

Oh, how beautiful she looked there in the flame! No angel out of heaven could have worn a greater loveliness. Even now my heart faints before the recollection of it, as naked in the naked fire she stood and smiled at our awed faces, and I would give half my remaining time upon this earth thus to see her once again.

But suddenly—more suddenly than I can tell—an indescribable change came over her countenance, a change which I could not define or explain, but none the less a change. The smile vanished, and in its stead there crept a dry, hard look; the rounded face seemed to grow pinched, as though some great anxiety was leaving its impress there. The glorious eyes, too, lost their light, and as I thought, the form its perfect shape and erectness.

I rubbed my eyes, thinking that I was the victim of some hallucination, or that the radiance of the intense light produced an optical delusion; and, as I marvelled, the flaming pillar slowly twisted and thundered on to whithersoever it passes in the bowels of the great earth, leaving Ayesha standing where it had been.

So soon as it was gone she stepped forward to Leo's side—it seemed to me that there was no spring in her step—and stretched out her hand to lay it upon his shoulder. I gazed at her arm. Where was its wonderful roundness and beauty? It looked thin and angular. And her face—by Heaven!—*her face was growing old before my eyes!* I suppose that Leo saw it also; certainly he recoiled a little.

"What is it, my Kallikrates?" she said, and her voice—what was wrong with those deep and thrilling notes? They sounded high and cracked.

"Why, what is it—what is it?" she said confusedly. "I am dazed. Surely the quality of the fire hath not altered. Can the principle of Life alter? Tell me, Kallikrates, is there aught wrong with my eyes? I see not clear," and she put her hand to her head and touched her hair—? and oh, *horror of horrors!*— it all fell upon the floor.

"*Look!—look!—look!*" shrieked Job, in a shrill falsetto of terror, his eyes starting from his head, and foam upon his lips. "*Look!—look!—look!* she's shrivelling up! she's turning into a monkey!" and down he fell upon the ground, foaming and gnashing in a fit.

True enough—I faint even as I write it in the living presence of that terrible recollection—Ayesha *was* shrivelling up; the golden snake that had encircled her gracious form slipped over her hips and to the ground. Smaller and smaller she grew; her skin changed colour, and in place of the perfect whiteness of its lustre it turned dirty brown and yellow, like to an old piece of withered parchment. She felt at her head: the delicate hand was nothing but a claw now, a human talon resembling that of a badly preserved Egyptian mummy. Then she seemed to understand what kind of change was passing over her, and she shrieked —ah, she shrieked!—Ayesha rolled upon the floor and shrieked.

Smaller she grew, and smaller yet, till she was no larger than a monkey. Now the skin had puckered into a million wrinkles, and on her shapeless face was the stamp of unutterable age. I never saw anything like it; nobody ever saw anything to equal the infinite age which was graven on that fearful countenance, no bigger now than that of a two-months' child, though the skull retained its same size; and let all men pray they never shall, if they wish to keep their reason.

At last she lay still, or only moving feebly. She, who but two minutes gone had gazed upon us—the loveliest, noblest, most splendid woman the world has ever seen—she lay still before us, near the masses of her own dark hair, no larger than a big ape, and hideous—ah, too hideous for words! And yet, think of this— at that very moment I thought of it—it was the *same* woman!

She was dying: we saw it, and thanked God—for while she lived she could feel, and what must she have felt? She raised herself upon her bony hands, and blindly gazed around her, swaying her head slowly from side to side as does a tortoise. She could not see, for her whitish eyes were covered with a horny film. Oh, the horrible pathos of the sight! But she could still speak.

"Kallikrates," she said in husky, trembling tones. "Forget me not, Kallikrates. Have pity on my shame; I die not. I shall come again, and shall once more be beautiful, I swear it—it is true! *Oh—h—h*" and she fell upon her face, and was still.

Yes, thus, on the very spot whence more than twenty centuries before she had slain Kallikrates the priest, Ayesha herself fell down and died.

Overcome with the extremity of horror, we too sank to the sandy floor of that dread place, and swooned away.

I know not how long we remained thus. Many hours, I suppose. When at last I opened my eyes the other two were still outstretched upon the floor. The rosy light yet beamed like a celestial dawn, and the thunder-wheels of the Spirit of Life yet rolled upon their accustomed track, for as I awoke the great pillar was passing away. There, too, lay the hideous little monkey frame, covered with crinkled yellow parchment, that once had been the glorious *She*. Alas! it was no hideous dream—it was an awful and unparalleled fact!

What had chanced to bring about this shocking change? Had the nature of the life-giving fire varied? Did it, perhaps, from time to time send forth an essence of Death instead of an essence of Life? Or was it that the frame once charged with its marvellous virtue could bear no more, so that were the process repeated —it mattered not at what lapse of time—the two impregnations neutralised each other, and left the body on which they acted as it was before ever it came into contact with the very spring of Being? This, and this alone, would account for the sudden and terrible ageing of Ayesha, as the whole length of her two thousand years took effect upon her. I had not the slightest doubt myself but that the shape now lying before me was just what the frame of a woman would be if by any extraordinary means life could be preserved in her till at length she died at the age of some two-and-twenty centuries.

But who can tell *what* happened? There was the fact. Often since this awful hour I have reflected that it requires no great stretch of imagination to see the finger of Providence in the matter. Ayesha locked up in her living tomb, waiting from age to age for the coming of her lover, worked but a small change in the order of the World. But Ayesha, strong and happy in her love, clothed with immortal youth, godlike beauty and power, and the wisdom of the centuries, would have revolutionised society, and even perchance have changed the destinies of Mankind. Thus she opposed herself to the eternal law, and, strong though she was, by it was swept back into nothingness—swept back with shame and hideous mockery!

For some minutes I lay, faintly turning these terrors over in my mind, while my physical strength came back to me, which it did quickly in that buoyant atmosphere. Then I bethought me of the others, and staggered to my feet, to see if I could arouse them. But first I took up Ayesha's kirtle and the gauzy scarf with which she had been wont to hide her dazzling loveliness from the eyes of men, and, averting my head so that I might not look upon it, I covered up that dreadful relic of the glorious dead, that shocking epitome of human beauty and human life. This I did hurriedly, fearing lest Leo should recover, and see it again.

Then, stepping over the perfumed masses of dark hair that were scattered upon the sand, I went to Job, who was lying upon his breast, and turned him over. As I lifted him his arm fell back in a way that I did not like—which sent a chill through me, indeed—and I glanced sharply at his face . One look was enough. Our old and faithful servant was dead. Already shattered by all he had seen and undergone, his nerves had utterly broken down beneath this last dire sight, and he had died of terror, or in a fit brought on by terror. I had only to look at his features to be assured of it.

This was another blow; but it may help people to understand how overwhelmingly awful was the experience through which we had passed when I say that we did not feel it much at the time. It seemed quite natural that the poor old fellow should be dead. When Leo came to himself, which he did with a groan and trembling of the limbs about ten minutes afterwards, and I told him that Job was dead, he merely said, *"Oh!"* and, mind you, this was from no heartlessness, for he and Job were much attached to each other; and he often talks of him now with the deepest regret and affection. It was only that his mind would bear no more. A harp can give out but a certain quantity of sound, however heavily it is smitten.

Well, I set myself to recovering Leo, who, to my infinite relief, I found was not dead, but only fainting, and in the end I succeeded, as I have said, and he sat up. Then I saw another dreadful thing. When we entered that awful place his curling hair had been of the ruddiest gold; now it was turning grey, and by the time we gained the outer air it was snow white. Besides, he looked twenty years older.

"What is to be done, old fellow?" he said in a hollow, dead sort of voice, when his brain cleared a little, and a recollection of what had happened forced itself upon him.

"Try and get out, I suppose," I answered; "that is, unless you would like to go in there," and I pointed to the column of fire, which was once more rolling by.

"I would if I were sure that it would kill me," he said with a little laugh. "It was my cursed hesitation that did this. If I had not been doubtful *She* might never have tried to show me the road. But I am *not* sure. The fire might have the opposite effect upon me.. It might make me immortal; and, old fellow, I have not the patience to wait a couple of thousand years for her to come back again as she did for me. I had rather die when my hour comes—and I should fancy that it isn't far off either—and go my ways to look for her. Do you try it, if you like."

But I merely shook my head; my excitement was as dead as ditch-water, and my distaste for the prolongation of our mortal span had come back upon me more strongly than ever. Besides, we neither of us knew what the effects of the essence might be. The result upon *She* had not been of an encouraging nature, and of the exact causes which produced that result we were, of course, ignorant.

"Well, my boy," I said, "we cannot stop here till we follow those two," and I pointed to the little heap under the white garment and to the stiffening corpse of poor Job. "If we are going we had better go. But, by the way, I expect that the lamps have burnt out," and I took one up to look at it, and sure enough it had.

"There is some more oil in the vase," said Leo indifferently—"if it is not broken, at least."

I examined the vessel in question—it was intact. With a trembling hand I filled the lamps—luckily there was still some of the linen wick unburnt. Then I lit them with one of our wax matches. While I did so we heard the pillar of fire approaching again as it went on in its never-ending journey, if, indeed, it was the same pillar that passed and repassed in a circle.

"Let us see it come once more," said Leo; "we shall never look upon its like again in this world."

It seemed but idle curiosity, yet somehow I shared it, and so we waited till, turning slowly upon its own axis, the burning cloud had flamed and thundered by; and I remember wondering for how many tens of thousands of years this phenomenon had recurred in the bowels of the earth, and for how many more thousands it would continue to recur. I wondered also if any mortal eyes would ever again mark its passage, or any mortal ears be thrilled and fascinated by the swelling volume of its majestic sound. I do not think so; I believe that we are the last human beings who will ever see that unearthly sight. Presently it had gone, and we too turned to go.

But before we went each of us took Job's cold hand and shook it. It seemed a ghastly ceremony, but it was the only means in our power of showing our respect to the faithful dead and of celebrating his obsequies. The heap beneath the white garment we did not uncover. We had no wish to look upon that terrible sight again. But we went to the pile of rippling hair that had fallen from her in the agony of the hideous change which was worse than a thousand natural deaths, and each of us drew from it a shining lock. These locks we still have, the sole memento that is left to us of Ayesha as we knew her in the fulness of her grace and glory. Leo pressed the perfumed hair to his lips.

"She called me not to forget her," he said hoarsely; "and swore that we should meet again. By Heaven! I never *will* forget her. Here I swear that, if we live to escape from this, I will not for all my days have aught to do with any other living woman, and that wherever I go I will wait for her as faithfully as she waited for me."

"Yes," I thought to myself, "if she comes back as beautiful as we knew her. But supposing she came back *like that!*"[1]

And then we went. We went, and left those two in the presence of the secret well and fount of Life, but gathered to the cold company of Death. How lonely they looked as they lay there, and how ill assorted! That little heap had been for two thousand years the wisest, loveliest, proudest creature—I can hardly call her woman—in the whole universe. She was wicked, too, in her way; but, alas! such is the frailty of the human heart, her wickedness had not detracted from her charm. Indeed, I am by no means certain that it did not add to it. After all it was of a grand order; there was nothing mean or small about Ayesha.

And poor Job! His presentiment had come true, and there was an end of him. Well, he has a strange burial-place—no Norfolk hind ever had a stranger, or ever will; and it is something to lie in the same sepulchre with the poor remains of the imperial *She*.

We looked our last upon them and the indescribable rosy glow in which they lay; then with hearts far too heavy for words we left them, and crept thence broken-down men—so broken down that we renounced the chance of practically immortal life, because all that made life valuable had gone from us, and we knew even then, that to prolong our days indefinitely would only be to prolong our sufferings. For we felt—yes, both of us— that having once looked Ayesha in the eyes, we could not forget her for ever and ever while memory and identity remained. We

---

[1]What a terrifying reflection it is, by the way, that nearly all our deep love for women who are not our kindred depends—at any rate, in the first instance—upon their personal appearance. If we lost them, and found them again dreadful to look on, though otherwise they were the very same, should we still love them?—L. H. H.

both loved her now and for all time; she was stamped and carven on our hearts, and no other woman or interest could ever raze that splendid die.

And I—there lies the sting—I had and have no right to think thus of her. As she told me, I was nothing to her, and never shall be through the unfathomed depth of Time, unless, indeed, conditions alter, and a day comes at last when two men may love one woman, and all three be happy in the fact. It is the only hope of my broken-heartedness, and a somewhat faint one. Beyond it I have nothing. I have paid down this heavy price, all that I am worth here and hereafter, and that is my sole reward. With Leo it is different, and often and often I bitterly envy him with happy lot, for if *She* was right, and her wisdom and knowledge did not fail her at the last, which, arguing from the precedent of her own case, I think most unlikely, he has some future to look forward to. But I have none, and yet—mark the folly and the feebleness of the human heart, and let him who is weak learn wisdom from it—yet I would not have it otherwise. I mean that I am content to give what I have given and must always give, and to take in payment those crumbs that fall from my mistress's table: the memory of a few kind words, the hope one day in the far undreamed future of a sweet smile or two of recognition, a little gentle friendship, and a little show of thanks for my devotion to her—and Leo.

If this does not constitute true love, I do not know what does, and all I have to say is, that it is a very bad state of mind for a man on the wrong side of middle age to fall into.

CHAPTER XXVII

WE LEAP

WE passed through the caves without trouble, but when we came to the slope of the inverted cone two obstacles stared us in the face. The first of these was the laborious nature of the ascent, and the next the extreme difficulty of finding our way. Indeed, had it not been for the mental notes that I had fortunately taken of the forms of various rocks, I am sure that we never should have managed it at all, but have wandered about in the dreadful womb of the volcano—for I suppose it must once have been something of the sort—until we died of exhaustion and despair. As it was we went wrong several times, and once nearly fell into a huge crack or crevasse. It was terrible work creeping about in the dense gloom and awful stillness from boulder to boulder, and examining them by the feeble light of the lamps to see if I could recognise their shapes. We rarely spoke; our hearts were too heavy for speech. We simply stumbled along in a dogged fashion, falling sometimes and cutting ourselves. The fact was that our spirits were utterly crushed, and we did not greatly care what happened to us. Only we felt bound to try to save our lives whilst we could, and indeed a natural instinct prompted us to it. So we blundered on for some three or four hours, I should think—I cannot tell exactly how long, for we had no watch left that would go. During the last two hours we were completely lost, and I began to fear we had wandered into the funnel of some subsidiary cone, when at length I suddenly recognised a very large rock which we had seen shortly after we began our descent. It is a marvel that I should have known it; indeed, we had already passed it going at right angles to the proper path, when something about it struck me, and I turned back and examined it in an idle sort of way, and, as it happened, this accident proved our salvation.

After this we gained the rocky natural stair without much difficulty, and in due course found ourselves again in the little chamber where the benighted Noot had lived and died.

But now a fresh terror confronted us. It will be remembered that owing to Job's fear and awkwardness the board upon which we walked from the huge spur to the rocking-stone had been whirled off into the tremendous gulf below.

How were we to cross without the plank

There was only one answer—we must try and *jump* it, or else perish where we were. The distance in itself was not so very great, between eleven and twelve feet I should think, and I have seen Leo jump over twenty when he was a young fellow at college; but then, think of the conditions! Two weary, worn-out men, one of them on the wrong side of forty, a rocking-stone to take off from, a trembling point of rock some few feet across to land upon, and a bottomless gulf to be cleared in a raging gale! It was bad enough, God knows; but when I pointed out these things to Leo, he put the whole matter in a nutshell by replying that, merciless as the choice was, we must choose between the certainty of a lingering death in the chamber and the risk of a swift one in the air.

There was no gainsaying this argument, but it was clear that we could not attempt to leap in the dark; the only thing to do was to wait for the ray of light which pierced through the gulf at sunset. How near to or how far from sunset we might be neither of us had the faintest notion; all we did know was, that when at last the light came it would not endure for more than two minutes at the outside, so that we must be prepared to meet it. Accordingly, we made up our minds to creep on to the top of the rocking-stone and lie there in readiness. We were the more easily reconciled to this course by the fact that our lamps were once more nearly exhausted—indeed, one had gone out bodily, and the other was jumping up and down as the flame of a lamp does when the oil is done. So, by the aid of its dying light, we hastened to crawl out of the little chamber and clamber up the side of the great stone.

At this moment the lamp expired.

The change in our situation was sufficiently remarkable. Below, in the little chamber, we had only heard the roaring of the gale overhead—here, lying face downwards on the swinging stone, we were exposed to its full force and fury, as the great draught drew first from this direction and then from that, howling against the mighty precipice and through the rocky cliffs like ten thousand despairing souls. We lay there hour after hour in terror and misery of mind so deep that I will not attempt to describe them, and listened to the wild storm-voices of that Tartarus, while, set to the deep undertone of the spur opposite, whereon the wind hummed as through some awful harp, they called to each other from precipice to precipice. No nightmare dreamed by man, no dark invention of the romancer, can ever equal the living horror of that place, and the weird crying of those voices of the night, as we clung like shipwrecked mariners to a raft, and tossed on the black, unfathomed wilderness of air. Fortunately the temperature was not a low one; indeed, the wind was warm, or we should have perished. So we clung and listened, and while we were stretched out upon the rock a thing chanced which was so curious and suggestive in itself, though doubtless a mere coincidence, that it added to, rather than lightened, the burden on our nerves.

It will be remembered that when Ayesha was standing on the spur, before we crossed to the stone, the wind tore her cloak from her, and whirled it away into the darkness of the gulf, we could not see whither. Well—I hardly like to tell the story; it is so strange—as we lay there upon the rocking-stone, this very cloak came floating out of black space, like a memory from the dead, and fell on Leo—so that it covered him almost from head to foot. At first we could not imagine what it was, but soon discovered by its texture and then, for the first time, poor Leo gave way, and I heard him sobbing there upon the stone. No doubt the cloak had been caught upon some pinnacle of the cliff, and thence was blown hither by a chance gust; at the least, it was a most curious and touching incident.

Shortly after this, suddenly, without the slightest previous warning, the red knife of light appeared stabbing the darkness through and through—struck the swaying stone on which we were, and rested its lurid point upon the spur opposite.

"Now for it," said Leo; "now or never."

We rose and stretched ourselves, looking first at the cloud-wreaths stained the colour of blood by that scarlet ray as they tore through the sickening depths beneath, then at the empty space between the swaying stone and the quivering rock, and, in our hearts, despaired, preparing for death. Surely we could not clear it—desperate though we were.

"Who is to go first?" said I.

"Do you, old fellow," answered Leo. "I will sit upon the other side of the stone to steady it. You must take as much run as you can, and jump high; and may God have mercy on us!"

I acquiesced with a nod, and then I did a thing I had never done since Leo was a little boy. I turned and put my arm round him, and kissed him on the forehead. It sounds rather French, but I was taking my last farewell of a man whom I could not have loved more if he had been my own son twice over.

"Good-bye, my boy," I said; "I hope we shall meet again, wherever it is that we go to."

The fact was I did not expect to live another two minutes.

Next I retreated to the far side of the rock, and waited till one of the chopping gusts of wind got behind me; then I ran the length of the huge stone, some three or four and thirty feet, and sprang wildly into the dizzy air. Oh! the sickening terrors which I felt as I launched myself at that little point of rock, and the horrible scene of despair which shot through my brain, as I real-ised that I had *jumped short!* But so it was; my feet never touched the point, they went down into space, only my hands and body came in contact with it. I gripped at it with a yell, but one hand slipped, and I swung right round, holding by the other, so that now I faced the stone from which I had sprung. In agony I clutched with my left hand, and this time managed to grasp a knob of rock, and there I hung in the fierce red light, with thou-sands of feet of empty air beneath me. My hands were holding to either side of the under part of the spur, so that its point was touching my head. Therefore, even had I found the strength, I could not have pulled myself up. The most that I could do would be to hang for about a minute, and then drop down, down into the bottomless pit. If any man can imagine a more hideous position, let him speak! All I know is that the torture of that half-minute nearly turned my brain.

I heard Leo give a cry, and then suddenly I saw him in mid air springing up and out like a chamois. It was a splendid leap that he took under the influence of his terror and despair. Clearing the horrible gulf as though it were nothing, and landing well on to the rocky point, he threw himself upon his face, to avoid pitching off into the depths. I felt the spur above me shake beneath the shock of his impact, and as it shook I saw the huge rocking-stone, that had been violently depressed by him as he sprang, fly back when relieved of his weight till, for the first time during all these centuries, it swung beyond its balance, falling with a most awful crash right into the rocky chamber which had once served the philosopher Noot for a hermitage, and, I have no doubt, for ever sealing the passage that leads to the Place of Life with some hundreds of tons of rock.

All this happened in a second, and, curiously enough, notwithstanding my terrible plight, I noted it, involuntarily as it were. I even remember thinking that no human being would go down that dread path again.

Next instant I felt Leo seize me by the right wrist with both hands. By lying flat on the point of rock he could just reach me.

"You must let go and swing yourself free," he said in a calm and collected voice, "and then I will try and pull you up, or we will both fall together. Are you ready?"

By way of answer I loosed the rock, first with my left hand, and then with the right, and, as a consequence, swayed out clear of the overshadowing point, my weight hanging upon Leo's arms. It was a dreadful moment. He was a very powerful man, I knew, but would his strength be equal to lifting me up till I could get a hold on the top of the spur, when owing to his position he had so little purchase?

For a few seconds I swung to and fro, while he gathered himself for the effort, and then I heard his sinews cracking above me, and felt myself lifted up as though I were a little child, till I hooked my left arm round the rock, and my body was supported by it. The rest was easy; in two or three more seconds I was up, and we lay panting side by side, trembling like leaves, with the cold perspiration of terror pouring from our skins.

Then, as before, the light went out like a lamp.

For some half-hour we rested thus without speaking a word, but at length we began to creep along the great spur as best we might in the dense gloom. As we drew towards the face of the cliff, from which the spur sprang out like a spike from a wall, the

light increased, however, though only very little, for it was night
overhead. After this the gusts of wind lessened, and we made
better progress, and at last reached the mouth of the first cave or
tunnel. But now a fresh trouble awaited us: our oil was gone,
and the lamps, no doubt, were crushed to powder beneath the
fallen rocking-stone. We were even without a drop of water to
stay our thirst, for we had drunk the last in the chamber of Noot.
How were we to see to make our way through this boulder-strewn
cavern?

Clearly all that we could do was to trust to our sense of touch,
and attempt the passage in the dark; so in we crept, fearing that
if we delayed to do so our exhaustion would overcome us, and we
should probably lie down and die where we were.

Oh, the horrors of that last tunnel! The place was strewn with
rocks, and we fell over them and knocked ourselves up against
them till we were bleeding from a score of wounds. Our only
guide was the side of the cave, which we kept touching, and so
bewildered did we grow in the darkness that thrice we were seized
with the terrifying thought that we had turned, and were travelling the wrong way. On we went, feebly, and still more feebly,
for hour after hour, stopping every few minutes to rest, for our
strength was spent. Once we fell asleep, and, I think, must have
slept for some hours, for, when we we woke, our limbs were quite
stiff, and the blood from our blows and scratches had caked, and
was hard and dry upon the skin. Then we dragged ourselves on
again, till at last, when despair was entering into our hearts, we
saw the light of day once more, and found ourselves outside the
tunnel in the rocky fold or lane that, it will be remembered, led
into it from the outer surface of the cliff.

It was early morning—that we could tell by the feel of the
sweet air and the look of the blessed sky, which we had never
hoped to see again. We entered the tunnel, so near as we knew,
an hour after sunset, so it followed that it had taken us the entire
night to crawl through this dreadful place.

"One more effort, Leo," I gasped, "and we shall reach the slope
where Billali is, if he has not gone. Come, don't give way" for he
had cast himself upon his face. He rose, and, leaning on each
other, we scrambled down that fifty feet or so of cliff—I have not
the least notion how. I only remember that we found ourselves
lying in a heap at the bottom, and then once more began to crawl
along upon our hands and knees towards the grove where *She* had
told Billali to wait her return, for we could not walk another foot.
We had not gone forty yards in this fashion when suddenly one
of the mutes emerged from some trees on our left, through which,

I presume, he had been taking a morning stroll, and ran to us to see what strange animals we were. He stared, and stared, then held up his hands in horror, and nearly fell to the ground. Next, he started as fast as he could go for the grove, which was some two hundred yards away. Small wonder that he was horrified at our appearance, for we must have been a shocking sight. To begin with, Leo, his golden curls turned to a snowy white, his clothes nearly rent from his body, his worn face, and his hands a mass of bruises, cuts, and blood-encrusted filth, was a sufficiently alarming spectacle, as he painfully dragged himself along the ground, and I have no doubt that I was little better to look on. I know that two days afterwards, when I inspected my face in some water, I scarcely recognised myself. I have never been famous for beauty, but there was something besides ugliness stamped upon my features that I have not lost to this day, something resembling that wild look with which a startled person awakes from deep sleep. And really it is not to be wondered at. What I do wonder at is that we escaped at all with our reason.

Presently, to my intense relief, I saw old Billali hurrying towards us, and even then I could scarcely help smiling at the expression of consternation on his dignified countenance.

"Oh, my Baboon! my Baboon!" he cried, "my dear son, is it indeed thou and the Lion? Why, his mane that was as ripe corn is white like the snow. Whence come ye? and where is the Pig, and where, too, is 'She-who-must-be-obeyed?'"

"Dead, both dead!" I answered; "but ask no questions; help us, and give us food and water, or we too shall die before thine eyes. Seest thou not that our tongues are black for want of water? How, then, can we talk?"

"Dead!" he gasped. "Impossible! She who never dies—dead, how can it be?" Then, perceiving, I think, that his face was being watched by the mutes who had hastened to us, he checked himself, and motioned to them to carry us to the camp, which they did.

Fortunately when we arrived some broth was boiling on the fire, and with this Billali fed us—for we were too weak to feed ourselves—thereby, I firmly believe, saving us from death by exhaustion. Then he bade the mutes wash the blood and grime from us with wet cloths, and after that we were laid down upon piles of aromatic grass, and instantly fell into the dead sleep which follows absolute prostration of mind and body.

CHAPTER XXVIII

OVER THE MOUNTAIN

THE next thing I recollect is a feeling of the most dreadful stiffness, and a curious, vague idea passing through my half-awakened brain that I was a carpet that had just been beaten. I opened my eyes, and the first object they fell on was the venerable countenance of our old friend Billali, who was seated by the side of the improvised bed upon which I was sleeping, and stroking his long beard thoughtfully. His presence at once brought back to my mind a memory of all that we had recently endured, which was accentuated by the vision of poor Leo lying opposite to me, his face black with bruises, and his beautiful curling hair turned from yellow to white.[1] At that sight I shut my eyes again and groaned.

"Thou hast slept long, my Baboon," said old Billali.

"How long, my father?" I asked.

"A round of the sun and a round of the moon, a day and a night hast thou slept, and the Lion also. See, he sleepeth yet."

"Blessed is sleep," I answered, "for it swallows up recollection."

"Tell me," he said, "what has befallen you, and what is this strange story of the death of Her who dieth not? Bethink thee, my son: if this be true, then is thy danger and the danger of the Lion very great—nay, almost is the pot red wherewith ye shall be potted, and the stomachs of those who shall eat you are already hungry for the feast. Knowest thou not that these Amahagger, my children, these dwellers in the caves, hate you? They hate you as strangers, and they hate you more because of their brethren whom *She* put to the torment for your sake. Assuredly, if once they learn that there is naught to fear from Hiya, from the terrible One-who-must-be-obeyed, they will slay you by the pot. But let me hear thy tale, my poor Baboon."

Thus adjured I began, and told him—not everything, indeed, as I did not think it desirable to do so, but sufficient for my purpose, which was to make him understand that *She* was in fact no more, having fallen into a volcanic fire, and—as I put it—been consumed therein; for the truth would have been incomprehensible to him. I also told him some of the horrors we had undergone in effecting our escape, which impressed him deeply. But I saw clearly that he did not believe in the report of Ayesha's death. He believed, indeed, that we thought that she was dead,

---

[1] Curiously enough, lately Leo's hair has to some extent regained its colour—that is to say, it is now a yellowish grey, and I am not without hopes that in time it will quite recover itself.— L. H. H.

but his explanation was that it had suited her to disappear for a while. Once, he said, in his father's time, she had vanished for twelve years, and there was a tradition in the country that many centuries back no one had seen her during a whole generation, when she reappeared suddenly, and destroyed a woman who had assumed the position of Queen. I said nothing to this, but only shook my head sadly. Alas! I knew too well that Ayesha would return no more, or at any rate that Billali would never see her again. Elsewhere we may find her, and, as I believe, shall find her, but not here.

"And now," concluded Billali, "what wouldst thou do, my Baboon?"

"Nay," I said, "I know not, my father. Can we not escape from this country?"

He shook his head.

" It is very difficult. By Kôr you cannot pass, for you would be seen, and so soon as those fierce ones found that you were alone—well," and he smiled significantly, lifting his hand as though he were placing a hat upon his head. "But there is that way over the cliff whereof once I spoke to thee, by which they drive the cattle out to pasture. Beyond these pastures are marshes, in width three days' journey, and after that I know not, but I have heard that seven days' march thence runs a mighty river, which flows down to the black water. If you could reach its banks, perchance you might escape, but how can you come thither?"

"Billali," I said, "once, thou knowest, I saved thy life. Now pay back the debt, my father, and save me mine and that of my son, the Lion. It shall be a pleasant thing for thee to think of when thine hour comes, and something to set in the scale against the evil doing of thy days, if perchance thou hast done any evil. Also, if thou art right, and if *She* does but hide herself, surely when she comes again she will reward thee."

"My son the Baboon," answered the old man, "think not that I have an ungrateful heart. Well do I remember how thou didst rescue me when those dogs stood by to see me drown. Measure for measure I will repay, and if thou canst be saved, surely I will save thee. Listen: by dawn to-morrow be prepared, for litters shall be here to bear you away across the mountains, and through the marshes beyond. This I will do, saying it is the word of *She* that it be done; and he who obeyeth not the word of *She,* food is he for the hyænas. Then, when you have crossed the marshes, must you strike with your own hands, so that perchance, if good fortune go with you, you may live to come to that black water whereof you told me. And now, see, the Lion wakes, and you must eat the food I have made ready for you."

Leo's condition, when once he was thoroughly aroused, proved not to be so bad as might have been expected from his appearance, and we both of us made a good meal, which, indeed, we needed sadly. After this we limped down to the spring and bathed, and then came back and slept again till evening, when once more we ate heartily. Billali was absent all that day, no doubt making arrangements about litters and bearers, for we were awakened in the middle of the night by the arrival of a considerable number of men in the little camp.

At dawn the old man himself appeared, and told us that by using *She's* dreadful name, though with some difficulty, he had succeeded in impressing the necessary men, and with them two guides to conduct us across the swamps. Also he urged us to start at once, at the same time announcing his intention of accompanying us, to protect us against treachery. I was much touched by this act of kindness on the part of that wily old barbarian towards two utterly defenceless strangers. A journey through those deadly swamps which, allowing for his return, would occupy six days was no light undertaking for a man of his age, but he consented to it cheerfully in order to promote our safety. This proves that even among those dreadful Amahagger —who with their gloom and their devilish and ferocious rites are certainly by far the most terrible savages that I ever heard of— there are people with kindly hearts. Of course self-interest may have had something to do with it. Billali may have thought that *She* would reappear suddenly and demand an account of us at his hands. Still, with all deductions, it was a great deal more than we could expect under the circumstances, and I can only say that for so long as I live I shall cherish a most affectionate remembrance of my nominal parent, Billali.

Accordingly, having breakfasted, we started in the litters, feeling, physically, almost recovered after our long rest and sleep. The condition of our minds I must leave to the imagination.

Then followed a terrible pull up the cliff. Sometimes the ascent was natural, more often it was a zigzag roadway, cut in the first instance, no doubt, by the old inhabitants of Kôr. The Amahagger say they drive their spare cattle over it once a year to pasture beyond; but if this is so, those cattle must be unusually active on their feet. Of course the litters were useless here, so we were obliged to walk.

By midday, however, we reached the great flat top of that mighty wall of rock, and grand indeed was the view from it, with the plain of Kôr, in the centre of which we could clearly discern the pillared ruins of the Temple of Truth, to the one side, and on the other the boundless and melancholy marsh. This wall of rock, which no doubt had once formed the lip of the crater, proved to be about a mile and a half thick, and was still covered with clinker. Nothing grew upon it; but here and there, wherever there was a little hollow, the eye was relieved by the sight of occasional pools of water, for rain had lately fallen. We clambered over the flat crest of this mighty rampart, and then came our downward march, which, if not so difficult a matter as the ascent, was still sufficiently break-neck, and took us till sunset to accomplish. That night, however, we camped in safety upon the wide slopes that rolled away to the marsh beneath.

On the following morning, about eleven o'clock, began our dreary journey across those awful seas of swamp which I have already described.

For three whole days, through stench and mire, and the all-prevailing flavour of fever, did our bearers struggle along, till at length, beyond that most desolate, and without guides utterly impracticable, district we came to open rolling ground, covered with game of all sorts, but quite uncultivated, and mostly treeless. And here on the following morning, not without some regret, we bade farewell to old Billali, who stroked his white beard and blessed us solemnly.

"Farewell, my son the Baboon," he said, "and farewell to thee too, O Lion. I can do no more to help you. But if ever you come to your country, be advised, and venture not again into lands that you know not, lest you never should return, but leave your white bones to mark the limit of your journeyings. Farewell once more; often shall I think of you; nor wilt thou forget me, my Baboon, for though thy face is ugly thy heart is true." Then he turned and went, and with him went the tall and sullen-looking bearers, and this was the last we saw of the Ama-hagger. We watched them winding away with their empty litters like a procession bearing dead men from a battle, till the mists of the marsh gathered round them and hid them, and then, left utterly desolate in the vast wilderness, we turned and gazed around us and at each other.

Three weeks ago four men had entered the swamps of Kôr, and now two of us were dead, and we who lived had suffered adventures and experiences so strange and terrible that Death

himself hath not a more fearful countenance. Three weeks—
and only three weeks! Truly time should be measured by events,
and not by the lapse of hours. It seemed like thirty years
since we were captured in our whale-boat.

"We must strike out for the Zambesi, Leo," I said, "but God
knows if we shall ever get there."

Leo nodded; he had become silent of late. So we started with
nothing but the clothes we stood in, a compass, our revolvers
and Express rifles, and about two hundred rounds of ammunition, and thus ended the history of our visit to the ancient ruins
of mighty and imperial Kôr.

As for the accidents and dangers that subsequently befell
us, strange and varied though they were, after deliberation
I have determined not to record them here. In these pages I
give only a short and clear account of an occurrence which I
believe to be unprecedented, and this I do, not with a view to
immediate publication, but merely to put on paper, while they
are yet fresh in my memory, the details of our journey and its
result, which will, I believe, prove interesting to the world
if ever we desire to make them public. It is not, however, our
present intention that this should be done during our joint lives.

For the rest, it is of no public interest, resembling as it does
the experience of more than one Central African traveller.
Suffice it to say that, after incredible hardships and privations,
we did reach the Zambesi, which proved to be about a hundred
and seventy miles south of the spot where Billali left us. There
for six months we were imprisoned by a savage tribe, who
believed us to be supernatural beings, chiefly on account of
Leo's youthful face and snow-white hair. From these people we
escaped, and, crossing the Zambesi, wandered southwards,
where, when on the point of starvation, we were sufficiently fortunate to fall in with a half-caste Portuguese hunter who had
followed a troop of elephants farther inland than he had ever
been before. This man treated us most hospitably, and, after
innumerable sufferings and adventures, ultimately, through his
assistance, we reached Delagoa Bay, more than eighteen months
from the time we emerged from the marshes of Kôr, and on the
next day were so fortunate as to catch one of the steamboats
that trade round the Cape to England. Our journey home was
prosperous, and we set foot on the quay at Southampton exactly
two years from the date of our departure upon our wild and
seemingly ridiculous quest. Now I write these last words with
Leo leaning over my shoulder in the old room in my College, the
same into which some two-and-twenty years ago my poor friend

Vincey stumbled on the memorable night of his death, bearing with him the iron chest.

Here ends this history so far as it concerns science and the outside world. What its end will be as regards Leo and myself is more than I can guess. But we feel that is not reached yet. A story that began more than two thousand years ago may stretch a long way into the dim and distant future.

Is Leo really a reincarnation of that ancient Kallikrates of whom the inscription tells? Or was Ayesha deceived by some strange hereditary resemblance? And, another question: In this play of reincarnations, had Ustane aught to do with the Amenartas of long ago? The reader must form his own opinion on these as on many other matters. I have mine, which is that, as regards Leo, *She* made no mistake.

Often I sit alone at night, staring with the eyes of my mind into the blackness of unborn time, and wondering in what shape and form the great drama will be finally developed, and where the scene of its next act will be laid. And when, ultimately, that *final* development occurs, as I have no doubt it must and will occur, in obedience to a fate that never swerves and a purpose which cannot be altered, what will be the part played therein by that beautiful Egyptian Amenartas, the Princess of the royal race of the Pharaohs, for the love of whom the Priest Kallikrates broke his vows to Isis, and, pursued by the inexorable vengeance of the outraged Goddess, fled down the coast of Libya to meet his doom at Kôr?

THE END

KING SOLOMON'S MINES

Now that this book is printed, and about to be given to the world, the sense of its shortcomings, both in style and contents, weighs very heavily upon me. As regards the latter, I can only say that it does not pretend to be a full account of everything we did and saw. There are many things connected with our journey into Kukuanaland which I should have liked to dwell upon at length, and which have, as it is, been scarcely alluded to. Among these are the curious legends which I collected about the chain armor that saved us from destruction in the great battle of Loo, and also about the "silent ones" or colossi at the mouth of the stalactite cave. Again, if I had given way to my own impulses I should have liked to go into the differences, some of which are to my mind very suggestive, between the Zulu and Kukuana dialects. Also a few pages might profitably have been given up to the consideration of the indigenous flora and fauna of Kukuanaland.* Then there remains the most interesting subject—that, as it is, has only been incidentally alluded to—of the magnificent system of military organization in force in that country, which is, in my opinion, much superior to that inaugurated by Chaka in Zululand, inasmuch as it permits of even more rapid mobilization and does not necessitate the employment of the pernicious system of forced celibacy. And, lastly, I have scarcely touched on the domestic and family customs of the Kukuanas, many of which are exceedingly quaint, or on their proficiency in the art of smelting and welding metals. This last they carry to considerable perfection, of which a good example is to be seen in their "tollas," or heavy throwing-knives, the backs of these knives being made of hammered iron, and the edges of beautiful steel welded with great skill on to the iron backs. The fact of the matter is that I thought (and so did Sir Henry Curtis and Captain Good) that the best plan would be to tell the story in a plain, straightforward manner, and leave these matters to be dealt with subsequently in whatever way may ultimately appear to be desirable. In the meanwhile I shall, of course, be delighted to give any information in my power to anybody interested in such things.

And now it only remains for me to offer my apologies for my blunt way of writing. I can only say in excuse for it that I am more accustomed to handle a rifle than a pen, and cannot make any pretence to the grand literary flights and flourishes which I see in novels—for I sometimes like to read a novel. I suppose

*I discovered eight varieties of antelope with which I was previously totally unacquainted, and many new species of plants, for the most part of the bulbous tribe.—A. Q.

they—the flights and flourishes—are desirable, and I regret not being able to supply them; but at the same time I cannot help thinking that simple things are always the most impressive, and books are easier to understand when they are written in plain language, though I have perhaps no right to set up an opinion on such a matter. "A sharp spear," runs the Kukuana saying, "needs no polish;" and on the same principle I venture to hope that a true story, however strange it may be, does not require to be decked out in fine words.

Allan Quatermain.

CHAPTER I.

I MEET SIR HENRY CURTIS.

IT is a curious thing that at my age—fifty-five last birthday
—I should find myself taking up a pen to try and write a
history. I wonder what sort of a history it will be when I have
done it, if I ever come to the end of the trip! I have done a
good many things in my life, which seems a long one to me,
owing to my having begun so young, perhaps. At an age when
other boys are at school I was earning my living as a trader
in the old Colony. I have been trading, hunting, fighting, or
mining ever since. And yet it is only eight months ago that I
made my pile. It is a big pile now I have got it—I don't yet
know how big—but I don't think I would go through the last
fifteen or sixteen months again for it; no, not if I knew that I
should come out safe at the end, pile and all. But then, I am
a timid man, and don't like violence, and am pretty sick of
adventure. I wonder why I am going to write this book; it is
not in my line. I am not a literary man, though very devoted
to the Old Testament and also to the "Ingoldsby Legends."
Let me try and set down my reasons, just to see if I have any.

First reason: Because Sir Henry Curtis and Captain John
Good asked me to.

Second reason: Because I am laid up here at Durban with
the pain and trouble in my left leg. Ever since that confounded
lion got hold of me I have been liable to it, and its being rather
bad just now makes me limp more than ever. There must be
some poison in a lion's teeth, otherwise how is it that when
your wounds are healed they break out again, generally, mark
you, at the same time of year that you got your mauling? It

is a hard thing that when one has shot sixty-five lions, as I have in the course of my life, that the sixty-sixth should chew your leg like a quid of tobacco. It breaks the routine of the thing, and, putting other considerations aside, I am an orderly man and don't like that. This is by the way.

Third reason: Because I want my boy Harry, who is over there at the hospital in London studying to become a doctor, to have something to amuse him and keep him out of mischief for a week or so. Hospital work must sometimes pall and get rather dull, for even of cutting-up dead bodies there must come satiety, and as this history won't be dull, whatever else it may be, it may put a little life into things for a day or two while he is reading it.

Fourth reason and last: Because I am going to tell the strangest story that I know of. It may seem a queer thing to say that, especially considering that there is no woman in it—except Foulata. Stop, though! there is Gagaoola, if she was a woman and not a fiend. But she was a hundred at least, and therefore not marriageable, so I don't count her. At any rate, I can safely say that there is not a *petticoat* in the whole history. Well, I had better come to the yoke. It's a stiff place, and I feel as though I were bogged up to the axle. But "sutjes, sutjes," as the Boers say (I'm sure I don't know how they spell it), softly does it. A strong team will come through at last, that is if they ain't too poor. You will never do anything with poor oxen. Now, to begin.

I, Allan Quatermain, of Durban, Natal, Gentleman, make oath and say—That's how I began my deposition before the magistrate about poor Khiva's and Ventvögel's sad deaths; but somehow it doesn't seem quite the right way to begin a book. And, besides, am I a gentleman? What is a gentleman? I don't quite know, and yet I have had to do with niggers— no, I'll scratch that word "niggers" out, for I don't like it. I've known natives who *are,* and so you'll say, Harry, my boy, before you're done with this tale, and I have known mean whites with lots of money and fresh out from home, too, who *ain't*. Well, at any rate I was born a gentleman, though I've been nothing but a poor travelling trader and hunter all my life. Whether I have remained so I know not; you must judge of that. Heaven knows I've tried. I've killed many men in my time, but I have never slain wantonly or stained my hand in innocent blood, only in self-defense. The Almighty gave us our lives, and I suppose he meant us to defend them; at least I have always acted on that, and I hope it won't be brought up against me when my clock strikes. There, there; it is a cruel and a wicked world, and, for a timid man, I have been mixed up in a deal of slaughter. I can't tell the rights of it, but at any rate I have never stolen, though I once cheated a Kaffir out of a herd of cattle. But, then, he had done me a dirty turn, and it has troubled me ever since into the bargain.

Well, it's eighteen months or so ago since I first met Sir Henry Curtis and Captain Good, and it was in this way. I had been up elephant hunting beyond Bamangwato, and had had bad luck. Everything went wrong that trip and to top up with I got the fever badly. So soon as I was well enough I trekked down to the Diamond Fields, sold such ivory as I had, and also my wagon and oxen, discharged my hunters, and took the post-cart to the Cape. After spending a week in Cape Town, finding that they overcharged me at the hotel, and having seen everything there was to see, including the botanical gardens, which seem to me likely to confer a great benefit on the country, and the new Houses of Parliament, which I expect will do nothing of the sort, I determined to go on back to Natal by the *Dunkeld*, then lying in the docks waiting for the *Edinburgh Castle* due in from England. I took my berth and went aboard, and that afternoon the Natal passengers from the *Edinburgh Castle* transshipped, and we weighed anchor and put out to sea.

Among the passengers who came on board there were two who excited my curiosity. One, a man of about thirty, was one of the biggest-chested and longest-armed men I ever saw. He had yellow hair, a big yellow beard, clear-cut features, and large gray eyes set deep into his head. I never saw a finer-looking man, and somehow he reminded me of an ancient Dane. Not that I know much of ancient Danes, though I remember a modern Dane who did me out of ten pounds; but I remember once seeing a picture of some of those gentry, who, I take it, were a kind of white Zulus. They were drinking out of big horns, and their long hair hung down their backs, and as I looked at my friend standing there by the companion-ladder, I thought that if one only let his hair grow a bit, put one of those chain shirts on to those great shoulders of his, and gave him a big battle-axe and a horn mug, he might have sat as a model for that picture. And, by the way, it is a curious thing, and just shows how the blood will show out, I found out afterwards that Sir Henry Curtis, for that was the big man's name, was of Danish blood.* He also reminded me strongly

*Mr. Quatermain's ideas about ancient Danes seem to be rather confused; we have always understood that they were dark-haired people. Probably he was thinking of Saxons.—*Editor.*

of somebody else, but at the time I could not remember who it was.

The other man, who stood talking to Sir Henry, was short, stout, and dark, and of quite a different cut. I suspected at once that he was a naval officer. I don't know why, but it is difficult to mistake a navy man. I have gone shooting trips with several of them in the course of my life, and they have always been just the best and bravest and nicest fellows I ever met, though given to the use of profane language.

I asked, a page or two back, what is a gentleman? I'll answer it now: a royal naval officer is, in a general sort of a way, though, of course there may be a black sheep among them here and there. I fancy it is just the wide sea and the breath of God's winds that washes their hearts and blows the bitterness out of their minds and makes them what men ought to be. Well, to return, I was right again; I found out that he *was* a naval officer, a lieutenant of thirty-one, who, after seventeen years' service, had been turned out of her majesty's employ with the barren honor of a commander's rank, because it was impossible that he should be promoted. This is what people who serve the queen have to expect: to be shot out into the cold world to find a living just when they are beginning to really understand their work, and to get to the prime of life. Well, I suppose they don't mind it, but for my part I had rather earn my bread as a hunter. One's half-pence are as scarce, perhaps, but you don't get so many kicks. His name I found out—by referring to the passengers' list—was Good—Captain John Good. He was broad, of medium height, dark, stout, and rather a curious man to look at. He was so very neat and so very clean shaved, and he always wore an eye-glass in his right eye. It seemed to grow there, for it had no string, and he never took it out except to wipe it. At first I thought he used to sleep in it, but I afterwards found that this was a mistake. He put it in his trousers pocket when he went to bed, together with his false teeth, of which he had two beautiful sets that have often, my own being none of the best, caused me to break the tenth Commandment. But I am anticipating.

Soon after we had got under way evening closed in, and brought with it very dirty weather. A keen breeze sprang up off land, and a kind of aggravated Scotch mist soon drove everybody from the deck. And as for that *Dunkeld*, she is a flat-bottomed punt, and, going up light as she was, she rolled very heavily. It almost seemed as though she would go right over, but she never did. It was quite impossible to walk about, so I stood near the engines, where it was warm, and amused myself with watching the pendulum, which was fixed opposite to me, swinging slowly backward and forward as the vessel rolled, and marking the angle she touched at each lurch.

"That pendulum's wrong; it is not properly weighted," suddenly said a voice at my shoulder, somewhat testily. Looking round I saw the naval officer I had noticed when the passengers came aboard.

"Indeed; now what makes you think so?" I asked.

"Think so. I don't think at all. Why there"—as she righted herself after a roll—"if the ship had really rolled to the degree that thing pointed to then she would never have rolled again, that's all. But it is just like these merchant skippers, they always are so confoundedly careless."

Just then the dinner-bell rang, and I was not sorry, for it is a dreadful thing to have to listen to an officer of the Royal Navy when he gets on to that subject. I only know one worse thing, and that is to hear a merchant skipper express his candid opinion of officers of the Royal Navy.

Captain Good and I went down to dinner together, and there we found Sir Henry Curtis already seated. He and Captain Good sat together, and I sat opposite to them. The captain and I soon got into talk about shooting and what not, he asking me many questions, and I answering as well as I could. Presently he got on to elephants.

"Ah, sir," called out somebody who was sitting near me, "you've got the right man for that; Hunter Quatermain should be able to tell you about elephants if anybody can."

Sir Henry, who had been sitting quiet listening to our talk, started visibly.

"Excuse me, sir," he said, leaning forward across the table, and speaking in a low, deep voice, a very suitable voice, it seemed to me, to come out of those great lungs. "Excuse me, sir, but is your name Allan Quatermain?"

I said it was.

The big man made no further remark, but I heard him mutter "fortunate" into his beard.

Presently dinner came to an end, and as we were leaving the saloon Sir Henry came up and asked me if I would come into his cabin and smoke a pipe. I accepted, and he led the way to the *Dunkeld* deck cabin, and a very good cabin it was.

It had been two cabins, but when Sir Garnet, or one of those big swells, went down the coast in the *Dunkeld* they had knocked away the partition and never put it up again. There was a sofa in the cabin, and a little table in front of it. Sir Henry sent the steward for a bottle of whiskey, and the three of us sat down and lit our pipes.

"Mr. Quatermain," said Sir Henry Curtis, when the steward had brought the whiskey and lit the lamp, "the year before last, about this time, you were, I believe, at a place called Bamangwato, to the north of the Transvaal."

"I was," I answered, rather surprised that this gentleman should be so well acquainted with my movements, which were not, so far as I was aware, considered of general interest.

"You were trading there, were you not?" put in Captain Good, in his quick way.

"I was. I took up a wagon-load of goods and made a camp outside the settlement, and stopped till I had sold them."

Sir Henry was sitting opposite to me in a Madeira chair, his arms leaning on the table. He now looked up, fixing his large gray eyes full upon my face. There was a curious anxiety in them, I thought.

"Did you happen to meet a man called Neville there?"

"Oh, yes; he outspanned alongside of me for a fortnight, to rest his oxen before going on to the interior. I had a letter from a lawyer, a few months back, asking me if I knew what had become of him, which I answered to the best of my ability at the time."

"Yes," said Sir Henry, "your letter was forwarded to me. You said in it that the gentleman called Neville left Bamangwato in the beginning of May, in a wagon, with a driver, a voorlooper, and a Kaffir hunter called Jim, announcing his intention of trekking, if possible, as far as Inyati, the extreme trading-post in the Matabele country, where he would sell his wagon and proceed on foot. You also said that he did sell his wagon, for, six months afterwards, you saw the wagon in the possession of a Portuguese trader, who told you that he had bought it at Inyati from a white man whose name he had forgotten, and that the white man, with a native servant, had started off for the interior on a shooting trip, he believed."

"Yes."

Then came a pause.

"Mr. Quatermain," said Sir Henry, suddenly, "I suppose you

know or can guess nothing more of the reasons of my—of Mr. Neville's journey to the northward, or as to what point that journey was directed?"

"I heard something," I answered, and stopped. The subject was one which I did not dare to discuss.

Sir Henry and Captain Good looked at each other, and Captain Good nodded.

"Mr. Quatermain," said the former, "I am going to tell you a story, and ask your advice, and perhaps your assistance. The agent who forwarded me your letter told me that I might implicitly rely upon it, as you were," he said, "well known and universally respected in Natal, and especially noted for your discretion."

I bowed, and drank some whiskey-and-water to hide my confusion, for I am a modest man; and Sir Henry went on.

"Mr. Neville was my brother."

"Oh," I said, starting; for now I knew who Sir Henry had reminded me of when I first saw him. His brother was a much smaller man and had a dark beard, but, now I thought of it, he possessed eyes of the same shade of gray and with the same keen look in them, and the features, too, were not unlike.

"He was," went on Sir Henry, "my only and younger brother, and till five years ago I do not suppose we were ever a month away from each other. But just about five years ago a misfortune befell us, as sometimes does happen in families. We had quarrelled bitterly, and I behaved very unjustly to my brother in my anger." Here Captain Good nodded his head vigorously to himself. The ship gave a big roll just then, so that the looking-glass, which was fixed opposite us to starboard, was for a moment nearly over our heads, and as I was sitting with my hands in my pockets and staring upward, I could see him nodding like anything.

"As I dare say you know," went on Sir Henry, "if a man dies intestate, and has no property but land—real property it is called in England—it all descends to his eldest son. It so happened that just at the time when we quarrelled our father died intestate. He had put off making his will until it was too late. The result was that my brother, who had not been brought up to any profession, was left without a penny. Of course it would have been my duty to provide for him, but at the time the quarrel between us was so bitter that I did not—to my shame I say it (and he sighed deeply)—offer to do anything. It was not that I grudged him anything, but I waited for him to make advances, and he made none. I am sorry to trouble you with all this, Mr. Quatermain, but I must, to make things clear; eh, Good?"

"Quite so, quite so," said the captain. "Mr. Quatermain will, I am sure, keep this history to himself."

"Of course," said I, for I rather pride myself on my discretion.

"Well," went on Sir Henry, "my brother had a few hundred pounds to his account at the time, and without saying anything to me he drew out this paltry sum, and, having adopted the name of Neville, started off for South Africa in the wild hope of making a fortune. This I heard afterwards. Some three years passed, and I heard nothing of my brother, though I wrote several times. Doubtless the letters never reached him. But as time went on I grew more and more troubled about him. I found out, Mr. Quatermain, that blood is thicker than water."

"That's true," said I, thinking of my boy Harry.

"I found out, Mr. Quatermain, that I would have given half my fortune to know that my brother George, the only relation I have, was safe and well, and that I should see him again."

"But you never did, Curtis," jerked out Captain Good, glancing at the big man's face.

"Well, Mr. Quatermain, as time went on I became more and more anxious to find out if my brother was alive or dead, and, if alive, to get him home again. I set inquiries on foot, and your letter was one of the results. So far as it went it was satisfactory, for it showed that till lately George was alive; but it did not go far enough. So, to cut a long story short, I made up my mind to come out and look for him myself, and Captain Good was so kind as to come with me."

"Yes," said the captain; "nothing else to do, you see. Turned out by my lords of the admiralty to starve on half-pay. And now, perhaps, sir, you will tell us what you know or have heard of the gentleman called Neville."

CHAPTER II.

THE LEGEND OF SOLOMON'S MINES.

"WHAT was it that you heard about my brother's journey at Bamangwato?" said Sir Henry, as I paused to fill my pipe before answering Captain Good.

"I heard this," I answered, "and I have never mentioned it

to a soul till to-day. I heard that he was starting for Solomon's Mines."

"Solomon's Mines!" ejaculated both my hearers at once. "Where are they?"

"I don't know," I said; "I know where they are said to be. I once saw the peaks of the mountains that border them, but there was a hundred and thirty miles of desert between me and them, and I am not aware that any white man ever got across it, save one. But perhaps the best thing I can do is to tell you the legend of Solomon's Mines as I know it, you passing your word not to reveal anything I tell you without my permission. Do you agree to that? I have my reasons for asking it."

Sir Henry nodded, and Captain Good replied, "Certainly, certainly."

"Well," I began, "as you may guess, in a general way elephant-hunters are a rough set of men, and don't trouble themselves with much beyond the facts of life and the ways of Kaffirs. But here and there you meet a man who takes the trouble to collect traditions from the natives, and tries to make out a little piece of the history of this dark land. It was such a man as this who first told me the legend of Solomon's Mines, now a matter of nearly thirty years ago. It was when I was on my first elephant-hunt in the Matabele country. His name was Evans, and he was killed next year, poor fellow, by a wounded buffalo, and lies buried near the Zambesi Falls. I was telling Evans one night, I remember, of some wonderful workings I had found while hunting koodoo and eland in what is now the Lydenburg district of the Transvaal. I see they have come across these workings again lately in prospecting for gold, but I knew of them years ago. There is a great wide wagon-road cut out of the solid rock, and leading to the mouth of the working or gallery. Inside the mouth of this gallery are stacks of gold quartz piled up ready for crushing, which shows that the workers, whoever they were, must have left in a hurry, and about twenty paces in the gallery is built across, and a beautiful bit of masonry it is.

" 'Ay,' said Evans, 'but I will tell you a queerer thing than that;' and he went on to tell me how he had found in the far interior a ruined city, which he believed to be the Ophir of the Bible—and, by the way, other more learned men have said the same long since poor Evans's time. I was, I remember, listening open-eared to all these wonders, for I was young at the time, and this story of an ancient civilization, and of the treasure which those old Jewish or Phœnician adventurers used to extract from a country long since lapsed into the darkest barbarism, took a great hold upon my imagination, when suddenly he said to me, 'Lad, did you ever hear of the Suliman Mountains up to the northwest of the Mashukulumbwe country?' I told him that I never had. 'Ah, well,' he said, 'that was where Solomon really had his mines—his diamond mines, I mean.'

" 'How do you know that?' I asked.

" 'Know it? why, what is "Suliman" but a corruption of Solomon?* and, besides, an old Isanusi (witch doctor) up in the Manica country told me all about it. She said that the people who lived across those mountains were a branch of the Zulus, speaking a dialect of Zulu, but finer and bigger men even; that there lived among them great wizards, who had learned their art from white men when "all the world was dark," and who had the secret of a wonderful mine of "bright stones." '

"Well, I laughed at this story at the time, though it interested me, for the diamond fields were not discovered then, and poor Evans went off and got killed, and for twenty years I never thought any more of the matter. But just twenty years afterwards—and that is a long time, gentlemen; an elephant-hunter does not often live for twenty years at his business—I heard something more definite about Suliman's Mountains and the country which lies beyond them. I was up beyond the Manica country at a place called Sitanda's Kraal, and a miserable place it was, for one could get nothing to eat there, and there was but little game about. I had an attack of fever, and was in a bad way generally, when one day a Portugee arrived with a single companion—a half-breed. Now I know your Delagoa Portugee well. There is no greater devil unhung, in a general way, battening as he does upon human agony and flesh in the shape of slaves. But this was quite a different type of man to the low fellows I had been accustomed to meet; he reminded me more of the polite dons I have read about. He was tall and thin, with large dark eyes and curling gray mustache. We talked together a little, for he could speak broken English, and I understood a little Portugee, and he told me that his name was José Silvestre, and that he had a place near Delagoa Bay; and when he went on next day, with his half-breed companion, he said, 'Good-bye,' taking off his hat quite in the old style. 'Good-bye, senor,' he said; 'if ever we meet again I shall be the richest man in the world, and I will remember you.' I

*Suliman is the Arabic form of Solomon.—*Editor.*

laughed a little—I was too weak to laugh much—and watched him strike out for the great desert to the west, wondering if he was mad, or what he thought he was going to find there.

"A week passed, and I got the better of my fever. One evening I was sitting on the ground in front of the little tent I had with me, chewing the last leg of a miserable fowl I had bought from a native for a bit of cloth worth twenty fowls, and staring at the hot, red sun sinking down into the desert, when suddenly I saw a figure, apparently that of a European, for it wore a coat, on the slope of the rising ground opposite to me, about three hundred yards away. The figure crept along on its hands and knees, then it got up and staggered along a few yards on its legs, only to fall and crawl along again. Seeing that it must be somebody in distress, I sent one of my hunters to help him, and presently he arrived, and who do you suppose it turned out to be?"

"José Silvestre, of course," said Captain Good.

"Yes, José Silvestre, or rather his skeleton and a little skin. His face was bright yellow with bilious fever, and his large, dark eyes stood nearly out of his head, for all his flesh had gone. There was nothing but yellow, parchment-like skin, white hair, and the gaunt bones sticking up beneath.

"'Water! for the sake of Christ, water!' he moaned. I saw that his lips were cracked, and his tongue, which protruded between them, was swollen and blackish.

"I gave him water with a little milk in it, and he drank it in great gulps, two quarts or more, without stopping. I would not let him have any more. Then the fever took him again, and he fell down and began to rave about Suliman's Mountains, and the diamonds, and the desert. I took him into the tent and did what I could for him, which was little enough; but I saw how it must end. About eleven o'clock he got quieter, and I lay down for a little rest and went to sleep. At dawn I woke again, and saw him in the half light sitting up, a strange, gaunt form, and gazing out towards the desert. Presently the first ray of the sun shot right across the wide plain before us till it reached the far-away crest of one of the tallest of the Suliman Mountains, more than a hundred miles away.

"'There it is!' cried the dying man in Portuguese, stretching out his long, thin arm, 'but I shall never reach it, never. No one will ever reach it!'

"Suddenly he paused, and seemed to take a resolution.

'Friend,' he said, turning towards me, 'are you there? My eyes grow dark.'

" 'Yes,' I said; 'yes, lie down now, and rest.'

" 'Ay,' he answered, 'I shall rest soon; I have time to rest—all eternity. Listen, I am dying! You have been good to me. I will give you the paper. Perhaps you will get there if you can live through the desert, which has killed my poor servant and me.'

"Then he groped in his shirt and brought out what I thought was a Boer tobacco-pouch of the skin of the Swartvet-pens (sable antelope). It was fastened with a little strip of hide, what we call a rimpi, and this he tried to untie, but could not. He handed it to me. 'Untie it,' he said. I did so, and extracted a bit of torn yellow linen, on which something was written in rusty letters. Inside was a paper.

"Then he went on feebly, for he was growing weak: 'The paper has it all, that is on the rag. It took me years to read. Listen: my ancestor, a political refugee from Lisbon and one of the first Portuguese who landed on these shores, wrote that when he was dying on those mountains which no white foot ever pressed before or since. His name was José da Silvestra, and he lived three hundred years ago. His slave, who waited for him on this side of the mountains, found him dead, and brought the writing home to Delagoa. It has been in the family ever since, but none have cared to read it till at last I did. And I have lost my life over it, but another may succeed, and become the richest man in the world—the richest man in the world. Only give it to no one; go yourself!' Then he began to wander again, and in an hour it was all over.

"God rest him! he died very quietly, and I buried him deep, with big boulders on his breast; so I do not think that the jackals can have dug him up. And then I came away."

"Ay, but the document," said Sir Henry, in a tone of deep interest.

"Yes, the document; what was in it?" added the captain.

"Well, gentlemen, if you like I will tell you. I have never showed it to anybody yet except my dear wife, who is dead, and she thought it was all nonsense, and a drunken old Portuguese trader who translated it for me, and had forgotten all about it next morning. The original rag is at my home in Durban, together with poor Don José's translation, but I have the English rendering in my pocket-book, and a fac-simile of the map, if it can be called a map. Here it is."

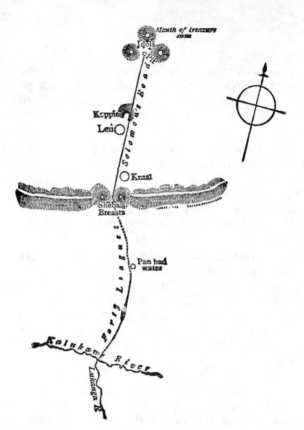

"I José da Silvestra, who am now dying of hunger in the little cave where no snow is on the north side of the nipple of the southernmost of the two mountains I have named Sheba's Breasts, write this in the year 1590 with a cleft bone upon a remnant of my raiment, my blood being the ink. If my slave should find it when he comes, and should bring it to Delagoa, let my friend (name illegible) bring the matter to the knowledge of the king, that he may send an army which, if they live through the desert and the mountains, and can overcome the brave Kukuanes and their devilish arts, to which end many priests should be brought, will make him the richest king since Solomon. With my own eyes have I seen the countless diamonds stored in Solomon's treasure-chamber behind the white Death; but through the treachery of Gagool the witch-finder I might bring nought away, scarcely my life. Let him who comes follow the map, and climb the snow of Sheba's left breast till he comes to the nipple, on the north side of which is the great road Solomon made, from whence three days' journey to the King's Place. Let him kill Gagool. Pray for my soul. Farewell. JOSE DA SILVESTRA."*

*"Eu José da Silvestra que estou morrendo de fome ná pequena cova onde não ha neve ao lado norte do bico mais ao sul das duas montanhas que chamei seio de Sheba; escrevo isto no anno 1590; escrevo isto com um pedaço d' ósso n' um farrapo de minha roupa e com sangue meu por tinta;

When I had finished reading the above and shown the copy of the map, drawn by the dying hand of the old don with his blood for ink, there followed a silence of astonishment.

"Well," said Captain Good, "I have been round the world twice, and put in at most ports, but may I be hung if I ever heard a yarn like that out of a story-book, or in it either, for the matter of that."

"It's a queer story, Mr. Quatermain," said Sir Henry. "I suppose you are not hoaxing us? It is, I know, sometimes thought allowable to take a greenhorn in."

"If you think that, Sir Henry," I said, much put out, and pocketing my paper, for I do not like to be thought one of those silly fellows who consider it witty to tell lies, and who are forever boasting to new-comers of extraordinary hunting adventures which never happened, "why there is an end of the matter," and I rose to go.

Sir Henry laid his large hand upon my shoulder. "Sit down, Mr. Quatermain," he said, "I beg your pardon; I see very well you do not wish to deceive us, but the story sounded so extraordinary that I could hardly believe it."

"You shall see the original map and writing when we reach Durban," I said, somewhat mollified; for really, when I came to consider the matter, it was scarcely wonderful that he should doubt my good faith. "But I have not told you about your brother. I knew the man Jim who was with him. He was a Bechuana by birth, a good hunter, and, for a native, a very clever man. The morning Mr. Neville was starting, I saw Jim standing by my wagon and cutting up tobacco on the disselboom.

" 'Jim,' said I, 'where are you off to this trip? Is it elephants?'

" 'No, Bass,' he answered, 'we are after something worth more than ivory.'

" 'And what might that be?' I said; for I was curious. 'Is it gold?'

" 'No, Baas, something worth more than gold,' and he grinned.

se o meu escravo dér com isto quando venha ao levar para Lourenzo Marquez, que o meu amigo (————) leve a cousa ao conhecimento d' El Rei, para que possa mandar um exercito que, se desfiler pelo deserto e pelas montanhas e mesmo sobrepujar os bravos Kukuanes e suas artes diabolicas, pelo que se deviam trazer muitos padres Fara o Rei mais rico depois de Salomão. Com meus proprios olhos vé os di amantes sem conto guardados nas camaras do thesouro de Salomão a traz da morte branca, mas pela traição de Gagoal a feiticeira achadora, nada poderia levar, e apenas a minha vida. Quem vier siga o mappa e trepe pela neve de Sheba peito à esquerda até chegar ao bico, do lado norte do qual está a grande estrada do Salomão por elle feita, donde ha tres dias de journada até ao Palacio do Rei. Mate Gagoal. Reze por minha alma. Adeos.

"JOSE DA SILVESTRA."

"I did not ask any more questions, for I did not like to lower my dignity by seeming curious, but I was puzzled. Presently Jim finished cutting his tobacco.

"'Baas,' said he.

"I took no notice.

"'Baas,' said he again.

"'Eh, boy, what is it?' said I.

"'Baas, we are going after diamonds.'

"'Diamonds! why, then, you are going in the wrong direction; you should head for the fields.'

"'Baas, have you ever heard of Suliman's Berg?' (Solomon's Mountains.)

"'Ay!'

"'Have you ever heard of the diamonds there?'

"'I have heard a foolish story, Jim.'

"'It is no story, Baas. I once knew a woman who came from there, and got to Natal with her child. She told me; she is dead now.'

"'Your master will feed the assvogels (vultures), Jim, if he tries to reach Suliman's country, and so will you, if they can get any pickings off your worthless old carcass,' said I.

"He grinned. 'Mayhap, Baas. Man must die; I'd rather like to try a new country myself; the elephants are getting worked out about here.'

"'Ah! my boy,' I said, 'you wait till the "pale old man" (death) gets a grip of your yellow throat, and then we'll hear what sort of a tune you sing.'

"Half an hour after that I saw Neville's wagon move off. Presently Jim came running back. 'Good-bye, Baas,' he said. 'I didn't like to start without bidding you good-bye, for I dare say you are right, and we shall never come back again.'

"'Is your master really going to Suliman's Berg, Jim, or are you lying?'

"'No,' says he; 'he is going. He told me he was bound to make his fortune somehow, or try to; so he might as well try the diamonds.'

"'Oh!' said I; 'wait a bit, Jim; will you take a note to your master, Jim, and promise not to give it to him until you reach Inyati?' (which was some hundred miles off).

"'Yes,' said he.

"So I took a scrap of paper and wrote on it, 'Let him who comes . . . climb the snow of Sheba's left breast, till he comes to the nipple, on the north side of which is Solomon's great road.'

"'Now, Jim,' I said, 'when you give this to your master, tell him he had better follow the advice implicitly. You are not to give it to him now, because I don't want him back asking me questions which I won't answer. Now be off, you idle fellow, the wagon is nearly out of sight.'

"Jim took the note and went, and that is all I know about your brother, Sir Henry; but I am afraid—"

"Mr. Quatermain," said Sir Henry, "I am going to look for my brother; I am going to trace him to Suliman's Mountains, and over them, if necessary, until I find him, or until I know that he is dead. Will you come with me?"

I am, as I think I have said, a cautious man, indeed a timid one, and I shrank from such an idea. It seemed to me that to start on such a journey would be to go to certain death, and, putting other things aside, as I had a son to support, I could not afford to die just then.

"No, thank you, Sir Henry, I think I had rather not," I answered. "I am too old for wild-goose chases of that sort, and we should only end up like my poor friend Silvestre. I have a son dependent on me, so cannot afford to risk my life."

Both Sir Henry and Captain Good looked very disappointed.

"Mr. Quatermain," said the former, "I am well off, and I am bent upon this business. You may put the remuneration for your services at whatever figure you like, in reason, and it shall be paid over to you before we start. Moreover, I will, before we start, arrange that in the event of anything happening to us or to you, your son shall be suitably provided for. You will see from this how necessary I think your presence. Also, if by any chance we should reach this place, and find diamonds, they shall belong to you and Good equally. I do not want them. But of course the chance is as good as nothing, though the same thing would apply to any ivory we might get. You may pretty well make your own terms with me, Mr. Quatermain; of course I shall pay all expenses."

"Sir Henry," said I, "this is the most liberal offer I ever had, and one not to be sneezed at by a poor hunter and trader. But the job is the biggest I ever came across, and I must take time to think it over. I will give you my answer before we get to Durban."

"Very good," answered Sir Henry, and then I said good-night and turned in, and dreamed about poor, long-dead Silvestre and the diamonds.

CHAPTER III.

UMBOPA ENTERS OUR SERVICE.

It takes from four to five days, according to the vessel and the state of the weather, to run up from the Cape to Durban. Sometimes, if the landing is bad at East London, where they have not yet got that wonderful harbor they talk so much of and sink such a mint of money in, one is delayed for twenty-four hours before the cargo boats can get out to take the goods off. But on this occasion we had not to wait at all, for there were no breakers on the bar to speak of, and the tugs came out at once with their long strings of ugly, flat-bottomed boats, into which the goods were bundled with a crash. It did not matter what they were, over they went, slap-bang! whether they were china or woolen goods they met with the same treatment. I saw one case containing four dozen of champagne smashed all to bits, and there was the champagne fizzing and boiling about in the bottom of the dirty cargo-boat. It was a wicked waste, and so evidently the Kaffirs in the boat thought, for they found a couple of unbroken bottles, and knocking the tops off drank the contents. But they had not allowed for the expansion caused by the fizz in the wine, and feeling themselves swelling, rolled about in the bottom of the boat, calling out that the good liquor was "tagati" (bewitched). I spoke to them from the vessel, and told them that it was the white man's strongest medicine, and that they were as good as dead men. They went on to the shore in a very great fright, and I do not think that they will touch champagne again.

Well, all the time we were running up to Natal I was thinking over Sir Henry Curtis's offer. We did not speak any more on the subject for a day or two, though I told them many hunting yarns, all true ones. There is no need to tell lies about hunting, for so many curious things happen within the knowledge of a man whose business it is to hunt; but this is by the way.

At last, one beautiful evening in January, which is our hottest month, we steamed along the coast of Natal, expecting to make Durban Point by sunset. It is a lovely coast all along from East London, with its red sandhills and wide sweeps of vivid green, dotted here and there with Kaffir kraals, and bordered by a ribbon of white surf which spouts up in pillars of foam where it hits the rocks. But just before you get to Durban there is a peculiar richness about it. There are the deep kloofs cut in the hills by the rushing rains of centuries, down which the rivers sparkle; there is the deepest green of the bush, growing as God planted it, and the other greens of the mealie-gardens and the sugar-patches, while here and there a white house, smiling out at the placid sea, puts a finish and gives an air of homeliness to the scene. For to my mind, however beautiful a view may be, it requires the presence of man to make it complete, but perhaps that is because I have lived so much in the wilderness, and therefore know the value of civilization, though, to be sure, it drives away the game. The Garden of Eden, no doubt, was fair before man was, but I always think it must have been fairer when Eve was walking about it. But we had miscalculated a little, and the sun was well down before we dropped anchor off the Point, and heard the gun which told the good folk that the English mail was in. It was too late to think of getting over the bar that night, so we went down comfortably to dinner, after seeing the mail carried off in the lifeboat.

When we came up again the moon was up, and shining so brightly over sea and shore that she almost paled the quick, large flashes from the lighthouse. From the shore floated sweet spicy odors that always remind me of hymns and missionaries, and in the windows of the houses on the Berea sparkle a hundred lights. From a large brig lying near came the music of the sailors as they worked at getting the anchor up to be ready for the wind. Altogether it was a perfect night, such a night as you only get in southern Africa, and it threw a garment of peace over everybody as the moon threw a garment of silver over everything. Even the great bulldog, belonging to a sporting passenger, seemed to yield to the gentle influences, and, giving up yearning to come to close quarters with the baboon in a cage on the fo'k'sle, snored happily in the door of the cabin, dreaming, no doubt, that he had finished him, and happy in his dream.

We all—that is, Sir Henry Curtis, Captain Good, and myself— went and sat by the wheel, and were quiet for a while.

"Well, Mr. Quatermain," said Sir Henry, presently, "have you been thinking about my proposals?"

"Ay," echoed Captain Good, "what do you think of them, Mr. Quatermain? I hope you are going to give us the pleasure of your company as far as Solomon's Mines, or wherever the gentleman you knew as Neville may have got to."

I rose and knocked out my pipe before I answered. I had not made up my mind, and wanted the additional moment to complete it. Before the burning tobacco had fallen into the sea it was completed; just that little extra second did the trick.

It is often the way when you have been bothering a long time over a thing.

"Yes, gentlemen," I said, sitting down again, "I will go, and by your leave I will tell you why and on what terms. First, for the terms which I ask.

"1. You are to pay all expenses, and any ivory or other valuables we may get is to be divided between Captain Good and myself.

"2. That you pay me £500 for my service on the trip before we start, I undertaking to serve you faithfully till you choose to abandon the enterprise, or till we succeed, or disaster overtakes us.

"3. That before we start you execute a deed agreeing in the event of my death or disablement, to pay my boy Harry, who is studying medicine over there in London at Guy's Hospital, a sum of £200 a year for five years, by which time he ought to be able to earn a living for himself. That is all, I think, and I dare say you will say quite enough, too."

"No," answered Sir Henry, "I accept them gladly. I am bent upon this project, and would pay more than that for your help, especially considering the peculiar knowledge you possess."

"Very well. And now that I have made my terms I will tell you my reasons for making up my mind to go. First of all, gentlemen, I have been observing you both for the last few days, and if you will not think me impertinent I will say that I like you, and think that we shall come up well to the yoke together. That is something, let me tell you, when one has a long journey like this before one.

"And now as to the journey itself, I tell you flatly, Sir Henry and Captain Good, that I do not think it probable that we can come out of it alive, that is, if we attempt to cross the Suliman Mountains. What was the fate of the old Don da Silvestra three hundred years ago? What was the fate of his descendant twenty years ago? What has been your brother's fate? I tell you frankly, gentlemen, that as their fate was so I believe ours will be."

I paused to watch the effect of my words. Captain Good looked a little uncomfortable; but Sir Henry's face did not change. "We must take our chance," he said.

"You may perhaps wonder," I went on, "why, if I think this, I, who am as I told you a timid man, should undertake such a journey. It is for two reasons. First, I am a fatalist, and believe that my time is appointed to come quite independ-

ently of my own movements, and that if I am to go to Suliman
Mountains to be killed, I shall go there and shall be killed there.
God Almighty, no doubt, knows his mind about me, so I need
not trouble on that point. Secondly, I am a poor man. For
nearly forty years I have hunted and traded, but I have never
made more than a living. Well, gentlemen, I don't know if
you are aware that the average life of an elephant-hunter from
the time he takes to the trade is from four to five years. So
you see I have lived through about seven generations of my
class, and I should think that my time cannot be far off, any
way. Now, if anything were to happen to me in the ordinary
course of business, by the time my debts were paid there would
be nothing left to support my son Harry while he was getting
in the way of earning a living, whereas now he would be provided
for for five years. There is the whole affair in a nutshell."

"Mr. Quatermain," said Sir Henry, who had been giving me
the most serious attention, "your motives for undertaking an
enterprise which you believe can only end in disaster reflect a
great deal of credit on you. Whether or not you are right, time
and the event, of course, alone can show. But whether you are
right or wrong, I may as well tell you at once that I am going
through with it to the end, sweet or bitter. If we are going to
be knocked on the head, all that I have to say is that I hope we
shall get a little shooting first—eh, Good?"

"Yes, yes," put in the captain. "We have all three of us been
accustomed to face danger, and hold our lives in our hands in
various ways, so it is no good turning back now."

"And now I vote we go down to the saloon and take an observation, just for luck, you know." And we did—through the
bottom of a tumbler.

Next day we went ashore, and I put Sir Henry and Captain
Good up at the little shanty I have on the Berea, and which I
call my home. There are only three rooms and a kitchen in it,
and it is built of green brick with a galvanized iron roof, but
there is a good garden, with the best loquot-trees in it that I
know, and some nice young mangoes, of which I hope great
things. The curator of the botanical gardens gave them to
me. It is looked after by an old hunter of mine named Jack,
whose thigh was so badly broken by a buffalo cow in Sikukunïs
country that he will never hunt again. But he can potter about
and garden, being a Griqua by birth. You can never get your
Zulu to take much interest in gardening. It is a peaceful art,
and peaceful arts are not in his line.

Sir Henry and Good slept in a tent pitched in my little grove of orange-trees at the end of the garden (for there was no room for them in the house), and what with the smell of the bloom and the sight of the green and golden fruit—for in Durban you will see all three on the tree together—I dare say it is a pleasant place enough (for we have few mosquitoes here unless there happens to come an unusually heavy rain).

Well, to get on—for unless I do you will be tired of my story before ever we fetch up at Suliman's Mountains—having once made up my mind to go, I set about making the necessary preparations. First I got the deed from Sir Henry, providing for my boy in case of accidents. There was some little difficulty about getting this legally executed, as Sir Henry was a stranger here, and the property to be charged was over the water; but it was ultimately got over with the help of a lawyer, who charged £20 for the job—a price that I thought outrageous. Then I got my check for £500. Having paid this tribute to my bump of caution, I bought a wagon and a span of oxen on Sir Henry's behalf, and beauties they were. It was a twenty-two-foot wagon with iron axles, very strong, very light, and built throughout of stink-wood. It was not quite a new one, having been to the Diamond Fields and back, but in my opinion it was all the better for that, for one could see that the wood was well-seasoned. If anything is going to give in a wagon, or if there is green wood in it, it will show out on the first trip. It was what we call a "half-tented" wagon—that is to say, it was only covered in over the after twelve feet, leaving all the front part free for the necessaries we had to carry with us. In this after part was a hide "cartle," or bed, on which two people could sleep, also racks for rifles, and many other little conveniences. I gave £125 for it, and think it was cheap at the price. Then I bought a beautiful team of twenty salted Zulu oxen, which I had had my eye on for a year or two. Sixteen oxen are the usual number for a team, but I had four extra to allow for casualties. These Zulu oxen are small and light, not more than half the size of the Africander oxen, which are generally used for transport purposes; but they will live where the Africander will starve, and with a light load will make five miles a day better going, being quicker and not so liable to get footsore. What is more, this lot were thoroughly "salted"—that is, they had worked all over South Africa, and so had become proof (comparatively speaking) against red water, which so frequently destroys whole teams of oxen when they get on to strange "veldt" (grass country). As for "lung sick," which is a dreadful form of pneumonia, very prevalent in this country, they had all been inoculated against it. This is done by cutting a slit in the tail of an ox, and binding in a piece of the diseased lung of an animal which has died of the sickness. The result is that the ox sickens, takes the disease in a mild form, which causes its tail to drop off, as a rule about a foot from the root, and becomes proof against future attacks. It seems cruel to rob the animal of his tail, especially in a country where there are so many flies, but it is better to sacrifice the tail and keep the ox than to lose both tail and ox, for a tail without an ox is not much good except to dust with. Still it does look odd to trek along behind twenty stumps, where there ought to be tails. It seems as though nature had made a trifling mistake, and stuck the stern ornaments of a lot of prize bulldogs on to the rumps of the oxen.

Next came the question of provisioning and medicines, one which required the most careful consideration, for what one had to do was to avoid lumbering the wagon up, and yet take everything absolutely necessary. Fortunately, it turned out that Good was a bit of a doctor, having at some period in his previous career managed to pass through a course of medical and surgical instruction, which he had more or less kept up. He was not, of course, qualified, but he knew more about it than many a man who could write M.D. after his name, as we found out afterwards, and he had a splendid travelling medicine-chest and a set of instruments. While we were at Durban he cut off a Kaffir's big toe in a way which it was a pleasure to see. But he was quite flabbergasted when the Kaffir, who had sat stolidly watching the operation, asked him to put on another, saying that a "white one" would do at a pinch.

There remained, when these questions were satisfactorily settled, two further important points for consideration, namely, that of arms and that of servants. As to the arms I cannot do better than to put down a list of those we finally decided on from among the ample store that Sir Henry had brought with him from England, and those which I had. I copy it from my pocket-book, where I made the entry at the time:

"Three heavy breechloading double-eight elephant guns, weighing about fifteen pounds each, with a charge of eleven drachms of black powder." Two of these were by a well-known London firm, most excellent makers, but I do not know by whom mine, which was not so highly finished, was made. I had used it on several trips, and shot a good many elephants with it, and it had always proved a most superior weapon, thoroughly to be relied on.

"Three double .500 expresses, constructed to carry a charge of six drachms," sweet weapons, and admirable for medium-sized game, such as eland or sable antelope, or for men, especially in an open country and with the semi-hollow bullet.

"One double No. 12 central-fire Keeper's shotgun, full choke both barrels." This gun proved of the greatest service to us afterwards in shooting game for the pot.

"Three Winchester repeating rifles (not carbines), spare guns.

"Three single-action Colt's revolvers, with the heavier pattern of cartridge."

This was our total armament, and the reader will doubtless observe that the weapons of each class were of the same make and calibre, so that the cartridges were interchangeable, a very important point. I make no apology for detailing it at length, for every experienced hunter will know how vital a proper supply of guns and ammunition is to the success of an expedition.

Now as to the men who were to go with us. After much consultation we decided that their number should be limited to five, namely, a driver, a leader, and three servants.

The driver and leader I got without much difficulty, two Zulus, named respectively Goza and Tom; but the servants were a more difficult matter. It was necessary that they should be thoroughly trustworthy and brave men, as in a business of this sort our lives might depend upon their conduct. At last I secured two, one a Hottentot called Ventvögel (wind-bird), and one a little Zulu named Khiva, who had the merit of speaking English perfectly. Ventvögel I had known before; he was one of the most perfect "spoorers" (game-trackers) I ever had to do with, and tough as whipcord. He never seemed to tire. But he had one failing, so common with his race, drink. Put him within reach of a bottle of grog and you could not trust him. But as we were going beyond the region of grog-shops this little weakness of his did not so much matter.

Having got these two men I looked in vain for a third to suit my purpose, so we determined to start without one, trusting to luck to find a suitable man on our way up country. But on the evening before the day we had fixed for our departure the Zulu Khiva informed me that a man was waiting to see me. Accordingly when we had done dinner, for we were at table at the time, I told him to bring him in. Presently a very tall, handsome-looking man, somewhere about thirty years of age, and very light-colored for a Zulu, entered and, lifting his knob-stick by way of salute, squatted himself down in the corner on his haunches and sat silent. I did not take any notice of him for a while, for it is a great mistake to do so. If you rush into conversation at once a Zulu is apt to think you are a person of little dignity or consideration. I observed, however, that he was a "Keshla" (ringed man), that is, that he wore on his head the black ring, made of a species of gum polished with fat and worked in with the hair, usually assumed by Zulus on attaining a certain age or dignity. Also it struck me that his face was familiar to me.

"Well," I said at last, "what is your name?"

"Umbopa," answered the man, in a slow, deep voice.

"I have seen your face before."

"Yes; the Inkoosi (chief) saw my face at the place of the Little Hand (Isandhlwana) the day before the battle."

Then I remembered. I had been one of Lord Chelmsford's guides in that unlucky Zulu war, and had had the good-fortune to leave the camp in charge of some wagons the day before the battle. While I had been waiting for the cattle to be inspanned I had fallen into conversation with this man, who held some small command among the native auxiliaries, and he had expressed to me his doubts of the safety of the camp. At the time I had told him to hold his tongue, and leave such matters to wiser heads; but afterwards I thought of his words.

"I remember," I said; "what is it you want?"

"It is this, 'Macumazahn' (that is my Kaffir name, and means the man who gets up in the middle of the night; or in vulgar English, he who keeps his eyes open). I hear that you go on a great expedition far into the north with the white chiefs from over the water. Is it a true word?"

"It is."

"I hear that you go even to the Lukanga River, a moon's journey beyond the Manica country. Is this so also, 'Macumazahn?' "

"Why do you ask whither we go? What is it to thee?" I answered, suspiciously, for the objects of our journey had been kept a dead secret.

"It is this, O white men, that if indeed you travel so far I would travel with you."

There was a certain assumption of dignity in the man's mode of speech, and especially in his use of the words "O white men," instead of "O Inkosis" (chiefs), which struck me.

"You forget yourself a little," I said. "Your words come out unawares. That is not the way to speak. What is your name, and where is your kraal? Tell us, that we may know with whom we have to deal."

"My name is Umbopa. I am of the Zulu people, yet not of them. The house of my tribe is in the far north; it was left behind when the Zulus came down here a 'thousand years ago,' long before Chaka reigned in Zululand. I have no kraal. I have wandered for many years. I came from the north as a child to Zululand. I was Cetywayo's man in the Nkomabakosi regiment. I ran away from Zululand and came to Natal because I wanted to see the white man's ways. Then I served against Cetywayo in the war. Since then I have been working in Natal. Now I am tired, and would go north again. Here is not my place. I want no money, but I am a brave man, and am worth my place and meat. I have spoken."

I was rather puzzled at this man and his way of speech. It was evident to me from his manner that he was in the main telling the truth, but he was somehow different from the ordinary run of Zulus, and I rather mistrusted his offer to come without pay. Being in a difficulty, I translated his words to Sir Henry and Good, and asked them their opinion. Sir Henry told me to ask him to stand up. Umbopa did so, at the same time slipping off the long military great-coat he wore, and revealing himself naked except for the moocha round his centre and a necklace of lion's claws. He certainly was a magnificent-looking man; I never saw a finer native. Standing about six foot three high, he was broad in proportion, and very shapely. In that light, too, his skin looked scarcely more than dark, except here and there where deep, black scars marked old assegai wounds. Sir Henry walked up to him and looked into his proud, handsome face.

"They make a good pair, don't they?" said Good; "one as big as the other."

"I like your looks, Mr. Umbopa, and I will take you as my servant," said Sir Henry in English.

Umbopa evidently understood him, for he answered in Zulu, "It is well;" and then, with a glance at the white man's great stature and breadth, "we are men, you and I."

CHAPTER IV.

AN ELEPHANT HUNT.

Now I do not propose to narrate at full length all the incidents of our long journey up to Sitanda's Kraal, near the junction of the Lukanga and Kalukwe rivers, a journey of more than a thousand miles from Durban, the last three hundred or so of which, owing to the frequent presence of the dreadful "tsetse" fly, whose bite is fatal to all animals except donkeys and men, we had to make on foot.

We left Durban at the end of January, and it was in the second week of May that we camped near Sitanda's Kraal. Our adventures on the way were many and various, but as they were of the sort which befall every African hunter, I shall not--with one exception to be presently detailed—set them down here, lest I should render this history too wearisome.

At Inyati, the outlying trading station in the Matabele country, of which Lobengula (a great scoundrel) is king, we with many regrets parted from our comfortable wagon. Only twelve oxen remained to us out of the beautiful span of twenty which I had bought at Durban. One we had lost from the bite of a cobra, three had perished from poverty and the want of water, one had been lost, and the other three had died from eating the poisonous herb called "tulip." Five more sickened from this cause, but we managed to cure them with doses of an infusion made by boiling down the tulip-leaves. If administered in time this is a very effective antidote. The wagon and oxen we left in the immediate charge of Goza and Tom, the driver and leader, both of them trustworthy boys, requesting a worthy Scotch missionary who lived in this wild place to keep an eye to it. Then, accompanied by Umbopa, Khiva, Ventvögel, and half a dozen bearers whom we hired on the spot, we started off on foot upon our wild quest. I remember we were all a little silent on the occasion of that departure, and I think that each of us was wondering if we should ever see that wagon again; for my part I never expected to. For a while we tramped on in silence, till Umbopa, who was marching in front, broke into a Zulu chant about how some brave men, tired of life and the tameness of things, started off into a great wilderness to find new things or die, and how, lo, and behold! when they had got far into the wilderness, they found it was not a wilderness at all, but a beautiful place full of young wives and fat cattle, of game to hunt and enemies to kill.

Then we all laughed and took it for a good omen. He was a cheerful savage, was Umbopa, in a dignified sort of way, when he had not got one of his fits of brooding, and had a wonderful knack of keeping one's spirits up. We all got very fond of him.

And now for the one adventure I am going to treat myself to, for I do heartily love a hunting yarn.

About a fortnight's march from Inyati we came across a

peculiarly beautiful bit of fairly-watered wooded country. The kloofs in the hills were covered with dense brush, "idoro" bush as the natives call it, and in some places with the "wacht-een-beche" (wait-a-little) thorn, and there were great quantities of the beautiful "machabell" tree, laden with refreshing yellow fruit with enormous stones. This tree is the elephant's favorite food, and there were not wanting signs that the great brutes were about, for not only was their spoor frequent, but in many places the trees were broken down and even uprooted. The elephant is a destructive feeder.

One evening, after a long day's march, we came to a spot of peculiar loveliness. At the foot of a bush-clad hill was a dry river-bed, in which, however, were to be found pools of crystal water all trodden round with the hoof-prints of game. Facing this hill was a parklike plain, where grew clumps of flat-topped mimosa, varied with occasional glossy-leaved machabells, and all round was the great sea of pathless, silent bush.

As we emerged into this river-bed path we suddenly started a troop of tall giraffes, who galloped, or, rather, sailed off, with their strange gait, their tails screwed up over their backs, and their hoofs rattling like castanets. They were about three hundred yards from us, and therefore practically out of shot, but Good, who was walking ahead and had an express loaded with solid ball in his hand, could not resist, but upped gun and let drive at the last, a young cow. By some extraordinary chance the ball struck it full on the back of the neck, shattering the spinal column, and that giraffe went rolling head over heels just like a rabbit. I never saw a more curious thing.

"Curse it!" said Good—for I am sorry to say he had a habit of using strong language when excited—contracted no doubt, in the course of his nautical career; "curse it, I've killed him."

"Ou, Bougwan," ejaculated the Kaffirs; "ou! ou!"

They called Good "Bougwan" (glass eye) because of his eyeglass.

"Oh, 'Bougwan!' " re-echoed Sir Henry and I; and from that day Good's reputation as a marvellous shot was established, at any rate among the Kaffirs. Really he was a bad one, but whenever he missed we overlooked it for the sake of that giraffe.

Having set some of the "boys" to cut off the best of the giraffe meat, we went to work to build a "scherm" near one of the pools about a hundred yards to the right of it. This is done by cutting a quantity of thorn bushes and laying them in the shape of a circular hedge. Then the space enclosed is smoothed, and dry tambouki grass, if obtainable, is made into a bed in the centre, and a fire or fires lighted.

By the time the "scherm" was finished the moon was coming up, and our dinner of giraffe steaks and roasted marrow-bones was ready. How we enjoyed those marrow bones, though it was rather a job to crack them! I know no greater luxury than giraffe marrow, unless it is elephant's heart, and we had that on the morrow. We ate our simple meal, pausing at times to thank Good for his wonderful shot, by the light of the full moon, and then we began to smoke and yarn, and a curious picture we must have made squatted there round the fire. I, with my short grizzled hair sticking up straight, and Sir Henry with his yellow locks, which were getting rather long, were rather a contrast, especially as I am thin and short and dark, weighing only nine stone and a half, and Sir Henry is tall and broad and fair, and weighs fifteen. But perhaps the most curious-looking of the three, taking all the circumstances into consideration, was Captain John Good, R.N. There he sat upon a leather bag, looking just as though he had come in from a comfortable day's shooting in a civilized country, absolutely clean, tidy, and well-dressed. He had on a shooting-suit of brown tweed, with a hat to match, and neat gaiters. He was, as usual, beautifully shaven, his eyeglass and his false teeth appeared to be in perfect order, and altogether he was the neatest man I ever had to do with in the wilderness. He even had on a collar, of which he had a supply, made of white gutta-percha.

"You see, they weigh so little," he said to me, innocently, when I expressed my astonishment at the fact; "I always liked to look like a gentleman."

Well, there we all sat yarning away in the beautiful moonlight, and watching the Kaffirs a few yards off sucking their intoxicating "daccha" in a pipe of which the mouthpiece was made of the horn of an eland, till they one by one rolled themselves up in their blankets and went to sleep by the fire, that is, all except Umbopa, who sat a little apart (I noticed he never mixed much with the other Kaffirs), his chin resting on his hand, apparently thinking deeply.

Presently, from the depths of the bush behind us came a loud "woof! woof!" "That's a lion," said I, and we all started up to listen. Hardly had we done so, when from the pool, about a hundred yards off, came the strident trumpeting of an elephant. "Unkungunklovo! Unkungunklovo!" (elephant! elephant!) whispered the Kaffirs; and a few minutes afterwards we saw a succession of vast shadowy forms moving slowly from the direction of the water towards the bush. Up jumped Good, burning for slaughter, and thinking, perhaps, that it was as easy to kill elephant as he had found it to shoot giraffe, but I caught him by the arm and pulled him down.

"It's no good," I said, "let them go."

"It seems that we are in a paradise of game. I vote we stop here a day or two, and have a go at them," said Sir Henry, presently.

I was rather surprised, for hitherto Sir Henry had always been for pushing on as fast as possible, more especially since we had ascertained at Inyati that about two years ago an Englishman of the name of Neville *had* sold his wagon there, and gone on up country; but I suppose his hunter instincts had got the better of him.

Good jumped at the idea, for he was longing to have a go at those elephants; and so, to speak the truth, did I, for it went against my conscience to let such a herd as that escape without having a pull at them.

"All right, my hearties," said I. "I think we want a little recreation. And now let's turn in, for we ought to be off by dawn, and then perhaps we may catch them feeding before they move on."

The others agreed, and we proceeded to make preparations. Good took off his clothes, shook them, put his eyeglass and his false teeth into his trousers' pocket, and, folding them all up neatly, placed them out of the dew under a corner of his mackintosh sheet. Sir Henry and I contented ourselves with rougher arrangements, and were soon curled up in our blankets and dropping off into the dreamless sleep that rewards the traveller.

Going, going, go—What was that?

Suddenly from the direction of the water came a sound of violent scuffling, and next instant there broke upon our ears a succession of the most awful roars. There was no mistaking what they came from; only a lion could make such a noise as that. We all jumped up and looked towards the water, in the direction of which we saw a confused mass, yellow and black in color, staggering and struggling towards us. We seized our rifles, and, slipping on our veldtschoons (shoes made of untanned hide), ran out of the scherm towards it. By this time it had fallen, and was rolling over and over on the ground, and by the time we reached it it struggled no longer, but was quite still.

And this was what it was. On the grass there lay a sable antelope bull—the most beautiful of all the African antelopes—

quite dead, and transfixed by its great curved horns was a magnificent black-maned lion, also dead. What had happened, evidently, was this. The sable antelope had come down to drink at the pool, where the lion—no doubt the same we had heard— had been lying in wait. While the antelope was drinking the lion had sprung upon him, but was received upon the sharp, curved horns and transfixed. I once saw the same thing happen before. The lion, unable to free himself, had torn and beaten at the back and neck of the bull, which, maddened with fear and pain, had rushed on till it dropped dead.

As soon as we had sufficiently examined the dead beasts we called the Kaffirs, and between us managed to drag their carcasses up to the scherm. Then we went in and laid down, to wake no more till dawn.

With the first light we were up and making ready for the fray. We took with us the three eight-bore rifles, a good supply of ammunition, and our large water-bottles filled with weak, cold tea, which I have always found the best stuff to shoot on. After swallowing a little breakfast we started, Umbopa, Khiva, and Ventvögel accompanying us. The other Kaffirs we left, with instructions to skin the lion and the sable antelope, and cut up the latter.

We had no difficulty in finding the broad elephant trail, which Ventvögel, after examination, pronounced to have been made by between twenty and thirty elephants, most of them full-grown bulls. But the herd had moved on some way during the night, and it was nine o'clock, and already very hot, before, from the broken trees, bruised leaves and bark, and smoking dung, we knew we could not be far off them.

Presently we caught sight of the herd, numbering, as Ventvögel had said, between twenty and thirty, standing in a hollow, having finished their morning meal, and flapping their great ears. It was a splendid sight.

They were about two hundred yards from us. Taking a handful of dry grass I threw it into the air to see how the wind was; for if once they winded us I knew they would be off before we could get a shot. Finding that, if anything, it blew from the elephants to us, we crept stealthily on, and, thanks to the cover, managed to get within forty yards or so of the great brutes. Just in front of us and broadside on stood three splendid bulls, one of them with enormous tusks. I whispered to the others that I would take the middle one; Sir Henry covered the one to the left, and Good the bull with the big tusks.

"Now," I whispered.

Boom! boom! boom! went the three heavy rifles, and down went Sir Henry's elephant, dead as a hammer, shot right through the heart. Mine fell on to its knees, and I thought he was going to die, but in another moment he was up and off, tearing along straight past me. As he went I gave him the second barrel in his ribs, and this brought him down in good earnest. Hastily slipping in two fresh cartridges, I ran up close to him, and a ball through the brain put an end to the poor brute's struggles. Then I turned to see how Good had fared with the big bull, which I had heard screaming with rage and pain as I gave mine its quietus. On reaching the captain I found him in a great state of excitement. It appeared that on receiving the bullet the bull had turned and come straight for his assailant, who had barely time to get out of his way, and then charged blindly on past him, in the direction of our encampment. Meanwhile the herd had crashed off in wild alarm in the other direction.

For a while we debated whether to go after the wounded bull or follow the herd, and finally decided for the latter alternative, and departed thinking that we had seen the last of those big tusks. I have often wished since that we had. It was easy work to follow the elephants, for they had left a trail like a carriage-road behind them, crushing down the thick bush in their furious flight as though it were tambouki grass.

But to come up with them was another matter, and we had struggled on under a broiling sun for over two hours before we found them. They were, with the exception of one bull, standing together, and I could see, from their unquiet way and the manner in which they kept lifting their trunks to test the air, that they were on the lookout for mischief. The solitary bull stood fifty yards or so this side of the herd, over which he was evidently keeping sentry, and about sixty yards from us. Thinking that he would see or wind us, and that it would probably start them all off again if we tried to get nearer, especially as the ground was rather open, we all aimed at this bull and, at my whispered word, fired. All three shots took effect, and down he went, dead. Again the herd started on, but, unfortunately for them, about a hundred yards farther on was a nullah, or dried water-track, with steep banks, a place very much resembling the one the Prince Imperial was killed in in Zululand. Into this the elephants plunged, and when we reached the edge we found them struggling in wild confusion to get up the other bank, and filling the air with their screams, and trumpeting as they pushed one another aside in their selfish panic, just like so many human beings. Now was our opportunity, and, firing away as quick as we could load, we killed five of the poor beasts, and no doubt should have bagged the whole herd had they not suddenly given up their attempts to climb the bank and rushed headlong down the nullah. We were too tired to follow them, and perhaps also a little sick of slaughter, eight elephants being a pretty good bag for one day.

So, after we had rested a little and the Kaffirs had cut out the hearts of two of the dead elephants for supper, we started homeward, very well pleased with ourselves, having made up our minds to send the bearers on the morrow to chop out the tusks.

Shortly after we had passed the spot where Good had wounded the patriarchal bull we came across a herd of eland, but did not shoot at them, as we had already plenty of meat They trotted past us, and then stopped behind a little patch of bush about a hundred yards away and wheeled round to look at us. As Good was anxious to get a near view of them, never having seen an eland close, he handed his rifle to Umbopa, and, followed by Khiva, strolled up to the patch of bush. We sat down and waited for him, not sorry of the excuse for a little rest.

The sun was just going down in its reddest glory, and Sir Henry and I were admiring the lovely scene, when suddenly we heard an elephant scream, and saw its huge and charging form with uplifted trunk and tail silhouetted against the great red globe of the sun. Next second we saw something else, and that was Good and Khiva tearing back towards us with the wounded bull (for it was he) charging after them. For a moment we did not dare to fire—though it would have been little use if we had at that distance—for fear of hitting one of them, and the next a dreadful thing happened: Good fell a victim to his passion for civilized dress. Had he consented to discard his trousers and gaiters as we had, and hunt in a flannel shirt and a pair of veldtschoons, it would have been all right, but as it was his trousers cumbered him in that desperate race, and presently, when he was about sixty yards from us, his boot, polished by the dry grass, slipped, and down he went on his face right in front of the elephant.

We gave a gasp, for we knew he must die, and ran as hard as we could towards him. In three seconds it had ended, but not as we thought. Khiva, the Zulu boy, had seen his master fall, and brave lad that he was, had turned and flung his assegai straight into the elephant's face. It stuck in his trunk.

With a scream of pain the brute seized the poor Zulu, hurled him to the earth, and, placing his huge foot on to his body about the middle, twined his trunk round his upper part and *tore him in two.*

We rushed up, mad with horror, and fired again and again, and presently the elephant fell upon the fragments of the Zulu.

As for Good, he got up and wrung his hands over the brave man who had given his life to save him; and myself, though an old hand, I felt a lump in my throat. Umbopa stood and contemplated the huge dead elephant and the mangled remains of poor Khiva.

"Ah, well," he said, presently, "he is dead, but he died like a man."

CHAPTER V.

OUR MARCH INTO THE DESERT.

WE had killed nine elephants, and it took us two days to cut out the tusks and get them home and bury them carefully in the sand under a large tree, which made a conspicuous mark for miles round. It was a wonderfully fine lot of ivory. I never saw a better, averaging as it did between forty and fifty pounds a tusk. The tusks of the great bull that killed poor Khiva scaled one hundred and seventy pounds the pair, as nearly as we could judge.

As for Khiva himself, we buried what remained of him in an ant-bear hole, together with an assegai to protect himself with on his journey to a better world. On the third day we started on, hoping that we might one day return to dig up our buried ivory, and in due course, after a long and wearisome tramp, and many adventures which I have not space to detail, reached Sitanda's Kraal, near the Lukanga River, the real starting-point of our expedition. Very well do I recollect our arrival at that place. To the right was a scattered native settlement with a few stone cattle kraals and some cultivated land down by the water, where these savages grew their scanty supply of grain, and beyond it great tracts of waving "veldt" covered with tall grass, over which herds of the smaller game were wandering. To the left was the vast desert. This spot appeared to be the outpost of the fertile country, and it would be difficult to say to what natural causes such an abrupt change in the character of the soil was due. But so it was. Just below our encampment flowed a little stream, on the farther side of which was a stony slope, the same down which I had twenty years before seen poor Silvestre creeping back after his attempt to reach Solomon's Mines, and beyond that slope began the waterless desert covered with a species of karoo shrub. It was evening when we pitched our camp, and the great fiery ball of the sun was sinking into the desert, sending glorious rays of many-colored light flying over all the vast expanse. Leaving Good to superintend the arrangement of our little camp, I took Sir Henry with me, and we walked to the top of the slope opposite and gazed out across the desert. The air was very clear, and far, far away I could distinguish the faint blue outlines, here and there capped with white, of the great Suliman Berg.

"There," I said, "there is the wall of Solomon's Mines, but God knows if we shall ever climb it."

"My brother should be there, and if he is I shall reach him somehow," said Sir Henry, in that tone of quiet confidence which marked the man.

"I hope so," I answered, and turned to go back to the camp, when I saw that we were not alone. Behind us, also gazing earnestly towards the far-off mountains, was the great Zulu, Umbopa.

The Zulu spoke when he saw that I had observed him, but addressed himself to Sir Henry, to whom he had attached himself.

"Is it to that land that thou wouldst journey, Incubu?" (a native word meaning, I believe, an elephant, and the name given to Sir Henry by the Kaffirs) he said, pointing towards the mountains with his broad assegai.

I asked sharply what he meant by addressing his master in that familiar way. It is very well for natives to have a name for one among themselves, but it is not decent that they should call one by their heathenish appellations to one's face. The man laughed a quiet little laugh which angered me.

"How dost thou know that I am not the equal of the Inkosi I serve?" he said. "He is of a royal house, no doubt; one can see it in his size and in his eye; so, mayhap, am I. At least I am as great a man. Be my mouth, oh, Macumazahn, and say my words to the Inkoos Incubu, my master, for I would speak to him and to thee."

I was angry with the man, for I am not accustomed to be talked to in that way by Kaffirs, but somehow he impressed me, and besides I was curious to know what he had to say, so I translated, expressing my opinion at the same time that he was an impudent fellow, and that his swagger was outrageous.

"Yes, Umbopa," answered Sir Henry, "I would journey there."

"The desert is wide and there is no water; the mountains are high and covered with snow, and man cannot say what is beyond them behind the place where the sun sets; how shalt thou come thither, Incubu, and wherefore dost thou go?"

I translated again.

"Tell him," answered Sir Henry, "that I go because I believe that a man of my blood, my brother, has gone there before me, and I go to seek him."

"That is so, Incubu; a man I met on the road told me that a white man went out into the desert two years ago towards those mountains with one servant, a hunter. They never came back."

"How do you know it was my brother?" asked Sir Henry.

"Nay, I know not. But the man, when I asked what the white man was like, said that he had your eyes and a black beard. He said, too, that the name of the hunter with him was Jim, that he was a Bechuana hunter and wore clothes."

"There is no doubt about it," said I; "I knew Jim well."

Sir Henry nodded. "I was sure of it," he said. "If George set his mind upon a thing he generally did it. It was always so from his boyhood. If he meant to cross the Suliman Berg he has crossed it, unless some accident has overtaken him, and we must look for him on the other side."

Umbopa understood English, though he rarely spoke it.

"It is a far journey, Incubu," he put in, and I translated his remark.

"Yes," answered Sir Henry, "it is far. But there is no journey upon this earth that a man may not make if he sets his heart to it. There is nothing, Umbopa, that he cannot do, there are no mountains he may not climb, there are no deserts he cannot cross, save a mountain and a desert of which you are spared the knowledge, if love leads him, and he holds his life in his hand counting it as nothing, ready to keep it or to lose it as Providence may order."

I translated.

"Great words, my father," answered the Zulu (I always called him a Zulu, though he was not really one), "great, swelling words, fit to fill the mouth of a man. Thou art right, my father Incubu. Listen! what is life? It is a feather; it is the seed of the grass, blown hither and thither, sometimes multiplying itself and dying in the act, sometimes carried away into the heavens. But if the seed be good and heavy it may perchance travel a little way on the road it will. It is well to try and journey one's road and to fight with the air. Man must die. At the worst he can but die a little sooner. I will go with thee across the desert and over the mountains, unless perchance I fall to the ground on the way, my father."

He paused awhile, and then went on with one of those strange bursts of rhetorical eloquence which Zulus sometimes indulge in, and which, to my mind, full as they are of vain repetitions, show that the race is by no means devoid of poetic instinct and of intellectual power.

"What is life? Tell me, O white men, who are wise, who know the secrets of the world of stars, and the world that lies above and around the stars; who flash their words from afar without a voice; tell me, white men, the secret of our life—whither it goes and whence it comes!

"Ye cannot answer; ye know not. Listen, I will answer. Out of the dark we came, into the dark we go. Like a storm-driven bird at night we fly out of the Nowhere! for a moment our wings are seen in the light of the fire, and, lo! we are gone again into the Nowhere. Life is nothing. Life is all. It is the hand with which we hold off death. It is the glow-worm that shines in the night-time and is black in the morning; it is the white breath of the oxen in winter; it is the little shadow that runs across the grass and loses itself at sunset."

"You are a strange man," said Sir Henry, when he ceased.

Umbopa laughed. "It seems to me that we are very much alike, Incubu. Perhaps *I* seek a brother over the mountains."

I looked at him suspiciously. "What dost thou mean?" I asked; "what dost thou know of the mountains?"

"A little; a very little. There is a strange land there, a land of witchcraft and beautiful things; a land of brave people and of trees and streams and white mountains and of a great white road. I have heard of it. But what is the good of talking? it grows dark. Those who live to see will see."

Again I looked at him doubtfully. The man knew too much.

"Ye need not fear me, Macumazahn," he said, interpreting my look. "I dig no holes for ye to fall in. I make no plots. If ever we cross those mountains behind the sun, I will tell what I know. But death sits upon them. Be wise, and turn back. Go and hunt elephant. I have spoken.

And without another word he lifted his spear in salutation and returned towards the camp, where shortly afterwards we found him cleaning a gun like any other Kaffir.

"That is an odd man," said Sir Henry.

"Yes," answered I, "too odd by half. I don't like his little ways. He knows something, and won't speak out. But I suppose it is no use quarrelling with him. We are in for a curious trip, and a mysterious Zulu won't make much difference one way or another."

Next day we made our arrangements for starting. Of course it was impossible to drag our heavy elephant rifles and other kit with us across the desert, so, dismissing our bearers, we made an arrangement with an old native who had a kraal close by to take care of them till we returned. It went to my heart to leave such things as those sweet tools to the tender mercies of an old thief, of a savage whose greedy eyes I could see gloating over them. But I took some precautions.

First of all I loaded all the rifles, and informed him that if he touched them they would go off. He instantly tried the experiment with my eight-bore, and it did go off, and blew a hole right through one of his oxen, which were just then being driven up to the kraal, to say nothing of knocking him head over heels with the recoil. He got up considerably startled, and not at all pleased at the loss of the ox, which he had the impudence to ask me to pay for, and nothing would induce him to touch them again.

"Put the live devils up there in the thatch," he said, "out of the way, or they will kill us all."

Then I told him that if, when we came back, one of those things was missing I would kill him and all his people by witchcraft; and if we died and he tried to steal the things, I would come and haunt him and turn his cattle mad and his milk sour till life was a weariness, and make the devils in the guns come out and talk to him in a way he would not like, and generally gave him a good idea of judgment to come. After that he swore he would look after them as though they were his father's spirit. He was a very superstitious old Kaffir and a great villain.

Having thus disposed of our superfluous gear we arranged the kit we five—Sir Henry, Good, myself, Umbopa, and the Hottentot Ventvögel—were to take with us on our journey. It was small enough, but do what we would we could not get it down under about forty pounds a man. This is what it consisted of:

The three express rifles and two hundred rounds of ammunition.

The two Winchester repeating rifles (for Umbopa and Ventvögel), with two hundred rounds of cartridge.

Three "Colt" revolvers and sixty rounds of cartridge.

Five Cochrane's water-bottles, each holding four pints.

Five blankets.

Twenty-five pounds' weight of biltong (sun-dried game flesh).

Ten pounds' weight of best mixed beads for gifts.

A selection of medicine, including an ounce of quinine, and

one or two small surgical instruments.

Our knives, a few sundries, such as a compass, matches, a pocket-filter, tobacco, a trowel, a bottle of brandy, and the clothes we stood in.

This was our total equipment, a small one, indeed, for such a venture, but we dared not attempt to carry more. As it was, that load was a heavy one per man to travel across the burning desert with, for in such places every additional ounce tells upon one. But try as we would we could not see our way to reducing it. There was nothing but what was absolutely necessary.

With great difficulty, and by the promise of a present of a good hunting-knife each, I succeeded in persuading three wretched natives from the village to come with us for the first stage, twenty miles, and to carry each a large gourd holding a gallon of water. My object was to enable us to refill our water-bottles after the first night's march, for we determined to start in the cool of the night. I gave out to these natives that we were going to shoot ostriches, with which the desert abounded. They jabbered and shrugged their shoulders, and said we were mad and should perish of thirst, which I must say seemed very probable; but being desirous of obtaining the knives, which were almost unknown treasures up there, they consented to come, having probably reflected that, after all, our subsequent extinction would be no affair of theirs.

All next day we rested and slept, and at sunset ate a hearty meal of fresh beef washed down with tea, the last, as Good sadly remarked, we were likely to drink for many a long day. Then, having made our final preparations, we lay down and waited for the moon to rise. At last, about nine o'clock, up she came in all her chastened glory, flooding the wild country with silver light, and throwing a weird sheen on the vast expanse of rolling desert before us, which looked as solemn and quiet and as alien to man as the star-studded firmament above. We rose up, and in a few minutes were ready, and yet we hesitated a little, as human nature is prone to hesitate on the threshold of an irrevocable step. We three white men stood there by ourselves. Umbopa, assegai in hand and the rifle across his shoulders, a few paces ahead of us, looked out fixedly across the desert; the three hired natives, with the gourds of water, and Ventvögel were gathered in a little knot behind.

"Gentlemen," said Sir Henry, presently, in his low, deep voice, "we are going on about as strange a journey as men can make in this world. It is very doubtful if we can succeed in it. But we are three men who will stand together for good or for evil to the last. And now before we start let us for a moment pray to the Power who shapes the destinies of men, and who ages since has marked out our paths, that it may please him to direct our steps in accordance with his will."

Taking off his hat he, for the space of a minute or so, covered his face with his hands, and Good and I did likewise.

I do not say that I am a first-rate praying-man; few hunters are; and as for Sir Henry, I never heard him speak like that before, and only once since, though deep down in his heart I believe he is very religious. Good, too, is pious, though very apt to swear. Anyhow I do not think I ever, excepting on one single occasion, put in a better prayer in my life than I did during that minute, and somehow I felt the happier for it. Our future was so completely unknown, and I think the unknown and the awful always brings a man nearer to his Maker.

"And now," said Sir Henry, "trek."

So we started.

We had nothing to guide ourselves by except the distant mountains and old José da Silvestra's chart, which, considering that it was drawn by a dying and half distraught man on a fragment of linen three centuries ago, was not a very satisfactory sort of thing to work on. Still, such as it was, our sole hope of success depended on it. If we failed in finding that pool of bad water which the old don marked as being situated in the middle of the desert, about sixty miles from our starting-point and as far from the mountains, we must in all probability perish miserably of thirst. And to my mind the chances of our finding it in that great sea of sand and karoo scrub seemed almost infinitesimal. Even supposing Da Silvestra had marked it right, what was there to prevent its having been generations ago dried up by the sun, or trampled in by game, or filled with drifting sand?

On we tramped silently as shades through the night and in the heavy sand. The karoo bushes caught our shins and retarded us, and the sand got into our veldtschoons and Good's shooting-boots, so that every few miles we had to stop and empty them; but still the night was fairly cool, though the atmosphere was thick and heavy, giving a sort of creamy feel to the air, and we made fair progress. It was very still and lonely there in the desert, oppressively so indeed. Good felt this, and once began to whistle the "Girl I left behind me," but the notes sounded lugubrious in that vast place, and he gave it up. Shortly afterwards a little incident occurred which, though it made us jump at the time, gave rise to a laugh. Good, as the holder of the compass, which, being a sailor, of course he thoroughly understood, was leading, and we were toiling along in single file behind him, when suddenly we heard the sound of an exclamation, and he vanished. Next second there arose all round us a most extraordinary hubbub, snorts, groans, wild sounds of rushing feet. In the faint light, too, we could descry dim, galloping forms half hidden by wreaths of sand. The natives threw down their loads and prepared to bolt, but, remembering that there was nowhere to bolt to, cast themselves upon the ground and howled out that it was the devil. As for Sir Henry and myself, we stood amazed; nor was our amazement lessened when we perceived the form of Good careering off in the direction of the mountains, apparently mounted on the back of a horse and halloing like mad. In another second he threw up his arms, and we heard him come to the earth with a thud. Then I saw what had happened: we had stumbled right on to a herd of sleeping quagga, on to the back of one of which Good had actually fallen, and the brute had naturally enough got up and made off with him. Singing out to the others that it was all right, I ran towards Good, much afraid lest he should be hurt, but to my great relief found him sitting in the sand, his eye-glass still fixed firmly in his eye, rather shaken and very much startled, but not in any way injured.

After this we travelled on without any further misadventure till after one o'clock, when we called a halt, and having drunk a little water, not much, for water was precious, and rested for half an hour, started on again.

On, on we went, till at last the east began to blush like the cheek of a girl. Then there came faint rays of primrose light that changed presently to golden bars, through which the dawn glided out across the desert. The stars grew pale and paler still till at last they vanished; the golden moon waxed wan, and her mountain ridges stood out clear against her sickly face like the bones on the face of a dying man; then came spear upon spear of glorious light flashing far away across the boundless wilderness, piercing and firing the veils of mist till the desert was draped in a tremulous golden glow, and it was day.

Still we did not halt, though by this time we should have been glad enough to do so, for we knew that when once the sun was fully up it would be almost impossible for us to travel in it. At length, about six o'clock, we spied a little pile of rocks rising out of the plain, and to this we dragged ourselves. As luck would have it, here we found an overhanging slab of rock carpeted beneath with smooth sand, which afforded a most grateful shelter from the heat. Underneath this we crept, and having drank some water each and eaten a bit of biltong, we lay down and were soon sound asleep.

It was three o'clock in the afternoon before we woke, to find our three bearers preparing to return. They had already had enough of the desert, and no number of knives would have tempted them to come a step farther. So we had a hearty drink, and, having emptied our water-bottles, filled them up again from the gourds they had brought with them, and then watched them depart on their twenty miles' tramp home.

At half-past four we also started on. It was lonely and desolate work, for, with the exception of a few ostriches, there was not a single living creature to be seen on all the vast expanse of sandy plain. It was evidently too dry for game, and, with the exception of a deadly-looking cobra or two, we saw no reptiles. One insect, however, was abundant, and that was the common or house fly. There they came, "not as single spies, but in battalions," as I think the Old Testament says somewhere. He is an extraordinary animal, is the house fly. Go where you will you find him, and so it must always have been. I have seen him enclosed in amber which must, I was told, have been half a million years old, looking exactly like his descendant of to-day, and I have little doubt that when the last man lies dying on the earth he will be buzzing round—if that event should happen to occur in summer—watching for an opportunity to settle on his nose.

At sunset we halted, waiting for the moon to rise. At ten she came up beautiful and serene as ever, and, with one halt about two o'clock in the morning, we trudged wearily on through the night, till at last the welcome sun put a period to our labors. We drank a little and flung ourselves down, thoroughly tired out, on the sand, and were soon all asleep. There was no need to set a watch, for we had nothing to fear from anybody or anything in that vast, untenanted plain. Our only enemies were heat, thirst, and flies, but far rather would I have faced any danger from man or beast than that awful trinity. This time we were not so lucky as to find a sheltering rock to guard us from the glare of the sun, with the result that about seven o'clock we woke up experiencing the exact sensations one would attribute to a beef-steak on a gridiron. We were literally being baked through and through. The burning sun seemed to be sucking our very blood out of us. We sat up and gasped.

"Phew!" said I, grabbing at the halo of flies which buzzed cheerfully round my head. The heat did not affect them.

"My word," said Sir Henry.

"It *is* hot!" said Good.

It was hot, indeed, and there was not a bit of shelter to be had. Look where we would there was no rock or tree; nothing but an unending glare, rendered dazzling by the hot air which danced over the surface of the desert as it does over a red-hot stove.

"What is to be done?" asked Sir Henry; "we can't stand this for long."

We looked at each other blankly.

"I have it," said Good; "we must dig a hole and get into it, and cover ourselves with the karoo bushes."

It did not seem a very promising suggestion, but at least it was better than nothing, so we set to work, and, with the trowel we had brought with us and our hands, succeeded in about an hour in delving out a patch of ground about ten feet long by twelve wide to the depth of two feet. Then we cut a quantity of low scrub with our hunting-knives, and, creeping into the hole, pulled it over us all, with the exception of Ventvögel, on whom, being a Hottentot, the sun had no particular effect. This gave us some slight shelter from the burning rays of the sun, but the heat in that amateur grave can be better imagined than described. The Black Hole of Calcutta must have been a fool to it; indeed, to this moment, I do not know how we lived through the day. There we lay panting, and every now and again moistening our lips from our scanty supply of water. Had we followed our inclinations we should have finished off all we had in the first two hours, but we had to exercise the most rigid care, for if our water failed us we knew that we must quickly perish miserably.

But everything has an end, if only you live long enough to see it, and somehow that miserable day wore on towards evening. About three o'clock in the afternoon we determined that we could stand it no longer. It would be better to die walking than to be slowly killed by heat and thirst in that dreadful hole. So, taking each of us a little drink from our fast diminishing supply of water now heated to about the same temperature as a man's blood, we staggered on.

We had now covered some fifty miles of desert. If my reader will refer to the rough copy and translation of old Da Silvestra's map he will see that the desert is marked as being forty leagues across, and the "pan bad water" is set down as being about in the middle of it. Now, forty leagues is one hundred and twenty miles; consequently, we ought at the most to be within twelve or fifteen miles of the water, if any should really exist.

Through the afternoon we crept slowly and painfully along, scarcely doing more than a mile and a half an hour. At sunset we again rested, waiting for the moon, and, after drinking a little, managed to get some sleep.

Before we lay down Umbopa pointed out to us a slight and indistinct hillock on the flat surface of the desert about eight miles away. At the distance it looked like an anthill, and as I was dropping off to sleep I fell to wondering what it could be.

With the moon we started on again, feeling dreadfully exhausted, and suffering tortures from thirst and prickly heat. Nobody who has not felt it can know what we went through. We no longer walked, we staggered, now and again falling from exhaustion, and being obliged to call a halt every hour or so. We had scarcely energy left in us to speak. Up to now Good had chatted and joked, for he was a merry fellow; but now he had not a joke left in him.

At last, about two o'clock, utterly worn out in body and mind, we came to the foot of this queer hill, or sand koppie, which did at first sight resemble a gigantic ant-heap about a hundred feet high, and covering at the base nearly a morgen (two acres) of ground.

Here we halted, and, driven by our desperate thirst, sucked down our last drops of water. We had but half a pint a head, and we could each have drank a gallon.

Then we lay down. Just as I was dropping off to sleep I heard Umbopa remark to himself in Zulu,

"If we cannot find water we shall all be dead before the moon rises tomorrow."

I shuddered, hot as it was. The near prospect of such an awful death is not pleasant, but even the thought of it could not keep me from sleeping.

CHAPTER VI.

WATER! WATER!

IN two hours' time, about four o'clock, I woke up. As soon as the first heavy demand of bodily fatigue had been satisfied the torturing thirst from which I was suffering asserted itself. I could sleep no more. I had been dreaming that I was bathing in a running stream with green banks, and trees upon them, and I awoke to find myself in that arid wilderness, and to remember that, as Umbopa had said, if we did not find water that day we must certainly perish miserably. No human creature could live long without water in that heat. I sat up and rubbed my grimy face with my dry and horny hands. My lips and eyelids were stuck together, and it was only after some rubbing and with an effort that I was able to open them. It was not far off the dawn, but there was none of the bright feel of dawn in the air which was thick with a hot murkiness I cannot describe. The others were still sleeping. Presently it began to grow light enough to read, so I drew out a little pocket copy of the "Ingoldsby Legends" I had brought with me, and read the "Jackdaw of Rheims." When I got to where

> "A nice little boy held a golden ewer,
> Embossed, and filled with water as pure
> As any that flows between Rheims and Namur,"

I literally smacked my cracked lips, or, rather, tried to smack them. The mere thought of that pure water made me mad. If the cardinal had been there with his bell, book, and candle, I would have whipped in and drank his water up, yes, even if he had already filled it with the suds of soap worthy of washing the hands of the pope, and I knew that the whole concentrated curse of the Catholic Church should fall upon me for so doing. I almost think I must have been a little light-headed with thirst and weariness and want of food; for I fell to thinking how astonished the cardinal and his nice little boy and the jackdaw would have looked to see a burned-up, brown-eyed, grizzle-haired little elephant-hunter suddenly bound in and put his dirty face into the basin and swallow every drop of the precious water. The idea amused me so that I laughed or rather cackled aloud, which woke the others up, and they began to rub *their* dirty faces and get *their* gummed-up lips and eyelids apart.

As soon as we were all well awake we fell to discussing the situation, which was serious enough. Not a drop of water was left. We turned the water-bottles upside down and licked the tops, but it was a failure; they were dry as a bone. Good, who had charge of the bottle of brandy, got it out and looked at it longingly; but Sir Henry promptly took it away from him, for to drink raw spirit would only have been to precipitate the end.

"If we do not find water we shall die," he said.

"If we can trust to the old don's map there should be some about," I said; but nobody seemed to derive much satisfaction from that remark, it was so evident that no great faith could be put in the map. It was now gradually growing light, and as we sat blankly staring at each other I observed the Hottentot Ventvögel rise and begin to walk about with his eyes on the ground. Presently he stopped short and, uttering a guttural exclamation, pointed to the earth.

"What is it?" we exclaimed, and simultaneously rose and went to where he was standing pointing at the ground.

"Well," I said, "it is pretty fresh Springbok spoor; what of it?"

"Sprinbucks do not go far from water," he answered in Dutch.

"No," I answered, "I forgot; and thank God for it."

This little discovery put new life into us; it is wonderful how, when one is in a desperate position, one catches at the slightest hope, and feels almost happy in it. On a dark night a single star is better than nothing.

Meanwhile Ventvögel was lifting his snub nose, and sniffing the hot air for all the world like an old Impala ram who scents danger. Presently he spoke again.

"I *smell* water," he said.

Then we felt jubilant, for we knew what a wonderful instinct these wild-bred men possess.

Just at that moment the sun came up gloriously and revealed so grand a sight to our astonished eyes that for a moment or two we forgot even our thirst.

For there, not more than forty or fifty miles from us, glittering like silver in the early rays of the morning sun, were Sheba's breasts; and stretching away for hundreds of miles on each side of them was the great Suliman Berg. Now that I, sitting here, attempt to describe the extraordinary grandeur and beauty of that sight, language seems to fail me. I am impotent even before its memory. There, straight before us, were two enormous mountains, the like of which are not, I believe, to be seen in Africa, if, indeed, there are any other such in the world, measuring each at least fifteen thousand feet in height, standing not more than a dozen miles apart, connected by a precipitous cliff of rock, and towering up in awful white solemnity straight into the sky. These mountains standing thus, like the pillars of a gigantic gateway, are shaped exactly like a woman's breasts. Their bases swelled gently up from the plain, looking, at that distance, perfectly round and smooth; and on the top of each was a vast round hillock covered with snow, exactly corresponding to the nipple on the female breast. The stretch of cliff which connected them appeared to be some thousand feet in height, and perfectly precipitous, and on each side of them, as far as the eye could reach, extended similar lines of cliff, broken only here and there by flat, table-topped mountains, something like the world-famed one at Cape Town; a formation, by the way, very common in Africa.

To describe the grandeur of the whole view is beyond my powers. There was something so inexpressibly solemn and over-powering about those huge volcanoes—for doubtless they are extinct volcanoes—that it fairly took our breath away. For a while the morning lights played upon the snow and the brown and swelling masses beneath, and then, as though to veil the majestic sight from our curious eyes, strange mists and clouds gathered and increased around them, till presently we could only trace their pure and gigantic outline swelling ghostlike through the fleecy envelope. Indeed, as we afterwards discovered, they were normally wrapped in this curious gauzy mist, which doubtless accounted for one not having made them out more clearly before.

Scarcely had the mountains vanished into cloud-clad privacy before our thirst—literally a burning question—reasserted itself.

It was all very well for Ventvögel to say he smelled water, but look which way we would we could see no signs of it. So far as the eye could reach there was nothing but arid, sweltering sand and karoo scrub. We walked round the hillock and gazed about anxiously on the other side, but it was the same story, not a drop of water was to be seen; there was no indication of a pan, a pool, or a spring.

"You are a fool," I said, angrily, to Ventvögel; "there is no water."

But still he lifted his ugly snub nose and sniffed.

"I smell it, Baas" (master), he answered; "it is somewhere in the air."

"Yes," I said, "no doubt it is in the clouds, and about two months hence it will fall and wash our bones."

Sir Henry stroked his yellow beard thoughtfully. "Perhaps it is on the top of the hill," he suggested.

"Rot," said Good; "who ever heard of water being found on the top of a hill?"

"Let us go and look," I put in, and hopelessly enough we scrambled up the sandy sides of the hillock, Umbopa leading. Presently he stopped as though he were petrified.

"Nanzia manzie!" (here is water), he cried, with a loud voice.

We rushed up to him, and there, sure enough, in a deep cup or indentation on the very top of the sand-koppie, was an undoubted pool of water. How it came to be in such a strange place we did

not stop to inquire, nor did we hesitate at its black and uninviting appearance. It was water, or a good imitation of it, and that
was enough for us. We gave a bound and a rush, and in another
second were all down on our stomachs sucking up the uninviting
fluid as though it were nectar fit for the gods. Heavens, how we
did drink! Then, when we had done drinking, we tore off our
clothes and sat down in it, absorbing the moisture through our
parched skins. You, my reader, who have only to turn on a
couple of taps and summon "hot" and "cold" from an unseen,
vasty boiler, can have little idea of the luxury of that muddy
wallow in brackish, tepid water.

After a while we arose from it, refreshed indeed, and fell to
on our biltong, of which we had scarcely been able to touch a
mouthful for twenty-four hours, and ate our fill. Then we smoked
a pipe, and lay down by the side of that blessed pool under the
overhanging shadow of the bank and slept till mid-day.

All that day we rested there by the water, thanking our stars
that we had been lucky enough to find it, bad as it was, and not
forgetting to render a due share of gratitude to the shade of the
long-departed Da Silvestra, who had corked it down so accurately
on the tail of his shirt. The wonderful thing to us was that it
should have lasted so long, and the only way that I can account
for it is by the supposition that it is fed by some spring deep
down in the sand.

Having filled both ourselves and our water-bottles as full as
possible, in far better spirits we started off again with the moon.
That night we covered nearly five-and-twenty miles, but, needless to say, found no more water, though we were lucky enough
on the following day to get a little shade behind some ant-heaps.
When the sun rose and, for a while, cleared away the mysterious
mists, Suliman's Berg and the two majestic breasts, now only
about twenty miles off, seemed to be towering right above us,
and looked grander than ever. At the approach of evening we
started on again, and, to cut a long story short, by daylight
next morning found ourselves upon the lowest slopes of Sheba's
left breast, for which we had been steadily steering. By this
time our water was again exhausted and we were suffering
severely from thirst, nor indeed could we see any chance of re-
lieving it till we reached the snow line, far, far above us. After
resting an hour or two, driven to it by our torturing thirst, we
went on again, toiling painfully in the burning heat up the lava
slopes, for we found that the huge base of the mountain was
composed entirely of lava-beds belched out in some far-past age.

By eleven o'clock we were utterly exhausted, and were,

generally speaking, in a very bad way indeed. The lava clinker, over which we had to make our way, though comparatively smooth compared with some clinker I have heard of, such as that on the island of Ascension, for instance, was yet rough enough to make our feet very sore, and this, together with our other miseries, had pretty well finished us. A few hundred yards above us were some large lumps of lava, and towards these we made with the intention of lying down beneath their shade. We reached them, and to our surprise, so far as we had a capacity for surprise left in us, on a little plateau or ridge close by we saw that the lava was covered with a dense green growth. Evidently soil formed from decomposed lava had rested there, and in due course had become the receptacle of seeds deposited by birds. But we did not take much further interest in the green growth, for one cannot live on grass, like Nebuchadnezzar. That requires a special dispensation of Providence and peculiar digestive organs. So we sat down under the rocks and groaned, and I, for one, heartily wished that we had never started on this fool's errand. As we were sitting there I saw Umbopa get up and hobble off towards the patch of green, and a few minutes afterwards, to my great astonishment, I perceived that usually uncommonly dignified individual dancing and shouting like a maniac, and waving something green. Off we all scrambled towards him as fast as our wearied limbs would carry us, hoping that he had found water.

"What is it, Umbopa, son of a fool?" I shouted in Zulu.

"It is food and water, Macumazahn," and again he waved the green thing.

Then I saw what he had got. It was a melon. We had hit upon a patch of wild melons, thousands of them, and dead ripe.

"Melons!" I yelled to Good, who was next me; and in another second he had his false teeth fixed in one.

I think we ate about six each before we had done, and, poor fruit as they were, I doubt if I ever thought anything nicer.

But melons are not very satisfying, and when we had satisfied our thirst with their pulpy substance, and set a stock to cool by the simple process of cutting them in two and setting them end on in the hot sun to get cold by evaporation, we began to feel exceedingly hungry. We had still some biltong left, but our stomachs turned from biltong, and, besides, we had to be very sparing of it, for we could not say when we should get more food. Just at this moment a lucky thing happened. Looking towards the desert I saw a flock of about ten large birds flying straight towards us.

"Skit, Baas, skit!" (shoot, master, shoot), whispered the Hottentot, throwing himself on his face, an example which we all followed.

Then I saw that the birds were a flock of pauw (bustards), and that they would pass within fifty yards of my head. Taking one of the repeating Winchesters, I waited till they were nearly over us, and then jumped on to my feet. On seeing me the pauw bunched up together, as I expected they would, and I fired two shots straight into the thick of them, and, as luck would have it, brought one down, a fine fellow, that weighed about twenty pounds. In half an hour we had a fire made of dry melon-stalks, and he was toasting over it, and we had such a feed as we had not had for a week. We ate that pauw—nothing was left of him but his bones and his beak—and felt not a little the better afterwards.

That night we again went on with the moon, carrying as many melons as we could with us. As we got higher up we found the air get cooler and cooler, which was a great relief to us, and at dawn, so far as we could judge, were not more than about a dozen miles from the snowline. Here we found more melons, so had no longer any anxiety about water, for we knew that we should soon get plenty of snow. But the ascent had now become very precipitous, and we made but slow progress, not more than a mile an hour. Also that night we ate our last morsel of biltong. As yet, with the exception of the pauw, we had seen no living thing on the mountain, nor had we come across a single spring or stream of water, which struck us as very odd, considering all the snow above us, which must, we thought, melt sometimes. But as we afterwards discovered, owing to some cause, which it is quite beyond my power to explain, all the streams flowed down upon the north side of the mountains.

We now began to grow very anxious about food. We had escaped death by thirst, but it seemed probable that it was only to die of hunger. The events of the next three miserable days are best described by copying the entries made at the time in my note-book.

21st May.—Started 11 A.M., finding the atmosphere quite cold enough to travel by day, carrying some water-melons with us. Struggled on all day, but saw no more melons, having, evidently, passed out of their district. Saw no game of any sort. Halted for the night at sundown, having had no food for many hours. Suffered much during the night from cold.

22d.—Started at sunrise again, feeling very faint and weak. Only made five miles all day; found some patches of snow, of which we ate, but nothing else. Camped at night under the edge of a great plateau. Cold bitter. Drank a little brandy each, and huddled ourselves together, each wrapped up in our blanket to keep ourselves alive. Are now suffering frightfully from starvation and weariness. Thought that Ventvögel would have died during the night.

23d.—Struggled forward once more as soon as the sun was well up, and had thawed our limbs a little. We are now in a dreadful plight, and I fear that unless we get food this will be our last day's journey. But little brandy left. Good, Sir Henry, and Umbopa bear up wonderfully, but Ventvögel is in a very bad way. Like most Hottentots, he cannot stand cold. Pangs of hunger not so bad, but have a sort of numb feeling about the stomach. Others say the same. We are now on a level with the precipitous chain, or wall of lava, connecting the two breasts, and the view is glorious. Behind us the great glowing desert rolls away to the horizon, and before us lies mile upon mile of smooth, hard snow almost level, but swelling gently upward, out of the centre of which the nipple of the mountain, which appears to be some miles in circumference, rises about four thousand feet into the sky. Not a living thing is to be seen. God help us, I fear our time has come.

And now I will drop the journal, partly because it is not very interesting reading, and partly because what followed requires perhaps rather more accurate telling.

All that day (the 23d May) we struggled slowly on up the incline of snow, lying down from time to time to rest. A strange, gaunt crew we must have looked, as, laden as we were, we dragged our weary feet over the dazzling plain, glaring round us with hungry eyes. Not that there was much use in glaring, for there was nothing to eat. We did not do more than seven miles that day. Just before sunset we found ourselves right under the nipple of Sheba's left breast, which towered up thousands of feet into the air above us, a vast, smooth hillock of frozen snow. Bad as we felt, we could not but appreciate the wonderful scene, made even more wonderful by the flying rays of light from the setting sun, which here and there stained the snow blood red, and crowned the towering mass above us with a diadem of glory.

"I say," gasped Good, presently, "we ought to be somewhere near the cave the old gentleman wrote about."

"Yes," said I, "if there is a cave."

"Come, Quatermain," groaned Sir Henry, "don't talk like that; I have every faith in the don; remember the water. We shall find the place soon."

"If we don't find it before dark we are dead men, that is all about it," was my consolatory reply.

For the next ten minutes we trudged on in silence, when suddenly Umbopa, who was marching along beside me, wrapped up in his blanket and with a leather belt strapped so tight round his stomach, to "make his hunger small," as he said, that his waist looked like a girl's, caught me by the arm.

"Look!" he said, pointing towards the springing slope of the nipple.

I followed his glance, and perceived, some two hundred yards from us, what appeared to be a hole in the snow.

"It is the cave," said Umbopa.

We made the best of our way to the spot, and found, sure enough, that the hole was the mouth of a cave, no doubt the same as that of which Da Silvestra wrote. We were none too soon, for just as we reached shelter the sun went down with startling rapidity, leaving the whole place nearly dark. In these latitudes there is but little twilight. We crept into the cave, which did not appear to be very big, and, huddling ourselves together for warmth, swallowed what remained of our brandy— barely a mouthful each—and tried to forget our miseries in sleep. But this the cold was too intense to allow us to do. I am convinced that at that great altitude the thermometer cannot have been less than fourteen or fifteen degrees below freezing-point. What this meant to us, enervated as we were by hardship, want of food, and the great heat of the desert, my reader can imagine better than I can describe. Suffice it to say that it was something as near death from exposure as I have ever felt. There we sat hour after hour through the bitter night, feeling the frost wander round and nip us now in the finger, now in the foot, and now in the face. In vain did we huddle up closer and closer; there was no warmth in our miserable, starved carcasses. Sometimes one of us would drop into an uneasy slumber for a few minutes, but we could not sleep long, and perhaps it was fortunate, for I doubt if we should ever have woke again. I believe it was only by force of will that we kept ourselves alive at all.

Not very long before dawn I heard the Hottentot Ventvögel, whose teeth had been chattering all night like castanets, give a deep sigh, and then his teeth stopped chattering. I did not think anything of it at the time, concluding that he had gone to sleep.

His back was resting against mine, and it seemed to grow colder and colder, till at last it was like ice.

At length the air began to grow gray with light, then swift golden arrows came flashing across the snow, and at last the glorious sun peeped up above the lava wall and looked in upon our half-frozen forms and upon Ventvögel, sitting there among us *stone dead*. No wonder his back had felt cold, poor fellow. He had died when I heard him sigh, and was now almost frozen stiff. Shocked beyond measure, we dragged ourselves from the corpse (strange the horror we all have of the companionship of a dead body), and left it still sitting there, with its arms clasped round its knees.

By this time the sunlight was pouring its cold rays (for here they were cold) straight in at the mouth of the cave. Suddenly I heard an exclamation of fear from some one, and turned my head down the cave.

And this was what I saw. Sitting at the end of it, for it was not more than twenty feet long, was another form, of which the head rested on the chest and the long arms hung down. I stared at it, and saw that it too was a *dead man*, and what was more, a white man.

The others saw it, too, and the sight proved too much for our shattered nerves. One and all we scrambled out of the cave as fast as our half-frozen limbs would allow.

CHAPTER VII.

SOLOMON'S ROAD.

OUTSIDE the cave we halted, feeling rather foolish.

"I am going back," said Sir Henry.

"Why?" asked Good.

"Because it has struck me that—what we saw—may be my brother."

This was a new idea, and we re-entered the cave to put it to the proof. After the bright light outside our eyes, weak as they were with staring at the snow, could not for a while pierce the gloom of the cave. Presently, however, we grew accustomed to the semi-darkness, and advanced on to the dead form.

Sir Henry knelt down and peered into its face.

"Thank God," he said, with a sigh of relief, "it is not my brother."

Then I went and looked. The corpse was that of a tall man in middle life, with acquiline features, grizzled hair, and a long black mustache. The skin was perfectly yellow, and stretched tightly over the bones. Its clothing, with the exception of what seemed to be the remains of a pair of woollen hose, had been removed, leaving the skeleton-like frame naked. Round the neck hung a yellow ivory crucifix. The corpse was frozen perfectly stiff.

"Who on earth can it be?" said I.

"Can't you guess?" asked Good.

I shook my head.

"Why, the old don, José da Silvestra, of course—who else?"

"Impossible," I gasped, "he died three hundred years ago."

"And what is there to prevent his lasting for three thousand years in this atmosphere I should like to know?" asked Good. "If only the air is cold enough flesh and blood will keep as fresh as New Zealand mutton forever, and Heaven knows it is cold enough here. The sun never gets in here; no animal comes here to tear or destroy. No doubt his slave, of whom he speaks on the map, took off his clothes and left him. He could not have buried him alone. Look here," he went on, stooping down and picking up a queer-shaped bone scraped at the end into a sharp point, "here is the 'cleft-bone' that he used to draw the map with."

We gazed astonished for a moment, forgetting our own miseries in the extraordinary and, as it seemed to us, semi-miraculous sight.

"Ay," said Sir Henry, "and here is where he got his ink from," and he pointed to a small wound on the dead man's left arm. "Did ever man see such a thing before?"

There was no longer any doubt about the matter, which I confess, for my own part, perfectly appalled me. There he sat, the dead man, whose directions, written some ten generations ago, had led us to this spot. There in my own hand was the rude pen with which he had written them, and there round his neck was the crucifix his dying lips had kissed. Gazing at him my imagination could reconstruct the whole scene: the traveller dying of cold and starvation, and yet striving to convey the great secret he had discovered to the world; the awful loneliness of his death, of which the evidence sat before us. It even seemed to me that I could trace in his strongly-marked features a likeness to those of my poor friend Silvestre, his descendant, who had died twenty years ago in my arms, but perhaps that was fancy. At any rate, there he sat, a sad memento of the fate that so often overtakes those who would penetrate into the unknown; and there probably he will still sit, crowned with the dread majesty of death, for centuries yet unborn, to startle the eyes of wanderers like ourselves, if any such should ever come again to invade his loneliness. The thing overpowered us, already nearly done to death as we were with cold and hunger.

"Let us go," said Sir Henry, in a low voice; "stay, we will give him a companion," and, lifting up the dead body of the Hottentot Ventvögel, he placed it near that of the old don. Then he stooped down and with a jerk broke the rotten string of the crucifix round his neck, for his fingers were too cold to attempt to unfasten it. I believe that he still has it. I took the pen, and it is before me as I write—sometimes I sign my name with it.

Then, leaving those two, the proud white man of a past age and the poor Hottentot, to keep their eternal vigil in the midst of the eternal snows, we crept out of the cave into the welcome sunshine and resumed our path, wondering in our hearts how many hours it would be before we were even as they are.

When we had gone about half a mile we came to the edge of the plateau, for the nipple of the mountain did not rise out of its exact centre, though from the desert side it seemed to do so. What lay below us we could not see, for the landscape was wreathed in billows of morning mist. Presently, however, the higher layers of mist cleared a little, and revealed, some five hundred yards beneath us, at the end of a long slope of snow, a patch of green grass, through which a stream was running. Nor was this all. By the stream, basking in the morning sun, stood and lay a group of from ten to fifteen *large antelopes*—at that distance we could not see what they were.

The sight filled us with an unreasoning joy. There was food in plenty if only we could get it. But the question was how to get it. The beasts were fully six hundred yards off, a very long shot, and one not to be depended on when one's life hung on the results.

Rapidly we discussed the advisability of trying to stalk the game, but finally reluctantly dismissed it. To begin with, the wind was not favorable, and further, we should be certain to be perceived, however careful we were, against the blinding background of snow which we should be obliged to traverse.

"Well, we must have a try from where we are," said Sir Henry. "Which shall it be, Quatermain, the repeating rifles or the expresses?"

Here again was a question. The Winchester repeaters—of which we had two, Umbopa carrying poor Ventvögel's as well as his own—were sighted up to a thousand yards, whereas the expresses were only sighted to three hundred and fifty, beyond which distance shooting with them was more or less guess-work.

On the other hand, if they did hit, the express bullets, being expanding, were much more likely to bring the game down. It was a knotty point, but I made up my mind that we must risk it and use the expresses.

"Let each of us take the buck opposite to him. Aim well at the point of the shoulder, and high up," said I; "and Umbopa, do you give the word, so that we may all fire together."

Then came a pause, each man aiming his level best, as indeed one is likely to do when one knows that life itself depends upon the shot.

"Fire!" said Umbopa, in Zulu, and at almost the same instant the three rifles rang out loudly; three clouds of smoke hung for a moment before us, and a hundred echoes went flying away over the silent snow. Presently the smoke cleared, and revealed— oh, joy!—a great buck lying on its back and kicking furiously in its death agony. We gave a yell of triumph; we were saved, we should not starve. Weak as we were, we rushed down the intervening slope of snow, and in ten minutes from the time of firing the animal's heart and liver were lying smoking before us. But now a new difficulty arose; we had no fuel, and therefore could make no fire to cook them at. We gazed at each other in dismay.

"Starving men must not be fanciful," said Good; "we must eat raw meat."

There was no other way out of the dilemma, and our gnawing hunger made the proposition less distasteful than it would otherwise have been. So we took the heart and liver and buried them for a few minutes in a patch of snow to cool them off. Then we washed them in the ice-cold water of the stream, and lastly ate them greedily. It sounds horrible enough, but, honestly, I never tasted anything so good as that raw meat. In a quarter of an hour we were changed men. Our life and our vigor came back to us, our feeble pulses grew strong again, and the blood went coursing through our veins. But, mindful of the results of over-feeding on starving stomachs, we were careful not to eat too much, stopping while we were still hungry.

"Thank God!" said Sir Henry; "that brute has saved our lives. What is it, Quatermain?"

I rose and went to look at the antelope, for I was not certain. It was about the size of a donkey, with large, curved horns. I had never seen one like it before, the species was new to me. It was brown, with faint red stripes and a thick coat. I afterwards discovered that the natives of that wonderful country called the species "Inco." It was very rare, and only found at a great altitude, where no other game would live. The animal was fairly shot high up in the shoulder, though whose bullet it was that brought it down we could not, of course, discover. I believe that Good, mindful of his marvellous shot at the giraffe, secretly set it down to his own prowess, and we did not contradict him.

We had been so busy satisfying our starving stomachs that we had hitherto not found time to look about us. But now, having set Umbopa to cut off as much of the best meat as we were likely to be able to carry, we began to inspect our surroundings. The mist had now cleared away, for it was eight o'clock, and the sun had sucked it up, so we were able to take in all the country before us at a glance. I know not how to describe the glorious panorama which unfolded itself to our enraptured gaze. I have never seen anything like it before, nor shall, I suppose, again.

Behind and over us towered Sheba's snowy breasts, and below, some five thousand feet beneath where we stood, lay league on league of the most lovely champaign country. Here were dense patches of lofty forest, there a great river wound its silvery way. To the left stretched a vast expanse of rich, undulating veldt or grass land, on which we could just make out countless herds of game or cattle, at that distance we could not tell which. This expanse appeared to be ringed in by a wall of distant mountains. To the right the country was more or less mountainous, that is, solitary hills stood up from its level, with stretches of culti-vated lands between, among which we could distinctly see groups of dome-shaped huts. The landscape lay before us like a map, in which rivers flashed like silver snakes, and Alplike peaks crowned with wildly-twisted snow-wreaths rose in solemn gran-deur, while over all was the glad sunlight and the wide breath of Nature's happy life.

Two curious things struck us as we gazed. First, that the country before us must lie at least five thousand feet higher than the desert we had crossed, and, secondly, that all the rivers flowed from south to north. As we had painful reason to know, there was no water at all on the southern side of the vast range on which we stood, but on the northern side were many streams, most of which appeared to unite with the great river we could trace winding away farther than we could follow it.

We sat down for a while and gazed in silence at this wonderful view. Presently Sir Henry spoke.

"Isn't there something on the map about Solomon's Great Road?" he said.

I nodded, my eyes still looking out over the far country.

"Well, look; there it is!" and he pointed a little to our right. Good and I looked accordingly, and there, winding away towards the plain, was what appeared to be a wide turnpike road. We had not seen it at first because it, on reaching the plain, turned behind some broken country. We did not say anything, at least not much; we were beginning to lose the sense of wonder. Somehow it did not seem particularly unnatural that we should find a sort of Roman road in this strange land. We accepted the fact, that was all.

"Well," said Good, "it must be quite near us if we cut off to the right. Hadn't we better be making a start?"

This was sound advice, and so soon as we had washed our faces and hands in the stream we acted on it. For a mile or so we made our way over boulders and across patches of snow, till suddenly, on reaching the top of the little rise, there lay the road at our feet. It was a splendid road cut out of the solid rock, at least fifty feet wide, and apparently well kept; but the odd thing about it was that it seemed to begin there. We walked down and stood on it, but one single hundred paces behind us, in the direction of Sheba's breasts, it vanished, the whole surface of the mountain being strewed with boulders interspersed with patches of snow.

"What do you make of that, Quatermain?" asked Sir Henry. I shook my head, I could make nothing of it.

"I have it!" said Good; "the road no doubt ran right over the range and across the desert the other side, but the sand of the desert has covered it up, and above us it has been obliterated by some volcanic eruption of molten lava."

This seemed a good suggestion; at any rate, we accepted it, and proceeded down the mountain It was a very different business travelling along down hill on that magnificent pathway with full stomachs, to what it had been travelling up hill over the snow quite starved and almost frozen. Indeed, had it not been for melancholy recollections of poor Ventvögel's sad fate, and of that grim cave where he kept company with the old don, we should have been positively cheerful, notwithstanding the sense of unknown dangers before us. Every mile we walked the atmosphere grew softer and balmier, and the country before us shone with a yet more luminous beauty. As for the road itself, I never saw such an engineering work, though Sir Henry said that the great road over the St. Gothard in Switzerland was very like it. No difficulty had been too great for the Old World engineer who designed it. At one place we came to a great ravine three hundred feet broad and at least a hundred deep. This vast gulf was actually filled in, apparently with huge blocks of dressed stone, with arches pierced at the bottom for a waterway, over which the road went sublimely on. At another place it was cut in zigzags out of the side of a precipice five hundred feet deep, and in a third it tunnelled right through the base of an intervening ridge a space of thirty yards or more.

Here we noticed that the sides of the tunnel were covered with quaint sculptures, mostly of mailed figures driving in chariots. One, which was exceedingly beautiful, represented a whole battle-scene with a convoy of captives being marched off in the distance.

"Well," said Sir Henry, after inspecting this ancient work of art, "it is very well to call this Solomon's Road, but my humble opinion is that the Egyptians have been here before Solomon's people ever set a foot on it. If that isn't Egyptian handiwork, all I have to say is it is very like it."

By midday we had advanced sufficiently far down the mountain to reach the region where wood was to be met with. First we came to scattered bushes which grew more and more frequent, till at last we found the road winding through a vast grove of silver-trees similar to those which are to be seen on the slopes of Table Mountain at Cape Town. I had never before met with them in all my wanderings, except at the Cape, and their appearance here astonished me greatly.

"Ah!" said Good, surveying these shining-leaved trees with evident enthusiasm, "here is lots of wood, let us stop and cook some dinner; I have about digested that raw meat."

Nobody objected to this, so, leaving the road, we made our way to a stream which was babbling away not far off, and soon had a goodly fire of dry boughs blazing. Cutting off some substantial hunks from the flesh of the inco which we had brought with us, we proceeded to toast them on the ends of sharp sticks, as one sees the Kaffirs do, and ate them with relish. After filling ourselves, we lit our pipes and gave ourselves up to enjoyment, which, compared to the hardships we had recently undergone, seemed almost heavenly.

The brook, of which the banks were clothed with dense masses of a gigantic species of maidenhair fern interspersed with feathery tufts of wild asparagus, babbled away merrily at our side, the soft air murmured through the leaves of the silver-trees, doves cooed around, and bright-winged birds flashed like living gems from bough to bough. It was like Paradise.

The magic of the place, combined with the overwhelming sense of dangers left behind and of the promised land reached at last, seemed to charm us into silence. Sir Henry and Umbopa sat conversing in a mixture of broken English and Kitchen Zulu in a low voice, but earnestly enough, and I lay, with my eyes half shut, upon that fragrant bed of fern and watched them. Presently I missed Good, and looked to see what had become of him. As I did so I observed him sitting by the bank of the stream, in which he had been bathing. He had nothing on but his flannel shirt, and, his natural habits of extreme neatness having reasserted themselves, was actively employed in making a most elaborate toilet. He had washed his gutta-percha collar, thoroughly shaken out his trousers, coat, and waistcoat, and was now folding them up neatly till he was ready to put them on, shaking his head sadly as he did so over the numerous rents and tears in them which had naturally resulted from our frightful journey. Then he took his boots, scrubbed them with a handful of fern, and finally rubbed them over with a piece of fat which he had carefully saved from the inco meat, till they looked, comparatively speaking, respectable. Having inspected them judiciously through his eyeglass, he put them on and began a fresh operation. From a little bag he carried he produced a pocket-comb in which was fixed a tiny looking-glass, and in this surveyed himself. Apparently he was not satisfied, for he proceeded to do his hair with great care. Then came a pause while he again contemplated the effect; still it was not satisfactory. He felt his chin, on which was now the accumulated scrub of a ten days' beard. "Surely," thought I, "he is not going to try and shave." But so it was. Taking the piece of fat with which he had greased his boots, he washed it carefully in the stream. Then diving again into the bag, he brought out a little pocket razor with a guard to it, such as are sold to people afraid of cutting themselves, or to those about to undertake a sea voyage. Then he vigorously scrubbed his face and chin with the fat and began. But it was evidently a painful process, for he groaned very much over it, and I was convulsed with inward laughter as I watched him struggling with that stubbly beard. It seemed so very odd that a man should take the trouble to shave himself with a piece of fat in such a place and under such circumstances. At last he succeeded in getting the worst of the scrub off the right side of his face and chin, when suddenly I, who was watching, became aware of a flash of light that passed just by his head.

Good sprang up with a profane exclamation (if it had not been a safety razor he would certainly have cut his throat), and so did I, without the exclamation, and this was what I saw. Standing there, not more than twenty paces from where I was, and ten from Good, was a group of men. They were very tall and copper-colored, and some of them wore great plumes of black feathers and short cloaks of leopard skins; this was all I noticed at the moment. In front of them stood a youth of about seventeen, his hand still raised and his body bent forward in the attitude of a Grecian statue of a spear-thrower. Evidently the flash of light had been a weapon, and he had thrown it.

As I looked an old, soldier-like looking man stepped forward out of the group, and catching the youth by the arm said something to him. Then they advanced upon us.

Sir Henry, Good, and Umbopa had by this time seized their rifles and lifted them threateningly. The party of natives still came on. It struck me that they could not know what rifles were, or they would not have treated them with such contempt.

"Put down your guns!" I halloed to the others, seeing that our only chance of safety lay in conciliation. They obeyed, and, walking to the front, I addressed the elderly man who had checked the youth.

"Greeting," I said, in Zulu, not knowing what language to use. To my surprise I was understood.

"Greeting," answered the man, not, indeed, in the same tongue, but in a dialect so closely allied to it that neither Umbopa nor myself had any difficulty in understanding it. Indeed, as we afterwards found out, the language spoken by this people was an old-fashioned form of the Zulu tongue, bearing about the same relationship to it that the English of Chaucer does to the English of the nineteenth century.

"Whence come ye?" he went on, "what are ye? and why are the faces of three of ye white, and the face of the fourth as the face of our mother's sons?" and he pointed to Umbopa. I looked at Umbopa as he said it, and it flashed across me that he was right. Umbopa was like the faces of the men before me; so was his great form. But I had not time to reflect on this coincidence.

"We are strangers, and come in peace," I answered, speaking very slow, so that he might understand me, "and this man is our servant."

"Ye lie," he answered, "no strangers can cross the mountains where all things die. But what do your lies matter; if ye are strangers then ye must die, for no strangers may live in the land of the Kukuanas. It is the king's law. Prepare then to die, O strangers!"

I was slightly staggered at this, more especially as I saw the hands of some of the party of men steal down to their sides, where hung on each what looked to me like a large and heavy knife.

"What does that beggar say?" asked Good.

"He says that we are going to be scragged," I answered, grimly.

"Oh, Lord," groaned Good; and, as was his way when perplexed, put his hand to his false teeth, dragging the top set down and allowing them to fly back to his jaw with a snap. It was a most fortunate move, for next second the dignified crowd of Kukuanas gave a simultaneous yell of horror, and bolted back some yards.

"What's up?" said I.

"It's his teeth," whispered Sir Henry, excitedly. "He moved them. Take them out, Good, take them out!"

He obeyed, slipping the set into the sleeve of his flannel shirt.

In another second curiosity had overcome fear, and the men advanced slowly. Apparently they had now forgotten their amiable intentions of doing for us.

"How is it, O strangers," asked the old man, solemnly, "that the teeth of the man" (pointing to Good, who had nothing on but a flannel shirt, and had only half finished his shaving) "whose body is clothed, and whose legs are bare, who grows hair on one side of his sickly face and not on the other, and who has one shining and transparent eye, move of themselves, coming away from the jaws and returning of their own will?"

"Open your mouth," I said to Good, who promptly curled up his lips and grinned at the old gentleman like an angry dog, revealing to their astonished gaze two thin red lines of gum as utterly innocent of ivories as a new-born elephant. His audience gasped.

"Where are his teeth?" they shouted; "with our eyes we saw them."

Turning his head slowly and with a gesture of ineffable contempt, Good swept his hand across his mouth. Then he grinned again, and lo! there were two rows of lovely teeth.

The young man who had flung the knife threw himself down on the grass and gave vent to a prolonged howl of terror; and as for the old gentleman, his knees knocked together with fear.

"I see that ye are spirits," he said, falteringly; "did ever man born of woman have hair on one side of his face and not on the other, or a round and transparent eye, or teeth which moved and melted away and grew again? Pardon us, O my lords."

Here was luck indeed, and, needless to say, I jumped at the chance

"It is granted," I said, with an imperial smile. "Nay, ye shall know the truth. We come from another world, though we are men such as ye; we come," I went on, "from the biggest star that shines at night."

"Oh! oh!" groaned the chorus of astonished aborigines.

"Yes," I went on, "we do, indeed;" and I again smiled benignly as I uttered that amazing lie. "We come to stay with you a little while, and bless you by our sojourn. Ye will see, O friends, that I have prepared myself by learning your language."

"It is so, it is so," said the chorus.

"Only, my lord," put in the old gentleman, "thou hast learned it very badly."

I cast an indignant glance at him and he quailed.

"Now, friends," I continued, "ye might think that after so long a journey we should find it in our hearts to avenge such a reception, mayhap to strike cold in death the impious hand that—that, in short—threw a knife at the head of him whose teeth come and go."

"Spare him, my lords," said the old man, in supplication, "he is the king's son, and I am his uncle. If anything befalls him his blood will be required at my hands."

"Yes, that is certainly so," put in the young man with great emphasis.

"You may perhaps doubt our power to avenge," I went on, heedless of this by-play. "Stay, I will show you. Here, you dog and slave" (addressing Umbopa in a savage tone), "give me the magic tube that speaks;" and I tipped a wink towards my express rifle.

Umbopa rose to the occasion, and with something as nearly resembling a grin as I have ever seen on his dignified face, handed me the rifle.

"It is here, O lord of lords," he said, with a deep obeisance.

Now, just before I asked for the rifle I had perceived a little klipspringer antelope standing on a mass of rock about seventy yards away, and determined to risk a shot at it.

"Ye see that buck," I said, pointing the animal out to the party before me. "Tell me, is it possible for man, born of woman, to kill it from here with a noise?"

"It is not possible, my lord," answered the old man.

"Yet shall I kill it," I said, quietly.

The old man smiled. "That my lord cannot do," he said.

I raised the rifle, and covered the buck. It was a small animal, and one which one might well be excused for missing, but I knew that it would not do to miss.

I drew a deep breath, and slowly pressed on the trigger. The buck stood still as stone.

"Bang! thud!" The buck sprang into the air and fell on the rock dead as a door-nail.

A groan of terror burst from the group before us.

"If ye want meat," I remarked, coolly, "go fetch that buck."

The old man made a sign and one of his followers departed, and presently returned bearing the klipspringer. I noticed, with satisfaction, that I had hit it fairly behind the shoulder. They gathered round the poor creature's body, gazing at the bullet-hole in consternation.

"Ye see," I said, "I do not speak empty words."

There was no answer.

"If ye yet doubt our power," I went on, "let one of ye go stand upon that rock, that I may make him as this buck."

None of them seemed at all inclined to take the hint, till at last the king's son spoke.

"It is well said. Do thou, my uncle, go stand upon the rock. It is but a buck that the magic has killed. Surely it cannot kill a man."

The old gentleman did not take the suggestion in good part. Indeed, he seemed hurt.

"No! no!" he ejaculated hastily; "my old eyes have seen enough. These are wizards, indeed. Let us bring them to the king. Yet if any should wish a further proof, let *him* stand upon the rock, that the magic tube may speak with him."

There was a most general and hasty expression of dissent.

"Let not good magic be wasted on our poor bodies," said one, "we are satisfied. All the witchcraft of our people cannot show the like of this."

"It is so," remarked the old gentleman, in a tone of intense relief; "without any doubt it is so. Listen, children of the stars, children of the shining eye and the movable teeth, who roar out in thunder and slay from afar. I am Infadoos, son of Kafa, once king of the Kukuana people. This youth is Scragga."

"He nearly scragged me," murmured Good.

"Scragga, son of Twala, the great king—Twala, husband of a thousand wives, chief and lord paramount of the Kukuanas, keeper of the great road, terror of his enemies, student of the Black Arts, leader of an hundred thousand warriors; Twala, the One-eyed, the Black, the Terrible."

"So," said I, superciliously, "lead us then to Twala. We do not talk with low people and underlings."

"It is well, my lords, we will lead you, but the way is long. We are hunting three days' journey from the place of the king. But let my lords have patience, and we will lead them."

"It is well," I said, carelessly, "all time is before us, for we do not die. We are ready; lead on. But Infadoos, and thou, Scragga, beware! Play us no tricks, make for us no snares, for before your brains of mud have thought of them we shall know them and avenge them. The light from the transparent eye of him with the bare legs and the half-haired face (Good) shall destroy you, and go through your land; his vanishing teeth shall fix themselves fast in you and eat you up, you and your wives and children; the magic tubes shall talk with you loudly, and make you as sieves. Beware!"

This magnificent address did not fail of its effect; indeed, it was hardly needed, so deeply were our friends already impressed with our powers.

The old man made a deep obeisance, and murmured the word "Koom, koom," which I afterwards discovered was their royal salute, corresponding to the Bayéte of the Zulus, and, turning, addressed his followers. These at once proceeded to lay hold of all our goods and chattels, in order to bear them for us, excepting only the guns, which they would on no account touch. They even seized Good's clothes, which were, as the reader may remember, neatly folded up beside him.

He at once made a dive for them, and a loud altercation ensued.

"Let not my lord of the transparent eye and the melting teeth touch them," said the old man. "Surely his slaves shall carry the things."

"But I want to put 'em on!" roared Good, in nervous English. Umbopa translated.

"Nay, my lord," put in Infadoos, "would my lord cover up his beautiful white legs (although he was so dark Good had a singularly white skin) from the eyes of his servants? Have we offended my lord that he should do such a thing?"

Here I nearly exploded with laughing; and meanwhile, one of the men started on with the garments.

"Damn it!" roared Good, "that black villain has got my trousers."

"Look here, Good," said Sir Henry, "you have appeared in this country in a certain character, and you must live up to it. It will never do for you to put on trousers again. Henceforth you must live in a flannel shirt, a pair of boots, and an eye-glass."

"Yes," I said, "and with whiskers on one side of your face and not on the other. If you change any of these things they will think that we are impostors. I am very sorry for you, but, seriously, you must do it. If once they begin to suspect us, our lives will not be worth a brass farthing."

"Do you really think so?" said Good, gloomily.

"I do, indeed. Your 'beautiful white legs' and your eye-glass are now *the* feature of the party, and, as Sir Henry says, you must live up to them. Be thankful that you have got your boots on, and that the air is warm."

Good sighed, and said no more, but it took him a fortnight to get accustomed to his attire.

CHAPTER VIII.

WE ENTER KUKUANALAND.

ALL that afternoon we travelled on along the magnificent roadway, which headed steadily in a northwesterly direction. Infadoos and Scragga walked with us, but their followers marched about one hundred paces ahead.

"Infadoos," I said at length, "who made this road?"

"It was made, my lord, of old time, none knew how or when, not even the wise woman, Gagool, who has lived for generations. We are not old enough to remember its making. None can make such roads now, but the king lets no grass grow upon it."

"And whose are the writings on the walls of the caves through which we have passed on the road?" I asked, referring to the Egyptian-like sculptures we had seen.

"My lord, the hands that made the road wrote the wonderful writings. We know not who wrote them."

"When did the Kukuana race come into this country?"

"My lord, the race came down here like the breath of a storm ten thousand moons ago, from the great lands which lie there beyond," and he pointed to the north. "They could travel no farther, so say the old voices of our fathers that have come down to us, the children, and so says Gagool, the wise woman, the smeller-out of witches, because of the great mountains which ring in the land," and he pointed to the snow-clad peaks. "The country, too, was good, so they settled here and grew strong and powerful, and now our numbers are like the sea sand, and when Twala the king calls up his regiments their plumes cover the plain as far as the eye of man can reach."

"And if the land is walled in with mountains, who is there for the regiments to fight with?"

"Nay, my lord, the country is open there," and again he pointed towards the north, "and now and again warriors sweep down upon us in clouds from a land we know not, and we slay them. It is the third part of the life of a man since there was a war. Many thousands died in it, but we destroyed those who came to eat us up. So, since then there has been no war."

"Your warriors must grow weary of resting on their spears."

"My lord, there was one war, just after we destroyed the people that came down upon us, but it was a civil war—dog eat dog."

"How was that?"

"My lord, the king, my half-brother, had a brother born at the same birth and of the same woman. It is not our custom, my lord, to let twins live; the weakest must always die. But the mother of the king hid away the weakest child, which was born the last, for her heart yearned over it, and the child is Twala the king. I am his younger brother born of another wife."

"Well?"

"My lord, Kafa, our father, died when we came to manhood, and my brother Imotu was made king in his place, and for a space reigned and had a son by his favorite wife. When the babe was three years old, just after the great war, during which no man could sow or reap, a famine came upon the land, and the people murmured because of the famine, and looked round like a starved lion for something to rend. Then it was that Gagool, the wise and terrible woman, who does not die, proclaimed to the people, saying, 'The king Imotu is no king.' And at the time Imotu was sick with a wound, and lay in his hut not able to move.

"Then Gagool went into a hut and led out Twala, my half-brother, and the twin brother of the king, whom she had hidden since he was born among the caves and rocks, and, stripping the 'moocha' (waist-cloth) off his loins, showed the people of the Kukuanas the mark of the sacred snake coiled round his waist, wherewith the eldest son of the king is marked at birth, and cried out loud, 'Behold, your king, whom I have saved for you even to this day!' And the people, being mad with hunger and altogether bereft of reason and the knowledge of truth, cried out, '*The king! The king!*' but I knew that it was not so, for Imotu, my brother, was the elder of the twins, and was the lawful king. And just as the tumult was at its height Imotu the king, though he was very sick, came crawling from his hut holding his wife by the hand, and followed by his little son Ignosi (the lightning).

"'What is this noise?' he asked; 'Why cry ye *The king! The king!*'

"Then Twala, his own brother, born of the same woman and

in the same hour, ran to him, and, taking him by the hair, stabbed him through the heart with his knife. And the people, being fickle, and ever ready to worship the rising sun, clapped their hands and cried, *'Twala is king!* Now we know that Twala is king!' "

"And what became of his wife and her son Ignosi? Did Twala kill them too?"

"Nay, my lord. When she saw that her lord was dead she seized the child with a cry, and ran away. Two days afterwards she came to a kraal very hungry, and none would give her milk or food, now that her lord the king was dead, for all men hate the unfortunate. But at nightfall a little child, a girl, crept out and brought her to eat, and she blessed the child, and went on towards the mountains with her boy before the sun rose again, where she must have perished, for none have seen her since, nor the child Ignosi."

"Then if this child Ignosi had lived, he would be the true king of the Kukuana people?"

"That is so, my lord; the sacred snake is round his middle. If he lives he is the king; but alas! he is long dead."

"See, my lord," and he pointed to a vast collection of huts surrounded with a fence, which was in its turn surrounded by a great ditch, that lay on the plain beneath us. "That is the kraal where the wife of Imotu was last seen with the child Ignosi. It is there that we shall sleep tonight, if, indeed," he added, doubtfully, "my lords sleep at all upon this earth."

"When we are among the Kukuanas, my good friend Infadoos, we do as the Kukuanas do," I said majestically, and I turned round suddenly to address Good, who was tramping along sullenly behind, his mind fully occupied with unsatisfactory attempts to keep his flannel shirt from flapping up in the evening breeze, and to my astonishment butted into Umbopa, who was walking along immediately behind me, and had very evidently been listening with the greatest interest to my conversation with Infadoos. The expression on his face was most curious, and gave the idea of a man who was struggling with partial success to bring something long ago forgotten back into his mind.

All this while we had been pressing on at a good rate down towards the undulating plain beneath. The mountains we had crossed now loomed high above us, and Sheba's breasts were modestly veiled in diaphanous wreaths of mist. As we went on the country grew more and more lovely. The vegetation was luxuriant without being tropical; the sun was bright and warm, but not burning, and a gracious breeze blew softly along the odorous slopes of the mountains. And indeed, this new land was little less than an earthly paradise; in beauty, in natural wealth, and in climate I have never seen its like. The Transvaal is a fine country, but it is nothing to Kukuanaland.

So soon as we started, Infadoos had despatched a runner on to warn the people of the kraal, which, by the way, was in his military command, of our arrival. This man had departed at an extraordinary speed, which Infadoos had informed me he would keep up all the way, as running was an exercise much practised among his people.

The result of this message now became apparent. When we got within two miles of the kraal we could see that company after company of men was issuing from its gates and marching towards us.

Sir Henry laid his hand upon my arm, and remarked that it looked as though we were going to meet with a warm reception. Something in his tone attracted Infadoo's attention.

"Let not my lords be afraid," he said, hastily, "for in my breast there dwells no guile. This regiment is one under my command, and comes out by my orders to greet you."

I nodded easily, though I was not quite easy in my mind.

About half a mile from the gates of the kraal was a long stretch of rising ground sloping gently upward from the road, and on this the companies formed. It was a splendid sight to see them, each company about three hundred strong, charging swiftly up the slope, with flashing spears and waving plumes, and taking their appointed place. By the time we came to the slope twelve such companies, or in all three thousand six hundred men, had passed out and taken up their positions along the road.

Presently we came to the first company, and were able to gaze in astonishment on the most magnificent set of men I have ever seen. They were all men of mature age, mostly veterans of about forty, and not one of them was under six feet in height, while many were six feet three or four. They wore upon their heads heavy black plumes of Sacaboola feathers, like those which adorned our guides. Round their waists and also beneath the right knee were bound circlets of white ox-tails, and in their left hands were round shields about twenty inches across. These shields were very curious. The framework consisted of an iron plate beaten out thin, over which was stretched milk-white ox-hide. The weapons that each man bore were simple, but most effective, consisting of a short and very heavy two-edged spear with a wooden shaft, the blade being about six inches across at the widest part. These spears were not used for throwing, but, like the Zulu "bangwan," or stabbing assegai, were for close quarters only, when the wound inflicted by them was terrible. In addition to these bangwans each man also carried three large and heavy knives, each knife weighing about two pounds. One knife was fixed in the ox-tail girdle, and the other two at the back of the round shield. These knives, which are called "tollas" by the Kukuanas, take the place of the throwing assegai of the Zulus. A Kukuana warrior can throw them with great accuracy at distances of fifty yards, and it is their custom on charging to hurl a volley of them at the enemy as they come to close quarters.

Each company stood like a collection of bronze statues till we were opposite to it, when, at a signal given by its commanding officer, who, distinguished by a leopard-skin cloak, stood some paces in front, every spear was raised into the air, and from three hundred throats sprang forth with a sudden roar the royal salute of "*Koom!*" Then, when we had passed, the company formed behind us and followed us towards the kraal, till at last the whole regiment of the "Grays" (so called from their white shields), the crack corps of the Kukuana people, was marching behind us with a tread that shook the ground.

At length, branching off from Solomon's Great Road, we came to the wide fosse surrounding the kraal, which was at least a mile round and fenced with a strong palisade of piles formed of the trunks of trees. At the gateway this fosse was spanned by a primitive drawbridge which was let down by the guard to allow us to pass in. The kraal was exceedingly well laid out. Through the centre ran a wide pathway intersected at right angles by other pathways so arranged as to cut the huts into square blocks, each block being the quarters of a company. The huts were dome-shaped, and built, like those of the Zulus, of a framework of wattle beautifully thatched with grass; but, unlike the Zulu huts, they had doorways through which one could walk. Also they were much larger, and surrounded with a veranda about six feet wide, beautifully paved with powdered lime trodden hard. All along each side of the wide pathway that pierced the kraal were ranged hundreds of women, brought out by curiosity to look at us. These women are, for a native race, exceedingly handsome. They are tall and graceful, and their figures are wonderfully fine. The hair, though short, is rather curly than woolly, the features are frequently aquiline, and their lips are not unpleasantly thick, as is the case in most African races. But what struck us most was their exceeding quiet, dignified air. They were as well-bred in their way as the *habitués* of a fashionable drawing-room, and in this respect differ from Zulu women, and their cousins, the Masai, who inhabit the district behind Zanzibar. Their curiosity had brought them out to see us, but they allowed no rude expression of wonder or savage criticism to pass their lips as we trudged wearily in front of them. Not even when old Infadoos with a surreptitious motion of the hand pointed out the crowning wonder of poor Good's "beautiful white legs," did they allow the feeling of intense admiration which evidently mastered their minds to find expression. They fixed their dark eyes upon their snowy loveliness (Good's skin exceedingly white), and that was all. But this was quite enough for Good, who is modest by nature.

When we got to the centre of the kraal Infadoos halted at the door of a large hut, which was surrounded at a distance by a circle of smaller ones.

"Enter, sons of the stars," he said, in a magniloquent voice, "and deign to rest awhile in our humble habitations. A little food shall be brought to you, so that ye shall have no need to draw your belts tight from hunger; some honey and some milk, and an ox or two, and a few sheep; not much, my lords, but still a little food."

"It is good," said I, "Infadoos, we are weary with travelling through realms of air; now let us rest."

Accordingly we entered into the hut, which we found amply prepared for our comfort. Couches of tanned skins were spread for us to rest on, and water was placed for us to wash in.

Presently we heard a shouting outside, and, stepping to the door, saw a line of damsels bearing milk and roasted mealies and honey in a pot. Behind these were some youths driving a fat young ox. We received the gifts, and then one of the young men took the knife from his girdle and dexterously cut the ox's throat. In ten minutes it was dead, skinned, and cut up. The best of the meat was then cut off for us, and the rest I, in the name of our party, presented to the warriors round us, who took it off and distributed the "white men's gift."

Umbopa set to work, with the assistance of an extremely prepossessing young woman, to boil our portion in a large earthenware pot over a fire which was built outside the hut, and when it was nearly ready we sent a message to Infadoos, and asked him, and Scragga the king's son, to join us.

Presently they came, and, sitting down upon little stools, of which there were several about the hut (for the Kukuanas do not in general squat upon their haunches like the Zulus), helped us to get through our dinner. The old gentleman was most affable and polite, but it struck us that the young one regarded us with suspicion. He had, together with the rest of the party, been overawed by our white appearance and by our magic properties; but it seemed to me that on discovering that we ate, drank, and slept like other mortals, his awe was beginning to wear off and be replaced by a sullen suspicion, which made us feel rather uncomfortable.

In the course of our meal Sir Henry suggested to me that it might be well to try and discover if our hosts knew anything of his brother's fate, or if they had ever seen or heard of him; but, on the whole, I thought that it would be wiser to say nothing of the matter at that time.

After supper we filled our pipes and lit them; a proceeding which filled Infadoos and Scragga with astonishment. The Kukuanas were evidently unacquainted with the divine use of tobacco-smoke. The herb was grown among them extensively; but, like the Zulus, they only used it for snuff, and quite failed to identify it in its new form.

Presently I asked Infadoos when we were to proceed on our journey, and was delighted to learn that preparations had been made for us to leave on the following morning, messengers having already left to inform Twala, the king, of our coming. It appeared that Twala was at his principal place, known as Loo, making ready for the great annual feast which was held in the first week of June. At this gathering all the regiments, with the exception of certain detachments left behind for garrison purposes, were brought up and paraded before the king, and the great annual witch-hunt, of which more by and by, was held.

We were to start at dawn; and Infadoos, who was to accompany us, expected that we should, unless we were detained by accident or by swollen rivers, reach Loo on the night of the second day.

When they had given us this information our visitors bade us good-night; and, having arranged to watch turn and turn about, three of us flung ourselves down and slept the sweet sleep of the weary, while the fourth sat up on the lookout for possible treachery.

CHAPTER IX.

TWALA, THE KING.

It will not be necessary for me to detail at length the incidents of our journey to Loo. It took two good days' travelling along

Solomon's Great Road, which pursued its even course right into the heart of Kukuanaland. Suffice it to say that as we went the country seemed to grow richer and richer, and the kraals, with their wide surrounding belts of cultivation, more and more numerous. They were all built upon the same principles as the first one we had reached, and were guarded by ample garrisons of troops. Indeed, in Kukuanaland, as among the Germans, the Zulus, and the Masai, every able-bodied man is a soldier, so that the whole force of the nation is available for its wars, offensive or defensive. As we travelled along we were overtaken by thousands of warriors hurrying up to Loo to be present at the great annual review and festival, and a grander series of troops I never saw. At sunset on the second day we stopped to rest awhile upon the summit of some heights over which the road ran, and there, on a beautiful and fertile plain before us, was Loo itself. For a native town it was an enormous place, quite five miles round, I should say, with outlying kraals jutting out from it, which served on grand occasions as cantonments for the regiments, and a curious horseshoe-shaped hill, with which we were destined to become better acquainted, about two miles to the north. It was beautifully situated, and through the centre of the kraal, dividing it into two portions, ran a river, which appeared to be bridged at several places, the same, perhaps, that we had seen from the slopes of Sheba's breasts. Sixty or seventy miles away three great snow-capped mountains, placed like the points of a triangle, started up out of the level plain. The conformation of these mountains was unlike that of Sheba's breasts, being sheer and precipitous, instead of smooth and rounded.

Infadoos saw us looking at them and volunteered a remark:

"The road ends there," he said, pointing to the mountains, known among the Kukuanas as the "Three Witches."

"Why does it end?" I asked.

"Who knows?" he answered, with a shrug; "the mountains are full of caves, and there is a great pit between them. It is there that the wise men of old time used to go to get whatever it was they came to this country for, and it is there now that our kings are buried in the Place of Death."

"What was it they came for?" I asked eagerly.

"Nay, I know not. My lords who come from the stars should know," he answered, with a quick look. Evidently he knew more than he chose to say.

"Yes," I went on, "you are right; in the stars we know many things. I have heard, for instance, that the wise men of old came to those mountans to get bright stones, pretty playthings, and yellow iron."

"My lord is wise," he answered, coldly; "I am but a child and cannot talk with my lord on such things. My lord must speak with Gagool the old, at the king's palace, who is wise even as my lord," and he turned away.

As soon as he was gone I turned to the others and pointed out the mountains. "There are Solomon's diamond mines," I said.

Umbopa was standing with them, apparently plunged in one of the fits of abstraction which were common to him, and caught my words.

"Yes, Macumazahn," he put in, in Zulu, "the diamonds are surely there, and you shall have them, since you white men are so fond of toys and money."

"How dost thou know that, Umbopa?" I asked, sharply, for I did not like his mysterious ways.

He laughed; "I dreamed it in the night, white men," and then he too turned upon his heel and went.

"Now what," said Sir Henry, "is our black friend at? He knows more than he chooses to say, that is clear. By the way, Quatermain, has he heard anything of—of my brother?"

"Nothing; he has asked every one he has got friendly with, but they all declare no white man has ever been seen in the country before."

"Do you suppose he ever got here at all?" suggested Good; "we have only reached the place by a miracle; is it likely he could have reached it at all without the map?"

"I don't know," said Sir Henry, gloomily, "but somehow I think that I shall find him."

Slowly the sun sank, and then suddenly darkness rushed down on the land like a tangible thing. There was no breathing-place between the day and the night, no soft transformation scene, for in these latitudes twilight does not exist. The change from day to night is as quick and as absolute as the change from life to death. The sun sank and the world was wreathed in shadows. But not for long, for see, in the east there is a glow, then a bent edge of silver light, and at last the full bow of the crescent moon peeps above the plain and shoots its gleaming arrows far and wide, filling the earth with a faint refulgence, as the glow of a good man's deeds shines for a while upon his little world after his sun has set, lighting the faint-hearted travellers who follow on towards a fuller dawn.

We stood and watched the lovely sight, while the stars grew pale before this chastened majesty, and felt our hearts lifted up in the presence of a beauty we could not realize, much less describe. Mine has been a rough life, my reader, but there are a few things I am thankful to have lived for, and one of them is to have seen that moon rise over Kukuanaland. Presently our meditations were broken in upon by our polite friend Infadoos.

" If my lords are ready we will journey on to Loo, where a hut is made ready for my lords to-night. The moon is now bright, so that we shall not fall on the way."

We assented, and in an hour's time were at the outskirts of the town, of which the extent, mapped out as it was by thousands of camp-fires, appeared absolutely endless. Indeed, Good, who was always fond of a bad joke, christened it "Unlimited Loo." Presently we came to a moat with a drawbridge, where we were met by the rattling of arms and the hoarse challenge of a sentry. Infadoos gave some password that I could not catch, which was met with a salute, and we passed on through the central street of the great grass city. After nearly half an hour's tramp past endless lines of huts, Infadoos at last halted at the gate of a little group of huts which surrounded a small courtyard of powdered limestone, and informed us that these were to be our "poor" quarters.

We entered, and found that a hut had been assigned to each of us. These huts were superior to any which we had yet seen, and in each was a most comfortable bed made of tanned skins spread upon mattresses of aromatic grass. Food, too, was ready for us, and as soon as we had washed ourselves with water, which stood ready in earthenware jars, some young women of handsome appearance brought us roasted meat and mealie cobs daintily served on wooden platters, and presented it to us with deep obeisances.

We ate and drank, and then, the beds having by our request been all moved into one hut, a precaution at which the amiable young ladies smiled, we flung ourselves down to sleep, thoroughly wearied out with our long journey.

When we woke, it was to find that the sun was high in the heavens, and that the female attendants, who did not seem to be troubled by any false shame, were already standing inside the hut, having been ordered to attend and help us to "make ready."

"Make ready, indeed," growled Good; "when one has only a flannel shirt and a pair of boots, that does not take long. I wish you would ask them for my trousers."

I asked accordingly, but was informed that those sacred relics had already been taken to the king, who would see us in the forenoon.

Having, somewhat to their astonishment and disappointment, requested the young ladies to step outside, we proceeded to make the best toilet that the circumstances admitted of. Good even went the length of again shaving the right side of his face; the left, on which now appeared a very fair crop of whiskers, we impressed upon him he must on no account touch. As for ourselves, we were contented with a good wash and combing our hair. Sir Henry's yellow locks were now almost down to his shoulders, and he looked more like an ancient Dane than ever, while my grizzled scrub was fully an inch long, instead of half an inch, which in a general way I considered my maximum length.

By the time that we had eaten our breakfast and smoked a pipe, a message was brought to us by no less a personage than Infadoos himself that Twala, the king, was ready to see us, if we would be pleased to come.

We remarked in reply that we should prefer to wait until the sun was a little higher, we were yet weary with our journey, etc. It is always well, when dealing with uncivilized people, not to be in too great a hurry. They are apt to mistake politeness for awe or servility. So, although we were quite as anxious to see Twala as Twala could be to see us, we sat down and waited for an hour, employing the interval in preparing such presents as our slender stock of goods permitted—namely, the Winchester rifle which had been used by poor Ventvögel, and some beads. The rifle and ammunition we determined to present to his royal highness, and the beads were for his wives and courtiers. We had already given a few to Infadoos and Scragga, and found that they were delighted with them, never having seen anything like them before. At length we declared that we were ready, and, guided by Infadoos, started off to the levée, Umbopa carrying the rifles and beads.

After walking a few hundred yards we came to an enclosure, something like that which surrounded the huts that had been allotted to us, only fifty times as big. It could not have been less than six or seven acres in extent. All round the outside fence was a row of huts, which were the habitations of the king's wives. Exactly opposite the gateway, on the farther side of the open space, was a very large hut, which stood by itself, in which his majesty resided. All the rest was open ground; that is to say, it would have been open had it not been filled by company after company of warriors, who were mustered there to the number of seven or eight thousand. These men stood still as statues as we advanced through them, and it would be impossible to give an idea of the grandeur of the spectacle which they presented, in their waving plumes, their glancing spears, and iron-backed ox-hide shields.

The space in front of the large hut was empty, but before it were placed several stools. On three of these, at a sign from Infadoos, we seated ourselves, Umbopa standing behind us. As for Infadoos, he took up a position by the door of the hut. So we waited for ten minutes or more in the midst of a dead silence, but conscious that we were the object of the concentrated gaze of some eight thousand pairs of eyes. It was a somewhat trying ordeal, but we carried it off as best we could. At length the door of the hut opened, and a gigantic figure, with a splendid tiger-skin karross flung over its shoulders, stepped out, followed by the boy Scragga, and what appeared to us to be a withered-up monkey wrapped in a fur cloak. The figure seated itself upon a stool, Scragga took his stand behind it, and the withered-up monkey crept on all fours into the shade of the hut and squatted down.

Still there was silence.

Then the gigantic figure slipped off the karross and stood up before us, a truly alarming spectacle. It was that of an enormous man with the most entirely repulsive countenance we had ever beheld. The lips were as thick as a negro's, the nose was flat, it had but one gleaming black eye (for the other was represented by a hollow in the face), and its whole expression was cruel and sensual to a degree. From the large head rose a magnificent plume of white ostrich feathers, the body was clad in a shirt of shining chain armor, while round the waist and right knee was the usual garnish of white ox-tails. In the right hand was a huge spear. Round the neck was a thick torque of gold, and bound on to the forehead was a single and enormous uncut diamond.

Still there was silence; but not for long. Presently the figure, whom we rightly guessed to be the king, raised the great spear in his hand. Instantly eight thousand spears were raised in answer, and from eight thousand throats rang out the royal salute of "*Koom!*" Three times this was repeated, and each time the earth shook with the noise, that can only be compared to the deepest notes of thunder.

"Be humble, O people," piped out a thin voice which seemed to come from the monkey in the shade; "it is the king."

"*It is the king,*" boomed out eight thousand throats, in answer. "*Be humble, O people; it is the king.*"

Then there was silence again—dead silence. Presently, however, it was broken. A soldier on our left dropped his shield, which fell with a clatter on the limestone flooring.

Twala turned his one cold eye in the direction of the noise. "Come hither, thou," he said, in a voice of thunder.

A fine young man stepped out of the ranks, and stood before him.

"It was thy shield that fell, thou awkward dog. Wilt thou make me a reproach in the eyes of strangers from the stars? What hast thou to say?"

And then we saw the poor fellow turn pale under his dusky skin.

"It was by chance, O calf of the black cow," he murmured.

"Then it is a chance for which thou must pay. Thou hast made me foolish; prepare for death."

"I am the king's ox," was the low answer.

"Scragga," roared the king, "let me see how thou canst use thy spear. Kill me this awkward dog."

Scragga stepped forward with an ill-favored grin, and lifted his spear. The poor victim covered his eyes with his hand and stood still. As for us, we were petrified with horror.

"Once, twice," he waved the spear and then struck, ah, God! right home—the spear stood out a foot behind the soldier's back. He flung up his hands and dropped dead. From the multitude around rose something like a murmur, it rolled round and round, and died away . The tragedy was finished; there lay the corpse, and we had not yet realized that it had been enacted. Sir Henry sprang up and swore a great oath, then, overpowered by the sense of silence, sat down again.

"The thrust was a good one," said the king; "take him away."

Four men stepped out of the ranks, and, lifting the body of the murdered man, carried it away.

"Cover up the blood-stains, cover them up," piped out the thin voice from the monkey-like figure; "the king's word is spoken, the king's doom is done."

Thereupon a girl came forward from behind the hut, bearing a jar filled with powdered lime, which she scattered over the red mark, blotting it from sight.

Sir Henry meanwhile was boiling with rage at what had happened; indeed, it was with difficulty that we could keep him still.

"Sit down, for Heaven's sake," I whispered; "our lives depend on it."

He yielded and remained quiet.

Twala sat still until the traces of the tragedy had been removed, then he addressed us.

"White people," he said, "who come hither, whence I know not, and why I know not, greeting."

"Greeting, Twala, king of the Kukuanas," I answered.

"White people, whence come ye, and what seek ye?"

"We come from the stars, ask us not how. We come to see this land."

"Ye come from far to see a little thing. And that man with ye," pointing to Umbopa, "does he too come from the stars?"

"Even so; there are people of thy color in the heavens above; but ask not of matters too high for thee, Twala, the king."

"Ye speak with a loud voice, people of the stars," Twala answered, in a tone which I scarcely liked. "Remember that the stars are far off, and ye are here. How if I make ye as him whom they bear away?"

I laughed out loud, though there was little laughter in my heart.

"Oh, king," I said; "be careful; walk warily over hot stones, lest thou shouldst burn thy feet; hold the spear by the handle, lest thou shouldst cut thy hands. Touch but one hair of our heads, and destruction shall come upon thee. What, have not these," pointing to Infadoos and Scragga (who, young villain that he was, was employed in cleaning the blood of the soldier off his spear), "told thee what manner of men we are? Hast thou ever seen the like of us?" and I pointed to Good, feeling quite sure that he had never seen anybody before who looked in the least like *him* as he then appeared.

"It is true, I have not," said the king.

"Have they not told thee how we strike with death from afar?" I went on.

"They have told me, but I believe them not. Let me see you kill. Kill me a man among those who stand yonder"—and he pointed to the opposite side of the kraal—"and I will believe."

"Nay," I answered; "we shed no blood of man except in just punishment; but if thou wilt see, bid thy servants drive in an ox through the kraal gates, and before he has run twenty paces I will strike him dead."

"Nay," laughed the king, "kill me a man, and I will believe."

"Good, O king, so be it," I answered coolly; "do thou walk across the open space, and before thy feet reach the gate thou shalt be dead; or, if thou wilt not, send thy son Scragga" (whom at that moment it would have given me much pleasure to shoot).

On hearing this suggestion Scragga gave a sort of howl, and bolted into the hut.

Twala frowned majestically; the suggestion did not please him.

"Let a young ox be driven in," he said.

Two men at once departed, running swiftly.

"Now, Sir Henry," said I, "do you shoot. I want to show this ruffian that I am not the only magician of the party."

Sir Henry accordingly took the "express," and made ready.

"I hope I shall make a good shot," he groaned.

"You must," I answered. "If you miss with the first barrel, let him have the second. Sight for one hundred and fifty yards, and wait till the beast turns broadside on."

Then came a pause, till presently we caught sight of an ox running straight for the kraal gate. It came on through the gate, and then, catching sight of the vast concourse of people, stopped stupidly, turned round, and bellowed.

"Now's your time," I whispered.

Up went the rifle.

Bang! thud! and the ox was kicking on his back, shot in the ribs. The semi-hollow bullet had done its work well, and a sigh of astonishment went up from the assembled thousands.

I turned coolly round—

"Have I lied, O king?"

"Nay, white man, it is truth," was the somewhat awed answer.

"Listen, Twala," I went on. "Thou hast seen. Now know we come in peace, not in war. See here" (and I held up the Winchester repeater); "here is a hollow staff that shall enable you to kill even as we kill, only this charm I lay upon it, thou shalt kill no man with it. If thou liftest it against a man, it shall kill thee. Stay, I will show thee. Bid a man step forty paces and place the shaft of a spear in the ground so that the flat blade looks towards us."

In a few seconds it was done.

"Now, see, I will break the spear."

Taking a careful sight, I fired. The bullet struck the flat of the spear and broke the blade into fragments.

Again the sigh of astonishment went up.

"Now, Twala" (handing him the rifle), "this magic tube we give to thee, and by and by I will show thee how to use it; but beware how thou usest the magic of the stars against a man of earth," and I handed him the rifle. He took it very gingerly, and laid it down at his feet. As he did so I observed the wizened, monkey-like figure creeping up from the shadow of the hut. It crept on all fours, but when it reached the place where the king sat it rose upon its feet, and, throwing the furry covering off its face, revealed a most extraordinary and weird countenance. It was (apparently) that of a woman of great age, so shrunken that in size it was no larger than that of a year-old child, and was made up of a collection of deep, yellow wrinkles. Set in the wrinkles was a sunken slit that represented the mouth, beneath which the chin curved outward to a point. There was no nose to speak of, indeed the whole countenance might have been taken for that of a sun-dried corpse had it not been for a pair of large black eyes, still full of fire and intelligence, which gleamed and played under the snow-white eyebrows and the projecting parchment-colored skull, like jewels in a charnel-house. As for the skull itself, it was perfectly bare, and yellow in hue, while its wrinkled scalp moved and contracted like the hood of a cobra.

The figure to whom this fearful countenance, which caused a shiver of fear to pass through us as we gazed on it, belonged stood still for a moment, and then suddenly projected a skinny claw armed with nails nearly an inch long, and laid it on the shoulder of Twala, the king, and began to speak in a thin, piercing voice:

"Listen, O king! Listen, O people! Listen, O mountains and plains and rivers, home of the Kukuana race! Listen, O skies and sun, O rain and storm and mist! Listen, all things that live and must die! Listen, all dead things that must live again—again to die! Listen, the spirit of life is in me, and I prophesy. I prophesy! I prophesy!"

The words died away in a faint wail, and terror seemed to seize upon the hearts of all who heard them, including ourselves. The old woman was very terrible.

"*Blood! blood! blood!* rivers of blood; blood everywhere. I see it, I smell it, I taste it—it is salt; it runs red upon the ground, it rains down from the skies.

"*Footsteps! footsteps! footsteps!* the tread of the white man coming from afar. It shakes the earth; the earth trembles before her master.

"Blood is good, the red blood is bright; there is no smell like the smell of new-shed blood. The lions shall lap it and roar, the vultures shall wash their wings in it and shriek in joy.

"I am old! I am old! I have seen much blood; but I shall see more ere I die, and be merry. How old am I, think ye? Your fathers knew me, and their fathers knew me, and their fathers' fathers. I have seen the white man, and known his desires. I am old, but the mountains are older than I. Who made the great road, tell me? Who wrote in pictures on the rocks, tell me? Who reared up the three silent ones yonder, who gaze across the pit, tell me?" (And she pointed towards the three precipitous mountains we had noticed on the previous night.)

"Ye know not, but I know. It was a white people who were before ye were, who shall be when ye are not, who shall eat ye up and destroy ye. Yea! yea! yea!

"And what came they for, the white ones, the terrible ones, the skilled in magic and all learning, the strong, the unswerving? What is that bright stone upon thy forehead, O king? Whose hands made the iron garments upon thy breast, O king? Ye know not, but I know. I the old one, I the wise one, I the Isanusi!" (witch doctress.)

Then she turned her bald, vulture head towards us.

"What seek ye, white men of the stars? Ah, yes, of the stars! Do ye seek a lost one? Ye shall not find him here. He is not here. Never for ages upon ages has a white foot pressed this land; never but once, and he left it but to die. Ye come for bright stones; I know it—I know it; ye shall find them when the blood is dry; but shall ye return whence ye came, or shall ye stop with me? Ha! ha! ha!

"And thou—thou with the dark skin and the proud bearing" (pointing her skinny finger at Umbopa), "who art *thou*, and what seekest *thou?* Not stones that shine; not yellow metal that gleams; that thou leavest to 'white men from the stars.' Methinks I know thee; methinks I can smell the smell of the blood in thy veins. Strip off the girdle—"

Here the features of this extraordinary creature became convulsed, and she fell to the ground foaming in an epileptic fit and was carried off into the hut.

The king rose up trembling, and waved his hand. Instantly the regiments began to file off, and in ten minutes, save for ourselves, the king, and a few attendants, the great space was left clear.

"White people," he said, "it passes in my mind to kill ye. Gagool has spoken strange words. What say ye?"

I laughed. "Be careful, O king, we are not easy to slay. Thou hast seen the fate of the ox; wouldst thou be as the ox?"

The king frowned. "It is not well to threaten a king."

"We threaten not, we speak what is true. Try to kill us, O king, and learn."

The great man put his hand to his forehead.

"Go in peace," he said, at length. "To-night is the great dance. Ye shall see it. Fear not that I shall set a snare for ye. Tomorrow I shall think."

"It is well, O king," I answered, unconcernedly, and then, accompanied by Infadoos, we rose and went back to our kraal.

CHAPTER X.

THE WITCH-HUNT.

On reaching our hut, I motioned to Infadoos to enter with us. "Now, Infadoos," I said, "we would speak with thee."

"Let my lords say on."

"It seems to us, Infadoos, that Twala, the king, is a cruel man."

"It is so, my lords. Alas! the land cries out with his cruelties. To-night ye will see. It is the great witch-hunt, and many will be smelt out as wizards and slain. No man's life is safe. If the king covets a man's cattle or a man's life, or if he fears a man that he should excite a rebellion against him, then Gagool, whom ye saw, or some of the witch-finding women whom she has taught, will smell that man out as a wizard, and he will be killed. Many will die before the moon grows pale to-night. It is ever so. Perhaps I too shall be killed. As yet I have been spared, because I am skilled in war and beloved by the soldiers; but I know not how long I shall live. The land groans at the cruelties of Twala, the king; it is wearied of him and his red ways."

"Then why is it, Infadoos, that the people do not cast him down?"

"Nay, my lords, he is the king, and if he were killed Scragga would reign in his place, and the heart of Scragga is blacker than the heart of Twala, his father. If Scragga were king the yoke upon our neck would be heavier than the yoke of Twala. If Imotu had never been slain, or if Ignosi, his son, had lived, it had been otherwise; but they are both dead."

"How know you that Ignosi is dead?" said a voice behind us. We looked round with astonishment to see who spoke. It was Umbopa.

"What meanest thou, boy?" asked Infadoos; "who told thee to speak?"

"Listen, Infadoos," was the answer, "and I will tell thee a story. Years ago the king Imotu was killed in this country, and his wife fled with the boy Ignosi. Is it not so?"

"It is so."

"It was said that the woman and the boy died upon the mountains. Is it not so?"

"It is even so."

"Well, it came to pass that the mother and the boy Ignosi did not die. They crossed the mountains, and were led by a tribe of wandering desert men across the sands beyond, till at last they came to water and grass and trees again."

"How knowest thou?"

"Listen. They travelled on and on, many months' journey, till they reached a land where a people called the Amazulu, who too are of the Kukuana stock, live by war, and with whom they tarried many years, till at length the mother died. Then the son, Ignosi, again became a wanderer, and went on into a land of wonders, where white people live, and for many more years learned the wisdom of the white people."

"It is a pretty story," said Infadoos, incredulously.

"For many years he lived there working as a servant and a soldier, but holding in his heart all that his mother had told him of his own place, and casting about in his mind to find how he might get back there to see his own people and his father's house before he died. For many years he lived and waited, and at last the time came, as it ever comes to him who can wait for it, and he met some white men who would seek this unknown land, and joined himself to them. The white men started and journeyed on and on, seeking for one who is lost. They crossed the burning desert, they crossed the snow-clad mountains, and reached the land of the Kukuanas, and there they met thee, oh Infadoos."

"Surely thou art mad to talk thus," said the astonished old soldier.

"Thou thinkest so; see, I will show thee, O my uncle. *I am Ignosi, rightful king of the Kukuanas!*"

Then, with a single movement, he slipped off the "moocha," or girdle round his middle, and stood naked before us.

"Look," he said; "what is this?" and he pointed to the mark of a great snake tattooed in blue round his middle, its tail disappearing in its open mouth just above where the thighs are set into the body.

Infadoos looked, his eyes starting nearly out of his head, and then fell upon his knees.

"*Koom! Koom!*" he ejaculated; "it is my brother's son; it is the king."

"Did I not tell thee so, my uncle? Rise; I am not yet the king, but with thy help, and with the help of these brave white men, who are my friends, I shall be. But the old woman Gagool was right; the land shall run with blood first, and hers shall run with it, for she killed my father with her words, and drove my mother forth. And now, Infadoos, choose thou. Wilt thou put thy hands between my hands and be my man? Wilt thou share the dangers that lie before me, and help me to overthrow this tyrant and murderer, or wilt thou not? Choose thou?"

The old man put his hand to his head and thought. Then he

rose, and, advancing to where Umbopa, or rather Ignosi, stood, knelt before him and took his hand.

"Ignosi, rightful king of the Kukuanas, I put my hand between thy hands, and am thy man till death. When thou wast a babe I dandled thee upon my knee; now shall my old arm strike for thee and freedom."

"It is well, Infadoos; if I conquer, thou shalt be the greatest man in the kingdom after the king. If I fail, thou canst only die, and death is not far off for thee. Rise, my uncle.

"And ye, white men, will ye help me? What have I to offer ye! The white stones, if I conquer and you can find them, ye shall have as many as ye can carry hence. Will that suffice ye?"

I translated this remark.

"Tell him," answered Sir Henry, "that he mistakes an Englishman. Wealth is good, and if it comes in our way we will take it; but a gentleman does not sell himself for wealth. But, speaking for myself, I say this: I have always liked Umbopa, and so far as in me lies, will stand by him in this business. It will be very pleasant to me to try and square matters with that cruel devil, Twala. What do you say, Good, and you, Quatermain?"

"Well," said Good, "to adopt the language of hyperbole, in which all these people seem to indulge, you can tell him that a row is surely good, and warms the cockles of the heart, and that so far as I am concerned, I'm his boy. My only stipulation is that he allows me to wear trousers."

I translated these answers.

"It is well, my friends," said Ignosi, late Umbopa; "and what say you, Macumazahn; art thou too with me, old hunter, cleverer than a wounded buffalo?"

I thought awhile and scratched my head.

"Umbopa, or Ignosi," I said, "I don't like revolutions. I am a man of peace, and a bit of a coward" (here Umbopa smiled), "but, on the other hand, I stick to my friends, Ignosi. You have stuck to us and played the part of a man, and I will stick to you. But, mind you, I am a trader, and have to make my living; so I accept your offer about those diamonds, in case we should ever be in a position to avail ourselves of it. Another thing: we came, as you know, to look for Incubu's (Sir Henry's) lost brother. You must help us to find him."

"That will I do," answered Ignosi. "Stay, Infadoos; by the sign of the snake round my middle, tell me the truth. Has any white man to thy knowledge set his foot within the land?"

"None, O Ignosi."

"If any white man had been seen or heard of, wouldst thou have known it?"

"I should certainly have known."

"Thou hearest, Incubu?" said Ignosi to Sir Henry; "he has not been here."

"Well, well," said Sir Henry, with a sigh; "there it is; I suppose he never got here. Poor fellow, poor fellow! So it has all been for nothing. God's will be done."

"Now for business," I put in, anxious to escape from a painful subject. "It is very well to be a king by right divine, Ignosi, but how dost thou propose to become a king indeed?"

"Nay, I know not. Infadoos, hast thou a plan?"

"Ignosi, son of the lightning," answered his uncle, "tonight is the great dance and witch-hunt. Many will be smelt out and perish, and in the hearts of many others there will be grief and anguish and anger against the king Twala. When the dance is over, then will I speak to some of the great chiefs, who in turn, if I can win them over, shall speak to their regiments. I shall speak to the chiefs softly at first, and bring them to see that thou art indeed the king, and I think that by to-morrow's light thou shalt have twenty thousand spears at thy command. And now must I go and think and hear and make ready. After the dance is done I will, if I am yet alive, and we are all alive, meet thee here, and we will talk. At the best there will be war."

At this moment our conference was interrupted by the cry that messengers had come from the king. Advancing to the door of the hut, we ordered that they should be admitted, and presently three men entered, each bearing a shining shirt of chain-armor and a magnificent battle-axe.

"The gifts of my lord, the king, to the white men from the stars!" exclaimed a herald who had come with them.

"We thank the king," I answered; "withdraw."

The men went, and we examined the armor with great interest. It was the most beautiful chain-work we had ever seen. A whole coat fell together so closely that it formed a mass of links scarcely too big to be covered with both hands.

"Do you make these things in this country, Infadoos?" I asked; "they are very beautiful."

"Nay, my lord; they come down to us from our forefathers. We know not who made them, and there are but few left. None but those of royal blood may wear them. They are magic coats through which no spear can pass. He who wears them is well-nigh safe in the battle. The king is well pleased or much afraid, or he would not have sent them. Wear them to-night, my lords."

The rest of the day we spent quietly resting and talking over the situation, which was sufficiently exciting. At last the sun went down, the thousand watch-fires glowed out, and through the darkness we heard the tramp of many feet and the clashing of hundreds of spears, as the regiments passed to their appointed places to be ready for the great dance. About ten the full moon came up in splendor, and as we stood watching her ascent Infadoos arrived, clad in full war toggery, and accompanied by a guard of twenty men to escort us to the dance. We had already, as he recommended, donned the shirts of chain armor which the king had sent us, putting them on under our ordinary clothing, and finding to our surprise that they were neither very heavy nor uncomfortable. These steel shirts, which had evidently been made for men of a very large stature, hung somewhat loosely upon Good and myself, but Sir Henry's fitted his magnificent frame like a glove. Then, strapping our revolvers round our waists, and taking the battle-axes which the king had sent with the armor in our hands, we started.

On arriving at the great kraal where we had that morning been interviewed by the king, we found that it was closely packed with some twenty thousand men arranged in regiments round it. The regiments were in turn divided into companies, and between each company was a little path to allow free passage to the witch-finders to pass up and down. Anything more imposing than the sight that was presented by this vast and orderly concourse of armed men it is impossible for one to conceive. There they stood perfectly silent, and the moonlight poured its light upon the forest of their raised spears, upon their majestic forms, waving plumes, and the harmonious shading of their various-colored shields. Wherever we looked was line upon line of set faces surmounted by range upon range of glittering spears.

"Surely," I said to Infadoos, "the whole army is here?"

"Nay, Macumazahn," he answered, "but a third part of it. One third part is present at this dance each year, another third part is mustered outside in case there should be trouble when the killing begins, ten thousand more garrison the outposts round Loo, and the rest watch at the kraals in the country. Thou seest it is a very great people."

"They are very silent," said Good; and, indeed, the intense stillness among such a vast concourse of living men was almost overpowering.

"What says Bougwan?" asked Infadoos.

I translated.

"Those over whom the shadow of death is hovering are silent," he answered, grimly.

"Will many be killed?"

"Very many."

"It seems," I said to the others, "that we are going to assist at a gladiatorial show arranged regardless of expense."

Sir Henry shivered, and Good said that he wished that we could get out of it.

"Tell me," I asked Infadoos, "are we in danger?"

"I know not, my lords—I trust not; but do not seem afraid. If ye live through the night all may go well. The soldiers murmur against the king."

All this while we had been advancing steadily towards the centre of the open space, in the midst of which were placed some stools. As we proceeded we perceived another small party coming from the direction of the royal hut.

"It is the king, Twala, and Scragga his son, and Gagool the old, and see, with them are those who slay," and he pointed to a little group of about a dozen gigantic and savage-looking men, armed with spears in one hand and heavy kerries in the other.

The king seated himself upon the centre stool, Gagool crouched at his feet, and the others stood behind.

"Greetings, white lords," he cried, as we came up; "be seated, waste not the precious time—the night is all too short for the deeds that must be done. Ye come in a good hour, and shall see a glorious show. Look round, white lords; look round," and he rolled his one wicked eye from regiment to regiment. "Can the stars show ye such a sight as this? See how they shake in their wickedness, all those who have evil in their hearts and fear the judgment of 'Heaven above.'"

"*Begin! begin!*" cried out Gagool, in her thin, piercing voice; "the hyenas are hungry, they howl for food. *Begin! begin!*" Then for a moment there was intense stillness, made horrible by a presage of what was to come.

The king lifted his spear, and suddenly twenty thousand feet were raised, as though they belonged to one man, and brought down with a stamp upon the earth. This was repeated three times, causing the solid ground to shake and tremble. Then from a far point of the circle a solitary voice began a wailing song, of which the refrain ran something as follows:

"*What is the lot of man born of woman?*"

Back came the answer rolling out from every throat in that vast company:

"*Death!*"

Gradually, however, the song was taken up by company after company, till the whole armed multitude was singing it, and I could no longer follow the words, except in so far as they appeared to represent various phases of human passions, fears, and joys. Now it seemed to be a love-song, now a majestic swelling war-chant, and last of all a death-dirge, ending suddenly in one heartbreaking wail that went echoing and rolling away in a volume of blood-curdling sound. Again the silence fell upon the place, and again it was broken by the king lifting up his hand. Instantly there was a pattering of feet, and from out of the masses of the warriors strange and awful figures came running towards us. As they drew near we saw that they were those of women, most of them aged, for their white hair, ornamented with small bladders taken from fish, streamed out behind them. Their faces were painted in stripes of white and yellow; down their backs hung snakeskins, and round their waists rattled circlets of human bones, while each held in her shrivelled hand a small forked wand. In all there were ten of them. When they arrived in front of us they halted, and one of them, pointing with her wand towards the crouching figure of Gagool, cried out:

"Mother, old mother, we are here."

"*Good! good! good!*" piped out that aged iniquity. "Are your eyes keen, Isanusis" (witch doctresses), "ye seers in dark places?"

"Mother, they are keen."

"*Good! good! good!* Are your ears open, Isanusis, ye who hear words that come not from the tongue?"

"Mother, they are open."

"*Good! good! good!* Are your senses awake, Isanusis—can ye smell blood, can ye purge the land of the wicked ones who compass evil against the king and against their neighbors? Are ye ready to do the justice of 'Heaven above,' ye whom I have taught, who have eaten of the bread of my wisdom and drunk of the water of my magic?"

"Mother, we can."

"Then go! Tarry not, ye vultures; see the slayers"—pointing to the ominous group of executioners behind—"make sharp their spears; the white men from afar are hungry to see. Go."

With a wild yell the weird party broke away in every direction, like the fragments from a shell, and, the dry bones round their waists rattling as they ran, made direct for various points of the dense human circle. We could not watch them all, so fixed our eyes upon the Isanusi nearest us. When she came within a few paces of the warriors, she halted and began to dance wildly, turning round and round with an almost incredible rapidity, and shrieking out sentences such as "I smell him, the evil-doer!" "He is near, he who poisoned his mother!" "I hear the thoughts of him who thought evil of the king!"

Quicker and quicker she danced, till she lashed herself into such a frenzy of excitement that the foam flew in flecks from her gnashing jaws, her eyes seemed to start from her head, and her flesh to quiver visibly. Suddenly she stopped dead, and stiffened all over, like a pointer dog when he scents game, and then with outstretched wand began to creep stealthily towards the soldiers before her. It seemed to us that as she came their stoicism gave way, and that they shrank from her. As for ourselves, we followed her movements with a horrible fascination. Presently, still creeping and crouching like a dog, she was before them. Then she stopped and pointed, and then again crept on a pace or two.

Suddenly the end came. With a shriek she sprang in and touched a tall warrior with the forked wand. Instantly two of his comrades, those standing immediately next to him, seized the doomed man, each by one arm, and advanced with him towards the king.

He did not resist, but we saw that he dragged his limbs as though they were paralyzed, and his fingers, from which the spear had fallen, were limp as those of a man newly dead.

As he came, two of the villainous executioners stepped forward to meet him. Presently they met, and the executioners turned round towards the king as though for orders.

"*Kill!*" said the king.

"*Kill!*" squeaked Gagool.

"*Kill!*" re-echoed Scragga, with a hollow chuckle.

Almost before the words were uttered, the horrible deed was done. One man had driven his spear into the victim's heart, and, to make assurance doubly sure, the other had dashed out his brains with his great club.

"*One*," counted Twala, the king, just like a black Madame Defarge, as Good said, and the body was dragged a few paces away and stretched out.

Hardly was this done before another poor wretch was brought up, like an ox to the slaughter. This time we could see, from the leopard-skin cloak, that the man was a person of rank. Again the awful syllables were spoken, and the victim fell dead.

"*Two*," counted the king.

And so the deadly game went on, till some hundred bodies were stretched in rows behind us. I have heard of the gladiatorial shows of the Cæsars, and of the Spanish bull-fights, but I take the liberty of doubting if they were either of them half as horrible as this Kukuana witch-hunt. Gladiatorial shows and Spanish bull-fights, at any rate, contributed to the public amusement, which certainly was not the case here. The most confirmed sensation-monger would fight shy of sensation if he knew that it was well on the cards that he would, in his own proper person, be the subject of the next "event."

Once we rose and tried to remonstrate, but were sternly repressed by Twala.

"Let the law take its course, white men. These dogs are magicians and evil-doers; it is well that they should die," was the only answer vouchsafed to us.

About midnight there was a pause. The witch-finders gathered themselves together, apparently exhausted with their bloody work, and we thought that the whole performance was done with. But it was not so, for presently, to our surprise, the old woman, Gagool, rose from her crouching position, and, supporting herself with a stick, staggered off into the open space. It was an extraordinary sight to see this frightful, vulture-headed old creature, bent nearly double with extreme age, gather strength by degrees till at last she rushed about almost as actively as her ill-omened pupils. To and fro she ran, chanting to herself, till suddenly she made a dash at a tall man standing in front of one of the regiments, and touched him. As she did so a sort of groan went up from the regiment, which he evidently commanded. But all the same two of its members seized him and brought him up for execution. We afterwards learned that he was a man of great wealth and importance, being, indeed, a cousin of the king's.

He was slain, and the king counted one hundred and three. Then Gagool again sprang to and fro, gradually drawing nearer and nearer to ourselves.

"Hang me if I don't believe she is going to try her games on us," ejaculated Good, in horror.

"Nonsense!" said Sir Henry.

As for myself, as I saw that old fiend dancing nearer and nearer, my heart positively sank into my boots. I glanced behind us at the long row of corpses, and shivered.

Nearer and nearer waltzed Gagool, looking for all the world like an animated crooked stick, her horrid eyes gleaming and glowing with a most unholy lustre.

Nearer she came, and nearer yet, every pair of eyes in that vast assemblage watching her movements with intense anxiety. At last she stood still and pointed.

"Which is it to be?" asked Sir Henry, to himself.

In a moment all doubts were set at rest, for the old woman had rushed in and touched Umbopa, alias Ignosi, on the shoulder.

"I smell him out," she shrieked. "Kill him, kill him, he is full of evil; kill him, the stranger, before blood flows for him. Slay him, O king."

There was a pause, which I instantly took advantage of.

"O king," I called out, rising from my seat, "this man is the servant of thy guests, he is their dog; whosoever sheds the blood of our dog sheds our blood. By the sacred law of hospitality I claim protection for him."

"Gagool, mother of the witch doctors, has smelled him out; he must die, white men," was the sullen answer.

"Nay, he shall not die," I replied; "he who tries to touch him shall die indeed."

"Seize him!" roared Twala, to the executioners, who stood around red to the eyes with the blood of their victims.

They advanced towards us, and then hesitated. As for Ignosi, he raised his spear, and raised it as though determined to sell his life dearly.

"Stand back, ye dogs," I shouted, "if ye would see to-morrow's light. Touch one hair of his head and your king dies," and I covered Twala with my revolver. Sir Henry and Good also drew their pistols, Sir Henry pointing his at the leading executioner, who was advancing to carry out the sentence, and Good taking a deliberate aim at Gagool.

Twala winced perceptibly, as my barrel came in a line with his broad chest.

"Well," I said, "what is it to be, Twala?"

Then he spoke.

"Put away your magic tubes," he said; "ye have adjured me in the name of hospitality, and for that reason, but not from fear of what ye can do, I spare him. Go in peace."

"It is well," I answered, unconcernedly; "we are weary of slaughter, and would sleep. Is the dance ended?"

"It is ended," Twala answered, sulkily. "Let these dogs," pointing to the long row of corpses, "be flung out to the hyenas and the vultures," and he lifted his spear.

Instantly the regiments began in perfect silence to defile off through the kraal gateway, a fatigue party only remaining behind to drag away the corpses of those who had been sacrificed.

Then we too rose, and, making our salaam to his majesty, which he hardly deigned to acknowledge, departed to our kraal.

"Well," said Sir Henry, as we sat down, having first lit a lamp of the sort used by the Kukuanas, of which the wick is made of the fibre of a species of palm leaf and the oil of clarified hippopotamus fat, "well, I feel uncommonly inclined to be sick."

"If I had any doubts about helping Umbopa to rebel against that infernal blackguard," put in Good, "they are gone now. It was as much as I could do to sit still while that slaughter was going on. I tried to keep my eyes shut, but they would open just at the wrong time. I wonder where Infadoos is. Umbopa, my friend, you ought to be grateful to us; your skin came near to having an air-hole made in it."

"I am grateful, Bougwan," was Umbopa's answer, when I had translated, "and I shall not forget. As for Infadoos, he will be here by and by. We must wait."

So we lit our pipes and waited.

CHAPTER XI.

WE GIVE A SIGN.

For a long while—two hours, I should think—we sat there in silence, for we were too overwhelmed by the recollection of the horrors we had seen to talk. At last, just as we were thinking of turning in—for already there were faint streaks of light in the eastern sky—we heard the sound of steps. Then came the challenge of the sentry who was posted at the kraal gate, which was apparently answered, though not in an audible tone, for the steps came on; and in another second Infadoos had entered the hut, followed by some half a dozen stately-looking chiefs.

"My lords," he said, "I have come, according to my word. My lords and Ignosi, rightful king of the Kukuanas, I have brought with me these men," pointing to the row of chiefs, "who are great men among us, having each one of them the command of three thousand soldiers, who live but to do their bidding, under the king's. I have told them of what I have seen, and what my ears have heard. Now let them also see the sacred snake around thee, and hear thy story, Ignosi, that they may say whether or no they will make cause with thee against Twala the king."

For answer, Ignosi again stripped off his girdle and exhibited the snake tattooed around him. Each chief in turn drew near and examined it by the dim light of the lamp, and without saying a word passed on to the other side.

Then Ignosi resumed his moocha and, addressing them, repeated the history he had detailed in the morning.

"Now ye have heard, chiefs," said Infadoos, when he had done, "what say ye; will ye stand by this man and help him to his father's throne, or will ye not? The land cries out against Twala, and the blood of the people flows like the waters in spring. Ye have seen to-night. Two other chiefs there were with whom I had it in my mind to speak, and where are they now? The hyenas howl over their corpses. Soon will ye be as they are if ye strike not. Choose, then, my brothers."

The eldest of the six men, a short, thick-set warrior, with white hair, stepped forward a pace and answered.

"Thy words are true, Infadoos; the land cries out. My own brother is among those who died tonight; but this is a great matter, and the thing is hard to believe. How know we that if we lift our spears it may not be for an impostor? It is a great matter, I say, and none may see the end of it. For of this be sure, blood will flow in rivers before the deed is done; many will still cleave to the king, for men worship the sun that still shines bright in the heavens, and not that which has not risen. These white men from the stars, their magic is great, and Ignosi is under the cover of their wing. If he be indeed the rightful king, let them give us a sign, and let the people have a sign, that all may see. So shall men cleave to us, knowing that the white man's magic is with them."

"Ye have the sign of the snake," I answered.

"My lord, it is not enough. The snake may have been placed there since the man's birth. Show us a sign. We will not move without a sign."

The others gave a decided assent, and I turned in perplexity to Sir Henry and Good, and explained the situation.

"I think I have it," said Good, exultingly; "ask them to give us a moment to think."

I did so, and the chiefs withdrew. As soon as they were gone, Good went to the little box in which his medicines were, unlocked it, and took out a note-book, in the front of which was an almanac. "Now, look here, you fellows, isn't to-morrow the fourth of June?"

We had kept a careful note of the days, so were able to answer that it was.

"Very good; then here we have it—'4 June, total eclipse of the sun commences at 11.15 Greenwich time, visible in these islands, *Africa*, etc.' There's a sign for you. Tell them that you will darken the sun to-morrow."

The idea was a splendid one; indeed, the only fear about it was a fear lest Good's almanac might be incorrect. If we made a false prophecy on such a subject, our prestige would be gone forever, and so would Ignosi's chance of the throne of the Kukuanas.

"Suppose the almanac is wrong?" suggested Sir Henry to Good, who was busily employed in working out something on the fly-leaf of the book.

"I don't see any reason to suppose anything of the sort," was his answer. "Eclipses always come up to time; at least, that is my experience of them, and it especially states that it will be visible in Africa. I have worked out the reckonings as well as I can without knowing our exact position; and I make out that the eclipse should begin here about one o'clock to-morrow, and last till half-past two. For half an hour or more there should be total darkness."

"Well," said Sir Henry, "I suppose we had better risk it."

I acquiesced, though doubtfully, for eclipses are queer cattle to deal with, and sent Umbopa to summon the chiefs back. Presently they came, and I addressed them thus:

"Great men of the Kukuanas, and thou, Infadoos, listen. We are not fond of showing our powers, since to do so is to interfere with the course of nature, and plunge the world into fear and confusion; but as this matter is a great one, and as we are angered against the king because of the slaughter we have seen, and because of the act of the Isanusi Gagool, who would have put our friend Ignosi to death, we have determined to do so, and to give such a sign as all men may see. Come thither," and I led them to the door of the hut and pointed to the fiery ball of the rising sun; "what see ye there?"

"We see the rising sun," answered the spokesman of the party.

"It is so. Now, tell me, can any mortal man put out that sun, so that night comes down on the land at midday?"

The chief laughed a little. "No, my lord, that no man can do. The sun is stronger than man who looks on him."

"Ye say so. Yet I tell you that this day, one hour after mid-day, will we put out that sun for a space of an hour, and darkness shall cover the earth, and it shall be for a sign that we are indeed men of honor, and that Ignosi is indeed king of the Kukuanas. If we do this thing will it satisfy ye?"

"Yea, my lords," answered the old chief with a smile, which was reflected on the faces of his companions; "*if* ye do this thing we will be satisfied indeed."

"It shall be done: we three, Incubu the Elephant, Bougwan the clear-eyed, and Macumazahn, who watches in the night, have said it, and it shall be done. Dost thou hear, Infadoos?"

"I hear, my lord, but it is a wonderful thing that ye promise, to put out the sun, the father of all things, who shines forever."

"Yet shall we do it, Infadoos."

"It is well, my lords. To-day, a little after midday, will Twala send for my lords to witness the girls dance, and one hour after the dance begins shall the girl whom Twala thinks the fairest be killed by Scragga, the king's son, as a sacrifice to the silent stone ones, who sit and keep watch by the mountains yonder," and he pointed to the three strange-looking peaks where Solomon's Road was supposed to end. "Then yet my lords darken the sun, and save the maiden's life, and the people will indeed believe."

"Ay," said the old chief, still smiling a little, "the people will believe, indeed."

"Two miles from Loo," went on Infadoos, "there is a hill curved like the new moon, a stronghold, where my regiment, and three other regiments which these men command, are stationed. This morning we will make a plan whereby other regiments, two or three, may be moved there also. Then, if my lords can indeed darken the sun, in the darkness I will take my lords by the hand and lead them out of Loo to this place, where they shall be safe, and thence can we make war upon Twala, the king."

"It is good," said I. "Now leave us to sleep awhile and make ready our magic."

Infadoos rose, and, having saluted us, departed with the chiefs.

"My friends," said Ignosi, as soon as they were gone, "can ye indeed do this wonderful thing, or were ye speaking empty words to the men?"

"We believe that we can do it, Umbopa—Ignosi, I mean."

"It is strange," he answered, "and had ye not been Englishmen I would not have believed it; but English 'gentlemen' tell no lies. If we live through the matter, be sure I will repay ye!"

"Ignosi," said Sir Henry, "promise me one thing."

"I will promise, Incubu, my friend, even before I hear it," answered the big man with a smile. "What is it?"

"This: that if you ever come to be king of this people you will do away with the smelling out of witches such as we have seen last night; and that the killing of men without trial shall not take place in the land."

Ignosi thought for a moment, after I had translated this, and then answered:

"The ways of black people are not as the ways of white men, Incubu, nor do we hold life so high as ye. Yet will I promise it. If it be in my power to hold them back, the witch-finders shall hunt no more, nor shall any man die the death without judgment."

"That's a bargain, then," said Sir Henry; "and now let us get a little rest."

Thoroughly wearied out, we were soon sound asleep, and slept till Ignosi woke us about eleven o'clock. Then we got up, washed, and ate a hearty breakfast, not knowing when we should get any more food. After that we went outside the hut and stared at the sun, which we were distressed to observe presented a remarkably healthy appearance without a sign of an eclipse anywhere about it.

"I hope it will come off," said Sir Henry, doubtfully. "False prophets often find themselves in painful positions."

"If it does not, it will soon be up with us," I answered, mournfully; "for so sure as we are living men, some of those chiefs will tell the whole story to the king, and then there will be another sort of eclipse, and one that we shall not like."

Returning to the hut, we dressed ourselves, putting on the mail shirts which the king had sent us as before. Scarcely had we done so when a messenger came from Twala to bid us to the great annual "dance of girls" which was about to be celebrated.

Taking our rifles and ammunition with us so as to have them handy in case we had to fly, as suggested by Infadoos, we started boldly enough, though with inward fear and trembling. The great space in front of the king's kraal presented a very different appearance from what it had done on the previous evening. In the place of the grim ranks of serried warriors were company after company of Kukuana girls, not overdressed, so far as clothing went, but each crowned with a wreath of flowers, and holding a palm leaf in one hand and a tall white lily (the arum) in the other. In the centre of the open space sat Twala, the king, with old Gagool at his feet, attended by Infadoos, the boy Scragga, and about a dozen guards. There were also present about a score of chiefs, among whom I recognized most of our friends of the night before.

Twala greeted us with much apparent cordiality, though I saw him fix his one eye viciously on Umbopa.

"Welcome, white men from the stars," he said; "this is a different sight from what your eyes gazed on by the light of last night's moon, but it is not so good a sight. Girls are pleasant, and were it not for such as these" (and he pointed round him) "we should none of us be here to-day; but men are better. Kisses and the tender words of women are sweet, but the sound of the clashing of men's spears, and the smell of men's blood, are sweeter far! Would ye have wives from among our people, white men?

If so, choose the fairest here, and ye shall have them, as many as ye will;" and he paused for an answer.

As the prospect did not seem to be without attractions to Good, who was, like most sailors, of a susceptible nature, I, being elderly and wise, and foreseeing the endless complications that anything of the sort would involve (for women bring trouble as surely as the night follows the day), put in a hasty answer:

"Thanks, O king, but we white men wed only with white women like ourselves. Your maidens are fair, but they are not for us!"

The king laughed. "It is well. In our land there is a proverb which says, 'Woman's eyes are always bright, whatever the color,' and another which says, 'Love her who is present, for be sure she who is absent is false to thee;' but perhaps these things are not so in the stars. In a land where men are white all things are possible. So be it, white men; the girls will not go begging! Welcome again; and welcome, too, thou black one; if Gagool here had had her way thou wouldst have been stiff and cold now. It is lucky that thou, too, camest from the stars; ha! ha!"

"I can kill thee before thou killest me, O king," was Ignosi's calm answer, "and thou shalt be stiff before my limbs cease to bend."

Twala started. "Thou speakest boldly, boy," he replied, angrily; "presume not too far."

"He may well be bold in whose lips are truth. The truth is a sharp spear which flies home and fails not. It is a message from 'the stars,' O king!"

Twala scowled, and his one eye gleamed fiercely, but he said nothing more.

"Let the dance begin," he cried, and next second the flower-crowned girls sprang forward in companies, singing a sweet song and waving the delicate palms and white flowers. On they danced, now whirling round and round, now meeting in mimic warfare, swaying, eddying here and there, coming forward, falling back in an ordered confusion delightful to witness. At last they paused, and a beautiful young woman sprang out of the ranks and began to pirouette in front of us with a grace and vigor which would have put most ballet-girls to shame. At length she fell back exhausted, and another took her place, then another and another, but none of them, either in grace, skill, or personal attractions, came up to the first.

At length the king lifted his hand.

"Which think ye the fairest, white men?" he asked.

"The first," said I, unthinkingly. Next second I regretted it, for I remembered that Infadoos had said that the fairest woman was offered as a sacrifice.

"Then is my mind as your minds, and my eyes as your eyes. She is the fairest; and a sorry thing it is for her, for she must die!"

"*Ay, must die!*" piped out Gagool, casting a glance from her quick eyes in the direction of the poor girl, who, as yet ignorant of the awful fate in store for her, was standing some twenty yards off in front of a company of girls, engaged in nervously picking a flower from her wreath to pieces, petal by petal.

"Why, O king?" said I, restraining my indignation with difficulty; "the girl has danced well and pleased us; she is fair, too; it would be hard to reward her with death."

Twala laughed as he answered:

"It is our custom, and the figures who sit in stone yonder" (and he pointed towards the three distant peaks) "must have their due. Did I fail to put the fairest girl to death to-day misfortune would fall upon me and my house. Thus runs the prophecy of my people: "If the king offer not a sacrifice of a fair girl on the day of the dance of maidens to the old ones who sit and watch on the mountains, then shall he fall and his house.' Look ye, white men, my brother who reigned before me offered not the sacrifice, because of the tears of the woman, and he fell, and his house, and I reign in his stead. It is finished; she must die!" Then, turning to the guards—"Bring her hither; Scragga, make sharp thy spear."

Two of the men stepped forward, and as they did so the girl, for the first time realizing her impending fate, screamed aloud and turned to fly. But the strong hands caught her fast, and brought her, struggling and weeping, up before us.

"What is thy name, girl?" piped Gagool. "What! wilt thou not answer; shall the king's son do his work at once?"

At this hint Scragga, looking more evil than ever, advanced a step and lifted his great spear, and as he did so I saw Good's hand creep to his revolver. The poor girl caught the glint of the cold steel through her tears, and it sobered her anguish. She ceased struggling, but merely clasped her hands convulsively, and stood shuddering from head to foot.

"See," cried Scragga, in high glee, "she shrinks from the sight of my little plaything even before she has tasted it," and he tapped the broad blade of the spear.

"If I ever get the chance, you shall pay for that, you young hound!" I heard Good mutter beneath his breath.

"Now that thou art quiet, give us thy name, my dear. Come, speak up, and fear not," said Gagool in mockery.

"O, mother," answered the girl in trembling accents, "my name is Foulata, of the house of Suko. Oh, mother, why must I die? I have done no wrong!"

"Be comforted," went on the old woman, in her hateful tone of mockery. "Thou must die, indeed, as a sacrifice to the old ones who sit yonder" (and she pointed to the peaks); "but it is better to sleep in the night than to toil in the day-time; it is better to die than to live, and thou shalt die by the royal hand of the king's own son."

The girl Foulata wrung her hands in anguish, and cried out aloud: "Oh, cruel; and I so young! What have I done that I should never again see the sun rise out of the night, or the stars come following on his track in the evening: that I should no more gather the flowers when the dew is heavy, or listen to the laughing of the waters! Woe is me, that I shall never see my father's hut again, nor feel my mother's kiss, nor tend the kid that is sick! Woe is me, that no lover shall put his arms around me and look into my eyes, nor shall men-children be born of me! Oh, cruel, cruel!" and again she wrung her hands and turned her tear-stained, flower-crowned face to heaven, looking so lovely in her despair—for she was indeed a beautiful woman—that it would assuredly have melted the hearts of any one less cruel than the three fiends before us. Prince Arthur's appeal to the ruffians who came to blind him was not more touching than this savage girl's.

But it did not move Gagool or Gagool's master, though I saw signs of pity among the guard behind and on the faces of the chiefs; and as for Good, he gave a sort of snort of indignation, and made a motion as though to go to her. With all a woman's quickness, the doomed girl interpreted what was passing in his mind, and with a sudden movement flung herself before him, and clasped his "beautiful white legs" with her hands.

"Oh, white father from the stars!" she cried, "throw over me the mantle of thy protection; let me creep into the shadow of thy strength, that I may be saved. Oh, keep me from these cruel men and from the mercies of Gagool!"

"All right, my hearty, I'll look after you," sang out Good, in nervous Saxon. "Come, get up, there's a good girl," and he stooped and caught her hand.

Twala turned and motioned to his son, who advanced with his spear lifted.

"Now's your time," whispered Sir Henry to me; "what are you waiting for?"

"I am waiting for the eclipse," I answered; "I have had my

eye on the sun for the last half-hour, and I never saw it look healthier."

"Well, you must risk it now or the girl will be killed. Twala is losing patience."

Recognizing the force of the argument, having cast one more despairing look at the bright face of the sun, for never did the most ardent astronomer with a theory to prove await a celestial event with such anxiety, I stepped, with all the dignity I could command, between the prostrate girl and the advancing spear of Scragga.

"King," I said; "this shall not be; we will not tolerate such a thing; let the girl go in safety."

Twala rose from his seat in his wrath and astonishment, and from the chiefs and serried ranks of girls, who had slowly closed in upon us in anticipation of the tragedy, came a murmur of amazement.

"*Shall not be*, thou white dog, who yaps at the lion in his cave; *shall not be!* Art thou mad? Be careful lest this chicken's fate overtake thee and those with thee. How canst thou prevent it? Who art thou, that thou standest between me and my will? Withdraw, I say. Scragga, kill her. Ho, guards! seize these men."

At his cry armed men came running swiftly from behind the hut, where they had evidently been placed beforehand.

Sir Henry, Good, and Umbopa arranged themselves alongside of me and lifted their rifles.

"Stop!" I shouted, boldly, though at the moment my heart was in my boots. "Stop! we, the white men from the stars, say that it shall not be. Come but one pace nearer and we will put out the sun and plunge the land in darkness. Ye shall taste of our magic."

My threat produced an effect; the men halted, and Scragga stood still before us, his spear lifted.

"Hear him! hear him!" piped Gagool; "hear the liar who says he will put out the sun like a lamp. Let him do it and the girl shall be spared. Yes, let him do it, or die with the girl, he and those with him."

I glanced up at the sun, and, to my intense joy and relief, saw that we had made no mistake. On the edge of its brilliant surface was a faint rim of shadow.

I lifted my hand solemnly towards the sky, an example which Sir Henry and Good followed, and quoted a line or two of the "Ingoldsby Legends" at it in the most impressive tones I could command. Sir Henry followed suit with a verse out of the Old Testament, while Good addressed the king of day in a volume of the most classical bad language that he could think of.

Slowly the dark rim crept on over the blazing surface, and as it did so I heard a deep gasp of fear rise from the multitude around.

"Look, O king! look, Gagool! Look, chiefs and people and women, and see if the white men from the stars keep their word, or if they be but empty liars!

"The sun grows dark before your eyes; soon there will be night—ay, night in the noon-time. Ye have asked for a sign; it is given to ye. Grow dark, O sun! withdraw thy light, thou bright one; bring the proud heart to the dust, and eat up the world with shadows."

A groan of terror rose from the onlookers. Some stood petrified with fear, others threw themselves upon their knees and cried out. As for the king, he sat still and turned pale beneath his dusky skin. Only Gagool kept her courage.

"It will pass," she cried; "I have seen the like before; no man can put out the sun; lose not heart; sit still—the shadow will pass."

"Wait, and ye shall see," I replied, hopping with excitement.

"Keep it up, Good; I can't remember any more poetry. Curse away, there's a good fellow."

Good responded nobly to the tax upon his inventive faculties. Never before had I the faintest conception of the breadth and depth and height of a naval officer's objurgatory powers. For ten minutes he went on without stopping, and he scarcely ever repeated himself.

Meanwhile the dark ring crept on. Strange and unholy shadows encroached upon the sunlight, an ominous quiet filled the place, the birds chirped out frightened notes and then were still; only the cocks began to crow.

On, yet on, crept the ring of darkness; it was now more than half over the reddening orb. The air grew thick and dusky. On, yet on, till we could scarcely see the fierce faces of the group before us. No sound now rose from the spectators, and Good stopped swearing.

"The sun is dying—the wizards have killed the sun," yelled out the boy Scragga at last. "We shall all die in the dark," and, animated by fear or fury, or both, he lifted his spear and drove it with all his force at Sir Henry's broad chest. But he had forgotten the mail shirts that the king had given us, and which we wore beneath our clothing. The steel rebounded harmless, and before he could repeat the blow Sir Henry had snatched the spear from his hand and sent it straight through him. He dropped dead.

At the sight, and driven mad with fear at the gathering gloom, the companies of girls broke up in wild confusion and ran screeching for the gateways. Nor did the panic stop there. The king himself, followed by the guards, some of the chiefs, and Gagool, who hobbled away after them with marvellous alacrity, fled for the huts, so that in another minute or so ourselves, the would-be victim, Foulata, Infadoos, and some of the chiefs who had interviewed us on the previous night, were left alone upon the scene with the dead body of Scragga.

"Now, chiefs," I said, "we have given you the sign. If ye are satisfied, let us fly swiftly to the place ye spoke of. The charm cannot now be stopped. It will work for an hour. Let us take advantage of the darkness."

"Come," said Infadoos, turning to go, an example which was followed by the awed chiefs, ourselves, and the girl Foulata, whom Good took by the hand.

Before we reached the gate of the kraal the sun went out altogether.

Holding each other by the hand we stumbled on through the darkness.

CHAPTER XII.

BEFORE THE BATTLE.

LUCKILY for us, Infadoos and the chiefs knew all the pathways of the great town perfectly, so that, notwithstanding the intense gloom, we made fair progress.

For an hour or more we journeyed on, till at length the eclipse began to pass, and that edge of the sun which had disappeared the first became again visible. In another five minutes there was sufficient light to see our whereabouts, and we then discovered that we were clear of the town of Loo, and approaching a large, flat-topped hill, measuring some two miles in circumference. This hill, which was of a formation very common in Southern Africa, was not very high; indeed, its greatest elevation was not more than two hundred feet, but it was shaped like a horseshoe, and its sides were rather precipitous and strewn with boulders. On the grass table-land at the top was ample camping-ground, which had been utilized as a military cantonment of no mean strength. Its ordinary garrison was one regiment of three thousand men, but as we toiled up the steep side of the hill in the returning daylight we perceived that there were many more warriors than that upon it.

Reaching the table-land at last, we found crowds of men huddled together in the utmost consternation at the natural phenomenon which they were witnessing. Passing through these without a word, we gained a hut in the centre of the ground, where we were astonished to find two men waiting, laden with our few goods and chattels, which, of course, we had been obliged to leave behind in our hasty flight.

"I sent for them," explained Infadoos; "also for these," and he lifted up Good's long-lost trousers.

With an exclamation of rapturous delight Good sprang at them, and instantly proceeded to put them on.

"Surely my lord will not hide his beautiful white legs!" exclaimed Infadoos, regretfully.

But Good persisted, and once only did the Kukuana people get the chance of seeing his beautiful legs again. Good is a very modest man. Henceforward they had to satisfy their æsthetic longings with one whisker, his transparent eye, and his movable teeth.

Still gazing with fond remembrance at Good's trousers, Infadoos next informed us that he had summoned the regiments to explain to them fully the rebellion which was decided on by the chiefs, and to introduce to them the rightful heir to the throne, Ignosi.

In half an hour the troops, in all nearly twenty thousand men, constituting the flower of the Kukuana army, were mustered on a large, open space, to which we proceeded. The men were drawn up in three sides of a dense square, and presented a magnificent spectacle. We took our station on the open side of the square, and were speedily surrounded by all the principal chiefs and officers.

These, after silence had been proclaimed, Infadoos proceeded to address. He narrated to them in vigorous and graceful language—for, like most Kukuanas of high rank, he was a born orator—the history of Ignosi's father, how he had been basely murdered by Twala, the king, and his wife and child driven out to starve. Then he pointed out how the land suffered and groaned under Twala's cruel rule, instancing the proceedings of the previous night, when, under pretence of their being evil-doers, many of the noblest in the land had been hauled forth and cruelly done to death. Next he went on to say that the white lords from the stars, looking down on the land, had perceived its trouble, and determined at great personal inconvenience, to alleviate its lot; how they had accordingly taken the real king of the country, Ignosi, who was languishing in exile, by the hand and led him over the mountains; how they had seen the wickedness of Twala's doings, and for a sign to the wavering, and to save the life of the girl Foulata, had actually, by the exercise of their high magic, put out the sun and slain the young fiend, Scragga; and how they were prepared to stand by them, and assist them to overthrow Twala, and set up the rightful king, Ignosi, in his place.

He finished his discourse amid a murmur of approbation, and then Ignosi stepped forward and began to speak. Having reiterated all that Infadoos, his uncle, had said, he concluded a powerful speech in these words:

"O chiefs, captains, soldiers, and people, ye have heard my words. Now must ye make choice between me and him who sits upon my throne, the uncle who killed his brother, and hunted his brother's child forth to die in the cold and the night. That I am indeed the king these"—pointing to the chiefs—"can tell ye, for they have seen the snake about my middle. If I were not the king, would these white men be on my side, with all their magic? Tremble, chiefs, captains, soldiers, and people! Is not the darkness they have brought upon the land to confound Twala, and cover our flight, yet before your eyes?"

"It is," answered the soldiers.

"I am the king; I say to ye, I am the king," went on Ignosi, drawing up his great stature to its full, and lifting his broad-bladed battle-axe above his head. "If there be any man among ye who says that it is not so, let him stand forth, and I will fight him now, and his blood shall be a red token that I tell ye true. Let him stand forth, I say;" and he shook the great axe till it flashed in the sunlight.

As nobody seemed inclined to respond to this heroic version of "Dilly, Dilly, come and be killed," our late henchman proceeded with his address.

"I am indeed the king, and if ye do stand by my side in the battle, if I win the day ye shall go with me to victory and honor. I will give ye oxen and wives, and ye shall take place of all the regiments; and if ye fall I will fall with ye.

"And behold, this promise do I give ye, that when I sit upon the seat of my fathers, bloodshed shall cease in the land. No longer shall ye cry for justice to find slaughter, no longer shall the witch-finder hunt ye out so that ye be slain without a cause. No man shall die save he who offendeth against the laws. The 'eating up' of your kraals shall cease; each shall sleep secure in his own hut and fear not, and justice shall walk blind throughout the land. Have ye chosen, chiefs, captains, soldiers, and people?"

"We have chosen, O king," came back the answer.

"It is well. Turn your heads and see how Twala's messengers go forth from the great town, east and west, and north and south, to gather a mighty army to slay me and ye, and these my friends and my protectors. To-morrow, or perchance the next day, will he come with all who are faithful to him. Then shall I see the man who is indeed my man, the man who fears not to die for his cause; and I tell ye he shall not be forgotten in the time of spoil. I have spoken, O chiefs, captains, soldiers, and people. Now go to your huts and make you ready for war."

There was a pause, and then one of the chiefs lifted his hand, and out rolled the royal salute, *"Koom!"* It was a sign that the regiments accepted Ignosi as their king. Then they marched off in battalions.

Half an hour afterwards we held a council of war, at which all the commanders of regiments were present. It was evident to us that before very long we should be attacked in overwhelming force. Indeed, from our point of vantage on the hill we could see troops mustering, and messengers going forth from Loo in every direction, doubtless to summon regiments to the king's assistance. We had on our side about twenty thousand men, composed of seven of the best regiments in the country. Twala had, so Infadoos and the chiefs calculated, at least thirty to thirty-five thousand on whom he could rely at present assembled in Loo, and they thought that by midday on the morrow he would be able to gather another five thousand or more to his aid. It was, of course, possible, that some of his troops would desert and come over to us, but it was not a contingency that could be reckoned on. Meanwhile, it was clear that active preparations were being made to subdue us. Already strong bodies of armed men were patrolling round and round the foot of the hill, and there were other signs of a coming attack.

Infadoos and the chiefs, however, were of opinion that no attack would take place that night, which would be devoted to preparation and to the removal by every possible means of the moral effects produced upon the minds of the soldiery by the supposed magical darkening of the sun. The attack would be on the morrow, they said, and they proved to be right.

Meanwhile, we set to work to strengthen the position as much as possible. Nearly the entire force was turned out, and in the two hours which yet remained to sundown wonders were done. The paths up the hill—which was rather a sanitarium than a fortress, being used generally as the camping-place of regiments suffering from recent service in unhealthy portions of the country —were carefully blocked with masses of stones, and every other possible approach was made as impregnable as time would allow. Piles of boulders were collected at various spots to be rolled down upon an advancing enemy, stations were appointed to the different regiments, and every other preparation which our joint ingenuity could suggest was taken.

Just before sundown we perceived a small company of men advancing towards us from the direction of Loo, one of whom bore a palm leaf in his hand as a sign that he came as a herald.

As he came, Ignosi, Infadoos, one or two chiefs, and ourselves went down to the foot of the mountain to meet him. He was a gallant-looking fellow, with the regulation leopard-skin cloak.

"Greeting!" he cried, as he came near; "the king's greeting to those who make unholy war against the king; the lion's greeting to the jackals who snarl around his heels."

"Speak," I said.

"These are the king's words. Surrender to the king's mercy ere a worse thing befall ye. Already the shoulder has been torn from the black bull, and the king drives him bleeding about the camp."[*]

"What are Twala's terms?" I asked, for curiosity.

"His terms are merciful, worthy of a great king. These are the words of Twala, the one-eyed, the mighty, the husband of a thousand wives, lord of the Kukuanas, keeper of the great road (Solomon's Road), beloved of the strange ones who sit in silence at the mountains yonder (the Three Witches), calf of the black cow, elephant whose tread shakes the earth, terror of the evil-doer, ostrich whose feet devour the desert, huge one, black one, wise one, king from generation to generation! these are the words of Twala: 'I will have mercy and be satisfied with a little blood. One in every ten shall die, the rest shall go free; but the white man Incubu, who slew Scragga, my son, and Infadoos, my brother, who brews rebellion against me, these shall die by torture as an offering to the silent ones.' Such are the merciful words of Twala."

After consulting with the others a little I answered him in a loud voice, so that the soldiers might hear, thus:

"Go back, thou dog, to Twala, who sent thee, and say that we, Ignosi, veritable king of the Kukuanas, Incubu, Bougwan, and

---

[*]This cruel custom is not confined to the Kukuanas, but is by no means uncommon among African tribes on the occasion of the outbreak of war or any other important public event.—A. Q.

Macumazahn, the wise white ones from the stars who make dark the sun, Infadoos, of the royal house, and the chiefs, captains, and people here gathered, make answer and say, 'That we will not surrender; that before the sun has twice gone down Twala's corpse shall stiffen at Twala's gate, and Ignosi, whose father Twala slew, shall reign in his stead.' Now go, ere we whip thee away, and beware how ye lift a hand against such as we."

The herald laughed loud. "Ye frighten not men with such swelling words," he cried out. "Show yourselves as bold to-morrow, O ye who darken the sun. Be bold, fight, and be merry, before the crows pick your bones till they are whiter than your faces. Farewell; perhaps we may meet in the fight; wait for me, I pray, white men." And with this shaft of sarcasm he retired, and almost immediately the sun sank.

That night was a busy one for us, for, as far as was possible by the moonlight, all preparations for the morrow's fight were continued. Messengers were constantly coming and going from the place where we sat in council. At last, about an hour after midnight, everything that could be done was done, and the camp, save for the occasional challenge of a sentry, sank into sleep. Sir Henry and I, accompanied by Ignosi and one of the chiefs, descended the hill and made the rounds of the vedettes. As we went, suddenly, from all sorts of unexpected places, spears gleamed out in the moonlight, only to vanish again as we uttered the password. It was clear to us that none were sleeping at their posts. Then we returned, picking our way through thousands of sleeping warriors, many of whom were taking their last earthly rest.

The moonlight flickered along their spears, and played upon their features and made them ghastly; the chilly night wind tossed their tall and hearselike plumes. There they lay in wild confusion, with arms outstretched and twisted limbs; their stern, stalwart forms looked weird and unhuman in the moonlight.

"How many of these do you suppose will be alive at this time to-morrow?" asked Sir Henry.

I shook my head and looked again at the sleeping men, and to my tired and yet excited imagination it seemed as though death had already touched them. My mind's eye singled out those who were sealed to slaughter, and there rushed in upon my heart a great sense of the mystery of human life, and an overwhelming sorrow at its futility and sadness. To-night these thousands slept their healthy sleep; to-morrow they, and many others with them, ourselves perhaps among them, would be stiffening in the cold; their wives would be widows, their children fatherless, and their place know them no more forever. Only the old moon would shine serenely on, the night wind would stir the grasses, and the wide earth would take its happy rest, even as it did æons before these were, and will do æons after they have been forgotten.

Yet man dies not while the world, at once his mother and his monument, remains. His name is forgotten, indeed, but the breath he breathed yet stirs the pine-tops on the mountains, the sound of the words he spoke yet echoes on through space; the thoughts his brain gave birth to we have inherited to-day; his passions are our cause of life; the joys and sorrows that he felt are our familiar friends—the end from which he fled aghast will surely overtake us also.

Truly the universe is full of ghosts; not sheeted, churchyard spectres, but the inextinguishable and immortal elements of life, which, having once been, can never *die*, though they blend and change and change again forever.

All sorts of reflections of this sort passed through my mind— for as I get older I regret to say that a detestable habit of thinking seems to be getting a hold of me—while I stood and stared at those grim yet fantastic lines of warriors sleeping, as their saying goes, "upon their spears."

"Curtis," I said to Sir Henry, "I am in a condition of pitiable funk."

Sir Henry stroked his yellow beard and laughed, as he answered:

"I've heard you make that sort of remark before, Quatermain."

"Well, I mean it now. Do you know, I very much doubt if one of us will be alive to-morrow night. We shall be attacked in overwhelming force, and it is exceedingly doubtful if we can hold this place."

"We'll give a good account of some of them, at any rate. Look here, Quatermain, the business is a nasty one, and one with which, properly speaking, we ought not to be mixed up; but we are in for it, so we must make the best of it. Speaking person- ally, I had rather be killed fighting than any other way, and now that there seems little chance of finding my poor brother, it makes the idea easier to me. But fortune favors the brave, and we may succeed. Anyway, the slaughter will be awful, and as we have a reputation to keep up, we shall have to be in the thick of it."

Sir Henry made this last remark in a mournful voice, but there was a gleam in his eye which belied it. I have a sort of idea that Sir Henry Curtis actually likes fighting.

After this we went and slept for a couple of hours.

Just about dawn we were awakened by Infadoos, who came to say that great activity was to be observed in Loo, and that parties of the king's skirmishers were driving in our vedettes.

We got up and dressed ourselves for the fray, each putting on his chain-armor shirt, for which at the present juncture we felt exceedingly thankful. Sir Henry went the whole length about the matter, and dressed himself like a native warrior. "When you are in Kukuanaland, do as the Kukuanas do," he remarked, as he drew the shining steel over his broad shoulders, which it fitted like a glove. Nor did he stop there. At his request, Infadoos had provided him with a complete set of war uniform. Round his throat he fastened the leopard-skin cloak of a commanding officer, on his brows he bound the plume of black ostrich feathers worn only by generals of high rank, and round his centre a magnificent moocha of white ox-tails. A pair of sandals, a leglet of goat's hair, a heavy battle-axe with a rhinoceros-horn handle, a round iron shield covered with white ox-hide, and the regulation number of tollas, or throwing knives, made up his equipment, to which, however, he added his revolver. The dress was, no doubt, a savage one; but I am bound to say I never saw a finer sight than Sir Henry Curtis presented in this guise. It showed off his magnificent physique to the greatest advantage, and when Ignosi arrived, presently, arrayed in a similar costume, I thought to myself that I never before saw two such splendid men. As for Good and myself, the chain armor did not suit us nearly so well. To begin with, Good insisted upon keeping on his trousers, and a stout, short gentleman with an eye-glass, and one half of his face shaved, arrayed in a mail shirt carefully tucked into a very seedy pair of corduroys, looks more striking than imposing. As for myself, my chain shirt being too big for me, I put it on over all my clothes, which caused it to bulge out in a somewhat ungainly fashion. I discarded my trousers, however, determined to go into battle with bare legs, in order to be the lighter in case it became necessary to retire quickly, retaining only my veldtschoons. This, a spear, a shield, which I did not know how to use, a couple of tollas, a revolver, and a huge plume, which I pinned into the top of my shooting-hat in order to give a bloodthirsty finish to my appearance, completed my modest equipment. In addition to all these articles, of course we had our rifles, but as ammunition was scarce, and they would be useless in case of a charge, we had arranged to have them carried behind us by bearers.

As soon as we had equipped ourselves we hastily swallowed some food, and then started out to see how things were progressing. At one point in the table-land of the mountain there was a little koppie of brown stone, which served for the double purpose of headquarters and a conning tower. Here we found Infadoos surrounded by his own regiment, the Grays, which was undoubtedly the finest in the Kukuana army, and the same which we had first seen at the outlying kraal. This regiment, now three thousand five hundred strong, was being held in reserve, and the men were lying down on the grass in companies, and watching the king's forces creep out of Loo in long, ant-like columns. There seemed to be no end to those columns—three in all, and each numbering at least eleven or twelve thousand men.

As soon as they were clear of the town, they formed up. Then one body marched off to the right, one to the left, and the third came slowly on towards us.

"Ah," said Infadoos, "they are going to attack us on three sides at once."

This was rather serious news, for as our position on the top of the mountain, which was at least a mile and a half in circumference, was an extended one, it was important to us to concentrate our comparatively small defending force as much as possible. But, as it was impossible for us to dictate in what way we should be attacked, we had to make the best of it, and accordingly sent orders to the various regiments to prepare to receive the separate onslaughts.

CHAPTER XIII.

THE ATTACK.

SLOWLY, and without the slightest appearance of haste or excitement, the three columns crept on. When within about five hundred yards of us, the main or centre column halted at the root of a tongue of open plain which ran up into the hill, to enable the other two to circumvent our position, which was shaped more or less in the form of a horseshoe, the two points being towards the town of Loo, their object being, no doubt, that the threefold assault should be delivered simultaneously.

"Oh, for a gatling!" groaned Good, as he contemplated the serried phalanxes beneath us. "I would clear the plain in twenty minutes."

"We have not got one, so it is no use yearning for it; but suppose you try a shot, Quatermain. See how near you can go to that tall fellow who appears to be in command. Two to one you miss him, and an even sovereign, to be honestly paid if ever we get out of this, that you don't drop the ball within ten yards."

This piqued me, so, loading the express with solid ball, I waited till my friend walked some ten yards out from his force, in order to get a better view of our position, accompanied only by an orderly, and then lying down and resting the express upon a rock, I covered him. The rifle, like all expresses, was only sighted to three hundred and fifty yards, so, to allow for the drop in trajectory, I took him half-way down the neck, which ought, I calculated, to find him in the chest. He stood quite still and gave me every opportunity, but whether it was the excitement or the wind, or the fact of the man being a long shot, I don't know, but this was what happened. Getting dead on, as I thought, a fine sight, I pressed, and when the puff of smoke had cleared away I, to my disgust, saw my man standing unharmed, while his orderly, who was at least three paces to the left, was stretched upon the ground, apparently dead. Turning swiftly, the officer I had aimed at began to run towards his force, in evident alarm.

"Bravo, Quatermain!" sang out Good; "you've frightened him."

This made me very angry, for if possible to avoid it, I hate to miss in public. When one can only do one thing well, one likes to keep up one's reputation in that thing. Moved quite out of myself at my failure, I did a rash thing. Rapidly covering the general as he ran, I let drive with the second barrel. The poor man threw up his arms and fell forward on his face. This time I had made no mistake; and—I say it as a proof of how little we think of others when our own pride or reputation are in question—I was brute enough to feel delighted at the sight.

The regiments who had seen the feat cheered wildly at this exhibition of the white man's magic, which they took as an omen of success, while the force to which the general had belonged— which, indeed, as we afterwards ascertained, he had commanded —began to fall back in confusion. Sir Henry and Good now took up their rifles and began to fire, the latter industriously "browning" the dense mass before him with a Winchester repeater, and I also had another shot or two, with the result that, so far as we could judge, we put some eight or ten men *hors de combat* before they got out of range.

Just as we stopped firing there came an ominous roar from our far right, then a similar roar from our left. The two other divisions were engaging us.

At the sound the mass of men before us opened out a little, and came on towards the hill up the spit of bare grass-land at a slow trot, singing a deep-throated song as they advanced. We kept up a steady fire from our rifles as they came, Ignosi joining in occasionally, and accounted for several men, but of course produced no more effect upon that mighty rush of armed humanity than he who throws pebbles does on the advancing wave.

On they came, with a shout and the clashing of spears; now they were driving in the outposts we had placed among the rocks at the foot of the hill. After that the advance was a little slower, for though as yet we had offered no serious opposition, the attacking force had to come up hill, and came slowly to save their breath. Our first line of defence was about half-way up the side, our second fifty yards farther back, while our third occupied the edge of the plain.

On they came, shouting their war-cry, *"Twala! Twala! Chielé! Chielé!"* (Twala! Twala! Smite! smite!). *"Ignosi! Ignosi! Chielé! Chielé!"* answered our people. They were quite close now, and the tollas, or throwing-knives, began to flash backward and forward, and now with an awful yell the battle closed in.

To and fro swayed the mass of struggling warriors, men falling thick as leaves in an autumn wind; but before long the superior weight of the attacking force began to tell, and our first line of defence was slowly pressed back, till it merged into the second. Here the struggle was very fierce, but again our people were driven back and up, till at length, within twenty minutes of the commencement of the fight, our third line came into action.

But by this time the assailants were much exhausted, and had, besides, lost many men killed and wounded, and to break through that third impenetrable hedge of spears proved beyond their powers. For a while the dense mass of struggling warriors swung backward and forward in the fierce ebb and flow of battle, and the issue was doubtful. Sir Henry watched the desperate struggle with a kindling eye, and then without a word he rushed off, followed by Good, and flung himself into the hottest of the fray. As for myself, I stopped where I was.

The soldiers caught sight of his tall form as he plunged into the battle, and there rose a cry of—

"Nanzia Incubu!" (Here is the elephant!) *"Chielé! Chielé!"*

From that moment the issue was no longer in doubt. Inch by inch, fighting with desperate gallantry, the attacking force was pressed back down the hillside, till at last it retreated upon its reserves in something like confusion. At that moment, too, a messenger arrived to say that the left attack had been repulsed, and I was just beginning to congratulate myself that the affair was over for the present, when, to our horror, we perceived our men who had been engaged in the right defence being driven towards us across the plain, followed by swarms of the enemy, who had evidently succeeded at this point.

Ignosi, who was standing by me, took in the situation at a glance, and issued a rapid order. Instantly the reserve regiment round us (the Grays) extended itself.

Again Ignosi gave a word of command, which was taken up and repeated by the captains, and in another second, to my intense disgust, I found myself involved in a furious onslaught upon the advancing foe. Getting as much as I could behind Ignosi's huge frame, I made the best of a bad job, and toddled along to be killed, as though I liked it. In a minute or two—the time seemed all too short to me—we were plunging through the flying groups of our men, who at once began to re-form behind us, and then I am sure I do not know what happened. All I can remember is a dreadful rolling noise of the meeting of shields, and the sudden apparition of a huge ruffian, whose eyes seemed literally to be starting out of his head, making straight at me with a bloody spear. But—I say it with pride—I rose to the occasion. It was an occasion before which most people would have collapsed once and for all. Seeing that if I stood where I was I must be done for, I, as the horrid apparition came, flung myself down in front of him so cleverly that, being unable to stop himself, he took a header right over my prostrate form. Before he could rise again I had risen and settled the matter from behind with my revolver.

Shortly after this somebody knocked me down, and I remember no more of the charge.

When I came to I found myself back at the koppie, with Good bending over me with some water in a gourd.

"How do you feel, old fellow?" he asked, anxiously.

I got up and shook myself before answering.

"Pretty well, thank you," I answered.

"Thank Heaven! when I saw them carry you in I felt quite sick; I thought you were done for."

"Not this time, my boy. I fancy I only got a rap on the head, which knocked me out of time. How has it ended?"

"They are repulsed at every point for the time. The loss is dreadfully heavy; we have lost quite two thousand killed and wounded, and they must have lost three. Look, there's a sight!" and he pointed to long lines of men advancing by fours. In the centre of, and being borne by, each group of four was a kind of hide tray, of which a Kukuana force always carried a quantity, with a loop for a handle at each corner. On these trays—and their number seemed endless—lay wounded men, who as they arrived were hastily examined by the medicine-men, of whom ten were attached to each regiment. If the wound was not of a fatal character the sufferer was taken away and attended to as carefully as circumstances would allow. But if, on the other hand, the wounded man's condition was hopeless, what followed was very dreadful, though doubtless it was the truest mercy. One of the doctors, under pretense of carrying out an examination, swiftly opened an artery with a sharp knife, and in a minute or two the sufferer expired painlessly. There were many cases that day in which this was done. In fact, it was done in most cases when the wound was in the body, for the gash made by the entry of the enormously broad spears used by the Kukuanas generally rendered recovery hopeless. In most cases the sufferers were already unconscious, and in others the fatal "nick" of the artery was done so swiftly and painlessly that they did not seem to notice it. Still it was a ghastly sight, and one from which we were glad to escape; indeed, I never remember one which affected me more than seeing those gallant soldiers thus put out of pain by the red-handed medicine-men, except, indeed, on an occasion when, after an attack, I saw a force of Swazis burying their hopelessly wounded *alive*.

Hurrying from this dreadful scene to the farther side of the koppie, we found Sir Henry (who still held a bloody battle-axe in his hand), Ignosi, Infadoos, and one or two of the chiefs in deep consultation.

"Thank heavens, here you are, Quatermain! I can't make out what Ignosi wants to do. It seems that, though we have beaten off the attack, Twala is now receiving large reinforcements, and is showing a disposition to invest us, with a view of starving us out."

"That's awkward."

"Yes; especially as Infadoos says that the water supply has given out."

"My lord, that is so," said Infadoos; "the spring cannot supply the wants of so great a multitude, and is failing rapidly. Before night we shall all be thirsty. Listen, Macumazahn. Thou art wise, and hast doubtless seen many wars in the lands from whence thou camest—that is if, indeed, they make wars in the stars. Now tell us, what shall we do? Twala has brought up many fresh men to take the place of those who have fallen. But Twala has learned a lesson; the hawk did not think to find the heron ready; but our beak has pierced his breast; he will not strike at us again. We, too, are wounded, and he will wait for us to die; he will wind himself round us like a snake round a buck, and fight the fight of 'sit down.' "

"I hear you," I said.

"So, Macumazahn, thou seest we have no water here, and but a little food, and we must choose between these three things—to languish like a starving lion in his den, or to strive to break away towards the north, or"—and here he rose and pointed towards the dense mass of our foes—"to launch ourselves straight at Twala's throat. Incubu, the great warrior—for to-day he fought like a buffalo in a net, and Twala's soldiers went down before his axe like corn before the hail; with these eyes I saw it—Incubu says 'charge;' but the Elephant is ever prone to charge. Now what says Macumazahn, the wily old fox, who has seen much and loves to bite his enemy from behind? The last word is in Ignosi, the king, for it is a king's right to speak of war; but let us hear thy voice, O Macumazahn, who watchest by night, and the voice too of him of the transparent eye."

What sayest thou, Ignosi?" I asked.

"Nay, my father," answered our quondam servant, who now, clad as he was in the full panoply of savage war, looked every inch a warrior king, "do thou speak, and let me, who am but a child in wisdom beside thee, hearken to thy words."

Thus abjured, I, after taking hasty counsel with Good and Sir Henry, delivered my opinion briefly to the effect that, being trapped, our best chance, especially in view of the failure of our water supply, was to initiate an attack upon Twala's forces, and then I recommended that the attack should be delivered at once, "before our wounds grow stiff," and also before the sight of Twala's overpowering force caused the hearts of our soldiers "to wax small like fat before a fire." Otherwise, I pointed out, some of the captains might change their minds, and, making peace with Twala, desert to him, or even betray us into his hands.

This expression of opinion seemed, on the whole, to be favorably received; indeed, among the Kukuanas my utterances met with a respect which has never been accorded to them before or since. But the real decision as to our course lay with Ignosi, who, since he had been recognized as rightful king, could exercise the almost unbounded rights of sovereignty, including, of course, the final decision on matters of generalship, and it was to him that all eyes were now turned.

At length, after a pause, during which he appeared to be thinking deeply, he spoke:

"Incubu, Macumazahn, and Bougwan, brave white men, and my friends; Infadoos, my uncle, and chiefs; my heart is fixed.

I will strike at Twala this day, and set my fortunes on the blow,
ay, and my life; my life and your lives also. Listen: thus will
I strike. Ye see how the hill curves round like the half-moon,
and how the plain runs like a green tongue towards us within
the curve?"

"We see," I answered.

"Good; it is now midday, and the men eat and rest after the
toil of battle. When the sun has turned and travelled a little
way towards the dark, let thy regiment, my uncle, advance with
one other down to the green tongue. And it shall be that when
Twala sees it he shall hurl his force at it to crush it. But the spot
is narrow, and the regiments can come against thee one at a time
only; so shall they be destroyed one by one, and the eyes of all
Twala's army shall be fixed upon a struggle the like of which
has not been seen by living man. And with thee, my uncle, shall
go Incubu, my friend, that when Twala sees his battle-axe flashing in the first rank of the 'Grays' his heart may grow faint. And
I will come with the second regiment, that which follows thee,
so that if ye are destroyed, as it may happen, there may yet be
a king left to fight for; and with me shall come Macumazahn
the wise."

"It is well, O King," said Infadoos, apparently contemplating
the certainty of the complete annihilation of his regiment with
perfect calmness. Truly these Kukuanas are a wonderful people.
Death has no terrors for them when it is incurred in the course
of duty.

"And while the eyes of the multitude of Twala's regiments
are thus fixed upon the fight," went on Ignosi, "behold, one third
of the men who are left alive to us" (*i.e.*.., about six thousand)
"shall creep along the right horn of the hill and fall upon the left
flank of Twala's force, and one third shall creep along the left
horn and fall upon Twala's right flank. And when I see that
the horns are ready to toss Twala, then will I, with the men who
are left to me, charge home in Twala's face, and if fortune goes
with us the day will be ours, and before Night drives her horses
from the mountains to the mountains we shall sit in peace at
Loo. And now let us eat and make ready; and, Infadoos, do thou
prepare, that the plan be carried out; and stay, let my white
father, Bougwan, go with the right horn, that his shining eye may
give courage to the men."

The arrangements for the attack thus briefly indicated were
set in motion with a rapidity that spoke well for the perfection
of the Kukuana military system. Within little more than an hour
rations had been served out to the men and devoured, the three

divisions were formed, the plan of attack explained to the leaders, and the whole force, with the exception of a guard left with the wounded, now numbering about eighteen thousand men in all, was ready to be put in motion.

Presently Good came up and shook hands with Sir Henry and myself.

"Good-bye, you fellows," he said, "I am off with the right wing, according to orders; and so I have come to shake hands in case we should not meet again, you know," he added, significantly.

We shook hands in silence, and not without the exhibition of as much emotion as Englishmen are wont to show.

"It is a queer business," said Sir Henry, his deep voice shaking a little, "and I confess I never expect to see to-morrow's sun. As far as I can make out, the Grays, with whom I am to go, are to fight until they are wiped out in order to enable the wings to slip round unawares and outflank Twala. Well, so be it; at any rate, it will be a man's death! Good-bye, old fellow. God bless you! I hope you will pull through and live to collar the diamonds; but if you do, take my advice and don't have anything more to do with pretenders!"

In another second Good had wrung us both by the hand and gone; and then Infadoos came up and led off Sir Henry to his place in the forefront of the Grays, while, with many misgivings, I departed with Ignosi to my station in the second attacking regiment.

CHAPTER XIV.

THE LAST STAND OF THE GRAYS.

In a few more minutes the regiments destined to carry out the flanking movements had tramped off in silence, keeping carefully under the lee of the rising ground in order to conceal the movement from the keen eyes of Twala's scouts.

Half an hour or more was allowed to elapse between the setting-out of the horns or wings of the army before any movement was made by the Grays and the supporting regiments, known as the Buffaloes, which formed its chest, and which were destined to bear the brunt of the battle.

Both of these regiments were almost perfectly fresh, and of full strength, the Grays having been in reserve in the morning, and having lost but a small number of men in sweeping back that part of the attack which had proved successful in breaking the line of defence on the occasion when I charged with them and got knocked silly for my pains. As for the Buffaloes, they had formed the third line of defence on the left, and as the attacking force at that point had not succeeded in breaking through the second, had scarcely come into action at all.

Infadoos, who was a wary old general, and knew the absolute importance of keeping up the spirits of his men on the eve of such a desperate encounter, employed the pause in addressing his own regiment, the Grays, in poetical language; in explaining to them the honor that they were receiving in being put thus in the forefront of the battle, and in having the great white warrior from the stars to fight with them in their ranks, and in promising large rewards of cattle and promotion to all who survived in the event of Ignosi's arms being successful.

I looked down the long lines of waving black plumes and stern faces beneath them, and sighed to think that within one short hour most, if not all, of those magnificent veteran warriors, not a man of whom was under forty years of age, would be laid dead or dying in the dust. It could not be otherwise; they were being condemned, with that wise recklessness of human life that marks the great general, and often saves his forces and attains his ends, to certain slaughter, in order to give the cause and the remainder of the army a chance of success. They were foredoomed to die, and they knew it. It was to be their task to engage regiment after regiment of Twala's army on the narrow strip of green beneath us, till they were exterminated, or till the wings found a favorable opportunity for their onslaught. And yet they never hesitated, nor could I detect a sign of fear upon the face of a single warrior. There they were—going to certain death, about to quit the blessed light of day forever, and yet able to contemplate their doom without a tremor. I could not, even at that moment, help contrasting their state of mind with my own, which was far from comfortable, and breathing a sigh of envy and admiration. Never before had I seen such an absolute devotion to the idea of duty, and such a complete indifference to its bitter fruits.

"Behold your king!" ended old Infadoos, pointing to Ignosi; "go fight and fall for him, as is the duty of brave men, and cursed and shameful forever be the name of him who shrinks from death for his king, or who turns his back to his enemy. Behold your king! chiefs, captains, and soldiers; now do your homage to the sacred snake, and then follow on, that Incubu and I may show ye the road to the heart of Twala's forces."

There was a moment's pause, then suddenly there rose from the serried phalanxes before us a murmur, like the distant whisper of the sea, caused by the gentle tapping of the handles of six thousand spears against their holders' shields. Slowly it swelled, till its growing volume deepened and widened into a roar of rolling noise, that echoed like thunder against the mountains, and filled the air with heavy waves of sound. Then it decreased and slowly died away into nothing, and suddenly out crashed the royal salute.

Ignosi, I thought to myself, might well be a proud man that day, for no Roman emperor ever had such a salutation from gladiators "about to die."

Ignosi acknowledged this magnificent act of homage by lifting his battle-axe, and then the Grays filed off in a triple-line formation, each line containing about one thousand fighting men, exclusive of officers. When the last line had gone some five hundred yards, Ignosi put himself at the head of the Buffaloes, which regiment was drawn up in a similar three-line formation, and gave the word to march, and off we went, I, needless to say, uttering the most heartfelt prayers that I might come out of that job with a whole skin. Many a queer position have I found myself in, but never before in one quite so unpleasant as the present, or one in which my chance of coming off safe was so small.

By the time that we reached the edge of the plateau the Grays were already half-way down the slope ending in the tongue of grass-land that ran up into the bend of the mountain, something as the frog of a horse's foot runs up into the shoe. The excitement in Twala's camp on the plain beyond was very great, and regiment after regiment was starting forward at a long swinging trot in order to reach the root of the tongue of land before the attacking force could emerge into the plain of Loo.

This tongue of land, which was some three hundred yards in depth, was, even at its root or widest part, not more than three hundred and fifty paces across, while at its tip it scarcely measured ninety. The Grays, who, in passing down the side of the hill and on to the tip of the tongue, had formed in column, on reaching the spot where it broadened out again reassumed their triple-line formation and halted dead.

Then we—that is, the Buffaloes—moved down the tip of the tongue and took our stand in reserve, about one hundred yards behind the last line of the Grays, and on slightly higher ground. Meanwhile we had leisure to observe Twala's entire force, which had evidently been reinforced since the morning attack, and could not now, notwithstanding their losses number less than forty thousand, moving swiftly up towards us. But as they drew near the root of the tongue they hesitated, having discovered that only one regiment could advance into the gorge at a time, and that there, some seventy yards from the mouth of it, unassailable except in front, on account of the high walls of boulder-strewn ground on either side, stood the famous regiment of Grays, the pride and glory of the Kukuana army, ready to hold the way against their forces as the three Romans once held the bridge against thousands. They hesitated, and finally stopped their advance; there was no eagerness to cross spears with those three lines of grim warriors who stood so firm and ready. Presently, however, a tall general, with the customary head-dress of nodding ostrich plumes, came running up, attended by a group of chiefs and orderlies, being, I thought, none other than Twala himself, and gave an order, and the first regiment raised a shout, and charged up towards the Grays, who remained perfectly still and silent until the attacking troops were within forty yards, and a volley of tollas, or throwing-knives, came rattling among their ranks.

Then suddenly, with a bound and a roar, they sprang forward with uplifted spears, and the two regiments met in deadly strife. Next second the roll of the meeting shields came to our ears like the sound of thunder, and the whole plain seemed to be alive with flashes of light reflected from the stabbing spears. To and fro swung the heaving mass of struggling, stabbing humanity, but not for long. Suddenly the attacking lines seemed to grow thinner, and then with a slow, long heave the Grays passed over them, just as a great wave heaves up and passes over a sunken ridge. It was done; that regiment was completely destroyed, but the Grays had but two lines left now; a third of their number were dead.

Closing up shoulder to shoulder once more, they halted in silence and awaited attack; and I was rejoiced to catch sight of Sir Henry's yellow beard as he moved to and fro, arranging the ranks. So he was yet alive!

Meanwhile we moved up on to the ground of the encounter, which was cumbered by about four thousand prostrate human beings, dead, dying, and wounded, and literally stained red with blood. Ignosi issued an order, which was rapidly passed down the ranks, to the effect that none of the enemy's wounded were to be killed, and, so far as we could see, this order was scrupulously carried out. It would have been a shocking sight, if we had had time to think of it.

But now a second regiment, distinguished by white plumes, kilts, and shields, was moving up to the attack of the two thousand remaining Grays, who stood waiting in the same ominous silence as before, till the foe was within forty yards or so, when they hurled themselves with irresistible force upon them. Again there came the awful roll of the meeting shields, and as we watched, the grim tragedy repeated itself. But this time the issue was left longer in doubt; indeed, it seemed for a while almost impossible that the Grays should again prevail. The attacking regiment, which was one formed of young men, fought with the utmost fury, and at first seemed by sheer weight to be driving the veterans back. The slaughter was something awful, hundreds falling every minute; and from among the shouts of the warriors and the groans of the dying, set to the clashing music of meeting spears, came a continuous hissing undertone of *"S'gee, s'gee,"* the note of triumph of each victor as he passed his spear through and through the body of his fallen foe.

But perfect discipline and steady and unchanging valor can do wonders, and one veteran soldier is worth two young ones, as soon became apparent in the present case, For just as we thought that it was all up with the Grays, and were preparing to take their place so soon as they made room by being destroyed, I heard Sir Henry's deep voice ringing out above the din, and caught a glimpse of his circling battle-axe as he waved it high above his plumes. Then came a change; the Grays ceased to give; they stood still as a rock, against which the furious waves of spearmen broke again and again, only to recoil. Presently they began to move again—forward this time; as they had no firearms there was no smoke, so we could see it all. Another minute and the onslaught grew fainter.

"Ah, they are *men* indeed; they will conquer again," called out Ignosi, who was grinding his teeth with excitement at my side. "See, it is done!"

Suddenly, like puffs of smoke from the mouth of a cannon, the attacking regiment broke away in flying groups, their white head-dresses streaming behind them in the wind, and left their opponents victors, indeed, but, alas! no more a regiment. Of the gallant triple-line, which, forty minutes before had gone into action three thousand strong, there remained at most some six hundred blood-bespattered men; the rest were under foot. And yet they cheered and waved their spears in triumph, and then, instead of falling back upon us as we expected, they ran forward, for a hundred yards or so, after the flying groups of foemen, took possession of a gently rising knoll of ground, and, resuming the old triple formation, formed a threefold ring around it. And then, thanks be to God, standing on the top of a mound for a minute, I saw Sir Henry, apparently unharmed, and with him our old friend Infadoos. Then Twala's regiments rolled down upon the doomed band, and once more the battle closed in.

As those who read this history will probably long ago have gathered, I am, to be honest, a bit of a coward, and certainly in no way given to fighting, though, somehow, it has often been my lot to get into unpleasant positions, and to be obliged to shed man's blood. But I have always hated it, and kept my own blood as undiminished in quantity as possible, sometimes by a judicious use of my heels. At this moment, however, for the first time in my life, I felt my bosom burn with martial ardor. Warlike fragments from the "Ingoldsby Legends," together with numbers of sanguinary verses from the Old Testament, sprang up in my brain like mushrooms in the dark; my blood, which hitherto had been half-frozen with horror, went beating through my veins, and there came upon me a savage desire to kill and spare not. I glanced round at the serried ranks of warriors behind us, and somehow, all in an instant, began to wonder if my face looked like theirs. There they stood, their heads craned forward over their shields, the hands twitching, the lips apart, the fierce features instinct with the hungry lust of battle, and in the eyes a look like the glare of a bloodhound when he sights his quarry.

Only Ignosi's heart seemed, to judge from his comparative self-possession, to all appearance, to beat as calmly as ever beneath his leopard-skin cloak, though even *he* still kept on grinding his teeth. I could stand it no longer.

"Are we going to stand here till we put out roots, Umbopa— Ignosi, I mean—while Twala swallows our brothers yonder?" I asked.

"Nay, Macumazahn," was the answer; "see, now is the ripe moment; let us pluck it."

As he spoke a fresh regiment rushed past the ring upon the little mound, and, wheeling round, attacked it from the hither side.

Then, lifting his battle-axe, Ignosi gave the signal to advance, and, raising the Kukuana battle-cry, the Buffaloes charged home with a rush like the rush of the sea.

What followed immediately on this it is out of my power to tell. All I can remember is a wild yet ordered rushing, that seemed to shake the ground; a sudden change of front and forming up on the part of the regiment against which the charge was directed; then an awful shock, a dull roar of voices, and a continuous flashing of spears, seen through a red mist of blood.

When my mind cleared I found myself standing inside the

remnant of the Grays near the top of the mound, and just behind
no less a person than Sir Henry himself. How I got there I had,
at the moment, no idea, but Sir Henry afterwards told me that
I was borne up by the first furious charge of the Buffaloes almost
to his feet, and then left, as they in turn were pressed back.
Thereon he dashed out of the circle and dragged me into it.

As for the fight that followed, who can describe it? Again and
again the multitudes surged up against our momentarily lessen-
ing circle, and again and again we beat them back.

> "The stubborn spearsmen still made good
> The dark impenetrable wood;
> Each stepping where his comrade stood
> The instant that he fell,"

as I think the "Ingoldsby Legends" beautifully puts it.

It was a splendid thing to see those brave battalions come on
time after time over the barriers of their dead, sometimes holding
corpses before them to receive our spear-thrusts, only to leave
their own corpses to swell the rising piles. It was a gallant sight
to see that sturdy old warrior, Infadoos, as cool as though he
were on parade, shouting out orders, taunts, and even jests, to
keep up the spirit of his few remaining men, and then, as each
charge rolled up, stepping forward to wherever the fighting was
thickest, to bear his share in repelling it. And yet more gallant
was the vision of Sir Henry, whose ostrich plumes had been
shorn off by a spear-stroke, so that his long yellow hair streamed
out in the breeze behind him. There he stood, the great Dane,
for he was nothing else, his hands, his axe, and his armor all red
with blood, and none could live before his stroke. Time after
time I saw it come sweeping down, as some great warrior ventured to give him battle, and as he struck he shouted, "Oh-hoy!
O-hoy!" like his Bersekir forefathers, and the blow went crashing
through shield and spear, through head-dress, hair, and skull,
till at last none would of their own will come near the great white
"tagati" (wizard), who killed and failed not.

But suddenly there rose a cry of "Twala, y' Twala," and out
of the press sprang forward none other than the gigantic one-eyed
king himself, also armed with battle-axe and shield, and clad in
chain armor.

"Where art thou, Incubu, thou white man, who slew Scragga,
my son—see if thou canst kill me!" he shouted, and at the same
time hurled a tolla straight at Sir Henry, who, fortunately, saw
it coming, and caught it on his shield, which transfixed it, remaining wedged in the iron plate behind the hide.

Then with a cry, Twala sprang forward straight at him, and

with his battle-axe struck him such a blow upon the shield that the mere force and shock of it brought Sir Henry, strong man as he was, down upon his knees.

But at the time the matter went no further, for at that instant there rose from the regiments pressing round us something like a shout of dismay, and on looking up I saw the cause.

To the right and to the left the plain was alive with the plumes of charging warriors. The outflanking squadrons had come to our relief. The time could not have been better chosen. All Twala's army had, as Ignosi had predicted would be the case, fixed their attention on the bloody struggle which was raging round the remnant of the Grays and the Buffaloes, who were now carrying on a battle of their own at a little distance, which two regiments had formed the chest of our army. It was not until the horns were about to close upon them that they had dreamed of their approach. And now, before they could even assume a proper formation for defence, the outflanking Impis had leaped, like greyhounds, on their flanks.

In five minutes the fate of the battle was decided. Taken on both flanks, and dismayed by the awful slaughter inflicted upon them by the Grays and Buffaloes, Twala's regiments broke into flight, and soon the whole plain between us and Loo was scattered with groups of flying soldiers, making good their retreat. As for the forces that had so recently surrounded us and the Buffaloes, they melted away as though by magic, and presently we were left standing there like a rock from which the sea has retreated. But what a sight it was! Around us the dead and dying lay in heaped-up masses, and of the gallant Grays there remained alive but ninety-five men. More than two thousand nine hundred had fallen in this one regiment, most of them never to rise again.

"Men," said Infadoos, calmly, as between the intervals of binding up a wound in his arm he surveyed what remained to him of his corps, "ye have kept up the reputation of your regiment, and this day's fighting will be spoken of by your children's children." Then he turned round and shook Sir Henry Curtis by the hand. "Thou art a great man, Incubu," he said, simply; "I have lived a long life among warriors, and known many a brave one, yet have I never seen a man like thee."

At this moment the Buffaloes began to march past our position on the road to Loo, and as they did so a message was brought to us from Ignosi requesting Infadoos, Sir Henry, and myself to join him. Accordingly, orders having been issued to the remaining ninety men of the Grays to employ themselves in collecting the wounded, we joined Ignosi, who informed us that he was pressing on to Loo to complete the victory by capturing Twala, if that should be possible. Before we had gone far we suddenly discovered the figure of Good sitting on an ant-heap about one hundred paces from us. Close beside him was the body of a Kukuana.

"He must be wounded," said Sir Henry, anxiously. As he made the remark, an untoward thing happened. The dead body of the Kukuana soldier, or rather what had appeared to be his dead body, suddenly sprang up, knocked Good head over heels off the ant-heap, and began to spear him. We rushed forward in terror, and as we drew near we saw the brawny warrior making dig after dig at the prostrate Good, who at each prod jerked all his limbs into the air. Seeing us coming, the Kukuana gave one final most vicious dig, and with a shout of "Take that, wizard," bolted off. Good did not move, and we concluded that our poor comrade was done for. Sadly we came towards him, and were indeed astonished to find him pale and faint indeed, but with a serene smile upon his face, and his eyeglass still fixed in his eye.

"Capital armor this," he murmured, on catching sight of our faces bending over him. "How sold he must have been," and then he fainted. On examination we discovered that he had been seriously wounded in the leg by a tolla in the course of the pursuit, but that the chain-armor had prevented his last assailant's spear from doing anything more than bruise him badly. It was a merciful escape. As nothing could be done for him at the moment, he was placed on one of the wicker shields used for the wounded, and carried along with us.

On arriving before the nearest gate of Loo we found one of our regiments watching it in obedience to orders received from Ignosi. The remaining regiments were in the same way watching the other exits to the town. The officer in command of this regiment coming up, saluted Ignosi as king, and informed him that Twala's army had taken refuge in the town, whither Twala himself had also escaped, but that he thought they were thoroughly demoralized, and would surrender. Thereupon Ignosi, after taking counsel with us, sent forward heralds to each gate ordering the defenders to open, and promising on his royal word life and forgiveness to every soldier who laid down his arms. The message was not without its effect. Presently, amid the shouts and cheers of the Buffaloes, the bridge was dropped across the fosse, and the gates upon the farther side flung open.

Taking due precautions against treachery, we marched on into the town. All along the roadways stood dejected warriors, their heads drooping and their shields and spears at their feet, who, as Ignosi passed, saluted him as king. On we marched, straight to Twala's kraal. When we reached the great space, where a day or two previously we had seen the review and the witch-hunt, we found it deserted. No, not quite deserted, for there, on the farther side, in front of his hut, sat Twala himself, with but one attendant—Gagool.

It was a melancholy sight to see him seated there, his battle-axe and shield by his side, his chin upon his mailed breast, with but one old crone for companion, and, notwithstanding his cruelties and misdeeds, a pang of compassion shot through me as I saw him thus "fallen from his high estate." Not a soldier of all his armies, not a courtier out of the hundreds who had cringed round him, not even a solitary wife, remained to share his fate or halve the bitterness of his fall. Poor savage! he was learning the lesson that fate teaches to most who live long enough, that the eyes of mankind are blind to the discredited, and that he who is defenceless and fallen finds few friends and little mercy. Nor, indeed, in this case did he deserve any.

Filing through the kraal gate, we marched straight across the open space to where the ex-king sat. When within about fifty yards the regiment was halted, and, accompanied only by a small guard, we advanced towards him, Gagool reviling us bitterly as we came. As we drew near, Twala, for the first time, lifted up his plumed head, and fixed his one eye, which seemed to flash with suppressed fury almost as brightly as the great diadem bound round his forehead, upon his successful rival—Ignosi.

"Hail, O king!" he said, with bitter mockery; "thou who hast eaten of my bread, and now by the aid of the white man's magic hast seduced my regiments and defeated mine army, hail! what fate hast thou for me, O king?"

"The fate thou gavest to my father, whose throne thou hast sat on these many years!" was the stern answer.

"It is well. I will show thee how to die, that thou mayest remember it against thine own time. See, the sun sinks in blood," and he pointed with his red battle-axe towards the fiery orb now going down; "it is well that my sun should sink with it. And now, O king! I am ready to die, but I crave the boon of the Kukuana royal house* to die fighting. Thou canst not refuse it, or even those cowards who fled to-day will hold thee shamed."

"It is granted. Choose—with whom wilt thou fight? Myself,

---

*It is a law among the Kukuanas that no man of the royal blood can be put to death unless by his own consent, which is, however, never refused. He is allowed to choose a succession of antagonists, to be approved by the king, with whom he fights until one of them kills him.

I cannot fight with thee, for the king fights not except in war."

Twala's sombre eye ran up and down our ranks, and I felt, as for a moment it rested on myself, that the position had developed a new horror. What if he chose to begin by fighting *me?* What chance should I have against a desperate savage six feet five high, and broad in proportion? I might as well commit suicide at once. Hastily I made up my mind to decline the combat, even if I were hooted out of Kukuanaland as a consequence. It is, I think, better to be hooted than to be quartered with a battle-axe.

Presently he spoke.

"Incubu, what sayest thou, shall we end what we began to-day, or shall I call thee coward, white—even to the liver?"

"Nay," interposed Ignosi, hastily; "thou shalt not fight with Incubu."

"Not if he is afraid," said Twala.

Unfortunately Sir Henry understood this remark, and the blood flamed up into his cheeks.

"I will fight him," he said; "he shall see if I am afraid."

"For God's sake," I entreated, "don't risk your life against that of a desperate man. Anybody who saw you to-day will know that you are not a coward."

"I will fight him," was the sullen answer. "No living man shall call me a coward. I am ready now!" and he stepped forward and lifted his axe.

I wrung my hands over this absurd piece of Quixotism; but if he was determined on fighting, of course I could not stop him.

"Fight not, my white brother," said Ignosi, laying his hand affectionately on Sir Henry's arm; "thou hast fought enough, and if aught befell thee at his hands it would cut my heart in twain."

"I will fight, Ignosi," was Sir Henry's answer.

"It is well, Incubu; thou art a brave man. It will be a good fight. Behold, Twala, the Elephant, is ready for thee."

The ex-king laughed savagely, and stepped forward and faced Curtis. For a moment they stood thus, and the setting sun caught their stalwart frames and clothed them both in fire. They were a well-matched pair.

Then they began to circle round each other, their battle-axes raised.

Suddenly Sir Henry sprang forward and struck a fearful blow at Twala, who stepped to one side. So heavy was the stroke that the striker half over-balanced himself, a circumstance of which his antagonist took a prompt advantage. Circling his heavy battle-axe round his head, he brought it down with tremendous force. My heart jumped into my mouth; I thought the affair was already finished. But no; with a quick upward movement of the left arm Sir Henry interposed his shield between himself and the axe, with the result that its outer edge was shorn clean off, the axe falling on his left shoulder, but not heavily enough to do any serious damage. In another second Sir Henry got in another blow, which was also received by Twala upon his shield. Then followed blow upon blow, which were, in turn, either received upon the shield or avoided. The excitement grew intense; the regiment which was watching the encounter forgot its discipline, and, drawing near, shouted and groaned at every stroke. Just at this time, too, Good, who had been laid upon the ground by me, recovered from his faint, and, sitting up, perceived what was going on. In an instant he was up, and, catching hold of my arm, hopped about from place to place on one leg, dragging me after him, yelling out encouragements to Sir Henry—

"Go it, old fellow!" he hallooed. "That was a good one! Give it him amidships," and so on.

Presently Sir Henry, having caught a fresh stroke upon his shield, hit out with all his force. The stroke cut through Twala's shield and through the tough chain armor behind it, gashing him in the shoulder. With a yell of pain and fury Twala returned the stroke with interest, and, such was his strength, shore right through the rhinoceros-horn handle of his antagonist's battle-axe, strengthened as it was with bands of steel, wounding Curtis in the face.

A cry of dismay rose from the Buffaloes as our hero's broad axe-head fell to the ground; and Twala, again raising his weapon, flew at him with a shout. I shut my eyes. When I opened them again, it was to see Sir Henry's shield lying on the ground, and Sir Henry himself with his great arms twined round Twala's middle. To and fro they swung, hugging each other like bears, straining with all their mighty muscles for dear life and dearer honor. With a supreme effort Twala swung the Englishman clean off his feet, and down they came together, rolling over and over on the lime paving, Twala striking out at Curtis's head with the battle-axe, and Sir Henry trying to drive the tolla he had drawn from his belt through Twala's armor.

It was a mighty struggle and an awful thing to see.

"Get his axe!" yelled Good; and perhaps our champion heard him.

At any rate, dropping the tolla, he made a grab at the axe, which was fastened to Twala's wrist by a strip of buffalo-hide, and, still rolling over and over, they fought for it like wildcats, drawing their breath in heavy gasps. Suddenly the hide string burst, and then, with a great effort, Sir Henry freed himself, the weapon remaining in his grasp. Another second and he was up on his feet, the red blood streaming from the wound in his face, and so was Twala. Drawing the heavy tolla from his belt, he staggered straight at Curtis and struck him upon the breast. The blow came home true and strong, but whoever it was made that chain armor understood his art, for it withstood the steel. Again Twala struck out with a savage yell, and again the heavy knife rebounded and Sir Henry went staggering back. Once more Twala came on, and as he came our great Englishman gathered himself together, and, swinging the heavy axe round his head, hit at him with all his force. There was a shriek of excitement from a thouasnd throats, and, behold! Twala's head seemed to spring from his shoulders, and then fell and came rolling and bounding along the ground towards Ignosi, stopping just at his feet. For a second the corpse stood upright, the blood spouting in fountains from the severed arteries; then with a dull crash it fell to the earth, and the gold torque from the neck went rolling away across the pavement. As it did so Sir Henry, overpowered by faintness and loss of blood, fell heavily across it.

In a second he was lifted up, and eager hands were pouring water on his face. Another minute, and the great gray eyes opened wide.

He was not dead.

Then I, just as the sun sank, stepping to where Twala's head lay in the dust, unloosed the diamond from the dead brows and handed it to Ignosi.

"Take it," I said, "lawful king of the Kukuanas."

Ignosi bound the diadem upon his brows, and then advancing placed his foot upon the broad chest of his headless foe and broke out into a chant, or rather a pæan of victory, so beautiful and yet so utterly savage, that I despair of being able to give an adequate idea of it. I once heard a scholar with a fine voice read aloud from the Greek poet Homer, and I remember that the sound of the rolling lines seemed to make my blood stand still. Ignosi's chant, uttered as it was in a language as beautiful and sonorous as the old Greek, produced exactly the same effect on me, although I was exhausted with toil and many emotions.

"Now," he began, "now is our rebellion swallowed up in victory, and our evil-doing justified by strength.

"In the morning the oppressors rose up and shook themselves; they bound on their plumes and made them ready for war.

"They rose up and grasped their spears: the soldiers called to the captains, 'Come, lead us'—and the captains cried to the king, 'Direct thou the battle.'

"They rose up in their pride, twenty thousand men, and yet a twenty thousand.

"Their plumes covered the earth as the plumes of a bird cover her nest; they shook their spears and shouted, yea, they hurled their spears into the sunlight; they lusted for the battle and were glad.

"They came up against me; their strong ones came running swiftly to crush me; they cried, 'Ha! ha! he is as one already dead.'

"Then breathed I on them, and my breath was as the breath of a storm, and lo! they were not.

"My lightnings pierced them; I licked up their strength with the lightning of my spears; I shook them to the earth with the thunder of my shouting.

"They broke—they scattered—they were gone as the mists of the morning.

"They are food for the crows and the foxes, and the place of battle is fat with their blood.

"Where are the mighty ones who rose up in the morning?

"Where are the proud ones who tossed their plumes and cried, 'He is as one already dead'?

"They bow their heads, but not in sleep; they are stretched out, but not in sleep.

"They are forgotten; they have gone into the blackness, and shall not return; yea, others shall lead away their wives, and their children shall remember them no more.

"And I—I! the king—like an eagle have I found my eyric.

"Behold! far have I wandered in the night-time, yet have I returned to my little ones at the daybreak.

"Creep ye under the shadow of my wings, O people, and I will comfort ye, and ye shall not be dismayed.

"Now is the good time, the time of spoil.

"Mine are the cattle in the valleys, the virgins in the kraals are mine also.

"The winter is overpast, the summer is at hand.

"Now shall Evil cover up her face, and prosperity shall bloom in the land like a lily.

"Rejoice, rejoice, my people! let all the land rejoice in that the tyranny is trodden down, in that I am the king."

He paused, and out of the gathering gloom there came back the deep reply:

"Thou art the king."

Thus it was that my prophecy to the herald came true, and within the forty-eight hours Twala's headless corpse was stiffening at Twala's gate.

CHAPTER XV.

GOOD FALLS SICK.

AFTER the fight was ended Sir Henry and Good were carried into Twala's hut, where I joined them. They were both utterly exhausted by exertion and loss of blood, and, indeed, my own condition was little better. I am very wiry, and can stand fatigue more than most men, probably on account of my light weight and long training; but that night I was fairly done up, and, as is always the case with me when exhausted, that old wound the lion gave me began to pain. Also my head was aching violently from the blow I had received in the morning, when I was knocked senseless. Altogether, a more miserable trio than we were that evening it would have been difficult to discover; and our only comfort lay in the reflection that we were exceedingly fortunate to be there to feel miserable, instead of being stretched dead upon the plain, as so many thousands of brave men were that night, who had risen well and strong in the morning. Somehow, with the assistance of the beautiful Foulata, who, since we had been the means of saving her life, had constituted herself our handmaiden, and especially Good's, we managed to get off the chain shirts, which had certainly saved the lives of two of us that day, when we found that the flesh underneath was terribly bruised, for though the steel links had prevented the weapons from entering, they had not prevented them from bruising. Both Sir Henry and Good were a mass of bruises, and I was by no means free. As a remedy Foulata brought us some pounded green leaves with an aromatic odor, which, when applied as a plaster, gave us considerable relief. But though the bruises were painful, they did not give us such anxiety as Sir Henry's and Good's wounds. Good had a hole right through the fleshy part of his "beautiful white legs," from which he had lost a great deal of blood; and Sir Henry had a deep cut over the jaw, inflicted by Twala's battle-axe. Luckily Good was a very decent surgeon, and as soon as his small box of medicines was forthcoming, he, having thoroughly cleansed the wounds, managed to stitch up first Sir Henry's and then his own pretty satisfactorily, considering the imperfect light given by the primitive Kukuana lamp in the hut. Afterwards he plentifully smeared the wounds with some antiseptic ointment, of which there was a pot in the little box, and we covered them with the remains of a pocket-handkerchief which we possessed.

Meanwhile Foulata had prepared us some strong broth, for we were too weary to eat. This we swallowed, and then threw ourselves down on the piles of magnificent karosses, or fur rugs, which were scattered about the dead king's great hut. By a very strange instance of the irony of fate, it was on Twala's own couch, and wrapped in Twala's own particular kaross, that Sir Henry, the man who had slain him, slept that night.

I say slept; but after that day's work sleep was indeed difficult. To begin with, in very truth the air was full

> "Of farewells to the dying
> And mournings for the dead."

From every direction came the sound of the wailing of women whose husbands, sons, and brothers had perished in the fight. No wonder that they wailed, for over twenty thousand men, or nearly a third of of the Kukuana army, had been destroyed in that awful struggle. It was heart-rending to lie and listen to their cries for those who would never return; and it made one realize the full horror of the work done that day to further man's ambition. Towards midnight, however, the ceaseless crying of the women grew less frequent, till at length the silence was only broken at intervals of a few minutes by a long, piercing howl that came from a hut in our immediate rear, and which I afterwards discovered proceeded from Gagool wailing for the dead king, Twala.

After that I got a little fitful sleep, only to wake from time to time with a start, thinking that I was once more an actor in the terrible events of the last twenty-four hours. Now I seemed to see that warrior, whom my hand had sent to his last account, charging at me on the mountain-top; now I was once more in that glorious ring of Grays, which made its immortal stand against all Twala's regiments, upon the little mound; and now again I saw Twala's plumed and gory head roll past my feet with gnashing teeth and glaring eye. At last, somehow or other, the night passed away; but when dawn broke I found that my companions had slept no better than myself. Good, indeed, was in a high fever, and very soon afterwards began to grow light-headed, and also, to my alarm, to spit blood, the result, no doubt, of some internal injury inflicted by the desperate efforts made by the Kukuana warrior on the previous day to get his big spear through the chain armor. Sir Henry, however, seemed pretty fresh, notwithstanding the wound on his face, which made eating difficult and laughter an impossibility, though he was so sore and stiff that he could scarcely stir.

About eight o'clock we had a visit from Infadoos, who seemed but little the worse—tough old warrior that he was—for his exertions on the previous day, though he informed us he had been up all night. He was delighted to see us, though much grieved at Good's condition, and shook hands cordially; but I noticed that he addressed Sir Henry with a kind of reverence, as though he were something more than man; and, indeed, as we afterwards found out, the great Englishman was looked on throughout Kukuanaland as a supernatural being. No man, the soldiers said, could have fought as he fought, or could, at the end of a day of such toil and bloodshed, have slain Twala, who, in addition to being the king, was supposed to be the strongest warrior in Kukuanaland, in single combat, sheering through his bull-neck at a stroke. Indeed, that stroke became proverbial in Kukuanaland, and any extraordinary blow or feat of strength was thenceforth known as "Incubu's blow."

Infadoos told us also that all Twala's regiments had submitted to Ignosi, and that like submissions were beginning to arrive from chiefs in the country. Twala's death at the hands of Sir Henry had put an end to all further chance of disturbance; for Scragga had been his only son, and there was no rival claimant left alive.

I remarked that Ignosi had swum to the throne through blood. The old chief shrugged his shoulders. "Yes," he answered; "but the Kukuana people can only be kept cool by letting the blood flow sometimes. Many were killed, indeed, but the women were left, and others would soon grow up to take the places of the fallen. After this the land would be quiet for a while."

Afterwards, in the course of the morning, we had a short visit from Ignosi, on whose brows the royal diadem was now bound. As I contemplated him advancing with kingly dignity, an obsequious guard following his steps, I could not help recalling to my mind the tall Zulu who had presented himself to us at Durban some few months back, asking to be taken into our service, and reflecting on the strange revolutions of the wheel of fortune.

"Hail, O king!" I said, rising.

"Yes, Macumazahn. King at last, by the grace of your three right hands," was the ready answer.

All was, he said, going on well; and he hoped to arrange a great feast in two weeks' time, in order to show himself to the people.

I asked him what he had settled to do with Gagool.

"She is the evil genius of the land," he answered, "and I shall kill her, and all the witch-doctors with her! She has lived so long that none can remember when she was not old, and always she it is who has trained the witch-hunters, and made the land evil in the sight of the heavens above."

"Yet she knows much," I replied; "it is easier to destroy knowledge, Ignosi, than to gather it."

"It is so," he said, thoughtfully. "She, and she only, knows the secret of the 'Three Witches' yonder, whither the great road runs, where the kings are buried, and the silent ones sit."

"Yes, and the diamonds are. Forget not thy promise, Ignosi; thou must lead us to the mines, even if thou hast to spare Gagool alive to show the way."

"I will not forget, Macumazahn, and I will think on what thou sayest."

After Ignosi's visit I went to see Good, and found him quite delirious. The fever from his wound seemed to have taken a firm hold of his system, and to be complicated by an internal injury. For four or five days his condition was most critical; indeed, I firmly believe that had it not been for Foulata's indefatigable nursing he must have died.

Women are women, all the world over, whatever their color. Yet somehow it seemed curious to watch this dusky beauty bending night and day over the fevered man's couch, and performing all the merciful errands of the sickroom as swiftly, gently, and with as fine an instinct as a trained hospital nurse. For the first night or two I tried to help her, and so did Sir Henry so soon as his stiffness allowed him to move, but she bore our interference with impatience, and finally insisted upon our leaving him to her, saying that our movements made him restless, which I think was true. Day and night she watched and tended him, giving him his only medicine, a native cooling drink made of milk, in which was infused the juice of the bulb of a species of tulip, and keeping the flies from settling on him. I can see the whole picture now as it appeared night after night by the light of our primitive lamp, Good tossing to and fro, his features emaciated, his eyes shining large and luminous, and jabbering nonsense by the yard; and seated on the ground by his side, her back resting against the wall of the hut, the soft-eyed, shapely Kukuana beauty, her whole face, weary as it was, animated by a look of infinite compassion—or was it something more than compassion?

For two days we thought that he must die, and crept about with heavy hearts. Only Foulata would not believe it.

"He will live," she said.

For three hundred yards or more around Twala's chief hut, where the sufferers lay, there was silence; for by the king's order all who lived in the habitations behind it had, except Sir Henry and myself, been removed, lest any noise should come to the sick man's ear. One night, it was the fifth night of his illness, as was my habit I went across to see how he was getting on before turning in for a few hours.

I entered the hut carefully. The lamp placed upon the floor showed the figure of Good, tossing no more, but lying quite still.

So it had come at last! and in the bitterness of my heart I gave something like a sob.

"Hush—h—h!" came from the patch of dark shadow behind Good's head.

Then, creeping closer, I saw that he was not dead, but sleeping soundly, with Foulata's taper fingers clasped tightly in his poor white hand. The crisis had passed, and he would live. He slept like that for eighteen hours; and I scarcely like to say it, for fear I should not be believed, but during that entire period did that devoted girl sit by him, fearing that if she moved and drew away her hand it would wake him. What she must have suffered from cramp, stiffness, and weariness, to say nothing of want of food, nobody will ever know; but it is a fact that, when at last he woke, she had to be carried away—her limbs were so stiff that she could not move them.

After the turn had once been taken, Good's recovery was rapid and complete. It was not till he was nearly well that Sir Henry told him of all he owed to Foulata; and when he came to the story of how she sat by his side for eighteen hours, fearing lest by moving she should wake him, the honest sailor's eyes filled with tears. He turned and went straight to the hut where Foulata was preparing the midday meal (we were back in our old quarters now), taking me with him to interpret in case he could not make his meaning clear to her, though I am bound to say she understood him marvellously as a rule, considering how extremely limited was his foreign vocabulary.

"Tell her," said Good, "that I owe her my life, and that I will never forget her kindness."

I interpreted, and under her dark skin she actually seemed to blush.

Turning to him with one of those swift and graceful motions that in her always reminded me of the flight of a wild bird, she answered softly, glancing at him with her large brown eyes:

"Nay, my lord; my lord forgets! Did he not save *my* life, and am I not my lord's handmaiden?"

It will be observed that the young lady appeared to have entirely forgotten the share which Sir Henry and myself had had in her preservation from Twala's clutches. But that is the way of women! I remember my dear wife was just the same. I retired from that little interview sad at heart. I did not like Miss Foulata's soft glances, for I knew the fatal amorous propensities of sailors in general, and Good in particular.

There are two things in the world, as I have found it, which cannot be prevented: you cannot keep a Zulu from fighting, or a sailor from falling in love upon the slightest provocation!

It was a few days after this last occurrence that Ignosi held his great "indaba" (council), and was formally recognized as king by the "indunas" (head men) of Kukuanaland. The spectacle was an imposing one, including, as it did, a great review of troops. On this day the remaining fragment of the Grays were formally paraded, and in the face of the army thanked for their splendid conduct in the great battle. To each man the king made a large present of cattle, promoting them one and all to the rank of officers in the new corps of Grays which was in process of formation. An order was also promulgated throughout the length and breadth of Kukuanaland that, while we honored the country with our presence, we three were to be greeted with the royal salute, to be treated with the same ceremony and respect that was by custom accorded to the king, and the power of life and death was publicly conferred upon us. Ignosi, too, in the presence of his people, reaffirmed the promises that he had made, to the effect that no man's blood should be shed without trial, and that witch-hunting should cease in the land.

When the ceremony was over we waited upon Ignosi, and informed him that we were now anxious to investigate the mystery of the mines to which Solomon's Road ran, asking him if he had discovered anything about them.

"My friends," he answered, "this have I discovered. It is there that the three great figures sit, who here are called the 'Silent Ones,' and to whom Twala would have offered the girl, Foulata, as a sacrifice. It is there, too, in a great cave deep in the mountain, that the kings of the land are buried; there ye shall find Twala's body, sitting with those who went before him. There, too, is a great pit which, at some time, long dead men dug out, mayhap for the stones ye speak of, such as I have heard men in Natal speak of at Kimberley. There, too, in the Place of Death is a secret chamber, known to none but the King and Gagool. But Twala, who knew it, is dead, and I know it not, nor know I what is in it. But there is a legend in the land that once, many generations gone, a white man crossed the mountains, and was led by a woman to the secret chamber and shown the wealth, but before he could take it she betrayed him, and he was driven by the king of the day back to the mountains, and since then no man has entered the chamber."

"The story is surely true, Ignosi, for on the mountains we found the white man," I said.

"Yes, we found him. And now I have promised ye that if ye can find that chamber, and the stones are there—"

"The stone upon thy forehead proves that they are there," I put in, pointing to the great diamond I had taken from Twala's dead brows.

"Mayhap; if they are there," he said, "ye shall have as many as ye can take hence—if, indeed, ye would leave me, my brothers."

"First we must find the chamber," said I.

"There is but one who can show it to thee—Gagool."

"And if she will not?"

"Then shall she die," said Ignosi, sternly. "I have saved her alive but for this. Stay, she shall choose," and, calling to a messenger, he ordered Gagool to be brought.

In a few minutes she came, hurried along by two guards, whom she was cursing as she walked.

"Leave her," said the king to the guards.

As soon as their support was withdrawn the withered old bundle, for she looked more like a bundle than anything else, sank into a heap on the floor, out of which her two bright, wicked eyes gleamed like a snake's.

"What will ye with me, Ignosi?" she piped. "Ye dare not touch me. If ye touch me I will blast ye as ye sit. Beware of my magic."

"Thy magic could not save Twala, old she-wolf, and it cannot hurt me," was the answer. "Listen: I will this of thee, that thou reveal where is the chamber where are the shining stones."

"Ha! ha!" she piped, "none know but I, and I will never tell thee. The white devils shall go hence empty-handed."

"Thou wilt tell me. I will make thee tell me."

"How, O king? Thou art great, but can thy power wring the truth from a woman?"

"It is difficult, yet will I do it."

"How, O king?"

"Nay, thus; if thou tellest not thou shalt slowly die."

"Die!" she shrieked, in terror and fury; "ye dare not touch me—man, ye know not who I am. How old think ye am I? I knew your fathers, and your fathers' fathers' fathers. When the country was young I was here, when the country grows old I shall still be here. I cannot die unless I be killed by chance, for none dare slay me."

"Yet will I slay thee. See, Gagool, mother of evil, thou art so old thou canst no longer love thy life. What can life be to such a hag as thee, who hast no shape, nor form, nor hair, nor teeth— hast naught, save wickedness and evil eyes? It will be mercy to slay thee, Gagool."

"Thou fool," shrieked the old fiend, "thou accursed fool, think - est thou that life is sweet only to the young? It is not so, and naught thou knowest of the heart of man to think it. To the young, indeed, death is sometimes welcome, for the young can feel. They love and suffer, and it wrings them to see their beloved pass to the land of shadows. But the old feel not, they love not, and, ha! ha! they laugh to see another go out into the dark; ha! ha! they laugh to see the evil that is done under the sun. All they love is life, the warm, warm sun, and the sweet, sweet air. They are afraid of the cold; afraid of the cold and the dark, ha! ha! ha!" and the old hag writhed in ghastly merriment on the ground.

"Cease thine evil talk and answer me," said Ignosi, angrily. "Wilt thou show the place where the stones are, or wilt thou not? If thou wilt not, thou diest, even now," and he seized a spear and held it over her.

"I will not show it; thou darest not kill me, darest not. He who slays me will be accursed forever."

Slowly Ignosi brought down the spear till it pricked the pros- trate heap of rags.

With a wild yell she sprang to her feet, and then again fell and rolled upon the floor.

"Nay; I will show it. Only let me live, let me sit in the sun and have a bit of meat to suck, and I will show thee."

"It is well. I thought I should find a way to reason with thee. To-morrow shalt thou go with Infadoos and my white brothers to the place, and beware how thou failest, for if thou showest it not, then shalt thou slowly die. I have spoken."

"I will not fail, Ignosi. I always keep my word: *ha! ha! ha!* Once a woman showed the place to a white man before, and behold evil befell him," and here her wicked eyes glinted. "Her name was Gagool, too. Perchance I was that woman."

"Thou liest," I said, "that was ten generations gone."

"Mayhap, mayhap; when one lives long one forgets. Perhaps it was my mother's mother who told me; surely her name was Gagool, also. But mark, ye will find in the place where the bright playthings are a bag of hide full of stones. The man filled that bag, but he never took it away. Evil befell him, I say; evil befell him! Perhaps it was my mother's mother who told me. It will be a merry journey—we can see the bodies of those who died in the battle as we go. Their eyes will be gone by now, and their ribs will be hollow. Ha! ha! ha!"

CHAPTER XVI.

THE PLACE OF DEATH.

It was already dark on the third day after the scene described in the previous chapter, when we camped in some huts at the foot of the "Three Witches," as the triangle of mountains was called to which Solomon's Great Road ran. Our party consisted of our three selves and Foulata, who waited on us—especially on Good —Infadoos, Gagool, who was borne along in a litter, inside which she could be heard muttering and cursing all day long, and a party of guards and attendants. The mountains, or rather the three peaks of the mountains, for the whole mass evidently consisted of a solitary upheaval, were, as I have said, in the form of a triangle, of which the base was towards us, one peak being on our right, one on our left, and one straight in front of us. Never shall I forget the sight afforded by those three towering peaks in the early sunlight of the following morning. High, high above us, up into the blue air, soared their twisted snow-wreaths. Beneath the snow the peaks were purple with heath, and so were the wild moors that ran up the slopes towards them. Straight before us the white ribbon of Solomon's Great Road stretched away up-hill to the foot of the centre peak, about five miles from us, and then stopped. It was its terminus.

I had better leave the feelings of intense excitement with which we set out on our march that morning to the imagination of those who read this history. At last we were drawing near to the wonderful mines that had been the cause of the miserable death of the old Portuguese don, three centuries ago, of my poor friend, his ill-starred descendant, and also, as we feared, of George Curtis, Sir Henry's brother. Were we destined, after all that we had gone through, to fare any better? Evil befell them, as that old fiend, Gagool, said; would it befall us? Somehow, as we were marching up that last stretch of beautiful road, I could not help feeling a little superstitious about the matter, and so, I think, did Good and Sir Henry.

For an hour and a half or more we tramped on up the heather-fringed road, going so fast in our excitement that the bearers with Gagool's hammock could scarcely keep pace with us, and its occupant piped out to us to stop.

"Go more slowly, white men," she said, projecting her hideous, shrivelled countenance between the curtains, and fixing her gleaming eyes upon us; "why will ye run to meet the evil that shall befall ye, ye seekers after treasure?" and she laughed that horrible laugh which always sent a cold shiver down my back, and which for a while quite took the enthusiasm out of us.

However, on we went, till we saw before us, and between ourselves and the peak, a vast circular hole with sloping sides, three hundred feet or more in depth, and quite half a mile round.

"Can't you guess what this is?" I said to Sir Henry and Good, who were staring in astonishment down into the awful pit before us.

They shook their heads.

"Then it is clear that you have never seen the diamond mines at Kimberley. You may depend on it that this is Solomon's diamond mine; look there," I said, pointing to the stiff blue clay which was yet to be seen among the grass and bushes which clothed the sides of the pit, "the formation is the same. I'll be bound that if we went down there we should find 'pipes' of soapy, brecciated rock. Look, too," and I pointed to a series of worn, flat slabs of rock which were placed on a gentle slope below the level of a watercourse which had in some past age been cut out of the solid rock; "if those are not tables once used to wash the 'stuff,' I'm a Dutchman."

At the edge of this vast hole, which was the pit marked on the old don's map, the great road branched into two and circumvented it. In many places this circumventing road was built entirely of vast blocks of stone, apparently with the object of supporting the edges of the pit and preventing falls of reef. Along this road we pressed, driven by curiosity to see what the three towering objects were which we could discern from the hither side of the great hole. As we got nearer we perceived that they were colossi of some sort or other, and rightly conjectured that these were the three "Silent Ones" that were held in such awe by the Kukuana people. But it was not until we got quite close that we recognized the full majesty of these "Silent Ones."

There, upon huge pedestals of dark rock, sculptured in unknown characters, twenty paces between each, and looking down the road which crossed some sixty miles of plain to Loo, were three colossal seated forms—two males and one female—each measuring about twenty feet from the crown of the head to the pedestal.

The female form, which was nude, was of great though severe beauty, but unfortunately the features were injured by centuries of exposure to the weather. Rising from each side of her head were the points of a crescent. The two male colossi were, on the contrary, draped, and presented a terrifying cast of features, especially the one to our right, which had the face of a devil. That to our left was serene in countenance, but the calm upon it was dreadful. It was the calm of inhuman cruelty, the cruelty, Sir Henry remarked, that the ancients attributed to beings potent for good, who could yet watch the sufferings of humanity, if not with rejoicing, at least without suffering themselves. The three formed a most awe-inspiring trinity, as they sat there in their solitude and gazed out across the plain forever. Contemplating these "Silent Ones," as the Kukuanas called them, an intense curiosity again seized us to know whose were the hands that had shaped them, who was it that had dug the pit and made the road. While I was gazing and wondering, it suddenly occurred to me (being familiar with the Old Testament) that Solomon went astray after strange gods, the names of three of whom I remembered—"Ashtoreth the goddess of the Zidonians, Chemosh the god of the Moabites, and Milcom the god of the children of Ammon"—and I suggested to my companions that the three figures before us might represent these false divinities.

"Hum," said Sir Henry, who was a scholar, having taken a high degree in classics at college, "there may be something in that; Ashtoreth of the Hebrews was the Astarte of the Phœnicians, who were the great traders of Solomon's time. Astarte, who afterwards was the Aphrodite of the Greeks, was represented with horns like the half-moon, and there on the brow of the female figure are distinct horns. Perhaps these colossi were designed by some Phœnician official who managed the mines. Who can say?"

Before we had finished examining these extraordinary relics of remote antiquity, Infadoos came up, and, having saluted the "Silent Ones" by lifting his spear, asked us if we intended entering the "Place of Death" at once, or if we would wait till after we had taken food at midday. If we were ready to go at once, Gagool had announced her willingness to guide us. As it was not more than eleven o'clock, we—driven to it by a burning curiosity—announced our intention of proceeding at once, and I suggested that, in case we should be detained in the cave, we should take some food with us. Accordingly Gagool's litter was brought up, and that lady herself assisted out of it; and meanwhile Foulata, at my request, stored some biltong, or dried game-flesh, together with a couple of gourds of water in a reed basket. Straight in front of us, at a distance of some fifty paces from the backs of the colossi, rose a sheer wall of rock, eighty feet or more in height, that gradually sloped up till it formed the base of the lofty snow-wreathed peak which soared up into the air three thousand feet above us. As soon as she was clear of her hammock Gagool cast one evil grin upon us, and then, leaning on a stick, hobbled off towards the sheer face of the rock. We followed her till we came to a narrow portal solidly arched, that looked like the opening of a gallery of a mine.

Here Gagool was waiting for us, still with that evil grin upon her horrid face.

"Now, white men from the stars," she piped; "great warriors, Incubu, Bougwan, and Macumazahn the wise, are ye ready? Behold, I am here to do the bidding of my lord the king, and to show ye the store of bright stones."

"We are ready," I said.

"Good! good! Make strong your hearts to bear what ye shall see. Comest thou too, Infadoos, who betrayed thy master?"

Infadoos frowned as he answered:

"Nay, I come not; it is not for me to enter there. But thou, Gagool, curb thy tongue, and beware how thou dealest with my lords. At thy hands will I require them, and if a hair of them be hurt, Gagool, be thou fifty times a witch, thou shalt die. Hearest thou?"

"I hear, Infadoos; I know thee, thou didst ever love big words; when thou wast a babe I remember thou didst threaten thine own mother. That was but the other day. But fear not, fear not; I live but to do the bidding of the king. I have done the bidding of many kings, Infadoos, till in the end they did mine. Ha! ha! I go to look upon their faces once more, and Twala's, too. Come on, come on, here is the lamp," and she drew a great gourd full of oil, and fitted with a rush wick, from under her fur cloak.

"Art thou coming, Foulata?" asked Good in his villainous kitchen Kukuana, in which he had been improving himself under that lady's tuition.

"I fear, my lord," the girl answered, timidly.

"Then give me the basket."

"Nay, my lord, whither thou goest, there will I go also."

"The deuce you will!" thought I to myself; "that will be rather awkward if ever we get out of this."

Without further ado Gagool plunged into the passage, which

was wide enough to admit of two walking abreast, and quite dark, we following her voice as she piped to us to come on, in some fear and trembling, which was not allayed by the sound of a sudden rush of wings.

"Hallo! what's that?" halloed Good; "somebody hit me in the face."

"Bats," said I; "on you go."

When we had, as far as we could judge, gone some fifty paces we perceived that the passage was growing faintly light. Another minute, and we stood in the most wonderful place that the eyes of living man ever lit on.

Let the reader picture to himself the hall of the vastest cathedral he ever stood in, windowless, indeed, but dimly lighted from above (presumably by shafts connected with the outer air and driven in the roof, which arched away a hundred feet above our heads), and he will get some idea of the size of the enormous cave in which we stood, with the difference that this cathedral designed of nature was loftier and wider than any built by man. But its stupendous size was the least of the wonders of the place, for, running in rows adown its length were gigantic pillars of what looked like ice, but were, in reality, huge stalactites. It is impossible for me to convey any idea of the overpowering beauty and grandeur of these pillars of white spar, some of which were not less than twenty feet in diameter at the base, and sprang up in lofty and yet delicate beauty sheer to the distant roof. Others again were in process of formation. On the rock floor there was in these cases what looked, Sir Henry said, exactly like a broken column in an old Grecian temple, while high above, depending from the roof, the point of a huge icicle could be dimly seen. And even as we gazed we could hear the process going on, for presently with a tiny splash a drop of water would fall from the far-off icicle on to the column below. On some columns the drops only fell once in two or three minutes, and in these cases it would form an interesting calculation to discover how long, at that rate of dripping, it would take to form a pillar, say eighty feet high by ten in diameter. That the process was, in at least one instance, incalculably slow, the following instance will suffice to show. Cut on one of these pillars we discovered a rude likeness of a mummy, by the head of which sat what appeared to be one of the Egyptian gods, doubtless the handiwork of some old-world laborer in the mine. This work of art was executed at about the natural height at which an idle fellow, be he Phœnician workman or British cad, is in the habit of trying to immortalize himself at the expense of nature's masterpieces, namely, about five feet from the ground; yet at the time that we saw it, which *must* have been nearly three thousand years after the date of the execution of the drawing, the column was only eight feet high, and was still in process of formation, which gives a rate of growth of a foot to a thousand years, or an inch and a fraction to a century. This we knew because, as we were standing by it, we heard a drop of water fall.

Sometimes the stalactites took strange forms, presumably where the dropping of the water had not always been on the same spot. Thus, one huge mass, which must have weighed a hundred tons or so, was in the form of a pulpit, beautifully fretted over outside with what looked like lace. Others resembled strange beasts, and on the sides of the cave were fan-like ivory tracings, such as the frost leaves upon a pane.

Out of the vast main aisle there opened here and there smaller caves, exactly, Sir Henry said, as chapels open out of great cathedrals. Some were large, but one or two—and this is a wonderful instance of how Nature carries out her handiwork by the same unvarying laws, utterly irrespective of size—were tiny. One little nook, for instance, was no larger than an unusually big doll's house, and yet it might have been the model of the whole place, for the water dropped, the tiny icicles hung, and the spar columns were forming in just the same way.

We had not time, however, to examine this beautiful place as thoroughly as we should have liked to do, for unfortunately Gagool seemed to be indifferent to stalactites, and only anxious to get her business over. This annoyed me the more, as I was particularly anxious to discover, if possible, by what system the light was admitted into the place, and whether it was by the hand of man or of nature that this was done; also if it had been used in any way in ancient times, as seemed probable. However, we consoled ourselves with the idea that we would examine it thoroughly on our return, and followed on after our uncanny guide.

On she led us, straight to the top of the vast and silent cave, where we found another doorway, not arched as the first was, but square at the top, something like the doorways of Egyptian temples.

"Are ye prepared to enter the Place of Death?" asked Gagool, evidently with a view to making us feel uncomfortable.

"Lead on, Macduff," said Good, solemnly, trying to look as though he was not at all alarmed, as indeed did we all except Foulata, who caught Good by the arm for protection.

"This is getting rather ghastly," said Sir Henry, peeping into the dark doorway. "Come on, Quatermain—*seniores priores*.

Don't keep the old lady waiting!" and he politely made way for me to lead the van, for which I inwardly did not bless him.

Tap, tap, went old Gagool's stick down the passage, as she trotted along, chuckling hideously; and, still overcome by some unaccountable presentiment of evil, I hung back.

"Come, get on, old fellow," said Good, "or we shall lose our fair guide."

Thus adjured, I started down the passage, and after about twenty paces found myself in a gloomy apartment some forty feet long by thirty broad and thirty high, which in some past age had evidently been hollowed, by hand-labor, out of the mountain. This apartment was not nearly so well lighted as the vast stalactite ante-cave, and at the first glance all I could make out was a massive stone table running its length, with a colossal white figure at its head, and life-sized white figures all round it. Next I made out a brown thing, seated on the table in the centre, and in another moment my eyes grew accustomed to the light, and I saw what all these things were, and I was tailing out of it as hard as my legs would carry me. I am not a nervous man, in a general way, and very little troubled with superstitions, of which I have lived to see the folly; but I am free to own that that sight quite upset me, and had it not been that Sir Henry caught me by the collar and held me, I do honestly believe that in another five minutes I should have been outside that stalactite cave, and that the promise of all the diamonds in Kimberley would not have induced me to enter it again. But he held me tight, so I stopped because I could not help myself. But next second his eyes got accustomed to the light, too, and he let go of me and began to mop the perspiration off his forehead. As for Good, he swore feebly, and Foulata threw her arms round his neck and shrieked.

Only Gagool chuckled loud and long.

It *was* a ghastly sight. There at the end of the long stone table, holding in his skeleton fingers a great white spear, sat *Death* himself, shaped in the form of a colossal human skeleton, fifteen feet or more in height. High above his head he held the spear, as though in the act of striking; one bony hand rested on the stone table before him, in the position a man assumes on rising from his seat, while his frame was bent forward so that the vertebræ of the neck and the grinning, gleaming skull projected towards us and fixed its hollow eye-places upon us, the jaws a little open, as though it were about to speak.

"Great heavens!" said I, faintly, at last, "what can it be?"

"And what are *those things?*" said Good, pointing to the white company round the table.

"And what on earth is *that thing?*" said Sir Henry, pointing to the brown creature seated on the table.

"Hee! hee! hee!" laughed Gagool. "To those who enter the Hall of the Dead, evil comes. Hee! hee! hee! ha! ha!"

"Come, Incubu, brave in battle, come and see him thou slewest;" and the old creature caught his coat in her skinny fingers, and led him away towards the table. We followed.

Presently she stopped and pointed at the brown object seated on the table. Sir Henry looked, and started back with an exclamation; and no wonder, for there seated, quite naked, on the table, the head which Sir Henry's battle-axe had shorn from the body resting on its knees, was the gaunt corpse of Twala, last king of the Kukuanas. Yes, there, the head perched upon the knees, it sat in all its ugliness, the vertebræ projecting a full inch above the level of the shrunken flesh of the neck, for all the world like a black double of Hamilton Tighe.* Over the whole surface of the corpse there was gathered a thin, glassy film, which made its appearance yet more appalling, and for which we were, at the moment, quite unable to account, till we presently observed that from the roof of the chamber the water fell steadily, *drip! drip! drip!* on to the neck of the corpse, from whence it ran down over the entire surface, and finally escaped into the rock through a tiny hole in the table. Then I guessed what it was—*Twala's body was being transformed into a stalactite.*

A look at the white forms seated on the stone bench that ran around that ghastly board confirmed this view. They were human forms, indeed, or rather had been human forms; now they were *stalactites*. This was the way in which the Kukuana people had from time immemorial preserved their royal dead. They petrified them. What the exact system was, if there was any beyond placing them for a long period of years under the drip, I never discovered, but there they sat, iced over and preserved forever by the silicious fluid. Anything more awe-inspiring than the spectacle of this long line of departed royalties, wrapped in a shroud of ice-like spar, through which the features could be dimly made out (there were twenty-seven of them, the last being Ignosi's father), and seated round that inhospitable board, with Death himself for a host, it is impossible to imagine. That the practice of thus preserving their kings must have been an ancient one is evident from the number, which, allowing for an average reign of fifteen years, would, supposing that every king who reigned

---

*"Now haste ye, my handmaidens, haste and see
   How he sits there and glowers with his head on his knee."

was placed here—an improbable thing, as some are sure to have perished in battle far from home—fix the date of its commencement at four and a quarter centuries back. But the colossal Death who sits at the head of the board is far older than that, and, unless I am much mistaken, owes his origin to the same artist who designed the three colossi. He was hewn out of a single stalactite, and, looked at as a work of art, was most admirably conceived and executed. Good, who understood anatomy, declared that, so far as he could see, the anatomical design of the skeleton was perfect down to the smallest bones.

My own idea is that this terrific object was a freak of fancy on the part of some old-world sculptor, and that its presence had suggested to the Kukuanas the idea of placing their royal dead under its awful presidency. Or perhaps it was placed there to frighten away any marauders who might have designs upon the treasure-chamber beyond. I cannot say. All I can do is to describe it as it is, and the reader must form his own conclusion.

Such, at any rate, was the white Death and such were the white dead!

CHAPTER XVII.

SOLOMON'S TREASURE-CHAMBER.

WHILE we had been engaged in getting over our fright, and in examining the grisly wonders of the place, Gagool had been differently occupied. Somehow or other—for she was marvellously active when she chose—she had scrambled on to the great table and made her way to where our departed friend Twala was placed under the drip, to see, suggested Good, how he was "pickling," or for some dark purpose of her own. Then she came hobbling back, stopping now and again to address a remark (the tenor of which I could not catch) to one or other of the shrouded forms, just as you or I might greet an old acquaintance. Having gone through this mysterious and horrible ceremony, she squatted herself down on the table immediately under the white Death, and began, so far as I could make out, to offer up prayers to it. The spectacle of this wicked old creature pouring out supplications (evil ones, no doubt) to the arch-enemy of mankind was so uncanny that it caused us to hasten our inspection.

"Now, Gagool," said I, in a low voice—somehow one did not dare to speak above a whisper in that place—"lead us to the chamber."

The old creature promptly scrambled down off the table.

"My lords are not afraid?" she said, leering up into my face. "Lead on."

"Good, my lords;" and she hobbled round to the back of the great Death. "Here is the chamber; let my lords light the lamp, and enter," and she placed the gourd full of oil upon the floor, and leaned herself against the side of the cave. I took out a match, of which we still had a few in a box, and lit the rush wick, and then looked for the doorway, but there was nothing before us but the solid rock. Gagool grinned. "The way is there, my lords."

"Do not jest with us," I said, sternly.

"I jest not, my lords. See!" and she pointed at the rock.

As she did so, on holding up the lamp we perceived that a mass of stone was slowly rising from the floor and vanishing into the rock above, where doubtless there was a cavity prepared to receive it. The mass was of the width of a good-sized door, about ten feet high and not less than five feet thick. It must have weighed at least twenty or thirty tons, and was clearly moved upon some simple balance principle, probably the same as that upon which the opening and shutting of an ordinary modern window is arranged. How the principle was set in motion, of course none of us saw; Gagool was careful to avoid that; but I have little doubt that there was some very simple lever, which was moved ever so little by pressure on a secret spot, thereby throwing additional weight on to the hidden counterbalances, and causing the whole huge mass to be lifted from the ground. Very slowly and gently the great stone raised itself, till at last it had vanished altogether, and a dark hole presented itself to us in the place which it had filled.

Our excitement was so intense, as we saw the way to Solomon's treasure-chamber at last thrown open, that I for one began to tremble and shake. Would it prove a hoax after all, I wondered, or was old Da Silvestra right? and were there vast hoards of wealth stored in that dark place, hoards which would make us the richest men in the whole world? We should know in a minute or two.

"Enter, white men from the stars," said Gagool, advancing into the doorway; "but first hear your servant, Gagoola the old. The bright stones that ye will see were dug out of the pit over which the Silent Ones are set, and stored here, I know not by whom. But once has this place been entered since the time that those who stored the stones departed in haste, leaving them behind. The report of the treasure went down among the people who lived in the country from age to age, but none knew where the chamber was, nor the secret of the door. But it happened that a white man reached this country from over the mountains, perchance he too came 'from the stars,' and was well received of the king of the day. He it is who sits yonder," and she pointed to the fifth king at the table of the dead. "And it came to pass that he and a woman of the country who was with him came to this place, and that by chance the woman learned the secret of the door—a thousand years might ye search, but ye should never find it. Then the white man entered with the woman and found the stones, and filled with stones the skin of a small goat, which the woman had with her to hold food. And as he was going from the chamber he took up one more stone, a large one, and held it in his hand." Here she paused.

"Well," I asked, breathless with interest, as we all were, "what happened to Da Silvestra?"

The old hag started at the mention of the name.

"How knowest thou the dead man's name?" she asked, sharply; and then, without waiting for an answer, went on—

"None knew what happened; but it came about that the white man was frightened, for he flung down the goat-skin with the stones, and fled out with only the one stone in his hand, and that the king took, and it is the stone that thou, Macumazahn, didst take from Twala's brows."

"Have none entered here since?" I asked, peering again down the dark passage.

"None, my lords. Only the secret of the door hath been kept, and every king hath opened it, though he hath not entered. There is a saying, that those who enter there will die within a moon, even as the white man died in the cave upon the mountain, where ye found him, Macumazahn. Ha! ha! mine are true words."

Our eyes met as she said it, and I turned sick and cold. How did the old hag know all these things?"

"Enter, my lords. If I speak truth the goat-skin with the stones will lie upon the floor; and if there is truth as to whether it is death to enter here, that will ye learn afterwards. Ha! ha! ha!" And she hobbled through the doorway, bearing the light with her; but I confess that once more I hesitated about following.

"Oh, confound it all!" said Good, "here goes. I am not going to be frightened by that old devil;" and, followed by Foulata, who, however, evidently did not at all like the job, for she was shivering with fear, he plunged into the passage after Gagool—an example which we quickly followed.

A few yards down the passage, in a narrow way hewn out of

the living rock, Gagool had paused, and was waiting for us.

"See, my lords," she said, holding the light before her, "those who stored the treasure here fled in haste, and bethought them to guard against any who should find the secret of the door, but had not the time," and she pointed to large square blocks of stone, which had, to the height of two courses (about two feet three), been placed across the passage with a view to walling it up. Along the side of the passage were similar blocks ready for use, and, most curious of all, a heap of mortar and a couple of trowels, which, so far as we had time to examine them, appeared to be of a similar shape and make to those used by workmen of this day.

Here Foulata, who had throughout been in a state of great fear and agitation, said that she felt faint and could go no farther, but would wait there. Accordingly we set her down on the unfinished wall, placing the basket of provisions by her side, and left her to recover.

Following the passage for about fifteen paces farther, we suddenly came to an elaborately painted wooden door. It was standing wide open. Whoever was last there had either not had the time, or had forgotten to shut it.

Across the threshold lay a skin bag, formed of a goat-skin, that appeared to be full of pebbles.

"Hee! hee! white men," sniggered Gagool, as the light from the lamp fell upon it. "What did I tell ye, that the white man who came here fled in haste, and dropped the woman's bag— behold it!"

Good stooped down and lifted it. It was heavy and jingled.

"By Jove! I believe it's full of diamonds," he said, in an awed whisper; and, indeed, the idea of a small goat-skin full of diamonds is enough to awe anybody.

"Go on," said Sir Henry, impatiently. "Here, old lady, give me the lamp," and, taking it from Gagool's hand, he stepped through the doorway and held it high above his head.

We pressed in after him, forgetful, for the moment, of the bag of diamonds, and found ourselves in Solomon's treasure-chamber.

At first, all that the somewhat faint light given by the lamp revealed was a room hewn out of the living rock, and apparently not more than ten feet square. Next there came into sight, stored one on the other as high as the roof, a splendid collection of elephant-tusks. How many of them there were we did not know, for of course we could not see how far they went back, but there could not have been less than the ends of four or five hundred tusks of the first quality visible to our eyes. There, alone, was enough ivory before us to make a man wealthy for life. Perhaps,

I thought, it was from this very store that Solomon drew his material for his "great throne of ivory," of which there was not the like made in any kingdom.

On the opposite side of the chamber were about a score of wooden boxes, something like Martini-Henry ammunition boxes, only rather larger, and painted red.

"There are the diamonds," cried I; "bring the light."

Sir Henry did so, holding it close to the top box, of which the lid, rendered rotten by time even in that dry place, appeared to have been smashed in, probably by Da Silvestra himself. Pushing my hand through the hole in the lid I drew it out full, not of diamonds, but of gold pieces, of a shape that none of us had seen before, and with what looked like Hebrew characters stamped upon them.

"Ah!" I said, replacing the coin, "we sha'n't go back empty-handed, anyhow. There must be a couple of thousand pieces in each box, and there are eighteen boxes. I suppose it was the money to pay the workmen and merchants."

"Well," put in Good, "I think that is the lot; I don't see any diamonds, unless the old Portuguese put them all into this bag."

"Let my lords look yonder where it is darkest, if they would find the stones," said Gagool, interpreting our looks. "There my lords will find a nook, and three stone chests in the nook, two sealed and one open."

Before interpreting this to Sir Henry, who had the light, I could not resist asking how she knew these things, if no one had entered the place since the white man, generations ago.

"Ah, Macumazahn, who watchest by night," was the mocking answer, "ye who live in the stars, do ye not know that some have eyes that can see through rock?"

"Look in that corner, Curtis," I said, indicating the spot Gagool had pointed out.

"Hallo, you fellows," he said, "here's a recess. Great heavens! look here."

We hurried up to where he was standing in a nook, something like a small bow-window. Against the wall of this recess were placed three stone chests, each about two feet square. Two were fitted with stone lids, the lid of the third rested against the side of the chest, which was open.

"*Look!*" he repeated, hoarsely, holding the lamp over the open chest. We looked, and for a moment could make nothing out, on account of a silvery sheen that dazzled us. When our eyes got used to it we saw that the chest was three-parts full of uncut diamonds, most of them of considerable size. Stooping, I picked some up. Yes, there was no mistake about it, there was the unmistakable soapy feel about them.

I fairly gasped as I dropped them.

"We are the richest men in the whole world," I said. "Monte Cristo is a fool to us."

"We shall flood the market with diamonds," said Good.

"Got to get them there first," suggested Sir Henry.

And we stood with pale faces and stared at each other, with the lantern in the middle, and the glimmering gems below, as though we were conspirators about to commit a crime, instead of being, as we thought, the three most fortunate men on earth.

"Hee! hee! hee!" went old Gagool behind us, as she flitted about like a vampire bat. "There are the bright stones that ye love, white men, as many as ye will; take them, run them through your fingers, *eat* of them, hee! hee! *drink* of them, ha! ha!"

There was something so ridiculous at that moment to my mind in the idea of eating and drinking diamonds, that I began to laugh outrageously, an example which the others followed, without knowing why. There we stood and shrieked with laughter over the gems which were ours, which had been found for *us* thousands of years ago by the patient delvers in the great hole yonder, and stored for *us* by Solomon's long-dead overseer, whose name, perchance, was written in the characters stamped on the faded wax that yet adhered to the lids of the chest. Solomon never got them, nor David, nor Da Silvestra, nor anybody else. *We* had got them; there before us were millions of pounds' worth of diamonds, and thousands of pounds' worth of gold and ivory, only waiting to be taken away.

Suddenly the fit passed off, and we stopped laughing.

"Open the other chests, white men, croaked Gagool, "there are surely more therein. Take your fill, white lords!"

Thus adjured, we set to work to pull up the stone lids on the other two, first—not without a feeling of sacrilege—breaking the seals that fastened them.

Hoorah! they were full too, full to the brim; at least the second one was; no wretched Da Silvestra had been filling goat-skins out of that. As for the third chest, it was only about a fourth full, but the stones were all picked ones; none less than twenty carats, and some of them as large as pigeon-eggs. Some of these biggest ones, however, we could see by holding them up to the light, were a little yellow, "off colored," as they call it at Kimberley.

What we did *not* see, however, was the look of fearful malevo-

lence that old Gagool favored us with as she crept, crept like a
snake, out of the treasure-chamber and down the passage towards
the massive door of solid rock.

Hark! Cry upon cry comes ringing up the vaulted path. It is
Foulata's voice!

"Oh, Bougwan! help! help! the rock falls!"

"Leave go, girl! Then—"

"Help! help! she has stabbed me!"

By now we are running down the passage, and this is what the
light from the lamp falls on. The door of rock is slowly closing
down; it is not three feet from the floor. Near it struggles Foulata and Gagool. The red blood of the former runs to her knees,
but still the brave girl holds the old witch, who fights like a wild-
cat. Ah! she is free! Foulata falls, and Gagool throws herself on
the ground, to twist herself like a snake through the crack of the
closing stone. She is under—ah, God! too late! too late! The
stone nips her, and she yells in agony. Down, down, it comes,
all the thirty tons of it, slowly pressing her old body against the
rock below. Shriek upon shriek, such as we never heard, then a
long, sickening *crunch*, and the door was shut just as we, rushing
down the passage, hurled ourselves against it.

It was all done in four seconds.

Then we turned to Foulata. The poor girl was stabbed in the
body, and could not, I saw, live long.

"Ah! Bougwan, I die!" gasped the beautiful creature. "She
crept out—Gagool; I did not see her, I was faint—and the door
began to fall; then she came back, and was looking up the path—
and I saw her come in through the slowly falling door, and caught
her and held her, and she stabbed me, and *I die*, Bougwan."

"Poor girl! poor girl!" Good cried; and then, as he could do
nothing else, he fell to kissing her.

"Bougwan," she said, after a pause, "is Macumazahn there? it
grows so dark, I cannot see."

"Here I am, Foulata."

"Macumazahn, be my tongue for a moment, I pray thee, for
Bougwan cannot understand me, and before I go into the darkness—I would speak a word."

"Say on, Foulata, I will render it."

"Say to my lord, Bougwan, that—I love him, and that I am
glad to die because I know that he cannot cumber his life with
such as me, for the sun cannot mate with the darkness nor the
white with the black.

"Say that at times I have felt as though there were a bird in my bosom, which would one day fly hence and sing elsewhere; even now, though I cannot lift my hand, and my brain grows cold, I do not feel as though my heart were dying; it is so full of love that could live a thousand years, and yet be young. Say that if I live again, mayhap I shall see him in the stars, and that—I will search them all, though perchance I should there still be black and he would—still be white. Say—nay, Macumazahn, say no more, save that I love—Oh, hold me closer, Bougwan, I cannot feel thine arms—*oh! oh!*"

"She is dead—she is dead!" said Good, rising in grief, the tears running down his honest face.

"You need not let that trouble you, old fellow," said Sir Henry.

"Eh!" said Good; "what do you mean?"

"I mean that you will soon be in a position to join her. *Man, don't you see that we are buried alive?*"

Until Sir Henry uttered these words, I do not think the full horror of what had happened had come home to us, preoccupied as we were with the sight of poor Foulata's end. But now we understood. The ponderous mass of rock had closed, probably forever, for the only brain which knew its secret was crushed to powder beneath it. This was a door that none could hope to force with anything short of dynamite in large quantities. And we were the wrong side of it!

For a few minutes we stood horrified there over the corpse of Foulata. All the manhood seemed to have gone out of us. The first shock of this idea of the slow and miserable end that awaited us was overpowering. We saw it all now; that fiend, Gagool, had planned this snare for us from the first. It would have been just the jest that her evil mind would have rejoiced in, the idea of the three white men, whom, for some reason of her own, she had always hated, slowly perishing of thirst and hunger in the company of the treasure they had coveted. I saw the point of that sneer of hers about eating and drinking the diamonds now. Perhaps somebody had tried to serve the poor old don in the same way, when he abandoned the skin full of jewels.

"This will never do," said Sir Henry, hoarsely; "the lamp will soon go out. Let us see if we can't find the spring that works the rock."

We sprang forward with desperate energy, and, standing in a bloody ooze, began to feel up and down the door and the sides of the passage. But no knob or spring could we discover.

"Depend on it," I said, "it does not work from the inside; if it did Gagool would not have risked trying to crawl underneath the stone. It was the knowledge of this that made her try to escape at all hazard, curse her."

"At all events," said Sir Henry, with a hard little laugh, "retribution was swift; hers was almost as awful an end as ours is likely to be. We can do nothing with the door; let us go back to the treasure-room." We turned and went, and as we did so I perceived by the unfinished wall across the passage the basket of food which poor Foulata had carried. I took it up and brought it with me back to that accursed treasure-chamber that was to be our grave. Then we went back and reverently bore in Foulata's corpse, laying it on the floor by the boxes of coin.

Next we seated ourselves, leaning our backs against the three stone chests of priceless treasures.

"Let us divide the food," said Sir Henry, "so as to make it last as long as possible." Accordingly we did so. It would, we reckoned, make four infinitesimally small meals for each of us; enough, say, to support life for a couple of days. Besides the biltong, or dried game-flesh, there were two gourds of water, each holding about a quart.

"Now," said Sir Henry, "let us eat and drink, for to-morrow we die."

We each ate a small portion of the biltong, and drank a sip of water. We had, needless to say, but little appetite, though we were sadly in need of food, and felt better after swallowing it. Then we got up and made a systematic examination of the walls of our prison-house, in the faint hope of finding some means of exit, sounding them and the floor carefully.

There was none. It was not probable that there would be one to a treasure-chamber.

The lamp began to burn dim. The fat was nearly exhausted.

"Quatermain," said Sir Henry, "what is the time—your watch goes?"

I drew it out and looked at it. It was six o'clock; we had entered the cave at eleven.

"Infadoos will miss us," I suggested. "If we do not return to-night he will search for us in the morning, Curtis."

"He may search in vain. He does not know the secret of the door, nor even where it is. No living person knew it yesterday, except Gagool. To-day no one knows it. Even if he found the door he could not break it down. All the Kukuana army could not break through five feet of living rock. My friends, I see nothing for it but to bow ourselves to the will of the Almighty. The search for treasure has brought many to a bad end; we shall go to swell their number."

The lamp grew dimmer yet.

Presently it flared up and showed the whole scene in strong relief, the great mass of white tusks, the boxes full of gold, the corpse of poor Foulata stretched before them, the goat-skin full of treasure, the dim glimmer of the diamonds, and the wild, wan faces of us three white men seated there awaiting death by starvation.

Suddenly it sank, and expired.

CHAPTER XVIII.

WE ABANDON HOPE.

I can give no adequate description of the horrors of the night which followed. Mercifully they were to some extent mitigated by sleep, for even in such a position as ours wearied nature will sometimes assert itself. But I, at any rate, found it impossible to sleep much. Putting aside the terrifying thought of our impending doom—for the bravest man on earth might well quail from such a fate as awaited us, and I never had any great pretensions to be brave—the *silence* itself was too great to allow of it. Reader, you may have lain awake at night and thought the silence oppressive, but I say with confidence that you can have no idea what a vivid, tangible thing perfect silence really is. On the surface of the earth there is always some sound or motion, and though it may in itself be imperceptible, yet does it deaden the sharp edge of absolute silence. But here there was none. We were buried in the bowels of a huge, snow-clad peak. Thousands of feet above us the fresh air rushed over the white snow, but no sound of it reached us. We were separated by a long tunnel and five feet of rock even from the awful chamber of the dead; and the dead make no noise. The crashing of all the artillery of earth and heaven could not have come to our ears in our living tomb. We were cut off from all echoes of the world—we were as already dead.

And then the irony of the situation forced itself upon me. There around us lay treasures enough to pay off a moderate national debt, or to build a fleet of iron-clads, and yet we would gladly have bartered them all for the faintest chance of escape. Soon, doubtless, we should be glad to exchange them for a bit of food or a cup of water, and, after that, even for the speedy close to our sufferings. Truly wealth, which men spend all their lives in acquiring, is a valueless thing at the last.

And so the night wore on.

"Good," said Sir Henry's voice at last, and it sounded awful in the intense stillness, "how many matches have you in the box?"

"Eight, Curtis."

"Strike one, and let us see the time."

He did so, and in contrast to the dense darkness the flame nearly blinded us. It was five o'clock by my watch. The beautiful dawn was now blushing on the snow-wreaths far over our heads, and the breeze would be stirring the night mists in the hollows.

"We had better eat something and keep up our strength," said I.

"What is the good of eating?" answered Good; "the sooner we die and get it over the better."

"While there is life there is hope," said Sir Henry.

Accordingly we ate and sipped some water, and another period of time passed, when somebody suggested that it might be as well to get as near to the door as possible and hallo, on the faint chance of somebody catching a sound outside. Accordingly Good, who, from long practice at sea, has a fine, piercing note, groped his way down the passage and began, and I must say he made a most diabolical noise. I never heard such yells; but it might have been a mosquito buzzing for all the effect it produced.

After a while he gave it up, and came back very thirsty, and had to have some water. After that we gave up yelling as it encroached on the supply of water.

So we all sat down once more against our chests of useless diamonds in that dreadful inaction which was one of the hardest circumstances of our fate; and I am bound to say that for my part, I gave way in despair. Laying my head against Sir Henry's broad shoulder, I burst into tears; and I think I heard Good gulping away on the other side, and swearing hoarsely at himself for doing so.

Ah, how good and brave that great man was! Had we been two frightened children, and he our nurse, he could not have treated us more tenderly. Forgetting his own share of miseries, he did all he could to soothe our broken nerves, telling stories of men who had been in somewhat similar circumstances and miraculously escaped; and when these failed to cheer us, pointing out how, after all, it was only anticipating an end that must come to us all, that it would soon be over, and that death from exhaustion was a merciful one (which is not true). Then, in a diffident sort of a way, as I had once before heard him do, he suggested that we should throw ourselves on the mercy of a higher Power, which, for my part, I did with great vigor.

His is a beautiful character, very quiet, but very strong.

And so somehow the day went as the night had gone (if, indeed, one can use the terms where all was densest night), and when I lit a match to see the time it was seven o'clock.

Once more we ate and drank, and as we did so an idea occurred to me.

"How is it," said I, "that the air in this place keeps fresh? It is thick and heavy, but it is perfectly fresh."

"Great heavens!" said Good, starting up, "I never thought of that. It can't come through the stone door, for it is air-tight, if ever a door was. It must come from somewhere. If there were no current of air in the place we should have been stifled when we first came in. Let us have a look."

It was wonderful what a change this mere spark of hope wrought in us. In a moment we were all three groping about the place on our hands and knees, feeling for the slightest indication of a draught. Presently my ardor received a check. I put my hand on something cold. It was poor Foulata's dead face.

For an hour or more we went on feeling about, till at last Sir Henry and I gave up in despair, having got considerably hurt by constantly knocking our heads against tusks, chests, and the sides of the chamber. But Good still persevered, saying with an approach to cheerfulness, that it was better than doing nothing.

"I say, you fellows," he said, presently, in a constrained sort of voice, "come here."

Needless to say we scrambled over towards him quick enough.

"Quatermain, put your hand here where mine is. Now, do you feel anything?"

"I *think* I feel air coming up."

"Now listen." He rose and stamped upon the place, and a flame of hope shot up in our hearts. *It rang hollow.*

With trembling hands I lit a match. I had only three left, and we saw that we were in the angle of the far corner of the chamber, a fact that accounted for our not having noticed the hollow ring of the place during our former exhaustive examination. As the match burned we scrutinized the spot. There was a join in the solid rock floor, and, great heavens! there, let in level with the rock, was a stone ring. We said no word; we were too excited, and our hearts beat too wildly with hope to allow us to speak. Good had a knife, at the back of which was one of those hooks that are made to extract stones from horses' hoofs. He opened it, and scratched away at the ring with it. Finally he got it under, and levered away gently for fear of breaking the hook. The ring began to move. Being of stone, it had not got set fast in all the centuries it had lain there, as would have been the case had it been of iron. Presently it was upright. Then he got his hands into it and tugged with all his force, but nothing budged.

"Let me try," I said, impatiently, for the situation of the stone, right in the angle of the corner, was such that it was impossible for two to pull at once. I got hold and strained away, but with no results.

Then Sir Henry tried and failed.

Taking the hook again, Good scratched all round the crack where we felt the air coming up.

"Now, Curtis," he said, "tackle on, and put your back into it; you are as strong as two. Stop," and he took off a stout black silk handkerchief, which, true to his habits of neatness, he still wore, and ran it through the ring. "Quatermain, get Curtis round the middle and pull for dear life when I give the word. *Now!*"

Sir Henry put out all his enormous strength, and Good and I did the same, with such power as nature had given us.

"Heave! heave! it's giving," gasped Sir Henry; and I heard the muscles of his great back cracking. Suddenly there came a parting sound, then a rush of air, and we were all on our backs on the floor with a great flag-stone on the top of us. Sir Henry's strength had done it, and never did muscular power stand a man in better stead.

"Light a match, Quatermain," he said, as soon as we had picked ourselves up and got one breath; "carefully now."

I did so, and there before us was, God be praised! the *first step of a stone stair*.

"Now what is to be done?" asked Good.

"Follow the stair, of course, and trust to Providence."

"Stop!" said Sir Henry; "Quatermain, get the bit of biltong and the water that is left; we may want them."

I went creeping back to our place by the chests for that purpose, and as I was coming away an idea struck me. We had not thought much of the diamonds for the last twenty-four hours or so; indeed, the idea of the diamonds was nauseous, seeing what they had entailed upon us; but, thought I, I may as well pocket a few in case we ever should get out of this ghastly hole. So I just stuck my fist into the first chest and filled all the available pockets of my shooting-coat, topping up—this was a happy thought—with a couple of handfuls of big ones out of the third chest.

"I say, you fellows," I sung out, "won't you take some diamonds with you? I've filled my pockets."

"Oh! hang the diamonds!" said Sir Henry. "I hope that I may never see another."

As for Good, he made no answer. He was, I think, taking a last farewell of all that was left of the poor girl who loved him so well. And, curious as it may seem to you, my reader, sitting at home at ease and reflecting on the vast, indeed, the immeasurable, wealth which we were thus abandoning, I can assure you that if you had passed some twenty-eight hours with next to nothing to eat and drink in that place, you would not have cared to cumber yourself with diamonds while plunging down into the unknown bowels of the earth, in the wild hope of escape from an agonizing death. If it had not, from the habits of a lifetime, become a sort of second nature with me never to leave anything worth having behind if there was the slightest chance of my being able to carry it away, I am sure I should not have bothered to fill my pockets.

"Come on, Quatermain," said Sir Henry, who was already standing on the first step of the stone stair. "Steady, I will go first."

"Mind where you put your feet; there may be some awful hole underneath," said I.

"Much more likely to be another room," said Sir Henry, as he slowly descended, counting the steps as he went.

When he got to "fifteen" he stopped. "Here's the bottom," he said. "Thank goodness! I think it's a passage. Come on down."

Good descended next, and I followed last, and on reaching the bottom lit one of the two remaining matches. By its light we could just see that we were standing in a narrow tunnel, which ran right and left at right angles to the staircase we had descended. Before we could make out any more the match burned my fingers and went out. Then arose the delicate question of which way to turn. Of course it was impossible to know what the tunnel was or where it ran to, and yet to turn one way might lead us to safety, and the other to destruction. We were utterly perplexed, till suddenly it struck Good that when I had lit the match the draught of the passage blew the flame to the left.

"Let us go against the draught," he said; "air draws inward, not outward."

We took this suggestion, and, feeling along the wall with the hand, while trying the ground before at every step, we departed from that accursed treasure-chamber on our terrible quest. If ever it should be entered again by living man, which I do not think it will be, he will find a token of our presence in the open chests of jewels, the empty lamp, and the white bones of poor Foulata.

When we had groped our way for about a quarter of an hour along the passage it suddenly took a sharp turn, or else was bisected by another, which we followed, only in course of time to be led into a third. And so it went on for some hours. We seemed to be in a stone labyrinth which led nowhere. What all these passages are, of course I cannot say, but we thought that they must be the ancient workings of a mine, of which the various shafts travelled hither and thither as the ore led them. This is the only way in which we could account for such a multitude of passages.

At length we halted, thoroughly worn out with fatigue, and with that hope deferred which maketh the heart sick, and ate up our poor remaining piece of biltong, and drank our last sup of water, for our throats were like lime-kilns. It seemed to us that we had escaped Death in the darkness of the chamber only to meet him in the darkness of the tunnels.

As we stood, once more utterly depressed, I thought I caught a sound, to which I called the attention of the others. It was very faint and very far off, but it *was* a sound, a faint, murmuring sound, for the others heard it too, and no words can describe the blessedness of it after all those hours of utter, awful stillness.

"By Heaven! it's running water," said Good. "Come on."

Off we started again in the direction from which the faint murmur seemed to come, groping our way as before along the rocky walls. As we went it got more and more audible, till at last it seemed quite loud in the quiet. On, yet on; now we could distinctly make out the unmistakable swirl of rushing water. And yet how could there be running water in the bowels of the earth? Now we were quite near to it, and Good, who was leading, swore that he could smell it.

"Go gently, Good," said Sir Henry, "we must be close." *Splash!* and a cry from Good.

He had fallen in.

"Good! Good! where are you?" we shouted, in terrified distress. To our intense relief, an answer came back in a choky voice.

"All right; I've got hold of a rock. Strike a light to show me where you are."

Hastily I lit the last remaining match. Its faint gleam discovered to us a dark mass of water running at our feet. How wide it was we could not see, but there, some way out, was the dark form of our companion, hanging on to a projecting rock.

"Stand clear to catch me," sung out Good. "I must swim for it."

Then we heard a splash and a great struggle. Another minute and he had grabbed at and caught Sir Henry's outstretched hand,

and we had pulled him high and dry into the tunnel.

"My word!" he said, between his gasps, "that was touch and go. If I hadn't caught that rock, and known how to swim, I should have been done. It runs like a mill-race, and I could feel no bottom."

It was clear that this would not do; so after Good had rested a little, and we had drunk our fill from the water of the subterranean river, which was sweet and fresh, and washed our faces, which sadly needed it, as well as we could, we started from the banks of this African Styx, and began to retrace our steps along the tunnel, Good dripping unpleasantly in front of us. At length we came to another tunnel leading to our right.

"We may as well take it," said Sir Henry, wearily; "all roads are alike here; we can only go on till we drop."

Slowly, for a long, long while, we stumbled, utterly weary, along this new tunnel, Sir Henry leading now.

Suddenly he stopped, and we bumped up against him.

"Look!" he whispered, "is my brain going, or is that light?"

We stared with all our eyes, and there, yes, there, far ahead of us, was a faint glimmering spot, no larger than a cottage window-pane. It was so faint that I doubt if any eyes, except those which, like ours, had for days seen nothing but blackness, could have perceived it at all.

With a sort of gasp of hope we pushed on. In five minutes there was no longer any doubt: it *was* a patch of faint light. A minute more and a breath of real live air was fanning us. On we struggled. All at once the tunnel narrowed. Sir Henry went on his knees. Smaller yet it grew, till it was only the size of a large fox's earth—it was *earth* now, mind you; the rock had ceased.

A squeeze, a struggle, and Sir Henry was out, and so was Good, and so was I, and there above us were the blessed stars, and in our nostrils was the sweet air; then suddenly something gave, and we were all rolling over and over and over through grass and bushes, and soft, wet soil.

I caught at something and stopped. Sitting up, I hallooed lustily. An answering shout came from just below, where Sir Henry's wild career had been stopped by some level ground. I scrambled to him, and found him unhurt, though breathless. Then we looked for Good. A little way off we found him, too, jammed in a forked root. He was a good deal knocked about, but soon came to.

We sat down together there on the grass, and the revulsion of feeling was so great that I really think we cried for joy. We had escaped from that awful dungeon, that was so near to becoming our grave. Surely some merciful Power must have guided our footsteps to the jackal-hole at the termination of the tunnel (for that is what it must have been). And see, there on the mountains, the dawn we had never thought to look upon again was blushing rosy red.

Presently the gray light stole down the slopes, and we saw that we were at the bottom, or, rather, nearly at the bottom, of the vast pit in front of the entrance to the cave. Now we could make out the dim forms of the three colossi who sat upon its verge. Doubtless those awful passages, along which we had wandered the livelong night, had originally been, in some way, connected with the great diamond mine. As for the subterranean river in the bowels of the mountain, Heaven only knows what it was, or whence it flows, or whither it goes. I, for one, have no anxiety to trace its course.

Lighter it grew, and lighter yet. We could see each other now, and such a spectacle as we presented I have never set eyes on before or since. Gaunt-cheeked, hollow-eyed wretches, smeared all over with dust and mud, bruised, bleeding, the long fear of imminent death yet written on our countenances, we were, indeed, a sight to frighten the daylight. And yet it is a solemn fact that Good's eye-glass was still fixed in Good's eye. I doubt whether he had ever taken it out at all. Neither the darkness, nor the plunge in the subterranean river, nor the roll down the slope, had been able to separate Good and his eye-glass.

Presently we rose, fearing that our limbs would stiffen if we stopped there longer, and commenced with slow and painful steps to struggle up the sloping sides of the great pit. For an hour or more we toiled steadfastly up the blue clay, dragging ourselves on by the help of the roots and grasses with which it was clothed.

At last it was done, and we stood on the great road, on the side of the pit opposite to the colossi.

By the side of the road, a hundred yards off, a fire was burning in front of some huts, and round the fire were figures. We made towards them, supporting one another, and halting every few paces. Presently, one of the figures rose, saw us, and fell on to the ground, crying out for fear.

"Infadoos, Infadoos! it is us, thy friends."

We rose; he ran to us, staring wildly, and still shaking with fear.

"Oh, my lords, my lords, it is indeed you come back from the dead!—come back from the dead!"

And the old warrior flung himself down before us, and clasped Sir Henry's knees, and wept aloud for joy.

CHAPTER XIX.

IGNOSI'S FAREWELL.

TEN days from that eventful morning found us once more in our old quarters at Loo; and, strange to say, but little the worse for our terrible experience, except that my stubbly hair came out of that cave about three shades grayer than it went in, and that Good never was quite the same after Foulata's death, which seemed to move him very greatly. I am bound to say that, looking at the thing from the point of view of an oldish man of the world, I consider her removal was a fortunate occurrence, since, otherwise, complications would have been sure to ensue. The poor creature was no ordinary native girl, but a person of great, I had almost said stately, beauty, and of considerable refinement of mind. But no amount of beauty or refinement could have made an entanglement between Good and herself a desirable occurrence; for, as she herself put it, "Can the sun mate with the darkness, or the white with the black?"

I need hardly state that we never again penetrated into Solomon's treasure-chamber. After we had recovered from our fatigues, a process which took us forty-eight hours, we descended into the great pit in the hope of finding the hole by which we had crept out of the mountain, but with no success. To begin with, rain had fallen, and obliterated our spoor; and what is more, the sides of the vast pit were full of ant-bear and other holes. It was impossible to say to which of these we owed our salvation. We also, on the day before we started back to Loo, made a further examination of the wonders of the stalactite cave, and, drawn by a kind of restless feeling, even penetrated once more into the Chamber of the Dead; and, passing beneath the spear of the white Death, gazed, with sensations which it would be quite impossible for me to describe, at the mass of rock which had shut us off from escape, thinking, the while, of the priceless treasures beyond, of the mysterious old hag whose flattened fragments lay crushed beneath it, and of the fair girl of whose tomb it was the portal. I say gazed at the "rock," for examine as we would we could find no traces of the join of the sliding door; nor, indeed, could we hit upon the secret, now utterly lost, that worked it, though we tried for an hour or more. It was certainly a marvellous bit of mechanism, characteristic, in its massive and yet inscrutable simplicity, of the age which produced it; and I doubt if the world has such another to show.

At last we gave it up in disgust; though, if the mass had suddenly risen before our eyes, I doubt if we should have screwed up courage to step over Gagool's mangled remains and once more enter the treasure-chamber, even in the sure and certain hope of unlimited diamonds. And yet I could have cried at the idea of leaving all that treasure, the biggest treasure probably that has ever in the world's history been accumulated in one spot. But there was no help for it. Only dynamite could force its way through five feet of solid rock. And so we left it. Perhaps, in some remote unborn century, a more fortunate explorer may hit upon the "Open Sesame," and flood the world with gems. But, myself, I doubt it. Somehow, I seem to feel that the millions of pounds' worth of gems that lie in the three stone coffers will never shine round the neck of an earthly beauty. They and Foulata's bones will keep cold company till the end of all things.

With a sigh of disappointment we made our way back, and next day started for Loo. And yet it was really very ungrateful of us to be disappointed; for, as the reader will remember, I had, by a lucky thought, taken the precaution to fill the pockets of my old shooting-coat with gems before we left our prison-house. A good many of these fell out in the course of our roll down the side of the pit, including most of the big ones, which I had crammed in on the top. But, comparatively speaking, an enormous quantity still remained, including eighteen large stones ranging from about one hundred to thirty carats in weight. My old shooting-coat still held enough treasure to make us all, if not millionaires, at least exceedingly wealthy men, and yet to keep enough stones each to make the three finest sets of gems in Europe. So we had not done so badly.

On arriving at Loo we were most cordially received by Ignosi, whom we found well, and busily engaged in consolidating his power and reorganizing the regiments which had suffered most in the great struggle with Twala.

He listened with breathless interest to our wonderful story; but when we told him of old Gagool's frightful end, he grew thoughtful.

"Come hither," he called, to a very old Induna (councillor), who was sitting with the others in a circle round the king, but out of ear-shot. The old man rose, approached, saluted, and seated himself.

"Thou art old," said Ignosi.

"Ay, my lord the king!"

"Tell me, when thou was little, didst thou know Gagool, the witch doctress?"

"Ay, my lord the king!"

"How was she then—young, like thee?"

"Not so, my lord, the king! She was even as now; old and dried, very ugly, and full of wickedness."

"She is no more; she is dead."

"So, O king! then is a curse taken from the land."

"Go!"

"*Koom!* I go, black puppy, who tore out the old dog's throat. *Koom!*"

"Ye see, my brothers," said Ignosi, "this was a strange woman, and I rejoice that she is dead. She would have let ye die in the dark place, and mayhap afterwards she had found a way to slay me, as she found a way to slay my father and set up Twala, whom her heart loved, in his place. Now go on with the tale; surely there never was the like!"

After I had narrated all the story of our escape, I, as we had agreed between ourselves that I should, took the opportunity to address Ignosi as to our departure from Kukuanaland.

"And now, Ignosi, the time has come for us to bid thee farewell, and start to seek once more our own land. Behold, Ignosi, with us thou camest a servant, and now we leave thee a mighty king. If thou art grateful to us, remember to do even as thou didst promise; to rule justly, to respect the law, and to put none to death without a cause. So shalt thou prosper. To-morrow, at break of day, Ignosi, wilt thou give us an escort who shall lead us across the mountains? Is it not so, O king?"

Ignosi covered his face with his hands for a while before answering.

"My heart is sore," he said at last; "your words split my heart in twain. What have I done to ye, Incubu, Macumazahn, and Bougwan, that ye should leave me desolate? Ye who stood by me in rebellion and battle, will ye leave me in the day of peace and victory? What will ye—wives? Choose from out the land! A place to live in? Behold, the land is yours as far as ye can see. The white man's houses? Ye shall teach my people how to build them. Cattle for beef and milk? Every married man shall bring ye an ox or a cow. Wild game to hunt? Does not the elephant walk through my forests, and the river-horse sleep in the reeds? Would ye make war? My Impis (regiments) wait your word. If there is anything more that I can give, that will I give ye."

"Nay, Ignosi, we want not these things," I answered; "we would seek our own place."

"Now do I perceive," said Ignosi, bitterly, and with flashing eyes, "that it is the bright stones that ye love more than me, your friend. Ye have the stones; now would ye go to Natal and across the black water and sell them, and be rich, as it is the desire of a white man's heart to be. Cursed for your sake be the stones, and cursed be he who seeks them. Death shall it be to him who sets foot in the Place of Death to seek them. I have spoken, white men; ye can go."

I laid my hand upon his arm. "Ignosi," I said, "tell us, when thou didst wander in Zululand, and among the white men in Natal, did not thine heart turn to the land thy mother told thee of, thy native land, where thou didst see the light, and play when thou wast little, the land where thy place was?"

"It was even so, Macumazahn."

"Then thus does our heart turn to our land and to our own place."

Then came a pause. When Ignosi broke it, it was in a different voice.

"I do perceive that thy words are, now as ever, wise and full of reason, Macumazahn; that which flies in the air loves not to run along the ground; the white man loves not to live on the level of the black. Well, ye must go, and leave my heart sore, because ye will be as dead to me, since from where ye will be no tidings can come to me.

"But listen, and let all the white men know my words. No other white man shall cross the mountains, even if any may live to come so far. I will see no traders with their guns and rum. My people shall fight with the spear and drink water, like their forefathers before them. I will have no praying-men to put fear of death into men's hearts, to stir them up against the king, and make a path for the white men who follow to run on. If a white man comes to my gates I will send him back; if a hundred come, I will push them back; if an army comes, I will make war on them with all my strength, and they shall not prevail against me. None shall ever come for the shining stones; no, not an army, for if they come I will send a regiment and fill up the pit, and break down the white columns in the caves and fill them with rocks, so that none can come even to that door of which ye speak, and whereof the way to move it is lost. But for ye three, Incubu, Macuma-zahn, and Bougwan, the path is always open; for behold, ye are dearer to me than aught that breathes.

"And ye would go. Infadoos, my uncle, and my Induna, shall take thee by the hand and guide thee, with a regiment. There is, as I have learned, another way across the mountains that he shall show ye. Farewell, my brothers, brave white men. See me no more, for I have no heart to bear it. Behold, I make a decree, and it shall be published from the mountains to the mountains, your names, Incubu, Macumazahn, and Bougwan, shall be as the names of dead kings, and he who speaks them shall die.* So shall your memory be preserved in the land forever.

"Go now, ere my eyes rain tears like a woman's. At times when ye look back down the path of life, or when ye are old and gather yourselves together to crouch before the fire, because the sun has no more heat, ye will think of how we stood shoulder to shoulder in that great battle that thy wise words planned, Macumazahn; of how thou wast the point of that horn that galled Twala's flank, Bougwan; whilst thou stoodst in the ring of the Grays, Incubu, and men went down before thine axe like corn before a sickle; ay, and of how thou didst break the wild bull's (Twala's) strength, and bring his pride to dust. Fare ye well forever, Incubu, Macumazahn, and Bougwan, my lords and my friends."

He rose, looked earnestly at us for a few seconds, and then threw the corner of his kaross over his head, so as to cover his face from us.

We went in silence.

Next day at dawn we left Loo, escorted by our old friend Infadoos, who was heart-broken at our departure, and the regiment of Buffaloes. Early as the hour was, all the main street of the town was lined with multitudes of people, who gave us the royal salute as we passed at the head of the regiment, while the women blessed us as having rid the land of Twala, throwing flowers before us as we went. It really was very affecting, and not the sort of thing one is accustomed to meet with from natives.

One very ludicrous incident occurred, however, which I rather welcomed, as it gave us something to laugh at.

Just as we got to the confines of the town a pretty young girl, with some beautiful lilies in her hand, came running forward and presented them to Good (somehow they all seemed to like Good; I think his eye-glass and solitary whisker gave him a fictitious value), and then said she had a boon to ask.

"Speak on."

"Let my lord show his servant his beautiful white legs, that his servant may look on them, and remember them all her days, and tell of them to her children; his servant has travelled four days' journey to see them, for the fame of them has gone throughout the land."

"I'll be hanged if I do!" said Good, excitedly.

*This extraordinary and negative way of showing intense respect is by no means unknown among African people, and the result is that if, as is usual, the name in question has a significance, the meaning has to be expressed by an idiom or another word. In this way a memory is preserved for generations, or until the new word supplants the old one.

"Come, come, my dear fellow," said Sir Henry, "you can't refuse to oblige a lady."

"I won't," said Good, obstinately; "it is positively indecent."

However, in the end he consented to draw up his trousers to the knee, amidst notes of rapturous admiration from all the women present, especially the gratified young lady, and in this guise he had to walk till we got clear of the town.

Good's legs will, I fear, never be so greatly admired again. Of his melting teeth, and even of his "transparent eye," they wearied more or less, but of his legs, never.

As we travelled, Infadoos told us that there was another pass over the mountains to the north of the one followed by Solomon's Great Road, or rather that there was a place where it was possible to climb down the wall of cliff that separated Kukuanaland from the desert, and was broken by the towering shapes of Sheba's breasts. It appeared, too, that rather more than two years previously a party of Kukuana hunters had descended this path into the desert in search of ostriches, whose plumes were much prized among them for war head-dresses, and that in the course of their hunt they had been led far from the mountains, and were much troubled by thirst. Seeing, however, trees on the horizon, they made towards them, and discovered a large and fertile oasis of some miles in extent, and plentifully watered. It was by way of this oasis that he suggested that we should return, and the idea seemed to us a good one, as it appeared that we should escape the rigors of the mountain pass, and as some of the hunters were in attendance to guide us to the oasis, from which, they stated, they could perceive more fertile spots far away in the desert.*

Travelling easily, on the night of the fourth day's journey we found ourselves once more on the crest of the mountains that separate Kukuanaland from the desert, which rolled away in sandy billows at our feet, and about twenty-five miles to the north of Sheba's breasts.

At dawn on the following day we were led to the commencement of a precipitous descent, by which we were to descend the

---

*It often puzzled all of us to understand how it was possible that Ignosi's mother, bearing the child with her, should have survived the dangers of the journey across the mountains and the desert, dangers which so nearly proved fatal to ourselves. It has since occurred to me, and I give the idea to the reader for what it is worth, that she must have taken this second route, and wandered out like Hagar into the desert. If she did so, there is no longer anything inexplicable about the story, since she may well, as Ignosi himself related, have been picked up by some ostrich-hunters before she or the child were exhausted, and led by them to the oasis, and thence by stages to the fertile country, and so on by slow degrees southward to Zululand.—A. Q.

precipice, and gain the desert two thousand and more feet below.

Here we bade farewell to that true friend and sturdy old warrior, Infadoos, who solemnly wished all good upon us, and nearly wept with grief. "Never, my lords," he said, "shall mine old eyes see the like of ye again. Ah! the way that Incubu cut his men down in the battle! Ah! for the sight of that stroke with which he swept off my brother Twala's head! It was beautiful—beautiful! I may never hope to see such another, except perchance in happy dreams."

We were very sorry to part from him; indeed, Good was so moved that he gave him as a souvenir—what do you think?—an *eye-glass*. (Afterwards we discovered that it was a spare one.) Infadoos was delighted, foreseeing that the possession of such an article would enormously increase his prestige, and after several vain attempts actually succeeded in screwing it into his own eye. Anything more incongruous than the old warrior looked with an eye-glass I never saw. Eye-glasses don't go well with leopard-skin cloaks and black ostrich plumes.

Then, having seen that our guides were well laden with water and provisions, and having received a thundering farewell salute from the Buffaloes, we wrung the old warrior's hand, and began our downward climb. A very arduous business it proved to be, but somehow that evening we found ourselves at the bottom without accident.

"Do you know," said Sir Henry that night, as we sat by our fire and gazed up at the beetling cliffs above us, "I think that there are worse places than Kukuanaland in the world, and that I have spent unhappier times than the last month or two, though I have never spent such queer ones. Eh! you fellows?"

"I almost wish I were back," said Good, with a sigh.

As for myself, I reflected that all's well that ends well; but in the course of a long life of shaves I never had such shaves as those I had recently experienced. The thought of that battle still makes me feel cold all over, and as for our experience in the treasure-chamber—!

Next morning we started on a toilsome march across the desert, having with us a good supply of water carried by our five guides, and camped that night in the open, starting again at dawn on the morrow.

By midday of the third day's journey we could see the trees of the oasis of which the guides spoke, and by an hour before sundown we were once more walking upon grass and listening to the sound of running water.

CHAPTER XX.

FOUND.

And now I come to perhaps the strangest thing that happened to us in all that strange business, and one which shows how wonderfully things are brought about.

I was walking quietly along, some way in front of the other two, down the banks of the stream which ran from the oasis till it was swallowed up in the hungry desert sands, when suddenly I stopped and rubbed my eyes, as well I might. There, not twenty yards in front, placed in a charming situation, under the shade of a species of fig-tree, and facing to the stream, was a cosey hut, built more or less on the Kaffir principle of grass and withes, only with a full-length door instead of a bee-hole.

"What the dickens," said I to myself, "can a hut be doing here!" Even as I said it, the door of the hut opened, and there limped out of it *a white man* clothed in skins, and with an enormous black beard. I thought that I must have got a touch of the sun. It was impossible. No hunter ever came to such a place as this. Certainly no hunter would ever settle in it. I stared and stared, and so did the other man, and just at that juncture Sir Henry and Good came up.

"Look here, you fellows," I said, "is that a white man, or am I mad?"

Sir Henry looked, and Good looked, and then all of a sudden the lame white man with the black beard gave a great cry, and came hobbling towards us. When he got close he fell down in a sort of faint.

With a spring Sir Henry was by his side.

"Great Powers!" he cried, *"it is my brother George!"*

At the sound of the disturbance another figure, also clad in skins, emerged from the hut with a gun in his hand, and came running towards us. On seeing me he too gave a cry.

"Macumazahn," he hallooed, "don't you know me, Baas? I'm Jim, the hunter. I lost the note you gave me to give to the Baas, and we have been here nearly two years." And the fellow fell at my feet and rolled over and over, weeping for joy.

"You careless scoundrel!" I said; "you ought to be well hided."

Meanwhile the man with the black beard had recovered and got up, and he and Sir Henry were pump-handling away at each other, apparently without a word to say. But whatever they had quarreled about in the past (I suspect it was a lady, though I never asked), it was evidently forgotten now.

"My dear old fellow," burst out Sir Henry at last, "I thought that you were dead. I have been over Solomon's Mountains to find you, and now I come across you perched in the desert, like an old Aasvögel (vulture)."

"I tried to go over Solomon's Mountains nearly two years ago," was the answer, spoken in the hesitating voice of a man who has had little recent opportunity of using his tongue, "but when I got here, a boulder fell on my leg and crushed it, and I have been able to go neither forward nor back."

Then I came up. "How do you do, Mr. Neville?" I said; "do you remember me?"

"Why," he said, "isn't it Quatermain, eh, and Good, too? Hold on a minute, you fellows, I am getting dizzy again. It is all so very strange, and, when a man has ceased to hope, so very happy."

That evening, over the camp-fire, George Curtis told us his story, which, in its way, was almost as eventful as our own, and amounted, shortly, to this. A little short of two years before, he had started from Sitanda's Kraal, to try and reach the mountains. As for the note I had sent him by Jim, that worthy had lost it, and he had never heard of it till to-day. But, acting upon information he had received from the natives, he made, not for Sheba's breasts, but for the ladder-like descent of the mountains down which we had just come, which was clearly a better route than that marked out in old Don Silvestra's plan. In the desert he and Jim suffered great hardships, but finally they reached this oasis, where a terrible accident befell George Curtis. On the day of their arrival he was sitting by the stream, and Jim was extracting the honey from the nest of a stingless bee, which is to be found in the desert, on the top of the bank immediately above him. In so doing he loosed a great boulder of rock, which fell upon George Curtis's right leg, crushing it frightfully. From that day he had been so dreadfully lame that he had found it impossible to go either forward or back, and had preferred to take the chances of dying on the oasis to the certainty of perishing in the desert.

As for food, however, they had got on pretty well, for they had a good supply of ammunition, and the oasis was frequented, especially at night, by large quantities of game, which came thither for water. These they shot, or trapped in pitfalls, using their flesh for food and, after their clothes wore out, their hides for covering.

"And so," he ended, "we have lived for nearly two years, like a second Robinson Crusoe and his man Friday, hoping against hope that some natives might come here and help us away, but none have come. Only last night we settled that Jim should leave me and try to reach Sitanda's Kraal and get assistance. He was to go to-morrow, but I had little hope of ever seeing him back again. And now *you*, of all the people in the world, *you* who I fancied had long ago forgotten all about me, and were living comfortably in old England, turn up in a promiscuous way and find me where you least expected. It is the most wonderful thing I ever heard of, and the most merciful, too."

Then Sir Henry set to work and told him the main facts of our adventures, sitting till late into the night to do it.

"By Jove!" he said, when I showed him some of the diamonds; "well, at least you have got something for your pains, besides my worthless self."

Sir Henry laughed. "They belong to Quatermain and Good. It was part of the bargain that they should share any spoils there might be."

This remark set me thinking, and, having spoken to Good, I told Sir Henry that it was our unanimous wish that he should take a third share of the diamonds, or, if he would not, that his share should be handed to his brother, who had suffered even more than ourselves on the chance of getting them. Finally, we prevailed upon him to consent to this arrangement, but George Curtis did not know of it till some time afterwards.

And here, at this point, I think I shall end this history. Our journey across the desert back to Sitanda's Kraal was most arduous, especially as we had to support George Curtis, whose right leg was very weak indeed, and continually throwing out splinters of bone; but we did accomplish it, somehow, and to give its details would only be to reproduce much of what happened to us on the former occasion.

Six months from the date of our re-arrival at Sitanda's, where we found our guns and other goods quite safe, though the old scoundrel in charge was much disgusted at our surviving to claim them, saw us all once more safe and sound at my little place on the Berea, near Durban, where I am now writing, and whence I bid farewell to all who have accompanied me throughout the strangest trip I ever made in the course of a long and varied experience.

Just as I had written the last word a Kaffir came up my avenue of orange-trees, with a letter in a cleft stick, which he had brought from the post. It turned out to be from Sir Henry, and, as it speaks for itself, I give it in full.

"BRAYLEY HALL, YORKSHIRE.

"MY DEAR QUATERMAN,—I sent you a line a few mails back to say that the three of us, George, Good, and myself, fetched up all right in England. We got off the boat at Southampton, and went up to town. You should have seen what a swell Good turned out the very next day, beautifully shaved, frock coat fitting like a glove, brand-new eye-glass, etc., etc. I went and walked in the park with him, where I met some people I know, and at once told them the story of his 'beautiful white legs.'

"He is furious, especially as some ill-natured person has printed it in a society paper.

"To come to business, Good and I took the diamonds to Streeter's to be valued, as we arranged, and I am really afraid to tell you what they put them at, it seems so enormous. They say that of course it is more or less guess-work, as such stones have never to their knowledge been put on the market in anything like such quantities. It appears that they are (with the exception of one or two of the largest) of the finest water, and equal in every way to the best Brazilian stones. I asked them if they would buy them, but they said that it was beyond their power to do so, and recommended us to sell by degrees, for fear we should flood the market. They offer, however, a hundred and eighty thousand for a small portion of them.

"You must come home, Quartermain, and see about these things, especially if you insist upon making the magnificent present of the third share, which does *not* belong to me, to my brother George. As for Good, he is *no good.* His time is too much occupied in shaving, and other matters connected with the vain adorning of his body. But I think he is still down on his luck about Foulata. He told me that since he had been home he hadn't seen a woman to touch her, either as regards her figure or the sweetness of her expression.

"I want you to come home, my dear old comrade, and buy a place near here. You have done your day's work, and have lots of money now, and there is a place for sale quite close which would suit you admirably. Do come; the sooner the better; you can finish writing the story of our adventures on board ship. We have refused to tell the story till it is written by you, for fear that we shall not be believed. If you start on receipt of this you will reach here by Christmas, and I book you to stay with me for that. Good is coming, and George, and so, by the way, is your boy Harry (there's a bribe for you). I have had him down for a week's shooting, and like him. He is a cool young hand; he shot me in the leg, cut out the pellets, and then remarked upon the advantage of having a medical student in every shooting party.

"Good-bye, old boy; I can't say any more, but I know that you will come, if it is only to oblige your sincere friend,   HENRY CURTIS.

"P.S.—The tusks of the great bull that killed poor Khiva have now been put up in the hall here, over the pair of buffalo-horns you gave me, and look magnificent; and the axe with which I chopped off Twala's head is stuck up over my writing-table. I wish we could have managed to bring away the coats of chain armor.   H. C."

To-day is Tuesday. There is a steamer going on Friday, and I really think I must take Curtis at his word, and sail by her for England, if it is only to see my boy Harry and see about the printing of this history, which is a task I do not like to trust to anybody else.

THE END.

ALLAN QUATERMAIN

INTRODUCTION.

'I have just buried my boy, my handsome boy of whom I was so proud, and my heart is broken. It is very hard having only one son to lose him thus, but God's will be done. Who am I that I should complain? The great wheel of Fate rolls on like a Juggernaut, and crushes us all in turn, some soon, some late—it does not matter when, in the end it crushes us all. We do not prostrate ourselves before it like the poor Indians; we fly hither and thither —we cry for mercy; but it is of no use, the black Fate thunders on and in its season reduces us to powder.

'Poor Harry to go so soon! just when his life was opening to him. He was doing so well at the hospital, he had passed his last examination with honours, and I was proud of them, much prouder than he was, I think. And then he must needs go to that small-pox hospital. He wrote to me that he was not afraid of small-pox and wanted to gain the experience; and now the disease has killed him, and I, old and grey and withered, am left to mourn over him, without a chick or child to comfort me. I might have saved him, too—I have money enough for both of us, and much more than enough—King Solomon's Mines provided me with that; but I said, "No, let the boy earn his living, let him labour that he may enjoy rest." But the rest has come to him before the labour. Oh, my boy, my boy!

'I am like the man in the Bible who laid up much goods and builded barns—goods for my boy and barns for him to store them in; and now his soul has been required of him, and I am left desolate. I would that it had been my soul and not my boy's!

'We buried him this afternoon under the shadow of the grey and ancient tower of the church of this village where my house is. It was a dreary December afternoon, and the sky was heavy with snow, but not much was falling. The coffin was put down by the grave, and a few big flakes lit upon it. They looked very white upon the black cloth! There was a little hitch about getting the coffin down into the grave—the necessary ropes had been forgotten: so we drew back from it, and waited in silence watching the big flakes fall gently one by one like heavenly benedictions to melt in tears on Harry's pall. But that was not all. A robin redbreast came as bold as could be and lit upon the coffin and began to sing. And then I am afraid that I broke down, and so did Sir Henry Curtis, strong man though he is; and as for Cap-

417

tain Good, I saw him turn away too; even in my own distress I could not help noticing it.'

The above, signed 'Allan Quatermain,' is an extract from my diary written two years and more ago. I copy it down here because it seems to me that it is the fittest beginning to the history which I am about to write, if it please God to spare me to finish it. If not, well it does not matter. That extract was penned seven thousand miles or so from the spot where I now lie painfully and slowly write this, with a pretty girl standing by my side fanning the flies from my august countenance. Harry is there and I am here, and yet somehow I cannot help feeling that I am not far from Harry.

When I was in England I used to live in a very fine house—at least I call it a fine house, speaking comparatively, and judging by the standard of the houses I have been accustomed to all my life in Africa—not five hundred yards from the old church where Harry is asleep, and thither I went after the funeral and ate some food; for it is no good starving even if one has just buried all one's earthly hopes. But I could not eat much, and soon I took to walking, or rather limping—being permanently lame from the bite of a lion—up and down, up and down the oak-panelled vestibule; for there is a vestibule in my house in England. On the four walls of this vestibule were placed pairs of horns—about a hundred pairs altogether, all of which I had shot myself. They are beautiful specimens, as I never keep any horns which are not in every way perfect, unless it may be now and again on account of the associations connected with them. In the centre of this room, however, over the wide fireplace, there was a clear space left on which I had fixed up all my rifles. Some of them I have had for forty years, old muzzle-loaders that nobody would look at nowadays. One was an elephant gun with strips of rimpi, or green hide, lashed round the stock and locks, such as used to be owned by the Dutchmen—a 'roer' they call it. The Boer I bought it from many years ago told me that gun had been used by his father at the battle of the Blood River, just after Dingaan swept into Natal and slaughtered six hundred men, women, and children. Then the Boers named the place where they died 'Weenen,' or the 'Place of Weeping;' and so it is called to this day, and always will be called. And many an elephant have I shot with that old gun. She always took a handful of black powder and a three-ounce ball, and kicked like the very deuce.

Well, up and down I walked, staring at the guns and the horns which the guns had brought low; and as I did so there rose up in me a great craving:—I would go away from this place where I lived idly and at ease, back again to the wild land where I had spent my life, where I met my dear wife and poor Harry was born, and so many things, good, bad, and indifferent had happened to me. The thirst for the wilderness was on me; I could tolerate this place no more; I would go and die as I had lived, among the wild game and the savages. Yes, as I walked, I began to long to see the moonlight gleaming silvery white over the wide veldt and mysterious sea of bush, and watch the lines of game travelling down the ridges to the water. The ruling passion is strong in death, they say, and my heart was dead that night. But, independently of my trouble, no man who has for forty years lived the life I have, can with impunity go coop himself in this prim English country, with its trim hedgerows and cultivated fields, its stiff formal manners, and its well-dressed crowds. He begins to long—ah, how he longs!—for the keen breath of the desert air; he dreams of the sight of Zulu impis breaking on their foes like surf upon the rocks, and his heart arises in rebellion against the strict limits of the civilised life.

Ah! this civilisation, what does it all come to? Full forty years and more I spent among savages, and studied them and their ways; and now for several years I have lived here in England, and in my own stupid manner have done my best to learn the ways of the children of light; and what do I find? A great gulf fixed? No, only a very little one, that a plain man's thought may spring across. I say that as the savage is, so is the white man, only the latter is more inventive, and possesses a faculty of combination; save and except also that the savage, as I have known him, is to a large extent free from the greed of money, which eats like a cancer into the heart of the white man. It is a depressing conclusion, but in all essentials the savage and the child of civilisation are identical. I dare to say that the highly civilised lady reading this will smile at an old fool of a hunter's simplicity when she thinks of her black bead-bedecked sister; and so will the superfine cultured idler scientifically eating a dinner at his club, the cost of which would keep a starving family for a week. And yet, my dear young lady, what are those pretty things round your own neck?—they have a strong family resemblance, especially when you wear that *very* low dress, to the savage woman's beads. Your habit of turning round and round to the sound of horns and tom-toms, your fondness for pigments and powders, the way in which you love to subjugate yourself to the rich warrior who has captured you in marriage, and the quickness with which your taste in feathered headdresses varies,—all these things suggest touches of kinship; and remember that in the fundamental principles of your nature you are quite identical. As for you, sir, who also laugh, let some man come and strike you in the face whilst you are enjoying that marvellous-looking dish, and we shall soon see how much of the savage there is in *you.*

There, I might go on for ever, but what is the good? Civilisation is only savagery silver-gilt. A vainglory is it, and, like a northern light, comes but to fade and leave the sky more dark. Out of the soil of barbarism it has grown like a tree, and, as I believe, into the soil like a tree, sooner or later, it will once more fall again, as the Egyptian civilisation fell, as the Hellenic civilisation fell, and as the Roman civilisation and maybe others of which the world has now lost count, fell also. Do not let me, however be understood as decrying our modern institutions, representing as they do the gathered experience of humanity applied for the good of all. Of course they have great advantages—hospitals for instance; but then, remember, we breed the sickly people who fill them. In a savage land they do not exist. Besides, the question will arise: How many of these blessings are due to Christianity as distinct from civilisation? And so the balance sways and the story runs—here a gain, there a loss, and Nature's great average struck across the two, whereof the sum total forms one of the factors in that mighty equation in which the result will equal the unknown quantity of her purpose.

I make no apology for this digression, especially as this is an introduction which all young people and those who never like to think (and it is a bad habit) will naturally skip. It seems to me very desirable that we should sometimes try to understand the limitations of our nature, so that we may not be carried away by the pride of knowledge. Man's cleverness is almost infinite, and stretches like an elastic band, but human nature is like an iron ring. You can go round and round it, you can polish it highly, you can even flatten it a little on one side, whereby you will make it bulge out on the other, but you will *never*, while the world endures and man is man, increase its total circumference. It is the one fixed unchangeable thing—fixed as the stars, more enduring than the mountains, unalterable as the way of the Eternal. Human nature is God's kaleidoscope, and the little bits of coloured glass which represent our passions, hopes, fears, joys, aspirations towards good and evil and what not, are turned in His mighty hand as surely and certainly as it turns the stars, to fall continually into new patterns and combinations. But the composing elements remain the same, nor will there be one more bit of coloured glass nor one less for ever and ever.

This being so, supposing for the sake of argument we divide ourselves into twenty parts, nineteen savage and one civilised, we must look to the nineteen savage portions of our nature, if we would really understand ourselves, and not to the twentieth, which, though so insignificant in reality, is spread all over the other nineteen, making them appear quite different from what they really are, as the blacking does a boot, or the veneer a table. It is on the nineteen rough serviceable savage portions that we fall back in emergencies, not on the polished but unsubstantial twentieth. Civilisation should wipe away our tears, and yet we weep and cannot be comforted. Warfare is abhorrent to her, and yet we strike out for hearth and home, for honour and fair fame, and can glory in the blow. And so on, through everything.

So, when the heart is stricken, and the head is humbled in the dust, civilisation fails us utterly. Back, back, we creep, and lay us like children on the great breast of Nature, that she perchance may soothe us and make us forget, or at least rid remembrance of its sting. Who has not in his great grief felt a longing to look upon the outward features of the universal Mother; to lie on the mountains and watch the clouds drive across the sky and hear the rollers break in thunder on the shore, to let his poor struggling life mingle a while with her life; to feel the slow beat of her eternal heart, and to forget his woes, and let his identity be swallowed in the vast imperceptibly moving energy of her in whom we are, from whom we came, and with whom we shall again be mingled, who gave us birth, and in a day to come will give us our burial also.

And so in my trouble, as I walked up and down the oak-panelled vestibule of my house there in Yorkshire, I longed once more to throw myself into the arms of Nature. Not the Nature which you know, the Nature that waves in well-kept woods and smiles out in corn-fields, but Nature as she was in the age when creation was complete, still undefiled by any sinks of struggling, sweltering humanity. I would go again where the wild game was, back to the land whereof none know the history, back to the savages, whom I love, although some of them are almost as merciless as Political Economy. There, perhaps, I should be able to learn to think of poor Harry lying in the churchyard, without feeling as though my heart would break in two.

And now there is an end of this egotistical talk, and there shall be no more of it. But if you whose eyes may perchance one day fall upon my written thoughts have got so far as this, I ask you to persevere, since what I have to tell you is not without its interest, and it has never been told before, nor ever will again.

CHAPTER I.

A WEEK had passed since the funeral of my poor boy Harry, and one evening I was in my room walking up and down and thinking, when there came a ring at the outer door. Going down the steps I opened it myself, and in walked my old friends Sir Henry Curtis and Captain John Good, R. N. They entered the vestibule and sat themselves down before the wide hearth, where, I remember, a particularly good fire of logs was burning.

'It is very kind of you to come round,' I said by way of making a remark; 'it must have been heavy walking in the snow.'

They said nothing, but Sir Henry slowly filled his pipe and lit it with a burning ember. As he leant forward to do so the fire got hold of a gassy bit of pine and flared up brightly, throwing the scene into a strong relief, and I thought, what a splendid-looking man he was. Calm, powerful face, clear-cut features, large grey eyes, yellow beard and hair—altogether a magnificent specimen of the higher type of humanity. Nor did his form belie his face. I have never seen wider shoulders or a deeper chest. Indeed, Sir Henry's girth is so great that, though he is six feet two high, he does not strike one as a tall man. As I looked at him I could not help thinking what a curious contrast my little dried-up self presented to his grand face and form. Imagine to yourself a small, withered, yellow-faced man of sixty-three, with thin hands, large brown eyes, a head of grizzled hair cut short and standing up like a half-worn scrubbing-brush—total weight in his clothes, nine stone six—and you will get a very fair idea of Allan Quatermain, commonly called Hunter Quatermain, or by the natives 'Macumazahn'—Anglicè, he who keeps a bright look-out at night, or, in vulgar English, a sharp fellow who is not to be taken in.

Then there was Good, who is not like either of us, being short, dark, stout—*very* stout—with twinkling black eyes, in one of which an eyeglass is fixed everlastingly. I say stout, but it is a mild term; I regret to state that of late years Good has been running to fat in a most disgraceful way. Sir Henry tells him that it comes from idleness and over-feeding, and Good does not like it at all, though he cannot deny it.

We sat for a while, and then I got a match and lit the lamp that stood ready on the table, for the half-light began to grow dreary, as it is apt to when a short week ago a man has buried the hope of his life. Next, I opened a cupboard in the wainscoting and found a bottle of whisky and some tumblers and water. I always like to do these things for myself: it is irritating to me to have somebody continually at my elbow, as though I were an eighteen-month-old baby. All this while Curtis and Good had been silent, feeling, I suppose, that they had nothing to say that could do me any good, and content to give me the comfort of their presence and unspoken sympathy; for it was only their second visit since the funeral. And it is, by the way, from the fact of the *presence* of others that we really derive support in our dark hours of grief, and not from their talk, which often only serves to irritate us. During a bad storm the game always herd together, but they cease their calling.

They sat and smoked and drank whisky and water, and I stood by the fire also smoking and looking at them.

At last I spoke. 'Old friends,' I said, 'how long is it since we got back from Kukuanaland?'

'Three years,' said Good. 'Why do you ask?'

'I ask because I think that I have had a long enough spell of civilisation. I am going back to the veldt.'

Sir Henry laid his head back in his arm-chair and laughed one of his deep laughs. 'How very odd,' he said, 'eh, Good?'

Good beamed at me mysteriously through his eyeglass and murmured, 'Yes, odd—very odd.'

'I don't quite understand,' said I, looking from one to the other, for I dislike mysteries.

'Don't you, old fellow?' said Sir Henry; 'then I will explain. As Good and I were walking up here we had a talk.'

'If Good was there you probably did,' I put in sarcastically, for Good is a great hand at talking. 'And what may it have been about?'

'What do you think?' asked Sir Henry.

I shook my head. It was not likely that I should know what Good might be talking about. He talks about so many things.

'Well, it was about a little plan that I have formed—namely, that if you were willing we should pack up our traps and go off to Africa on another expedition.'

I fairly jumped at his words. 'You don't say so!' I said.

'Yes, I do, though, and so does Good; don't you Good?'

'Rather,' said that gentleman.

'Listen, old fellow,' went on Sir Henry, with considerable animation of manner. 'I'm tired of it too, dead-tired of doing nothing except play the squire in a country that is sick of squires. For a year or more I have been getting as restless as an old elephant who scents danger. I am always dreaming of Kukuanaland and Gagool and King Solomon's Mines. I can assure you I have become the victim of an almost unaccountable craving. I am sick of shooting pheasants and partridges, and want to have a go at some large game again. There, you know the feeling—when once one has tasted brandy and water, milk becomes insipid to the palate. That year we spent together up in Kukuanaland seems to me worth all the other years of my life put together. I dare say that I am a fool for my pains, but I can't help it; I long to go, and, what is more, I mean to go.' He paused, and then went on again. 'And, after all, why should I not go? I have no wife or parent, no chick or child to keep me. If anything happens to me the baronetcy will go to my brother George and his boy, as ultimately it would do in any case. I am of no importance to any one.'

'Ah!' I said, 'I thought you would come to that sooner or later. And now, Good, what is your reason for wanting to trek; have you got one?'

'I have,' said Good, solemnly. 'I never do anything without a reason; and it isn't a lady—at least, if it is, it's several.'

I looked at him again. Good is so overpoweringly frivolous. 'What is it?' I said.

'Well, if you really want to know, though I'd rather not speak of a delicate and strictly personal matter, I'll tell you: I'm getting too fat.'

'Shut up, Good!' said Sir Henry. 'And now, Quatermain, tell us, where do you propose going to?'

I lit my pipe, which had gone out, before answering.

'Have you people ever heard of Mt. Kenia?' I asked.

'Don't know the place,' said Good.

'Did you ever hear of the Island of Lamu?' I asked again.

'No. Stop, though—isn't it a place about 300 miles north of Zanzibar?'

'Yes. Now listen. What I have to propose is this. That we go to Lamu and thence make our way about 250 miles inland to Mt. Kenia; from Mt. Kenia onwards to Mt. Lekakisera, another 200 miles, or thereabouts, beyond which to the best of my belief no white man has ever been; and then if we get so far, right on into the unknown interior. What do you say to that, my friends?'

'It's a big order,' said Sir Henry, reflectively.

'You are right,' I answered, 'it is; but I take it that we are all three of us in search of a big order. We want a change of scene, and we are likely to get one—a thorough change. All my life I have longed to visit those parts, and I mean to do it before I die. My poor boy's death has broken the last link between me and civilisation, and I'm off to my native wilds. And now I'll tell you another thing, and that is, that for years and years I have heard rumours of a great white race which is supposed to have its home somewhere up in this direction, and I have a mind to see if there is any truth in them. If you fellows like to come, well and good; if not, I'll go alone.'

'I'm your man, though I don't believe in your white race,' said Sir Henry Curtis, rising and placing his arm upon my shoulder.

'Ditto,' remarked Good; 'I'll go into training at once. By all means let's go to Mt. Kenia and the other place with an unpronounceable name, and look for a white race that does not exist. It's all one to me.'

'When do you propose to start?' asked Sir Henry.

'This day month,' I answered, 'by the British India steamboat; and don't you be so certain that things have no existence because you do not happen to have heard of them, Good. Remember King Solomon's Mines!'

.   .   .   .

Some fourteen weeks or so had passed since the date of this conversation, and this history goes on its way in very different surroundings.

After much deliberation and inquiry we came to the conclusion that our best starting-point for Mt. Kenia would be from the neighbourhood of the mouth of the Tana River, and not from Mombasa, a place over 100 miles nearer Zanzibar. This conclusion we arrived at from information given to us by a German trader whom we met upon the steamer at Aden. I think that he was the dirtiest German I ever knew; but he was a good fellow, and gave us a great deal of valuable information. 'Lamu,' said he, 'you goes to Lamu—oh ze beautiful place!' and he turned up his fat face and beamed with mild rapture. 'One year and a half I live there and never change my shirt—never at all.'

And so it came to pass that on arriving at the island we disembarked with all our goods and chattels, and, not knowing where to go, marched boldly up to the house of Her Majesty's Consul, where we were most hospitably received.

Lamu is a very curious place, but the things which stand out most clearly in my memory in connection with it are its exceeding dirtiness and its smells. These last are simply awful. Just below the Consulate is the beach, or rather a mud bank that is called a beach. It is left quite bare at low tide, and serves as a repository for all the filth, offal, and refuse of the town. Here it is, too, that the women come to bury cocoanuts in the mud, leaving them there till the outer husk is quite rotten, when they dig them up again and use the fibres to make mats with, and for various other purposes. As this process has been going on for generations, the condition of the shore can be better imagined than described. I have smelt many evil odours in the course of my life, but the concentrated essence of stench which arose from that beach at Lamu as we sat in the moonlit night—not under, but *on* our friend the Consul's hospitable roof—and sniffed it, makes the remembrance of them very poor and faint. No wonder people get fever at Lamu. And yet the place was not without a certain quaintness and charm of its own, though possibly—indeed probably—it was one which would quickly pall.

'Well, where are you gentlemen steering for?' asked our friend the hospitable Consul, as we smoked our pipes after dinner.

'We propose to go to Mt. Kenia and then on to Mt. Lekakisera,' answered Sir Henry. 'Quatermain has got hold of some yarn about there being a white race up in the unknown territories beyond.'

The Consul looked interested, and answered that he had heard something of that, too.

'What have you heard?' I asked.

'Oh, not much. All I know about it is that a year or so ago I had a letter from Mackenzie, the Scotch missionary, whose station, "The Highlands," is placed at the highest navigable point of the Tana River, in which he said something about it.'

'Have you the letter?' I asked.

'No, I destroyed it; but I remember that he said that a man had arrived at his station who declared that two months' journey beyond Mt. Lekakisera, which no white man has yet visited— at least, so far as I know—he found a lake called Laga, and that then he went off to the north-east, a month's journey, over desert and thorn veldt and great mountains, till he came to a country where the people are white and live in stone houses. Here he was hospitably entertained for a while, till at last the priests of the country set it about that he was a devil, and the people drove him away, and he journeyed for eight months and reached Mackenzie's place, as I heard, dying. That's all I know; and if you ask me, I believe that it is a lie; but if you want to find out more about it, you had better go up the Tana to Mackenzie's place and ask him for information.'

Sir Henry and I looked at each other. Here was something tangible.

'I think that we will go to Mr. Mackenzie's,' I said.

'Well,' answered the Consul, 'that is your best way, but I warn you that you are likely to have a rough journey, for I hear that the Masai are about, and, as you know, they are not pleasant customers. Your best plan will be to choose a few picked men for personal servants and hunters, and to hire bearers from village to village. It will give you an infinity of trouble, but perhaps on the whole it will prove a cheaper and more advantageous course than engaging a caravan, and you will be less liable to desertion '

Fortunately there were at Lamu at this time a party of Wakwafi Askari (soldiers). The Wakwafi, who are a cross between the Masai and the Wataveta, are a fine manly race, possessing many of the good qualities of the Zulu, and a larger capacity for civilisation. They are also great hunters. As it happened, these particular men had recently been on a long trip with an Englishman named Jutson, who had started from Mombasa, a port about 150 miles below Lamu, and journeyed right round Kilimanjairo, one of the highest known mountains in Africa. Poor fellow, ie had died of fever when on his return journey, and within a day's march of Mombasa. It seems most hard that he should have gone off thus when within a few hours of safety, and after having survived so many perils, but so it was. His hunters buried him, and then came on to Lamu in a dhow. Our friend the Consul suggested to us that we had better try to hire these men, and accordingly on the following morning we started to interview the party, accompanied by an interpreter.

In due course we found them in a mud hut on the outskirts of the town. Three of the men were sitting outside the hut, and fine frank-looking fellows they were, having a more or less civilised appearance. To them we cautiously opened the object of our visit, at first with very scant success. They declared that they could not entertain any such idea, that they were worn and weary with long travelling, and that their hearts were sore at the loss of their master. They meant to go back to their homes and rest awhile. This did not sound very promising, so by way of effecting a diver-

sion I asked where the remainder of them were. I was told there
were six, and I saw but three. One of the men said that they
slept in the hut, and were yet resting after their labours—'sleep
weighed down their eyelids, and sorrow made their hearts as lead:
it was best to sleep, for with sleep came forgetfulness. But the
men should be awakened.'

Presently they came out of the hut, yawning—the first two
men being evidently of the same race and style as those already
before us; but the appearance of the third and last nearly made
me jump out of my skin. He was a very tall, broad man, quite
six foot three, I should say, but gaunt, with lean, wiry-looking
limbs. My first glance at him told me that he was no Wakwafi:
he was a pure bred Zulu. He came out with his thin aristocratic-
looking hand placed before his face to hide a yawn, so I could
only see that he was a 'Keshla,' or ringed man,[1] and that he had a
great three-cornered hole in his forehead. In another second he
removed his hand, revealing a powerful-looking Zulu face, with
a humorous mouth, a short woolly beard, tinged with grey, and
a pair of brown eyes keen as hawk's. I knew my man at once,
although I had not seen him for twelve years. 'How do you do,
Umslopogaas?' I said quietly in Zulu.

The tall man, of whose origin and history strange tales were
current in Zululand, and who among his own people was commonly known as the 'Woodpecker,' and also as the 'Slaughterer,'
started, almost letting the long-handled battle-axe he held in his
hand fall in his astonishment. Next second he had recognised me,
and was saluting me.

'Koos' (chief), he began, 'Koos-y-Pagate! Koos-y-umcool!
(Chief from of old—mighty chief) Koos! Baba! (father) Macumazahn, old hunter, slayer of elephants, eater up of lions, clever
one! watchful one! brave one! quick one! whose shot never misses,
who strikes straight home, who grasps a hand and holds it to the
death (i.e. is a true friend) Koos! Baba! Wise is the voice of
our people that says, "Mountain never meets with mountain, but
at daybreak or at even man shall meet again with man." Behold!
a messenger came up from Natal, "Macumazahn is dead!" cried
he. "The land knows Macumazahn no more." That was years ago.
And now, behold, now in this strange place of stinks I find Macumazahn, my friend. There is no room for doubt. The brush of

[1] Among the Zulus a man assumes the ring, which is made of a species of
black gum twisted in with the hair, and polished a brilliant black, when he
has reached a certain dignity and age, or is the husband of a sufficient
number of wives. Till he is in a position to wear a ring he is looked on as
a boy, though he may be thirty-five years of age, or even more.—A. Q.

the old jackal has gone a little grey; but is not his eye as keen,
and are not his teeth as sharp? Ha! ha! Macumazahn, mindest
thou how thou didst plant the ball in the eye of the charging buffalo—mindest thou——'

I had let him run on thus because I saw that his enthusiasm
was producing a marked effect upon the minds of the five Wakwafi, who appeared to understand something of his talk; but now
I thought it time to put a stop to it, for there is nothing that I
hate so much as this Zulu system of extravagant praising—'bong-
ering' as they call it. 'Silence!' I said. 'Has all thy noisy talk
been stopped up since last I saw thee that it breaks out thus, and
sweeps us away? What doest thou here with these men—thou
whom I left a chief in Zululand? How is it that thou art far from
thine own place, and gathered together with strangers?'

Umslopogaas leant himself upon the head of his long battle-
axe, which was nothing else but a pole-axe, with a beautiful
handle of rhinoceros horn, and his grim face grew sad.

'My Father,' he answered, 'I have a word to tell thee, but I
cannot speak it before these low people (umfagozana),' and he
glanced at the Wakwafi Askari; 'it is for thine own ear. My
Father, this will I say,' and here his face grew stern again, 'a
woman betrayed me to the death, and covered my name with
shame—ay, my own wife, a round-faced girl, betrayed me; but I
escaped from death; ay, I broke from the very hands of those who
came to slay me. I struck but three blows with this mine axe
Inkosikaas—surely my Father will remember it—one to the right,
one to the left, and one in front, and yet I left three men dead.
And then I fled, and, as my Father knows, even now that I am
old, my feet are as the feet of the Sassaby,[1] and there breathes
not the man who, by running, can touch me again when once I
have bounded from his side. On I sped, and after me came the
messengers of death, and their voice was as the voice of dogs that
hunt. From my own kraal I flew, and, as I passed, she who had
betrayed me was drawing water at the spring. I fleeted by her
like the shadow of Death, and as I went I smote with mine axe,
and lo! her head fell: it fell into the water pan. Then I fled
north. Day after day I journeyed on; for three moons I journeyed, resting not, stopping not, but running on towards forgetfulness, till I met the party of the white hunter who is now dead,
and am come hither with his servants. And nought have I brought
with me. I who am high-born, ay, of the blood of Chaka, the great
king—a chief, and captain of the regiment of the Nkomabakosi—
I am a wanderer, a man without a kraal. Nought have I brought

[1]One of the fleetest of the African antelopes.—A. Q.

save this mine axe; in right of which once I ruled the people of the axe. They have divided my cattle; they have taken my wives; and my children know my face no more. Yet with this axe'—and he swung the formidable weapon round his head, making the air hiss as he clove it—'will I cut another path to fortune. I have spoken.'

I shook my head at him. 'Umslopogaas,' I said, 'I know thee from of old. Ever ambitious, born of the Blood, I fear me that thou hast overreached thyself at last. Years ago, when thou wouldst have plotted against Cetywayo, son of Panda, I warned thee, and thou didst listen. But now, when I was not by thee to stay thy hand, thou hast dug a pit for thine own feet to fall in. Is it not so? But what is done is done. Who can make the dead tree green, or gaze again upon last year's light? Who can recall the spoken word, or bring back the spirit of the fallen? That which Time swallows comes not up again. Let thy story be forgotten!

'And now, behold, Umslopogaas, I know thee for a great warrior of the blood royal, faithful to the death. Even in Zululand, where all men are brave, they called thee the "Slaughterer," and at night told stories round the fire of thy strength and deeds. Hear me now. Thou seest this tall man, my friend'—and I pointed to Sir Henry; 'he also is a warrior as great as thou, and, strong as thou art, he could throw thee over his shoulder. Incubu is his name. And thou seest this one also; him with the round stomach, the shining eye, and the pleasant face. Bougwan (glass eye) is his name, and a good man is he and a true, being of a curious tribe who pass their life upon the water, and live in floating kraals.

'Now, we three whom thou seest would travel inland, past Dongo Egere, the great white mountain (Mt. Kenia), and far into the unknown beyond. We know not what we shall find there; we go to hunt and seek adventures, and new places, being tired of sitting still, with the same old things around us. Wilt thou come with us? To thee shall be given command of all our servants; but what shall befall thee, that I know not. Once before we three journeyed thus, in search of adventure, and we took with us a man such as thou—one Umbopa; and, behold, we left him the king of a great country, with twenty Impis (regiments), each of 3,000 plumed warriors, waiting on his word. How it shall go with thee, I know not; mayhap death awaits thee and us. Wilt thou throw thyself to Fortune and come, or fearest thou, Umslopogaas?'

The old chief smiled. 'Thou art not altogether right, Macumazahn,' he said; 'I have plotted in my time, but it was not ambition that led to my fall; but, shame on me that I should have to say it, a fair woman's face. Let it pass. So we are going to see something like the old times again, Macumazahn, when we fought and hunted in Zululand? Ay, I will come. Come life, come death, what care I, so that the blows fall fast and the blood runs red? I grow old, I grow old, and I have not fought enough! And yet am I a warrior among warriors; see my scars'—and he pointed to countless cicatrices, stabs and cuts, that marked the skin of his chest and legs and arms. 'See the hole in my head; the brains gushed out therefrom, yet did I slay him who smote, and live. Knowest thou how many men I have slain, in fair hand-to-hand combat, Macumazahn? See, here is the tale of them'—and he pointed to long rows of notches cut in the rhinoceros-horn handle of his axe. 'Number them, Macumazahn—one hundred and three —and I have never counted but those whom I have ripped open,[1] nor have I reckoned those whom another man had struck.'

'Be silent,' I said, for I saw that he was getting the blood-fever on him; 'be silent; well art thou called the "Slaughterer." We would not hear of thy deeds of blood. Remember, if thou comest with us, we fight not save in self-defence. Listen, we need servants. These men,' and I pointed to the Wakwafi, who had retired a little way during our 'indaba' (talk), 'say they will not come.'

'Will not come!' shouted Umslopogaas; 'where is the dog who says he will not come when my Father orders? Here, thou'—and with a single bound he sprang upon the Wakwafi with whom I had first spoken, and, seizing him by the arm, dragged him towards us. 'Thou dog!' he said, giving the terrified man a shake, 'didst thou say that thou wouldst not go with my Father? Speak it once more and I will choke thee'—and his long fingers closed round his throat as he said it—'thee, and those with thee. Hast thou forgotten how I served thy brother?'

'Nay, we will come with the white man,' gasped the man.

'White man!' went on Umslopogaas, in simulated fury, which a very little provocation would have made real enough; 'of whom speakest thou, insolent dog?'

'Nay, we will go with the great chief.'

'So!' said Umslopogaas, in a quiet voice, as he suddenly released his hold, so that the man fell backward. 'I thought you would.'

'That man Umslopogaas seems to have a curious *moral* ascendancy over his companions,' Good afterwards remarked thoughtfully.

---

[1]Alluding to the Zulu custom of opening the stomach of a dead foe. They have a superstition that, if this is not done, as the body of their enemy swells up so will the bodies of those who killed him swell up.—A. Q.

CHAPTER II.

THE BLACK HAND.

In due course we left Lamu, and ten days afterwards we found ourselves at a spot called Charra, on the Tana River, having gone through many adventures which need not be recorded here. Amongst other things we visited a ruined city, of which there are many on this coast, and which must once, to judge from their extent and the numerous remains of mosques and stone houses, have been very populous places. These ruined cities are immeasurably ancient, having, I believe, been places of wealth and importance so far back as the Old Testament times, when they were centres of trade with India and elsewhere. But their glory has departed now—the slave trade has finished them—and where once wealthy merchants from all parts of the then civilised world stood and bargained in the crowded market-places, the lion holds his court at night, and instead of the chattering of slaves and the eager voices of the bidders, his awful note goes echoing down the ruined corridors. At this particular place we discovered on a mound, covered up with rank growth and rubbish, two of the most beautiful stone doorways that it is possible to conceive. The carving on them was simply exquisite, and I only regret that we had no means of getting them away. No doubt they had once been the entrances to a palace, of which, however, no traces were now to be seen, though probably its ruins lay under the rising mound.

Gone! quite gone! the way that everything must go. Like the nobles and the ladies who lived within their gates, these cities have had their day, and now they are as Babylon and Nineveh, and as London and Paris will one day be. Nothing may endure. That is the inexorable law. Men and women, empires and cities, thrones, principalities, and powers, mountains, rivers, and unfathomed seas, worlds, spaces, and universes, all have their day, and all must go. In this ruined and forgotten place the moralist may behold a symbol of the universal destiny. For this system of ours allows no room for standing still—nothing can loiter on the road and check the progress of things upwards towards Life, or the rush of things downward towards Death. The stern policeman Fate moves us and them on, on, uphill and downhill and across the level; there is no resting-place for weary feet, till at last the abyss swallows us, and we are hurled into the sea of the Eternal.

At Charra we had a violent quarrel with the headman of the bearers we had hired to go as far as this, and who now wished to extort large extra payments from us. In the result he threatened to set the Masai—about whom more anon—on to us. That night with all our hired bearers, he ran away, stealing most of the goods which had been entrusted to them to carry. Luckily, however, they had not happened to steal our rifles, ammunition, and personal effects; not because of any delicacy of feeling on their part, but owing to the fact that they chanced to be in the charge of the five Wakwafis. After that, it was clear to us that we had borne enough from caravans and bearers. Indeed, we had not much left for a caravan to carry. And yet, how were we to get on?

It was Good who solved the question. 'Here is water,' he said, pointing to the Tana River; 'and yesterday I saw a party of natives hunting hippopotami in canoes. I understand that Mr. Mackenzie's mission station is on the Tana River. Why not get into canoes and paddle up to it?'

This brilliant suggestion, needless to say, was received with acclamation; and I instantly set to work to buy suitable canoes from the surrounding natives. I succeeded after a delay of three days in obtaining two large ones, each hollowed out of a single log of some light wood, and capable of holding six people and baggage. For these two canoes we had to pay nearly all our remaining cloth, and also many other articles.

On the day following our purchase of the two canoes we effected a start. In the first canoe were Good, Sir Henry, and three of our Wakwafi followers; in the second myself, Umslopogaas, and the other two Wakwafis. As our course lay up stream, we had to keep four paddles at work in each canoe, which meant that the whole lot of us, except Good, had to row away like galley-slaves; and very exhausting work it was. I say, except Good, for, of course, the moment that Good got into a boat his foot was on his native heath, and he took command of the party. And certainly he worked us. On shore Good is a gentle, mild-mannered man, and given to jocosity; but, as we found to our cost, Good in a boat was a perfect demon. To begin with, he knew all about it, and we didn't. On all nautical subjects, from the torpedo fittings of a man-of-war down to the best way of handling the paddle of an African canoe, he was a perfect mine of information, which, to say the least of it, we were not. Also his ideas of discipline were of the sternest, and, in short, he came the royal naval officer over us pretty considerably, and paid us out amply for all the chaff we were wont to treat him to on land; but, on the other hand, I am bound to say that he managed the boats admirably.

After the first day Good succeeded, with the help of some cloth and a couple of poles, in rigging up a sail in each canoe, which lightened our labours not a little. But the current ran very strong against us, and at the best we were not able to make more than twenty miles a day. Our plan was to start at dawn, and paddle along till about half-past ten, by which time the sun got too hot to allow of further exertion. Then we moored our canoes to the bank, and ate our frugal meal; after which we slept or otherwise amused ourselves till about three o'clock, when we started again, and rowed till within an hour of sundown, when we called a halt for the night. On landing in the evening, Good would at once set to work, with the help of the Askari, to build a little 'scherm,' or small enclosure, fenced with thorn bushes, and to light a fire. I, with Sir Henry and Umslopogaas, would go out to shoot something for the pot. Generally this was an easy task, for all sorts of game abounded on the banks of the Tana. One night Sir Henry shot a young cow-giraffe, of which the marrow-bones were excellent; on another I got a couple of waterbuck right and left; and once, to his own intense satisfaction, Umslopogaas, who, like most Zulus, was a vile shot with a rifle, managed to kill a fine fat eland with a Martini I had lent him. Sometimes we varied our food by shooting some guinea-fowl, or bush-bustard (paau)—both of which were numerous—with a shot-gun, or by catching a supply of beautiful yellow fish, with which the waters of the Tana swarmed, and are, as I believe, one of the chief food-supplies of the crocodiles.

Three days after our start an ominous incident occurred. We were just drawing in to the bank to make our camp as usual for the night, when we caught sight of a figure standing on a little knoll not forty yards away, and intently watching our approach. One glance was sufficient—although I was personally unacquainted with the tribe—to tell me that he was a Masai Elmoran, or young warrior. Indeed, had I felt any doubts, they would have been quickly dispelled by the terrified ejaculation of 'Masai!' that burst simultaneously from the lips of our Wakwafi followers, who are, as I think I have said, themselves bastard Masai.

And what a figure he presented as he stood there in his savage war-gear! Accustomed as I have been to savages all my life, I do not think that I have ever before seen anything quite so ferocious or awe-inspiring. To begin with, the man was enormously tall, quite as tall as Umslopogaas, I should say, and beautifully, though somewhat slightly, shaped; but with the face of a devil. In his right hand he held a spear about five and a half feet long, the blade being two and a half feet in length, by nearly three inches in width, and having an iron spike at the end of the handle that measured more than a foot. On his left arm was a large and well-made elliptical shield of buffalo hide, on which were painted strange heraldic-looking devices. On his shoulders was a huge cape of hawk's feathers, and round his neck was a 'naibere,' or strip of cotton, about seventeen feet long, by one and a half broad, with a stripe of colour running down the middle of it. The tanned goatskin robe, which formed his ordinary attire in times of peace, was tied lightly round his waist, so as to serve the purposes of a belt, and through it were stuck, on the right and left sides respectively, his short pear-shaped sime, or sword, which is made of a single piece of steel, and carried in a wooden sheath, and an enormous knobkerrie. But perhaps the most remarkable feature of his attire consisted of a headdress of ostrich-feathers, which was fixed on the chin, and passed in front of the ears to the forehead, and, being shaped like an ellipse, completely framed the face, so that the diabolical countenance appeared to project from a sort of feather fire-screen. Round the ankles he wore black fringes of hair, and, projecting from the upper portion of the calves, to which they were attached, were long spurs like spikes, from which flowed down tufts of the beautiful black and waving hair of the Colobus monkey. Such was the elaborate array of the Masai Elmoran who stood watching the approach of our two canoes, but it is one which, to be appreciated, must be seen; only those who see it do not often live to describe it. Of course, I could not discover all these details of his full dresss on the occasion of this my first introduction, being, indeed, amply taken up with the consideration of the general effect, but I had plenty of subsequent opportunities of becoming acquainted with the items that went to make it up.

Whilst we were hesitating what to do, the Masai warrior drew himself up in a dignified fashion, shook his huge spear at us, and, turning, vanished on the further side of the slope.

'Hulloa!' holloaed Sir Henry from the other boat; 'our friend the caravan leader has been as good as his word, and set the Masai after us. Do you think that it will be safe to go ashore?'

I did not think it would be at all safe; but, on the other hand, we had no means of cooking in the canoes, and nothing that we could eat raw, so it was difficult to know what to do. At last Umslopogaas simplified matters by volunteering to go and reconnoitre, which he did, creeping off into the bush like a snake, while we hung off in the stream waiting for him. In half an hour he returned, and told us that there was not a Masai to be seen anywhere about, but he had discovered a spot where they had recently been encamped, and from various indications he judged that they must have moved on an hour or so before; the man we saw, no doubt, having been left to report upon our movements.

Thereupon we landed; and, having posted a sentry, proceeded to cook and eat our evening meal. This done, we took the situation into our serious consideration. Of course, it was possible that the apparition of a Masai warrior had nothing to do with us, that he was merely one of a band bent upon some marauding and murdering expedition against another tribe. Our friend the Consul had told us that such expeditions were about. But when we recalled the threat of the caravan leader, and reflected on the ominous way in which the warrior had shaken his spear at us, this did not appear very probable. On the contrary, what did seem probable was that the party were after us and awaiting a favourable opportunity to attack us. This being so, there were two things that we could do—one of which was to go on, and the other to go back. The latter idea, however, was rejected at once, it being obvious that we should encounter as many dangers in retreat as in advance; and, besides, we had made up our minds to journey onwards at any price. Under these circumstances, however, we did not consider it safe to sleep ashore, so we got into our canoes, and, paddling out into the middle of the stream, which was not very wide, we managed to anchor them by means of big stones fastened to ropes made of cocoanut-fibre, of which there were several fathoms in each canoe.

Here the musquitoes nearly ate us up alive, and this, combined with anxiety as to our position, effectually prevented me from sleeping as the others were doing, notwithstanding the attacks of the aforesaid Tana musquitoes. And so I lay awake, smoking and reflecting on many things, but, being of a practical turn of mind, chiefly on how we were to give those Masai villains the slip. It was a beautiful moonlight night, and, notwithstanding the musquitoes, and the great risk we were running of fever from sleeping in such a spot, and forgetting that I had the cramp very badly in my right leg from squatting in a constrained position in the canoe, and that the Wakwafi who was sleeping by me smelt horribly, I really began to enjoy myself. The moonbeams played upon the surface of the running water that speeded unceasingly past us towards the sea, like men's lives towards the grave, till it glittered like a wide sheet of silver, that is in the open where the trees threw no shadows. Near the banks, however, it was very dark, and the night wind sighed sadly in the reeds. To our left, on the further side of the river, was a little sandy bay which was clear of trees, and here I could make out the forms of numerous antelopes advancing to the water, till suddenly there came an ominous roar, whereupon they all made off hurriedly. Then after a pause I caught sight of the massive form of His Majesty the Lion, coming down to drink his fill after meat. Presently he moved on, then came a crashing of the reeds about fifty yards above us, and a few minutes later a huge black mass rose out of the water, about twenty yards from me, and snorted. It was the head of a hippopotamus. Down it went without a sound, only to rise again within five yards of where I sat. This was decidedly too near to be comfortable, more especially as the hippopotamus was evidently animated by intense curiosity to know what on earth our canoes were. He opened his great mouth, to yawn, I suppose, and gave me an excellent view of his ivories; and I could not help reflecting how easily he could crunch up our frail canoe with a single bite. Indeed, I had half a mind to give him a ball from my eight-bore, but on reflection determined to let him alone unless he actually charged the boat. Presently he sank again as noiselessly as before, and I saw no more of him. Just then, on looking towards the bank on our right, I fancied that I caught sight of a dark figure flitting between the tree trunks. I have very keen sight, and I was almost sure that I saw something, but whether it was bird, beast, or man I could not say. At this moment, however, a dark cloud passed over the moon, and I saw no more of it. Just then, too, although all the other sounds of the forest had ceased, a species of horned owl with which I was well acquainted began to hoot with great persistency. After that, save for the rustling of trees and reeds when the wind caught them, there was complete silence.

But somehow, in the most unaccountable way, I had suddenly become nervous. There was no particular reason why I should be, beyond the ordinary reasons which surround the Central African traveller, and yet undoubtedly I was. If there is one thing more than another of which I have the most complete and entire scorn and disbelief, it is of presentiments, and yet here I was all of a sudden filled with and possessed by a most undoubted presentiment of approaching evil. I would not give way to it, however, although I felt the cold perspiration stand out upon my forehead. I would not arouse the others. Worse and worse I grew, my pulse fluttered like a dying man's, my nerves thrilled with the horrible sense of impotent terror which anybody who is subject to nightmare will be familiar with, but still my will triumphed over my fears, and I lay quiet (for I was half sitting, half lying in the bow of the canoe), only turning my face so as to command a view of Umslopogaas and the two Wakwafi who were sleeping alongside of and beyond me.

In the distance I heard a hippopotamus splash faintly, then the owl hooted again in a kind of unnatural screaming note,[1] and the wind began to moan plaintively through the trees, making a heart-chilling music. Above was the black bosom of the cloud, and beneath me swept the black flood of the water, and I felt as though I and Death were utterly alone between them. It was very desolate.

Suddenly my blood seemed to freeze in my veins, and my heart to stand still. Was it fancy, or were we moving? I turned my eyes to look for the other canoe which should be alongside of us. I could not see it, but instead I saw a lean and clutching black hand lifting itself above the gunwale of the little boat. Surely it was a nightmare! At the same instant a dim but devilish-looking face appeared to rise out of the water, and then came a lurch of the canoe, the quick flash of a knife, and an awful yell from the Wakwafi who was sleeping by my side (the same poor fellow whose odour had been annoying me), and something warm spurted into my face. In an instant the spell was broken; I knew that it was no nightmare, but that we were attacked by swimming Masai. Snatching at the first weapon that came to hand, that happened to be Umslopogaas' battle-axe, I struck with all my force in the direction in which I had seen the flash of the knife. The blow fell upon a man's arm, and, catching it against the thick wooden gunwale of the canoe, completely severed it from the body just above the wrist. As for its owner, he uttered no sound or cry. Like a ghost he came, and like a ghost he went, leaving behind him a bloody hand still gripping a great knife, or rather a short sword, that was buried in the heart of our poor servant.

Instantly there arose a hubbub and confusion, and I fancied, rightly or wrongly, that I made out several dark heads gliding away towards the right-hand bank, whither we were rapidly drifting, for the rope by which we were moored had been severed with a knife. As soon as I had realised this fact, I also understood that the scheme had been to cut the boat loose so that it should drift on to the right bank, as it would have done with the natural swing of the current, where no doubt a party of Masai were waiting to dig their shovel-headed spears into us. Seizing one paddle myself, I told Umslopogaas to take another, for the remaining Askari was too frightened and bewildered to be of any use, and together we rowed vigorously out towards the middle of the stream; and not an instant too soon, for in another minute we

[1] No doubt this owl was a wingless bird. I afterwards learnt that the hooting of an owl is a favourite signal among the Masai tribes.—A. Q.

should have been aground, and then there would have been an end of us.

As soon as we were well out, we set to work to paddle the canoe up stream again to where the other was moored; and very hard and dangerous work it was in the dark, and with nothing but the notes of Good's stentorian shouts, which he kept firing off at intervals like a fog-horn, to guide us. But at last we fetched up, and were thankful to find that they had not been molested at all. No doubt the owner of the same hand that severed our rope should have severed theirs also, but was led away from his purpose by an irresistible inclination to murder when he got the chance, which, whilst it cost us a man and him his hand, undoubtedly saved all the rest of us from massacre. Had it not been for that ghastly apparition over the side of the boat—an apparition that I shall never forget till my dying hour—the canoe would undoubtedly have drifted ashore before I knew what had happened, and this history would never have been written by me.

CHAPTER III.

THE MISSION STATION.

WE made the remains of our rope fast to the other canoe, and sat waiting for the dawn and congratulating ourselves upon our merciful escape, which really seemed to result more from the special favour of Providence than from our own care or prowess. At last it came, and I have not often been more grateful to see the light, though so far as my canoe was concerned it revealed a ghastly sight. There in the bottom of the little boat lay the unfortunate Askari, the sime, or sword, in his bosom, and the severed hand gripping the handle. I could not bear the sight, so hauling up the stone which had served as an anchor to the other canoe, we made it fast to the murdered man and dropped him overboard, and down he went to the bottom, leaving nothing but a train of bubbles behind him. Alas! when our time comes, most of us like him leave nothing but bubbles behind, to show that we have been, and the bubbles soon burst. The hand of his murderer we threw into the stream, where it sank slowly. The sword, of which the handle was ivory, inlaid with gold, evidently Arab work, I kept and used as a hunting-knife, and very useful it proved.

Then, a man having been transferred to my canoe, we once more started on in very low spirits and not feeling at all comfortable as to the future, but fondly hoping to arrive at the 'Highlands' station by night. To make matters worse, within an hour of sunrise it came on to rain in torrents, wetting us to the skin, and even necessitating the occasional baling of the canoes, and as the rain beat down the wind we could not use the sails, and had to get along as best we could with our paddles.

At eleven o'clock we halted on an open piece of ground on the left bank of the river, and, the rain abating a little, managed to make a fire and catch and broil some fish. We did not dare to wander about to search for game. At two o'clock we got off again, taking a supply of broiled fish with us, and shortly afterwards the rain came on harder than ever. Also the river began to get exceedingly difficult to navigate on account of the numerous rocks, reaches of shallow water, and the increased force of the current; so that it soon became clear to us that we should not reach the Rev. Mackenzie's hospitable roof that night—a prospect that did not tend to enliven us. Toil as we would, we could not make more than an average of a mile an hour, and at five o'clock in the afternoon, by which time we were all utterly worn out, we reckoned that we were still quite ten miles below the station. This being so, we set to work to make the best arrangements we could for the night. After our recent experience, we simply did not dare to land, more especially as the banks of the Tana were here clothed with dense bush that would have given cover to five thousand Masai, and at first I thought that we were destined to pass another night in the canoes. Fortunately, however, we espied a little rocky islet, not more than fifteen yards or so square, situated nearly in the middle of the river. For this we paddled, and, making fast the canoes, landed and made ourselves as comfortable as circumstances would permit, which was very uncomfortable indeed. As for the weather, it continued to be simply vile, the rain coming down in sheets till we were chilled to the marrow, and utterly preventing us from lighting a fire. There was, however, one consoling circumstance about this rain; our Askari declared that nothing would induce the Masai to make an attack in it, as they disliked moving about in the wet intensely, perhaps, as Good suggested, because they hate the idea of washing. We ate some insipid and sodden cold fish—that is, with the exception of Umslopogaas, who, like most Zulus, cannot bear fish—and took a pull of brandy, of which we fortunately had a few bottles left, and then began what, with one exception—when we same three white men nearly perished of cold on the snow of Sheba's Breast in the course of our journey to Kukuanaland—was, I think, the most trying night I ever experienced. It seemed absolutely endless, and once or twice I feared that two of the Askari would have died of the wet, cold, and exposure. Indeed, had it not been for timely doses of brandy I am sure that they would have died, for no African people can stand much exposure, which first paralyses and then kills them. I could see that even that iron old warrior Umslopogaas felt it keenly; though, in strange contrast to the Wakwafis, who groaned and bemoaned their fate unceasingly, he never uttered a single complaint. To make matters worse, about one in the morning we again heard the owl's ominous hooting, and had at once to prepare ourselves for another attack; though, if it had been attempted, I do not think that we could have offered a very effective resistance. But either the owl was a real one this time, or else the Masai were themselves too miserable to think of offensive operations, which, indeed, they rarely, if ever, undertake in bush veldt. At any rate, we saw nothing of them.

At last the dawn came gliding across the water, wrapped in wreaths of ghostly mist, and, with the daylight, the rain ceased; and then, out came the glorious sun, sucking up the mists and warming the chill air. Benumbed, and utterly exhausted, we dragged ourselves to our feet, and went and stood in the bright rays, and were thankful for them. I can quite understand how it is that primitive people become sun worshippers, especially if their conditions of life render them liable to exposure.

In half an hour more we were once again making fair progress with the help of a good wind. Our spirits had returned with the sunshine, and we were ready to laugh at difficulties and dangers that had been almost crushing on the previous day.

And so we went on cheerily till about eleven o'clock. Just as we were thinking of halting as usual, to rest and try to shoot something to eat, a sudden bend in the river brought us in sight of a substantial-looking European house with a verandah round it, splendidly situated upon a hill, and surrounded by a high stone wall with a ditch on the outer side. Right against and overshadowing the house was an enormous pine, the top of which we had seen through a glass for the last two days, but of course without knowing that it marked the site of the mission station. I was the first to see the house, and could not restrain myself from giving a hearty cheer, in which the others, including the natives, joined lustily. There was no thought of halting now. On we laboured, for, unfortunately, though the house seemed quite near, it was still a long way off by river, until at last, by one o'clock, we found ourselves at the bottom of the slope on which the building stood. Running the canoes to the bank, we disembarked, and were just hauling them up on to the shore, when we perceived three figures, dressed in ordinary English-looking clothes, hurrying down through a grove of trees to meet us.

'A gentleman, a lady, and a little girl,' ejaculated Good, after surveying the trio through his eyeglass, 'walking in a civilised fashion, through a civilised garden, to meet us in this place. Hang me, if this isn't the most curious thing we have seen yet!'

Good was right: it certainly did seem odd and out of place—more like a scene out of a dream or an Italian opera than a real tangible fact; and the sense of unreality was not lessened when we heard ourselves addressed in good broad Scotch, which, however, I cannot reproduce.

'How do you do, sirs,' said Mr. Mackenzie, a grey-haired, angular man, with a kindly face and red cheeks; 'I hope I see you very well. My natives told me an hour ago they spied two canoes with white men in them coming up the river; so we have just come down to meet you.'

'And it is very glad that we are to see a white face again, let me tell you,' put in the lady—a charming and refined-looking person.

We took off our hats in acknowledgment, and proceeded to introduce ourselves.

'And now,' said Mr. Mackenzie, 'you must all be hungry and weary; so come on, gentlemen, come on, and right glad we are to see you. The last white who visited us was Alphonse—you will see Alphonse presently—and that was a year ago.'

Meanwhile we had been walking up the slope of the hill, the lower portion of which was fenced off, sometimes with quince fences and sometimes with rough stone walls, into Kaffir gardens, just now full of crops of mealies, pumpkins, potatoes, &c. In the corners of these gardens were groups of neat mushroom-shaped huts, occupied by Mr. Mackenzie's mission natives, whose women and children came pouring out to meet us as we walked. Through the centre of the gardens ran the roadway up which we were walking. It was bordered on each side by a line of orange trees, which, although they had only been planted ten years, in the lovely climate of the uplands below Mt. Kenia, the base of which is about 5,000 feet above the coast line level, had already grown to imposing proportions, and were positively laden with golden fruit. After a stiffish climb of a quarter of a mile or so—for the hill-side was steep—we came to a splendid quince fence, also covered with fruit, which enclosed, Mr. Mackenzie told us, a space of about four acres of ground that contained his private garden, house, church, and outbuildings, and, indeed, the whole hill-top. And what a garden it was! I have always loved a good garden, and

I could have thrown up my hands for joy when I saw Mr. Mackenzie's. First there were rows upon rows of standard European fruit-trees, all grafted; for on the top of this hill the climate was so temperate that very nearly all the English vegetables, trees, and flowers flourished luxuriantly, even including several varieties of the apple, which, generally speaking, runs to wood in a warm climate and obstinately declines to fruit. Then there were strawberries and tomatoes, such tomatoes! melons and cucumbers, and, indeed, every sort of vegetable and fruit.

'Well, you have something like a garden!' I said, overpowered with admiration not untouched by envy.

'Yes,' answered the missionary, 'it is a very good garden, and has well repaid my labour; but it is the climate that I have to thank. If you stick a peach-stone into the ground it will bear fruit the fourth year, and a rose-cutting will bloom in a year. It is a lovely clime.'

Just then we came to a ditch about ten feet wide, and full of water, on the other side of which was a loopholed stone wall eight feet high, and with sharp flints plentifully set in mortar on the coping.

'There,' said Mr. Mackenzie, pointing to the ditch and wall, 'this is my *magnum opus*; at least, this and the church, which is the other side of the house. It took me and twenty natives two years to dig the ditch and build the wall, but I never felt safe till it was done; and now I can defy all the savages in Africa, for the spring that fills the ditch is inside the wall, and bubbles out at the top of the hill winter and summer alike, and I always keep a store of four months' provisions in the house.'

Crossing over a plank and through a very narrow opening in the wall, we entered into what Mrs. Mackenzie called *her* domain—namely the flower garden, the beauty of which it is really beyond my power to describe. I do not think I ever saw such roses, gardenias, or camellias (all reared from seeds or cuttings sent from England); and there was also a patch given up to a collection of bulbous roots mostly collected by Miss Flossie, Mr. Mackenzie's little daughter, from the surrounding country, some of which were surpassingly beautiful. In the middle of this garden, and exactly opposite the verandah, a beautiful fountain of clear water bubbled up from the ground, and fell into a stonework basin which had been carefully built to receive it, whence the overflow found its way by means of a drain to the moat round the outer wall, this moat in its turn serving as a reservoir, whence an unfailing supply of water was available to irrigate all the gardens below. The house itself, a massively built single-storied building, was roofed with slabs of stone, and had a handsome verandah in front. It was built on three sides of a square, the fourth side being taken up by the kitchens, which stood separate from the house—a very good plan in a hot country. In the centre of this square thus formed was, perhaps, the most remarkable object that we had yet seen in this charming place, and that was a single tree of the conifer tribe, varieties of which grow freely on the highlands of this part of Africa. This splendid tree, which Mr. Mackenzie informed us was a landmark for fifty miles round, and which we had ourselves seen for the last forty miles of our journey, must have been nearly three hundred feet in height, the trunk measuring about sixteen feet in diameter at a yard from the ground. For some seventy feet it rose a beautiful tapering brown pillar without a single branch, but at that height splendid dark green boughs, which, looked at from below, had the appearance of gigantic fern-leaves, sprang out horizontally from the trunk, projecting right over the house and flower-garden, to both of which they furnished a grateful proportion of shade, without— being so high up—offering any impediment to the passage of light and air.

'What a beautiful tree!' exclaimed Sir Henry.

'Yes, you are right; it is a beautiful tree. There is not another like it in all the country round, that I know of,' answered Mr. Mackenzie. 'I call it my watch tower. As you see, I have a rope ladder fixed to the lowest bough; and if I want to see anything that is going on within fifteen miles or so all I have to do is to run up it with a spyglass. But you must be hungry, and I am sure the dinner is cooked. Come in, my friends; it is a rough place, but well enough for these savage parts; and I can tell you what, we have got—a French cook.' And he led the way on to the verandah.

As I was following him, and wondering what on earth he could mean by this, there suddenly appeared, through the door that opened on to the verandah from the house, a dapper little man, dressed in a neat blue cotton suit, with shoes made of tanned hide, remarkable for a bustling air and most enormous black mustachios, shaped into an upward curve, and coming to a point for all the world like a pair of buffalo-horns.

'Madame bids me for to say that dinnar is sarved. Messieurs, my compliments;' then suddenly perceiving Umslopogaas, who was loitering along after us and playing with his battle-axe, he threw up his hands in astonishment. *'Ah! mais quel homme!'* he ejaculated in French, *'quel sauvage affreux!* Take but note of his huge *choppare* and the great pit in his head.'

'Ay,' said Mr. Mackenzie; 'what are you talking about, Alphonse?'

'Talking about!' replied the little Frenchman, his eyes still fixed upon Umslopogaas, whose general appearance seemed to fascinate him; 'why I talk of him'—and he rudely pointed—'of *ce monsieur noir.*'

At this everybody began to laugh, and Umslopogaas, perceiving that he was the object of remark, frowned ferociously, for he had a most lordly dislike of anything like a personal liberty.

'*Parbleu!*' said Alphonse, 'he is angered—he makes the grimace. I like not his air. I vanish.' And he did with considerable rapidity.

Mr. Mackenzie joined heartily in the shout of laughter which we indulged in. 'He is a queer character—Alphonse,' he said. 'By-and-by I will tell you his history; in the meanwhile let us try his cooking.'

'Might I ask,' said Sir Henry, after we had eaten a most excellent dinner, 'how you came to have a French cook in these wilds?'

'Oh,' answered Mrs. Mackenzie, 'he arrived here of his own accord about a year ago, and asked to be taken into our service. He had got into some trouble in France, and fled to Zanzibar, where he found an application had been made by the French Government for his extradition. Whereupon he rushed off up-country, and when nearly starved, fell in with our caravan of men, who were bringing us our annual supply of goods, and was brought on here. You should get him to tell you the story.'

When dinner was over we lit our pipes, and Sir Henry proceeded to give our host a description of our journey, over which he looked very grave.

'It is evident to me,' he said, 'that those rascally Masai are following you, and I am very thankful that you have reached this house in safety. I do not think that they will dare to attack you here. It is unfortunate, though, that nearly all my men have gone down to the coast with ivory and goods. There are two hundred of them in the caravan, and the consequence is that I have not more than twenty men available for defensive purposes in case they should attack us. But, still, I will just give a few orders;' and, calling a black man who was loitering about outside in the garden, he went to the window, and addressed him in a Swahili dialect. The man listened, then saluted and departed.

'I am sure I devoutly hope that we shall bring no such calamity upon you,' said I, anxiously, when he had taken his seat again.

'Rather than set those bloodthirsty villains about your ears, we will move on and take our chance.'

'You will do nothing of the sort. If the Masai come, they come, and there is an end on it; and I think we can give them a pretty warm greeting. I would not show any man the door for all the Masai in the world.'

'That reminds me,' I said, 'the Consul at Lamu told me that he had a letter from you, in which you said that a man arrived here who reported that he had come across a white people in the interior. Do you think that there was any truth in his story? I ask, because I have once or twice in my life heard rumours from natives who have come down from the far north of the existence of such a race.

Mr. Mackenzie, by way of answer, went out of the room and returned, bringing with him a most curious sword. It was long, and all the blade, which was very thick and heavy, was worked to within a quarter of an inch of the cutting edge into an ornamental pattern exactly as we work soft wood with a fret-saw, the steel, however, being invariably pierced in such a way as not to interfere with the strength of the sword. This in itself was sufficiently curious, but what was still more so was that all the edges of the hollow spaces cut through the substance of the blade were most beautifully inlaid with gold, which in some way that I cannot understand was welded on to the steel.[1]

'There,' said Mr. Mackenzie, 'did you ever see a sword like that?'

We all examined it and shook our heads.

'Well, I have got it to show you, because this is what the man who said he had seen the white people brought with him, and because it does more or less give an air of truth to what I should otherwise have set down as a lie. Look here; I will tell you all that I know about the matter, which is not much. One afternoon, just before sunset, I was sitting on the verandah, when a poor, miserable, starved-looking man came limping up and squatted down before me. I asked him where he came from and what he wanted, and thereon he plunged into a long rambling narrative about how he belonged to a tribe far in the north, and how his tribe was destroyed by another tribe, and he with a few other survivors driven still further north past a lake named Laga. Thence, it appears, he made his way to another lake that lay up in the mountains, "a lake without a bottom" he called it, and here his

[1] Since I saw the above I have examined hundreds of these swords, but have never been able to discover how the gold plates were inlaid in the fretwork. The armourers who make them in Zu-vendis bind themselves by oath not to reveal the secret.—A. Q.

wife and brother died of an infectious sickness—probably small-pox—whereon the people drove him out of their villages into the wilderness, where he wandered miserably over mountains for ten days, after which he entered dense thorn forest, and was one day found there by some *white men* who were hunting, and who took him to a place where all the people were white and live in stone houses. Here he remained a week shut up in a house, till one night a man with a white beard, whom he understood to be a "medicine-man," came and inspected him, after which he was led off and taken through the thorn forest to the confines of the wilderness, and given food and this sword, at least so he said, and turned loose.'

'Well,' said Sir Henry, who had been listening with breathless interest, 'and what did he do then?'

'Oh! he seems, according to his acount, to have gone through sufferings and hardships innumerable, and to have lived for weeks on roots and berries, and such things as he could catch and kill. But somehow he did live, and at last by slow degrees made his way south and reached this place. What the details of his journey were I never learnt, for I told him to return on the morrow, bidding one of my headmen look after him for the night. The headman took him away, but the poor man had the itch so badly that the headman's wife would not have him in the hut for fear of catching it, so he was given a blanket and told to sleep outside. As it happened, we had a lion hanging about here just then, and most unhappily he winded this unfortunate wanderer, and, springing on him, bit his head almost off without the people in the hut knowing anything about it, and there was an end of him and his story about the white people; and whether or no there is any truth in it is more than I can tell you. What do you think, Mr. Quatermain?'

I shook my head, and answered, 'I don't know. There are so many queer things hidden away in the heart of this great continent that I should be sorry to assert that there was no truth in it. Anyhow, we mean to try and find out. We intend to journey to Lekakisera, and thence, if we live to get so far, to this Lake Laga; and, if there are any white people beyond, we will do our best to find them.'

'You are very venturesome people,' said Mr. Mackenzie, with a smile, and the subject dropped.

CHAPTER IV.

ALPHONSE AND HIS ANNETTE.

AFTER dinner we thoroughly inspected all the outbuildings and grounds of the station, which I consider the most successful as well as the most beautiful place of the sort that I have seen in Africa. We then returned to the verandah, where we found Umslopogaas taking advantage of this favourable opportunity to clean all the rifles thoroughly. This was the only *work* that he ever did or was asked to do, for as a Zulu chief it was beneath his dignity to work with his hands; but such as it was he did it very well. It was a curious sight to see the great Zulu sitting there upon the floor, his battle-axe resting against the wall behind him, whilst his long aristocratic-looking hands were busily employed, delicately and with the utmost care, cleaning the mechanism of the breechloaders. He had a name for each gun. One—a double four-bore belonging to Sir Henry—was the Thunderer; another, my 500 Express, which had a peculiarly sharp report, was 'the little one who spoke like a whip;' the Winchester repeaters were 'the women, who talked so fast that you could not tell one word from another;' the six Martinis were 'the common people;' and so on with them all. It was very curious to hear him addressing each gun as he cleaned it, as though it were an individual, and in a vein of the quaintest humour. He did the same with his battle-axe, which he seemed to look upon as an intimate friend, and to which he would at times talk by the hour, going over all his old adventures with it—and dreadful enough some of them were. By a piece of grim humour, he had named this axe 'Inkosi-kaas,' which is the Zulu word for chieftainess. For a long while I could not make out why he gave it such a name, and at last I asked him, when he informed me that the axe was evidently feminine, because of her womanly habit of prying very deep into things, and that she was clearly a chieftainess because all men fell down before her, struck dumb at the sight of her beauty and power. In the same way he would consult 'Inkosi-kaas' if in any dilemma; and when I asked him why he did so, he informed me it was because she must needs be wise, having 'looked into so many people's brains.'

I took up the axe and closely examined this formidable weapon. It was, as I have said, of the nature of a pole-axe. The haft, made out of an enormous rhinoceros horn, was three feet three inches long, about an inch and a quarter thick, and with a knob at the end as large as a Maltese orange, left there to prevent the hand from slipping. This horn haft though so massive, was as flexible as cane, and practically unbreakable; but, to make assurance doubly sure, it was whipped round at intervals of a few inches with copper wire—all the parts where the hands grip being thus treated. Just above where the haft entered the head were scored a number of little nicks, each nick representing a man killed in battle with the weapon. The axe itself was made of the most beautiful steel, and very curiously worked, though Umslopogaas did not know where it came from originally, having taken it from the hand of a chief he had killed in battle many years before.[1] It was not very heavy, the head weighing two and a half pounds, so nearly as I could judge. The cutting part was slightly concave in shape—not convex, as is generally the case with savage battle-axes—and sharp as a razor, measuring five and three-quarter inches across the widest part. From the back of the axe sprang a stout spike four inches long, for the last two of which it was hollow, and shaped like a leather punch, with an opening for anything forced into the hollow at the punch end to be pushed out above—in fact, in this respect it exactly resembled a butcher's pole-axe. It was with this punch end, as we afterwards discovered, that Umslopogaas usually struck when fighting, driving a neat round hole in his adversary's skull, and only using the broad cutting edge for a circular sweep, or sometimes in a *mêlée*. I think he considered the punch a neater and more sportsmanlike tool, and it was from his habit of pecking at his enemy with it that he got his name of 'Woodpecker.' Certainly in his hands it was a terribly efficient one.

Such was Umslopogaas' axe, Inkosi-kaas, the most remarkable and fatal hand-to-hand weapon that I ever saw, and one which he cherished as much as his own life. It scarcely ever left his hand except when he was eating, and then he always sat with it under his leg.

Just as I returned his axe to Umslopogaas Miss Flossie came up and took me to see her collection of flowers, African liliums, and blooming shrubs, some of which are very beautiful, many of the varieties being quite unknown to me and also, I believe, to botanical science. I asked her if she had ever seen or heard of the 'Goya' lily, which Central African explorers have told me they have occasionally met with and whose wonderful loveliness has filled them with astonishment. This lily, which the natives say blooms only once in ten years, flourishes in the most arid soil.

[1] I afterwards discovered that the original name of this axe was 'The Groanmaker.' It was owned by a chief whose history I do not know, but who was called 'The Unconquered.'—A. Q.

Compared to the size of the bloom, the bulb is small, generally weighing about four pounds. As for the flower itself, which I afterwards first saw under circumstances likely to impress its appearance fixedly in my mind, I know not how to describe its beauty and splendour, or the indescribable sweetness of its perfume. The flower—for it only has one bloom—rises from the crown of the bulb on a thick fleshy and flat-sided stem, the specimen that I saw measured fourteen inches in diameter, and is somewhat trumpet-shaped like the bloom of an ordinary 'longiflorum' set vertically. First there is the green sheath, which in its early stage is not unlike that of a water-lily, but which as the bloom opens splits into four portions and curls back gracefully towards the stem. Then comes the bloom itself, a single dazzling arch of white enclosing another cup of richest velvety crimson, from the heart of which rises a golden-coloured pistil. I have never seen anything to equal this bloom in beauty or fragrance, and as I believe it is but little known, I take the liberty to describe it at length. Looking at it for the first time I well remember that I realised how even in a flower there dwells something of the majesty of its Maker. To my great delight Miss Flossie told me that she knew the flower well and had tried to grow it in her garden, but without success, adding, however, that as it should be in bloom at this time of year she thought that she could procure me a specimen.

After that I fell to asking her if she was not lonely up here among all these savage people and without any companions of her own age.

'Lonely?' she said. 'Oh, indeed no! I am as happy as the day is long, and besides I have my own companions. Why, I should hate to be buried in a crowd of white girls all just like myself so that nobody could tell the difference! Here,' she said, giving her head a little toss, 'I am *I*; and every native for miles round knows the "Waterlily,"—for that is what they call me—and is ready to do what I want, but in the books that I have read about little girls in England it is not like that. Everybody thinks them a trouble, and they have to do what their schoolmistress likes. Oh! it would break my heart to be put in a cage like that and not to be free—free as the air.'

'Would you not like to learn?' I asked.

'So I do learn. Father teaches me Latin and French and arithmetic.'

'And are you never afraid among all these wild men?'

'Afraid? Oh, no! they never interfere with me. I think they believe that I am "Ngai" (of the Divinity) because I am so white and have fair hair. And look here,' and diving her little hand into the bodice of her dress she produced a double-barrelled nickel-plated Derringer, 'I always carry that loaded, and if anybody tried to touch me I should shoot him. Once I shot a leopard that jumped upon my donkey as I was riding along. It frightened me very much, but I shot it in the ear and it fell dead, and I have its skin upon my bed. Look there!' she went on in an altered voice, touching me on the arm and pointing to some far-away object, 'I said just now that I had companions; there is one of them.'

I looked, and for the first time there burst upon my sight the glory of Mt. Kenia. Hitherto the mountain had always been hidden in mist, but now its radiant beauty was unveiled for many thousand feet, although the base was still wrapped in vapour so that the lofty peak or pillar, towering nearly twenty thousand feet into the sky, appeared to be a fairy vision, hanging between earth and heaven, and based upon the clouds. The solemn majesty and beauty of this white peak are together beyond the power of my poor pen to describe. There it rose straight and sheer—a glittering white glory, its crest piercing the very blue of heaven. As I gazed at it with that little girl I felt my whole heart lifted up in an indescribable emotion, and for a moment great and wonderful thoughts seemed to break upon my mind, even as the arrows of the setting sun were breaking on Kenia's snows. Mr. Mackenzie's natives call the mountain the 'Finger of God,' and to me it did seem eloquent of immortal peace and of the pure high calm that surely lies above this fevered world. Somewhere I had heard a line of poetry,

A thing of beauty is a joy for ever,

and now it came into my mind, and for the first time I thoroughly understood what the poet meant. Base, indeed, would be the man who could look upon that mighty snow-wreathed pile—that white old tombstone of the years, and not feel his own utter insignificance, and, by whatsoever name he calls Him, worship God in his heart. Such sights are like visions of the spirit; they throw wide the windows of the chamber of our small selfishness and let in a breath of that air that rushes round the rolling spheres, and for a while illumines our darkness with a gleam of the white light which beats upon the Throne.

Yes, such things of beauty are indeed a joy for ever, and I can well understand what little Flossie meant when she talked of Kenia as her companion. As Umslopogaas, savage old Zulu that he was, said when I pointed out to him the peak hanging in the glittering air: 'A man might look thereon for a thousand years and yet be hungry to see.' But he gave rather another colour to his poetical idea when he added in a sort of chant, and with a touch of that weird imagination for which the man was remarkable, that when he was dead he should like his spirit to sit upon yon snow-clad peak for ever, and to rush down the steep white sides in the breath of the whirlwind, or on the flash of the lightning, and 'slay, and slay, and slay.'

'Slay what, old bloodhound?' I asked.

This rather puzzled him, but at length he answered—

'The other shadows.'

'So thou wouldst continue thy murdering even after death?' I said.

'I murder not,' he answered hotly; 'I kill in fair fight. Man is born to kill. He who kills not when his blood is hot is a woman, and no man. The people who kill not are slaves. I say I kill in fair fight; and when I am "in the shadow," as you white men say, I hope to go on killing in fair fight. May my shadow be accursed and chilled to the bone for ever if it should fall to murdering like a bushman with his poisoned arrows!' And he stalked away with much dignity, and left me laughing.

Just then the spies whom our host had sent out in the morning to find out if there were any traces of our Masai friends about, returned, and reported that the country had been scoured for fifteen miles round without a single Elmoran being seen, and they believed that those gentry had given up the pursuit and returned whence they came. Mr. Mackenzie gave a sigh of relief when he heard this, and so indeed did we, for we had seen quite enough of the Masai to last us for some time. Indeed, the general opinion was that, finding we had reached the mission station in safety, knowing its strength, they had given up the pursuit of us as a bad job. How ill-judged that view was the sequel will show.

After the spies were gone, and Mrs. Mackenzie and Flossie had retired for the night, Alphonse, the little Frenchman, came out, and Sir Henry, who is a very good French scholar, got him to tell us how he came to visit Central Africa, which he did in a most extraordinary lingo, that for the most part I shall not attempt to reproduce.

'My grandfather,' he began, 'was a soldier of the Guard, and served under Napoleon. He was in the retreat from Moscow, and lived for ten days on his own leggings and a pair he stole from a comrade. He used to get drunk—he died drunk, and I remember playing at drums on his coffin. My father——'

Here we suggested that he might skip his ancestry and come to the point.

'Bien, messieurs!' replied this comical little man, with a polite bow. 'I did only wish to demonstrate that the military principle is not hereditary. My grandfather was a splendid man, six feet two high, broad in proportion, a swallower of fire and gaiters. Also he was remarkable for his moustache. To me there remains the moustache and—nothing more.

'I am, messieurs, a cook, and I was born at Marseilles. In that dear town I spent my happy youth. For years and years I washed the dishes at the Hôtel Continental. Ah, those were golden days!' and he sighed. 'I am a Frenchman. Need I say, messieurs, that I admire beauty? Nay, I adore the fair. Messieurs, we admire all the roses in a garden, but we pluck one. *I* plucked one, and, alas, messieurs, it pricked my finger. She was a chambermaid, her name Annette, her figure ravishing, her face an angel's, her heart —alas, messieurs, that I should have to own it!—black and slippery as a patent leather boot. I loved to desperation, I adored her to despair. She transported me—in every sense; she inspired me. Never have I cooked as I cooked (for I had been promoted at the hotel) when Annette, my adored Annette, smiled on me. Never'— and here his manly voice broke into a sob—'never shall I cook so well again.' Here he melted into tears.

'Come, cheer up!' said Sir Henry in French, smacking him smartly on the back. 'There's no knowing what may happen, you know. To judge from your dinner to-day, I should say you were in a fair way to recovery.'

Alphonse stopped weeping, and began to rub his back. 'Monsieur,' he said, 'doubtless means to console, but his hand is heavy. To continue: we loved, and were happy in each other's love. The birds in their little nest could not be happier than Alphonse and his Annette. Then came the blow—sapristi!—when I think of it. Messieurs will forgive if I wipe away a tear. Mine was an evil number; I was drawn for the conscription. Fortune would be avenged on me for having won the heart of Annette.

'The evil moment came; I had to go. I tried to run away, but I was caught by brutal soldiers, and they banged me with the butt-end of muskets till my mustachios curled with pain. I had a cousin a linendraper, well-to-do, but very ugly. He had drawn a good number, and sympathised when they thumped me. "To thee, my cousin," I said, "to thee, in whose veins flows the blue blood of our heroic grandparent, to thee I consign Annette. Watch over her whilst I hunt for glory in the bloody field."

' "Make your mind easy," said he; "I will." As the sequel shows, he did!

'I went. I lived in barracks on black soup. I am a refined man and a poet by nature, and I suffered tortures from the coarse horror of my surroundings. There was a drill sergeant, and he had a cane. Ah, that cane, how it curled! Alas, never can I forget it!

'One morning came the news; my battalion was ordered to Tonquin. The drill sergeant and the other coarse monsters rejoiced. I—I made inquiries about Tonquin. They were not satisfactory. In Tonquin are savage Chinese who rip you open. My artistic tastes—for I am also an artist—recoiled from the idea of being ripped open. The great man makes up his mind quickly. I made up my mind. I determined not to be ripped open. I deserted.

'I reached Marseilles disguised as an old man. I went to the house of my cousin—he in whom runs my grandfather's heroic blood—and there sat Annette. It was the season of cherries. They took a double stalk. At each end was a cherry. My cousin put one into his mouth, Annette put the other in hers. Then they drew the stalks in till their lips met—and alas, alas that I should have to say it!—they kissed. The game was a pretty one, but it filled me with fury. The heroic blood of my grandfather boiled up in me. I rushed into the kitchen. I struck my cousin with the old man's crutch. He fell—I had slain him. Alas, I believe that I did slay him. Annette screamed. The gendarmes came. I fled. I reached the harbour. I hid aboard a vessel. The vessel put to sea. The captain found me and he beat me. He took an opportunity. He posted a letter from a foreign port to the police. He did not put me ashore because I cooked so well. I cooked for him all the way to Zanzibar. When I asked for payment he kicked me. The blood of my heroic grandfather boiled within me, and I shook my fist in his face and vowed to have my revenge. He kicked me again. At Zanzibar there was a telegram. I cursed the man who invented telegraphs. Now I curse him again. I was to be arrested for desertion, for murder, and *que sais-je?* I escaped from the prison. I fled, I starved. I met the men of Monsieur le Curé. They brought me here. I am here full of woe. But I return not to France. Better to risk my life in these horrible places than to know the Bagne.'

He paused, and we nearly choked with laughter, having to turn our faces away.

'Ah! you weep, messieurs,' he said. 'No wonder—it is a sad story.'

'Perhaps,' said Sir Henry, 'the heroic blood of your grandparent will triumph after all; perhaps you will still be great. At any rate we shall see. And now I vote we go to bed. I am dead

tired, and we had not much sleep on that confounded rock last
night.'

And so we did, and very strange the tidy rooms and clean white
sheets seemed to us after our recent experiences.

CHAPTER V.

UMSLOPOGAAS MAKES A PROMISE.

NEXT morning at breakfast I missed Flossie and asked where
she was.

'Well,' said her mother, 'when I got up this morning I found a
note put outside my door in which——But here it is, you can read
it for yourself, and she gave me the slip of paper on which the
following was written:—

'Dearest M——,—It is just dawn, and I am off to the hills to
get Mr. Q——a bloom of the lily he wants, so don't expect me
till you see me. I have taken the white donkey; and nurse and a
couple of boys are coming with me—also something to eat, as I
may be away all day, for I am determined to get the lily if I have
to go twenty miles for it.—FLOSSIE.'

'I hope she will be all right,' I said a little anxiously; 'I never
meant her to trouble after the flower.'

'Ah, Flossie can look after herself,' said her mother; 'she often
goes off in this way like a true child of the wilderness.' But Mr.
Mackenzie, who came in just then and saw the note for the first
time, looked rather grave, though he said nothing.

After breakfast was over I took him aside and asked him if it
would not be possible to send after the girl and get her back, having in view the possibility of there still being some Masai hanging
about, at whose hands she might come to harm.

'I fear it would be of no use,' he answered. 'She may be fifteen
miles off by now, and it is impossible to say what path she has
taken. There are the hills;' and he pointed to a long range of
rising ground stretching almost parallel with the course followed
by the river Tana, but gradually sloping down to a dense bush-
clad plain about five miles short of the house.

Here I suggested that we might get up the great tree over the
house and search the country round with a spyglass; and this we
did after Mr. Mackenzie had given some orders to his people to
try and follow Flossie's spoor.

The ascent of the mighty tree was rather an alarming perform-ance, even with a sound rope ladder fixed at both ends to climb up, at least to a landsman; but Good came up like a lamplighter.

On reaching the height at which the first fern-shaped boughs sprang from the bole, we stepped without any difficulty upon a platform made of boards, nailed from one bough to another, and large enough to accommodate a dozen people. As for the view, it was simply glorious. In every direction the bush rolled away in great billows for miles and miles, as far as the glass would show, only here and there broken by the brighter green of patches of cultivation, or by the glittering surfaces of lakes. To the north-west, Kenia reared his mighty head, and we could trace the Tana River curling like a silver snake almost from his feet, and far away beyond us towards the ocean. It is a glorious country, and only wants the hand of civilised man to make it a most productive one.

But look as we would, we could see no signs of Flossie and her donkey, so at last had to come down disappointed. On reaching the verandah I found Umslopogaas sitting there, slowly and lightly sharpening his axe with a small whetstone which he always carried with him.

"What doest thou, Umslopogaas?' I asked.

'I smell blood,' was the answer; and I could get no more out of him.

After dinner again we went up the tree and searched the sur-rounding country with a spyglass, but without result. When we came down Umslopogaas was still sharpening Inkosi-kaas, al-though she already had an edge like a razor. Standing in front of him, and regarding him with a mixture of fear and fascination, was Alphonse. And certainly he did seem an alarming object—sitting there, Zulu fashion, on his haunches, a wild look upon his intensely savage and yet intellectual face, sharpening, sharpening, sharpening at the murderous-looking axe.

'Oh, the monster, the horrible man!' said the little French cook, lifting his hands in amazement. 'See but the hole in his head; the skin beats on it up and down like a baby's! Who would nurse such a baby?' and he burst out laughing at the idea.

For a moment Umslopogaas looked up from his sharpening, and a sort of evil light played in his dark eyes.

'What does the little "buffalo-heifer" say? [so named by Um-slopogaas, on account of his mustachios and feminine character-istics]. Let him be careful, or I will cut his horns. Beware, little man monkey, beware!'

Unfortunately Alphonse, who was getting over his fear of him, went on laughing at '*ce drôle d'un monsieur noir.*' I was about to warn him to desist, when suddenly the huge Zulu bounded off the verandah on to the open space where Alphonse was standing, his features alive with a sort of malicious enthusiasm, and began swinging the axe round and round over the Frenchman's head.

'Stand still,' I shouted; 'do not move as you value your life—he will not hurt you;' but I doubt if Alphonse heard me, being, fortunately for himself, almost petrified with horror.

Then followed the most extraordinary display of sword, or rather of axemanship, that I ever saw. First of all the axe went flying round and round over the top of Alphonse's head, with an angry whirl and such extraordinary swiftness that it looked like a continuous band of steel, ever getting nearer and yet nearer to that unhappy individual's skull, till at last it grazed it as it flew. Then suddenly the motion was changed, and it seemed to literally flow up and down his body and limbs, never more than an eighth of an inch from them, and yet never striking them. It was a wonderful sight to see the little man fixed there, having apparently realised that to move would be to run the risk of sudden death, while his black tormentor towered over him, and wrapped him round with the quick flashes of the axe. For a minute or more this went on, till suddenly I saw the moving brightness travel down the side of Alphonse's face, and then outwards and stop. As it did so a tuft of something black fell to the ground; it was the tip of one of the little Frenchman's curling mustachios.

Umslopogaas leant upon the handle of Inkosi-kaas, and broke into a long, low laugh; and Alphonse, overcome with fear, sank into a sitting posture on the ground, whilst we stood astonished at this exhibition of almost superhuman skill and mastery of a weapon. 'Inkosi-kaas is sharp enough,' he shouted; 'the blow that clipped the "buffalo-heifer's" horn would have split a man from the crown to the chin. Few could have struck it but I; none could have struck it and not taken off the shoulder too. Look, thou little heifer! Am I a good man to laugh at, thinkest thou? For a space hast thou stood within a hair's-breadth of death. Laugh not again, lest the hair's-breadth be wanting. I have spoken.'

'What meanest thou by such mad tricks?' I asked of Umslopogaas, indignantly. 'Surely thou art mad. Twenty times didst thou go near to slaying the man.'

'And yet, Macumazahn, I slew not. Thrice as Inkosi-kaas flew the spirit entered into me to end him, and send her crashing through his skull; but I did not. Nay, it was but a jest; but tell the "heifer" that it is not well to mock at such as I. Now I go to make a shield, for I smell blood, Macumazahn—of a truth I smell blood. Before the battle hast thou not seen the vultures grow of a sudden in the sky? They smell the blood, Macumazahn, and my scent is more keen than theirs. There is a dry ox-hide down yonder; I go to make a shield.'

'That is an uncomfortabe sort of retainer of yours,' said Mr. Mackenzie, who had witnessed this extraordinary scene. 'He has frightened Alphonse out of his wits; look!' and he pointed to the Frenchman, who, with a scared white face and trembling limbs, was making his way into the house. 'I don't think that he will ever laugh at "le monsieur noir" again.'

'Yes,' answered I, 'it is ill jesting with such as he. When he is roused he is like a fiend, and yet he has a kind heart in his own fierce way. I remember years ago seeing him nurse a sick child for a week. He is a strange character, but true as steel, and a strong stick to rest on in danger.'

'He says he smells blood,' said Mr. Mackenzie. 'I only trust he is not right. I am getting very fearful about my little girl. She must have gone far, or she would be home by now. It is half-past three o'clock.'

I pointed out that she had taken food with her, and very likely in the ordinary course of events would not return till nightfall; but I myself felt very anxious, and fear that my anxiety betrayed itself.

Shortly after this, the people whom Mr. Mackenzie had sent out to search for Flossie returned, stating that they had followed the spoor of the donkey for a couple of miles and had then lost it on some stony ground, nor could they discover it again. They had, however, scoured the country far and wide, but without success.

After this the afternoon wore on drearily, and towards evening, there still being no signs of Flossie, our anxiety grew very keen. As for the poor mother, she was quite prostrated by her fears, and no wonder, but the father kept his head wonderfully well. Everything that could be done was done: people were sent out in all directions, shots were fired, and a continuous outlook kept from the great tree, but without avail.

And then at last it grew dark, and still no sign of fair-haired little Flossie.

At eight o'clock we had supper. It was but a sorrowful meal, and Mrs. Mackenzie did not appear at it. We three also were very silent, for in addition to our natural anxiety as to the fate of the child, we were weighed down by the sense that we had brought this trouble on the head of our kind host. When supper was nearly at an end I made an excuse to leave the table. I wanted to get outside and think the situation over. I went on to the verandah and, having lit my pipe, sat down on a seat about a dozen feet from the right-hand end of the structure, which, as the reader may remember, was exactly opposite one of the narrow doors of the protecting wall that enclosed the house and flower garden. I had been sitting there perhaps six or seven minutes when I thought I heard the door move. I looked in that direction and listened, but, being unable to make out anything, concluded that I must have been mistaken. It was a darkish night, the moon not having yet risen.

Another minute passed, when suddenly something round fell with a soft but heavy thud upon the stone flooring of the verandah, and came bounding and rolling along past me. For a moment I did not rise, but sat wondering what it could be. Finally, I concluded it must have been an animal. Just then, however, another idea struck me, and I got up quick enough. The thing lay quite still a few feet beyond me. I put down my hand towards it and it did not move: clearly it was not an animal. My hand touched it. It was soft and warm and heavy. Hurriedly I lifted it and held it up against the faint starlight.

It was a newly severed human head!

I am an old hand and not easily upset, but I own that this ghastly sight made me feel sick. How had the thing come there? Whose was it? I put it down and ran to the little doorway. I could see nothing, hear nobody. I was about to go out into the darkness beyond, but remembering that to do so was to expose myself to the risk of being stabbed, I drew back, shut the door, and bolted it. Then I returned to the verandah, and in as careless a voice as I could command called Curtis. I fear, however, that my tones must have betrayed me, for not only Sir Henry but also Good and Mackenzie rose from the table and came hurrying out.

'What is it?' said the clergyman, anxiously.

Then I had to tell them.

Mr. Mackenzie turned pale as death under his red skin. We were standing opposite the hall door, and there was a light in it so that I could see. He snatched the head up by the hair and held it against the light.

'It is the head of one of the men who accompanied Flossie,' he said with a gasp. 'Thank God it is not hers!'

We all stood and stared at each other aghast. What was to be done?

Just then there was a knocking at the door that I had bolted, and a voice cried, 'Open, my father, open!'

The door was unlocked, and in sped a terrified man. He was one of the spies who had been sent out.

'My father,' he cried, 'the Masai are on us! A great body of them have passed round the hill and are moving towards the old stone kraal down by the little stream. My father, make strong thy heart! In the midst of them I saw the white ass, and on it sat the Waterlily [Flossie]. An Elmoran [young warrior] led the ass, and by its side walked the nurse weeping. The men who went with her in the morning I saw not.'

'Was the child alive?' asked Mr. Mackenzie, hoarsely.

'She was white as the snow, but well, my father. They passed quite close to me, and looking up from where I lay hid I saw her face against the sky.'

'God help her and us!' groaned the clergyman.

'How many are there of them?' I asked.

'More than two hundred—two hundred and half a hundred.'

Once more we looked one on the other. What was to be done? Just then there rose a loud insistent cry outside the wall.

'Open the door, white man; open the door! A herald—a herald to speak with thee.' Thus cried the voice.

Umslopogaas ran to the wall, and, reaching with his long arms to the coping, lifted his head above it and gazed over.

'I see but one man,' he said. 'He is armed, and carries a basket in his hand.'

'Open the door,' I said. 'Umslopogaas, take thine axe and stand thereby. Let one man pass. If another follows, slay.'

The door was unbarred. In the shadow of the wall stood Umslopogaas, his axe raised above his head to strike. Just then the moon came out. There was a moment's pause, and then in stalked a Masai Elmoran, clad in the full war panoply that I have already described, but bearing a large basket in his hand. The moonlight shone bright upon his great spear as he walked. He was a splendid man, physically, apparently about thirty-five years of age. Indeed, none of the Masai that I saw were under six feet high, though mostly quite young. When he was opposite to us he halted, put down the basket, and stuck the spike of his spear into the ground, so that it stood upright.

'Let us talk,' he said. 'The first messenger we sent to you could not talk;' and he pointed to the head which lay upon the paving of the stoep—a ghastly sight in the moonlight; 'but I have words to speak if ye have ears to hear. Also I bring presents;' and he pointed to the basket and laughed with an air of swaggering insolence that is perfectly indescribable, and yet which one could not but admire, seeing that he was surrounded by enemies.

'Say on,' said Mr. Mackenzie.

'I am the "Lygonani" [war captain] of a part of the Masai of the Guasa Amboni. I and my men followed these three white men,' and he pointed to Sir Henry, Good, and myself, 'but they were too clever for us, and escaped hither. We have a quarrel with them, and are going to kill them.'

'Are you, my friend?' I said to myself.

'In following these men this morning we caught two black men, one black woman, a white donkey, and a white girl. One of the black men we killed—there is his head upon the pavement; the other ran away. The black woman, the little white girl, and the white ass we took and brought with us. In proof thereof have I brought this basket that she carried. Is it not thy daughter's basket?'

Mr. Mackenzie nodded, and the warrior went on.

'Good! With thee and thy daughter we have no quarrel nor do we wish to harm thee, save as to thy cattle, which we have already gathered, two hundred and forty head—a beast for every man's father.'[1]

Here Mr. Mackenzie gave a groan, as he greatly valued this herd of cattle, which he bred with much care and trouble.

'So, save for the cattle, thou mayst go free; more especially,' he added frankly, glancing at the wall, 'as this place would be a difficult one to take. But as to these men it is otherwise; we have followed them for nights and days, and must kill them. Were we to return to our kraal without having done so, all the girls would make a mock of us. So, however troublesome it may be, they must die.

'Now I have a proposition for thine ear. We would not harm the little girl; she is too fair to harm, and has besides a brave spirit. Give us one of these three men—a life for a life—and we will let her go, and throw in the black woman with her also. This is a fair offer, white man. We ask but for one, not for the three; we must take another opportunity to kill the other two. I do not even pick my man, though I should prefer the big one,' pointing to Sir Henry; 'he looks strong, and would die more slowly.'

'And if I say I will not yield the man?" said Mr. Mackenzie.

'Nay, say not so, white man,' answered the Masai, 'for then thy daughter dies at dawn, and the woman with her says thou hast no other child. Were she older I would take her for a servant; but as she is so young I will slay her with my own hand—ay, with this very spear. Thou canst come and see, an' thou wilt. I give thee a safe conduct;' and the fiend laughed aloud at his brutal jest.

[1] The Masai Elmoran or young warriors can own no property, so all the booty they may win in battle belongs to their fathers alone.—A. Q.

Meanwhile I had been thinking rapidly, as one does in emergencies, and had come to the conclusion that I would exchange myself against Flossie. I scarcely like to mention the matter for fear it should be misunderstood. Pray do not let any one be misled into thinking that there was anything heroic about this, or any such nonsense. It was merely a matter of common sense and common justice. My life was an old and worthless one, hers was young and valuable. Her death would pretty well kill her father and mother also, whilst nobody would be much the worse for mine; indeed, several charitable institutions would have cause to rejoice thereat. It was indirectly through me that the dear little girl was in her present position. Lastly, a man is better fitted to meet death in such a peculiarly awful form than a sweet young girl. Not, however, that I meant to let these gentry torture me to death—I am far too much of a coward to allow that, being naturally a timid man; my plan was to see the girl safely exchanged and then to shoot myself, trusting that the Almighty would take the peculiar circumstances of the case into consideration and pardon the act. All this and more went through my mind in very few seconds.

'All right, Mackenzie,' I said, 'you can tell the man that I will exchange myself against Flossie, only I stipulate that she shall be safely in the house before they kill me.'

'Eh?' said Sir Henry and Good simultaneously. 'That you don't.'

'No, no,' said Mr. Mackenzie, 'I will have no man's blood upon my hands. If it please God that my daughter die this awful death, His will be done. You are a brave man (which I am not by any means) and a noble man, Quatermain, but you shall not go.'

'If nothing else turns up I shall go,' I said decidedly.

'This is an important matter,' said Mackenzie, addressing the Lygonani, 'and we must think it over. You shall have our answer at dawn.'

'Very well, white man,' answered the savage indifferently; 'only remember if thy answer is late thy little white bud will never grow into a flower, that is all, for I shall cut it with this,' and he touched the spear. 'I should have thought that thou wouldst play a trick and attack us at night, but I know from the woman with the girl that thy men are down at the coast, and that thou hast but twenty left here. It is not wise, white man,' he added with a laugh, 'to keep so small a garrison for thy "boma" [kraal]. Well, good night, and good night to you also, other white men, whose eyelids I shall soon close once and for all. At dawn thou wilt bring me word. If not, remember it shall be as I have said.' Then turning to Umslopogaas, who had been standing behind him all the while and shepherding him as it were, 'Open the door for me, fellow, quick now.'

This was too much for the old chief's patience. For the last ten minutes, figuratively speaking, his lips had been positively watering over the Masai Lygonani, and this he could not stand. Placing his long hand on the Elmoran's shoulder Umslopogaas gave him such a twist as brought him face to face with himself. Then, thrusting his fierce countenance to within a few inches of the Masai's evil feather-framed features, he said in a low growling voice:—

'Seest thou me?'

'Ay, fellow, I see thee.'

'And seest thou this?' and he held Inkosi-kaas before his eyes.

'Ay, fellow, I see the toy; what of it?'

'Thou Masai dog, thou boasting windbag, thou capturer of little girls, with this "toy" will I hew thee limb from limb. Well for thee that thou art a herald, or even now would I strew thy members about the grass.'

The Masai shook his great spear and laughed long and loud as he answered, 'I would that thou stoodst against me man to man, and we could see,' and again he turned to go, still laughing.

'Thou shalt stand against me man to man, be not afraid,' replied Umslopogaas, still in the same ominous voice. 'Thou shalt stand face to face with Umslopogaas, of the blood of Chaka, of the people of the Amazulu, captain of the regiment of the Nkomabakosi, as many have done before, and bow thyself to Inkosi-kaas, as many have done before. Ay, laugh on, laugh on! to-morrow night shall the jackals laugh as they crunch thy ribs.'

When the Lygonani had gone, one of us thought of opening the basket he had brought as proof that Flossie was really their prisoner. On lifting the lid it was found to contain a most lovely specimen of both bulb and flower of the Goya lily, which I have already described, in full bloom and quite uninjured, and what was more a note in Flossie's childish hand written in pencil upon a greasy piece of paper that had been used to wrap up some food in:—

'DEAREST FATHER AND MOTHER,' ran the note,—'The Masai caught us when we were coming home with the lily. I tried to escape but could not. They killed Tom: the other man ran away. They have not hurt nurse and me, but say that they mean to exchange us against one of Mr. Quatermain's party. *I will have nothing of the sort.* Do not let anybody give his life for me. Try

and attack them at night; they are going to feast on three bul-
locks they have stolen and killed. I have my pistol, and if no help
comes by dawn I will shoot myself. They shall not kill me. If so,
remember me always, dearest father and mother. I am very
frightened, but I trust in God. I dare not write any more as they
are beginning to notice. Good-bye.—FLOSSIE.'

Scrawled across the outside of this was 'Love to Mr. Quatermain. They are going to take up the basket, so he will get the
lily.'

When I read those words, written by that brave little girl in
an hour of danger sufficiently near and horrible to have turned the
brain of a strong man, I own I wept, and once more in my heart
I vowed that she should not die while my life could be given to
save her.

Then eagerly, quickly, almost fiercely, we fell to discussing the
situation. Again I said that I would go, and again Mackenzie
negatived it, and Curtis and Good, like the true men that they
are, vowed that, if I did, they would go with me, and die back to
back with me.

'It is,' I said at last, 'absolutely necessary that an effort of some
sort should be made before the morning.'

'Then let us attack them with what force we can muster, and
take our chance,' said Sir Henry.

'Ay, ay,' growled Umslopogaas, in Zulu; 'spoken like a man,
Incubu. What is there to be afraid of? Two hundred and fifty
Masai, forsooth! How many are we? The chief there [Mr. Mac-
kenzie] has twenty men, and thou, Macumazahn, hast five men,
and there are also five white men—that is, thirty men in all—
enough, enough. Listen now, Macumazahn, thou who art very
clever and old in war. What says the maid? These men eat and
make merry; let it be their funeral feast. What said the dog
whom I hope to hew down at daybreak? That he feared no
attack because we were so few. Knowest thou the old kraal where
the men have camped? I saw it this morning; it is thus:' and he
drew an oval on the floor; 'here is the big entrance, filled up with
thorn bushes, and opening on to a steep rise. Why, Incubu, thou
and I with axes will hold it against an hundred men striving to
break out! Look, now; thus shall the battle go. Just as the light
begins to glint upon the oxen's horns—not before, or it will be too
dark, and not later, or they will be awakening and perceive us—
let Bougwan creep round with ten men to the top end of the kraal,
where the narrow entrance is. Let them silently slay the sentry
there so that he makes no sound, and stand ready. Then, Incubu,

let us two and one of the Askari—the one with the broad chest—
he is a brave man—creep to the wide entrance that is filled with
thorn bushes, and there cut down the sentry, and armed with
battle-axes take our stand also one on each side of the pathway,
and one a few paces beyond to deal with such as pass the twain
at the gate. It is there that the rush will come. That will leave
sixteen men. Let these men be divided into two parties, with one
of which shalt thou go, Macumazahn, and with one the "praying
man" [Mr. Mackenzie], and, all armed with rifles, let them make
their way one to the right side of the kraal and one to the left;
and when thou, Macumazahn, lowest like an ox, all shall open fire
with the guns upon the sleeping men, being very careful not to hit
the little maid. Then shall Bougwan at the far end and his ten
men raise their war-cry, and, springing over the wall, put the
Masai there to the sword. And it shall happen that, being yet
heavy with food and sleep, and bewildered by the firing of the
guns, the falling of men, and the spears of Bougwan, the soldiers
shall rise and rush like wild game towards the thorn-stopped entrance, and there the bullets from either side shall plough through
them, and there shall Incubu and the Askari and I wait for
those who break across. Such is my plan, Macumazahn; if thou
hast a better, name it.'

When he had done, I explained to the others such portions of
this scheme as they had failed to understand, and they all joined
with me in expressing the greatest admiration of the acute and
skilful programme devised by the old Zulu, who was indeed, in
his own savage fashion, the finest general I ever knew. After
some discussion we determined to accept the scheme, as it stood,
it being the only one possible under the circumstances, and giving
the best chance of success that such a forlorn hope would admit
of—which, however, considering the enormous odds and the character of our foe, was not very great.

'Ah, old lion!' I said to Umslopogaas, 'thou knowest how to lie
in wait as well as how to bite, when to seize as well as where to
hang on.'

'Ay, ay, Macumazahn,' he answered. 'For forty years have I
been a warrior, and have seen many things. It will be a good
fight. I smell blood—I tell thee, I smell blood.'

CHAPTER VI.

THE NIGHT WEARS ON.

As may be imagined, at the very first sign of a Masai the entire population of the Mission Station had sought refuge inside the stout stone wall, and were now to be seen—men, women, and countless children—huddled up together in little groups, and all talking at once in awed tones of the awfulness of Masai manners and customs, and of the fate that they had to expect if those bloodthirsty savages succeeded in getting over the stone wall.

Immediately after we had settled upon the outline of our plan of action as suggested by Umslopogaas, Mr. Mackenzie sent for four sharp boys of from twelve to fifteen years of age, and despatched them to various points whence they could keep an outlook upon the Masai camp, with orders to report from time to time what was going on. Other lads and even women were stationed at intervals along the wall in order to guard against the possibility of surprise.

After this the twenty men who formed his whole available fighting force were summoned by our host into the square formed by the house, and there, standing by the bole of the great conifer, he earnestly addressed them and our four Askari. Indeed, it formed a very impressive scene—one not likely to be forgotten by anybody who witnessed it. Immediately by the tree stood the angular form of Mr. Mackenzie, one arm outstretched as he talked, and the other resting against the giant bole, his hat off, and his plain but kindly face clearly betraying the anguish of his mind. Next to him came his poor wife, who was seated on a chair, her face hidden in her hand. On the other side of her was Alphonse, looking exceedingly uncomfortable, and behind him stood the three of us, with Umslopogaas' grim form towering in the background, resting, as usual, on his axe. In front stood and squatted the group of armed men—some with rifles in their hands, and others with spears and shields—following with eager attention every word that fell from the speaker's lips. The white light of the moon peering in beneath the lofty boughs threw a certain glamour over the scene, whilst the melancholy soughing of the night wind passing through the millions of pine needles overhead added its own sadness to what was already a sufficiently tragic occasion.

'Men,' said Mr. Mackenzie, after he had put all the circumstances of the case fully and clearly before them, and explained to them the proposed plan of our forlorn hope—'men, for years I have been a good friend to you, protecting you, teaching you, guarding you and yours from harm, and ye have prospered with me. Ye have seen my child—the Waterlily, as ye call her—grow year by year, from tenderest infancy to tender childhood, and from childhood on towards maidenhood. She has been your children's playmates, she has helped to nurse you when sick, and ye have loved her.'

'We have,' said a deep voice, 'and we will die to save her.'

'I thank you from my heart—I thank you. Sure am I that now, in this hour of darkest trouble; now that her young life is to be cut off by cruel and savage men—who of a truth "know not what they do"—ye will strive your best to save her, and to save me and her mother from broken hearts. Think, too, of your own wives and children. If she dies, her death will be followed by an attack upon us here, and at the best, even if we hold our own, your houses and gardens will be destroyed, and your goods and cattle swept away. I am, as ye well know, a man of peace. Never in all these years have I lifted my hand to shed man's blood; but now I say strike, strike, in the name of God, Who bade us protect our lives and homes. Swear to me,' he went on with added fervour—'swear to me that whilst a man of you remains alive ye will strive your uttermost with me and with these brave white men to save the child from a bloody and a cruel death.'

'Say no more, my father,' said the same deep voice, that belonged to a stalwart elder of the Mission; 'we swear it. May we and ours die the death of dogs, and our bones be thrown to the jackals and the kites, if we break the oath! It is a fearful thing to do, my father, so few to strike at so many, yet will we do it or die in the doing. We swear!'

'Ay, thus say we all,' chimed in the others.

'Thus say we all,' said I.

'It is well,' went on Mr. Mackenzie. 'Ye are true men and not broken reeds to lean on. And now, friends—white and black together—let us kneel and offer up our humble supplication to the Throne of Power, praying that He in the hollow of Whose hand lie all our lives, Who giveth life and giveth death, may be pleased to make strong our arms that we may prevail in what awaits us at the morning's light.'

And he knelt down, an example that we all followed except Umslopogaas, who still stood in the background, grimly leaning on Inkosi-kaas. The fierce old Zulu had no gods and worshipped nought, unless it were his battle-axe.

'Oh, God of gods!' began the clergyman, his deep voice, tremulous with emotion, echoing up in the silence even to the leafy roof; 'Protector of the oppressed, Refuge of those in danger, Guardian of the helpless, hear Thou our prayer! Almighty Father, to Thee we come in supplication. Hear Thou our prayer! Behold, one child hast Thou given us—an innocent child, nurtured in Thy knowledge—and now she lies beneath the shadow of the sword, in danger of a fearful death at the hands of savage men. Be with her now, O God, and comfort her! Save her, O Heavenly Father! O God of battle, Who teachest our hands to war and our fingers to fight, in Whose strength are hid the destinies of men, be Thou with us in the hour of strife. When we go forth into the shadow of death, make Thou us strong to conquer. Breathe Thou upon our foes and scatter them; turn Thou their strength to water, and bring their high-blown pride to nought; compass us about with Thy protection; throw over us the shield of Thy power; forget us not now in the hour of our sore distress; help us now that the cruel man would dash our little ones against the stones! Hear Thou our prayer! And for those of us who, kneeling now on earth in health before Thee, shall at the sunrise adore Thy Presence on the Throne, hear our prayer! Make them clean, O God; wash away their offences in the blood of the Lamb; and when their spirits pass, receive Thou them into the haven of the just. Go forth, O Father, go forth with us into the battle, as with the Israelites of old. O God of battles, hear Thou our prayer!'

He ceased, and after a moment's silence we all rose, and then began our preparations in good earnest. As Umslopogaas said, it was time to stop 'talking' and get to business. The men who were to form each little party were carefully selected, and still more carefully and minutely instructed as to what was to be done. After much consideration it was agreed that the ten men led by Good, whose duty it was to stampede the camp, were not to carry firearms; that is, with the exception of Good himself, who had a revolver as well as a short sword—the Masai 'sime' which I had taken from the body of our poor servant who was murdered in the canoe. We feared that if they had firearms the result of three cross-fires carried on at once would be that some of our own people would be shot; besides, it appeared to all of us that the work they had to do would best be carried out with cold steel—especially to Umslopogaas, who was, indeed, a great advocate of cold steel. We had with us four Winchester repeating rifles, besides half a dozen Martinis. I armed myself with one of the repeaters—my own; an excellent weapon for this kind of work, where great rapidity of fire is desirable, and fitted with ordinary flap-sights instead of the cumbersome sliding mechanism which they generally carry. Mr. Mackenzie took another, and the remaining ones were given to two of his men who understood the use of them and

were noted shots. The Martinis and some rifles of Mr. Mackenzie's were served out, together with a plentiful supply of ammunition, to the other natives who were to form the two parties
whose duty it was to be to open fire from separate sides of the
kraal on the sleeping Masai, and who were fortunately all more
or less accustomed to the use of a gun.

As for Umslopogaas, we know how he was armed—with an axe.
It may be remembered that he, Sir Henry, and the strongest of
the Askari were to hold the thorn-stopped entrance to the kraal
against the anticipated rush of men striving to escape. Of course,
for such a purpose as this guns were useless. Therefore Sir Henry
and the Askari proceeded to arm themselves in like fashion. It
so happened that Mr. Mackenzie had in his little store a selection
of the very best steel English-made hammer-backed axe-heads.
Sir Henry selected one of these weighing about two and a half
pounds and very broad in the blade, and the Askari took another
a size smaller. After Umslopogaas had put an extra edge on these
two axe-heads, we fixed them to three feet six helves, of which
Mr. Mackenzie fortunately had some in stock, made of a light
but exceedingly tough native wood, something like English ash,
only more springy. When two suitable helves had been selected
with great care and the ends of the hafts notched to prevent the
hand from slipping, the axe-heads were fixed on them as firmly
as possible, and the weapons immersed in a bucket of water for
half an hour. The result of this was to swell the wood into the
socket in such a fashion that nothing short of burning would get
it out again. When this important matter had been attended to
by Umslopogaas, I went into my room and proceeded to open a
little tin-lined deal case, which had not been undone since we left
England, and which contained—what do you think?—nothing
more nor less than four mail shirts.

It had happened to us three on a previous journey that we took
in another part of Africa to owe our lives to iron shirts of native
make, and remembering this, I suggested before we started on
our present hazardous expedition that we should have some made
to fit us. There was a little difficulty about this, as armour-
making is almost an extinct art, but they can do most things in
the way of steel work in Birmingham if they are put to it and
you will pay the price, and the end of it was that they turned us
out the loveliest steel shirts it is possible to see. The workmanship
was exceedingly fine, the web being composed of thousands upon
thousands of stout but tiny rings of the very best steel. These
shirts, or rather steel-sleeved and high-necked jerseys, were lined
with ventilated wash leather, were not bright, but browned like

the barrel of a gun; and mine weighed exactly seven pounds and fitted me so well that I found I could wear it for days next my skin without being chafed. Sir Henry had two, one of the ordinary make, viz. a jersey with little dependent flaps meant to afford some protection to the upper part of the thighs, and another of his own design fashioned on the pattern of the garments advertised as 'combinations' and weighing twelve pounds. This combination shirt, of which the seat was made of wash-leather, protected the whole body down to the knees, but was rather more cumbersome, inasmuch as it had to be laced up the back and, of course, involved some extra weight. With these shirts were what looked like four brown cloth travelling caps with ear pieces. Each of these caps was, however, quilted with steel links so as to afford a most valuable protection for the head.

It seems almost laughable to talk of steel shirts in these days of bullets, against which they are of course quite useless; but where one has to do with savages, armed with cutting arms such as assegais or battle-axes, they are of service, being, if well made, quite invulnerable to such weapons. I have often thought that if only the English Government in our savage wars, and more especially in the Zulu war, had thought fit to serve out light steel shirts, there would be many a man alive to-day who, as it is, is dead and forgotten.

To return: on the present occasion we blessed our foresight in bringing these shirts, and also our good luck, in that they had not been stolen by our rascally bearers when they ran away with our goods. As Curtis had two, and, after considerable deliberation, made up his mind to wear his 'combination' himself—the extra three or four pounds' weight being a matter of no account to one so strong, and the protection afforded to the thighs being a very important matter to a fighting man not armed with a shield of any kind—I suggested that he should lend the other to Umslopogaas, who was to share the danger and the glory of his post. He readily consented, and called the Zulu, who came bearing with him Sir Henry's axe, which he had now fixed up to his satisfaction. When we showed him the steel shirt, and then explained that we wanted him to wear it, he at first declined, saying that he had fought in his own skin for forty years, and that he was not going to begin now to fight in an iron one. Thereupon I took a heavy spear, and, spreading the shirt upon the floor, drove the spear down upon it with all my strength, the weapon rebounding without leaving a mark upon the tempered steel. This exhibition half converted him; and when I pointed out to him how necessary it was that he should not let any old-fashioned prejudices he

might possess stand in the way of a precaution which might preserve a valuable life at a time when men were scarce, and also
that if he wore this shirt he might dispense with a shield, and so
have both hands free, he yielded at once, and proceeded to invest
his frame with the 'iron skin.' And indeed, although made for Sir
Henry, it fitted the great Zulu like a skin. The two men were
almost of a height; and, though Curtis looked the bigger man, I
am inclined to think that the difference was more imaginary than
real, the fact being, although he was plumper and rounder, that
he was not really bigger, except in the arm. Umslopogaas had,
comparatively speaking, thin arms, but they were as strong as
wire ropes. At any rate, when, axe in hand, they both stood clad
in the brown mail, which clung to their mighty forms like a web
garment, showing the swell of every muscle and the curve of
every line, they seemed a pair that any ten men might shrink
from meeting.

It was now nearly one o'clock in the morning, and the spies
reported that, after having drunk the blood of the oxen and eaten
enormous quantities of meat, the Masai were going to sleep round
their watchfires; but that sentries had been posted at each opening of the kraal. Flossie, they added, was sitting not far from
the wall in the centre of the western side of the kraal, and by her
were the nurse and the white donkey, which was tethered to a
peg. Her feet were bound with a rope, and warriors were lying
about all round her.

As there was absolutely nothing further that could be done
then we all took some supper, and went to lie down for a couple
of hours. I could not help admiring the ease with which old Umslopogaas flung himself upon the floor, and, unmindful of what
was hanging over him, instantly sank into a deep sleep. I do not
know how it was with the others, but I could not do as much.
Indeed, as is usual with me on these occasions, I am sorry to say
that I felt rather frightened; and, now that some of the enthusiasm had gone out of me, and I began calmly to contemplate
what we had undertaken to do, truth compels me to add that I
did not like it. We were but thirty men all told, a good many of
whom were no doubt quite unused to fighting, and we were going
to engage two hundred and fifty of the fiercest, bravest, and most
formidable savages in Africa, who, to make matters worse, were
protected by a stone wall. It was, indeed, a mad undertaking,
and what made it even madder was the exceeding improbability
of our being able to take up our positions without attracting the
notice of the sentries. Of course if once we did that—and any
slight accident, such as the chance discharge of a gun, might do

it—we were destroyed, for the whole camp would be up in a second, and our only hope lay in a surprise.

The bed whereon I lay indulging in these uncomfortable reflections was near an open window that looked on to the verandah, through which came an extraordinary sound of groaning and weeping. For a time I could not make out what it was, but at last I got up and, putting my head out of the window, stared about. Presently I saw a dim figure kneeling on the end of the verandah and beating his breast—in which I recognised Alphonse. Not being able to understand his French talk or what on earth he was at, I called to him and asked him what he was doing.

'Ah, monsieur,' he sighed, 'I do make prayer for the souls of those whom I shall slay to-night.'

'Indeed,' I said, 'then I wish that you would pray a little more quietly.'

Alphonse retreated, and I heard no more of his groans. And so the time passed, till at length Mr. Mackenzie called me in a whisper through the window, for of course everything must now be done in the most absolute silence. 'Three o'clock,' he said: 'we should begin to move at half-past.'

I told him to come in, and presently he entered, and I am bound to say that if it had not been that just then I had not a laugh anywhere about me, I should have exploded as the sight he presented as armed for battle. To begin with, he wore a clergyman's black swallow-tail and a kind of broad-rimmed black felt hat, both of which he had donned on account, he said, of their dark colour. In his hand was the Winchester repeating rifle we had lent him; and stuck in an elastic cricketing belt, like those worn by English boys, were, first, a huge buckhorn-handled carving knife with a guard to it, and next a long-barrelled Colt's revolver.

'Ah, my friend,' he said, seeing me staring at his belt, 'you are looking at my "carver." I thought it might be very handy if we came to close quarters; it is excellent steel, and many is the pig I have killed with it.'

By this time everybody was up and dressing. I put on a light Norfolk jacket over my mail shirt in order to have a pocket handy to hold my cartridges, and buckled on my revolver. Good did the same, but Sir Henry put on nothing except his mail-shirt, steel-lined cap, and a pair of 'veldtschoons' or soft hide shoes, his legs being bare from the knees down. His revolver he strapped on round his middle outside the armoured shirt.

Meanwhile Umslopogaas was mustering the men in the square under the big tree and going the rounds to see that each was properly armed, etc. At the last moment we made one change.

Finding that two of the men who were to have gone with the firing parties knew little or nothing of guns, but were good spearsmen, we took away their rifles, supplied them with shields and long spears of the Masai pattern, and told them off to join Curtis, Umslopogaas, and the Askari in holding the wide opening; it having become clear to us that three men, however brave and strong, were too few for the work.

CHAPTER VII.

A SLAUGHTER GRIM AND GREAT.

THEN there was a pause, and we stood still in the chilly silent darkness waiting till the moment came to start. It was, perhaps, the most trying time of all—that slow, slow quarter of an hour. The minutes seemed to drag along with leaden feet, and the quiet, the solemn hush, that brooded over all—big, as it were, with a coming fate, was most oppressive to the spirits. I once remember having to get up before dawn to see a man hanged, and I then went through a very similar set of sensations, only in the present instance my feelings were animated by that more vivid and personal element which naturally appertains rather to the person to be operated on than to the most sympathetic spectator. The solemn faces of the men, well aware that the short passage of an hour would mean for some, and perhaps all of them, the last great passage to the unknown or oblivion; the bated whispers in which they spoke; even Sir Henry's continuous and thoughtful examination of his woodcutter's axe and the fidgety way in which Good kept polishing his eyeglass, all told the same tale of nerves stretched pretty nigh to breaking point. Only Umslopogaas, leaning as usual upon Inkosi-kaas and taking an occasional pinch of snuff, to all appearance was perfectly and completely unmoved. Nothing could touch his iron nerves.

The moon went down, for a long while she had been getting nearer and nearer to the horizon, now she finally sank and left the world in darkness save for a faint grey tinge in the eastern sky that palely heralded the dawn.

Mr. Mackenzie stood, watch in hand, his wife clinging to his arm and striving to stifle her sobs.

'Twenty minutes to four,' he said; 'it ought to be light enough to attack at twenty minutes past four. Captain Good had better be moving, he will want three or four minutes' start.'

Good gave one final polish to his eyeglass, nodded to us in a jocular sort of way—which I could not help feeling it must have cost him something to muster up. Then, ever polite, he took off his steel-lined cap to Mrs. Mackenzie and started for his position at the head of the kraal, to reach which he must make a detour by some paths known to the natives.

Just then one of the boys came in and reported that everybody in the Masai camp appeared to be fast asleep, with the exception of the two sentries who were walking up and down in front of the respective entrances. Then the rest of us took the road. First came the guide, next Sir Henry, Umslopogaas, the Wakwafi Askari, and Mr. Mackenzie's two mission natives armed with long spears and shields. I followed immediately after with Alphonse and five natives all armed with guns, and Mr. Mackenzie brought up the rear with the six remaining natives.

The cattle kraal where the Masai were camped lay at the foot of the hill on which the house stood, or, roughly speaking, about eight hundred yards from the Mission buildings. The first five hundred yards of this distance we traversed quietly indeed, but at a good pace; after that we crept forward as silently as a leopard on his prey, gliding like ghosts from bush to bush and stone to stone. When I had gone a little way I chanced to look behind me, and saw the redoubtable Alphonse staggering along with white face and trembling knees, and his rifle, which was at full cock, pointed directly at the small of my back. Having halted and carefully put the rifle at 'safety,' we started again, and all went well till we were within one hundred yards or so of the kraal, when his teeth began to chatter in the most aggressive way.

'If you don't stop that I will kill you,' I whispered savagely; for the idea of seeing all our lives sacrificed to a tooth-chattering cook was too much for me. I began to fear that he would betray us, and heartily wished we had left him behind.

'But, monsieur, I cannot help it,' he answered, 'it is the cold.'

Here was a dilemma, but fortunately I devised a plan. In the pocket of the coat I wore was a small piece of dirty rag that I had used some time before to clean a gun with. 'Put this in your mouth,' I whispered again, giving him the rag; 'and if I hear another sound you are a dead man.' I knew that it would stifle the clatter of his teeth. I must have looked as if I meant what I said, for Alphonse instantly obeyed me, and continued his journey in silence.

Then we crept on again.

At last we were within fifty yards of the kraal. Between us and it was an open space of sloping grass with only one mimosa bush and a couple of tussocks of a sort of thistle for cover. We were still hidden in fairly thick bush. It was beginning to grow light. The stars had paled and a sickly gleam played about the east and was reflected on the earth. We could see the outline of the kraal clearly enough, and could also make out the faint glimmer of the dying embers of the Masai camp fires. We halted and watched, for we knew the sentry was posted at the opening. Presently he appeared, a fine tall fellow, walking idly up and down within five paces of the thorn-stopped entrance. We had hoped to catch him napping, but it was not to be. He seemed particularly wide awake. If we could not kill that man, and kill him silently, we were lost. There we crouched and watched him. Presently Umslopogaas, who was a few paces ahead of me, turned and made a sign, and next second I saw him go down on his stomach like a snake, and, taking an opportunity when the sentry's head was turned, begin to work his way through the grass without a sound.

The unconscious sentry commenced to hum a little tune, and Umslopogaas crept on. He reached the shelter of the mimosa bush unperceived and there waited. Still the sentry walked up and down. Presently he turned and looked over the wall into the camp. Instantly the human snake who was stalking him glided on ten yards and got behind one of the tussocks of the thistle-like plant, reaching it as the Elmoran turned again. As he did so his eye fell upon this patch of thistles, and it seemed to strike him that it did not look quite right. He advanced a pace towards it—halted, yawned, stooped down, picked up a little pebble and threw it at it. It hit Umslopogaas upon the head, luckily not upon the armour shirt. Had it done so the clink would have betrayed us. Luckily, too, the shirt was browned and not bright steel, which would certainly have been detected. Apparently satisfied that there was nothing wrong, he then gave over his investigations and contented himself with leaning on his spear and in gazing idly at the tuft. For at least three minutes did he stand thus, plunged apparently in a gentle reverie, and there we lay in the last extremity of anxiety, expecting every moment that we should be discovered or that some untoward accident would happen. I could hear Alphonse's teeth going like anything on the oiled rag, and turning my head round made an awful face at him. But I am bound to state that my own heart was at much the same game as the Frenchman's castanets, while the perspiration poured from my body, causing the washleather-lined shirt to stick to me unpleasantly, and altogether I was in the pitiable state known by school boys as a 'blue fright.'

At last the ordeal came to an end. The sentry glanced at the east, and appeared to note with satisfaction that his period of duty was coming to an end—as indeed it was, once and for all—

for he rubbed his hands and began to walk again briskly to warm himself.

The moment his back was turned the long black snake glided on again, and reached the other thistle tuft, which was within a couple of paces of his return beat.

Back came the sentry and strolled right past the tuft, utterly unconscious of the presence that was crouching behind it. Had he looked down he could scarcely have failed to see, but he did not do so.

He passed, and then his hidden enemy erected himself, and with outstretched hand followed in his tracks.

A moment more, and, just as the Elmoran was about to turn, the great Zulu made a spring, and in the growing light we could see his long lean hands close round the Masai's throat. Then followed a convulsive twining of the two dark bodies, and in another second I saw the Masai's head bent back, and heard a sharp crack, something like that of a dry twig snapping, and he fell down upon the ground, his limbs moving spasmodically.

Umslopogaas had put out all his iron strength and broken the warrior's neck.

For a moment he knelt upon his victim, still gripping his throat till he was sure that there was nothing more to fear from him, then he rose and beckoned us to advance, which we did on all fours, like a colony of huge apes. On reaching the kraal we saw that the Masai had still further choked this entrance, which was about ten feet wide—no doubt in order to guard against attack— by dragging four or five tops of mimosa trees up to it. So much the better for us, I reflected; the more obstruction there was the slower would they be able to come through. Here we separated; Mackenzie and his party creeping up under the shadow of the wall to the left, while Sir Henry and Umslopogaas took their stations one on each side of the thorn fence, the two spearmen and the Askari lying down in front of it. I and my men crept on up the right side of the kraal, which was about fifty paces long.

When I was two-thirds up I halted, and placed my men at distances of four paces from one another, keeping Alphonse close to me, however. Then I peeped for the first time over the wall. It was getting fairly light now, and the first thing I saw was the white donkey, exactly opposite to me, and close by it I could make out the pale face of little Flossie, who was sitting as the lad had described, some ten paces from the wall. Round her lay many warriors, sleeping. At distances all over the surface of the kraal were the remains of fires, round each of which slept some five-and-twenty Masai, for the most part gorged with food. Now and then a man would raise himself, yawn, and look at the east, which was turning primrose; but none got up. I determined to wait another five minutes, both to allow the light to increase, so that we could make better shooting, and to give Good and his party—of whom I could see or hear nothing—every opportunity to make ready.

The quiet dawn began to throw her ever-widening mantle over plain and forest and river—mighty Kenia, wrapped in the silence of eternal snows, looked out across the earth—till presently a beam from the unrisen sun lit upon his soaring pinnacle and purpled it with blood; the sky above grew blue, and tender as a mother's smile; a bird began to pipe his morning song, and a little breeze passing through the bush shook down the dewdrops in millions to refresh the waking world. Everywhere was peace and the happiness of arising strength, everywhere save in the heart of man!

Suddenly, just as I was nerving myself for the signal, having already selected my man on whom I meant to open fire—a great fellow sprawling on the ground within three feet of little Flossie—Alphonse's teeth began to chatter again like the hoofs of a galloping giraffe, making a great noise in the silence. The rag had dropped out in the agitation of his mind. Instantly a Masai within three paces of us woke, and, sitting up, gazed about him, looking for the cause of the sound. Moved beyond myself, I brought the butt-end of my rifle down on to the pit of the Frenchman's stomach. This stopped his chattering; but, as he doubled up, he managed to let off his gun in such a manner that the bullet passed within an inch of my head.

There was no need for a signal now. From both sides of the kraal broke out a waving line of fire, in which I myself joined, managing with a snap shot to knock over my Masai by Flossie, just as he was jumping up. Then from the top end of the kraal there rang an awful yell, in which I rejoiced to recognise Good's piercing note rising clear and shrill above the din, and in another second followed such a scene as I have never seen before nor shall again. With an universal howl of terror and fury the brawny crowd of savages within the kraal sprang to their feet, many of them to fall again beneath our well-directed hail of lead before they had moved a yard. For a moment they stood undecided, but then hearing the cries and curses that rose unceasingly from the top end of the kraal, and bewildered by the storm of bullets, as by one impulse they rushed down towards the thorn-stopped entrance. As they went we kept pouring our fire with terrible effect into the thickening mob as fast as we could load. I had

emptied my repeater of the ten shots it contained and was just
beginning to slip in some more when I bethought me of little
Flossie. Looking up, I saw that the white donkey was lying
kicking, having been knocked over either by one of our bullets or
a Masai spear-thrust. There were no living Masai near, but the
black nurse was on her feet and with a spear cutting the rope
that bound Flossie's feet. Next second she ran to the wall of the
kraal and began to climb over it, an example which the little
girl followed. But Flossie was evidently very stiff and cramped,
and could only go slowly, and as she went two Masai flying down
the kraal caught sight of her and rushed towards her to kill her.
The first fellow came up just as the poor little girl, after a desperate effort to climb the wall, fell back into the kraal. Up flashed
the great spear, and as it did so a bullet from my rifle found its
home in the holder's ribs, and over he went like a shot rabbit. But
behind him was the other man, and, alas, I had only that one
cartridge in the magazine! Flossie had scrambled to her feet and
was facing the second man, who advanced with raised spear. I
turned my head aside and felt sick as death. I could not bear to
see him stab her. Glancing up again, to my surprise I saw the
Masai's spear lying on the ground, while the man himself was
staggering about with both hands to his head. Suddenly I saw
a puff of smoke, proceeding apparently from Flossie, and the man
fell down headlong. Then I remembered the Derringer pistol she
carried, and saw that she had fired both barrels of it at him,
thereby saving her life. In another instant she had made an
effort, and assisted by the nurse, who was lying on the top, had
scrambled over the wall, and I knew that, comparatively speaking, she was safe.

All this takes some time to tell, but I do not suppose that it
took more than fifteen seconds to enact. I soon got the magazine
of the repeater filled again with cartridges, and once more opened
fire, not on the seething black mass which was gathering at the
end of the kraal, but on fugitives who bethought them to climb
the wall. I picked off several of these men, moving down towards
the end of the kraal as I did so, and arriving at the corner, or
rather the bend of the oval, in time to see, and by means of my
rifle to assist in, the mighty struggle that took place there.

By this time some two hundred Masai—allowing that we had
up to the present accounted for fifty—had gathered together in
front of the thorn-stopped entrance, driven thither by the spears
of Good's men, whom they doubtless supposed were a large force
instead of being but ten strong. For some reason it never occurred
to them to try and rush the wall, which they could have scrambled

over with comparative ease; they all made for the fence, which was really a strongly interwoven fortification. With a bound the first warrior went at it, and even before he touched the ground on the other side I saw Sir Henry's great axe swing up and fall with awful force upon his feather head-piece, and he sank into the middle of the thorns. Then with a yell and a crash they began to break through as they might, and ever as they came the great axe swung and Inkosi-kaas flashed and they fell dead one by one, each man thus helping to build up a barrier against his fellows. Those who escaped the axes of the pair fell at the hands of the Askari and the two Mission Kaffirs, and those who passed scatheless from them were brought low by my own and Mackenzie's fire.

Faster and more furious grew the fighting. Single Masai would spring upon the dead bodies of their comrades, and engage one or other of the axemen with their long spears; but, thanks chiefly to the mail shirts, the result was always the same. Presently there was a great swing of the axe, a crashing sound, and another dead Masai. That is, if the man was engaged with Sir Henry. If it was Umslopogaas that he fought with the result indeed would be the same, but it would be differently attained. It was but rarely that the Zulu used the crashing double-handed stroke; on the contrary, he did little more than tap continually at his adversary's head, pecking at it with the pole-axe end of the axe as a woodpecker[1] pecks at rotten wood. Presently a peck would go home, and his enemy would drop down with a neat little circular hole in his forehead or skull, exactly similar to that which a cheese-scoop makes in cheese. He never used the broad blade of the axe except when hard pressed, or when striking at a shield. He told me afterwards that he did not consider it sportsmanlike.

Good and his men were quite close by now, and our people must cease firing into the mass for fear of killing some of them (as it was, one of them was slain in this way). Mad and desperate with fear, the Masai by a frantic effort burst through the thorn fence and piled-up dead, and, sweeping Curtis, Umslopogaas, and the other three before them, broke into the open. And now it was that we began to lose men fast. Down went our poor Askari who was armed with the axe, a great spear standing out a foot behind his back; and before long the two spearsmen who had stood with him went down too, dying fighting like tigers; and others of our

[1]As I think I have already said, one of Umslopogaas's Zulu names was the 'Woodpecker.' I could never make out why he was called so until I saw him in action with Inkosi-kaas, when I at once recognised the resemblance.—A. Q.

party shared their fate. For a moment I feared the fight was lost—certainly it trembled in the balance. I shouted to my men to cast down their rifles, and to take spears and throw themselves into the *mêlée*. They obeyed, their blood being now thoroughly up, and Mr. Mackenzie's people followed their example.

This move had a momentary good result, but still the fight hung in the balance.

Our people fought magnificently, hurling themselves upon the dark mass of Elmoran, hewing, thrusting, slaying, and being slain. And ever above the din rose Good's awful yell of encouragement as he plunged to wherever the fight was thickest; and ever, with an almost machine-like regularity, the two axes rose and fell, carrying death or disablement at every stroke. But I could see that the strain was beginning to tell upon Sir Henry, who was bleeding from several flesh wounds: his breath was coming in gasps, and the veins stood out on his forehead like blue and knotted cords. Even Umslopogaas, man of iron that he was, was hard pressed. I noticed that he had given up 'woodpecking,' and was now using the broad blade of Inkosi-kaas, 'browning' his enemy wherever he could hit him, instead of drilling scientific holes in his head. I myself did not go into the *mêlée*, but hovered outside like the swift 'back' in a football scrimmage, putting a bullet through a Masai whenever I got a chance. I was of more use so. I fired forty-nine cartridges that morning, and I did not miss many shots.

Presently, do as we would, the beam of the balance began to rise against us. We had not more than fifteen or sixteen effectives left now, and the Masai had at least fifty. Of course if they had kept their heads, and shaken themselves together, they could soon have made an end of the matter; but that is just what they did not do, not having yet recovered from their start, and some of them having actually fled from the sleeping-places without their weapons. Still by now many individuals were fighting with their normal courage and discretion, and this alone was sufficient to defeat us. To make matters worse just then, when Mackenzie's rifle was empty, a brawny savage armed with a 'sime,' or sword, made a rush for him. The clergyman flung down his gun, and drawing his huge carver from his elastic belt (his revolver had dropped out in the fight), they closed in desperate struggle. Presently, locked in a close embrace, missionary and Masai rolled on to the ground behind the wall, and for some time, being amply occupied with my own affairs, and in keeping my skin from being pricked, I remained in ignorance of his fate or how the duel had ended.

To and fro surged the fight, slowly turning round like the vortex of a human whirlpool, and the matter began to look very bad for us. Just then, however, a fortunate thing happened. Umslopogaas, either by accident or design, broke out of the ring and engaged a warrior at some few paces from it. As he did so, another man ran up and struck him with all his force between the shoulders with his great spear, which, falling on the tough steel shirt, failed to pierce it and rebounded. For a moment the man stared aghast—protective armour being unknown among these tribes—and then he yelled out at the top of his voice—

'*They are devils—bewitched, bewitched!*' And seized by a sudden panic, he threw down his spear, and began to fly. I cut short his career with a bullet, Umslopogaas brained his man, and then the panic spread to the others.

'*Bewitched, bewitched!*' they cried, and tried to escape in every direction, utterly demoralised and broken-spirited, for the most part even throwing down their shields and spears.

On the last scene of that dreadful fight I need not dwell. It was a slaughter great and grim, in which no quarter was asked or given. One incident, however, is worth detailing. Just as I was hoping that it was all done with, suddenly from under a heap of slain where he had been hiding, an unwounded warrior sprang up, and, clearing the piles of dying and dead like an antelope, sped like the wind up the kraal towards the spot where I was standing at the moment. But he was not alone, for Umslopogaas came gliding on his tracks with the peculiar swallow-like motion for which he was noted, and as they neared me I recognised in the Masai the herald of the previous night. Finding that, run as he would, his pursuer was gaining on him, the man halted and turned round to give battle. Umslopogaas also pulled up.

'Ah, ah,' he cried, in mockery, to the Elmoran, 'it is thou whom I talked with last night—the Lygonani! the Herald! the capturer of little girls—he who would kill a little girl! And thou didst hope to stand man to man and face to face with Umslopogaas, an Induna of the tribe of the Maquilisini, of the people of the Amazulu? Behold, thy prayer is granted! And I did swear to hew thee limb from limb, thou insolent dog. Behold, I will do it even now!'

The Masai ground his teeth with fury, and charged at the Zulu with his spear. As he came, Umslopogaas deftly stepped aside, and, swinging Inkosi-kaas high above his head with both hands, brought the blade down with such fearful force from behind upon the Masai's shoulder just where the neck is set into the frame, that its razor edge shore right through bone and flesh and muscle, almost severing the head and one arm from the body.

'*Ou!*' ejaculated Umslopogaas, contemplating the corpse of his foe; 'I have kept my word. It was a good stroke.'

CHAPTER VIII.

ALPHONSE EXPLAINS.

AND so the fight was ended. On turning from the shocking scene it struck me suddenly that I had seen nothing of Alphonse since the moment, some twenty minutes before—for though this fight has taken a long while to describe, it did not take long in reality—when I had been forced to hit him in the wind with the result of nearly getting myself shot. Fearing that the poor little man had perished in the battle, I began to hunt about among the dead for his body, but, not being able either to see or hear anything of it, I concluded that he must have survived, and walked down the side of the kraal where we had first taken our stand, calling him by name. Now some fifteen paces back from the stone wall stood a very ancient tree of the banyan species. So ancient was it that all the inside had in the course of ages decayed away, leaving nothing but a shell of bark.

'Alphonse,' I called, as I walked down the wall, 'Alphonse!'

'Oui, monsieur,' answered a voice. 'Here am I.'

I looked round but could see nobody. 'Where?' I cried.

'Here am I, monsieur, in the tree.'

I looked, and there, peering out of a hole in the trunk of the banyan about five feet from the ground I saw a pale face and a pair of large mustachios, one clipped short and the other as lamentably out of curl as the tail of a newly whipped pug. Then, for the first time, I realised what I had suspected before—namely, that Alphonse was an arrant coward. I walked up to him. 'Come out of that hole,' I said.

'Is it finished, monsieur?' he asked anxiously; 'quite finished? Ah, the horrors I have undergone, and the prayers that I have uttered!'

'Come out, you little wretch,' I said, for I did not feel amiable; 'it is all over.'

'So, monsieur, then my prayers have prevailed? I emerge,' and he did.

As we were walking down together to join the others, who were gathered in a group by the wide entrance to the kraal, which now resembled a veritable charnel-house, a Masai, who had escaped so far and been hiding under a bush, suddenly sprang up and charged furiously at us. Off went Alphonse with a howl of terror, and after him flew the Masai, bent upon doing some execution before he died. He soon overtook the poor little Frenchman, and would have finished him then and there had I not managed to plant a bullet between the Elmoran's broad shoulders, which brought matters to a satisfactory conclusion so far as the Frenchman was concerned, just as Alphonse made a last agonised double in the vain hope of avoiding the yard of steel that was flashing in his immediate rear. But just then he tripped and fell flat, and the body of the Masai fell right on the top of him, moving convulsively in the death struggle. Thereupon there arose such a series of piercing howls that I concluded that before he died the savage must have managed to stab poor Alphonse. I ran up in a hurry and pulled the Masai off, and there beneath him lay Alphonse covered with blood and jerking himself about like a galvanised frog. Poor fellow! thought I, he is done for, and kneeling down by him I began to search for his wound as well as his struggles would allow.

'Oh, the hole in my back!' he yelled. 'I am murdered. I am dead.

I searched again, but could see no wound. Then the truth dawned on me—the man was frightened, not hurt.

'Get up!' I shouted, 'get up. Aren't you ashamed of yourself? You are not touched.'

Thereupon he rose, not a penny the worse. 'But, monsieur, I thought I was,' he said apologetically; 'I did not know that I had conquered.' Then, giving the body of the Masai a kick, he ejaculated triumphantly, 'Ah, dog of a black savage, thou art dead; what victory!'

Thoroughly disgusted, I left Alphonse to look after himself, which he did by following me like a shadow, and proceeded to join the others by the large entrance. The first thing that I saw was Mackenzie, seated on a stone with a handkerchief twisted round his thigh, from which he was bleeding freely, having, indeed, received a spear-thrust that passed right through it, and still holding in his hand his favourite carving-knife now bent nearly double, from which I gathered that he had been successful in his rough and tumble with the Elmoran.

'Ah, Quatermain!' he sang out in a trembling, excited voice, 'so we have conquered; but it is a sorry sight, a sorry sight;' and then breaking into broad Scotch and glancing at the bent knife in his hand, 'It fashes me sair to hae bent my best carver on the breast-bane of a savage,' and he laughed hysterically. Poor fellow, what between his wound and the killing excitement he had undergone his nerves were much shaken, and no wonder! It is hard upon a man of peace and kindly heart to be called upon to join in such a gruesome business. But there, fate puts us sometimes into very ironical positions!

At the kraal entrance the scene was a strange one. The slaughter was over by now, and the wounded men had been put out of their pain, for no quarter was given. The bush-closed entrance was trampled flat, and in place of bushes it was filled with the bodies of dead men. Dead men, everywhere dead men—they lay about in knots, they were flung by ones and twos in every position upon the open spaces, for all the world like the people on the grass in one of the London parks on a particularly hot Sunday in August. In front of this entrance, on a space which had been cleared of dead and of the shields and spears which were scattered in all directions as they had fallen or been thrown from the hands of their owners, stood and lay the survivors of the awful struggle, and at their feet were four wounded men. We had gone into the fight thirty strong, and of the thirty but fifteen remained alive, and five of them (including Mr. Mackenzie) were wounded, two mortally. Of those who held the entrance, Curtis and the Zulu alone remained. Good had lost five men killed, I had lost two killed, and Mackenzie no less than five out of the six with him. As for the survivors, with the exception of myself who had never come to close quarters, they were red from head to foot—Sir Henry's armour might have been painted that colour—and utterly exhausted, except Umslopogaas, who, as he stood grimly on a little mound above a heap of dead, leaning as usual upon his axe, did not seem particularly distressed, although the skin over the hole in his head palpitated violently.

'Ah, Macumazahn!' he said to me as I limped up, feeling very sick, 'I told thee that it would be a good fight, and it has. Never have I seen a better, or one more bravely fought. As for this iron shirt, surely it is "tagati" [bewitched]; nothing could pierce it. Had it not been for the garment I should have been *there*,' and he nodded towards the great pile of dead men beneath him.

'I give it thee; thou art a gallant man,' said Sir Henry, briefly.

'Koos!' answered the Zulu, deeply pleased both at the gift and the compliment. 'Thou, too, Incubu, didst bear thyself as a man, but I must give thee some lessons with the axe; thou dost waste thy strength.'

Just then Mackenzie asked about Flossie, and we were all greatly relieved when one of the men said he had seen her flying towards the house with the nurse. Then bearing such of the wounded as could be moved at the moment with us, we slowly made our way towards the Mission-house, spent with toil and bloodshed, but with the glorious sense of victory against overwhelming odds glowing in our hearts. We had saved the life of the little maid, and taught the Masai of those parts a lesson that they will not forget for ten years—but at what a cost!

Painfully we made our way up the hill which, but a little more than an hour before, we had descended under such different circumstances. At the gate of the wall stood Mrs. Mackenzie waiting for us. When her eyes fell upon us, however, she shrieked out, and covered her face with her hands, crying, 'Horrible, horrible!' Nor were her fears allayed when she discovered her worthy husband being borne upon an improvised stretcher; but her doubts as to the nature of his injury were soon set at rest. Then when in a few brief words I had told her the upshot of the struggle (of which Flossie, who had arrived in safety, had been able to explain something) she came up to me and solemnly kissed me on the forehead.

'God bless you all, Mr. Quatermain; you have saved my child's life,' she said simply.

Then we went in and got our clothes off and doctored our wounds; I am glad to say I had none, and Sir Henry's and Good's, thanks to those invaluable chain shirts, were of a comparatively harmless nature, and to be dealt with by means of a few stitches and sticking-plaster. Mackenzie's, however, was serious, though fortunately the spear had not severed any large artery. After that we took a bath, and what a luxury it was! and having clad ourselves in ordinary clothes, proceeded to the dining-room, where breakfast was set as usual. It was curious sitting down there, drinking tea and eating toast in an ordinary nineteenth-century sort of a way just as though we had not employed the early hours in a regular primitive hand-to-hand middle-ages kind of struggle. As Good said, the whole thing seemed more as though one had enjoyed a nightmare just before being called, than as a deed done. When we were finishing our breakfast the door opened, and in came little Flossie, very pale and tottery, but quite unhurt. She kissed us all and thanked us. I congratulated her on the presence of mind she had shown in shooting the Masai with her Derringer pistol, and thereby saving her own life.

'Oh, don't talk of it!' she said, beginning to cry hysterically; 'I shall never forget his face as he went turning round and round, never—I can see it now.'

I advised her to go to bed and get some sleep, which she did, and awoke in the evening quite recovered, so far as her strength was concerned. It struck me as an odd thing that a girl who could find the nerve to shoot a huge black ruffian rushing to kill her with a spear should have been so affected at the thought of it afterwards; but it is, after all, characteristic of the sex. Poor Flossie! I fear that her nerves will not get over that night in the Masai camp for many a long year. She told me afterwards that it was the suspense that was so awful, having to sit there hour after hour through the livelong night utterly ignorant as to whether or no any attempt was to be made to rescue her. She said that on the whole she did not expect it, knowing how few there were of us, and how many of the Masai—who, by the way, came continually to stare at her, most of them never having seen a white person before, and handled her arms and hair with their filthy paws. She said also that she had made up her mind that if she saw no signs of succour by the time the first rays of the rising sun reached the kraal she would kill herself with the pistol, for the nurse had heard the Lygonani say that they were to be tortured to death as soon as the sun was up if one of the white men did not come in their place. It was an awful resolution to have to take, but she meant to act on it, and I have little doubt but what she would have done so. Although she was at an age when in England girls are in the schoolroom and come down to dessert, this 'child of the wilderness' had more courage, discretion, and power of mind than many a woman of mature age nurtured in idleness and luxury, with minds carefully drilled and educated out of any originality or self-resource that nature may have endowed them with.

When breakfast was over we all turned in and had a good sleep, only getting up in time for dinner; after which meal we once more adjourned, together with all the available population—men, women, youths, and girls—to the scene of the morning's slaughter, our object being to bury our own dead and get rid of the Masai by flinging them into the Tana River, which ran within fifty yards of the kraal. On reaching the spot we disturbed thousands upon thousands of vultures and a sort of brown bush eagle, which had been flocking to the feast from miles and miles away. Often have I watched these great and repulsive birds, and marvelled at the extraordinary speed with which they arrive on a scene of slaughter. A buck falls to your rifle, and within a minute high in the blue ether appears a speck that gradually grows into a vulture, then another, and another. I have heard many theories advanced to account for the wonderful power of perception nature has given these birds. My own, founded on a good deal of observation, is that the vultures, gifted as they are with powers of sight greater than those given by the most powerful glass, quarter out the heavens among themselves, and hanging in mid-air at a vast height—probably from two to three miles above the earth—keep watch, each of them, over an enormous stretch of country. Presently one of them spies food, and instantly begins to sink towards it. Thereon his next neighbour in the airy heights sailing leisurely through the blue gulf, at a distance perhaps of some miles, follows his example, knowing that food has been sighted. Down he goes, and all the vultures within sight of him follow after, and so do all those in sight of them. In this way the vultures for twenty miles round can be summoned to the feast in a few minutes.

We buried our dead in solemn silence, Good being selected to read the Burial Service over them (in the absence of Mr. Mackenzie, confined to bed), as he was generally allowed to possess the best voice and most impressive manner. It was melancholy in the extreme, but, as Good said, it might have been worse, for we might have had 'to bury ourselves.' I pointed out that this would have been a difficult feat, but I knew what he meant.

Next we set to work to load an ox-wagon which had been brought round from the Mission with the dead bodies of the Masai, having first collected the spears, shields, and other arms. We loaded the wagon five times, about fifty bodies to the load, and emptied it into the Tana. From this it was evident that very few of the Masai could have escaped. The crocodiles must have been well fed that night. One of the last bodies we picked up was that of the sentry at the upper end. I asked Good how he managed to kill him, and he told me that he had crept up much as Umslopogaas had done, and stabbed him with his sword. He groaned a good deal, but fortunately nobody heard him. As Good said, it was a horrible thing to have to do, and most unpleasantly like cold-blooded murder.

And so with the last body that floated away down the current of the Tana ended the incident of our attack on the Masai camp. The spears and shields and other arms we took up to the Mission, where they filled an outhouse. One incident, however, I must not forget to mention. As we were returning from performing the obsequies of our Masai friends we passed the hollow tree where Alphonse had secreted himself in the morning. It so happened that the little man himself was with us assisting in our unpleasant task with a far better will than he had shown where live Masai were concerned. Indeed, for each body that he handled he found an appropriate sarcasm. Alphonse throwing dead Masai into the Tana was a very different creature from Alphonse flying for dear life from the spear of a live Masai. He was quite merry and gay, he clapped his hands and warbled snatches of French songs as the grim dead warriors went 'splash' into the running waters to carry a message of death and defiance to their kindred a hundred miles below. In short, thinking that he wanted taking down a peg, I suggested holding a court-martial on him for his conduct in the morning.

Accordingly we brought him to the tree where he had hidden, and proceeded to sit in judgment on him, Sir Henry explaining to him in the very best French the unheard-of cowardice and enormity of his conduct, more especially in letting the oiled rag out of his mouth, whereby he nearly aroused the Masai camp with teeth-chattering and brought about the failure of our plans: ending up with a request for an explanation.

But if we expected to find Alphonse at a loss and put him to open shame we were destined to be disappointed. He bowed and scraped and smiled, and acknowledged that his conduct might at first blush appear strange, but really it was not, inasmuch as his teeth were chattering not from fear—oh, dear no! oh, certainly not! he marvelled how the 'messieurs' could think of such a thing —but from the chill air of the morning. As for the rag, if monsieur could have but tasted its evil flavour, being compounded indeed a mixture of stale paraffin oil, grease, and gunpowder, monsieur himself would have spat it out. But he did nothing of the sort; he determined to keep it there till, alas! his stomach 'revolted,' and the rag was ejected in an access of involuntary sickness.

'Oh, get along with you, you little cur!' broke out Sir Henry, with a shout of laughter, and giving Alphonse a good kick which sent him flying off with a rueful face.

In the evening I had an interview with Mr. Mackenzie, who was suffering a good deal from his wounds, which Good, who was a skilful though unqualified doctor, was treating him for. He told me that this occurrence had taught him a lesson, and that, if he recovered safely, he meant to hand over the Mission to a younger man, who was already on his road to join him in his work, and return to England.

'You see, Quatermain,' he said, 'I made up my mind to it, this very morning, when we were creeping down upon those benighted savages. If we live through this and rescue Flossie alive,' I said to myself, 'I will go home to England; I have had enough of savages. Well, I did not think that we should live through it at the time; but thanks be to God and you four, we have lived through it, and I mean to stick to my resolution, lest a worse thing befall us. Another such time would kill my poor wife, And besides, Quatermain, between you and me, I am well off; it is thirty thousand pounds I am worth to-day, and every farthing of it made by honest trade and savings in the bank of Zanzibar, for living here costs me next to nothing. So though it will be hard to leave this place, which I have made to blossom like a rose in the wilderness, and harder still to abandon the people I have taught, I shall go.'

'I congratulate you on your decision,' answered I, 'for two reasons. The first is, that you owe a duty to your wife and daughter, and more especially to the latter, who should receive some education and mix with girls of her own race, otherwise she will grow up wild, shunning her kind. The other is, that as sure as I am standing here, sooner or later the Masai will try to avenge the slaughter inflicted on them to-day. Some few men are sure to have escaped in the confusion who will carry the story back to their people, and the result will be that a great expedition will one day be sent against you. It might be delayed for a year, but sooner or later it will come. Therefore, if only for that reason, I should go. When once they have learnt that you are no longer here they may perhaps leave the place alone.'[1]

'You are quite right,' answered the clergyman. 'I will turn my back upon this place in a month. But it will be a wrench, it will be a wrench.'

CHAPTER IX.

INTO THE UNKNOWN.

A WEEK had passed, and we all sat at supper one night in the Mission dining-room, feeling very much depressed in spirits, for the reason that we were going to say good-bye to our kind friends, the Mackenzies, and depart upon our way at dawn on the morrow. Nothing more had been seen or heard of the Masai, and save for a spear or two which had been overlooked and lay rusting in the grass, and a few empty cartridges where we had stood outside the wall, it would have been difficult to tell that the old cattle kraal at the foot of the slope had been the scene of so desperate a struggle. Mackenzie, thanks chiefly to his being so temperate a man, was rapidly recovering from his hurt, and could get about on a pair of crutches; and as for the other wounded

[1] By a sad coincidence, since the above was written by Mr. Quatermain, the Masai, in April 1886, have massacred a missionary and his wife—Mr. and Mrs. Houghton—on this very Tana River, and at the spot described. These are, I believe, the first white people who are known to have fallen victims to this cruel tribe.—EDITOR.

men, one had died of gangrene, and the rest were in a fair way to recovery. Mr. Mackenzie's caravan of men had also returned from the coast, so that the station was now amply garrisoned.

Under these circumstances we concluded, warm and pressing as were the invitations for us to stay, that it was time to move on, first to Mt. Kenia, and thence into the unknown in search of the mysterious white race which we had set our hearts on discovering. This time we were going to progress by means of the humble but useful donkey, of which we had collected no less than a dozen, to carry our goods and chattels, and, if necessary, ourselves. We had now but two Wakwafis left for servants, and found it quite impossible to get other natives to venture with us into the unknown parts we proposed to explore—and small blame to them. After all, as Mr. Mackenzie said, it was odd that three men, each of whom possessed many of those things that are supposed to make life worth living—health, sufficient means, and position, &c.—should of their own pleasure start out upon a wild goose chase, from which the chances were they never would return. But then that is what Englishmen are, adventurers to the backbone; and all our magnificent muster-roll of colonies, each of which will in time become a great nation, testify to the extraordinary value of the spirit of adventure which at first sight looks like a mild form of lunacy. 'Adventurer'—he who goes out to meet whatever may come. Well, that is what we all do in the world one way or another, and, speaking for myself, I am proud of the title, because it implies a brave heart and a trust in Providence. Besides, when many and many a noted Crœsus, at whose feet the people worship, and many and many a time-serving and word-coining politician are forgotten, the names of those grand-hearted old adventurers who have made England what she is, will be remembered and taught with love and pride to little children whose unshaped spirits yet slumber in the womb of centuries to be. Not that we three can expect to be numbered with such as these, yet have we done something—enough, perhaps, to throw a garment over the nakedness of our folly.

That evening, whilst we were sitting on the verandah, smoking a pipe before turning in, who should come up to us but Alphonse, and, with a magnificent bow, announce his wish for an interview. Being requested to 'fire away,' he explained at some length that he was anxious to attach himself to our party—a statement that astonished me not a little, knowing what a coward the little man was. The reason, however, soon appeared. Mr. Mackenzie was going down to the coast, and thence on to England. Now, if he went down country, Alphonse was persuaded that he would be seized, extradited, sent to France, and to penal servitude. This was the idea that haunted him, as King Charles's head haunted Mr. Dick, and he brooded over it till his imagination exaggerated the danger ten times. As a matter of fact, the probability is that his offence against the laws of his country had long ago been forgotten, and that he would have been allowed to pass unmolested anywhere except in France; but he could not be got to see this. Constitutional coward as the little man was, he infinitely preferred to face the certain hardships and great risks and dangers of such an expedition as ours, than to expose himself, notwithstanding his intense longing for his native land, to the possible scrutiny of a police officer—which is after all only another exemplification of the truth that, to the majority of men, a far-off foreseen danger, however shadowy, is much more terrible than the most serious present emergency. After listening to what he had to say, we consulted among ourselves, and finally agreed, with Mr. Mackenzie's knowledge and consent, to accept his offer. To begin with, we were very short-handed, and Alphonse was a quick, active fellow, who could turn his hand to anything, and cook—ah, he *could* cook! I believe that he would have made a palatable dish of those gaiters of his heroic grandfather which he was so fond of talking about. Then he was a good-tempered little man, and merry as a monkey, whilst his pompous, vainglorious talk was a source of infinite amusement to us; and what is more, he never bore malice. Of course, his very pronounced cowardice was a great drawback to him, but now that we knew his weakness we could more or less guard against it. So, after warning him of the undoubted risks he was exposing himself to, we told him that we would accept his offer on condition that he would promise implicit obedience to our orders. We also undertook to give him wages at the rate of ten pounds a month should he ever return to a civilised country to receive them. To all of this he agreed with alacrity, and retired to write a letter to his Annette, which Mr. Mackenzie promised to post when he got down country. He read it to us afterwards, Sir Henry translating, and a wonderful composition it was. I am sure the depth of his devotion and the narration of his sufferings in a barbarous country, 'far, far from thee, Annette, for whose adored sake I endure such sorrow,' ought to have touched the feelings of the stoniest-hearted chambermaid.

Well, the morrow came, and by seven o'clock the donkeys were all loaded, and the time of parting was at hand. It was a melancholy business, especially the saying good-bye to little Flossie. She and I were great friends, and often used to have talks together —but her nerves had never got over the shock of that awful night when she lay in the power of those bloodthirsty Masai. 'Oh, Mr. Quatermain,' she cried, throwing her arms round my neck and bursting into tears, 'I can't bear to say good-bye to you. I wonder when we shall meet again?'

'I don't know, my dear little girl,' I said. 'I am at one end of life and you are at the other. I have but a short time before me at best, and most things lie in the past, but I hope that for you there are many long and happy years, and everything lies in the future. By-and-by you will grow into a beautiful woman, Flossie, and all this wild life will be like a far-off dream to you; but I hope, even if we never do meet again, that you will think of your old friend and remember what I say to you now. Always try to be good, my dear, and to do what is right, rather than what happens to be pleasant, for in the end, whatever sneering people may say, what is good and what is happy are the same. Be unselfish, and whenever you can, give a helping hand to others—for the world is full of suffering, my dear, and to alleviate it is the noblest end that we can set before us. If you do that you will become a sweet and God-fearing woman, and make many people's lives a little brighter, and then you will not have lived, as so many of your sex do, in vain. And now I have given you a lot of old-fashioned advice, and so I am going to give you something to sweeten it with. You see this little piece of paper. It is what is called a cheque. When we are gone give it to your father with this note—not before, mind. You will marry one day, my dear little Flossie, and it is to buy you a wedding present which you are to wear, and your daughter after you, if you have one, in remembrance of Hunter Quatermain.'

Poor little Flossie cried very much, and gave me a lock of her bright hair in return, which I still have. The cheque I gave her was for a thousand pounds (which, being now well off, and having no calls upon me except those of charity, I could well afford), and in the note I directed her father to invest it for her in Government security, and when she married or came of age to buy her the best diamond necklace he could get for the money and accumulated interest. I chose diamonds because I think that now that King Solomon's Mines are lost to the world, their price will never be much lower than it is at present, so that if in after-life she should ever be in pecuniary difficulties, she will be able to turn them into money.

Well, at last we got off, after much hand-shaking, hat-waving, and also farewell saluting from the natives, Alphonse weeping copiously, for he has a warm heart, at parting with his master and mistress; and I was not sorry for it at all, for I hate those goodbyes. Perhaps the most affecting thing of all was to witness Umslopogaas' distress at parting with Flossie, for whom the grim old warrior had conceived a strong affection. He used to say that she was as sweet to see as the only star on a dark night, and was never tired of loudly congratulating himself on having killed the Lygonani who had threatened to murder her. And that was the last we saw of the pleasant Mission-house—a true oasis in the desert—and of European civilisation. But I often think of the Mackenzies, and wonder how they got down country, and if they are now safe and well in England, and will ever see these words. Dear little Flossie! I wonder how she fares now where there are no black folk to do her imperious bidding, and no sky-piercing snow-clad Kenia for her to look at when she gets up in the morning. And so good-bye to Flossie.

After leaving the Mission-house we made our way, comparatively unmolested, by the base of Mount Kenia, which the Masai call 'Dongo Egere,' or the 'speckled mountain,' on account of the black patches of rock that appear upon its mighty spire, where the sides are too precipitous to allow of the snow lying on them; then on past the lonely lake Baringo, where one of our two remaining Askari, having unfortunately trodden upon a puff-adder, died of snake-bite, in spite of all our efforts to save him. Thence we proceeded a distance of about a hundred and fifty miles to another magnificent snow-clad mountain called Lekakisera, which has never, to the best of my belief, been visited before by a European, but which I cannot now stop to describe. There we rested a fortnight, and then started out into the trackless and uninhabited forest of a vast district called Elgumi. In this forest alone exist more elephants than I ever met with or heard of before. The mighty mammals literally swarm there entirely unmolested by man, and only kept down by the natural law that prevents any animals increasing beyond the capacity of the country they inhabit to support them. Needless to say, however, we did not shoot many of them, first because we could not afford to waste ammunition, of which our stock was getting perilously low, a donkey loaded with it having been swept away in fording a flooded river; and secondly, because we could not carry away the ivory, and did not wish to kill for the mere sake of slaughter. So we let the great brutes be, only shooting one or two in self-protection. In this district, the elephants, being unacquainted with the hunter and his tender mercies, would allow one to walk up to within twenty yards of them in the open, while they stood, with their great ears cocked for all the world like puzzled and gigantic puppy-dogs, and stared at that new and extraordinary phenomenon—man. Occasionally, when the inspection did not prove satisfactory, the staring ended in a trumpet and a charge, but this did not often happen. When it did we had to use our rifles. Nor were elephants the only wild beasts in the great El-gumi forest. All sorts of large game abounded, including lions—confound them! I have always hated the sight of a lion since one bit my leg and lamed me for life. As a consequence, another thing that abounded was the dreaded tsetse fly, whose bite is death to domestic animals. Donkeys have, together with men, hitherto been supposed to enjoy a peculiar immunity from its attacks; but all I have to say, whether it was on account of their poor condition, or because the tsetse in those parts is more poison-ous than usual, I do not know, but ours succumbed to its on-slaught. Fortunately, however, that was not till two months or so after the bites had been inflicted, when suddenly, after a two days' cold rain, they all died, and on removing the skins of sev-eral of them, I found the long yellow streaks upon the flesh which are characteristic of death from bites of the tsetse, marking the spot where the insect had inserted his proboscis. On emerging from the great Elgumi forest, still steering northwards, in accord-ance with the information Mr. Mackenzie had collected from the unfortunate wanderer who reached him only to die so tragically, we struck the base in due course of the large lake, called Laga by the natives, which is about fifty miles long by twenty broad, and of which, it may be remembered, he made mention. Thence we pushed on nearly a month's journey over great rolling uplands, something like those in the Transvaal, but diversified by patches of bush country.

All this time we were continually ascending at the rate of about one hundred feet every ten miles. Indeed the country was on a slope which appeared to terminate at a mass of snow-tipped mountains, for which we were steering, and where we learnt the second lake was situated, of which the wanderer had spoken as the water without a bottom. At length we arrived there, and, hav-ing ascertained that there *was* a large lake on the top of the mountains, ascended three thousand feet more till we came to a precipitous cliff or edge, to find a great sheet of water some twenty miles square lying fifteen hundred feet below us, and evi-dently occupying an extinct volcanic crater or craters of vast ex-tent. Perceiving villages on the border of this lake, we descended with great difficulty through forests of pine-trees, which now clothed the precipitous sides of the crater, and were well received by the people, a simple, unwarlike folk, who had never seen or even heard of a white man before, and treated us with great reverence and kindness, supplying us with as much food and milk as we could eat and drink. This wonderful and beautiful lake lay, according to our aneroid, at a height of no less than 11,450 feet above sea level, and its climate was quite cold, and not at all unlike that of England. Indeed, for the first three days of our stay there we saw little or nothing of the scenery on account of an unmistakable Scotch mist which prevailed. It was this rain that set the tsetse poison working in our remaining donkeys, so that they all died.

This disaster left us in a very awkward position, as we had now no means of transport whatever, though on the other hand we had not much to carry. Ammunition, too, was very short, amounting to but one hundred and fifty rounds of rifle cartridges and some fifty shot-gun cartridges. How to get on we did not know; indeed it seemed to us that we had about reached the end of our tether. Even if we had been inclined to abandon the object of our search, which, shadow as it was, was by no means the case, it was ridiculous to think of forcing our way back some seven hundred miles to the coast in our present plight; so we came to the conclusion that the only thing to be done was to stop where we were—the natives being so well disposed and food plentiful— for the present, and abide events, while trying to collect information as to the countries beyond.

Accordingly, having purchased a capital log canoe, large enough to hold us all and our baggage, from the headman of the village we were staying in, presenting him with three empty colddrawn brass cartridges by way of payment, with which he was perfectly delighted, we set out to make a tour of the lake in order to find the most favourable place to set a camp. As we did not know if we should return to this village, we put all our gear into the canoe, and also a quarter of cooked water-buck, which when young is delicious eating, and off we went, natives having already gone before us in light canoes to warn the inhabitants of the other villages of our approach.

As we were paddling leisurely along Good remarked upon the extraordinary deep blue colour of the water, and said that he understood from the natives, who were great fishermen—fish, indeed, being their principal food—that the lake was supposed to be wonderfully deep, and to have a hole at the bottom through which the water escaped and put out some great fire that was raging below.

I pointed out to him that what he had heard was probably a legend arising from a tradition among the people which dated back to the time when one of the extinct parasitic volcanic cones was in activity. We saw several round the borders of the lake which had no doubt been working at a period long subsequent to the volcanic death of the central crater that now formed the bed of the lake itself. When it became finally extinct the people would imagine that the water from the lake had run down and put out the big fire below, more especially as there was no visible exit to it, though it was constantly fed by streams running from the snow-tipped peaks about.

The farther shore of the lake we found, on approaching it, to consist of a vast perpendicular wall of rock, which held the water without any intermediate sloping bank, as elsewhere. Accordingly we paddled parallel with this precipice, at a distance of about a hundred paces from it, shaping our course for the end of the lake, where we knew that there was a large village.

As we went we began to pass a considerable accumulation of floating rushes, weed, boughs of trees, and other rubbish, brought, Good supposed, to this spot by some current, which he was much puzzled to account for. Whilst we were speculating about this, Sir Henry pointed out a large flock of large white swans, which were feeding on the drift some little way ahead of us. Now I had already noticed swans flying about this lake, and, having never come across them before in Africa, was exceedingly anxious to obtain a specimen. I had questioned the natives about them, and learnt that they came from over the mountain, always arriving at certain periods of the year in the early morning, when it was very easy to catch them, on account of their exhausted condition. I also asked them what country they came from, when they shrugged their shoulders, and said that on the top of the great black precipice was stony inhospitable land, and beyond that were mountains with snow, and full of wild beasts, where no people lived, and beyond the mountains were hundreds of miles of dense thorn forest, so thick that even the elephants could not get through it, much less men. Next I asked them if they had ever heard of white people like ourselves living on the farther side of the mountains and the thorn forest, whereat they laughed. But afterwards a very old woman came and told me that when she was a little girl her grandfather had told her that in his youth *his* grandfather had crossed the desert and the mountains, and pierced the thorn forest, and seen a white people who lived in stone kraals beyond. Of course, as this took the tale back some two hundred and fifty years, the information was very indefinite; but still there it was again, and on thinking it over I grew firmly convinced that there was some truth in all these rumours, and equally firmly determined to solve the mystery. Little did I guess in what an almost miraculous way my desire was to be gratified.

Well, we set to work to stalk the swans, which kept drawing, as they fed, nearer and nearer to the precipice, and at last we pushed the canoe under shelter of a patch of drift within forty yards of them. Sir Henry had the shot-gun, loaded with No. 1, and, waiting for a chance, got two in a line, and, firing at their necks, killed them both. Up rose the rest, thirty or more of them, with a mighty splashing; and, as they did so, he gave them the other barrel. Down came one fellow with a broken wing, and I saw the leg of another drop and a few feathers start out of his back; but he went on quite strong. Up went the swans, circling ever higher till at last they were mere specks level with the top of the frowning precipice, when I saw them form into a triangle and head off for the unknown north-east. Meanwhile we had picked up our two dead fowl, and beautiful birds they were, weighing not less than about thirty pounds each, and were chasing the winged one, which had scrambled over a mass of driftweed into a pool of clear water beyond. Finding a difficulty in forcing the canoe through the rubbish, I told our only remaining Wakwafi servant, whom I knew to be an excellent swimmer, to jump over, dive under the drift, and catch him, knowing that as there were no crocodiles in this lake he could come to no harm. Entering into the fun of the thing, the man obeyed, and soon was dodging about after the winged swan in fine style, as he did so getting gradually nearer to the rock wall, against which the water washed.

Presently he gave up swimming after the swan, and began to cry out that he was being carried away; and, indeed, we saw, though he was swimming with all his strength towards us, that he was being drawn slowly towards the precipice. With a few desperate strokes of our paddles we pushed the canoe through the crust of drift and rowed towards the man as hard as we could, but, fast as we went, he was drawn faster towards the rock. Suddenly I saw that before us, just rising eighteen inches or so above the surface of the lake, was what looked like the top of the arch of a submerged cave or railway tunnel. Evidently, from the water-mark on the rock several feet above it, it was generally quite submerged; but there had been a dry season, and the great cold prevented the snow from melting as freely as usual; so the lake was low and the arch showed. Towards this arch our poor servant was being sucked with frightful rapidity. He was not more than ten fathoms from it, and we were about twenty when I saw it, and with little help from us the canoe flew along after him. He struggled bravely, and I thought that we should have saved him, when suddenly I perceived an expression of despair come upon his face, and there before our eyes he was sucked down into the swirling depths, and vanished from sight. At the some moment I felt our canoe seized as by a mighty hand, and propelled with resistless force towards the rock.

We realised our danger now and rowed, or rather paddled, furiously in our attempt to get out of the vortex. In vain; in another second we were flying straight for the arch like an arrow, and I thought that we were lost. Luckily I retained sufficient presence of mind to shout out, instantly setting the example by throwing myself into the bottom of the canoe, 'Down on your faces—down!' and the others had the sense to take the hint. In another instant there was a grinding noise, and the boat was pushed down till the water began to trickle over the sides, and I thought that we were gone. But no, suddenly the grinding ceased, and we could again feel the canoe flying along. I turned my head a little—I dared not lift it—and looked up. By the feeble light that yet reached the canoe, I could make out that a dense arch of rock hung just over our heads, and that was all. In another minute I could not even see as much as that, for the faint light had merged into shadow, and the shadows were swallowed up in darkness, utter and complete.

For an hour or so we lay there, not daring to lift our heads for fear lest the brains should be dashed out of them, and scarcely able to speak even, on account of the noise of the rushing water which drowned our voices. Not, indeed, that we had much inclination to speak, seeing that we were overwhelmed by the awfulness of our position and the imminent fear of instant death, either by being dashed against the sides of the cavern, or on a rock, or sucked down into the raging waters, or perhaps asphyxiated by want of air. All of these and many other modes of death presented themselves to my imagination as I lay at the bottom of the canoe, listening to the swirl of the hurrying waters which ran whither we knew not. One only other sound could I hear, and that was Alphonse's intermittent howl of terror coming from the centre of the canoe, and even that seemed faint and unreal. Indeed, the position overpowered my brain, and I began to believe that I was the victim of some ghastly nightmare.

CHAPTER X.

THE ROSE OF FIRE.

On we flew, drawn by the mighty current, till at last I noticed that the sound of the water was not half so deafening as it had been, and concluded that this must be because there was more room for the echoes to disperse in. I could now hear Alphonse's howls much more distinctly; they were made up of the oddest mixture of invocations to the Supreme Power and the name of his beloved Annette that it is possible to conceive; and, in short, though their evident earnestness saved them from profanity, were, to say the least, very remarkable. Taking up a paddle, I managed to drive it into his ribs, whereon, thinking that the end had come, he howled louder than ever. Then I slowly and cautiously raised myself on my knees and stretched my hand upwards, but could touch no roof. Next I took the paddle and lifted it above my head as high as I could, but with the same result. I also thrust it out laterally to the right and left, but could touch nothing except water. Then I bethought me that there was in the boat, amongst our other remaining possessions, a bull's-eye lantern and a tin of oil. I groped about and found it, and having a match on me carefully lit it, and so soon as the flame had got a hold of the wick I turned it on down the boat. As it happened, the first thing the light lit on was the white and scared face of Alphonse, who, believing it was all over at last, and that he was witnessing a preliminary celestial phenomenon, gave a terrific yell and was with difficulty reassured with the paddle. As for the other three, Good was lying on the flat of his back, his eyeglass still fixed in his eye, and gazing blankly into the upper darkness. Sir Henry had his head resting on the thwarts of the canoe, and with his hand was trying to test the speed of the water. But when the beam of light fell upon old Umslopogaas I could really have laughed. I think I have said that we had put a roast quarter of waterbuck into the canoe. Well, it so happened that when we all prostrated ourselves to avoid being swept out of the boat and into the water by the rock roof, Umslopogaas's head had come down uncommonly near this roast buck, and so soon as he had recovered a little from the first shock of our position it occurred to him that he was hungry. Thereupon he coolly cut off a chop with Inkosi-kaas, and was now employed in eating it with every appearance of satisfaction. As he afterwards explained, he thought that he was going 'on a long journey,' and preferred to

start on a full stomach. It reminded me of the people who are
going to be hanged, and who are generally reported in the English
daily papers to have made 'an excellent breakfast.'

As soon as the others saw that I had managed to light the
lamp, we bundled Alphonse into the farther end of the canoe
with a threat which calmed him wonderfully, that if he would
insist upon making the darkness hideous with his cries we would
put him out of suspense by sending him to join the Wakwafi and
wait for Annette in another spere. Then we discussed the situation as well as we could. First, however, at Good's suggestion,
we bound two paddles mast-fashion in the bows so that they
might give us warning against any sudden lowering of the roof
of the cave or waterway. It was clear to us that we were in an
underground river or, as Alphonse defined it, 'main drain,' which
carried off the superfluous waters of the lake. Such rivers are
well known to exist in many parts of the world, but it has not
often been the evil fortunes of explorers to travel by them. That
the river was wide we could clearly see, for the light from the
bull's-eye lantern failed to reach from shore to shore, although
occasionally, when the current swept us either to one side or the
other, we could distinguish the rock wall of the tunnel, which,
so far as we could make out, appeared to arch about twenty-five
feet above our heads. As for the current, itself, it ran, Good
estimated, at least eight knots, and, fortunately for us, as is usual,
fiercest in the middle of the stream. Still, our first act was to
arrange that one of us, with the lantern and a pole which lay in
the canoe, should always be in the bows ready, if possible, to
prevent us from being stove in against the side of the cave or
any projecting rock. Umslopogaas, having already dined, took
the first turn. This was absolutely, with one exception, all that we
could do towards preserving our safety. The exception was that
another of us took up a position in the stern with a paddle by
means of which it was possible to steer the canoe more or less and
to keep her from the sides of the cave. These matters attended
to, we made a somewhat sparing meal off the cold buck's meat
(for we did not know how long it might have to last us), and then
feeling in rather better spirits I gave my opinion that, serious
as it undoubtedly was, I did not consider our position altogether
without hope, unless, indeed, the natives were right, and the
river plunged straight down into the bowels of the earth. If not,
it was clear that it must emerge somewhere, probably on the other
side of the mountains, and in that case all we had to think of was
to keep ourselves alive till we got there, wherever 'there' might
be. But, of course, as Good lugubriously pointed out, on the other

hand we might fall victims to a hundred unsuspected horrors—
or the river might go winding away inside the earth till it dried
up, in which case our fate would indeed be an awful one.

'Well, let us hope for the best and prepare ourselves for the
worst,' said Sir Henry, who is always cheerful and even spirited
—a very tower of strength in the time of trouble. 'We have come
out of so many queer scrapes together, that somehow I almost
fancy we shall come out of this,' he added.

This was excellent advice, and we proceeded to take it each in
our separate way—that is, except Alphonse, who had by now
sunk into a sort of terrified stupor. Good was at the helm and
Umslopogaas in the bows, so there was nothing left for Sir Henry
and myself to do except to lie down in the canoe and think. It
certainly was a curious, and indeed almost a weird, position to
be placed in—rushing along, as we were, through the bowels of
the earth, borne on the bosom of a Stygian river, something after
the fashion of souls being ferried by Charon, as Curtis said. And
how dark it was! the feeble ray from our little lamp did but
serve to show the darkness. There in the bows sat old Umslopogaas, like Pleasure in the poem,[1] watchful and untiring, the pole
ready to his hand, and behind in the shadow I could just make out
the form of Good peering forward at the ray of light in order to
make out how to steer with the paddle that he held and now and
again dipped in the water.

'Well, well,' thought I, 'you have come in search of adventures,
Allan my boy, and you have certainly got them. At your time of
life, too! you ought to be ashamed of yourself; but somehow you
are not, and, awful as it all is, perhaps you will pull through
after all; and if you don't, why, you cannot help it, you see!
And when all's said and done an underground river will make
a very appropriate burying-place.'

At first, however, I am bound to say that the strain upon the
nerves was very great. It is trying to the coolest and most experienced person not to know from one hour to another if he
has five more minutes to live, but there is nothing in this world
that one cannot get accustomed to, and in time we began to get
accustomed even to that. And, after all, our anxiety, though no
doubt natural, was, strictly speaking, illogical, seeing that we
never know what is going to happen to us the next minute, even
when we sit in a well-drained house with two policemen patrolling
under the window—nor how long we have to live. It is all
arranged for us, my sons, so what is the use of bothering?

It was nearly midday when we made our dive into darkness,

[1]Mr. Allan Quatermain misquotes—Pleasure sat at the helm.—EDITOR.

and we had set our watch (Good and Umslopogaas) at two, having agreed that it should be of a duration of five hours. At seven o'clock, accordingly, Sir Henry and I went on, Sir Henry at the bow and I at the stern, and the other two lay down and went to sleep. For three hours all went well, Sir Henry only finding it necessary once to push us off from the side; and I that but little steering was required to keep us straight, as the violent current did all that was needed, though occasionally the canoe showed a tendency which had to be guarded against to veer and travel broadside on. What struck me as the most curious thing about this wonderful river was: how did the air keep fresh? It was muggy and thick, no doubt, but still not sufficiently so to render it bad or even remarkably unpleasant. The only explanation that I can suggest is that the water of the lake had sufficient air in it to keep the atmosphere of the tunnel from absolute stagnation, this air being given out as the stream went its headlong way. Of course I only give this solution of the mystery for what it is worth, which perhaps is not much.

When I had been for three hours or so at the helm, I began to notice a decided change in the temperature, which was getting warmer. At first I took no notice of it, but when, at the expiration of another half-hour, I found that it was growing hotter and hotter, I called to Sir Henry and asked him if he noticed it, or if it was only my imagination. 'Noticed it!' he answered; 'I should think so. I am in a sort of Turkish bath.' Just about then the others woke up gasping, and were obliged to begin to discard their clothes. Here Umslopogaas had the advantage, for he did not wear any to speak of, except a moocha.

Hotter it grew, and hotter yet, till at last we could scarcely breathe, and the perspiration poured out of us. Half an hour more, and though we were all now stark naked, we could hardly bear it. The place was like an antechamber of the infernal regions proper. I dipped my hand into the water and drew it out almost with a cry; it was nearly boiling. We consulted a little thermometer we had—the mercury stood at 123°. From the surface of the water rose a dense cloud of steam. Alphonse groaned out that we were already in purgatory, which indeed we were, though not in the sense that he meant it. Sir Henry suggested that we must be passing near the seat of some underground fire, and I am inclined to think, especially in the light of what subsequently occurred, that he was right. Our sufferings for some time after this really pass my powers of description. We no longer perspired, for all the perspiration had been sweated out of us. We simply lay in the bottom of the boat, which we were now physically incapable of directing, feeling like hot embers, and I fancy under-going very much the same sensations that the poor fish do when they are dying on land—namely, those of slow suffocation. Our skins began to crack, and the blood to throb in our heads like the beating of a steam-engine.

This had been going on for some time, when suddenly the river turned a little, and I heard Sir Henry call out from the bows in a hoarse, startled voice, and, looking up, saw a most wonderful and awful sight. About half a mile ahead of us, and a little to the left of the centre of the stream—which we could now see was about ninety feet broad—a huge pillar-like jet of almost white flame rose from the surface of the water and sprang fifty feet into the air, when it struck the roof and spread out some forty feet in diameter, falling back in curved sheets of fire shaped like the petals of a full-blown rose. Indeed this awful gas jet resembled nothing so much as a great flaming tower rising out of the black water. Below was the straight stalk, a foot or more thick, and above the dreadful bloom. And as for the fearfulness of it and its fierce and awesome beauty, who can describe it? Certainly I cannot. Although we were now some five hundred yards away, notwithstanding the steam, it lit up the whole cavern as clear as day, and we could see that the roof was here about forty feet above us, and washed perfectly smooth with water. The rock was black, and here and there I could make out long shining lines of ore running through it like great veins, but of what metal they were I know not.

On we rushed towards this pillar of fire, which gleamed fiercer than any furnace ever lit by man.

'Keep the boat to the right, Quatermain—to the right,' shouted Sir Henry, and a minute afterwards I saw him fall forward senseless. Alphonse had already gone. Good was the next to go. There they lay as though dead: only Umslopogaas and I kept our senses. We were within fifty yards of it now, and I saw the Zulu's head fall forward on his hands. He had gone too, and I was alone. I could not breathe; the fierce heat dried me up. For yards and yards round the great rose of fire the rock-roof was red-hot. The wood of the boat was almost burning. I saw the feathers on one of the dead swans begin to twist and shrivel up; but I would not give in. I knew that if I did we should pass within three or four yards of the gas jet and perish miserably. I set the paddle so as to turn the canoe as far from it as possible, and held on grimly.

My eyes seemed to be bursting from my head, and through my closed lids I could see the fierce light. We were nearly opposite now; it roared like all the fires of hell, and the water boiled furiously around it. Five seconds more. We were past; I heard the roar behind me.

Then I too fell senseless. The next thing that I recollect is feeling a breath of air upon my face. My eyes opened with great difficulty. I looked up. Far, far above me there was light, though around me was deep gloom. Then I remembered and looked. The canoe still floated down the river, and in the bottom of it lay the naked forms of my companions. 'Were they dead?' I wondered. 'Was I left alone in this awful place?' I knew not. Next I became conscious of a burning thirst. I put my hand over the edge of the boat into the water and drew it up again with a cry. No wonder: nearly all the skin was burnt off the back of it. The water, however, was cold, or nearly so, and I drank pints and splashed myself all over. My body seemed to suck up the fluid as one may see a brick wall suck up rain after a drought; but where I was burnt the touch of it caused intense pain. Then I bethought myself of the others, and, dragging myself towards them with difficulty, I sprinkled them with water, and to my joy they began to recover—Umslopogaas first, then the others. Next they drank, absorbing water like so many sponges. Then, feeling chilly—a queer contrast to our recent sensations—we began as best we could to get into our clothes. As we did so Good pointed to the port side of the canoe: it was all blistered with heat, and in places actually charred. Had it been built like our civilised boats, Good said that the planks would have certainly warped and let in enough water to sink us; but fortunately it was dug out of the soft, willowy wood of a single great tree, and had sides nearly three inches and a bottom four inches thick. What that awful flame was we never discovered, but I suppose that there is at this spot a crack or hole in the bed of the river through which a vast volume of gas forced its way from its volcanic home in the bowels of the earth towards the upper air. How it first became ignited it is, of course, impossible to say—probably, I should think, from some spontaneous explosion of mephitic gases.

As soon as we had put some clothes on and shaken ourselves together a little, we set to work to make out where we were now. I have said that there was light above, and on examination we found that it came from the sky. Our river that was, Sir Henry said, a literal realisation of the wild vision of the poet,[1] was no longer underground, but was running on its darksome way, not

[1] Where Alph the sacred river ran
Through caverns measureless to man
Down to a sunless sea.

now through 'caverns measureless to man,' but between most frightful cliffs which cannot have been less than two thousand feet high. So high were they, indeed, that though the sky shone above us, where we were was dense gloom—not darkness indeed, but the gloom of a room closely shuttered in the daytime. Up on either side rose the great straight cliffs, grim and forbidding, till the eye grew dizzy with trying to measure their sheer height. The little space of sky that marked where they ended lay like a thread of blue upon their soaring blackness, which was unrelieved by any tree or creeper. Here and there, however, grew ghostly patches of a long grey lichen, hanging motionless to the rock as the white beard to the chin of a dead man. It seemed as though only the dregs or heavier part of the light had sunk to the bottom of this awful place. No bright winged sunbeam could fall so low: they died far, far above our heads.

By the river's edge was a little shore formed of round fragments of rock washed into this shape by the constant action of water, and giving the place an appearance of being strewn with thousands of fossil cannon balls. Evidently when the water of the underground river is high there is no beach at all, or very little, between the border of the stream and the precipitous cliffs; but now there was a space of seven or eight yards. And here, on this beach, we determined to land, in order to rest ourselves a little after all that we had gone through and to stretch our limbs. It was a dreadful place, but it would give an hour's respite from the terrors of the river, and also allow of our repacking and arranging the canoe. Accordingly we selected what looked like a favourable spot, and with some little difficulty managed to beach the canoe and scramble out on to the round, inhospitable pebbles.

'My word,' called out Good, who came on shore the first, 'what an awful place! it's enough to give one a fit.' And he laughed.

Instantly a thundering voice took up his words, magnifying them a hundred times. '*Give one a fit—Ho! ho! ho!*'—'*A fit, Ho! ho! ho!*' answered another voice in wild accents from far up the cliff—*a fit! a fit! a fit!* chimed in voice after voice—each flinging the words to and fro with shouts of awful laughter to the invisible lips of the other till the whole place echoed with the words and with shrieks of fiendish merriment, which at last ceased as suddenly as they had begun.

'Oh, mon Dieu!' yelled Alphonse, startled quite out of such self-command as he possessed.

'*Mon Dieu! Mon Dieu! Mon Dieu!*' the Titanic echoes thundered, shrieked, and wailed in every conceivable tone.

'Ah,' said Umslopogaas calmly, 'I clearly perceive that devils live here. Well, the place looks like it.'

I tried to explain to him that the cause of all the hubbub was a very remarkable and interesting echo, but he would not believe it.

'Ah,' he said, 'I know an echo when I hear one. There was one lived opposite my kraal in Zululand, and the Intombis [maidens] used to talk with it. But if what we hear is a full-grown echo, mine at home can only have been a baby. No, no—they are devils up there. But I don't think much of them, though,' he added, taking a pinch of snuff. 'They can copy what one says, but they don't seem to be able to talk on their own account, and they dare not show their faces,' and he relapsed into silence, apparently paying no further attention to such contemptible fiends.

After this we found it necessary to keep our conversation down to a whisper—for it was really unbearable to have every word one uttered tossed to and fro like a tennis-ball, as precipice called to precipice.

But even our whispers ran up the rocks in mysterious murmurs till at last they died away in long-drawn sighs of sound. Echoes are delightful and romantic things, but we had more than enough of them in that dreadful gulf.

As soon as we had settled ourselves a little on the round stones, we went on to wash and dress our burns as well as we could. As we had but a little oil for the lantern, we could not spare any for this purpose, so we skinned one of the swans, and used the fat off its breast, which proved an excellent substitute. Then we re-packed the canoe, and finally began to take some food, of which I need scarcely say we were in need, for our insensibility had endured for many hours, and it was, as our watches showed, midday. Accordingly we seated ourselves in a circle, and were soon engaged in discussing our cold meat with such appetite as we could muster, which, in my case at any rate, was not much, as I felt sick and faint after my sufferings of the previous night, and had besides a racking headache. It was a curious meal. The gloom was so intense that we could scarcely see the way to cut the food and convey it to our mouths. Still we got on pretty well, although the meat was tainted by the heat through which it had passed, till I happened to look behind me—my attention being attracted by a noise of something crawling over the stones, and perceived sitting upon a rock in my immediate rear a huge species of black freshwater crab only it was five times the size of any crab I ever saw. This hideous and loathsome-looking animal had projecting eyes that seemed to glare at one, very long and flexible antennæ or feelers, and gigantic claws. Nor was I especially favoured with its company. From every quarter dozens of these horrid brutes were creeping up, drawn, I suppose, by the smell of the food, from between the round stones and out of holes in the precipice. Some were already quite close to us. I stared quite fascinated by the unusual sight, and as I did so I saw one of the beasts stretch out its huge claw and give the unsuspecting Good such a nip behind that he jumped up with a howl, and set the 'wild echoes flying' in sober earnest. Just then, too, another, a very large one, got hold of Alphonse's leg, and declined to part with it, and, as may be imagined, a considerable scene ensued. Umslopogaas took his axe and cracked the shell of a great crab with it, whereon it set up a horrid screaming which the echoes multiplied a thousandfold, and began to foam at the mouth, a proceeding that drew hundreds more of its friends out of unsuspected holes and corners. Those on the spot perceiving that the animal was hurt fell upon it like creditors on a bankrupt, and literally rent it limb from limb with their huge pincers and devoured it, using their claws to convey the fragments to their mouths. Seizing whatever weapons were handy, such as stones or paddles, we commenced a war upon the monsters—whose numbers were increasing by 'leaps and bounds,' and whose stench was overpowering. So fast as we cracked their armour others seized the injured ones and devoured them, foaming at the mouth, and screaming as they did so. Nor did the brutes stop at that. When they could they nipped hold of us—and awful nips they were— or tried to steal the meat. One enormous fellow got hold of the swan we had skinned and began to drag it off. Instantly a score of others flung themselves upon the prey, and then began a ghastly and disgusting scene. How the monsters foamed and screamed, and rent the flesh, and each other! It was a sickening unnatural sight, and one that will haunt all who saw it till their dying day—enacted as it was in the deep, oppressive gloom, and set to the unceasing music of the many-toned nerve-shaking echoes. Strange as it may seem to say so, there was something so shockingly human about these fiendish creatures—it was as though all the most evil passions and desires of man had entered the shell of a magnified crab and gone mad. They were so dreadfully courageous and intelligent, and they looked as if they *understood*. The whole scene might have furnished material for another canto of Dante's 'Inferno,' as Curtis said.

'I say, you fellows, let's get out of this or we shall all go off our heads,' sung out Good; and we were not slow to take the hint.

Pushing the canoe, around which the animals were now crawling by hundreds and making vain attempts to climb, off the rocks, we bundled into it and got out into mid-stream, leaving behind us the fragments of our meal and the screaming, foaming, stinking mass of monsters in full possession of the ground.

'Those are the devils of the place,' said Umslopogaas with the air of one who has solved a problem, and upon my word I felt almost inclined to agree with him.

Umslopogaas's remarks were like his axe—very much to the point.

'What's to be done next?' said Sir Henry blankly.

'Drift, I suppose,' I answered, and we drifted accordingly. All the afternoon and well into the evening we floated on in the gloom beneath the far-off line of blue sky, scarcely knowing when day ended and night began, for down in that vast gulf the difference was not marked, till at length Good pointed out a star hanging right above us, which, having nothing better to do, we observed with great interest. Suddenly it vanished, the darkness became intense, and a familiar murmuring sound filled the air. 'Underground again,' I said with a groan, holding up the lamp. Yes, there was no doubt about it. I could just make out the roof. The chasm had come to an end and the tunnel had recommenced. And then began another long, long night of danger and horror. To describe all its incidents would be too wearisome, so I will simply say that about midnight we struck on a flat projecting rock in mid-stream and were as nearly as possible overturned and drowned. However, at last we got off, and went upon the uneven tenor of our way. And so the hours passed till it was nearly three o'clock. Sir Henry, Good, and Alphonse were asleep, utterly worn out; Umslopogaas was at the bow with the pole, and I was steering, when I perceived that the rate at which we were travelling had increased perceptibly. Then, suddenly, I heard Umslopogaas make an exclamation, and next second came a sound as of parting branches, and I became aware that the canoe was being forced through hanging bushes or creepers. Another minute, and a breath of sweet open air fanned my face, and I felt that we had emerged from the tunnel and were floating upon clear water. I say felt, for I could see nothing, the darkness being absolutely pitchy, as it often is just before the dawn. But even this could scarcely damp my joy. We were out of that dreadful river, and wherever we might have got to this at least was something to be thankful for. And so I sat down and inhaled the sweet night air and waited for the dawn with such patience as I could command.

CHAPTER XI.

THE FROWNING CITY.

For an hour or more I sat waiting, Umslopogaas having meanwhile gone to sleep also, till at length the east turned grey, and huge misty shapes moved over the surface of the water like ghosts of long-forgotten dawns. They were the vapours rising from their watery bed to greet the sun. Then the grey turned to primrose, and the primrose grew to red. Next, glorious bars of light sprang up across the eastern sky, and now between them the messengers of dawn came speeding upon their arrowy way, scattering the ghostly vapours and touching the distant mountain tops, as they flew from range to range and longitude to longitude. Another moment, and the golden gates were open and the sun himself came forth gloriously, with pomp and splendour and a flashing as of ten million spears, and covered up the night with brightness, and it was day.

But as yet I could see nothing save the beautiful blue sky above, for over the water was a thick layer of mist exactly as though the whole surface had been spread with billows of cotton wool. By degrees, however, the sun sucked up the mists, and then I saw that we were afloat upon a lovely sheet of blue water of which I could not make out the shore. Some eight or ten miles behind us, however, there stretched as far as the eye could reach a range of precipitous hills that formed a retaining wall of the lake, and I have no doubt but that it was through some entrance in these hills that the subterranean river found its way into the open water. Indeed, I afterwards ascertained this to be the fact, and it will be some indication of the extraordinary strength and directness of the current of this mysterious river that the canoe, even at this distance, was still answering to it. Presently, too, I, or rather Umslopogaas, who woke up just then, discovered another indication, and a very unpleasant one it was. Perceiving some whitish object upon the water, Umslopogaas called my attention to it, and with a few strokes of the paddle brought the canoe to the spot, whereupon we discovered that the object was the body of a man floating face downwards. This was bad enough, but imagine my horror when Umslopogaas having turned him on to his back with the paddle, we recognised in the sunken features the lineaments of——whom do you suppose? None other than our poor servant who had been sucked down two days before in the waters of the subterranean river. It quite frightened me. I thought that we had left him behind for ever, and behold!

borne by the current, he had made the awful journey with us, and with us had reached its end. His appearance also was dreadful, for he bore traces of having touched the pillar of fire—one arm being completely shrivelled up and all his hair being burnt off. The features were, as I have said, sunken, and yet they preserved upon them that awful look of despair which I had seen upon his living face as the poor fellow was sucked down. Really the sight unnerved me, weary and shaken as I felt with all that we had gone through, and I was heartily glad when suddenly and without any warning the body began to sink, just as though, its pre-destined mission having been accomplished, it retired; the real reason no doubt being that turning it on its back allowed a free passage to the gas . Down it went into the transparent depths —fathom after fathom we could trace its course till at last a long line of bright air-bubbles, swiftly chasing each other to the surface, alone remained where it had passed. At length these, too, were gone, and that was an end of our poor servant. Umslopogaas watched the body vanish thoughtfully.

'What did he follow us for?' he asked. "Tis an ill omen for thee and me, Macumazahn.' And he laughed.

I turned on him angrily, for I dislike these unpleasant suggestions. If people have such ideas, they ought in common decency to keep them to themselves. I detest individuals who make one the subject of their disagreeable presentiments, or who, when they dream that they saw you hanged as a common felon, or some such horror, will insist upon telling you all about it at breakfast, even if they have to get up early to do so.

Just then, however, the others woke up, and began to rejoice exceedingly at finding that we were out of that dreadful river and once more beneath the blue sky. Then followed a babel of talk and suggestions as to what we were to do next, the upshot of all of which was that, as we were excessively hungry, and had nothing whatsoever left to eat except a few scraps of biltong (dried game-flesh), having abandoned what remained of our provisions to those horrible freshwater crabs, we determined to make for the shore. But now a new difficulty arose. We did not know where the shore was, and, with the exception of the cliffs through which the subterranean river made its entry, could see nothing but a wide expanse of sparkling blue water. Observing, however, that the long flights of aquatic birds kept flying from our left, we concluded that they were advancing from their feeding-grounds on shore to pass the day in the lake, and accordingly headed the boat towards the quarter whence they came, and began to paddle. Before long, however, a stiffish breeze sprang up, blowing directly in the direction we wanted, so we improvised a sail with a blanket and the pole, which took us along merrily. This done, we devoured the remnants of our biltong, washed down with the sweet lake water, and then lit our pipes and awaited whatever might turn up.

When we had been sailing for an hour, Good, who was searching the horizon with the spy-glass, suddenly announced joyfully that he saw land, and pointed out that, from the change in the colour of the water, he thought that we must be approaching the mouth of a river. In another minute we perceived a great golden dome, not unlike that of St. Paul's, piercing the morning mists, and while we were wondering what in the world it could be, Good reported another and still more important discovery, namely, that a small sailing-boat was advancing towards us. This bit of news, which we were very shortly able to verify with our own eyes, threw us into a considerable flutter. That the natives of this unknown lake should understand the art of sailing seemed to suggest that they possessed some degree of civilisation. In a few more minutes it became evident that the occupant or occupants of the advancing boat had made us out. For a moment or two she hung in the wind as though in doubt, and then came tacking towards us with great swiftness. In ten more minutes she was within a hundred yards, and we saw that she was a neat little boat—not a canoe 'dug out,' but built more or less in the European fashion with planks, and carrying a singularly large sail for her size. But our attention was soon diverted from the boat to her crew, which consisted of a man and woman, *nearly as white as ourselves.*

We stared at each other in amazement, thinking that we must be mistaken: but no, there was no doubt about it. They were not fair, but the two people in the boat were decidedly of a white as distinguished from a black race, as white, for instance, as Spaniards or Italians. It was a patent fact. So it was true, after all; and, mysteriously led by a most strange chance, we had discovered this wonderful people. I could have shouted for joy when I thought of the glory and the wonder of the thing; and as it was, we all shook hands and congratulated each other on the unexpected success of our wild search. All my life had I heard rumours of a white race that existed in the highlands of the interior of this vast continent, and longed to put them to the proof, and now here I saw it with my own eyes, and was dumbfounded. Truly, as Sir Henry said, the old Roman was right when he wrote 'Ex Africa semper aliquid novi,' which he tells me means that out of Africa there always comes some new thing.

The man in the boat was of a good but not particularly fine physique, and possessed straight black hair, regular aquiline features, and an intelligent face. He was dressed in a brown cloth garment, something like a flannel shirt without the sleeves, and in an unmistakable kilt of the same material. The legs and feet were bare. Round the right arm and left leg he wore thick rings of yellow metal that I judged to be gold. The woman had a sweet face, wild and shy, with large eyes and curling brown hair. Her dress was made of the same material as the man's, and consisted, as we afterwards discovered, first of a linen under-garment that hung down to her knee, and then of a single long strip of cloth, about four feet wide by fifteen long, which was wound round the body in graceful folds and finally flung over the left shoulder so that the end, which was dyed blue or purple or some other colour, according to the social standing of the wearer, hung down in front, the right arm and breast being, however, left quite bare. A more becoming dress, especially when, as in the present case, the wearer was young and pretty, it is quite impossible to conceive. Good, who has an eye for such things, was greatly struck with it, and so indeed was I. It was so simple and yet so effective.

Meanwhile, if we had been astonished at the appearance of the man and woman, it was clear that they were far more astonished at us. As for the man, he appeared to be overcome with fear and wonder, and for a while hovered round our canoe, but would not approach. At last, however, he came within hailing distance, and called to us in a language that sounded soft and pleasing enough, but of which we could not understand one word. So we hailed back in English, French, Latin, Greek German, Zulu, Dutch, Sisutu, Kukuana, and a few other native dialects that I am acquainted with, but our visitor did not understand any of these tongues; indeed, they appeared to bewilder him. As for the lady, she was busily employed in taking stock of us, and Good was returning the compliment by staring at her hard through his eye-glass, a proceeding that she seemed rather to enjoy than otherwise. At length, the man, being unable to make anything out of us, suddenly headed his boat round and began to head off for the shore, his little boat skimming away before the wind like a swallow. As she passed across our bows the man turned to attend to the large sail, and Good promptly took the opportunity to kiss his hand to the young lady. I was horrified at this proceeding, both on general grounds and because I feared that she might take offence, but to my delight she did not, for, first glancing round and seeing that her husband, or brother, or whoever he was, was engaged, she promptly kissed hers back.

'Ah!' said I. 'It seems that we have at last found a language that the people of this country understand.'

'In which case,' said Sir Henry, 'Good will prove an invaluable interpreter.'

I frowned, for I do not approve of Good's frivolities, and he knows it, and I turned the conversation to more serious subjects. 'It is very clear to me,' I said, 'that the man will be back before long with a host of his fellows, so we had best make up our minds as to how we are going to receive them.'

'The question is how will they receive us?' said Sir Henry.

As for Good he made no remark, but began to extract from under a pile of baggage a small square tin case that had accompanied us in all our wanderings. Now we had often remonstrated with Good about this tin case, inasmuch as it was a most awkward thing to carry, and he had never given any very explicit account as to its contents; but always insisted on keeping it, saying mysteriously that its contents might come in very useful one day.

'What on earth are you going to do, Good?' asked Sir Henry.

'Do—why dress, of course! You don't expect me to appear in a new country in these things, do you?' and he pointed to his soiled and worn garments, which were however, like all Good's things, very tidy, and with every tear neatly mended.

We said no more, but watched his proceedings with breathless interest. His first step was to make Alphonse, who was thoroughly competent in such matters, trim his hair and beard in the most approved fashion. I think that if he had had some hot water and a cake of soap at hand he would have shaved off the latter; but he had none. This done, he suggested that we should lower the sail of the canoe and all take a bath, which we did, greatly to the horror and astonishment of Alphonse, who lifted his hands and ejaculated that these English were indeed a wonderful people. Umslopogaas, who, though, like most high-bred Zulus, he was scrupulously cleanly in his person, did not see the fun of swimming about in a lake, also regarded the proceeding with mild amusement. We returned to the canoe much refreshed by the cold water and sat to dry in the sun, whilst Good undid his tin box, and produced a most beautiful clean white shirt, just as it had left a London steam laundry, and then some garments wrapped first in brown, then in white, and finally in silver paper. We watched this undoing with the tenderest interest and much speculation. One by one Good removed the dull husks that hid their splendours, carefully folding and replacing each piece of paper as he did so; and there at last lay, in all the majesty of its gold epaulettes, lace, and buttons, a Commander of the Royal Navy's full-dress uniform—dress sword, cocked hat, shiny patent leather boots and all. We literally gasped.

'*What!*' we said, '*what!* Are you going to put those things on?'

'Certainly,' he answered composedly; 'you see so much depends upon a first impression, especially,' he added, 'as I observe that there are ladies about. One at least of us ought to be decently dressed.

We said no more; we were simply dumbfounded, especially when we considered the artful way in which Good had concealed the contents of that box for all these months. Only one suggestion did we make—namely, that he should wear his mail-shirt next his skin. He replied that he feared it would spoil the set of his coat, now carefully spread in the sun to take the creases out, but finally consented to this precautionary measure. The most amusing part of the affair, however, was to see old Umslopogaas's astonishment and Alphonse's delight at Good's transformation. When at last he stood up in all his glory, even down to the medals on his breast, and contemplated himself in the still waters of the lake, after the fashion of the young gentleman in ancient history, whose name I cannot remember, but who fell in love with his own shadow, the old Zulu could no longer restrain his feelings.

'Oh, Bougwan!' he said. 'Oh, Bougwan! I always thought thee an ugly little man, and fat—fat as the cows at calving time; and now thou art like a blue jay when he spreads his tail out. Surely, Bougwan, it hurts my eyes to look at thee.'

Good did not much like this allusion to his fat, which, to tell the truth, was not very well deserved, for hard exercise had brought him down three inches; but on the whole he was pleased at Umslopogaas's admiration. As for Alphonse, he was quite delighted.

'Ah! but Monsieur has the beautiful air—the air of the warrior. It is the ladies who will say so when we come to get ashore. Monsieur is complete; he puts me in mind of my heroic grand——'

Here we stopped Alphonse.

As we gazed upon the beauties thus revealed by Good, a spirit of emulation filled our breasts, and we set to work to get ourselves up as well as we could. The most, however, that we were able to do was to array ourselves in our spare suits of shooting clothes, of which we each had one, keeping on our mail shirts underneath. As for my appearance, all the fine clothes in the world could never make it otherwise than scrubby and insignificant; but Sir Henry looked what he is, a magnificent man in his nearly new tweed suit, gaiters, and boots. Alphonse also got

himself up to kill, giving an extra turn to his enormous mous-
taches. Even old Umslopogaas, who was not in a general way
given to the vain adorning of his body, took some oil out of the
lantern and a bit of tow, and polished up his head-ring with it
till it shone like Good's patent leather boots. Then he put on the
mail shirt Sir Henry had given him and his 'moocha,' and, having
cleaned up Inkosi-kaas a little, stood forth complete.

All this while, having hoisted the sail again as soon as we had
finished bathing, we had been progressing steadily for the land,
or, rather, for the mouth of a great river. Presently—in all about
an hour and a half after the little boat had left us—we saw
emerging from the river or harbour a large number of boats,
ranging up to ten or twelve tons burden. One of these was propelled by twenty-four oars, and most of the rest sailed. Looking
through the glass we soon made out that the row-boat was an
official vessel, her crew being all dressed in a sort of uniform,
whilst on the half-deck forward stood an old man of venerable
appearance, with a flowing white beard, and a sword strapped to
his side, who was evidently the commander of the craft. The
other boats were occupied apparently by people brought out by
curiosity, and were rowing or sailing towards us as quickly as
they could.

'Now for it,' said I. 'What is the betting? Are they going to
be friendly or to put an end to us?'

Nobody could answer this question, and, not liking the warlike appearance of the old gentleman and his sword, we felt a
little anxious.

Just then Good spied a school of hippopotami on the water
about two hundred yards off us, and suggested that it would not
be a bad plan to impress the natives with a sense of our power
by shooting some of them if possible. Unluckily enough, this
struck us as a good idea, and accordingly we at once got out our
eight-bore rifles, for which we still had a few cartridges left, and
prepared for action. There were four of the animals, a big bull,
a cow, and two large calves, one three parts grown. We got up to
them without difficulty, the great animals contenting themselves
with sinking down into the water and rising again a few yards
farther on; indeed, their excessive tameness struck me as being
peculiar. When the advancing boats were about five hundred
yards away, Sir Henry opened the ball by firing at the three-parts
grown young one. The heavy bullet struck it fair between the
eyes, and, crashing through the skull, killed it, and it sank, leaving a long train of blood behind it. At the same moment I fired
at the cow, and Good at the old bull. My shot took effect, but

not fatally, and down went the hippopotamus with a prodigious splashing, only to rise again presently blowing and grunting furiously, dyeing all the water round her crimson, when I killed her with the left barrel. Good, who is an execrable shot, missed the head of the bull altogether, the bullet merely cutting the side of his face as it passed. On glancing up, after I had fired my second shot, I perceived that the people we had fallen among were evidently ignorant of the nature of firearms, for the consternation caused by our shots and their effect upon the animals was prodigious. Some of the parties in the boats began to cry out with fear; others turned and made off as hard as they could; and even the old gentleman with the sword looked greatly puzzled and alarmed, and halted his big row-boat. We had, however, but little time for observation, for just then the old bull, rendered furious by the wound he had received, rose fair within forty yards of us, glaring savagely. We all fired, and hit him in various places, and down he went, badly wounded. Curiosity now began to overcome the fear of the onlookers, and some of them sailed on up close to us, amongst these being the man and woman whom we had first seen a couple of hours or so before, who drew up almost alongside. Just then the great brute rose again within ten yards of their boat, and instantly with a roar of fury made at it open-mouthed. The woman shrieked, and the man tried to give the boat way, but without success. In another second I saw the huge red jaws and gleaming ivories close with a crunch on the frail craft, taking an enormous mouthful out of its side and capsizing it. Down went the boat, leaving its occupants struggling in the water. Next moment, before we could do anything towards saving them, the huge and furious creature was up again and making open-mouthed at the poor girl, who was struggling in the water. Lifting my rifle just as the grinding jaws were about to close on her, I fired over her head right down the hippopotamus's throat. Over he went, and commenced turning round and round, snorting and blowing red streams of blood through his nostrils. Before he could recover himself, however, I let him have the other barrel in the side of the throat, and that finished him. He never moved or struggled again, but sank instantly. Our next effort was directed towards saving the girl, the man having swum off towards another boat, and in this we were fortunately successful, pulling her into the canoe, amidst the shouts of the spectators, considerably exhausted and frightened, but otherwise unhurt.

Meanwhile the boats had gathered together at a distance, and we could see that their occupants, who were evidently much frightened, were consulting what to do. Without giving them time for further consideration, which we thought might result unfavourably to ourselves, we instantly took our paddles and advanced towards them, Good standing in the bow and taking off his cocked hat politely in every direction, his amiable features suffused by a bland but intelligent smile. Most of the craft retreated as we advanced, but a few held their ground, while the big row-boat came on to meet us. Presently we were alongside, and I could see that our appearance—and especially Good's and Umslopogaas's—filled the venerable-looking commander with astonishment, not unmixed with awe. He was dressed after the same fashion as the man we first met, except that his shirt was not made of brown cloth, but of pure white linen hemmed with purple. The kilt, however, was identical, and so were the thick rings of gold around the arm and beneath the left knee. The rowers wore only a kilt, their bodies being naked to the waist. Good took off his hat to the old gentleman with an extra flourish, and inquired after his health in the purest English, to which he replied by laying the first two fingers of his right hand horizontally across his lips and holding them there for a moment, which we took to be his mode of salutation. Then he also addressed some remarks to us in the same soft accents that had distinguished our first interviewer, which we were forced to indicate we did not understand by shaking our heads and shrugging our shoulders. This last Alphonse, being to the manner born, did to perfection, and in so polite a way that nobody could take any offence. Then we came to a standstill, till I, being exceedingly hungry, thought I might as well call attention to the fact, and did so first by opening my mouth and pointing down it, and then rubbing my stomach. These signals the old gentleman clearly understood, for he nodded his head vigorously, and pointed towards the harbour; and at the same time one of the men on his boat threw us a line and motioned to us to make it fast, which we did. The row-boat then took us in tow, and went with great rapidity towards the mouth of the river, accompanied by all the other boats. In about twenty minutes more we reached the entrance to the harbour, which was crowded with boats full of people who had come out to see us. We observed that all the occupants were more or less of the same type, though some were fairer than others. Indeed, we noticed certain ladies whose skin was of a most dazzling whiteness; and the darkest shade of colour which we saw was like that of a rather swarthy Spaniard. Presently the river gave an inward sweep, and when it did so an exclamation of astonishment and delight burst from our lips as we caught our first view of the place that we afterwards knew as Milosis, or the Frowning City (from *mi*, which means city, and *losis*, a frown).

At a distance of some five hundred yards from the river's bank rose a sheer precipice of granite, two hundred feet or so in height, which once no doubt had formed the bank itself—the intermediate space of land now utilised as docks and roadways having been gained by draining, and deepening and embanking the stream.

On the brow of this precipice stood a great building of the same granite that formed the cliff, built on three sides of a square, the fourth side being open, save for a kind of battlement pierced at its base by a little door. We afterwards discovered this imposing place was the palace of the queen, or rather of the queens. At the back of the palace the town sloped gently upwards to a flashing building of white marble, crowned by the golden dome which we had already observed. The city, with the exception of this one building, was entirely built of red granite, and laid out in regular blocks with splendid roadways between. So far as we could see also the houses were all one-storied and detached, with gardens round them, which gave some relief to the eye wearied with the vista of red granite. At the back of the palace a road of extraordinary width stretched away up the hill for a distance of a mile and a half or so, and appeared to terminate at an open space surrounding the gleaming building that crowned the hill. But right in front of us was the wonder and glory of Milosis—the great staircase of the palace, the magnificence of which fairly took our breath away. Let the reader imagine, if he can, a splendid stairway, sixty-five feet from balustrade to balustrade, consisting of two vast flights, each of one hundred and twenty-five steps of eight inches in height by three feet broad, connected by a flat resting-place sixty feet in length, and running from the palace wall on the edge of the precipice down to meet a waterway or canal cut to its foot from the river. This marvellous staircase was supported upon a single enormous granite arch, of which the resting-place between the two flights formed the crown; that is, the connecting open space lay upon it. From this archway sprang a subsidiary flying arch, or rather something that resembled a flying arch in shape, such as none of us had seen in any other country, and of which the beauty and wonder surpassed all that we had ever imagined. Three hundred feet from point to point, and no less than five hundred and fifty round the curve, that half-arc soared touching the bridge it supported for a space of fifty feet only, one end resting on and built into the parent archway, and the other embedded in the solid granite of the side of the precipice.

This staircase with its supports was, indeed, a work of which any living man might have been proud, both on account of its magnitude and its surpassing beauty. Four times, as we afterwards learnt, did the work, which was commenced in remote antiquity, fail, and was then abandoned for three centuries when half-finished, till at last there rose a youthful engineer named Rademas, who said that he would complete it successfully, and staked his life upon it. If he failed he was to be hurled from the precipice he had undertaken to scale; if he succeeded, he was to be rewarded by the hand of the king's daughter. Five years was given to him to complete the work, and an unlimited supply of labour and material. Three times did his arch fall, till at last, seeing failure to be inevitable, he determined to commit suicide on the morrow of the third collapse. That night, however, a beautiful woman came to him in a dream and touched his forehead, and of a sudden he saw a vision of the completed work, and saw too through the masonry and how the difficulties connected with the flying arch that had hitherto baffled his genius were to be overcome. Then he awoke and once more commenced the work, but on a different plan, and at length achieved it, and on the last day of the five years he led the princess his bride up the stair and into the palace. And in due course he became king by right of his wife, and founded the present Zu-Vendi dynasty, which is to this day called the 'House of the Stairway,' thus proving once more how energy and talent are the natural stepping stones to grandeur. To commemorate his triumph he fashioned a statue of himself dreaming, and of the fair woman who touched him on the forehead, and placed it in the great hall of the palace, and there it stands to this day.

Such is the great stair of Milosis, and such the city beyond. No wonder they named it the 'Frowning City,' for certainly those mighty works in solid granite did seem to frown down upon our littleness in their sombre splendour. This was so even in the sunshine, but when the storm-clouds gathered on her imperial brow Milosis looked more like a supernatural dwelling-place, or some imagining of a poet's brain, than what she is—a mortal city, carven by the patient genius of generations out of the silence of the mountain side.

CHAPTER XII.

THE SISTER QUEENS.

THE big rowing-boat glided on up the cutting that ran almost to the foot of the vast stairway, and then halted at a flight of steps leading to the landing-place. Here the old gentleman disembarked, and invited us to do so likewise, which, having no alternative, and being nearly starved, we did without hesitation —taking our rifles with us, however. As each of us landed, our guide again laid his fingers on his lips in salutation and bowed deeply, at the same time ordering back the crowds who had assembled to gaze on us. The last to leave the canoe was the girl we had picked out of the water, for whom her companion was waiting. Before she went away she kissed my hand, I suppose as a token of gratitude for having saved her from the fury of the hippopotamus; and it seemed to me that she had by this time quite got over any fear she might have had of us, and was by no means anxious to return in such a hurry to her lawful owners. At any rate, she was going to kiss Good's hand as well as mine, when the young man interfered and led her off. As soon as we were on shore, a number of the men who had rowed the big boat took possession of our few goods and chattels, and started with them up the splendid staircase, our guide indicating to us by means of motions that the things were perfectly safe. This done, he turned to the right and led the way to a small house, which was, as I afterwards discovered, an inn. Entering into a good-sized room, we saw that a wooden table was already furnished with food, presumably in preparation for us. Here our guide motioned us to be seated on a bench that ran the length of the table. We did not require a second invitation, but at once fell to ravenously on the viands before us, which were served on wooden platters, and consisted of cold goat's-flesh, wrapped up in some kind of leaf that gave it a delicious flavour, green vegetables resembling lettuces, brown bread, and red wine poured from a skin into horn mugs. This wine was peculiarly soft and good, having something of the flavour of Burgundy. Twenty minutes after we sat down at that hospitable board we rose from it, feeling like new men. After all that we had gone through we needed two things, food and rest, and the food of itself was a great blessing to us. Two girls of the same charming cast of face as the first whom we had seen waited on us while we ate, and very nicely they did it. They were also dressed in the same fashion namely,—in a white linen petticoat coming to the knee, and with the toga-like garment of brown cloth, leaving bare the right arm and breast. I afterwards found out that this was the national dress, and regulated by an iron custom, though of course subject to variations. Thus, if the petticoat was pure white, it signified that the wearer was unmarried; if white, with a straight purple stripe round the edge, that she was married and a first or legal wife; if with a wavy purple stripe, that she was a second or other wife; if with a black stripe, that she was a widow. In the same way the toga, or 'kaf,' as they call it, was of different shades of colour, from pure white to the deepest brown, according to the rank of the wearer, and embroidered at the end in various ways. This also applies to the 'shirts' or tunics worn by the men, which varied in material and colour; but the kilts were always the same except as regards quality. One thing, however, every man and woman in the country wore as the national insignia, and that was the thick band of gold round the right arm above the elbow, and the left leg beneath the knee. People of high rank also wore a torque of gold round the neck, and I observed that our guide had one on.

So soon as we had finished our meal our venerable conductor, who had been standing all the while, regarding us with inquiring eyes, and our guns with something as like fear as his pride would allow him to show, bowed towards Good, whom he evidently took for the leader of the party on account of the splendour of his apparel, and once more led the way through the door and to the foot of the great staircase. Here we paused for a moment to admire two colossal lions, each hewn from a single block of pure black marble, and standing rampant on the terminations of the wide balustrades of the staircase. These lions are magnificently executed, and it is said were sculptured by Rademas, the great prince who designed the staircase, and who was without doubt, to judge from the many beautiful examples of his art that we saw afterwards, one of the finest sculptors who ever lived, either in this or any other country. Then we climbed almost with a feeling of awe up that splendid stair, a work executed for all time and that will, I do not doubt, be admired thousands of years hence by generations unborn unless an earthquake should throw it down. Even Umslopogaas, who as a general rule made it a point of honour not to show astonishment, which he considered undignified, was fairly startled out of himself, and asked if the 'bridge had been built by men or devils,' which was his vague way of alluding to any supernatural power. But Alphonse did not care about it. Its solid

grandeur jarred upon the frivolous little Frenchman, who said
that it was all 'très magnifique, mais triste—ah, triste!' and
went on to suggest that it would be improved if the balustrades
were *gilt*.

On we went up the first flight of one hundred and twenty
steps, across the broad platform joining it to the second flight,
where we paused to admire the glorious view of one of the most
beautiful stretches of country that the world can show, edged by
the blue waters of the lake. Then we passed on up the stair till
at last we reached the top, where we found a large standing space
to which there were three entrances, all of small size. Two of
these opened on to rather narrow galleries or roadways cut in
the face of the precipice that ran round the palace walls and led
to the principal thoroughfares of the city, and were used by the
inhabitants passing up and down from the docks. These were
defended by gates of bronze, and also, as we afterwards learnt,
it was possible to let down a portion of the roadways themselves
by withdrawing certain bolts, and thus render it quite impracticable for an enemy to pass. The third entrance consisted of a
flight of ten curved black marble steps leading to a doorway cut
in the palace wall. This wall was in itself a work of art, being
built of huge blocks of granite to the height of forty feet, and so
fashioned that its face was concave, whereby it was rendered
practically impossible for it to be scaled. To this doorway our
guide led us. The door, which was very massive, and made of
wood protected by an outer gate of bronze, was closed; but on our
approach it was thrown wide, and we were met by the challenge
of a sentry, who was armed with a heavy triangular-bladed spear,
not unlike a bayonet in shape, and a cutting sword, and protected
by breast and back plates of skilfully prepared hippopotamus
hide, and a small round shield fashioned of the same tough
material. The sword instantly attracted our attention; it was
practically identical with the one in the possession of Mr. Mackenzie which he had obained from the ill-starred wanderer.
There was no mistaking the gold-lined fretwork cut in the thickness of the blade. So the man had told the truth, after all. Our
guide instantly gave a password, which the soldier acknowledged
by letting the iron shaft of his spear fall with a ringing sound
upon the pavement, and we passed on through the massive wall
into the courtyard of the palace. This was about forty yards
square, and laid out in flower-beds full of lovely shrubs and
plants, many of which were quite new to me. Through the centre
of this garden ran a broad walk formed of powdered shells
brought from the lake in the place of gravel. Following this we

came to another doorway with a round heavy arch, which is hung with thick curtains, for there are no doors in the palace itself. Then came another short passage, and we were in the great hall of the palace, and once more stood astonished at the simple and yet overpowering grandeur of the place.

The hall is, as we afterwards learnt, one hundred and fifty feet long by eighty wide, and has a magnificent arched roof of carved wood. Down the entire length of the building there are on either side, and at a distance of twenty feet from the wall, slender shafts of black marble springing sheer to the roof, beautifully fluted, and with carved capitals. At one end of this great place which these pillars support is the group of which I have already spoken as executed by the King Rademas to commemorate his building of the staircase; and really, when we had time to admire it, its loveliness almost struck us dumb. The group, of which the figures are in white, and the rest in black marble, is about half as large again as life, and represents a young man of noble countenance and form sleeping heavily upon a couch. One arm is carelessly thrown over the side of this couch, and his head reposes upon the other, its curling locks partially hiding it. Bending over him, her hand resting on his forehead, is a draped female form of such white loveliness as to make the beholder's breath stand still. And as for the calm glory that shines upon her perfect face—well, I can never hope to describe it. But there it rests like the shadow of an angel's smile; and power, love, and divinity all have their part in it. Her eyes are fixed upon the sleeping youth, and perhaps the most extraordinary thing about this beautiful work is the success with which the artist has succeeded in depicting on the sleeper's worn and weary face the sudden rising of a new and spiritual thought as the spell begins to work within his mind. You can see that an inspiration is breaking in upon the darkness of the man's soul as the dawn breaks in upon the darkness of the night. It is a glorious piece of statuary, and none but a genius could have conceived it. Between each of the black marble columns is some such group of figures, some allegorical, and some representing the persons and wives of deceased monarchs or great men; but none of them, in our opinion, come up to the one I have described, although several are from the hand of the great sculptor and engineer, King Rademas.

In the exact centre of the hall was a solid mass of black marble about the size of a baby's arm-chair, which it rather resembled in appearance. This, as we afterwards learnt, was the sacred stone of this remarkable people, and on it their monarchs laid their hand after the ceremony of coronation, and swore by the sun to safeguard the interests of the empire, and to maintain its customs, traditions, and laws. This stone was evidently exceedingly ancient, as indeed all stones are, and was scored down its sides with long marks or lines which Sir Henry said proved it to have been a fragment that at some remote period in its history had been ground in the iron jaws of glaciers. There was a curious prophecy about this block of marble, which was reported among the people to have fallen from the sun, to the effect that when it was shattered into fragments a king of alien race should rule over the land. As the stone, however, looked remarkably solid, the native princes seemed to have a fair chance of keeping their own for many a long year.

At the end of the hall is a däis spread with rich carpets, on which two thrones are set side by side. These thrones are shaped like great chairs, and made of solid gold. The seats are richly cushioned, but the backs are left bare, and on each is carved the emblem of the sun, shooting out his fiery rays in all directions. The footstools are golden lions couchant, with yellow topazes set in them for eyes. There are no other gems about them.

The place is lighted by numerous but narrow windows placed high up, cut on the principle of the loopholes to be seen in ancient castles, but innocent of glass, which was evidently unknown here.

Such is a brief description of this splendid hall in which we now found ourselves, compiled of course from our subsequent knowledge of it. On this occasion we had but little time for observation, for when we entered we perceived that a large number of men were gathered together in front of the two thrones, which were unoccupied. The principal among them were seated on carved wooden chairs ranged to the right and the left of the thrones, but not in front of them, and were dressed in white tunics, with various embroideries and different coloured edgings, and armed with the usual pierced and gold-inlaid swords. To judge from the dignity of their appearance, they seemed one and all to be individuals of very great importance. Behind each of these great men stood a small knot of followers and attendants.

Seated by themselves, in a little group to the left of the throne, were six men of a different stamp. Instead of wearing the ordinary kilt, they were clothed in long robes of pure white linen, with the same symbol of the sun that is to be seen on the back of the chairs, emblazoned in gold thread upon the breast. This garment was girt up at the waist with a simple golden curb-like chain, from which hung long elliptical plates of the same metal, fashioned in shiny scales like those of a fish, that, as their

wearer moved, jingled and reflected the light. They were all men
of mature age and of a severe and impressive cast of features,
which was rendered still more imposing by the long beards they
wore.

The personality of one individual among them, however, impressed us at once. He seemed to stand out among his fellows
and refuse to be overlooked. He was very old—eighty at least—
and extremely tall, with a long snow-white beard that hung
nearly to his waist. His features were aquiline and deeply cut,
and his eyes were grey and cold-looking. The heads of the others
were bare, but this man wore a round cap entirely covered with
gold embroidery, from which we judged that he was a person of
great importance; and indeed we afterwards discovered that he
was Agon, the High Priest of the country. As we approached, all
these men, including the priests, rose and bowed to us with the
greatest courtesy, at the same time placing the two fingers across
the lips in salutation. Then soft-footed attendants advanced
from between the pillars, bearing seats, which were placed in a
line in front of the thrones. We three sat down, Alphonse and
Umslopogaas standing behind us. Scarcely had we done so when
there came a blare of trumpets from some passage to the right,
and a similar blare from the left. Next a man with a long white
wand of ivory appeared just in front of the right-hand throne,
and cried out something in a loud voice, ending with the word
Nyleptha, repeated three times; and another man, similarly
attired, called out a similar sentence before the other throne,
but ending with the word *Sorais*, also repeated thrice. Then
came the tramp of armed men from each side entrance, and in
filed about a score of picked and magnificently accoutred guards,
who formed up on each side of the thrones, and let their heavy
iron-handled spears fall simultaneously with a clash upon the
black marble flooring. Another double blare of trumpets, and
from either side, each attended by six maidens, in swept the two
Queens of Zu-Vendis, everybody in the hall rising to greet them
as they came.

I have seen beautiful women in my day, and am no longer
thrown into transports at the sight of a pretty face; but language
fails me when I try to give some idea of the blaze of loveliness
that then broke upon us in the persons of these sister Queens.
Both were young—perhaps five-and-twenty years of age—both
were tall and exquisitely formed; but there the likeness stopped.
One, Nyleptha, was a woman of dazzling fairness; her right
arm and breast, bare after the custom of her people, showed like
snow even against her white and gold-embroidered 'kaf,' or toga.

And as for her sweet face, all I can say is, that it was one that few men could look on and forget. Her hair, a veritable crown of gold, clustered in short ringlets over her shapely head, half hiding the ivory brow, beneath which eyes of deep and glorious grey flashed out in tender majesty. I cannot attempt to describe her other features, only the mouth was most sweet, and curved like Cupid's bow, and over the whole countenance there shone an indescribable look of loving kindness, lit up by a shadow of delicate humour that lay upon her face like a touch of silver on a rosy cloud.

She wore no jewels, but on her neck, arm, and knee were the usual torques of gold, in this instance fashioned like a snake; and her dress was of pure white linen of excessive fineness, plentifully embroidered with gold and with the familiar symbols of the sun.

Her twin sister, Sorais, was of a different and darker type of beauty. Her hair was wavy like Nyleptha's but coal-black, and fell in masses on her shoulders; her complexion was olive, her eyes large, dark, and lustrous; the lips were full, and I thought rather cruel. Somehow her face, quiet and even cold as it was, gave an idea of passion in repose, and caused me to wonder involuntarily what its aspect would be if anything occurred to break the calm. It reminded me of the deep sea, that even on the bluest days never loses its visible stamp of power, and in its murmuring sleep is yet instinct with the spirit of the storm. Her figure, like her sister's, was almost perfect in its curves and outlines, but a trifle more rounded, and her dress was absolutely the same.

As this lovely pair swept onwards to their respective thrones, amid the deep attentive silence of the Court, I was bound to confess to myself that they did indeed fulfil my idea of royalty. Royal they were in every way—in form, in grace, and queenly dignity, and in the barbaric splendour of their attendant pomp. But methought that they needed no guards or gold to proclaim their power and bind the loyalty of wayward men. A glance from those bright eyes or a smile from those sweet lips, and while the blood runs in the veins of youth women such as these will never lack subjects ready to do their biddings to the death.

But after all they were women first and queens afterwards and therefore not devoid of curiosity. As they passed to their seats I saw both of them glance swiftly in our direction. I saw, too, that their eyes passed by me, seeing nothing to charm them in the person of an insignificant and grizzled old man. Then they looked with evident astonishment on the grim form of old Um-slopogaas, who raised his axe in salutation. Attracted next by the splendour of Good's apparel, for a second their glance rested on him like a humming moth upon a flower, then off it darted to where Sir Henry Curtis stood, the sunlight from a window playing upon his yellow hair and peaked beard, and marking the outlines of his massive frame against the twilight of the somewhat gloomy hall. He raised his eyes, and they met the fair Nyleptha's full, and thus for the first time the goodliest man and woman that it has ever been my lot to see looked one upon another. And why it was I know not, but I saw the swift blood run up beneath Nyleptha's skin as the pink lights run up the morning sky. Red grew her fair bosom and shapely arm, red the swanlike neck; the rounded cheek blushed red as the petals of a rose, and then the crimson flood sank back to whence it came and left her pale and trembling.

I glanced at Sir Henry. He, too, had coloured up to the eyes.

'Oh, my word' thought I to myself, 'the ladies have come on the stage, and now we may look to the plot to develop itself.' And I sighed and shook my head, knowing that the beauty of a woman is like the beauty of the lightning—a destructive thing and a cause of desolation. By the time that I had finished my reflections both the Queens were on the thrones, for all this had happened in about six seconds. Once more the unseen trumpets blared out, and then the Court seated itself, and Queen Sorais motioned to us to do likewise.

Next from among the crowd whither he had withdrawn stepped forward our guide, the old gentleman who had towed us ashore, holding by the hand the girl whom we had seen first and afterwards rescued from the hippopotamus. Having made obeisance he proceeded to address the Queens, evidently describing to them the way and place where we had been found. It was most amusing to watch the astonishment, not unmixed with fear, reflected upon their faces as they listened to his tale. Clearly they could not understand how we had reached the lake and been found floating on it, and were inclined to attribute our presence to supernatural causes. Then the narrative proceeded, as I judged from the frequent appeals that our guide made to the girl, to the point where we had shot the hippopotami, and we at once perceived that there was something very wrong about those hippopotami, for the history was frequently interrupted by indignant exclamations from the little group of white-robed priests and even from the courtiers, while the two Queens listened with an amazed expression, especially when our guide pointed to the rifles in our hands as being the means of destruction. And here, to make matters clear, I may as well explain at once that the inhabitants of Zu-Vendis are sun-worshippers, and that for some reason or other the hippopotamus is a sacred animal among them. Not that they do not kill it, because at a certain season of the year they slaughter thousands—which are specially preserved in large lakes up the country—and use their hides for armour for soldiers; but this does not prevent them from considering these animals as sacred to the sun.[1] Now, as ill luck would have it, the particular hippopotami we had shot were a family of tame animals that were kept at the mouth of the port and daily fed by priests whose special duty it was to attend to them. When we shot them I thought that the brutes were suspiciously tame, and as we afterwards ascertained, this was the cause of it. Thus it came about that in attempting to show off we had committed sacrilege of a most aggravated nature.

When our guide had finished his tale, the old man with the long beard and round cap, whose appearance I have already described, and who was, as I have said, the High Priest of the country, and known by the name of Agon, rose and commenced an impassioned harangue. I did not like the look of his cold grey eye as he fixed it on us. I should have liked it still less had I known that in the name of the outraged majesty of his god he was demanding that the whole lot of us should be offered up as a sacrifice by means of being burnt alive.

After he had finished speaking the Queen Sorais addressed him in a soft and musical voice, and appeared, to judge from his gestures of dissent, to be putting the other side of the question before him. Then Nyleptha spoke in liquid accents. Little did we know that she was pleading for our lives. Finally, she turned and addressed a tall, soldierlike man of middle age with a black beard and a long plain sword, whose name, as we afterwards learnt, was Nasta, and who was the greatest lord in the country; apparently appealing to him for support. Now when Sir Henry had caught her eye and she had blushed so rosy red, I had seen that the incident had not escaped this man's notice, and, what is more, that it was eminently disagreeable to him, for he bit his lip and his hand tightened on his sword-hilt. Afterwards we learnt that he was an aspirant for the hand of this Queen in marriage, which accounted for it. This being so, Nyleptha could not have appealed to a worse person, for, speaking in slow, heavy tones, he appeared to confirm all that the High Priest Agon said. As he spoke, Sorais put her elbow on her knee, and, resting her

---

[1] Mr. Quatermain does not seem to have been aware that it is common for animal-worshipping people to annually sacrifice the beasts they adore. See Herodotus ii. 42.—EDITOR.

chin on her hand, looked at him with a suppressed smile upon her lips, as though she saw through the man, and was determined to be his match; but Nyleptha grew very angry. Her cheek flushed, her eyes flashed, and she did indeed look lovely. Finally she turned to Agon and seemed to give some sort of qualified assent, for he bowed at her words; and as she spoke she moved her hands as though to emphasise what she said; while all the time Sorais kept her chin on her hand and smiled. Then suddenly Nyleptha made a sign, the trumpets blew again, and everybody rose to leave the hall save ourselves and the guards, whom she motioned to stay.

When they were all gone she bent forward and, smiling sweetly, partially by signs and partially by exclamations made it clear to us that she was very anxious to know where we came from. The difficulty was how to explain, but at last an idea struck me. I had my large pocket-book in my pocket and a pencil. Taking it out, I made a little sketch of a lake, and then as best I could I drew the underground river and the lake at the other end. When I had done this I advanced to the steps of the throne and gave it to her. She understood it at once and clapped her hands with delight, and then descending from the throne took it to her sister Sorais, who also evidently understood. Next she took the pencil from me, and after examining it with curiosity proceeded to make a series of delightful little sketches, the first representing herself holding out both hands in welcome, and a man uncommonly like Sir Henry taking them. Next she drew a lovely little picture of a hippopotamus rolling about dying in the water, and of an individual, in whom we had no difficulty in recognising Agon the High Priest, holding up his hands in horror on the bank. Then followed a most alarming picture of a dreadful fiery furnace and of the same figure, Agon, poking us into it with a forked stick. This picture perfectly horrified me, but I was a little reassured when she nodded sweetly and proceeded to make a fourth drawing—of a man again uncommonly like Sir Henry, and of two women, in whom I recognised Sorais and herself, each with one arm around him, and holding a sword in protection over him. To all of these Sorais, who I saw was employed in carefully taking us all in—especially Curtis—signified her approval by nodding.

At last Nyleptha drew a final sketch of a rising sun, indicating that she must go, and that we should meet on the following morning; whereat Sir Henry looked so disappointed that she saw it, and, I suppose by way of consolation, extended her hand to him to kiss, which he did with pious fervour. At the same time

Sorais, off whom Good had never taken his eyeglass during the whole indaba [interview], rewarded him by giving him her hand to kiss, though, while she did so, her eyes were fixed upon Sir Henry. I am glad to say that I was not implicated in these proceedings: neither of them gave *me* her hand to kiss.

Then Nyleptha turned and addressed the man who appeared to be in command of the bodyguard, apparently from her manner and his frequent obeisances, giving him very stringent and careful orders; after which, with a somewhat coquettish nod and smile, she left the hall, followed by Sorais and most of the guards.

When the Queens had gone, the officer whom Nyleptha had addressed came forward and with many tokens of deep respect led us from the hall through various passages to a sumptuous set of apartments opening out of a large central room lighted with brazen swinging lamps (for it was now dusk) and richly carpeted and strewn with couches. On a table in the centre of the room was set a profusion of food and fruit, and, what is more, flowers. There was delicious wine also in ancient-looking sealed earthenware flagons, and beautifully chased golden and ivory cups to drink it from. Servants, male and female, also were there to minister to us, and whilst we ate, from some recess outside the apartment

> 'The silver lute did speak between
> The trumpet's lordly blowing;'

and altogether we found ourselves in a sort of earthly paradise which was only disturbed by the vision of that disgusting High Priest who intended to commit us to the flames. But so very weary were we with our labours that we could scarcely keep ourselves awake through the sumptuous meal, and as soon as it was over we indicated that we desired to sleep. So they led us off, and would have given us a room each, but we made it clear that we would sleep two in a room. As a further precaution against surprise we left Umslopogaas with his axe to sleep in the main chamber near the curtained doorways leading to the apartments which we occupied respectively, Good and I in the one, and Sir Henry and Alphonse in the other. Then throwing off our clothes, with the exception of the mail shirts, which we considered it safer to keep on, we flung ourselves down upon the low and luxurious couches, and drew the silk-embroidered coverlids over us.

In two minutes I was just dropping off when I was aroused by Good's voice.

'I say, Quatermain,' he said, 'did you ever see such eyes?'

'Eyes!' I said, crossly; 'what eyes?'

'Why, the Queen's, of course! Sorais, I mean—at least I think that is her name.'

'Oh, I don't know,' I yawned; 'I suppose they are good eyes,' and again I dropped off.

Five minutes or so elapsed, and I was once more awakened.

'I say, Quatermain,' said the voice.

'Well,' I answered testily, 'what is it now?'

'Did you notice her ankle? The shape——'

This was more than I could stand. By my bed stood the veldt-schoons I had been wearing. Moved quite beyond myself, I took them up and threw them straight at Good's head—and hit it.

After that I slept the sleep of the just, and a very heavy sleep it must be. As for Good, I don't know if he went to sleep or if he continued to pass Sorais' beauties in mental review, and, what is more, I don't care.

CHAPTER XIII.

ABOUT THE ZU-VENDI PEOPLE.

And now the curtain is down for a few hours, and the actors in this novel drama are plunged in dewy sleep. Perhaps we should except Nyleptha, whom the reader, if poetically inclined, may imagine lying in her bed of state encompassed by her maidens, tiring women, guards, and all the other people and appurtenances that surround a throne, and yet not able to slumber for thinking of the strangers who had visited a country where no such strangers had ever come before, and wondering, as she lay awake, who they were and what their past had been, and if she was ugly compared to the women of their native place. I, however, not being poetically inclined, will take advantage of the lull to give some account of the people among whom we found ourselves, compiled, needless to state, from information which we subsequently collected.

The name of this country, to begin at the beginning, is Zu-Vendis, from Zu, 'yellow,' and Vendis, 'place or country.' Why it is called the Yellow Country I have never been able to ascertain accurately, nor do the inhabitants themselves know. Three reasons are, however, given, each of which would suffice to account for it. The first is that the name owes its origin to the great quantity of gold that is found in the land. Indeed, in this respect Zu-Vendis is a veritable Eldorado, the precious metal being extraordinarily plentiful. At present it is collected from purely alluvial diggings, which we subsequently inspected, and which are situated within a day's journey from Milosis, being mostly found in pockets and in nuggets weighing from an ounce up to six or seven pounds in weight. But other diggings of a similar nature are known to exist, and I have besides seen great veins of gold-bearing quartz. In Zu-Vendis gold is a much commoner metal than silver, and thus it has curiously enough come to pass that silver is the legal tender of the country.

The second reason is, that at certain seasons of the year the native grasses of the country, which are very sweet and good, turn as yellow as ripe corn; and the third arises from a tradition that the people were originally yellow skinned, but grew white after living for many generations upon these high lands. Zu-Vendis is a country about the size of France, is, roughly speaking, oval in shape, and on every side cut off from the surrounding territory by illimitable forests of impenetrable thorn, beyond which are said to be hundreds of miles of morasses, deserts, and great mountains. It is, in short, a huge, high tableland rising up in the centre of the dark continent, much as in southern Africa flat-topped mountains rise from the level of the surrounding veldt. Milosis itself lies, according to my aneroid, at a level of about nine thousand feet above the sea, but most of the land is even higher, the greatest elevation of the open country being, I believe, about eleven thousand feet. As a consequence the climate is, comparatively speaking, a cold one, being very similar to that of southern England, only brighter and not so rainy. The land is, however, exceedingly fertile, and grows all cereals and temperate fruits and timber to perfection; and in the lower-lying parts even produces a hardy variety of sugar-cane. Coal is found in great abundance, and in many places crops out from the surface; and so is pure marble, both black and white. The same may be said of almost every metal except silver, which is scarce, and only to be obtained from a range of mountains in the north.

Zu-Vendis comprises in her boundaries a great variety of scenery, including two ranges of snow-clad mountains, one on the western boundary beyond the impenetrable belt of thorn forest, and the other piercing the country from north to south, and passing at a distance of about eighty miles from Milosis, from which town its higher peaks are distinctly visible. This range forms the chief watershed of the land. There are also three large lakes—the biggest, namely that whereon we emerged, and which is named Milosis after the city, covering some two hundred square miles of country—and numerous small ones, some of them salt.

The population of this favoured land is, comparatively speaking, dense, numbering at a rough estimate from ten to twelve millions. It is almost purely agricultural in its habits, and divided into great classes as in civilised countries. There is a territorial nobility, a considerable middle class, formed principally of merchants, officers of the army, &c.; but the great bulk of the people are well-to-do peasants who live upon the lands of the lords, from whom they hold under a species of feudal tenure. The best bred people in the country, are, as I think I have said, pure whites with a somewhat southern cast of countenance; but the common herd are much darker, though they do not show any negro or other African characteristics. As to their descent I can give no certain information. Their written records, which extend back for about a thousand years, give no hint of it. One very ancient chronicler does indeed, in alluding to some old tradition that existed in his day, talk of it as having probably originally 'come down with the people from the coast,' but that may mean little or nothing. In short, the origin of the Zu-Vendi is lost in the mists of time. Whence they came or of what race they are no man knows. Their architecture and some of their sculptures suggest an Egyptian or possibly an Assyrian origin; but it is well known that their present remarkable style of building has only sprung up within the last eight hundred years, and they certainly retain no traces of Egyptian theology or customs. Again, their appearance and some of their habits are rather Jewish; but here again it seems hardly conceivable that they should have utterly lost all traces of the Jewish religion. Still, for aught I know, they may be one of the lost ten tribes whom people are so fond of discovering all over the world, or they may not. I do not know, and so can only describe them as I find them, and leave wiser heads than mine to make what they can out of it, if indeed this account should ever be read at all, which is exceedingly doubtful.

And now after I have said all this, I am, after all, going to hazard a theory of my own, though it is only a very little one, as the young lady said in mitigation of her baby. This theory is founded on a legend which I have heard among the Arabs on the east coast, which is to the effect that 'more than two thousand years ago' there were troubles in the country which was known as Babylonia, and that thereon a vaste horde of Persians came down to Bushire, where they took ship and were driven by the northeast monsoon to the east coast of Africa, where, according to the legend, 'the sun and fire worshippers' fell into conflict with the belt of Arab settlers who even then were settled on the east coast, and finally broke their way through them, and, vanishing into the interior, were no more seen. Now, I ask, is it not at least possible that the Zu-Vendis people are the descendants of these 'sun and fire worshippers' who broke through the Arabs and vanished? As a matter of fact, there is a good deal in their characters and customs that tallies with the somewhat vague ideas that I have of Persians. Of course we have no books of reference here, but Sir Henry says that if his memory does not fail him, there was a tremendous revolt in Babylon about 500 B.C., whereon a vast multitude were expelled from the city. Anyhow, it is a well-established fact that there have been many separate emigrations of Persians from the Persian Gulf to the east coast of Africa up to as lately as seven hundred years ago. There are Persian tombs at Kilwa, on the east coast, still in good repair, which bear dates showing them to be just seven hundred years old.[1]

In addition to being an agricultural people, the Zu-Vendi are, oddly enough, excessively warlike, and as they cannot from the exigencies of their position make war upon other nations, they fight among each other like the famed Kilkenny cats, with the happy result that the population never outgrows the power of the country to support it. This habit of theirs is largely fostered by the political condition of the country. The monarchy is nominally an absolute one, save in so far as it is tempered by the power of the priests and the informal council of the great lords; but, as in many other such institutions, the king's writ does not run unquestioned throughout the length and breadth of the land. In short, the whole system is a purely feudal one, though absolute serfdom or slavery is unknown, all the great lords holding nominally from the throne, but a number of them being practically independent, having the power of life and death, waging war against and making peace with their neighbours as the whim or their interests lead them, and even on occasion rising in open

[1]There is another theory which might account for the origin of the Zu-Vendi which does not seem to have struck my friend Mr. Quatermain and his companions, and that is, that they are descendants of the Phœnicians. The cradle of the Phœnician race is supposed to have been on the western shore of the Persian Gulf. Thence, as there is good evidence to show, they emigrated in two streams, one of which took possession of the shores of Palestine, while the other is supposed by savants to have immigrated down the coast of Eastern Africa where, near Mozambique, signs and remains of their occupation of the country are not wanting. Indeed, it would have been very extraordinary if they did not, when leaving the Persian Gulf, make straight for the East Coast, seeing that the north-east monsoon blows for six months in the year dead in that direction, while for the other six months it blows back again. And, by way of illustrating the probability, I may add that to this day a very extensive trade is carried on between the Persian Gulf and Lamu and other East African ports as far south as Madagascar, which is of course the ancient Ebony Isle of the 'Arabian Nights.'—EDITOR.

rebellion against their royal master or mistress, and, safely shut up in their castles and fenced cities, far from the seat of government, successfully defying them for years.

Zu-Vendis has had its king-makers as well as England, a fact that will be appreciated when I state that eight different dynasties have sat upon the throne during the last one thousand years, every one of which took its rise from some noble family that succeeded in grasping the purple after a sanguinary struggle. At the date of our arrival in the country things were a little better than they had been for some centuries, the last king, the father of Nyleptha and Sorais, having been an exceptionally able and vigorous ruler, and, as a consequence, he kept down the power of the priests and nobles. On his death, two years before we reached Zu-Vendis, the twin sisters, his children, following an ancient precedent, were called to the throne, since an attempt to exclude either would instantly have provoked a sanguinary civil war; but it was generally felt in the country that this measure was a most unsatisfactory one, and could hardly be expected to be permanent. Indeed, as it was, the various intrigues that were set on foot by ambitious nobles to obtain the hand of one or other of the queens in marriage had disquieted the country, and the general opinion was that there would be bloodshed before long.

I will now pass on to the question of the Zu-Vendi religion, which is nothing more or less than sun-worship of a pronounced and highly developed character. Around this sun-worship is grouped the entire social system of the Zu-Vendi. It sends its roots through every institution and custom of the land. From the cradle to the grave the Zu-Vendi follows the sun in every sense of the saying. As an infant he is solemnly held up in its light and dedicated to 'the symbol of good, the expression of power, and the hope of Eternity,' the ceremony answering to our baptism. Whilst yet a tiny child, his parents point out the glorious orb as the presence of a visible and beneficent god, and he worships it at its up-rising and down-setting. Then when still quite small, holding fast to the pendent end of his mother's 'kaf' (toga), he goes up to the temple of the Sun of the nearest city, and there, when at midday the bright beams strike down upon the golden central altar and beat back the fire that burns thereon, he hears the white-robed priests raise their solemn chant of praise and sees the people fall down to adore, and then, amidst the blowing of the golden trumpets, watches the sacrifice thrown into the fiery furnace beneath the altar. Here he comes again to be declared a 'man' by the priests, and consecrated to war and to good works; here before the solemn altar he leads his bride; and here too, if differences shall unhappily arise, he divorces her.

And so on, down life's long pathway till the last mile is travelled, and he comes again armed indeed, and with dignity, but no longer a man. Here they bear him dead and lay his bier upon the falling brazen doors before the eastern altar, and when the last ray from the setting sun falls upon his white face the bolts are drawn and he vanishes into the raging furnace beneath and is ended.

The priests of the Sun do not marry, but are recruited by young men specially devoted to the work by their parents and supported by the State. The nomination to the higher offices of the priesthood lies with the Crown, but once appointed the nominees cannot be dispossessed, and it is scarcely too much to say that they really rule the land. To begin with, they are a united body sworn to obedience and secrecy, so that an order issued by the High Priest at Milosis will be instantly and unhesitatingly acted upon by the resident priest of a little country town three or four hundred miles off. They are the judges of the land, criminal and civil, an appeal lying only to the lord paramount of the district, and from him to the king; and they have, of course, practically unlimited jurisdiction over religious and moral offences, together with a right of excommunication, which, as in the faiths of more highly civilised lands, is a very effective weapon. Indeed, their rights and powers are almost unlimited; but I may as well state here that the priests of the Sun are wise in their generation, and do not push things too far. It is but very seldom that they go to extremes against anybody, being more inclined to exercise the prerogative of mercy than run the risk of exasperating the powerful and vigorous-minded people on whose neck they have set their yoke, lest it should rise and break it off altogether.

Another source of the power of the priests is their practical monopoly of learning, and their very considerable astronomical knowledge, which enables them to keep a hold on the popular mind by predicting eclipses and even comets. In Zu-Vendis only a few of the upper classes can read and write, but nearly all the priests have this knowledge, and are therefore looked upon as learned men.

The law of the country is, on the whole, mild and just, but differs in several respects from our civilised law. For instance, the law of England is much more severe upon offences against property than against the person, as becomes a people whose ruling passion is money. A man may half kick his wife to death or inflict horrible sufferings upon his children at a much cheaper rate of punishment than he can compound for the theft of a pair of old boots. In Zu-Vendis this is not so, for there they rightly or wrongly look upon the person as of more consequence than goods and chattels, and not, as in England, as a sort of necessary appendage to the latter. For murder the punishment is death, for treason death, for defrauding the orphan and the widow, for sacrilege, and for attempting to quit the country (which is looked on as a sacrilege) death. In each case the method of execution is the same, and a rather awful one. The culprit is thrown alive into the fiery furnace beneath one of the altars to the Sun. For all other offences, including the offence of idleness, the punishment is forced labour upon the vast national buildings which are always going on in some part of the country, with or without periodical floggings, according to the crime.

The social system of the Zu-Vendi allows considerable liberty to the individual, provided he does not offend against the laws and customs of the country. They are polygamous in theory, though most of them have only one wife on account of the expense. By law a man is bound to provide a separate establishment for each wife. The first wife also is the legal wife, and her children are said to be 'of the house of the Father.' The children of the other wives are of the houses of their respective mothers. This does not, however, imply any slur upon either mother or children. Again, a first wife can, on entering into the married state, make a bargain that her husband shall marry no other wife. This, however, is very rarely done, as the women are the great upholders of polygamy, which not only provides for their surplus numbers but gives greater importance to the first wife, who is thus practically the head of several households. Marriage is looked upon as primarily a civil contract, and, subject to certain conditions and to a proper provision for children, is dissoluble at the will of both contracting parties, the divorce, or 'unloosing,' being formally and ceremoniously accomplished by going through certain portions of the marriage ceremony backwards.

The Zu-Vendi are on the whole a very kindly, pleasant, and light-hearted people. They are not great traders and care little about money, only working to earn enough to support themselves in that class of life in which they were born. They are exceedingly conservative, and look with disfavour on changes. Their legal tender is silver, cut into little squares of different weights; gold is the baser coin, and is about of the same value as our silver. It is, however, much prized for its beauty, and largely used for ornaments and decorative purposes. Most of the trade, however, is carried on by means of sale and barter, payment being made in kind. Agriculture is the great business of the country, and is really well understood and executed, most of the available acreage being under cultivation. Great attention is also given to the breeding of cattle and horses, the latter being unsurpassed by any I have ever seen either in Europe or Africa.

The land belongs theoretically to the Crown, and under the Crown to the great lords, who again divide it among smaller lords, and so on down to the little peasant farmer who works his forty 'reestu' (acres) on a system of half-profits with his immediate lord. In fact the whole method is, as I have said, distinctly feudal, and it interested us much to meet with such an old friend far in the unknown heart of Africa.

The taxes are very heavy. The State takes a third of a man's total earnings, and the priesthood about five per cent. on the remainder. But on the other hand, if a man through any cause falls into *bonâ fide* misfortune the State supports him in the position of life to which he belongs. If he is idle, however, he is sent to work on the Government undertakings, and the State looks after his wives and children. The State also makes all the roads and builds all town houses, about which great care is shown, letting them out to families at a small rent. It also keeps up a standing army of about twenty thousand men, and provides watchmen, &c. In return for their five per cent. the priests attend to the service of the temples, carry out all religious ceremonies, and keep schools, where they teach whatever they think desirable, which is not very much. Some of the temples also possess private property, but priests as individuals cannot hold property.

And now comes a question which I find some difficulty in answering. Are the Zu-Vendi a civilised or a barbarous people? Sometimes I think the one, sometimes the other. In some branches of art they have attained the very highest proficiency. Take for instance their buildings and their statuary. I do not think that the latter can be equalled either in beauty or imaginative power anywhere in the world, and as for the former it may have been rivalled in ancient Egypt, but I am sure that it has never been since. But, on the other hand, they are totally ignorant of many other arts. Till Sir Henry, who happened to know something about it, showed them how to do it by mixing silica and lime, they could not make a piece of glass, and their crockery is rather primitive. A water-clock is their nearest approach to a watch; indeed, ours delighted them exceedingly. They know nothing about steam, electricity, or gunpowder, and mercifully for themselves nothing about printing or the penny post. Thus they are spared many evils, for of a truth our age has learnt the wisdom of the old-world saying, 'He who increaseth knowledge, increaseth sorrow.'

As regards their religion, it is a natural one for imaginative people who know no better, and might therefore be expected to turn to the sun and worship him as the all-Father, but it cannot justly be called elevating or spiritual. It is true that they do sometimes speak of the sun as the 'garment of the Spirit,' but it is a vague term, and what they really adore is the fiery orb himself. They also call him the 'hope of eternity,' but here again the meaning is vague, and I doubt if the phrase conveys any very clear impression to their minds. Some of them do indeed believe in a future life for the good—I know that Nyleptha does firmly—but it is a private faith arising from the promptings of the spirit, not an essential of their creed. So on the whole I cannot say that I consider this sun-worship as a religion indicative of a civilised people, however magnificent and imposing its ritual, or however moral and high-sounding the maxims of its priests, many of whom , I am sure, have their own opinions on the whole subject; though of course they have nothing but praise for a system which provides them with so many of the good things of this world.

There are now only two more matters to which I need allude—namely, the language and the system of calligraphy. As for the former, it is soft-sounding, and very rich and flexible. Sir Henry says that it sounds something like modern Greek, but of course it has no connection with it. It is easy to acquire, being simple in its construction, and a peculiar quality about it is its euphony, and the way in which the sound of the words adapts itself to the meaning to be expressed. Long before we mastered the language, we could frequently make out what was meant by the ring of the sentence. It is on this account that the language lends itself so well to poetical declamation, of which these remarkable people are very fond. The Zu-Vendi alphabet seems, Sir Henry says, to be derived, like every other known system of letters, from a Phœnician source, and therefore more remotely still from the ancient Egyptian hieratic writing. Whether this is a fact I cannot say, not being learned in such matters. All I know about it is that their alphabet consists of twenty-two characters, of which a few, notably B, E, and O, are not very unlike our own. The whole affair is, however, clumsy and puzzling.[1] But as the people of Zu-Vendis are not given to the writing of novels, or of anything except business documents and records of the briefest character, it answers their purpose well enough.

CHAPTER XIV.

THE FLOWER TEMPLE.

It was half-past eight by my watch when I woke on the morning following our arrival at Milosis, having slept almost exactly twelve hours, and I must say that I did indeed feel better. Ah, what a blessed thing is sleep! and what a difference twelve hours of it or so makes to us after days and nights of toil and danger. It is like going to bed one man and getting up another.

I sat up upon my silken couch—never had I slept upon such a bed before—and the first thing that I saw was Good's eyeglass fixed on me from the recesses of his silken couch. There was nothing else of him to be seen except his eyeglass, but I knew from the look of it that he was awake, and waiting till I woke up to begin.

'I say, Quatermain,' he commenced sure enough, 'did you observe her skin? It is as smooth as the back of an ivory hair-brush.'

'Now look here, Good,' I remonstrated, when there came a sound at the curtain, which, on being drawn, admitted a functionary, who signified by signs that he was there to lead us to the bath. We consented gladly, and were conducted to a delightful marble chamber, with a pool of running crystal water in the centre of it, into which we plunged. When we had bathed, we returned to our apartment and dressed, and then went into the central room where we had supped on the previous evening, to find a morning meal already prepared for us, and a capital meal it was, though I should be puzzled to describe the dishes. After breakfast we lounged round and admired the tapestries and carpets and some pieces of statuary that were placed about, wondering the while what was going to happen next. Indeed, by this time our minds were in such a state of complete bewilderment that we were, as a matter of fact, ready for anything that might arrive. As for our sense of astonishment, it was pretty well obliterated. Whilst we were still thus engaged, our friend

---

[1]There are twenty-two letters in the Phœnician alphabet (*see* Appendix, Maspero's *Histoire ancienne des peuples de l'Orient,* p. 746, &c.). Unfortunately Mr. Quatermain gives us no specimen of the Zu-Vendi writing, but what he here states seems to go a long way towards substantiating the theory advanced in the note on p. 151.—Editor.

the captain of the guard presented himself, and with many obeisances signified that we must follow him, which we did, not without doubts and heart-searchings—for we guessed that the time had come when we should have to settle the bill for those confounded hippopotami with our cold-eyed friend Agon, the High Priest. However, there was no help for it, and personally I took great comfort in the promise of the protection of the sister Queens, knowing that if ladies have a will they can generally find a way; so off we started as though we liked it. A minute's walk through a passage and an outer court brought us to the great double gates of the palace that open on to the wide highway which runs up hill through the heart of Milosis to the Temple of the Sun a mile away, and thence down the slope on the farther side of the temple to the outer wall of the city.

These gates are very large and massive, and an extraordinarily beautiful work in metal. Between them—for one set is placed at the entrance to an interior, and one at that of the exterior wall—is a fosse, forty-five feet in width. This fosse is filled with water and spanned by a drawbridge, which when lifted makes the palace nearly impregnable to anything except siege guns. As we came, one half of the wide gates were flung open, and we passed over the draw bridge and presently stood gazing up one of the most imposing, if not the most imposing, roadways in the world. It is a hundred feet from curb to curb, and on either side, not cramped and crowded together, as is our European fashion, but each standing in its own grounds, and built equidistant from and in similar style to the rest, are a series of splendid, single-storied mansions, all of red granite. These are the town houses of the nobles of the Court, and stretch away in unbroken lines for a mile or more till the eye is arrested by the glorious vision of the Temple of the Sun that crowns the hill and heads the roadway.

As we stood gazing at this splendid sight, of which more anon, there suddenly dashed up to the gateway four chariots, each drawn by two white horses. These chariots are two-wheeled, and made of wood. They are fitted with a stout pole, the weight of which is supported by leathern girths that form a portion of the harness. The wheels are made with four spokes only, are tired with iron, and quite innocent of springs. In the front of the chariot, and immediately over the pole, is a small seat for the driver, railed round to prevent him from being jolted off. Inside the machine itself are three low seats, one at each side, and one with the back to the horses, opposite to which is the door. The whole vehicle is lightly and yet strongly made, and, owing to the grace of the curves, though primitive, not half so ugly as might be expected.

But if the chariots left something to be desired, the horses did not. They were simply splendid, not very large but strongly built, and well ribbed up, with small heads, remarkably large and round hoofs, and a great look of speed and blood. I have often and often wondered whence this breed, which presents many distinct characteristics, came, but, like that of its owners, its history is obscure. Like the people the horses have always been there. The first and last of these chariots were occupied by guards, but the centre two were empty, except for the driver, and to these we were conducted. Alphonse and I got into the first, and Sir Henry, Good, and Umslopogaas into the one behind, and then suddenly off we went. And we did go! Among the Zu-Vendi it is not usual to trot horses either riding or driving, especially when the journey to be made is a short one—they go at full gallop. As soon as we were seated the driver called out, the horses sprang forward, and we were whirled away at a speed sufficient to take one's breath, and which, till I got accustomed to it, kept me in momentary fear of an upset. As for the wretched Alphonse, he clung with a despairing face to the side of what he called this 'devil of a fiacre,' thinking that every moment was his last. Presently it occurred to him to ask where we were going, and I told him that, as far as I could ascertain, we were about to be sacrificed by burning. You should have seen his face as he grasped the side of the vehicle and cried out in his terror.

But the wild-looking charioteer only leant forward over his flying steeds and shouted and the air, as it went singing past, bore away the sound of Alphonse's lamentations.

And now before us, in all its marvellous splendour and daz-zling loveliness, shone out the Temple of the Sun—the peculiar pride of the Zu-Vendi, to whom it was what Solomon's, or rather Herod's, Temple was to the Jews. The wealth, and skill, and labour of generations had been given to the building of this wonderful place, which had been only finally completed within the last fifty years. Nothing was spared that the country could produce, and the result was indeed worthy of the effort, not so much on account of its size—for there are larger fanes in the world—as because of its perfect proportions, the richness and beauty of its materials, and the wonderful workmanship. The building, that stands by itself on a space of some eight acres of garden ground on the hill top, around which are the dwelling-places of the priests, is built in the shape of a sunflower, with a dome-covered central hall, from which radiate twelve petal-shaped courts, each dedicated to one of the twelve months, and serving as the repositories of statues reared in memory of the illustrious dead. The width of the circle beneath the dome is three hundred feet, the height of the dome is four hundred feet, and the length of the rays is one hundred and fifty feet, and the height of their roofs three hundred feet, so that they run into the central dome exactly as the petals of the sunflower run into the great raised heart. Thus the exact measurement from the midst of the central altar to the extreme point of any one of the rounded rays would be three hundred feet (the width of the circle itself), or a total of six hundred feet from the rounded extremity of one ray or petal to the extremity of the opposite one.[1]

The building itself is of pure and polished white marble, which shows out in marvellous contrast to the red granite of the frowning city, on whose brow it glistens indeed like an imperial diadem upon the forehead of a dusky queen. The outer surface of the dome and of the twelve petal courts is covered entirely with thin sheets of beaten gold; and from the extreme point of the roof of each of these petals a glorious golden form with a trumpet in its hand and widespread wings is figured in the very act of soaring into space. I really must leave whoever reads this to imagine the surpassing glory of these golden roofs flashing when the sun strikes—flashing like a thousand fires aflame on a mountain of polished marble—so fiercely that the reflection can be clearly seen from the great peaks of the range a hundred miles away.

It is a marvellous sight—this golden flower upborne upon the cool white marble walls, and I doubt if the world can show such another. What makes the whole effect even more gorgeous is that a belt of a hundred and fifty feet around the marble wall of the temple is planted with an indigenous species of sunflower, which were at the time when we first saw them a sheet of golden bloom.

The main entrance to this wonderful place is between the two northernmost of the rays or petal courts, and is protected first by the usual bronze gates, and then by doors made of solid marble, beautifully carved with allegorical subjects and overlaid with gold. When these are passed there is only the thickness of the wall, which is, however, twenty-five feet (for the Zu-Vendi build for all time), and another slight door also of white marble, introduced in order to avoid causing a visible gap in the inner skin of the wall, and you stand in the circular hall under the great dome. Advancing to the central altar you look upon as beautiful a sight as the imagination of man can conceive. You are in the

[1]These are internal measurements.—A. Q.

middle of the holy place, and above you the great white marble dome, for the inner skin, like the outer, is of polished marble throughout, arches away in graceful curves something like that of St. Paul's in London, only at a slighter angle, and from the funnel-like opening at the exact apex a bright beam of light pours down upon the golden altar. At the east and the west are other altars, and other beams of light stab the sacred twilight to the heart. In every direction, 'white, mystic, wonderful,' open out the ray-like courts, each pierced through by a single arrow of light that serves to illumine its lofty silence and dimly to reveal the monuments of the dead.[1]

Overcome at so awe-inspiring a sight, the vast loveliness of which thrills the nerves like the scene of Kenia's snows, you turn to the central golden altar, in the midst of which, though you cannot see it now, there burns a pale but steady flame crowned with curls of faint blue smoke. It is of marble overlaid with pure gold, in shape round like the sun, four feet in height, and thirty-six in circumference. Here also, hinged to the foundations of the altar, are twelve petals of beaten gold. All night and, except at one hour, all day also, these petals are closed over the altar it-self exactly as the petals of a water-lily close over the yellow crown in stormy weather; but when the sun at mid-day pierces through the funnel in the dome and lights upon the golden flower, the petals open and reveal the hidden mystery, only to close again when the ray has passed.

Nor is this all. Standing in semicircles at equal distances from each other on the north and south of the sacred place are ten golden angels, or female winged forms, exquisitely shaped and draped. These figures, which are slightly larger than life-size, stand with bent heads in an attitude of adoration, their faces shadowed by their wings, and are most imposing and of exceed-ing beauty.

There is but one thing further which calls for description in this altar, which is, that to the east the flooring in front of it is not of pure white marble, as elsewhere throughout the building, but of solid brass, and this is also the case in front of the other two altars.

The eastern and western altars, which are semicircular in shape, and placed against the wall of the building, are much less imposing, and are not enfolded in golden petals. They are, how-ever, also of gold, the sacred fire burns on each, and a golden-winged figure stands on either side of them. Two great golden

[1] Light was also admitted by sliding shutters under the eaves of the dome and in the roof.—A. Q.

rays run up the wall behind them, but where the third or middle one should be is an opening in the wall, wide on the outside, but narrow within, like a loophole turned inwards. Through the eastern loophole stream the first beams of the rising sun, and strike right across the circle, touching the folded petals of the great gold flower as they pass till they impinge upon the western altar. In the same way at night the last rays of the sinking sun rest for a while on the eastern altar before they die away into darkness. It is the promise of the dawn to the evening and the evening to the dawn.

With the exception of these three altars and the winged figures about them, the whole space beneath the vast white dome is utterly empty and devoid of ornamentation—a circumstance that to my fancy adds greatly to its grandeur.

Such is a brief description of this wonderful and lovely building, to the glories of which, to my mind so much enhanced by their complete simplicity, I only wish I had the power to do justice. But I cannot, so it is useless talking more about it. But when I compare this great work of genius to some of the tawdry buildings and tinsel ornamentation produced in these latter days by European ecclesiastical architects, I feel that even highly civilised art might learn something from the Zu-Vendi masterpieces. I can only say that the exclamation which sprang to my lips as soon as my eyes first became accustomed to the dim light of that glorious building, and its white and curving beauties, perfect and thrilling as those of a naked goddess, grew upon me one by one, was, 'Well! a dog would feel religious here.' It is vulgarly put, but perhaps it conveys my meaning more clearly than any polished utterance.

At the temple gates our party was received by a guard of soldiers, who appeared to be under the orders of a priest; and by them we were conducted into one of the ray or 'petal' courts, as the priests call them, and there left for at least half-an-hour. Here we conferred together, and realising that we stood in great danger of our lives, determined, if any attempt should be made upon us, to sell them as dearly as we could—Umslopogaas announcing his fixed intention of committing sacrilege on the person of Agon, the High Priest, by splitting his venerable head with Inkosi-kaas. From where we stood we could perceive that an immense multitude were pouring into the temple, evidently in expectation of some unusual event, and I could not help fearing that we had to do with it. And here I may explain that every day, when the sunlight falls upon the central altar, and the trumpets sound, a burnt sacrifice is offered to the Sun, consisting generally of the carcase of a sheep or an ox, or sometimes of fruit or corn. This event comes off about midday; of course, not always exactly at that hour, but as Zu-Vendis is situated not far from the Line, although—being so high above the sea it is very temperate— midday and the falling of the sunlight on the altar were generally simultaneous. To-day the sacrifice was to take place at about eight minutes past twelve.

Just at twelve o'clock a priest appeared, and made a sign, and the officer of the guard signified to us that we were expected to advance, which we did with the best grace that we could muster, all except Alphonse, whose fears were written on his countenance. In a few seconds we were out of the court and looking at a vast sea of human faces stretching away to the farthest limits of the great circle, all straining to catch a glimpse of the mysterious strangers who had committed sacrilege; the first strangers, mind you, who, to the knowledge of the multitude, had ever set foot in Zu-Vendis since such time that the memory of man runneth not to the contrary.

As we appeared there was a murmur throughout the vast crowd that went echoing away up the great dome, and we saw a visible blush of excitement grow on the thousands of faces, like a pink light on a stretch of pale cloud, and a very curious effect it was. On we passed down a lane cut through the heart of the human mass, till presently we stood upon the brazen patch of flooring to the east of the central altar, and immediately facing it. For some thirty feet around the golden-winged figures the space was roped off, and the multitudes stood outside the ropes. Within were a circle of white-robed gold-cinctured priests holding long golden trumpets in their hands, and immediately in front of us was our friend Agon, the High Priest, with his curious cap upon his head. His was the only covered head in that vast assemblage. We took our stand upon the brazen space, little knowing what was prepared for us beneath, but I noticed a curious hissing sound proceeding apparently from the floor for which I could not account. Then came a pause, and I looked round to see if there was any sign of the two Queens, Nyleptha and Sorais, but they were not there. To the right of us, however, was a bare space that I guessed was reserved for them.

We waited, and presently a far-off trumpet blew, apparently high up in the dome. Then came another murmur from the mul- titude, and up a long lane, leading to the open space to our right, we saw the two Queens walking side by side. Behind them were some nobles of the Court, among whom I recognised the great lord Nasta, and behind them again a body of about fifty guards.

These last I was very glad to see. Presently they had all arrived and taken their stand, the two Queens in the front, the nobles to the right and left, and the guards in a double semicircle behind them.

Then came another silence and Nyleptha looked up and caught my eye; it seemed to me that there was meaning in her glance; and I watched it narrowly. From my eye it travelled down to the brazen flooring, on the outer edge of which we stood. Then followed a slight and almost imperceptible sidelong movement of the head. I did not understand it, and it was repeated. Then I guessed that she meant us to move back off the brazen floor. One more glance and I was sure of it—there was danger in stand-ing on the floor. Sir Henry was placed on one side of me, Um-slopogaas on the other. Keeping my eyes fixed straight before me, I whispered to them, first in Zulu and then in English, to draw slowly back inch by inch till half their feet were resting on the marble flooring where the brass ceased. Sir Henry whispered on to Good and Alphonse, and slowly, very very slowly, we shifted backwards; so slowly indeed that nobody, except Nyleptha and Sorais, who saw everything, seemed to notice the movement. Then I glanced again at Nyleptha, and saw that, by an almost imperceptible nod, she indicated approval. All the while Agon's eyes were fixed upon the altar before him apparently in an ec-stasy of contemplation, and mine were fixed upon the small of his back in another sort of ecstasy. Suddenly he flung up his long arms, and in a solemn and resounding voice commenced a chant, of which for convenience' sake I append a rough, a *very* rough translation here, though, of course, I did not then com-prehend its meaning. It was an invocation to the Sun, and ran somewhat as follows:—

There is silence upon the face of the Earth and the waters thereof!
Yea, the silence doth brood on the waters like a nesting bird;
The silence sleepeth also upon the bosom of the profound darkness.
Only high up in the great spaces star doth speak unto star.
The Earth is faint with longing and wet with the tears of her desire;
The star-girdled night doth embrace her, but she is not comforted.
She lies enshrouded in mists like a corpse in the grave-clothes.
And stretches her pale hands to the East.

Lo! away in the farthest East there is the shadow of a light;
The Earth seeth and lifts herself. She looks out from beneath the hollow of her hand.
Then thy great angels fly forth from thy Holy Place, O Sun,
They shoot their fiery swords into the darkness and shrivel it up.
They climb the heavens and cast down the pale stars from their thrones;
Yea, they hurl the changeful stars back into the womb of the night,
They cause the moon to become wan as the face of a dying man,
And behold Thy glory comes, O Sun!

O, Thou beautiful one, Thou drapest thyself in fire.
The wide heavens are thy pathway: Thou rollest o'er them as a chariot.
The Earth is thy bride. Thou dost embrace her and she brings forth
   children;
Yea, Thou favourest her, and she yields her increase.
Thou art the All Father and the giver of life, O Sun.
The young children stretch out their hands and grow in thy brightness;
The old men creep forth and seeing remember their strength.
Only the dead forget Thee, O Sun!

When Thou art wroth then Thou dost hide Thy face;
Thou drawest around Thee a thick curtain of shadows.
Then the Earth grows cold and the Heavens are dismayed;
They tremble, and the sound thereof is the sound of thunder:
They weep, and their tears are outpoured in the rain;
They sigh, and the wild winds are the voice of their sighing.
The flowers die, the fruitful fields languish and turn pale;
The old men and the little children go unto their appointed place
When Thou withdrawest thy light, O Sun!

Say, what art Thou, O Thou matchless Splendour—
Who set Thee on high, O Thou flaming Terror?
When didst Thou begin, and when is the day of Thy ending?
Thou art the raiment of the living Spirit.[1]
None did place Thee on high, for Thou wast the Beginning.
Thou shalt not be ended when thy children are forgotten;
Nay, Thou shalt never end, for thy hours are eternal.
Thou sittest on high within thy golden house and measurest out the centuries.
O Father of Life! O dark-dispelling Sun!

He ceased this solemn chant, which, though it seems a poor
enough thing after going through my mill, is really beautiful and
impressive in the original; and then, after a moment's pause, he
glanced up towards the funnel-sloped opening in the dome and
added—

O Sun, descend upon thine Altar!

As he spoke a wonderful and a beautiful thing happened.
Down from on high flashed a splendid living ray of light, cleav-
ing the twilight like a sword of fire. Full upon the closed petals
it fell and ran shimmering down their golden sides, and then the
glorious flower opened as though beneath the bright influence.
Slowly it opened, and as the great petals fell wide and revealed
the golden altar on which the fire ever burns, the priests blew a
blast upon the trumpets, and from all the people there rose a
shout of praise that struck against the domed roof and came
echoing down the marble walls. And now the flower altar was
open, and the sunlight fell full upon the tongue of sacred flame
and beat it down, so that it wavered, sank, and vanished into
the hollow recesses whence it rose. As it vanished, the mellow

[1]This line is interesting as being one of the few allusions to be found in
the Zu-Vendri ritual to a vague divine essence independent of the material
splendour of the orb they worship. '*Taia,*' the word used here, has a very
indeterminate meaning, and signifies *essence, vital principle, spirit,* or even
God.

notes of the trumpets rolled out once more. Again the old priest
flung up his hands and called aloud—

We sacrifice to thee, O Sun!

Once more I caught Nyleptha's eye; it was fixed upon the
brazen flooring.

'Look out,' I said, aloud; and as I said it, I saw Agon bend
forward and touch something on the altar. As he did so, the
great white sea of faces around us turned red and then white
again, and a deep breath went up like a universal sigh. Nyleptha
leant forward, and with an involuntary movement covered her
eyes with her hand. Sorais turned and whispered to the officer
of the royal bodyguard, and then with a rending sound the
whole of the brazen flooring slid from before our feet, and there
in its place was suddenly revealed a smooth marble shaft, terminating in a most awful raging furnace beneath the altar, big
enough and hot enough to heat the iron stern-post of a man-
of-war.

With a cry of terror we sprang backwards, all except the
wretched Alphonse, who was paralysed with fear, and would
have fallen into the fiery furnace which had been prepared for us,
had not Sir Henry caught him in his strong hand as he was
vanishing and dragged him back.

Instantly there arose the most fearful hubbub, and we four got
back to back, Alphonse dodging frantically round our little circle
in his attempts to take shelter under our legs. We all had our
revolvers on—for though we had been politely disarmed of our
guns on leaving the palace, of course these people did not know
what a revolver was. Umslopogaas, too, had his axe, of which
no effort had been made to deprive him, and now he whirled it
round his head and sent his piercing Zulu war-shout echoing up
the marble walls in fine defiant fashion. Next second, the priests,
baffled of their prey, had drawn swords from beneath their white
robes and were leaping on us like hounds upon a stag at bay. I
saw that, dangerous as action might be, we must act or be lost,
so as the first man came bounding along—and a great tall fellow
he was—I sent a heavy revolver ball through him, and down he
fell at the mouth of the shaft, and slid, shrieking frantically,
into the fiery gulf that had been prepared for us.

Whether it was his cries, or the, to them, awful sound and effect
of the pistol shot, or what, I know not, but the other priests
halted, paralysed and dismayed, and before they could come on
again Sorais had called out something, and, together with the
two Queens and most of the courtiers, we were being surrounded
with a wall of armed men. In a moment it was done, and still

the priests hesitated, and the people hung in the balance like a herd of startled buck as it were, making no sign one way or the other.

The last yell of the burning priest had died away, the fire had finished him, and a great silence fell upon the place.

Then the High Priest Agon turned, and his face was as the face of a devil. 'Let the sacrifice be sacrificed,' he cried to the Queens. 'Has not sacrilege enough been done by these strangers, and would ye, as Queens, throw the cloak of your majesty over evil-doers? Are not the creatures sacred to the Sun dead? and is not a priest of the Sun also dead, but now slain by the magic of these strangers, who come as the winds out of heaven, whence we know not, and who are what we know not? Beware, O Queens, how ye tamper with the great majesty of the God, even before His high altar! There is a Power that is more than your power; there is a Justice that is higher than your justice. Beware how ye lift an impious hand against it! Let the sacrifice be sacrificed, O Queens.'

Then Sorais made answer in her deep quiet tones, that always seemed to me to have a suspicion of mockery about them, how-ever serious the theme: 'O Agon, thou hast spoken according to thy desire, and thou hast spoken truth. But it is thou who wouldst lift an impious hand against the justice of thy God. Be-think thee the midday sacrifice is accomplished; the Sun hath claimed his priest as a sacrifice.'

This was a novel idea, and the people applauded it.

'Bethink thee what are these men? They are strangers found floating on the bosom of a lake. Who brought them there? How came they there? How know you that they also are not servants of the Sun? Is this the hospitality that ye would have our nation show to those whom chance brings to them, to throw them to the flames? Shame on you! shame on you! What is hospitality? To receive the stranger and show him favour. To bind up his wounds, and find a pillow for his head, and food for him to eat. But thy pillow is the fiery furnace, and thy food the hot savour of the flame. Shame on thee, I say!'

She paused a little to watch the effect of her speech upon the multitude, and seeing that it was favourable, changed her tone from one of remonstrance to one of command.

'Ho! place there,' she cried; 'place, I say; make way for the Queens, and those whom the Queens cover with their "kaf" (mantle).'

'And if I refuse, O Queen?' said Agon between his teeth.

'Then will I cut a path with my guards,' was the proud

answer; 'ay, even in the presence of the sanctuary, and through the bodies of thy priests.'

Agon turned livid with baffled fury. He glanced at the people as though meditating an appeal to them, but saw clearly that their sympathies were all the other way. The Zu-Vendi are a very curious and sociable people, and great as was their sense of the enormity that we had committed in shooting the sacred hippopotami, they did not like the idea of the only real live strangers they had seen or heard of being consigned to a fiery furnace, thereby putting an end for ever to their chance of extracting knowledge and information from, and gossiping about us. Agon saw this and hesitated, and then for the first time Nyleptha spoke in her soft sweet voice.

'Bethink thee, Agon,' she said, 'as my sister Queen hath said, these men may also be servants of the Sun. For themselves they cannot speak, for their tongues are tied. Let the matter be adjourned till such time as they have learnt our language. Who can be condemned without a hearing? When these men can plead for themselves, then it will be time to put them to the proof.'

Here was a clever loophole of escape, and the vindictive old priest took it, little as he liked it.

'So be it, O Queens,' he said. 'Let the men go in peace, and when they have learnt our tongue then let them speak. And I, even I, will make humble supplication at the altar lest pestilence fall on the land by cause of the sacrilege.'

These words were received with a murmur of applause, and in another minute we were marching out of the temple surrounded by the royal guards.

But it was not till long afterwards that we learnt the exact substance of what had passed, and how hardly our lives had been wrung out of the cruel grip of the Zu-Vendi priesthood, in the face of which even the Queens were practically powerless. Had it not been for their strenuous efforts to protect us we should have been slain even before we set foot in the Temple of the Sun. The attempt to drop us bodily into the fiery pit as an offering was a last artifice to attain this end when several others quite unsuspected by us had already failed.

CHAPTER XV.

SORAIS' SONG.

AFTER our escape from Agon and his pious crew we returned to our quarters in the palace and had a very good time. The two Queens, the nobles and the people vied with each other in doing us honour and showering gifts upon us. As for that painful little incident of the hippopotami it sank into oblivion, where we were quite content to leave it. Every day deputations and individuals waited on us to examine our guns and clothing, our chain shirts, and our instruments, especially our watches, with which they were much delighted. In short, we became quite the rage, so much so that some of the fashionable young swells among the Zu-Vendi began to copy the cut of some of our clothes, notably Sir Henry's shooting jacket. One day, indeed, a deputation waited on us and, as usual, Good donned his full-dress uniform for the occasion. This deputation seemed somehow to be of a different class to those who came to visit us generally. They were little insignificant-looking men of an excessively polite, not to say servile, demeanour; and their attention appeared to be chiefly taken up with observing the details of Good's full-dress uniform, of which they took copious notes and measurements. Good was much flattered at the time, not suspecting that he had to deal with the six leading tailors of Milosis. A fortnight afterwards, however, when on attending court as usual he had the pleasure of seeing some seven or eight Zu-Vendi 'mashers' arrayed in all the glory of a very fair imitation of his full-dress uniform, he changed his mind. I shall never forget his face of astonishment and disgust. It was after this, chiefly in order to avoid remark, and also because our clothes were wearing out and had to be saved up, that we resolved to adopt the native dress; and a very comfortable one we found it, though I am bound to say that I looked sufficiently ludicrous in it, and as for Alphonse! Only Umslopogaas would have none of these things; when his moocha was worn out the fierce old Zulu made him a new one, and went about unconcerned, as grim and naked as his own battle-axe.

Meanwhile we pursued our study of the language steadily and made very good progress. On the morning following our adventure in the temple three grave and reverend signiors presented themselves armed with manuscript books, ink-horns, and feather pens, and indicated that they had been sent to teach us. So, with the exception of Umslopogaas, we all buckled to with a will, doing four hours a day. As for Umslopogaas, he would have none of that either. He did not wish to learn that 'woman's talk,' not he; and when one of the teachers advanced on him with a book and an ink-horn and waved them before him in a mild persuasive way, much as a churchwarden invitingly shakes the offertory bag under the nose of a rich but niggardly parishioner, he sprang up with a fierce oath and flashed Inkosi-kaas before the eyes of our learned friend, and there was an end of the attempt to teach Umslopogaas Zu-Vendi.

Thus we spent our mornings in useful occupation which grew more and more interesting as we proceeded, and the afternoons were given up to recreation. Sometimes we made trips, notably one to the gold mines and another to the marble quarries, both of which I wish I had space and time to describe; and sometimes we went out hunting buck with dogs trained for that purpose, and a very exciting sport it is, as the country is full of agricultural enclosures and our horses were magnificent. This is not to be wondered at, seeing that the royal stables were at our command, in addition to which we had four splendid saddle horses given to us by Nyleptha.

Sometimes, again, we went hawking, a pastime that is in great favour among the Zu-Vendi, who generally fly their birds at a species of partridge which is remarkable for the swiftness and strength of its flight. When attacked by the hawk this bird appears to lose its head, and, instead of seeking cover, flies high into the air, thus offering wonderful sport. I have seen one of these partridges soar up almost out of sight when followed by the hawk. Still better sport is offered by a variety of solitary snipe as big as a small woodcock, which is plentiful in this country, and which is flown at with a very small, agile, and highly-trained hawk with an almost red tail. The zigzagging of the great snipe and the lightning rapidity of the flight and movements of the red-tailed hawk make the pastime a delightful one. Another variety of the same amusement is the hunting of a very small species of antelope with trained eagles; and it certainly is a marvellous sight to see the great bird soar and soar till he is nothing but a black speck in the sunlight, and then suddenly come dashing down like a cannon-ball upon some cowering buck that is hidden in a patch of grass from everything except that piercing eye. Still finer is the spectacle when the eagle takes the buck running.

On other days we would pay visits to the country seats at some of the great lords' beautiful fortified places, and the villages clustering beneath their walls. Here we saw vineyards and corn-fields and well-kept park-like grounds, with such timber in them as filled me with delight, for I do love a good tree. There it stands so strong and sturdy, and yet so beautiful, a very type of the best sort of man. How proudly it lifts its bare head to the winter storms, and with what a full heart it rejoices when the spring has come again! How grand its voice is, too, when it talks with the wind: a thousand æolian harps cannot equal the beauty of the sighing of a great tree in leaf. All day it points to the sunshine and all night to the stars, and thus passionless, and yet full of life, it endures through the centuries, come storm, come shine, drawing its sustenance from the deep bosom of its mother earth, and as the slow years roll by, learning the great mysteries of growth and of decay. And so on and on through generations, outliving individuals, customs, dynasties—all save the landscape it adorns and human nature—till the appointed day when the wind wins the long battle and rejoices over a reclaimed space, or decay puts the last stroke to his lingering work.

Ah, one should always think twice before one cuts down a tree!

In the evening it was customary for Sir Henry, Good, and myself to dine, or rather sup, with their majesties—not every night, indeed, but about three or four times a week, whenever they had not much company, or the affairs of state would allow of it. And I am bound to say that those little suppers were quite the most charming things of their sort that I ever had to do with. How true is the saying that the very highest in rank are always the most simple and kindly. It is in your half-and-half sort of people that you find pompousness and vulgarity, the difference between the two being very much what one sees every day in England between the old, out-at-elbows, broken-down county family, and the overbearing, purse-proud people who come and 'take the place.' I really think that Nyleptha's greatest charm is her sweet simplicity, and her kindly genuine interest even in little things. She is the simplest woman I ever knew, and where her passions are not involved, one of the sweetest; but she can look queenly enough when she likes, and be as fierce as any savage too.

For instance, never shall I forget that scene when for the first time I was sure that she was really in love with Curtis. It came about in this way—all through Good's weakness for ladies' society. When we had been employed for some three months in learning Zu-Vendi, it struck Captain Good that he was growing rather tired of the old gentleman who did us the honour to lead us in the way that we should go, so without saying a word to anybody else, he proceeded to inform them that it was a peculiar fact, but that we could not make any real progress in the deeper intricacies of a foreign language unless we were taught by ladies —young ladies, he was careful to explain. In his own country, he pointed out, it was habitual to choose the very best-looking and most charming girls who could be found to instruct any strangers who happened to come that way, &c.

All of this the old gentlemen swallowed open-mouthed. There was, they admitted, reason in what he said, since the contemplation of the beautiful, as their philosophy taught, induced a certain porosity of mind similar to that produced upon the physical body by the healthful influences of sun and air. Consequently it was probable that we might absorb the Zu-Vendi tongue a little faster if suitable teachers could be found. Another thing was that, as the female sex was naturally loquacious, good practice would be gained in the *vivâ voce* departments of our studies.

To all of this Good gravely assented, and the learned gentlemen departed, assuring him that their orders were to fall in with our wishes in every way, and that, if possible, our views should be met.

Imagine, therefore, the surprise and disgust of myself, and I trust and believe Sir Henry, when, on entering the room where we were accustomed to carry on our studies the following morning, we found, instead of our usual venerable tutors, three of the best-looking young women that Milosis could produce—and this is saying a good deal—who blushed and smiled and curtseyed, and gave us to understand that they were there to carry on our instruction. Then Good, as we gazed at one another in bewilderment, thought fit to explain, saying that it had slipped his memory before—but the old gentlemen had told him, on the previous evening, that it was absolutely necessary that our further education should be carried on by the other sex. I was overwhelmed, and appealed to Sir Henry for advice in such a crisis.

'Well,' he said, 'you see the ladies are here, ain't they? If we sent them away, don't you think it might hurt their feelings, eh? One doesn't like to be rough, you see; and they look regular *blues*, don't they, eh?'

By this time Good had already begun his lessons with the handsomest of the three, and so with a sigh I yielded. That day everything went very well: the young ladies were certainly very clever, and they only smiled when we blundered. I never saw Good so attentive to his books before, and even Sir Henry appeared to tackle Zu-Vendi with a renewed zest. 'Ah,' thought I, 'will it always be thus?'

Next day we were much more lively, our work was pleasingly interspersed with questions about our native country, what the ladies were like there, &c., all of which we answered as best we could in Zu-Vendi, and I heard Good assuring his teacher that her loveliness was to the beauties of Europe as the sun to the moon, to which she replied with a little toss of the head, that she was a plain teaching woman and nothing else, and that it was not kind 'to deceive a poor girl so.' Then we had a little singing that was really charming, so natural and unaffected. The Zu-

Vendi love-songs are most touching. On the third day we were all quite intimate. Good narrated some of his previous love affairs to his fair teacher, and so moved was she that her sighs mingled with his own. I discoursed with mine, a merry blue-eyed girl, upon Zu-Vendian art, and never saw that she was waiting for an opportunity to drop a specimen of the cockroach tribe down my back, whilst in the corner Sir Henry and his governess appeared, so far as I could judge, to be going through a lesson framed on the great educational principles laid down by Wackford Squeers, Esq., though in a very modified or rather spiritualised form. The lady softly repeated the Zu-Vendian word for 'hand,' and he took hers; 'eyes,' and he gazed deep into her brown orbs; 'lips,' and—but just at that moment *my* young lady dropped the cockroach down my back and ran away laughing. Now if there is one thing I loathe more than another it is cockroaches, and moved quite beyond myself, and yet laughing at her impudence, I took up the cushion she had been sitting on and threw it after her. Imagine then my shame—my horror, and my distress—when the door opened, and, attended by two guards only, in walked *Nyleptha*. The cushion could not be recalled (it missed the girl and hit one of the guards on the head), but I instantly and ineffectually tried to look as though I had not thrown it. Good ceased his sighing, and began to murder Zu-Vendi at the top of his voice, and Sir Henry whistled and looked silly. As for the poor girls, they were utterly dumbfounded.

And Nyleptha! she drew herself up till her frame seemed to tower even above that of the tall guards, and her face went first red, and then pale as death.

'Guards,' she said in a quiet choked voice, and pointing at the fair but unconscious disciple of Wackford Squeers, 'slay me that woman.'

The men hesitated, as well they might.

'Will ye do my bidding,' she said again in the same voice, 'or will ye not?'

Then they advanced upon the girl with uplifted spears. By this time Sir Henry had recovered himself, and saw that the comedy was likely to turn into a tragedy.

'Stand back,' he said in an angry voice, at the same time getting in front of the terrified girl. 'Shame on thee, Queen—shame! Thou shalt not kill her.'

'Doubtless thou hast good reason to try to protect her. Thou couldst hardly do less in honour,' answered the infuriated Queen; 'but she shall die—she shall die,' and she stamped her little foot.

'It is well,' he answered; 'then I will die with her. I am thy servant, O Queen; do with me even as thou wilt.' And he bowed towards her, and fixed his clear eyes contemptuously on her face.

'I could wish to slay thee too,' she answered; 'for thou dost make a mock of me;' and then feeling that she was mastered, and I suppose not knowing what else to do, she burst into such a storm of tears, and looked so royally lovely in her passionate distress, that, old as I am, I must say I envied Curtis his task of supporting her. It was rather odd to see him holding her in his arms considering what had just passed—a thought that seemed to occur to herself, for presently she wrenched herself free and went, leaving us all much disturbed.

Presently, however, one of the guards returned with a message to the girls that on pain of death, they were to leave the city and return to their homes in the country, and that no further harm would come to them. Accordingly they went, one of them remarking philosophically that it could not be helped, and that it was a satisfaction to know that they had taught us a little serviceable Zu-Vendi. Mine was an exceedingly nice girl, and, overlooking the cockroach, I made her a present of my favourite lucky sixpence with a hole in it when she went away. After that our former masters resumed their course of instruction, needless to say to my great relief.

That night, when in fear and trembling we attended the royal supper table, we found that Nyleptha was laid up with a bad headache. This headache lasted for three whole days; but on the fourth she was present at supper as usual, and with the most gracious and sweet smile gave Sir Henry her hand to lead her to the table. No allusion was made to the little affair described above beyond her saying, with a charming air of innocence, that when she came to see us at our studies the other day she had been seized with a giddiness from which she had only now recovered. She supposed, she added with a touch of the humour that was common to her, that it was the sight of people working so hard which had affected her.

In reply Sir Henry said, dryly, that he had thought she did not look quite herself on that day, whereat she flashed one of those quick glances of hers at him, which if he had the feelings of a man must have gone through him like a knife, and the subject dropped entirely. Indeed, after supper was over Nyleptha condescended to put us through an examination to see what we had learnt, and to express herself well satisfied with the results. Indeed, she proceeded to give us, especially Sir Henry, a lesson on her own account, and very interesting we found it.

And all the while that we talked, or rather tried to talk, and laughed, Sorais would sit there in her carven ivory chair, and look at us and read us all like a book, only from time to time saying a few words, and smiling that quick ominous smile of hers which was more like a flash of summer lightning on a dark cloud than anything else. And as near to her as he dared would sit Good, worshipping through his eyeglass, for he was really growing seriously devoted to this sombre beauty, of whom, speaking personally, I felt terribly afraid. I watched her keenly, and soon I found out that for all her apparent impassibility she was at heart bitterly jealous of Nyleptha. Another thing I found out, and the discovery filled me with dismay, and it was, that she *also* was growing devoted to Sir Henry Curtis. Of course I could not be sure; it is not easy to read so cold and haughty a woman; but I noticed one or two little things, and, as elephant hunters know, dried grass shows which way the wind has set.

And so another three months passed over us, by which time we had all attained to a very considerable mastery of the Zu-Vendi language, which is an easy one to learn. And as the time went on we became great favourites with the people, and even with the courtiers, gaining an enormous reputation for cleverness, because, as I think I have said, Sir Henry was able to show them how to make glass, which was a national want, and also, by the help of a twenty-year almanac that we had with us, to predict various heavenly combinations which were quite unsuspected by the native astronomers. We even succeeded in demonstrating the principle of the steam-engine to a gathering of the learned men, who were filled with amazement; and several other things of the same sort we did. And so it came about that the people made up their minds that we must on no account be allowed to go out of the country, which was indeed an apparent impossibility even if we had wished it. Also we were advanced to great honour and made officers of the bodyguards of the sister Queens, permanent quarters being assigned to us in the palace, and our opinion asked upon all questions of national policy.

But blue as the sky seemed, there was a cloud, and a big one, on the horizon. We had indeed heard no more of those confounded hippopotami, but it is not on that account to be supposed that our sacrilege was forgotten, or the enmity of the great and powerful priesthood headed by Agon appeased. On the contrary, it was burning the more fiercely because it was necessarily suppressed, and what had perhaps begun in bigotry was ending in downright direct hatred born of jealousy. Hitherto, the priests had been the wise men of the land, and on this account, as well as from superstitious causes, were looked on with peculiar veneration. But our arrival, with our outlandish wisdom and our strange inventions and hints of unimagined things, dealt a serious blow to this state of affairs, and, among the educated Zu-Vendi, went far towards destroying the priestly prestige. A still worse affront to them, however, was the favour with which we were regarded, and the trust that was reposed in us. All these things tended to make us excessively obnoxious to the great sacerdotal clan, the most powerful because the most united faction in the kingdom.

Another source of imminent danger to us was the rising envy of some of the great lords headed by Nasta, whose antagonism to us at best had been but thinly veiled, and which now threatened to break out into open flame. Nasta for some years had been a candidate for Nyleptha's hand in marriage, and when we appeared on the scene I fancy, from all I could gather, that though there were still many obstacles in his path, success was by no means out of his reach. But now all this had changed; the coy Nyleptha smiled no more in his direction, and he was not slow to guess the cause. Infuriated and alarmed, he turned his attention to Sorais, only to find that he might as well try to woo a mountain side. With a bitter jest or two about his fickleness, that door was closed on him for ever. So Nasta bethought him of the thirty thousand wild swordsmen who would pour down at his bidding through the northern mountain passes, and no doubt vowed to adorn the gates of Milosis with our heads.

But first he determined, as we learned, to make one more attempt and to demand the hand of Nyleptha in the open Court after the formal annual ceremony of the signing of the laws that had been proclaimed by the Queens during the year.

Of this astounding fact Nyleptha heard with simulated nonchalance, and with a little trembling of the voice herself informed us of it as we sat at supper on the night preceding the great ceremony of the law-signing.

Sir Henry bit his lip, and do what he could to prevent it plainly showed his agitation.

'And what answer will the Queen be pleased to give to the great lord?' asked I, in a jesting manner.

'Answer, Macumazahn' (for we had elected to pass by our Zulu names in Zu-Vendis), she said, with a pretty shrug of her ivory shoulder. 'Nay, I know not; what is a poor woman to do, when the wooer has thirty thousand swords wherewith to urge his love?' And from under her long lashes she glanced at Curtis.

Just then we rose from the table to adjourn into another room. 'Quatermain, a word, quick,' said Sir Henry to me. 'Listen. I have never spoken about it, but surely you have guessed: I love Nyleptha. What am I to do?'

Fortunately, I had more or less already taken the question into consideration, and was therefore able to give such answer as seemed the wisest to me.

'You must speak to Nyleptha to-night,' I said. 'Now is your time, now or never. Listen. In the sitting-chamber get near to her, and whisper to her to meet you at midnight by the Rademas statue at the end of the great hall. I will keep watch for you there. Now or never, Curtis.'

We passed on into the other room. Nyleptha was sitting, her hands before her, and a sad anxious look upon her lovely face. A little way off sat Sorais talking to Good in her slow measured tones.

The time went on; in another quarter of an hour I knew that, according to their habit, the Queens would retire. As yet, Sir Henry had had no chance of saying a word in private: indeed, though we saw much of the royal sisters, it was by no means easy to see them alone. I racked my brains, and at last an idea came to me.

'Will the Queen be pleased,' I said, bowing low before Sorais, 'to sing to her servants? Our hearts are heavy this night; sing to us, O Lady of the Night' (Sorais' favourite name among the people).

'My songs, Macumazahn, are not such as to lighten the heavy heart, yet will I sing if it pleases thee,' she answered; and she rose and went a few paces to a table whereon lay an instrument not unlike a zither, and struck a few wandering chords.

Then suddenly, like the notes of some deep-throated bird, her rounded voice rang out in song so wildly sweet, and yet with so eerie and sad a refrain, that it made the very blood stand still. Up, up soared the golden notes, that seemed to melt far away, and then to grow again and travel on, laden with all the sorrow of the world and all the despair of the lost. It was a marvellous song, but I had not time to listen to it properly. However, I got the words of it afterwards, and here is a translation of its burden, so far as it admits of being translated at all.

SORAIS' SONG.

As a desolate bird that through darkness its lost way is winging,
As a hand that is helplessly raised when Death's sickle is swinging,
So is life! ay, the life that lends passion and breath to my singing.

As the nightingale's song that is full of a sweetness unspoken,
As a spirit unbarring the gates of the skies for a token,
So is love! ay, the love that shall fall when his pinion is broken.

As the tramp of the legions when trumpets their challenge are sending,
As the shout of the Storm-god when lightnings the black sky are rending,
So is power! ay, the power that shall lie in the dust at its ending.

So short is our life; yet with space for all things to forsake us,
A bitter delusion, a dream from which nought can awake us,
Till Death's dogging footsteps at morn or at eve shall o'ertake us.

REFRAIN.

Oh, the world is fair at the dawning—dawning—dawning,
But the red sun sinks in blood—the red sun sinks in blood.

I only wish that I could write down the music too.

'Now, Curtis, now,' I whispered, when she began the second verse, and turned my back.

'Nyleptha,' he said—for my nerves were so much on the stretch that I could hear every word, low as it was spoken, even through Sorais' divine notes—'Nyleptha, I must speak with thee this night, upon my life I must. Say me not nay, I pray thee!'

'How can I speak with thee?' she answered, looking fixedly before her; 'queens are not like other people. I am surrounded and watched.'

'Listen, Nyleptha, thus. I will be before the statue of Rademas in the great hall at midnight. I have the countersign and can pass in. Macumazahn will be there to keep guard, and with him the Zulu. Oh come, my Queen, deny me not.'

'It is not seemly,' she murmured, 'and to-morrow——'

Just then the music began to die in the last wail of the refrain, and Sorais slowly turned her round.

'I will be there,' said Nyleptha, hurriedly; 'on thy life see that thou fail me not.'

CHAPTER XVI.

BEFORE THE STATUE.

IT was night—dead night—and the silence lay on the Frowning City like a cloud.

Secretly, as evildoers, Sir Henry Curtis, Umslopogaas, and myself threaded our way through the passages towards a by-entrance to the great Throne Chamber. Once we were met by the fierce rattling challenge of the sentry. I gave the countersign, and the man grounded his spear and let us pass. Also we were officers of the Queens' bodyguard, and in that capacity had a right to come and go unquestioned.

We gained the hall in safety. So empty and so still was it, that even when we had passed the sound of our footsteps yet echoed up the lofty walls, vibrating faintly and still more faintly against the carven roof, like ghosts of the footsteps of dead men haunting the place that once they trod.

It was an eerie spot, and it oppressed me. The moon was full, and threw great pencils and patches of light through the high windowless openings in the walls, that lay pure and beautiful upon the blackness of the marble floor, like white flowers on a coffin. One of these silver arrows fell upon the statue of the sleeping Rademas, and of the angel form bent over him, illumining it, and a small circle round it, with a soft clear light, reminding me of that with which Catholics illumine the altars of their cathedrals.

Here by the statue we took our stand, and waited. Sir Henry and I close together, Umslopogaas some paces off in the darkness, so that I could only just make out his towering outline leaning on the outline of an axe.

So long did we wait that I almost fell asleep resting against the cold marble, but was aroused suddenly by hearing Curtis give a quick catching breath. Then from far far away there came a little sound as though the statues that lined the walls were whispering to each other some message of the ages.

It was the faint sweep of a lady's dress. Nearer it grew, and nearer yet. We could see a figure steal from patch to patch of moonlight, and even hear the soft fall of sandalled feet. Another second and I saw the black silhouette of the old Zulu raise its arm in mute salute, and Nyleptha was before us.

Oh, how beautiful she looked as she paused a moment just within the circle of the moonlight! Her hand was pressed upon her heart, and her white bosom heaved beneath it. Round her hear a broidered scarf was loosely thrown, partially shadowing the perfect face, and thus rendering it even more lovely; for beauty, dependent as it is to a certain extent upon the imagination, is never so beautiful as when it is half hid. There she stood radiant but half doubting, stately and yet so sweet. It was but a moment, but I then and there fell in love with her myself, and have remained so to this hour; for, indeed, she looked more like an angel out of heaven than a loving, passionate, mortal woman. Low we bowed before her, and then she spoke.

'I have come,' she whispered, 'but it was at great risk. Ye know not how I am watched. The priests watch me. Sorais watches me with those great eyes of hers. My very guards are spies upon me. Nasta watches me too. Oh, let him be careful!' and she stamped her foot. 'Let him be careful; I am a woman, and therefore hard to drive. Ay, and I am a Queen, too, and can still avenge. Let him be careful, I say, lest in place of giving him my hand I take his head,' and she ended the outburst with a little sob, and then smiled up at us bewitchingly and laughed.

'Thou didst bid me come hither, my lord Incubu,' (Curtis had taught her to call him so). 'Doubtless it is about business of the State, for I know that thou art ever full of great ideas and plans for my welfare and my people's. So even as a Queen should I have come, though I greatly fear the dark alone,' and again she laughed and gave him a glance from her grey eyes.

At this point I thought it wise to move a little, since secrets 'of the State' should not be made public property; but she would not let me go far, peremptorily stopping me within five yards or so, saying that she feared surprise. So it came to pass that, however unwillingly, I heard all that passed.

'Thou knowest, Nyleptha,' said Sir Henry, 'that it was for none of these things that I asked thee to meet me at this lonely place. Nyleptha, waste not the time in pleasantry, but listen to me, for—I love thee.'

As he said the words I saw her face break up, as it were, and change. The coquetry went out of it, and in its place there shone a great light of love which seemed to glorify it, and make it like that of the marble angel overhead. I could not help thinking that it must have been a touch of prophetic instinct which made the long dead Rademas limn, in the features of the angel of his inspiring vision, so strange a likeness of his own descendant. Sir Henry, also, must have observed and been struck by the likeness, for, catching the look upon Nyleptha's face, he glanced quickly from it to the moonlit statue, and then back again at his beloved.

'Thou sayest thou dost love me,' she said in a low voice, 'and thy voice rings true, but how am I to know that thou dost speak the truth?'

'Though,' she went on with proud humility, and in the stately third person which is so largely used by the Zu-Vendi, 'I be as nothing in the eyes of my lord,' and she curtseyed towards him, 'who comes from among a wonderful people, to whom my people are but children, yet here am I a queen and a leader of men, and if I would go to battle a hundred thousand spears shall sparkle in my train like stars glimmering down the path of the bent moon. And although my beauty be a little thing in the eyes of my lord,' and she lifted her broidered skirt and curtseyed again, 'yet here among my own people am I held right fair, and ever since I was a woman the great lords of my kingdom have made quarrel concerning me, as though forsooth,' she added with a flash of passion, 'I were a deer to be pulled down by the hungriest wolf, or a horse to be sold to the highest bidder. Let my lord pardon me if I weary my lord, but it hath pleased my lord to say that he loves me, Nyleptha, a Queen of the Zu-Vendi, and therefore would I say that though my love and my hand be not much to my lord, yet to me are they all.'

'Oh!' she cried, with a sudden and thrilling change of voice, and modifying her dignified mode of address. 'Oh, how can I know that thou lovest but me? How can I know that thou wilt not weary of me and seek thine own place again, leaving me desolate? Who is there to tell me but that thou lovest some other woman, some fair woman unknown to me, but who yet draws breath beneath this same moon that shines on me to-night? Tell me *how* am I to know?' And she clasped her hands and stretched them out towards him and looked appealingly into his face.

'Nyleptha,' answered Sir Henry, adopting the Zu-Vendi way of speech; 'I have told thee that I love thee; how am I to tell thee how much I love thee? Is there then a measure for love? Yet will I try. I say not that I have never looked upon another woman with favour, but this I say that I love thee with all my life and with all my strength; that I love thee now and shall love thee till I grow cold in death, ay, and as I believe beyond my death, and on and on for ever: I say that thy voice is music to my ear, and thy touch as water to a thirsty land, that when thou art there the world is beautiful, and when I see thee not it is as though the light was dead. Oh, Nyleptha, I will never leave thee; here and now for thy dear sake I will forget my people and my father's house, yea, I renounce them all. By thy side will I live, Nyleptha, and at thy side will I die.'

He paused and gazed at her earnestly, but she hung her head like a lily, and said never a word.

'Look!' he went on, pointing to the statue on which the moonlight played so brightly. 'Thou seest that angel woman who rests her hand upon the forehead of the sleeping man, and thou seest how at her touch his soul flames up and shines out through his flesh, even as a lamp at the touch of the fire, so is it with me and thee, Nyleptha. Thou hast awakened my soul and called it forth, and now, Nyleptha, it is not mine, not mine, but *thine* and thine only. There is no more for me to say; in thy hands is my life.' And he leaned back against the pedestal of the statue, looking very pale, and his eyes shining, but proud and handsome as a god.

Slowly Nyleptha raised her head, and fixed her wonderful eyes, all alight with the greatness of her passion, full upon his face, as though to read his very soul. Then at last she spoke, low indeed, but clearly as a silver bell.

'Of a truth, weak woman that I am, I do believe thee. Ill shall be the day for thee and for me also if it be my fate to learn that I have believed a lie. And now hearken unto me, O man, who hast wandered here from far to steal my heart and make me all thine own. I put my hand upon thy hand thus, and thus I, whose lips have never kissed before, do kiss thee on the brow; and now by my hand and by that first and holy kiss, ay, by my people's weal and by my throne that like enough I shall lose for thee—by the name of my high House, by the sacred Stone and by the eternal majesty of the Sun, I swear that for thee will I live and die. And I swear that I will love thee and thee only till death, ay, and beyond, if as thou sayest there be a beyond, and that thy will shall be my will, and thy ways my ways.'

'Oh see, see, my lord! thou knowest not how humble is she who loves; I, who am a Queen, I kneel before thee, even at thy feet I do my homage;' and the lovely impassioned creature flung herself down on her knees on the cold marble before him. And after that I really do not know what happened, for I could stand it no longer, and cleared off to refresh myself with a little of old Umslopogaas's society, leaving them to settle it their own way, and a very long time they were about it.

I found the old warrior leaning on Inkosi-kaas as usual, and surveying the scene in the patch of moonlight with a grim smile of amusement.

'Ah, Macumazahn,' he said, 'I suppose it is because I am getting old, but I don't think that I shall ever learn to understand the ways of you white people. Look there now, I pray thee, they are a pretty pair of doves, but what is all the fuss about, Macumazahn? He wants a wife, and she wants a husband, then why does he not pay his cows down[1] like a man and have done with it? It would save a deal of trouble, and we should have had our night's sleep. But there they go, talk, talk, talk, and kiss, kiss, kiss, like mad things. Eugh!'

Some three-quarters of an hour afterwards the 'pair of doves' came strolling towards us, Curtis looking slightly silly, and Nyleptha remarking calmly that the moonlight made very pretty effects on the marble. Then, for she was in a most gracious mood, she took my hand and said that I was 'her Lord's' dear friend, and therefore most dear to her—not a word for my own sake, you see. Next she lifted Umslopogaas' axe, and examined it curiously, saying significantly as she did so that he might soon have cause to use it in defence of her.

After that she nodded prettily to us all, and casting one tender

[1]Alluding to the Zulu custom.—A. Q.

glance at her lover, glided off into the darkness like a beautiful vision.

When we got back to our quarters, which we did without acciden, Curtis asked me jocularly what I was thinking about.

'I am wondering,' I answered, 'on what principle it is arranged that some people should find beautiful queens to fall in love with them, while others find nobody at all, or worse than nobody; and I am also wondering how many brave men's lives this night's work will cost.' It was rather nasty of me, perhaps, but somehow all the feelings do not evaporate with age, and I could not help being a little jealous of my old friend's luck. Vanity, my sons; vanity of vanities!

On the following morning Good was informed of the happy occurrence, and positively rippled with smiles that, originating somewhere about the mouth, slowly travelled up his face like the rings in a duckpond, till they flowed over the brim of his eyeglass and went where sweet smiles go. The fact of the matter, however, was that not only was Good rejoiced about the thing on its own merits but also for personal reasons. He adored Sorais quite as earnestly as Sir Henry adored Nyleptha, and his adoration had not altogether prospered. Indeed, it had seemed to him and to me also that the dark Cleopatra-like queen favoured Curtis in her own curious inscrutable way much more than Good. Therefore it was a relief to him to learn that his unconscious rival was permanently and satisfactorily attached in another direction. His face fell a little, however, when he was told that the matter was to be kept as secret as the dead, above all from Sorais for the present, inasmuch as the political convulsion which would follow such an announcement at the moment would be altogether too great to face and would very possibly, if prematurely made, shake Nyleptha from her throne.

That morning we again attended in the Throne Hall, and I could not help smiling to myself when I compared the visit to our last, and reflecting that, if the walls could speak, they would have strange tales to tell.

What actresses women are! There, high upon her golden throne, draped in her blazoned 'kaf' or robe of state, sat the fair Nyleptha, and when Sir Henry came in a little late, dressed in the full uniform of an officer of her guard and humbly bent himself before her, she merely acknowledged his salute with a careless nod and turned her head coldly aside. It was a very large Court, for not only did the ceremony of the signing of the laws attract many outside of those whose duty it was to attend, but also the rumour that Nasta was going to publicly ask the hand of Nyleptha in marriage had gone abroad, with the result that the great hall was crowded to its utmost capacity. There were our friends the priests in force, headed by Agon, who regarded us with a vindictive eye; and a most imposing band they were, with their long white embroidered robes girt with golden chains from which hung the fish-like scales. There, too, were a number of the lords, each with a band of brilliantly attired attendants, and prominent among them was Nasta, stroking his black beard meditatively and looking unusually unpleasant. It was a splendid and impressive sight, especially when the officer having read out each law it was handed to the Queens to sign, whereupon the trumpets blared out and the Queens' guard grounded their spears with a crash in salute. This reading and signing of the laws took a long time, but at length it came to an end, the last one reciting that 'whereas certain distinguished strangers, &c.,' and proceeding to confer on the three of us the rank of 'lords,' together with certain military commands and large estates bestowed by the Queens. When it was read the trumpets blared and the spears clashed down as usual, but I saw some of the lords turn and whisper to each other, while Nasta ground his teeth. They did not like the favour that was shown to us, which under all the circumstances was not perhaps unnatural.

Then there came a pause, and Nasta stepped forwards and bowing humbly, though with no humility in his eye, craved a boon at the hands of the Queen Nyleptha.

Nyleptha turned a little pale, but bowed graciously, and prayed the 'well-beloved lord' to speak on, whereon in a few straightforward soldier-like words he asked her hand in marriage.

Then, before she could find words to answer, the high priest Agon took up the tale, and in a speech of real eloquence and power pointed out the many advantages of the proposed alliance; how it would consolidate the kingdom, for Nasta's dominions, of which he was virtually king, were to Zu-Vendis much what Scotland used to be to England; how it would gratify the wild mountaineers and be popular among the soldiery, for Nasta was a famous general; how it would set her dynasty firmly on the throne, and would gain the blessing and approval of the 'Sun,' i.e. of the office of the High Priest, and so on. Many of his arguments were undoubtedly valid, and, looking at it from a political point of view, there was everything to be said for the marriage. But unfortunately it is difficult to play the game of politics with the persons of young and lovely queens as though they were ivory effigies of themselves on a chessboard. Nyleptha's face, while Agon spouted away, was a perfect study; she smiled indeed, but beneath the smile it set like a stone, and her eyes began to flash ominously.

At last he stopped, and she prepared herself to answer. Before she did so, however, Sorais leant towards her and said in a voice sufficiently loud for me to catch what she said, 'Bethink thee well, my sister, ere thou dost speak, for methinks that our thrones may hang upon thy words.'

Nyleptha made no answer, and with a shrug and a smile Sorais leant back again and listened.

'Of a truth a great honour has been done to me,' she said, 'that my poor hand should not only have been asked in marriage, but that Agon here should be so swift to pronounce the blessing of the Sun upon my union. Methinks that in another minute he would have wed us fast ere the bride had said her say. Nasta, I thank thee, and I will bethink me of thy words, but now as yet I have no mind for marriage, that as a cup of which none know the taste until they begin to drink it. Again I thank thee, Nasta,' and she made as though she would rise.

The great lord's face turned almost as black as his beard with fury, for he knew that the words amounted to a final refusal of his suit.

'Thanks be to the Queen for her gracious words,' he said, restraining himself with difficulty and looking anything but grateful, 'my heart shall surely treasure them. And now I crave another boon, namely, the royal leave to withdraw myself to my own poor cities in the north till such time as the Queen shall say my suit nay or yea. Mayhap,' he added, with a sneer, 'the Queen will be pleased to visit me there, and to bring with her these stranger lords,' and he scowled darkly towards us. 'It is but a poor country and a rough, but we are a hardy race of mountaineers, and there shall be gathered thirty thousand swordsmen to shout a welcome to her.'

This speech, which was almost a declaration of rebellion, was received in complete silence, but Nyleptha flushed up and answered it with spirit.

'Oh, surely, Nasta, I will come, and the strange lords in my train, and for every man of thy mountaineers who calls thee Prince, will I bring two from the lowlands who call me Queen, and we will see which is the staunchest breed. Till then farewell.'

The trumpets blared out, the Queens rose, and the great assembly broke up in murmuring confusion, and for myself I went home with a heavy heart foreseeing civil war.

After this there was quiet for a few weeks. Curtis and the Queen did not often meet, and exercised the utmost caution not

to allow the true relation in which they stood to each other to
leak out; but do what they would, rumours as hard to trace as a
buzzing fly in a dark room, and yet quite as audible, began to
hum round and round, and at last to settle on her throne.

CHAPTER XVII.

THE STORM BREAKS.

AND now it was that the trouble which at first had been but a
cloud as large as a man's hand began to loom very black and big
upon our horizon, namely, Sorais' preference for Sir Henry. I
saw the storm drawing nearer and nearer; and so, poor fellow,
did he. The affection of so lovely and highly-placed a woman
was not a thing that could in a general way be considered a
calamity by any man, but, situated as Curtis was, it was a
grievous burden to bear.

To begin with, Nyleptha, though altogether charming, was, it
must be admitted, of a rather jealous disposition, and was somewhat apt to visit on her lover's head her indignation at the marks
of what Alphonse would have called the 'distinguished consideration' with which her royal sister favoured him. Then the enforced
secrecy of his relation to Nyleptha prevented Curtis from taking
some opportunity of putting a stop, or trying to put a stop, to
this false condition of affairs, by telling Sorais, in a casual but
confidential way, that he was going to marry her sister. A third
sting in Sir Henry's honey was that he knew that Good was honestly and sincerely attached to the ominous-looking but most
attractive Lady of the Night. Indeed, poor Bougwan was wasting
himself to a shadow of his fat and jolly self about her, his face
getting so thin that his eyeglass would scarcely stick in it; while
she, with a sort of careless coquetry, just gave him encouragement
enough to keep him going, thinking, no doubt, that he might be
useful as a stalking-horse. I tried to give him a hint, in as delicate a way as I could, but he flew into a huff and would not
listen to me, so I determined to let ill alone, for fear of making
it worse. Poor Good, he really was very ludicrous in his distress,
and went in for all sorts of absurdities, under the belief that he
was advancing his suit. One of them was the writing—with the
assistance of one of the grave and reverend signiors who instructed us, and who, whatever may have been the measure of
his erudition, did not understand how to scan a line—of a most
interminable Zu-Vendi love song, of which the continually recurring refrain was something about 'I will kiss thee; oh yes, I will

kiss thee!' Now among the Zu-Vendi it is a common and most harmless thing for young men to serenade ladies at night, as I believe they do in the southern countries of Europe, and sing all sorts of nonsensical songs to them. The young man may or may not be serious; but no offence is meant and none is taken, even by ladies of the highest rank, who accept the whole thing as an English girl would a gracefully-turned compliment.

Availing himself of this custom, Good bethought him that he would serenade Sorais, whose private apartments, together with those of her maidens, were exactly opposite our own, on the further side of a narrow courtyard which divided one section of the great palace from another. Accordingly, having armed himself with a native zither, on which, being an adept with the light guitar, he had easily learned to strum, he proceeded at midnight— the fashionable hour for this sort of caterwauling, to make night hideous with his amorous yells. I was fast asleep when they began, but they soon woke me up—for Good possesses a tremendous voice and has no notion of time—and I ran to my window-place to see what was the matter. And there, standing in the full moonlight in the courtyard, I perceived Good, adorned with an enormous ostrich feather headdress and a flowing silken cloak, which it is the right thing to wear upon these occasions, and shouting out the abominable song which he and the old gentleman had evolved, to a jerky, jingling accompaniment. From the direction of the quarters of the maid of honour came a succession of faint sniggerings; but the apartments of Sorais herself—whom I devoutly pitied if she happened to be there—were silent as the grave. There was absolutely no end to that awful song, with its eternal 'I will kiss thee!' and at last neither I nor Sir Henry, whom I had summoned to enjoy the sight, could bear it any longer; so, remembering the dear old story, I put my head to the window opening, and shouted, 'For Heaven's sake, Good, don't go on talking about it, but *kiss* her and let's all go to sleep!' That choked him off, and we had no more serenading.

This diversion was a laughable incident in a tragic business. How deeply thankful we ought to be that even the most serious matters have generally a silver lining about them in the shape of a joke, if only people could see it. The sense of humour is a very valuable possession in life, and ought to be cultivated in the Board schools—especially in Scotland.

Well, the more Sir Henry held off the more Sorais came on, as is not uncommon in such cases, till at last things were very queer indeed. Evidently, by some strange perversity of mind, she was quite blinded to the true state of the case; and I, for one, greatly dreaded the moment of her awakening. Sorais was a dangerous woman to be mixed up with, either with or without one's own consent. At last the evil moment came, as I saw it must come. One fine day, Good having gone out hawking, Sir Henry and I were sitting quietly talking over the situation, especially with reference to Sorais, when a Court messenger arrived with a written note, which we deciphered with some difficulty, and which was to the effect that 'the Queen Sorais commanded the attendance of the Lord Incubu in her private apartments, whither he would be conducted by the bearer.'

'Oh my word!' groaned Sir Henry. 'Can't you go instead, old fellow?'

'Not if I know it,' I said with vigour. 'I had rather face a wounded elephant with a shot-gun. Take care of your own business, my boy. If you will be so fascinating you must take the consequences. I would not be in your place for an empire.'

'You remind me of when I was going to be flogged at school and the other boys came to console me,' he said gloomily. 'What right has this Queen to command my attendance, I should like to know? I won't go.'

'But you must; you are one of her officers and bound to obey her, and she knows it. And after all it will soon be over.'

'That's just what they used to say,' he said again. 'I only hope she won't put a knife into me. I believe that she is quite capable of it.' And off he started very faintheartedly, and no wonder.

I sat and waited, and at the end of about forty-five minutes he returned, looking a great deal worse than when he went.

'Give me something to drink,' he said hoarsely.

I got him a cup of wine, and asked what was the matter.

'What is the matter? Why if ever there was trouble there's trouble now. You know when I left you? Well, I was shown straight into Sorais' private chamber, and a wonderful place it is; and there she sat, quite alone, upon a silken couch at the end of the room, playing gently upon that zither of hers. I stood before her, and for a while she took no notice of me, but kept on playing and singing a little, and very sweet music it was. At last she looked up and smiled.

' "So thou art come," she said. "I thought that perhaps thou hadst gone about the Queen Nyleptha's business. Thou art ever on her business, and I doubt not a good servant and a true."

'To this I merely bowed, and said I was there to receive the Queen's word.

' "Ah yes, I would talk with thee, but be thou seated. It wearies me to look so high," and she made room for me beside her on the couch, placing herself with her back against the end, so as to have a view of my face.

'"It is not meet," I said, "that I should make myself equal with the Queen."

'"I said be seated," was her answer, so I sat down, and she began to look at me with those dark eyes of hers. There she sat like an incarnate spirit of beauty, hardly talking at all, and when she did, very low, but all the while looking at me. There was a white flower in her black hair, and I tried to keep my eyes on it and count the petals, but it was of no use. At last, whether it was her gaze, or the perfume on her hair, or what I do not know, but I almost felt as though I was being mesmerised. At last she roused herself.

'"Incubu," she said, "lovest thou power?"

'I replied that I supposed all men loved power of one sort or another.

'"Thou shalt have it," she said. "Lovest thou wealth?"

'I said I liked wealth for what it brought.

'"Thou shalt have it," she said. "And lovest thou beauty?"

'To this I replied that I was very fond of statuary and architecture, or something silly of that sort, at which she frowned, and there was a pause. By this time my nerves were on such a stretch that I was shaking like a leaf. I knew that something awful was going to happen, but she held me under a kind of spell, and I could not help myself.

'"Incubu," she said at length, "wouldst thou be a king? Listen, wouldst thou be a king? Behold, stranger, I am minded to make thee king of all Zu-Vendis, ay and husband of Sorais of the Night. Nay, peace and hear me. To no man among my people had I thus opened out my secret heart, but thou art an outlander and therefore do I speak without shame, knowing all I have to offer and how hard it had been to thee to ask. See, a crown lies at thy feet, my lord Incubu, and with that fortune a woman whom some have wished to woo. Now mayst thou answer, O my chosen, and soft shall thy words fall upon mine ears."

'"O Sorais," I said, "I pray thee speak not thus"—you see I had not time to pick and choose my words—"for this thing cannot be. I am betrothed to thy sister Nyleptha, Sorais, and I love her and her alone."

'Next moment it struck me that I had said an awful thing, and I looked up to see the results. When I spoke, Sorais' face was hidden in her hands, and as my words reached her she slowly raised it, and I shrank back dismayed. It was ashy white, and her eyes were flaming. She rose to her feet and seemed to be choking, but the awful thing was that she was so quiet about it all. Once she looked at a side table, on which lay a dagger, and from it to me, as though she thought of killing me; but she did not take it up. At last she spoke one word, and one only—

' "Go!"

'And I went, and glad enough to get out of it, and here I am. Give me another cup of wine, there's a good fellow, and tell me, what is to be done?'

I shook my head, for the affair was indeed serious. As one of the poets says,

'Hell hath no fury like a woman scorned,'

more especially if the woman is a queen and a Sorais, and indeed I feared the very worst, including imminent danger to ourselves.

'Nyleptha must be told of all this at once,' I said, 'and perhaps I had better tell her; she might receive your account with suspicion.'

'Who is captain of her guard to-night?' I went on.

'Good.'

'Very well then, there will be no chance of her being got at. Don't look surprised. I don't think that her sister would stick at that. I suppose one must tell Good of what has happened.'

'Oh, I don't know,' said Sir Henry. 'It would hurt his feelings, poor fellow! You see, he takes a lively personal interest in Sorais.'

'That's true; and after all, perhaps there is no need to tell him. He will find out the truth soon enough. Now, you mark my words, Sorais will throw in her lot with Nasta, who is sulking up in the North there, and there will be such a war as has not been known in Zu-Vendis for centuries. Look there!' and I pointed to two Court messengers, who were speeding away from the door of Sorais' private apartments. 'Now follow me,' and I ran up a stairway into an outlook tower that rose from the roof of our quarters, taking the spyglass with me, and looked out over the palace wall. The first thing we saw was one of the messengers speeding towards the Temple, bearing without any doubt, the Queen's word to the high priest Agon, but for the other I searched in vain. Presently, however, I spied a horseman riding furiously through the northern gate of the city, and in him I recognised the other messenger.

'Ah!' I said, 'Sorais is a woman of spirit. She is acting at once, and will strike quick and hard. You have insulted her, my boy, and men's blood will flow in rivers before the stain is washed away, and yours with it, if she can get hold of you. Well, I'm off to Nyleptha. Just you stop where you are, old fellow, and try

to get your nerves straight again. You'll need them all, I can tell
you, unless I have observed human nature in the rough for fifty
years for nothing.' And off I went accordingly.

I gained audience of the Queen without trouble. She was
expecting Curtis, and was not best pleased to see my mahogany-
coloured face instead.

'Is there aught wrong with my Lord, Macumazahn, that he
waits not upon me? Say, is he sick?'

I said that he was well enough, and then, without further ado,
I plunged into my story and told it from beginning to end. Oh,
what a rage she flew into! It was a sight to see her, she looked
so lovely.

'How darest thou come to me with such a tale?' she cried. 'It
is a lie to say that my Lord was making love to Sorais, my sister.'

'Pardon me, O Queen,' I answered, 'I said that Sorais was
making love to thy lord.'

'Spin me no spiders' webs of words. Is not the thing the same
thing? The one giveth, the other taketh; but the gift passes, and
what matters it which is the most guilty? Sorais! oh, I hate her—
Sorais is a queen and my sister. She had not stooped so low had
he not shown the way. Oh, truly hath the poet said that man is
like a snake, whom to touch is poison, and whom none can hold.'

'The remark, O Queen, is excellent, but methinks thou hast
misread the poet. Nyleptha,' I went on, 'thou knowest well that
thy words are empty foolishness, and that this is no time for
folly.'

'How darest thou?' she broke in, stamping her foot. 'Has my
false lord sent thee to me to insult me also? Who art thou,
stranger, that thou shouldst speak to me, the Queen, after this
sort? How darest thou?'

'Yea, I dare. Listen. The moments which thou dost waste in
idle anger may well cost thee thy crown and all of us our lives.
Already Sorais' horsemen go forth and call to arms. In three
days' time Nasta will rouse himself in his fastness like a lion
in the evening, and his growling will be heard throughout the
North. The "Lady of the Night" (Sorais) hath a sweet voice, and
she will not sing in vain. Her banner will be borne from range
to range and valley to valley, and warriors will spring up in its
track like dust beneath a whirlwind; half the army will echo her
war-cry; and in every town and hamlet of this wide land the
priests will call out against the foreigner and will preach her
cause as holy. I have spoken, O Queen!'

Nyleptha was quite calm now; her jealous anger had passed;
and putting off the character of a lovely headstrong lady, with

a rapidity and completeness that distinguished her, she put on that of a queen and a woman of business. The transformation was sudden but entire.

'Thy words are very wise, Macumazahn. Forgive me my folly. Ah, what a Queen I should be if only I had no heart! To be heartless—that is to conquer all. Passion is like the lightning, it is beautiful, and it links the earth to heaven, but alas it blinds!

'And thou thinkest that my sister Sorais would levy war upon me. So be it. She shall not prevail against me. I, too, have my friends and my retainers. There are many, I say, who will shout "Nyleptha!" when my pennon runs up on peak and pinnacle, and the light of my beacon fires leaps to-night from crag to crag, bearing the message of my war. I will break her strength and scatter her armies. Eternal night shall be the portion of Sorais of the Night. Give me that parchment and the ink. So. Now summon me the officer in the ante-room. He is a trusty man.'

I did as I was bid! and the man, a veteran and quiet-looking gentleman of the guard, named Kara, entered, bowing low.

'Take this parchment,' said Nyleptha; 'it is thy warrant; and guard every place of in and outgoing in the apartments of my sister Sorais, the "Lady of the Night," and a Queen of the Zu-Vendi. Let none come in and none go out, or thy life shall pay the cost.'

The man looked startled, but he merely said, 'The Queen's word be done,' and departed. Then Nyleptha sent a messenger to Sir Henry, and presently he arrived looking uncommonly uncomfortable. I thought that another outburst was about to follow, but wonderful are the ways of women; she said not a word about Sorais and his supposed inconstancy, greeting him with a friendly nod, and stating simply that she required his advice upon high matters. All the same there was a look in her eye, and a sort of suppressed energy in her manner towards him, that makes me think that she had not forgotten the affair, but was keeping it for a private occasion.

Just after Curtis arrived the officer returned, and reported that Sorais was *gone*. The bird had flown to the Temple, stating that, as was sometimes the custom among Zu-Vendi ladies of rank, she was going to spend the night in meditation before the altar. We looked at each other significantly. The blow had fallen very soon.

Then we set to work.

Generals who could be trusted were summoned from their quarters, and as much of the State affairs as was thought desirable was told to each, strict injunctions being given to them to get all

their available force together. The same was done with such of
the more powerful lords as Nyleptha knew she could rely on,
several of whom left that very day for distant parts of the country to gather up their tribesmen and retainers. Sealed orders
were dispatched to the rulers of far-off cities, and some twenty
messengers were sent off before nightfall with instructions to
ride early and late till they reached the distant chiefs to whom
their letters were addressed: also many spies were set to work.
All the afternoon and evening we laboured, assisted by some confidential scribes, Nyleptha showing an energy and resource of
mind that astonished me, and it was eight o'clock before we got
back to our quarters. Here we heard from Alphonse, who was
deeply aggrieved because our non-return had spoilt his dinner, for
he had turned cook again now, that Good had come back from
his hawking and gone on duty. As instructions had already been
given to the officer of the outer guard to double the sentries at
the gate, and as we had no reason to fear any immediate danger,
we did not think it worth while to hunt him up and tell him anything of what had passed, which at best, under the peculiar
circumstances of the case, was one of those tasks one prefers to
postpone, so after swallowing our food we turned in to get some
much-needed rest. Before we did so, however, it occurred to
Curtis to tell old Umslopogaas to keep a look-out in the neighbourhood of Nyleptha's private apartments. Umslopogaas was
now well known about the place, and by the Queen's order
allowed to pass whither he would by the guards, a permission of
which he often availed himself by roaming about the palace
during the still hours in a nocturnal fashion that he favoured,
and which is by no means uncommon amongst black men generally. His presence in the corridors would not, therefore, be
likely to excite remark. Without any comment the Zulu took up
his axe and departed, and we also departed to bed.

I seemed to have been asleep but a few minutes when I was
awakened by a peculiar sensation of uneasiness. I felt that somebody was in the room and looking at me, and instantly sat up, to
see to my surprise that it was already dawn, and that there,
standing at the foot of my couch and looking peculiarly grim and
gaunt in the grey light, was Umslopogaas himself.

'How long hast thou been there?' I asked testily, for it is not
pleasant to be aroused in such a fashion.

'Mayhap the half of an hour, Macumazahn. I have a word
for thee.'

'Speak on,' I said, now wide enough awake.

'As I was bid I went last night to the place of the White Queen and hid myself behind a pillar in the second anteroom, beyond which is the sleeping-place of the Queen. Bougwan (Good) was in the first anteroom alone, and outside the curtain of that room was a sentry, but I had a mind to see if I could pass in unseen, and I did, gliding behind them both. There I waited for many hours, when suddenly I perceived a dark figure coming secretly towards me. It was the figure of a woman, and in her hand she held a dagger. Behind that figure crept another, unseen by the woman. It was Bougwan following in her tracks. His shoes were off, and for so fat a man he followed very well. The woman passed me, and the starlight shone upon her face.'

'Who was it?' I asked impatiently.

'The face was the face of the "Lady of the Night," and of a truth she is well named.

'I waited, and Bougwan passed me also. Then I followed. So we went slowly and without a sound up the long chamber. First the woman, then Bougwan, and then I; and the woman saw not Bougwan, and Bougwan saw not me. At last the "Lady of the Night" came to the curtains that shut off the sleeping place of the White Queen, and put out her left hand to part them. She passed through, and so did Bougwan, and so did I. At the far end of the room is the bed of the Queen, and on it she lay very fast asleeep. I could hear her breathe, and see one white arm lying on the coverlid like a streak of snow on the dry grass. The "Lady of the Night" doubled herself thus, and with the long knife lifted crept towards the bed. So straight did she gaze thereat that she never thought to look behind her. When she was quite close Bougwan touched her on the arm, and she caught her breath and turned, and I saw the knife flash, and heard it strike. Well was it for Bougwan that he had the skin of iron on him, or he had been pierced. Then for the first time he saw who the woman was, and without a word he fell back astonished, and unable to speak. She, too, was astonished, and spoke not, but suddenly she laid her finger on her lips, thus, and walked towards and through the curtain, and with her went Bougwan. So close did she pass to me that her dress touched me, and I was nigh to slaying her as she went. In the first outer room she spoke to Bougwan in a whisper and, clasping her hands thus, she pleaded with him, but what she said I know not. And so they passed on to the second outer room, she pleading and he shaking his head, and saying, "Nay, nay, nay." And it seemed to me that he was about to call the guard, when she stopped talking and looked at him with great eyes, and I saw that he was bewitched by her beauty. Then she stretched out her hand and he kissed it, whereon I gathered myself together to advance and take her, seeing that now had Bougwan become a woman, and no longer knew the good from the evil, when behold! she was gone.'

'Gone!' I ejaculated.

'Ay, gone, and there stood Bougwan staring at the wall like one asleep, and presently he went too, and I waited a while and came away also.'

'Art thou sure, Umslopogaas,' said I, 'that thou hast not been a dreamer this night?'

In reply he opened his left hand and produced about three inches of the blade of a dagger of the finest steel. 'If I be, Macumazahn, behold what the dream left with me. The knife broke upon Bougwan's bosom, and as I passed I picked this up in the sleeping-place of the White Queen.'

CHAPTER XVIII.

WAR! RED WAR!

TELLING Umslopogaas to wait, I tumbled into my clothes and went off with him to Sir Henry's room, where the Zulu repeated his story word for word. It was a sight to watch Curtis's face as he heard it.

'Great Heavens!' he said: 'here have I been sleeping away while Nyleptha was nearly murdered—and all through me, too. What a fiend that Sorais must be! It would have served her well if Umslopogaas had cut her down in the act.'

'Ay,' said the Zulu. 'Fear not; I should have slain her ere she struck. I was but waiting the moment.'

I said nothing; but I could not help thinking that many a thousand doomed lives would have been saved if he had meted out to Sorais the fate she meant for her sister. And, as the issue proved, I was right.

After he had told his tale Umslopogaas went off unconcernedly to eat his morning meal, and Sir Henry and I fell to talking.

At first he was very bitter against Good, who, he said, was no longer to be trusted, having designedly allowed Sorais to escape by some secret stair when it was his duty to have handed her over to justice. Indeed, he spoke in the most unmeasured terms on the matter. I let him run on awhile, reflecting to myself how easy we find it to be hard on the weaknesses of others, and how tender we are to our own.

'Really, my dear fellow,' I said at length, 'one would never think to hear you talk, that you were the man who had an interview with this same lady yesterday, and found it rather difficult to resist her fascinations, notwithstanding your ties to one of the loveliest and most loving women in the whole world. Now suppose that it was Nyleptha who had tried to murder Sorais, and *you* had caught her, and she had pleaded with *you*, would you have been so very eager to hand her over to an open shame, and to death by fire? Just look at the matter through Good's eyeglass for a minute before you denounce an old friend as a scoundrel.'

He listened to this jobation submissively, and then frankly acknowledged that he had spoken hardly. It is one of the best points in Sir Henry's character that he is always ready to admit it when he is in the wrong.

But, though I spoke up thus for Good, I was not blind to the fact that, however natural his behaviour might be, it was obvious that he was being involved in a very awkward and disgraceful complication. A foul and wicked murder had been attempted, and he had let the murderess escape, and thereby, among other things, allowed her to gain a complete ascendancy over himself. In fact, he was in a fair way to become her tool—and no more dreadful fate can befall a man than to become the tool of an unscrupulous woman, or indeed of any woman. There is but one end to it: when he is broken, or has served her purpose, he is thrown away— turned out on the world to hunt for his lost self-respect. Whilst I was pondering thus, and wondering what was to be done—for the whole subject was a thorny one—I suddenly heard a great clamour in the courtyard outside, and distinguished the voices of Umslopogaas and Alphonse, the former cursing furiously, and the latter yelling in terror.

Hurrying out to see what was the matter, I was met by a ludicrous sight. The little Frenchman was running up the courtyard at an extraordinary speed, and after him sped Umslopogaas like a great greyhound. Just as I came out he caught him, and, lifting him right off his legs, carried him some paces to a beautiful but very dense flowering shrub which bore a flower not unlike the gardenia, but was covered with short thorns. Next, despite his howls and struggles, with one mighty thrust he plunged poor Alphonse head first into the bush, so that nothing but the calves of his legs and his heels remained in evidence. Then, satisfied with what he had done, the Zulu folded his arms and stood grimly contemplating the Frenchman's kicks, and listening to his yells, which were awful.

'What art thou doing?' I said, running up. 'Wouldst thou kill the man? Pull him out of the bush!'

With a savage grunt he obeyed, seizing the wretched Alphonse by the ankle, and with a jerk that must have nearly dislocated it, tearing him out of the heart of the shrub. Never did I see such a sight as he presented, his clothes half torn off his back, and bleeding as he was in every direction from the sharp thorns. There he lay and yelled and rolled, and there was no getting anything out of him.

At last, however, he got up and, ensconcing himself behind me, cursed old Umslopogaas by every saint in the calendar, vowing by the blood of his heroic grandfather that he would poison him, and 'have his revenge.'

At last I got to the truth of the matter. It appeared that Alphonse habitually cooked Umslopogaas's porridge, which the latter ate for breakfast in the corner of the courtyard, just as he would have done at home in Zululand, from a gourd, and with a wooden spoon. Now Umslopogaas, like many Zulus, had a great horror of fish, which he considered a species of water-snake; so Alphonse, who was as fond of playing tricks as a monkey, and who was also a consummate cook, determined to make him eat some. Accordingly he grated up a quantity of white fish very finely, and mixed it with the Zulu's porridge, who swallowed it nearly all down in ignorance of what he was eating. But, unfortunately for Alphonse, he could not restrain his joy at this sight, and came capering and peering round, till at last Umslopogaas, who was very clever in his way, suspected something, and, after a careful examination of the remains of his porridge, discovered 'the buffalo heifer's trick,' and, in revenge, served him as I have said. Indeed, the little man was fortunate not to get a broken neck for his pains; for, as one would have thought, he might have learnt from the episode of his display of axemanship that 'le Monsieur noir' was an ill person to play practical jokes upon.

This incident was unimportant enough in itself, but I narrate it because it led to serious consequences. As soon as he had staunched the bleeding from his scratches and washed himself, Alphonse went off still cursing, to recover his temper, a process which I knew from experience would take a very long time. When he had gone I gave Umslopogaas a jobation and told him that I was ashamed of his behaviour.

'Ah, well, Macumazahn,' he said, 'you must be gentle with me, for here is not my place. I am weary of it, weary to death of eating and drinking, of sleeping and giving in marriage. I love not this soft life in stone houses that takes the heart out of a man,

and turns his strength to water and his flesh to fat. I love not
the white robes and the delicate women, the blowing of trumpets
and the flying of hawks. When we fought the Masai at the kraal
yonder, ah, then life was worth the living, but here is never a
blow struck in anger, and I begin to think I shall go the way of
my fathers and lift Inkosi-kaas no more,' and he held up the axe
and gazed at it in sorrow.

'Ah,' I said, 'that is thy complaint, is it? Thou hast the blood-
sickness, hast thou? and the Woodpecker wants a tree. And at
thy age, too. Shame on thee! Umslopogaas.

'Ay, Macumazahn, mine is a red trade, yet it is better and
more honest than some. Better is it to slay a man in fair fight
than to suck out his heart's blood in buying and selling and usury
after your white fashion. Many a man have I slain, yet is there
never a one that I should fear to look in the face again, ay, many
are there who once were friends, and whom I should be right glad
to snuff with. But there! there! thou hast thy ways, and I mine:
each to his own people and his own place. The high-veldt ox
will die in the fat bush country, and so is it with me, Macumazahn. I am rough, I know it, and when my blood is warm I know
not what I do, but yet wilt thou be sorry when the night swallows
me and I am utterly lost in blackness, for in thy heart thou lovest
me, my father, Macumazahn the fox, though I be nought but a
broken-down Zulu war-dog—a chief for whom there is no room
in his own kraal, an outcast and a wanderer in strange places:
ay, I love thee, Macumazahn, for we have grown grey together,
and there is that between us that cannot be seen, and yet is too
strong for breaking;' and he took his snuff-box, which was made
of an old brass cartridge, from the slit in his ear where he always
carried it, and handed it to me for me to help myself.

I took the pinch of snuff with some emotion. It was quite true,
I was much attached to the bloodthirsty old ruffian. I do not
know what was the charm of his character, but it had a charm;
perhaps it was its fierce honesty and directness; perhaps one
admired his almost superhuman skill and strength, or it may
have been simply that he was so absolutely unique. Frankly,
with all my experience of savages, I never knew a man quite
like him, he was so wise and yet such a child with it all; and
though it seems laughable to say so, like the hero of the Yankee
parody, he 'had a tender heart.' Anyway, I was very fond of
him, though I should never have thought of telling him so.

'Ay, old wolf,' I said, 'thine is a strange love. Thou wouldst
split me to the chin if I stood in thy path to-morrow.'

'Thou speakest truth, Macumazahn, that would I if it came in the way of duty, but I should love thee all the same when the blow had gone fairly home. Is there any chance of some fighting here, Macumazahn?' he went on in an insinuating voice. 'Me-thought that what I saw last night did show that the two great Queens were vexed one with another. Else had the "Lady of the Night" not brought that dagger with her.'

I agreed with him that it showed that more or less pique and irritation existed between the ladies, and told him how things stood, and that they were quarrelling over Incubu.

'Ah, is it so?' he exclaimed, springing up in delight; 'then will there be war as surely as the rivers rise in the rains—war to the end. Women love the last blow as well as the last word, and when they fight for love they are pitiless as a wounded buffalo. See thou, Macumazahn, a woman will swim through blood to her desire, and think nought of it. With these eyes have I seen it once, and twice also. Ah, Macumazahn, we shall see this fine place of houses burning yet, and hear the battle cries come ringing up the street. After all, I have not wandered for nothing. Can this folk fight, think ye?'

Just then Sir Henry joined us, and Good arrived, too, from another direction, looking very pale and hollow-eyed. The mo-ment Umslopogaas saw the latter he stopped his bloodthirsty talk and greeted him.

'Ah, Bougwan,' he cried, 'greeting to thee, Inkoos! Thou art surely weary. Didst thou hunt too much yesterday?' Then, with-out waiting for an answer, he went on—

'Listen, Bougwan, and I will tell thee a story; it is about a woman, therefore wilt thou hear it, is it not so?'

'There was a man and he had a brother, and there was a woman who loved the man's brother and was beloved of the man. But the man's brother had a favourite wife and loved not the woman, and he made a mock of her. Then the woman, being very cun-ning and fierce-hearted for revenge, took counsel with herself and said to the man, "I love thee, and if thou wilt make war upon thy brother I will marry thee." And he knew it was a lie, yet because of his great love of the woman, who was very fair, did he listen to her words and made war. And when many people had been killed his brother sent to him, saying, "Why slayest thou me? What hurt have I done unto thee? From my youth up have I not loved thee? When thou wast troubled did I not succour thee, and have we not gone down to war together and divided the cattle, girl by girl, ox by ox, and cow by cow? Why slayest thou me, my brother, whom I have loved?"

'Then the man's heart was heavy, and he knew that his path was evil, and he put aside the tempting of the woman and ceased to make war on his brother, and lived at peace in the same kraal with him. And after a time the woman came to him and said, "I have lost the past, I will be thy wife." And in his heart he knew that it was a lie and that she thought the evil thing, yet because of his love did he take her to wife.

'And the very night that they were wed, when the man was plunged into a deep sleep, did the woman arise and take his axe from his hand and creep into the hut of his brother and slay him in his rest. Then did she slink back like a gorged lioness and place the thong of the red axe back upon his wrist and go her ways.

'And at the dawning the people came shouting, "Lousta is slain in the night," and they came into the hut of the man, and there he lay asleep and by him was the red axe. Then did they remember the war and say, "Lo! he hath of a surety slain his brother," and they would have taken him and killed him, but he rose and fled swiftly, and as he fleeted by he slew the woman.

'But death could not wipe out the evil she had done, and on him rested the weight of all her sin. Therefore is he an outcast and his name a scorn among his own people; for on him, and him only, resteth the burden of her who betrayed. And, therefore, does he who was a great chief wander afar, without a kraal or a wife, and therefore will he die afar like a stricken buck and his name be accursed from generation to generation, in that the people say that he slew his brother, Lousta, by treachery in the night-time.'

The old Zulu paused, and I saw that he was deeply agitated by his own story. Presently he lifted his head, which he had bowed to his breast, and went on:

'I was that man, Bougwan. Ou! *I* was that man, and now hark thou! Even as I am so wilt thou be—a tool, a plaything, an ox of burden to carry the evil deeds of another. Listen! When thou didst creep after the "Lady of the Night" *I* was hard upon thy track. When she struck thee with the knife in the sleeping place of the White Queen *I* was there also; when thou didst let her slip away like a snake in the stones *I* saw thee, and I knew that she had bewitched thee and that a true man had abandoned the truth, and he who aforetime loved a straight path had taken a crooked way. Forgive me, my father, if my words are sharp, but out of a full heart are they spoken. See her no more, so shalt thou go down with honour to the grave. Else because of the beauty of a woman that weareth as a garment of fur shalt thou be even as I am, and perchance with more cause. I have said.'

Throughout this long and eloquent address Good had been perfectly silent, but when the tale began to shape itself so aptly to his own case, he coloured up, and when he learnt that what had passed between him and Sorais had been overseen he was evidently much distressed. And now, when at last he spoke, it was in a tone of humility quite foreign to him.

'I must say,' he said, with a bitter little laugh, 'that I scarcely thought that I should live to be taught my duty by a Zulu; but it just shows what we can come to. I wonder if you fellows can understand how humiliated I feel, and the bitterest part of it is that I deserve it all. Of course I should have handed Sorais over to the guard, but I could not, and that is a fact. I let her go and I promised to say nothing, more is the shame to me. She told me that if I would side with her she would marry me and make me king of this country, but thank goodness I did find the heart to say that even to marry her I could not desert my friends. And now you can do what you like, I deserve it all. All I have to say is that I hope that you may never love a woman with all your heart and then be so sorely tempted of her,' and he turned to go.

'Look here, old fellow,' said Sir Henry, 'just stop a minute. I have a little tale to tell you too.' And he went on to narrate what had taken place on the previous day between Sorais and himself.

This was a finishing stroke to poor Good. It is not pleasant to any man to learn that he has been made a tool of, but when the circumstances are as peculiarly atrocious as in the present case, it is about as bitter a pill as anybody can be called on to swallow.

'Do you know,' he said, 'I think that between you, you fellows have about worked a cure,' and he turned and walked away, and I for one felt very sorry for him. Ah, if the moths would always carefully avoid the candle, how few burnt wings there would be!

That day was a Court day, when the Queens sat in the great hall and received petitions, discussed laws, money grants, and so forth, and thither we adjourned shortly afterwards. On our way we were joined by Good, who was looking exceedingly depressed.

When we got into the hall Nyleptha was already on her throne and proceeding with business as usual, surrounded by councillors, courtiers, lawyers, priests, and an unusually strong guard. It was, however, easy to see from the air of excitement and expectation on the faces of everybody present that nobody was paying much attention to ordinary affairs, the fact being that the knowledge that civil war was imminent had now got abroad. We saluted Nyleptha and took our accustomed places, and for a little while things went on as usual, when suddenly the trumpets began to call outside the palace, and from the great crowd that was gathered there in anticipation of some unusual event there rose a roar of 'Sorais! Sorais!'

Then came the roll of many chariot wheels, and presently the great curtains at the end of the hall were drawn wide and through them entered the 'Lady of the Night' herself. Nor did she come alone. Preceding her was Agon, the high priest, arrayed in his most gorgeous vestments, and on either side were other priests. The reason for their presence was obvious—coming with them it would have been sacrilege to attempt to detain her. Behind her were a number of the great lords, and behind them a small body of picked guards. A glance at Sorais herself was enough to show that her mission was of no peaceful kind, for in place of her gold-embroidered 'kaf' she wore a shining tunic formed of golden scales, and on her head a little golden helmet. In her hand, too, she bore a toy spear, beautifully made and fashioned of solid silver. Up the hall she came looking like a lioness in her conscious pride and beauty, and as she came the spectators fell back bowing and made a path for her. By the sacred stone she halted, and laying her hand on it, she cried out with a loud voice to Nyleptha on the throne, 'Hail, O Queen!'

'All hail, my royal sister!' answered Nyleptha. 'Draw thou near. Fear not, I give thee safe conduct.'

Sorais answered with a haughty look, and swept on up the hall till she stood right before the thrones.

'A boon, O Queen!' she cried again.

'Speak on, my sister; what is there that I can give thee who hast half our kingdom?'

'Thou canst tell me a true word—me and the people of Zu-Vendis. Art thou, or art thou not, about to take this foreign wolf,' and she pointed to Sir Henry with her toy spear, 'to be a husband to thee, and share thy bed and throne?'

Curtis winced at this, and turning towards Sorais, said to her in a low voice, 'Methinks that yesterday thou hadst other names than wolf to call me by, O Queen!' and I saw her bite her lips as, like a danger flag, the blood flamed red upon her face. As for Nyleptha, who is nothing if not original, seeing that the thing was out, and that there was nothing further to be gained by concealment, she answered the question in a novel and effectual manner, inspired thereto, as I firmly believe, by coquetry and a desire to triumph over her rival.

Up she rose and, descending from the throne, swept in all the glory of her royal grace on to where her lover stood. There she stopped and untwined the golden snake that was wound around her arm. Then she bade him kneel, and he dropped on one knee on the marble before her, and next, taking the golden snake with both her hands, she bent the pure soft metal round his neck, and when it was fast, deliberately kissed him on the brow and called him her 'dear lord.'

'Thou seest,' she said, when the excited murmur of the spectators had died away, addressing her sister as Sir Henry rose to his feet, 'I have put my collar round the "wolf's" neck, and behold! he shall be my watchdog, and that is my answer to thee, Queen Sorais, my sister, and to those with thee. Fear not,' she went on, smiling sweetly on her lover, and pointing to the golden snake she had twined round his massive throat, 'if my yoke be heavy, yet is it of pure gold, and it shall not gall thee.'

Then, turning to the audience, she continued in a clear proud tone, 'Ay, Lady of the Night, Lords, Priests, and People here gathered together, by this sign do I take the foreigner to husband, even here in the face of you all. What, am I a Queen, and yet not free to choose the man whom I will love? Then should I be lower than the meanest girl in all my provinces. Nay, he hath won my heart, and with it goes my hand, and throne, and all I have—ay, had he been a beggar instead of a great lord fairer and stronger than any here, and having more wisdom and knowledge of strange things, I had given him all, how much more so then being what he is!' And she took his hand and gazed proudly on him, and holding it, stood there boldly facing the people. And such was her sweetness and the power and dignity of her person, and so beautiful she looked standing hand in hand there at her lover's side, so sure of him and of herself, and so ready to risk all things and endure all things for him, that most of those who saw the sight, which I am sure no one of them will ever forget, caught the fire from her eyes and the happy colour from her blushing face, and cheered her like wild things. It was a bold stroke for her to make, and it appealed to the imagination; but human nature in Zu-Vendis, as elsewhere, loves that which is bold and not afraid to break a rule, and is moreover peculiarly susceptible to appeals to its poetical side.

And so the people cheered till the roof rang; but Sorais of the Night stood there with downcast eyes, for she could not bear to see her sister's triumph, which robbed her of the man whom she had hoped to win, and in the awfulness of her jealous anger she trembled and turned white like an aspen in the wind. I think I have said somewhere of her that she reminded me of the sea on a calm day, having the same aspect of sleeping power about her. Well, it was all awake now, and like the face of the furious ocean it awed and yet fascinated me. A really handsome woman in a royal rage is always a beautiful sight, but such beauty and such a rage I never saw combined before, and I can only say that the effect produced was well worthy of the two.

She lifted her white face, the teeth were set, and there were purple rings beneath her glowing eyes. Thrice she tried to speak and thrice she failed, but at last her voice came. Raising her silver spear, she shook it, and the light glanced from it and from the golden scales of her cuirass.

'And thinkest thou, Nyleptha,' she said in notes which pealed through the great hall like a clarion, 'thinkest thou that I, Sorais, a Queen of the Zu-Vendi, will brook that this base outlander shall sit upon my father's throne and rear up half-breeds to fill the place of the great House of the Stairway? Never! never! while there is life in my bosom and a man to follow me and a spear to strike with. Who is on my side? Who?

'Now hand thou over this foreign wolf and those who came hither to prey with him to the doom of fire, for have they not committed the deadly sin against the Sun? or, Nyleptha, I give thee War—red War! Ay, I say to thee that the path of thy passion shall be marked out by the blazing of thy towns and watered with the blood of those who cleave to thee. On thy head rest the burden of the deed, and in thy ears ring the groans of the dying and the cries of the widows and those who are left fatherless for ever and for ever.

'I tell thee I will tear thee, Nyleptha, the White Queen, from thy throne, and that thou shalt be hurled—ay, hurled even from the topmost stair of the great way to the foot thereof, in that thou hast covered the name of the House of him who built it with black shame. And I tell ye strangers—all save thou Bougwan, whom because thou didst do me a service I will save alive if thou wilt leave these men and follow me' (here poor Good shook his head vigorously and ejaculated 'Can't be done' in English)—'that I will wrap you in sheets of gold and hang you yet alive in chains from the four golden trumpets of the four angels that fly east and west and north and south from the giddiest pinnacles of the Temple, so that ye may be a token and a warning to the land. And as for thee, Incubu, thou shalt die in yet another fashion that I will not tell thee now.'

She ceased, panting for breath, for her passion shook her like a storm, and a murmur, partly of horror and partly of admiration, ran through the hall. Then Nyleptha answered calmly and with dignity:

'Ill would it become my place and dignity, O sister, so to speak as thou hast spoken and so to threat as thou hast threatened. Yet if thou wilt make war, then will I strive to bear up against thee, for if my hand seem soft, yet shalt thou find it of iron when it grips thine armies by the throat. Sorais, I fear thee not. I weep for that which thou wilt bring upon our people and on thyself, but for myself I say—I fear thee not. Yet thou, who but yesterday didst strive to win my lover and my lord from me, whom to-day thou dost call a "foreign wolf," to be *thy* lover and *thy* lord' (here there was an immense sensation in the hall), 'thou who but last night, as I have learnt but since thou didst enter here, didst creep like a snake into my sleeping-place—ay, even by a secret way, and wouldst have foully murdered me, thy sister, as I lay asleep——'

'It is false, it is false!' rang out Agon's and a score of other voices.

'It is *not* false' said I, producing the broken point of the dagger and holding it up. 'Where is the haft from which this flew, O Sorais?'

'It is not false,' cried Good, determined at last to act like a loyal man. 'I took the Lady of the Night by the White Queen's bed, and on my breast the dagger broke.'

'Who is on my side?' cried Sorais, shaking her silver spear, for she saw that public sympathy was turning against her. 'What, Bougwan, thou comest not?' she said, addressing Good, who was standing close to her, in a low, concentrated voice. 'Thou pale-souled fool, for a reward thou shalt eat out thy heart with love of me and not be satisfied, and thou mightest have been my husband and a king! At least I hold *thee* in chains that cannot be broken.'

'*War! War! War!*' she cried. 'Here, with my hand upon the sacred stone that shall endure, so runs the prophecy, till the Zu-Vendi set their necks beneath an alien yoke, I declare war to the end. Who follows Sorais of the Night to victory and honour?'

Instantly the whole concourse began to break up in indescribable confusion. Many present hastened to throw in their lot with the 'Lady of the Night,' but some came from her following to us. Amongst the former was an under officer of Nyleptha's own guard, who suddenly turned and made a run for the doorway through which Sorais' people were already passing. Umslopogaas, who was present and had taken the whole scene in, seeing with admirable presence of mind that if this soldier got away others would follow his example, seized the man, who drew his sword and struck at him. Thereon the Zulu sprang back with a wild shout, and, avoiding the sword cuts, began to peck at his foe with his terrible axe, till in a few seconds the man's fate overtook him and he fell with a clash heavily and quite dead upon the marble floor.

This was the first blood spilt in the war.

'Shut the gates,' I shouted, thinking that we might perhaps catch Sorais so, and not being troubled with the idea of committing sacrilege. But the order came too late, her guards were already passing through them, and in another minute the streets echoed with the furious galloping of horses and the rolling of her chariots.

So, drawing half the people after her, Sorais was soon passing like a whirlwind through the Frowning City on her road to her headquarters at M'Arstuna, a fortress situated a hundred and thirty miles to the north of Milosis.

And after that the city was alive with the endless tramp of regiments and preparations for the gathering war, and old Umslopogaas once more began to sit in the sunshine and go through a show of sharpening Inkosi-kaas's razor edge.

CHAPTER XIX.

A STRANGE WEDDING.

ONE person, however, did not succeed in getting out in time before the gates were shut, and that was the high priest Agon, who, as we had every reason to believe, was Sorais' great ally, and the heart and soul of her party. This cunning and ferocious old man had not forgiven us for those hippopotami, or rather that was what he said. What he meant was that he would never brook the introduction of our wider ways of thought and foreign learning and influence while there was a possibility of stamping us out. Also he knew that we possessed a different system of religion, and no doubt was in daily terror of our attempting to introduce it into Zu-Vendis. One day he asked me if we had any religion in our country, and I told him that so far as I could remember we had ninety-five different ones. You might have knocked him down with a feather, and really it is difficult not to pity a high priest of a well-established cult who is haunted by the possible approach of one or all of ninety-five new religions.

When we knew that Agon was caught, Nyleptha, Sir Henry, and I discussed what was to be done with him. I was for closely incarcerating him, but Nyleptha shook her head, saying that it would produce a disastrous effect throughout the country. 'Ah!' she added, with a stamp of her foot, 'if I win and am once really Queen, I will break the power of those priests, with their rites and revels and dark secret ways.' I only wished that old Agon could have heard her, it would have frightened him.

'Well,' said Sir Henry, 'if we are not to imprison him, I suppose that we may as well let him go. He is of no use here.'

Nyleptha looked at him in a curious sort of way, and said in a dry little voice, 'Thinkest thou so, my lord?'

'Eh?' said Curtis. 'No, I do not see what is the use of keeping him.'

She said nothing, but continued looking at him in a way that was as shy as it was sweet.

Then at last he understood.

'Forgive me, Nyleptha,' he said, rather tremulously. 'Dost thou mean that thou wilt marry me, even now?'

'Nay, I know not; let my lord say,' was her rapid answer; 'but if my lord wills, the priest is there and the altar is there'—pointing to the entrance to a private chapel—'and am I not ready to do the will of my lord? Listen, O my lord! in eight days or less thou must leave me and go down to war, for thou shalt lead my armies, and in war—men sometimes fall, and if so I would for a little space have had thee all my own, if only for memory's sake;' and the tears overflowed her lovely eyes and rolled down her face like heavy drops of dew down the red heart of a rose.

'Mayhap, too,' she went on, 'I shall lose my crown, and with my crown my life and thine also. Sorais is very strong and very bitter, and if she prevails she will not spare. Who can read the future? Happiness is the world's White Bird, that alights seldom, and flies fast and far till one day he is lost in the clouds. Therefore we should hold him fast if by any chance he rests for a little space upon our hand. It is not wise to neglect the present for the future, for who knows what the future will be, Incubu? Let us pluck our flowers while the dew is on them, for when the sun is up they wither and on the morrow will others bloom that we shall never see.' And she lifted her sweet face to him and smiled into his eyes, and once more I felt a curious pang of jealousy and turned and went away. They never took much notice of whether I was there or not, thinking, I suppose, that I was an old fool, and that it did not matter one way or the other, and really I believe they were right.

So I went back to our quarters and ruminated over things in general, and watched old Umslopogaas whetting his axe outside the window as a vulture whets his beak beside a dying ox.

And in about an hour's time Sir Henry came tearing over, looking very radiant and wildly excited, and found Good and myself and even Umslopogaas, and asked us if we should like to assist at a real wedding. Of course we said yes, and off we went to the chapel, where we found Agon looking as sulky as any high priest possibly could, and no wonder. It appeared that he and Nyleptha had had a slight difference of opinion about the coming ceremony. He had flatly refused to celebrate it, or to allow any of his priests to do so, whereupon Nyleptha became very angry and told him that she, as Queen, was head of the Church, and meant to be obeyed. Indeed, she played the part of a Zu-Vendi Henry the Eighth to perfection and insisted that, if she wanted to be married, she would be married, and that he should marry her.[1]

He still refused to go through the ceremony, so she clinched her argument thus—

'Well, I cannot execute a High Priest, because there is an absurd prejudice against it, and I cannot imprison him because all his subordinates would raise a crying that would bring the stars down on Zu-Vendis and crush it; but I *can* leave him to contemplate the altar of the Sun without anything to eat, because that is his natural vocation, and if thou wilt not marry me, O Agon! thou shalt be placed before the altar yonder with nought but a little water till such time as thou hast reconsidered the matter.'

Now, as it happened, Agon had been hurried away that morning without his breakfast, and was already exceedingly hungry, so he presently modified his views and consented to marry them, saying at the same time that he washed his hands of all responsibility in the matter.

So it chanced that presently, attended only by two of her favourite maidens, came the Queen Nyleptha, with happy blushing face and downcast eyes, dressed in pure white, without embroidery of any sort, as seems to be the fashion on these occasions in most countries of the world. She did not wear a single ornament, even her gold circlets were removed, and I thought that if possible she looked more lovely than ever without them, as really superbly beautiful women do.

She came, curtseyed low to Sir Henry, and then took his hand and led him up before the altar, and after a little pause, in a slow, clear voice uttered the following words, which are customary in Zu-Vendis if the bride desires and the man consents:—

---

[1]In Zu-Vendis members of the Royal House can only be married by the High Priest or a formally appointed deputy.—A. Q.

'Thou dost swear by the Sun that thou wilt take no other woman to wife unless I lay my hand upon her and bid her come?'

'I swear it,' answered Sir Henry; adding in English, 'One is quite enough for me.'

Then Agon, who had been sulking in a corner near the altar, came forward and gabbled off something into his beard at such a rate that I could not follow it, but it appeared to be an invocation to the Sun to bless the union and make it fruitful. I observed that Nyleptha listened very closely to every word, and afterwards discovered that she was afraid lest Agon should play her a trick, and by going through the invocations backwards divorce instead of marry them. At the end of the invocations they were asked, as in our service, if they took each other for husband and wife, and on their assenting they kissed each other before the altar, and the service was over, so far as their rites were concerned. But it seemed to me that there was yet something wanting, and so I produced a Prayer-Book, which, together with the 'Ingoldsby Legends,' that I often read when I lie awake at night, has accompanied me in all my later wanderings. I gave it to my poor boy Harry years ago, and after his death I found it among his things and took it back again.

'Curtis,' I said, 'I am not a clergyman, and I do not know if what I am going to propose is allowable—I know it is not legal— but if you and the Queen have no objection I should like to read the English marriage service over you. It is a solemn step which you are taking, and I think that you ought, so far as circumstances will allow, to give it the sanction of your own religion.'

'I have thought of that,' he said, 'and I wish you would. I do not feel half married yet.'

Nyleptha raised no objection, fully understanding that her husband wished to celebrate the marriage according to the rites prevailing in his own country, and so I set to work and read the service, from 'Dearly beloved' to 'amazement,' as well as I could; and when I came to 'I, Henry, take thee, Nyleptha,' I translated, and also 'I, Nyleptha, take thee, Henry,' which she repeated after me very well. Then Sir Henry took a plain gold ring from his little finger and placed it on hers, and so on to the end. The ring had been Curtis' mother's wedding-ring, and I could not help thinking how astonished the dear old Yorkshire lady would have been if she could have foreseen that her wedding-ring was to serve a similar purpose for Nyleptha, a Queen of the Zu-Vendi.

As for Agon, he was kept calm with difficulty while this second ceremony was going on, for he soon understood that it was religious in its nature, and doubtless bethought him of the ninety-five new faiths which loomed so ominously in his eyes. Indeed, he set me down at once as a rival High Priest, and hated me accordingly. However, in the end off he went, positively bristling with indignation, and I knew that we might look out for danger from his direction.

And off went Good and I, and old Umslopogaas also, leaving the happy pair to themselves, and very low we all felt. Marriages are supposed to be cheerful things, but my experience is that they are very much the reverse to everybody, except perhaps the two people chiefly interested. They mean the breaking-up of so many old ties as well as the undertaking of so many new ones, and there is always something sad about the passing away of the old order. Now to take this case for instance: Sir Henry Curtis is the best and kindest fellow and friend in the world, but he has never been quite the same since that little scene in the chapel. It is always Nyleptha this and Nyleptha that—Nyleptha, in short, from morning till night in one way or another, either expressed or understood. And as for the old friends—well, of course they have taken the place that old friends ought to take, and which ladies are as a rule very careful to see they do take when a man marries, and that is, the second place. Yes, he would be angry if anybody said so, but it is a fact for all that. He is not quite the same, and Nyleptha is very sweet and very charming, but I think that she likes him to understand that she has married *him,* and not Quatermain, Good, and Co. But there! what is the use of grumbling? It is all very right and proper, as any married lady would have no difficulty in explaining, and I am a selfish, jealous old man, though I hope that I never show it.

So Good and I went and ate in silence and then indulged in an extra fine flagon of old Zu-Vendian to keep our spirits up, and presently one of our attendants came and told a story that gave us something to think about.

It may, perhaps, be remembered that, after his quarrel with Umslopogaas, Alphonse had gone off in an exceedingly ill temper to sulk over his scratches. Well, it appears that he walked straight past the Temple to the Sun, down the wide road on the further side of the slope it crowns, and thence on into the beautiful park, or pleasure gardens, which are laid out just beyond the outer wall. After wandering about there for a little he started to return, but was met near the outer gate by Sorais' train of chariots, which were galloping furiously along the great northern road. When she caught sight of Alphonse, Sorais halted her train and called to him. On approaching he was instantly seized and dragged into one of the chariots and carried off, 'crying out loudly,' as our informant said, and as from my general knowledge of him I can well believe.

At first I was much puzzled to know what object Sorais could have had in kidnapping the poor little Frenchman. She could hardly stoop so low as to try to wreak her fury on one whom she knew was only a servant. It would not be in keeping with her character to do so. At last, however, an idea occurred to me. We three, as I think I have said, were much revered by the people of Zu-Vendis at large, both because we are the first strangers they had ever seen, and because we were supposed to be the possessors of almost supernatural wisdom. Indeed, though Sorais' cry against the 'foreign wolves'—or, to translate it more accurately, 'foreign hyenas'—was sure to go down very well with the nobles and the priests, it was not, as we learnt, likely to be particularly effectual amongst the bulk of the population. The Zu-Vendi people, like the Athenians of old, are ever seeking for some new thing, and just because we were so new our presence was on the whole acceptable to them. Again, Sir Henry's magnificent personal appearance made a deep impression upon a race who possess a greater love of beauty than any other I have ever been acquainted with. Beauty may be prized in other countries, but in Zu-Vendis it is almost worshipped, as indeed the national love of statuary shows. The people said openly in the market-places that there was not a man in the country to touch Curtis in personal appearance, as with the exception of Sorais there was no woman who could compete with Nyleptha, and that it was meet therefore that they should marry; and that he had been sent by the Sun as a husband for their Queen. Now, from all this it will be seen that the outcry against us was to a considerable extent fictitious, and nobody knew it better than Sorais herself. Consequently it struck me that it might have occurred to her that down in the country and among the country people, it would be better to place the reason of her conflict with her sister upon other and more general grounds than Nyleptha's marriage with the stranger. It would be easy in a land where there had been so many civil wars to rake out some old cry that would stir up the recollection of buried feuds, and, indeed, she soon found an effectual one. This being so, it was of great importance to her to have one of the strangers with her whom she could show to the common people as a great Outlander, who had been so struck by the justice of her cause that he had elected to leave his companions and follow her standard.

This no doubt was the cause of her anxiety to get a hold of Good, whom she would have used till he ceased to be of service and then cast off. But Good having drawn back she grasped at the opportunity of securing Alphonse, who was not unlike him in personal appearance though smaller, no doubt with the object of showing him off in the cities and country as the great Bougwan himself. I told Good that I though this to be her plan, and his face was a sight to see—he was so horrified at the idea.

'What,' he said, 'dress up that little wretch to represent me? Why, I shall have to get out of the country! My reputation will be ruined for ever.'

I consoled him as well as I could but it is not pleasant to be personated all over a strange country by an arrant little coward, and I can quite sympathise with his vexation.

Well, that night, as I have said, Good and I messed in solitary grandeur, feeling very much as though we had just returned from burying a friend instead of marrying one, and next morning the work began in good earnest. The messages and orders which had been despatched by Nyleptha two days before now began to take effect, and multitudes of armed men came pouring into the city. We saw, as may be imagined, but very little of Nyleptha and not too much of Curtis during those next few days, but Good and I sat daily with the council of generals and loyal lords, drawing up plans of action, arranging commissariat matters, the distribution of commands, and a hundred and one other things. Men came in freely, and all the day long the great roads leading to Milosis were spotted with the banners of lords arriving from their distant places to rally round Nyleptha.

After the first two days it became clear that we should be able to take the field with about forty thousand infantry and twenty thousand cavalry, a very respectable force considering how short was the time we had to collect it, and also that about half of the regular army had elected to follow Sorais.

But if our force was large, Sorais', according to the reports brought in day by day by our spies, was much larger. She had taken up her headquarters at a very strong town called M'Arstuna, situated, as I have said, to the north of Milosis, and all the country-side was flocking to her standard. Nasta had poured down from his highlands and was on his way to join her with no less than twenty-five thousand of his mountaineers, the most terrible soldiers to face in all Zu-Vendis. Another mighty lord, named Belusha, who lived in the great horse-breeding district, had come in with twelve thousand cavalry, and so on. Indeed, what between one thing and another, it seemed certain that she would gather a fully armed host of nearly one hundred thousand men.

And then came news that Sorais was proposing to break up her camp and march on the Frowning City itself, desolating the country as she came. Thereon arose the question whether it would be best to meet her at Milosis or to go out and give her battle. When our opinion was asked upon the subject, Good and I unhesitatingly gave it in favour of an advance. If we were to shut ourselves up in the city and wait to be attacked, it seemed to us that our inaction would be set down to fear. It is so important, especially on an occasion of this sort, when a very little will suffice to turn men's opinions one way or the other, to be up and doing something. Ardour for a cause will soon evaporate if the cause does not move but sits down to conquer. Therefore we cast our vote for moving out and giving battle in the open, instead of waiting till we were drawn from our walls like a badger from a hole.

Sir Henry's opinion coincided with ours, and so, heedless to say, did that of Nyleptha, who, like a flint, was always ready to flash out fire. A great map of the country was brought and spread out before her. About thirty miles this side of M'Arstuna, where Sorais lay, and ninety odd miles from Milosis, the road ran over a neck of land some two and a half miles in width, and flanked on either side by forest-clad hills which, without being lofty, if the path were blocked, would be quite impracticable for a great baggage-laden army to cross. She looked earnestly at the map, and then, with a quickness of perception that in some women amounts almost to an instinct, she laid her finger upon this neck of rising ground, and turning to her husband, said, with a proud air of confidence and a toss of the golden head—

'Here shalt thou meet Sorais' armies. I know the spot, here shalt shou meet them, and drive them before thee like dust before the storm.'

But Curtis looked grave and answered nothing.

CHAPTER XX.

THE BATTLE OF THE PASS.

It was on the third morning after this incident of the map that Sir Henry and I started. With the exception of a small guard, all the great host had moved on the night before, leaving the Frowning City very silent and empty. Indeed, it was found impossible to spare any garrison with the exception of a personal guard for Nyleptha, and about a thousand men who from sickness or one cause or another were unable to proceed with the army; but as Milosis was practically impregnable, and as our enemy was in front of and not behind us, this did not so much matter.

Good and Umslopogaas had gone on with the army, but Nyleptha accompanied Sir Henry and myself to the city gates, riding a magnificent white horse called Daylight, which was supposed to be the fleetest and most enduring animal in Zu-Vendis. Her face bore traces of recent weeping, but there were no tears in her eyes now, indeed she was bearing up bravely against what must have been a bitter trial to her. At the gate she reined in her horse and bade us farewell. On the previous day she had reviewed and addressed the officers of the great army, speaking to them such high, eloquent words, and expressing so complete a confidence in their valour and in their ultimate victory, that she quite carried their hearts away, and as she rode from rank to rank they cheered her till the ground shook. And now to-day the same mood seemed to be on her.

'Fare thee well, Macumazahn!' she said. 'Remember, I trust to thy wits, which are as a needle to a spear-handle compared to those of my people, to save us from Sorais. I know that thou wilt do thy duty.'

I bowed and explained to her my horror of fighting, and my fear lest I should lose my head, at which she laughed gently and turned to Curtis.

'Fare thee well, my lord!' she said. 'Come back with victory, and as a king, or on thy soldiers' spears.'[1]

Sir Henry said nothing, but turned his horse to go; perhaps he had a bit of a lump in his throat. One gets over it afterwards, but these sort of partings are trying when one has only been married a week.

'Here,' added Nyleptha, 'will I greet ye when ye return in triumph. And now, my lords, once more, farewell!'

Then we rode on, but when we had gone a hundred and fifty yards or so, we turned and perceived her still sitting on her horse at the same spot, and looking out after us beneath her hand, and that was the last we saw of her. About a mile farther on, however, we heard galloping behind us, and looking round, saw a mounted soldier coming towards us leading Nyleptha's steed—Daylight.

'The Queen sends the white stallion as a farewell gift to her Lord Incubu, and bids me tell my lord that he is the fleetest and the most enduring horse in all the land,' said the soldier, bending to his saddle-bow before us.

At first Sir Henry did not want to take the horse, saying that he was too good for such rough work, but I persuaded

[1] Alluding to the Zu-Vendi custom of carrying dead officers on a framework of spears.—A. Q.

him to do so, thinking that Nyleptha would be hurt if he did not. Little did I guess at the time what service that noble horse would render in our sorest need. It is curious to look back and realise upon what trivial and apparently accidental circumstances great events frequently turn as easily and naturally as a door on its hinges.

Well, we took the horse, and he was a beauty, it was a perfect pleasure to see him move. Then Curtis having sent back his greetings and thanks, we proceeded on our journey.

By mid-day we overtook the rear-guard of the great army of which Sir Henry now formally took over the command. It was a heavy responsibility, and it oppressed him very much, but the Queen's injunctions on the point were such as did not admit of being trifled with. He was beginning to find out that greatness has its responsibilities as well as its glories.

Then we marched on without meeting with any opposition, almost indeed without seeing anybody, for the populations of the towns and villages along our route had fled for the most part, fearing lest they should be caught between the two rival armies and ground to powder like grain between the upper and the nether stones.

On the evening of the fourth day, for the progress of so great a multitude necessarily was slow, we camped two miles this side of the neck or ridge I have spoken of, and our outposts brought us word that Sorais with all her power was rolling down upon us, and had pitched her camp that night ten miles from the farther side of the neck.

Accordingly before dawn we sent forward fifteen hundred cavalry to seize the position. Scarcely had they occupied it, however, before they were attacked by about as many of Sorais' horsemen, and a very smart little cavalry fight ensued, with a loss to us of about thirty men killed. On the advance of our supports, however, Sorais' force drew off, carrying their dead and wounded with them.

The main body of the army reached the neck about dinner-time, and I must say that Nyleptha's judgment had not failed her, it was an admirable place to give battle in, especially against a superior force.

The road ran down a mile or more, through ground too broken to admit of the handling of any considerable force, till it reached the crest of a great green wave of land, that rolled down a gentle slope to the banks of a little stream, and then rolled away again up a still gentler slope to the plain beyond, the distance from the crest of the land-wave down to the stream being a little over half a mile, and from the stream up to the plain beyond a trifle less. The length of this wave of land at its highest point, which corresponded exactly with the width of the neck of land between the wooded hills, was about two miles and a quarter, and it was protected on either side by dense, rocky, bush-clad ground, that afforded a most valuable cover to the flanks of the army and rendered it almost impossible for them to be turned.

It was on the hither slope of this rocky neck that Curtis encamped his army in the same formation that, after consultation with the various generals, Good, and myself, he had determined that they should occupy in the great pitched battle which now appeared to be imminent.

Our force of sixty thousand men, roughly speaking, was divided as follows. In the centre was a dense body of twenty thousand foot-soldiers, armed with spears, swords, and hippopotamus-hide shields, breast and back plates.[1] These formed the chest of the army, and were supported by five thousand foot, and three thousand horse in reserve. On either side of this chest were stationed seven thousand horse arranged in deep, majestic squadrons; and beyond and on either side but slightly in front of them again were two bodies, each numbering about seven thousand five hundred spearmen, forming the right and left wings of the army, and each supported by a contingent of some fifteen hundred cavalry. This makes in all sixty thousand men.

Curtis commanded in chief, I was in command of the seven thousand horse between the chest and right wing, which was commanded by Good, the other battalions and squadrons being entrusted to Zu-Vendi generals.

Scarcely had we taken up our positions before Sorais' vast army began to swarm on the opposite slope about a mile in front of us, till the whole place seemed alive with the multitude of her spear-points, and the ground shook with the tramp of her battalions. It was evident that the spies had not exaggerated; we were outnumbered by at least a third. At first we expected that Sorais was going to attack us at once, as the clouds of cavalry which hung upon her flanks executed some threatening demonstrations, but she thought better of it, and there was no fight that day. As for the formation of her great forces I cannot now describe it with accuracy, and it would only serve to bewilder if I did, but I may say, generally, that in its leading features it resembled our own, only her reserve was much greater.

Opposite our right wing, and forming Sorais' left wing, was

[1]The Zu-Vendi people do not use bows.—A. Q.

a great army of dark, wild-looking men, armed with sword and shield, only, which, I was informed, was composed of Nasta's twenty-five thousand savage hillsmen.

'My word, Good,' said I, when I saw them, 'you will catch it to-morrow when those gentlemen charge!' whereat Good not unnaturally looked rather anxious.

All day we watched and waited, but nothing happened, and at last night fell, and a thousand watch-fires twinkled brightly on the slopes, to wane and die one by one like the stars they resembled. As the hours wore on, the silence gradually gathered more deeply over the opposing hosts.

It was a very wearying night, for in addition to the endless things that had to be attended to, there was our gnawing suspense to reckon with. The fray which to-morrow would witness would be so vast, and the slaughter so awful, that stout indeed must the heart have been that was not overwhelmed at the prospect. And when I thought of all that hung upon it, I own I felt ill, and it made me very sad to reflect that these mighty forces were gathered for destruction, simply to gratify the jealous anger of a woman. This was the hidden power which was to send those dense masses of cavalry, flashing like human thunderbolts across the plain, and to roll together the fierce battalions as clouds when hurricane meets hurricane. It was a dreadful thought, and set one wondering about the responsibilities of the great ones of the earth. Deep into the night we sat, with pale faces and heavy hearts, and took counsel, whilst the sentries tramped up and down, down and up, and the armed and plumed generals came and went, grim and shadow-like.

And so the time wore away, till everything was ready for the coming slaughter; and I lay down and thought, and tried to get a little rest, but could not sleep for fear of the morrow— for who could say what the morrow would bring forth? Misery and death, this was certain; beyond that we knew not, and I confess I was very much afraid. But as I realised then, it is useless to question that eternal Sphinx, the future. From day to day she reads aloud the riddles of the yesterday, of which the puzzled worldlings of all ages have not answered one, nor ever will, guess they never so wildly or cry they never so loud.

And so at length I gave up wondering, being forced humbly to leave the issue in the balancing hands of Providence and the morrow.

And at last up came the red sun, and the huge camps awoke with a clash, and a roar, and gathered themselves together for battle. It was a beautiful and awe-inspiring scene, and old

Umslopogaas, leaning on his axe, contemplated it with grim delight.

'Never have I seen the like, Macumazahn, never,' he said. 'The battles of my people are as the play of children to what this will be. Thinkest thou that they will fight it out?'

'Ay,' I answered sadly, 'to the death. Content thyself, "Woodpecker," for once shalt thou peck thy fill.'

Time went on, and still there was no sign of an attack. A force of cavalry crossed the brook, indeed, and rode slowly along our front, evidently taking stock of our position and numbers. With this we did not attempt to interfere, as our decision was to stand strictly on the defensive, and not to waste a single man. The men breakfasted and stood to their arms, and the hours wore on. About mid-day, when the men were eating their dinner, for we thought they would fight better on full stomachs, a shout of '*Sorais, Sorais,*' arose like thunder from the enemy's extreme right, and taking the glass, I was able clearly to distinguish the 'Lady of the Night,' herself, surrounded by a glittering staff, and riding slowly down the lines of her battalions. And as she went, that mighty, thundering shout rolled along before her like the rolling of ten thousand chariots, or the roaring of the ocean when the gale turns suddenly and carries the noise of it to a listeners' ears, till the earth shook, and the air was full of the majesty of sound.

Guessing that this was a prelude to the beginning of the battle, we remained still and made ready.

We had not long to wait. Suddenly, like flame from a cannon's mouth, out shot two great tongue-like forces of cavalry, and came charging down the slope towards the little stream, slowly at first, but gathering speed as they went. Before they got to the stream, orders reached me from Sir Henry, who evidently feared that the shock of such a charge, if allowed to fall unbroken upon our infantry, would be too much for them, to send five thousand sabres to meet the force opposite to me, at the moment when it began to mount the stiffest of the rise about four hundred yards from our lines. This I did, remaining behind myself with the rest of my men.

Off went the five thousand horsemen, drawn up in a wedge-like form, and I must say that the general in command handled them very ably. Starting at a hand gallop, for the first three hundred yards he rode straight at the tip of the tongue-shaped mass of cavalry which, numbering, so far as I could judge, about eight thousand sabres, was advancing to charge us. Then he suddenly swerved to the right and put on the pace, and I saw the great wedge curl round, and before the foe could check himself and turn to meet it, strike him about halfway down his length, with a crashing rending sound, like that of the breaking-up of vast sheets of ice. In sank the great wedge, into his heart, and as it cut its way hundreds of horsemen were thrown up on either side of it, just as the earth is thrown up by a ploughshare, or more like still, as the foaming water curls over beneath the bows of a rushing ship. In, yet in, vainly does the tongue twist its ends round in agony, like an injured snake, and strive to protect its centre; still farther in, by Heaven! right through, and so, amid cheer after cheer from our watching thousands, back again upon the severed ends, beating them down, driving them as a gale drives spray, till at last, amidst the rushing of hundreds of riderless horses, the flashing of swords, and the victorious clamour of their pursuers, the great force crumples up like an empty glove, then turns and gallops pell-mell for safety back to its own lines.

I do not think it reached them more than two-thirds as strong as it went out ten minutes before. The lines which were now advancing to the attack, opened and swallowed them up, and my force returned, having only suffered a loss of about five hundred men—not much, I thought, considering the fierceness of the struggle. I could also see that the opposing bodies of cavalry on our left wing were drawing back, but how the fight went with them I do not quite know. It is as much as I can do to describe what took place immediately around me.

By this time the dense masses of the enemy's left, composed almost entirely of Nasta's swordsmen, were across the little stream, and with alternate yells of 'Nasta' and 'Sorais,' with dancing banners and gleaming swords, were swarming up towards us like ants.

Again I received orders to try and check this movement, and also the main advance against the chest of our army, by means of cavalry charges, and this I did to the best of my ability, by continually sending squadrons of about a thousand sabres out against them. These squadrons did the enemy much damage, and it was a glorious sight to see them flash down the hill-side, and bury themselves like a living knife in the heart of the foe. But, also, we lost many men, for after the experience of a couple of these charges, which had drawn a sort of bloody St. Andrew's cross of dead and dying through the centre of Nasta's host, our foes no longer attempted to offer an unyielding front to their irresistible weight, but opened out to let the rush go through, throwing themselves on the ground and hamstringing hundreds of horses as they passed.

And so, notwithstanding all that we could do, the enemy drew nearer, till at last he hurled himself upon Good's force of seven thousand five hundred regulars, who were drawn up to receive them in three strong squares. About the same time, too, an awful and heartshaking roar told me that the main battle had closed in on the centre and extreme left. I raised myself in my stirrups and looked down to my left; so far as the eye could see there was a long dazzling shimmer of steel as the sun glanced upon falling sword and thrusting spear.

To and fro swung the contending lines in that dread struggle, now giving way, now gaining a little in the mad yet ordered confusion of attack and defence. But it was as much as I could do to keep count of what was happening to our own wing; and, as for the moment the cavalry had fallen back under cover of Good's three squares, I had a fair view of this.

Nasta's wild swordsmen were now breaking in red waves against the sullen rock-like squares. Time after time did they yell out their war-cries, and hurl themselves furiously against the long triple ridges of spear points, only to be rolled back as billows are when they meet the cliff.

And so for four long hours the battle raged almost without a pause, and at the end of that time, if we had gained nothing we had lost nothing. Two attempts to turn our left flank by forcing a way through the wood by which it was protected had been defeated; and as yet Nasta's swordsmen, notwithstanding their desperate efforts, had entirely failed to break Good's three squares, though they had thinned their numbers by quite a third.

As for the chest of the army where Sir Henry was with his staff and Umslopogaas, it had suffered dreadfully, but it still held its own with honour, and the same may be said of our left battle.

At last the attacks slackened, and Sorais' army drew back, having, I began to think, had enough of it. On this point, however, I was soon undeceived, for splitting up her cavalry into comparatively small squadrons she charged us furiously with them, all along the line, and then once more sullenly rolled her tens of thousands of sword and spearmen down upon our weakened squares and squadrons; Sorais herself directing the movement, and fearless as a lioness heading the main attack. On they came like an avalanche—I saw her golden helm gleaming in the van—our counter charges of cavalry entirely failing to check their forward sweep. Now they had struck us, and our centre bent in like a bow beneath the weight of their rush—it parted, and had not the ten thousand men in reserve charged down to its support it must have been utterly destroyed. As for Good's three squares, they were swept backwards like boats upon an incoming tide, and the foremost one was burst into and lost half its remaining men. But the effort was too fierce and terrible to last. Suddenly the battle came, as it were, to a turning-point, and for a minute or two stood still.

Then it began to move towards Sorais' camp. Just then, too, Nasta's fierce and almost invincible highlanders, either because they were disheartened by their losses or by way of a ruse, fell back, and the remains of Good's gallant squares, leaving the positions they had held for so many hours, cheered wildly, and rashly followed them down the slope, whereon the swarms of swordsmen turned to envelop then, and once more flung themselves upon them with a yell. Taken thus on every side, what remained of the first square was quickly destroyed, and I perceived that the second, in which I could see Good himself mounted on a large horse, was on the point of annihilation. A few more minutes and it was broken, its streaming colours sank, and I lost sight of Good in the confused and hideous slaughter that ensued.

Presently, however, a cream-coloured horse with a snow-white mane and tail burst from the ruins of the square and came rushing past me riderless and with wide streaming reins, and in it I recognised the charger that Good had been riding. Then I hesitated no longer, but taking with me half my effective cavalry force, which now amounted to between four and five thousand men, I commended myself to God, and without waiting for orders, I charged straight down upon Nasta's swordsmen. Seeing me coming, and being warned by the thunder of my horses' hoofs, the majority of them faced round, and gave us a right warm welcome. Not an inch would they yield; in vain did we hack and trample them down as we ploughed a broad red furrow through their thousands; they seemed to re-arise by hundreds, driving their terrible sharp swords into our horses, or severing their hamstrings, and then hacking the troopers who came to the ground with them almost into pieces. My horse was speedily killed under me, but luckily I had a fresh one, my own favourite, a coal-black mare Nyleptha had given me, being held in reserve behind, and on this I afterwards mounted. Meanwhile I had to get along as best I could, for I was pretty well lost sight of by my men in the mad confusion of the moment. My voice, of course, could not be heard in the midst of the clanging of steel and the shrieks of rage and agony. Presently I found myself mixed up with the remnants of the square, which had formed round its leader Good, and was fighting desperately for existence. I stumbled against somebody, and glancing down, caught sight of Good's eyeglass. He had been beaten to his knee. Over him stood a great fellow swinging a heavy sword. Somehow I managed to run the man through with the sime I had taken from the Masai whose hand I had cut off; but as I did so, he dealt me a frightful blow on the left side and breast with his sword, and though my chain shirt saved my life, I felt that I was badly hurt. For a minute I fell on to my hands and knees among the dead and dying, and turned sick and faint. When I came to again I saw that Nasta's spearmen, or rather those of them who remained, were retreating back across the stream, and that Good was there by me smiling sweetly.

'Near go that,' he shouted; 'but all's well that ends well.'

I assented, but I could not help feeling that it had not ended well for me. I was sorely hurt.

Just then we saw the smaller bodies of cavalry stationed on our extreme right and left, and which were now reinforced by the three thousand sabres which we had held in reserve, flash out like arrows from their posts and fall upon the disordered flanks of Sorais' forces, and that charge decided the issue of the battle. In another minute or two the enemy was in slow and sullen retreat across the little stream, where they once more re-formed. Then came another lull, during which I managed to get my second horse, and received my orders to advance from Sir Henry, and then with one fierce deep-throated roar, with a waving of banners and a wide flashing of steel, the remains of our army took the offensive and began to sweep down, slowly indeed, but irresistibly from the positions they had so gallantly held all day.

At last it was our turn to attack.

On we moved, over the piled-up masses of dead and dying, and were approaching the stream, when suddenly I perceived an extraordinary sight. Galloping wildly towards us, his arms tightly clasped around his horse's neck, against which his blanched cheek was tightly pressed, was a man arrayed in the full costume of a Zu-Vendi general, but in whom, as he came nearer, I recognised none other than our lost Alphonse. It was impossible even then to mistake those curling black mustachios. In a minute he was tearing through our ranks and narrowly escaped being cut down, till at last somebody caught his horse's bridle, and he was brought to me just as a momentary halt occurred in our advance to allow what remained of our shattered squares to form into line.

'Ah, monsieur,' he gasped out in a voice that was nearly inarticulate with fright, 'grace to the sky, it is you! Ah, what I have endured! But you win, monsieur, you win; they fly, the laches. But listen, monsieur—I forget, it is no good; the Queen is to be murdered to-morrow at the first light in the palace of Milosis; her guards will leave their posts, and the priests are going to kill her. Ah yes! they little thought it, but I was ensconced beneath a banner, and I heard it all.'

'What?' I said, horror-struck; 'what do you mean?'

'What I say, monsieur; that devil of a Nasta he went last night to settle the affair with the Archbishop [Agon]. The guard will leave open the little gate leading from the great stair and go away, and Nasta and Agon's priests will come in and kill her. Themselves they would not kill her.'

'Come with me,' I said, and, shouting to the staff-officer next me to take over the command, I snatched his bridle and galloped as hard as I could for the spot, between a quarter and half a mile off, where I saw the royal pennon flying, and where I knew that I should find Curtis if he were still alive. On we tore, our horses clearing heaps of dead and dying men, and splashing through pools of blood, on past the long broken lines of spearmen to where, mounted on the white stallion Nyleptha had sent to him as a parting gift, I saw Sir Henry's form towering above the generals who surrounded him.

Just as we reached him the advance began again. A bloody cloth was bound round his head, but I saw that his eye was as bright and keen as ever. Beside him was old Umslopogaas, his axe red with blood, but looking quite fresh and uninjured.

'What's wrong, Quatermain?' he shouted.

'Everything. There is a plot to murder the Queen to-morrow at dawn. Alphonse here, who has just escaped from Sorais, has overheard it all,' and I rapidly repeated to him what the Frenchman had told me.

Curtis' face turned deadly pale and his jaw dropped.

'At dawn,' he gasped, 'and it is now sunset; it dawns before four and we are nearly a hundred miles off—nine hours at the outside. What is to be done?'

An idea entered into my head. 'Is that horse of yours fresh?' I said.

'Yes, I have only just got him—when my last was killed, and he has been fed.'

'So is mine. Get off him, and let Umslopogaas mount; he can ride well. We will be at Milosis before dawn, or if we are not—well, we cannot help it. No, no; it is impossible for you to leave now. You would be seen, and it would turn the fate of the battle. It is not half won yet. The soldiers would think you were making a bolt of it. Quick now.'

In a moment he was down, and at my bidding Umslopogaas sprang into the empty saddle.

'Now farewell,' I said. 'Send a thousand horsemen with re-mounts after us in an hour if possible. Stay, despatch a general to the left wing to take over command and explain my absence.'

'You will do your best to save her, Quatermain?' he said in a broken voice.

'Ay, that I will. Go on; you are being left behind.'

He cast one glance at us, and accompanied by his staff galloped off to join the advance, which by this time was fording the little brook that now ran red with the blood of the fallen.

As for Umslopogaas and myself, we left that dreadful field as arrows leave a bow, and in a few minutes had passed right out of the sight of slaughter, the smell of blood, and the turmoil and shouting, which only came to our ears as a faint, far-off roaring like the sound of distant breakers.

CHAPTER XXI.

AWAY! AWAY!

AT the top of the rise we halted for a second to breathe our horses; and, turning, glanced at the battle beneath us, which, illumined as it was by the fierce rays of the sinking sun staining the whole scene red, looked from where we stood more like some wild titanic picture than an actual hand-to-hand combat. The distinguishing scenic effect from that distance was the countless distinct flashes of light reflected from the swords and spears, otherwise the panorama was not so grand as might have been expected. The great green lap of sward in which the struggle was being fought out, the bold round outline of the hills behind, and the wide sweep of the plain beyond, seemed to dwarf it; and what was tremendous enough when one was in it, grew insignif-icant when viewed from the distance. But is it not thus with all the affairs and doings of our race about which we blow the loud trumpet and make such a fuss and a worry? How utterly antlike, and morally and physically insignificant, must they seem to the calm eyes that watch them from the arching depths above!

'We win the day, Macumazahn,' said old Umslopogaas, taking in the whole situation with a glance of his practised eye. 'Look, the Lady of the Night's forces give on every side, there is no

stiffness left in them, they bend like hot iron, they are fighting
with but half a heart. But alas! the battle will in a manner be
drawn, for the darkness gathers, and the regiments will not be
able to follow and slay!'—and he shook his head sadly. 'But,'
he added, 'I do not think that they will fight again, we have fed
them with too strong a meat. Ah! it is well to have lived! At
last I have seen a fight worth seeing, and I have seen many
fights.'

By this time we were on our way again, and as we went side
by side I told him what our mission was, and how that, if it failed,
all the lives that had been lost that day would have been lost
in vain.

'Ah!' he said, 'nigh on a hundred miles and no horses but these,
and to be there before the dawn! Well—away! away! man can
but try, Macumazahn; and mayhap we shall be there in time to
split that old "witch-finder's" [Agon's] skull for him. Once he
wanted to burn us, the old "rain-maker," did he? And now he
would set a snare for my mother [Nyleptha], would he? Good!
So sure as my name is the name of the Woodpecker, so surely,
be my mother alive or dead, will I split him to the beard. Ay, by
T'Chaka's head I swear it!' and he shook Inkosi-kaas as he galloped. By now the darkness was closing in, but fortunately there
would be a moon later, and the road was good.

On we sped through the twilight, the two splendid horses we
bestrode had got their wind by this, and were sweeping along
with a wide steady stride that neither failed nor varied for mile
upon mile. Down the sides of slopes we galloped, across wide
vales that stretched to the foot of far-off hills. Nearer and nearer
grew the blue hills; now we were travelling up their steeps, and
now we were over and passing towards others that sprang up like
visions in the far, faint distance beyond.

On, never pausing or drawing rein, through the perfect quiet
of the night, that was set like a song to the falling music of our
horses' hoofs; on, past deserted villages, where only some forgotten starving dog howled a melancholy welcome; on, past
lonely moated dwellings; on, through the white patchy moonlight,
that lay coldly upon the wide bosom of the earth, as though there
was no warmth in it; on, knee to knee, for hour after hour!

We spake not, but bent us forward on the necks of those two
glorious horses, and listened to their deep, long-drawn breaths
as they filled their great lungs, and to the regular unfaltering
ring of their round hoofs. Grim and black indeed did old Umslopogaas look beside me, mounted upon the great white horse, like
Death in the Revelation of St. John, as now and again lifting his

fierce set face he gazed out along the road, and pointed with his axe towards some distant rise or house.

And so on, still on, without break or pause for hour after hour.

At last I felt that even the splendid animal which I rode was beginning to give out. I looked at my watch; it was nearly midnight, and we were considerably more than half way. On the top of a rise was a little spring, which I remembered because I had slept by it a few nights before, and here I motioned to Umslopogaas to pull up, having determined to give the horses and ourselves ten minutes to breathe in. He did so, and we dismounted—that is to say, Umslopogaas did, and then helped me off, for what with fatigue, stiffness, and the pain of my wound, I could not do so for myself; and the gallant horses stood panting there, resting first one leg and then another, while the sweat fell drip, drip, from them, and the steam rose and hung in pale clouds in the still night air.

Leaving Umslopogaas to hold the horses, I hobbled to the spring and drank deep of its sweet waters. I had had nothing but a single mouthful of wine since mid-day, when the battle began, and I was parched up, though my fatigue was too great to allow me to feel hungry. Then, having laved my fevered head and hands, I returned, and the Zulu went and drank. Next we allowed the horses to take a couple of mouthfuls each—no more; and oh, what a struggle we had to get the poor beasts away from the water! There were yet two minutes, and I employed it in hobbling up and down to try and relieve my stiffness, and in inspecting the condition of the horses. My mare, gallant animal though she was, was evidently much distressed; she hung her head, and her eye looked sick and dull; but Daylight, Nyleptha's glorious horse—who, if he is served aright, like the steeds who saved the great Rameses in his need, should feed for the rest of his days out of a golden manger—was still comparatively speaking fresh, notwithstanding that he had by far the heavier weight to carry. He was 'tucked up,' indeed, and his legs were weary, but his eye was bright and clear, and he held his shapely head up and gazed out into the darkness round him in a way that seemed to tell us whoever failed *he* was good for those five-and-forty miles that yet lay between us and Milosis. Then Umslopogaas helped me into the saddle and—vigorous old savage that he was!—vaulted into his own without touching a stirrup, and we were off once more, slowly at first, till the horses got into their stride, and then more swiftly. So we passed over another ten miles, and then came a long, weary rise of some six or seven miles, and three times did my poor black mare nearly come to the ground with me. But on the top she seemed to gather herself together, and rattled down the slope with long, convulsive strides, breathing in gasps. We did that three or four miles more swiftly than any since we had started on our wild ride, but I felt it to be a last effort, and I was right. Suddenly my poor horse took the bit between her teeth and bolted furiously along a stretch of level ground for some three or four hundred yards, and then, with two or three jerky strides, pulled herself up and fell with a crash right on to her head, I rolling myself free as she did so. As I struggled on to my feet the brave beast raised her head and looked at me with piteous bloodshot eyes, and then her head dropped with a groan and she was dead. Her heart was broken.

Umslopogaas pulled up beside the carcase, and I looked at him in dismay. There were still more than twenty miles to do by dawn, and how were we to do it with one horse? It seemed hopeless, but I had forgotten the old Zulu's extraordinary running powers.

Without a single word he sprang from the saddle and began to hoist me into it.

'What wilt thou do?' I asked.

'Run,' he answered, seizing my stirrup-leather.

Then off we went again, almost as fast as before; and oh, the relief it was to me to get that change of horses! Anybody who has ever ridden against time will know what it meant.

Daylight sped along at a long stretching hand-gallop, giving the gaunt Zulu a lift at every stride. It was a wonderful thing to see old Umslopogaas run mile after mile, his lips slightly parted and his nostrils agape like the horse's. Every five miles or so we stopped for a few minutes to let him get his breath, and then flew on again.

'Canst thou go farther,' I said at the third of these stoppages, 'or shall I leave thee to follow me?'

He pointed with his axe to a dim mass before us. It was the Temple of the Sun, now not more than five miles away.

'I reach it or I die,' he gasped.

Oh, that last five miles! The skin was rubbed from the inside of my legs, and every movement of my horse gave me anguish. Nor was that all. I was exhausted with toil, want of food and sleep, and also suffering very much from the blow I had received on my left side; it seemed as though a piece of bone or something was slowly piercing into my lung. Poor Daylight, too, was pretty nearly finished, and no wonder. But there was a smell of dawn in the air, and we might not stay; better that all three of us should die upon the road than that we should linger while there was

life in us. The air was thick and heavy, as it sometimes is before
the dawn breaks, and—another infallible sign in certain parts
of Zu-Vendis that sunrise is at hand—hundreds of little spiders
pendant on the end of long tough webs were floating about in it.
These early-rising creatures, or rather their webs, caught upon
the horse's and our own forms by scores, and, as we had neither
the time nor the energy to brush them off, we rushed along
covered with hundreds of long grey threads that streamed out a
yard or more behind us—and a very strange appearance they
must have given us.

And now before us are the huge brazen gates of the outer wall
of the Frowning City, and a new and horrible doubt strikes me:
What if they will not let us in?

'*Open! open!*' I shout imperiously, at the same time giving
the royal password. '*Open! open!* a messenger, a messenger with
tidings of the war!'

'What news?' cried the guard. 'And who art thou that ridest
so madly, and who is that whose tongue lolls out'—and it actually
did—'and who runs by thee like a dog by a chariot?'

It is the Lord Macumazahn, and with him is his dog, his black
dog. *Open! open!* I bring tidings.'

The great gates ran back on their rollers, and the drawbridge
fell with a rattling crash, and we dashed on through the one and
over the other.

'What news, my lord, what news?' cried the guard.

'Incubu rolls Sorais back, as the wind a cloud,' I answered, and
was gone.

One more effort, gallant horse, and yet more gallant man!

So, fall not now, Daylight, and hold thy life in thee for fifteen
short minutes more, old Zulu war-dog, and ye shall both live for
ever in the annals of the land.

On, clattering through the sleeping streets. We are passing
the Flower Temple now—one mile more, only one little mile—
hold on, keep your life in ye, see the houses run past of themselves. Up, good horse, up, there—but fifty yards now. Ah! you
see your stables and stagger on gallantly.

'Thank God, the palace at last!' and see, the first arrows of the
dawn are striking on the temple's golden dome.[1] But shall I get
in here, or is the deed done and the way barred?

Once more I give the password and shout '*Open! open!*'

No answer, and my heart grows very faint.

Again I call, and this time a single voice replies, and to my

---

[1] Of course, the roof of the Temple, being so high, caught the light some
time before the breaking of the dawn.—A. Q.

joy I recognise it as belonging to Kara, a fellow-officer of Nyleptha's guards, a man I know to be as honest as the light—indeed, the same whom Nyleptha had sent to arrest Sorais on the day she fled to the temple.

'Is it thou, Kara?' I cry; 'I am Macumazahn. Bid the guard let down the bridge and throw wide the gate. Quick, quick!'

Then followed a space that seemed to me endless, but at length the bridge fell and one half of the gate opened and we entered the courtyard, where at last poor Daylight fell down beneath me, as I thought dead. I struggled free, and leaning against a post looked around. Except Kara, there was nobody to be seen, and his look was wild, and his garments were all torn. He had opened the gate and let down the bridge alone, and was now getting them up and shut again as, owing to a very ingenious arrangement of cranks and levers, one man could easily do, and indeed generally did do.

'Where are the guard?' I gasped, fearing his answer as I never feared anything before.

'I know not,' he answered; 'two hours ago, as I slept, was I seized and bound by the watch under me, and but now, this very moment, have I betrayed myself with my teeth. I fear, I greatly fear, that we are betrayed.'

His words gave me fresh energy. Catching him by the arm, I staggered, followed by Umslopogaas, who reeled after us like a drunken man, through the courtyards, up the great hall, which was silent as the grave, towards the Queen's sleeping-place.

We reached the first ante-room—no guards; the second, still no guards. Oh, surely the thing was done! we were too late after all, too late! The silence and solitude of those great chambers was dreadful, and weighed me down like an evil dream. On, right into Nyleptha's chamber we rushed and staggered, sick at heart, fearing the very worst; we saw there was a light in it, ay, and a figure bearing the light. Oh, thank God, it is the White Queen herself, the Queen unharmed! There she stands in her night gear, roused from her bed by the clatter of our coming, the heaviness of sleep yet in her eyes, and a red flush of fear and shame mantling her lovely breast and cheek.

'Who is it?' she cries. 'What means this? Oh, Macumazahn, is it thou? Why lookest thou so wildly? Thou comest as one bearing evil tidings—and my lord—oh, tell me not my lord is dead—not dead!' she wailed, wringing her white hands.

'I left Incubu wounded, but leading the advance against Sorais last night at sundown; therefore let thy heart have rest. Sorais is beaten back all along her lines, and thy arms prevail.'

'I knew it,' she cried in triumph. 'I knew that he would win; and they called him Outlander, and shook their wise heads when I gave him the command! Last night at sundown, sayest thou, and it is not yet dawn? Surely——'

'Throw a cloak around thee, Nyleptha,' I broke in, 'and give us wine to drink; ay, and call thy maidens quick if thou wouldst save thyself alive. Nay, stay not.'

Thus adjured she ran and called through the curtains towards some room beyond, and then hastily put on her sandals and a thick cloak, by which time a dozen or so of half-dressed women were pouring into the room.

'Follow us and be silent,' I said to them as they gazed with wondering eyes, clinging one to another. So we went into the first ante-room.

'Now,' I said, 'give us wine to drink and food, if ye have it, for we are near to death.'

The room was used as a mess-room for the officers of the guards, and from a cupboard some flagons of wine and some cold flesh were brought forth, and Umslopogaas and I drank, and felt life flow back into our veins as the good red wine went down.

'Hark to me, Nyleptha,' I said, as I put down the empty tankard. 'Hast thou here among these the waiting-ladies any two of discretion?'

'Ay,' she said, 'surely.'

'Then bid them go out by the side entrance to any citizens whom thou canst bethink thee of as men loyal to thee, and pray them come armed, with all honest folk that they can gather, to rescue thee from death. Nay, question not; do as I say, and quickly. Kara here will let out the maids.'

She turned, and selecting two of the crowd of damsels, repeated the words I had uttered, giving them besides a list of the names of the men to whom each should run.

'Go swiftly and secretly; go for your very lives,' I added.

In another moment they had left with Kara, whom I told to rejoin us at the door leading from the great courtyard on to the stairway as soon as he had made fast behind the girls. Thither, too, Umslopogaas and I made our way, followed by the Queen and her women. As we went we tore off mouthfuls of food, and between them I told her what I knew of the danger which encompassed her, and how we had found Kara, and how all the guards and menservants were gone, and she was alone with her women in that great place. She told me, too, that a rumour had spread through the town that our army had been utterly destroyed, and that Sorais was marching in triumph on Milosis, and how in consequence thereof all men had fallen away from her.

Though all this takes some time to tell, we had now been but six or seven minutes in the palace; and, notwithstanding that the golden roof of the temple being very lofty was ablaze with the rays of the rising sun, it was not yet dawn, nor would be for another ten minutes. We were in the courtyard now, and here my wound pained me so that I had to take Nyleptha's arm, while Umslopogaas rolled along after us, eating as he went.

Now we were across, and had reached the narrow doorway through the palace wall that opened on to the mighty stair.

I looked through and stood aghast, as well I might. The door was gone, and so were the outer gates of bronze—entirely gone. They had been taken from their hinges, and, as we found afterwards, hurled from the stairway to the ground two hundred feet beneath. There in front of us was the semi-circular standing-space, about twice the size of a large oval dining-table, and the ten curved black marble steps leading on to the main stair—and that was all.

CHAPTER XXII.

HOW UMSLOPOGAAS HELD THE STAIR.

WE looked one at another.

'Thou seest,' I said, 'they have taken away the door. Is there aught with which we may fill the place? Speak quickly, for they will be on us ere the daylight.' I spoke thus, because I knew that we must hold this place or none, as there were no inner doors in the palace, the rooms being separated one from another by curtains. I also knew that if we could by any means defend this doorway the murderers could get in nowhere else; for the palace is absolutely impregnable, that is, since the secret door by which Sorais had entered on that memorable night of attempted murder by Nyleptha's order had been closed up with masonry.

'I have it,' said Nyleptha, who, as usual with her, rose to the emergency in a wonderful way. 'On the farther side of the courtyard are blocks of cut marble—the workmen brought them there for the bed of the new statue of Incubu, my lord; let us block the door with them.'

I jumped at the idea; and having despatched one of the remaining maidens down the great stair to see if she could obtain assistance from the docks below, where her father, who was a great merchant employing many men, had his dwelling-place, and set another to watch through the doorway, we made our way back across the courtyard to where the hewn marble lay; and here we met Kara returning, having despatched the first two messengers. There were the marble blocks, sure enough, broad, massive lumps, some six inches thick, and weighing about eighty pounds each, and there, too, were a couple of implements like small stretchers, that the workmen used to carry them on. Without delay we set some of the blocks on the stretchers, and four of the girls carried them to the doorway.

'Listen, Macumazahn,' said Umslopogaas, 'if these low fellows come, it is I who will hold the stair against them till the door is built. Nay, it will be a man's death: gainsay me not, old friend, for this end was foretold me by one long dead. It has been a good day, now let it be good night. See, I throw myself down to rest yonder; when their footsteps are nigh, wake thou me, not before, for I need my strength,' and without a word he went outside and flung himself down on the marble, and was instantly asleep.

At this time, I, too was overcome, and was forced to sit down by the doorway, and content myself with directing operations. The girls brought the blocks, while Kara and Nyleptha built them up across the six-foot-wide doorway, a triple row of them, for less would be useless. But the marble had to be brought forty yards, and then there were forty yards to run back, and though the girls laboured gloriously, even staggering along alone, each with a block in her arms, it was slow work, dreadfully slow.

The light was growing now, and, presently, in the silence, we heard a commotion at the far-off bottom of the stair, and the faint clanking of armed men. As yet the wall was only two feet high, and we had been eight minutes at the building of it. So they had come. Alphonse had heard aright.

The clanking sound came nearer, and in the ghostly grey of the dawning we could make out long files of men, some fifty or so in all, slowly creeping up the stair. They were now at the half-way standing-place that rested on the great flying arch; and here, perceiving that something was going on above, to our great gain, they halted for three or four minutes and consulted, then slowly and cautiously advanced again.

We had been nearly a quarter of an hour at the work now, and it was almost three feet high.

Then I woke Umslopogaas. The great man rose, stretched himself, and swung Inkosi-kaas round his head.

'It is well,' he said. 'I feel as a young man once more. My strength has come back to me, ay, even as a lamp flares up before it dies. Fear not, I shall fight a good fight; the wine and the sleep have put a new heart into me.

'Macumazahn, I have dreamed a dream. I dreamed that thou and I stood together on a star, and looked down to the world, and thou wast as a spirit, Macumazahn, for light flamed through thy flesh, but I could not see what was the fashion of mine own face. The hour has come for us, old hunter. So be it: we have had our time, but I would that in it I had seen some more such fights as yesterday's.

'Let them bury me after the fashion of my people, Macumazahn, and set my eyes towards Zululand;' and he took my hand and shook it, and then turned to face the advancing foe.

Just then, to my astonishment, the Zu-Vendi officer Kara clambered over our improvised wall in his quiet, determined sort of way, and took his stand by the Zulu, unsheathing his sword as he did so.

'What, comest thou too?' laughed out the old warrior. 'Welcome—a welcome to thee, brave heart! Ow! for the man who can die like a man; ow! for the death grip and the ringing of steel. Ow! we are ready. We wet our beaks like eagles, our spears flash in the sun; we shake our assegais, and are hungry to fight. Who comes to give greeting to the Chieftainess [Inkosi-kaas]? Who would taste her kiss, whereof the fruit is death? I, the Woodpecker, I, the Slaughterer, I the Swiftfooted! I, Umslopogaas, holder of the axe, of the people of Amazulu, captain of the regiment of the Nkomabakosi: I, Umslopogaas, the son of the King's Tongue, the son of Makedama, I of the royal blood of T'Chaka, I, conqueror of the Unconquered, I the Ringed Man, I the Wolf-Man, I call to them as a buck calls, I challenge them, I await them. Ow! it is thou, it is thou!'

As he spake, or rather chanted, his wild war-song, the armed men, among whom in the growing light I recognised both Nasta and Agon, streamed along the stair with a rush, and one big fellow, armed with a heavy spear, dashed up the ten semicircular steps ahead of his comrades and struck at the great Zulu with a spear. Umslopogaas moved his body but not his legs, so that the blow missed him, and next instant Inkosi-kaas crashed through headpiece, hair and skull, and the man's corpse was rattling down the steps. As he dropped, his round hippopotamus-hide shield fell from his hand on to the marble, and the Zulu stooped down and seized it, still chanting as he did so.

In another second the sturdy Kara had also slain a man, and then began a scene the like of which has not been known to me. Up rushed the assailants, one, two, three at a time, and as fast as they came, the axe crashed and the sword swung, and down they rolled again, dead or dying. And ever as the fight thickened, the old Zulu's eye seemed to get quicker and his arm stronger. He shouted out his war-cries and the names of chiefs whom he had slain, and the blows of his awful axe rained straight and true, shearing through everything they fell on. There was none of the scientific method he was so fond of about this last immortal fight of his; he had no time for it, but struck with his full strength, and at every stroke a man sank in his tracks, and went rattling down the marble steps.

They hacked and hewed at him with swords and spears, wounding him in a dozen places till he streamed red with blood; but the shield protected his head and the chain-shirt his vitals, and for minute after minute, aided by the gallant Zu-Vendi, he still held the stair.

At last Kara's sword broke, and he grappled with a foe, and they rolled down together, and he was cut to pieces, dying like the brave man that he was.

Umslopogaas never blenched or turned. 'Galazi! Oh that thou wert here my brother Galazi!' he cried, and beat down a foe, ay, and another, and another, till at last they drew back from the slippery blood-stained steps, and stared at him in amazement, thinking that he was no mortal man.

The wall of marble block was four feet six high now, and hope rose in my heart as I leaned there against it a miserable helpless log, grinding my teeth, and watched that glorious struggle. I could do no more for I had lost my revolver in the battle.

And old Umslopogaas, he leaned too on his good axe, and, faint as he was with wounds, he mocked them, he called them 'women'—the grand old warrior, standing there one against so many! And for a breathing space none would come against him, notwithstanding Nasta's exhortations, till at last old Agon, who, to do him justice, was a brave man, mad with baffled rage, and seeing that the wall would soon be built and his plans defeated, shook the great spear he held, and rushed up the dripping steps.

'Ah, ah!' shouted the Zulu, as he recognised the priest's flowing white beard, 'it is thou, old "witch-finder!" Come on! I await thee, white "medicine man;" come on! come on! I have sworn to slay thee, and I ever keep my faith.'

On came Agon, taking him at his word, and drave the big spear with such force at Umslopogaas that it sunk right through the tough shield and pierced him in the neck. The Zulu cast down the transfixed shield, and that moment was Agon's last, for before he could free his spear and strike again, with a shout of

'*There's for thee, Rainmaker!*' Umslopogaas gripped Inkosi-kaas with both hands and whirled her on high and drove her right on to his venerable head, so that Agon rolled down dead among the corpses of his fellow-murderers, and there was an end of him and his plots together. And even as he fell, a great cry rose from the foot of the stair, and looking out through the portion of the doorway that was yet unclosed, we saw armed men rushing up to the rescue, and called an answer to their shouts. Then the would-be murderers who yet remained on the stairway, and amongst whom I saw several priests, turned to fly, but, having nowhere to go, were butchered as they fled. Only one man stayed, and he was the great lord Nasta, Nyleptha's suitor, and the father of the plot. For a moment the black-bearded Nasta stood with bowed face leaning on his long sword as though in despair, and then, with a dreadful shout, he too rushed up at the Zulu, and swinging the glittering sword around his head, dealt him such a mighty blow beneath his guard, that the keen steel of the heavy blade bit right through the chain armour and deep into Umslopogaas' side, for a moment paralysing him and causing him to drop his axe.

Raising the sword again, Nasta sprang forward to make an end of him but little he knew his foe. With a shake and a yell of fury, the Zulu gathered himself together and sprang straight at Nasta's throat, as I have sometimes seen a wounded lion spring. He struck him full as his foot was on the topmost stair, and his long arm closing round him like iron bands, down they rolled together struggling furiously. Nasta was a strong man and a desperate, but he could not match the strongest man in Zululand, sore wounded though he was, whose strength was as the strength of a bull. In a minute the end came. I saw old Umslopogaas stagger to his feet—ay, and saw him swing up the struggling Nasta by a single gigantic effort, and with a shout of triumph hurl him straight over the parapet of the bridge, to be crushed to powder on the rocks two hundred feet below.

The succour which had been summoned by the girl who had passed down the stair before the assassins passed up was at hand, and the loud shouts which reached us from the outer gates told us that the town was also aroused, and the men awakened by the women were calling to be admitted. Some of Nyleptha's brave ladies, who in their night-shifts and with their long hair streaming down their backs, just as they had been aroused from rest, had worked so gallantly at blocking the passage through the wall, went off to admit them at the side entrance, whilst others, assisted by the rescuing party outside, pushed and pulled down the marble blocks they had placed there with so much labour.

Soon the wall was down again, and through the doorway, followed by a crowd of rescuers, staggered old Umslopogaas, an awful and, in a way, a glorious figure. The man was a mass of wounds, and a glance at his wild eye told me that he was dying. The 'keshla' gum-ring upon his head was severed in two places by sword-cuts, one just over the curious hole in his skull, and the blood poured down his face from the gashes. Also on the right side of his neck was a stab from a spear, inflicted by Agon; there was a deep cut on his left arm just below where the mail-shirt stopped, and on the right side of his body the armour was severed by a gash six inches long, where Nasta's mighty sword had bitten through it and deep into its wearer's vitals.

On, axe in hand, he staggered, that dreadful-looking, splendid savage, and the ladies forgot to turn faint at the scene of blood, and cheered him, as well they might, but he never stayed or heeded. With outstretched arms and tottering gait he pursued his way, followed by us all along the broad shell-strewn walk that ran through the courtyard, past the spot where the blocks of marble lay, through the round arched doorway and the thick curtains that hung within it, down the short passage and into the great hall, which was now filling with hastily-armed men, who poured through the side entrance. Straight up the hall he went, leaving behind him a track of blood on the marble pavement, till at last he reached the sacred stone, which stood in the centre of it, and here his strength seemed to fail him, for he stopped and leaned upon his axe. Then suddenly he lifted up his voice and cried aloud:

'I die, I die—but it was a kingly fray. Where are they who came up the great stair? I see them not. Art thou there, Macumazahn, or art thou gone before to wait for me in the dark whither I go? The blood blinds me—the place turns round—I hear the voice of waters; Galazi calls me!'[1]

Next as though a new thought had struck him, he lifted the red axe and kissed the blade.

'Farewell, Inkosi-kaas,' he cried. 'Nay, nay, we will go together; we cannot part, thou and I. We have lived too long one with another, thou and I. None other shall hold thee.

'One more stroke, only one! A good stroke! a straight stroke! a strong stroke!' and, drawing himself to his full height, with a

<hr/>

[1] I do not know who Galazi was; Umslopogaas never spoke of him to me.—A. Q.

For the history of the life and death of Galazi see *Nada the Lily.*—ED.

wild heart-shaking shout, with both hands he began to whirl the axe round his head till it looked like a circle of flaming steel. Then, suddenly, with awful force he brought it down straight on to the crown of the mass of sacred stone. A shower of sparks flew up, and such was the almost superhuman strength of the blow, that the massive marble split with a rending sound into a score of pieces, whilst of Inkosi-kaas there remained but some fragments of steel and a fibrous rope of shattered horn that had been the handle. Down with a crash on to the pavement fell the fragments of the holy stone, and down with a crash on to them, still grasping the knob of Inkosi-kaas, fell the brave old Zulu—dead.

And thus the hero died.

A gasp of wonder and astonishment rose from all those who witnessed the extraordinary sight, and then somebody cried, *'The prophecy! the prophecy!* He has shattered the sacred stone!' and at once a murmuring arose.

'Ay,' said Nyleptha, with that quick wit which distinguishes her. 'Ay, my people, he has shattered the stone, and behold the prophecy is fulfilled, for a stranger king rules in Zu-Vendis. Incubu, my lord, hath beat Sorais back, and I fear her no more, and to him who hath saved the Crown it shall surely be. And this man,' she said, turning to me and laying her hand upon my shoulder, 'wot ye that, though wounded in the fight of yesterday, he rode, with that old warrior who lies there, one hundred miles 'twixt sun set and rise to save me from the plots of cruel men. Ay, and he has saved me, by a very little, and therefore because of the deeds that they have done—deeds of glory such as our history cannot show the like—therefore I say that the name of Macumazahn and the name of dead Umslopogaas, ay, and the name of Kara, my servant, who aided him to hold the stair, shall be blazoned in letters of gold above my throne, and shall be glorious for ever while the land endures. I, the Queen, have said it.'

This spirited speech was met with loud cheering, and I said that after all we had only done our duty, as it is the fashion of both Englishmen and Zulus to do, and there was nothing to make an outcry about; at which they cheered still more, and then I was supported across the outer court-yard to my old quarters, in order that I might be put to bed. As I went, my eyes lit upon the brave horse Daylight that lay there, his white head outstretched on the pavement, exactly as he had fallen on entering the yard; and I bade those who supported me take me near him, that I might look on the good beast once more before he was dragged away. And as I looked, to my astonishment, he opened his eyes and, lifting his head a little, whinnied faintly. I could have shouted for joy to find that he was not dead, only unfortunately I had not a shout left in me; but as it was, grooms were sent for and he was lifted up and wine poured down his throat, and in a fortnight he was as well and strong as ever, and is the pride and joy of all the people of Milosis, who, whenever they see him, point him out to the little children as the 'horse which saved the White Queen's life.'

Then I went on and got into bed, and was washed and had my mail shirt removed. They hurt me a good deal in getting it off, and no wonder, for on my left breast and side was a black bruise the size of a saucer.

The next thing that I remember was the tramp of horsemen outside the palace wall, some ten hours later. I raised myself and asked what was the news, and they told me that a large body of cavalry sent by Curtis to assist the Queen had arrived from the scene of the battle, which they had left two hours after sundown. When they left, the wreck of Sorais' army was in full retreat upon M'Arstuna, followed by all our effective cavalry. Sir Henry was encamping the remains of his worn-out forces on the site (such is the fortune of war) that Sorais had occupied the night before, and proposed marching on to M'Arstuna on the morrow. Having heard this, I felt that I could die with a light heart, and then everything became a blank.

When next I awoke the first thing I saw was the round disc of a sympathetic eye-glass, behind which was Good.

'How are you getting on, old chap?' said a voice from the neighbourhood of the eye-glass.

'What are you doing here?' I asked faintly. 'You ought to be at M'Arstuna—have you run away, or what?'

'M'Arstuna,' he replied cheerfully. 'Ah, M'Arstuna fell last week—you've been unconscious for a fortnight, you see—with all the honours of war, you know—trumpets blowing, flags flying, just as though they had had the best of it; but for all that, weren't they glad to go? Israel made for his tents, I can tell you—never saw such a sight in my life.'

'And Sorais?' I asked.

'Sorais—oh, Sorais is a prisoner; they gave her up, the scoundrels,' he added, with a change of tone—'sacrificed the Queen to save their skins, you see. She is being brought up here, and I don't know what will happen to her, poor soul' and he sighed.

'Where is Curtis?' I asked.

'He is with Nyleptha. She rode out to meet us to-day, and

there was a grand to do, I can tell you. He is coming to see you to-morrow; the doctors (for there is a medical "faculty" in Zu-Vendis as elsewhere) thought that he had better not come to-day.'

I said nothing, but somehow I thought to myself that notwith-standing the doctors he might have given me a look; but there, when a man is newly married and has just gained a great victory, he is apt to listen to the advice of doctors, and quite right too.

Just then I heard a familiar voice informing me that 'Monsieur must now couch himself,' and looking up perceived Alphonse's enormous black mustachios curling away in the distance.

'So you are here?' I said.

'Mais oui, Monsieur; the war is now finished, my military instincts are satisfied, and I return to nurse Monsieur.'

I laughed, or rather tried to; but whatever may have been Alphonse's failings as a warrior, and I fear that he did not come up to the level of his heroic grandfather in this particular, show-ing thereby how true is the saying that it is a bad thing to be overshadowed by some great ancestral name, a better or a kinder nurse never lived. Poor Alphonse! I hope he will always think of me as kindly as I think of him.

On the morrow I saw Curtis and Nyleptha with him, and he told me the whole history of what had happened since Umslopo-gaas and I galloped wildly away from the battle to save the life of the Queen. It seemed to me that he had managed the thing exceedingly well, and showed great ability as a general. Of course, however, our loss had been dreadfully heavy—indeed, I am afraid to say how many perished in the desperate battle I have described, but I know that the slaughter has appreciably affected the male population of the country. He was very pleased to see me, dear fellow that he is, and thanked me with tears in his eyes for the little I had been able to do. I saw him, however, start violently when his eyes fell upon my face.

As for Nyleptha, she was positively radiant now that 'her dear lord' had come back with no other injury than an ugly scar on his forehead. I do not believe that she allowed all the fearful slaughter that had taken place to weigh ever so little in the balance against this one fact, or even greatly to diminish her joy; and I cannot blame her for it, seeing that it is the nature of loving woman to look at all things through the spectacles of her love, and little does she reck of the misery of the many if the happiness of the *one* be assured. That is human nature, which the Positivists tell us is just perfection; so no doubt it is all right.

'And what art thou going to do with Sorais?' I asked her.

Instantly her bright brow darkened to a frown.

'Sorais,' she said, with a little stamp of the foot; 'ah, but Sorais!'

Sir Henry hastened to turn the subject.

'You will soon be about and all right again now, old fellow,' he said.

I shook my head and laughed.

'Don't deceive yourselves,' I said. 'I may be about for a little, but I shall never be all right again. I am a dying man, Curtis. I may die slow, but die I must. Do you know I have been spitting blood all the morning? I tell you there is something working away into my lung; I can feel it. There, don't look distressed; I have had my day, and am ready to go. Give me the mirror, will you? I want to look at myself.'

He made some excuse, but I saw through it and insisted, and at last he handed me one of the discs of polished silver set in a wooden frame like a hand-screen, which serve as looking-glasses in Zu-Vendis. I looked and put it down.

'Ah,' I said quietly, 'I thought so; and you talk of my getting all right!' I did not like to let them see how shocked I really was at my own appearance. My grizzled stubby hair was turned snow-white, and my yellow face was shrunk like an aged woman's, and two deep purple rings were painted beneath the eyes.

Here Nyleptha began to cry, and Sir Henry again turned the subject, telling me that the artists had taken a cast of the dead body of old Umslopogaas, and that a great statue in black marble was to be erected of him in the act of splitting the sacred stone, which was to be matched by another statue in white marble of myself and the horse Daylight as he appeared when, at the termination of that wild ride, he sank beneath me in the courtyard of the palace. I have since seen these statues, which at the time of writing this, six months after the battle, are nearly finished; and very beautiful they are, especially that of Umslopogaas, which is exactly like him. As for that of myself, it is good, but they have idealised my ugly face a little, which is perhaps as well, seeing that thousands of people will probably look at it in the centuries to come, and it is not pleasant to look at unsightly things.

Then they told me that Umslopogaas' last wish had been carried out, and that, instead of being cremated, as I shall be, after the usual custom here, he had been tied up, Zulu fashion, with his knees beneath his chin, and, having been wrapped in a thin sheet of beaten gold, entombed in a hole hollowed out of the masonry of the semicircular space at the top of the stair he defended so splendidly, which faces, as far as we can judge, almost exactly towards Zululand. There he sits, and will sit for ever, for they embalmed him with spices, and put him in an air-tight stone coffer, keeping his grim watch beneath the spot he held alone against a multitude; and the people say that at night his ghost rises and stands shaking the phantom of Inkosi-kaas at phantom foes. Certainly they fear during the dark hours to pass the place where the hero is buried.

Oddly enough, too, a new legend or prophecy has arisen in the land in that unaccountable way by which such things do arise among barbarous and semi-civilised people, blowing, like the wind, no man knows whence. According to this saying, so long as the old Zulu sits there, looking down the stairway he defended when alive, so long will the new House of the Stairway, springing from the union of the Englishman and Nyleptha, endure and flourish; but when he is taken from thence, or when, ages after, his bones at last crumble into dust, the House shall fall, and the Stairway shall fall, and the Nation of the Zu-Vendi shall cease to be a Nation.

CHAPTER XXIII.

I HAVE SPOKEN.

It was a week after Nyleptha's visit, when I had begun to get about a little in the middle of the day, that a message came to me from Sir Henry to say that Sorais would be brought before them in the Queen's first ante-chamber at midday, and request-ing my attendance if possible. Accordingly, greatly drawn by curiosity to see this unhappy woman once more, I made shift, with the help of that kind little fellow Alphonse, who is a perfect treasure to me, and that of another waiting-man, to reach the ante-chamber. I got there, indeed, before anybody else, except a few of the great Court officials who had been bidden to be pres-ent, but I had scarcely seated myself before Sorais was brought in by a party of guards, looking as beautiful and defiant as ever, but with a worn expression on her proud face. She was dressed, as usual, in her royal 'kaf,' emblazoned with the emblem of the Sun, and in her right hand she still held the toy spear of silver. A pang of admiration and pity went through me as I looked at her, and struggling to my feet I bowed deeply, at the same time expressing my sorrow that, owing to my condition, I was not able to remain standing before her.

She coloured a little and then laughed bitterly. 'Thou dost forget, Macumazahn,' she said, 'I am no more a Queen, save in blood; I am an outcast and a prisoner, one whom all men should scorn, and none show deference to.'

'At least,' I replied, 'thou art still a lady, and therefore one to whom deference is due. Also, thou art in an evil case, and therefore it is doubly due.'

'Ah!' she answered, with a little laugh, 'thou dost forget that I would have wrapped thee in a sheet of gold and hung thee to the angel's trumpet at the topmost pinnacle of the temple.'

'No,' I answered, 'I assure thee I forgot it not; indeed, I often thought of it when it seemed to me that the battle of the Pass was turning against us; but the trumpet is there, and I am still here, though perchance not for long, so why talk of it now?'

'Ah!' she went on, 'the battle! the battle! Oh, would that I were once more a Queen, if only for one little hour, and I would take such a vengeance on those accursed jackals who deserted me in my need; that it should only be spoken of in whispers; those women, those pigeon-hearted half-breeds who suffered themselves to be overcome!' and she choked in her wrath.

'Ay, and that little coward beside thee,' she went on, pointing at Alphonse with the silver spear, whereat he looked very uncomfortable; 'he escaped and betrayed my plans. I tried to make a general of him, telling the soldiers it was Bougwan, and to scourge valour into him' (here Alphonse shivered at some unhappy recollection), 'but it was of no avail. He hid beneath a banner in my tent and thus overheard my plans. I would that I had slain him, but, alas! I held my hand.

'And thou, Macumazahn, I have heard of what thou didst; thou art brave, and hast a loyal heart. And the black one too, ah, he was a *man*. I would fain have seen him hurl Nasta from the stairway.'

'Thou art a strange woman, Sorais,' I said; 'I pray thee now plead with the Queen Nyleptha, that perchance she may show mercy unto thee.'

She laughed out loud. '*I* plead for mercy!' she said, and at that moment the Queen entered, accompanied by Sir Henry and Good, and took her seat with an impassive face. As for poor Good, he looked intensely ill at ease.

'Greetings, Sorais!' said Nyleptha, after a short pause. 'Thou hast rent the kingdom like a rag, thou hast put thousands of my people to the sword, thou hast twice basely plotted to destroy my life by murder, thou hast sworn to slay my lord and his companions and to hurl me from the Stairway. What hast thou to say why thou shouldst not die? Speak, O Sorais!'

'Methinks my sister the Queen hath forgotten the chief count of the indictment,' answered Sorais in her slow musical tones. 'It runs thus: "Thou didst strive to win the love of my lord Incubu." It is for this crime that my sister will slay me, not because I levied war. It is perchance happy for thee, Nyleptha, that I fixed my mind upon his love too late.

'Listen,' she went on, raising her voice. 'I have nought to say save that I would I had won instead of lost. Do thou with me even as thou wilt, O Queen, and let my lord the King there' (pointing to Sir Henry)—'for now will he be King—carry out the sentence, as it is meet he should, for as he is the beginning of the evil, let him also be the end.' And she drew herself up and shot one angry glance at him from her deep fringed eyes, and then began to toy with her spear.

Sir Henry bent towards Nyleptha and whispered something that I could not catch, and then the Queen spoke.

'Sorais, ever have I been a good sister to thee. When our father died, and there was much talk in the land as to whether thou shouldst sit upon the throne with me, I being the elder, I gave my voice for thee and said, "Nay, let her sit. She is twin with me; we were born at a birth; wherefore should the one be preferred before the other?" And so has it ever been 'twixt thee and me, my sister. But now thou knowest in what sort thou hast repaid me, but I have prevailed, and thy life is forfeit, Sorais. And yet art thou my sister, born at a birth with me, and we played together when we were little and loved each other much, and at night we slept in the same cot with our arms each around the other's neck, and therefore, even now does my heart go out to thee, Sorais.

'But not for that would I spare thy life, for thy offence has been too heavy; it doth drag down the wide wings of my mercy even to the ground. Also, while thou dost live the land will never be at peace.

'Yet shalt thou not die, Sorais, because my dear lord here hath begged thy life of me as a boon; therefore as a boon and as a marriage gift give I it to him, to do with even as he wills, knowing that, though thou dost love him, he loves thee not, Sorais, for all thy beauty. Nay, though thou art lovely as the night in all her stars, O Lady of the Night, yet is it me his wife whom he loves, and not thee, and therefore do I give thy life to him.'

Sorais flushed up to her eyes and said nothing, and I do not think that I ever saw a man look more miserable than did Sir

Henry at that moment. Somehow, Nyleptha's way of putting the thing, though true and forcible enough, was not altogether pleasant.

'I understood,' stammered Curtis, looking at Good, 'I understood that you were attached—eh—attached to—to the Queen Sorais. I am—eh—not aware what the—in short, the state of your feelings may be just now; but if they happened to be that way inclined, it has struck me that—in short, it might put a satisfactory end to an unpleasant business. The lady also has ample private estates, where I am sure she would be at liberty to live unmolested so far as we are concerned, eh, Nyleptha? Of course, I only suggest.'

'So far as I am concerned,' said Good, colouring up, 'I am quite willing to forget the past; and if the Lady of the Night thinks me worth the taking I will marry her to-morrow, or when she likes, and try to make her a good husband.'

All eyes were now turned to Sorais, who stood with that same slow smile upon her beautiful face which I had noticed the first time that I ever saw her. She paused a little while, and cleared her throat, and then thrice she curtseyed low, once to Nyleptha, once to Curtis, and once to Good, and began to speak in measured tones.

'I thank thee, most gracious Queen and royal sister, for the loving-kindness thou hast shown me from my youth up, and especially in that thou hast been pleased to give my person and my fate as a gift to the Lord Incubu—the King that is to be. May prosperity, peace and plenty deck the life-path of one so merciful and so tender, even as flowers do. Long mayst thou reign, O great and glorious Queen, and hold thy husband's love in both thy hands, and many be the sons and the daughters of thy beauty. And I thank thee, my Lord Incubu—the King that is to be—I thank thee a thousand times in that thou hast been pleased to accept that gracious gift, and to pass it on to thy comrade in arms and in adventure, the Lord Bougwan. Surely the act is worthy of thy greatness, my Lord Incubu. And now, lastly, I thank thee also, my Lord Bougwan, who in thy turn hast deigned to accept me and my poor beauty. I thank thee a thousand times, and I will add that thou art a good and honest man, and I put my hand upon my heart and swear that I would that I could say thee "yea." And now that I have rendered thanks to all in turn'—and again she smiled—'I will add one short word.'

'Little can you understand of me, Queen Nyleptha and my Lords, if ye know not that for me there is no middle path; that I scorn your pity and hate you for it; that I cast off your forgiveness as though it were a serpent's sting; and that standing here, betrayed, deserted, insulted, and alone, I yet triumph over you, mock you, and defy you, one and all, and *thus* I answer you.' And then of a sudden, before anybody guessed what she intended to do she drove the little silver spear she carried in her hand into her side with such a strong and steady aim that the keen point projected through her back, and fell prone upon the pavement.

Nyleptha shrieked, and poor Good almost fainted at the sight, while the rest of us rushed towards her. But Sorais of the Night lifted herself upon her hands, and for a moment fixed her glorious eyes intently on Curtis's face, as though there were some message in the glance, then dropped her head and sighed, and with a sob her dark but splendid spirit passed.

Well, they gave her a royal funeral, and there was an end of her.

.   .   .   .

It was a month after the last act of the Sorais' tragedy that a great ceremony was held in the Flower Temple, and Curtis was formally declared King-Consort of Zu-Vendis. I was too ill to go myself; and, indeed, I hate all that sort of thing, with the crowds and the trumpet-blowing and banner-waving; but Good, who was there (in his full-dress uniform), came back much impressed, and told me that Nyleptha had looked lovely, and Curtis had borne himself in a right royal fashion, and had been received with acclamations that left no doubt as to his popularity. Also he told me that when the horse Daylight was led along in the procession, the populace had shouted '*Macumazahn, Macumazahn!*' till they were hoarse, and would only be appeased when he, Good, rose in his chariot and told them that I was too ill to be present.

Afterwards, too, Sir Henry, or rather the King, came to see me, looking very tired, and vowing that he had never been so bored in his life; but I dare say that that was a slight exaggeration. It is not in human nature that a man should be altogether bored on such an extraordinary occasion; and, indeed, as I pointed out to him, it was a marvellous thing that a man, who but little more than one short year before had entered a great country as an unknown wanderer, should to-day be married to its beautiful and beloved Queen, and lifted, amidst public rejoicings, to its throne. I even went the length to exhort him not to be carried away in the future by the pride and pomp of absolute power, but always to strive to remember that he was first a Christian gentleman, and next a public servant, called by Providence to a great and almost unprecedented trust. These remarks, which he might fairly have resented, he was so good as to receive with patience, and even to thank me for making them.

It was immediately after this ceremony that I caused myself to be moved to the house where I am now writing. It is a very pleasant country-seat, situated about two miles from the Frowning City, on to which it looks. That was five months ago, during the whole of which time, being confined to a kind of couch, I have employed my leisure in compiling this history of our wanderings from my journal and our joint memories. It is probable that it will never be read, but it does not much matter whether it is or not; at any rate, it has served to while away many hours of suffering, for I have suffered a deal of pain lately. Thank God, however, there will not be much more of it.

.   .   .   .   .   .

It is a week since I wrote the above, and now I take up my pen for the last time, for I know that the end is at hand. My brain is still clear and I can manage to write, though with difficulty. The pain in my lung, which has been very bad during the last week, has suddenly quite left me, and been succeeded by a feeling of numbness of which I cannot mistake the meaning. And just as the pain has gone, so with it all fear of that end has departed, and I feel only as though I were about to sink into the arms of an unutterable rest. Happily, contentedly, and with the same sense of security with which an infant lays itself to sleep in its mother's arms, do I lay myself down in the arms of the Angel Death. All the tremors, all the heart-shaking fears which have haunted me through a life that seems long as I look back upon it, have left me now; the storms have passed, and the Star of our Eternal Hope shines clear and steady on the horizon that seems so far from man, and yet is so very near to me to-night.

And so this is the end of it— a brief space of troubling, a few restless, fevered, anguished years, and then the arms of that great Angel Death. Many times have I been near to them, many and many a comrade have they embraced even at my side, and now it is my turn at last, and it is well. Twenty-four hours more and the world will be gone from me, and with it all its hopes and all its fears. The air will close in over the space that my form filled and my place know me no more; for the dull breath of the world's forgetfulness will first dim the brightness of my memory, and then blot it out for ever, and of a truth I shall be dead. So is it with us all. How many millions have lain as I lie, and thought these thoughts and been forgotten!—thousands upon thousands of years ago they thought them, those dying men of the dim past; and thousands on thousands of years hence will their descendants think them and be in their turn forgotten. 'As the breath of the oxen in winter, as the quick star that runs along the sky, as a little shadow that loses itself at sunset,' as I once heard a Zulu called Ignosi put it, such is the order of our life, the order that passeth away.

Well, it is not a good world—nobody can say that it is, save those who wilfully blind themselves to facts. How can a world be good in which Money is the moving power, and Self-interest the guiding star? The wonder is not that it is so bad, but that there should be any good left in it.

Still, now that my life is over, I am glad to have lived, glad to have known the dear breath of woman's love, and that true friendship which can even surpass the love of woman, glad to have heard the laughter of little children, to have seen the sun and the moon and the stars, to have felt the kiss of the salt sea on my face, and watched the wild game trek down to the water in the moonlight. But I should not wish to live again!

Everything is changing to me. The darkness draws near, and the light departs. And yet it seems to me that through that darkness I can already see the shining welcome of many a long-lost face. Harry is there, and others; one above all, to my mind the sweetest and most perfect woman that ever gladdened this grey earth. But of her I have already written elsewhere, and at length, so why speak of her now? Why speak of her after this long silence, now that she is again so near to me, now that I go where she has gone?

The sinking sun is turning the golden roof of the great Temple to a fiery flame, and my fingers tire.

So to all who have known me, or known of me, to all who can think one kindly thought of the old hunter, I stretch out my hand from the far-off shore and bid a long farewell.

And now into the hands of Almighty God, who sent it, do I commit my spirit.

'I have spoken,' as the Zulus say.

CHAPTER XXIV.

BY ANOTHER HAND.

A year has elapsed since our most dear friend Allan Quatermain wrote the words 'I have spoken' at the end of his record of our adventures. Nor should I have ventured to make any additions to the record had it not happened that by a most strange accident a chance has arisen of its being conveyed to England. The chance is but a faint one, it is true; but, as it is not probable that another will arise in our lifetimes, Good and myself think that we may as well avail ourselves of it, such as it is. During the last six months several Frontier Commissions have been at work on the various boundaries of Zu-Vendis, with a view of discovering whether there exists any possible means of ingress or egress from the country, with the result that a channel of communication with the outer world hitherto overlooked has been discovered. This channel, apparently the only one (for I have discovered that it was by it that the native who ultimately reached Mr. Mackenzie's mission station, and whose arrival in the country, together with the fact of his expulsion—for he *did* arrive about three years before ourselves—was for reasons of their own kept a dead secret by the priests to whom he was brought), is about to be effectually closed. But before this is done, a messenger is to be despatched bearing with him this manuscript, and also one or two letters from Good to his friends, and from myself to my brother George, whom it deeply grieves me to think I shall never see again, informing them, as our next heirs, that they are welcome to our effects in England, if the Court of Probate will allow them to take them,[1] inasmuch as we have made up our minds never to return to Europe. Indeed, it would be impossible for us to leave Zu-Vendis even if we wished to do so.

The messenger who is to go—and I wish him joy of his journey—is Alphonse. For a long while he has been wearied to death of Zu-Vendis and its inhabitants. 'Oh, oui, c'est beau,' he says, with an expressive shrug; 'mais je m'ennuie; ce n'est pas chic.' Again, he complains dreadfully of the absence of cafés and theatres, and moans continually for his lost Annette, of whom he says he dreams three times a week. But I fancy his secret cause of disgust at the country, putting aside the homesickness to which every Frenchman is subject, is that the people here laugh at him so dreadfully about his conduct on the occasion of the great battle of the Pass about eighteen months ago, when he hid beneath a banner in Sorais's tent in order to avoid being sent forth to fight, which he says would have gone against his conscience. Even the little boys call out at him in the streets, thereby offending his pride and making his life unbearable. At any rate, he has determined to brave the horrors of a journey of almost unprecedented difficulty and danger, and also to run the risk of falling into the hands of the French police to answer for a certain

[1] Of course the Court of Probate would allow nothing of the sort.—EDITOR.

little indiscretion of his own some years old (though I do not consider that a very serious matter), rather than remain in *ce triste pays*. Poor Alphonse! we shall be very sorry to part with him; but I sincerely trust, for his own sake and also for the sake of this history, which is, I think, worth giving to the world, that he may arrive in safety. If he does, and can carry the treasure we have provided him with in the shape of bars of solid gold, he will be, comparatively speaking, a rich man for life, and well able to marry his Annette, if she is still in the land of the living and willing to marry her Alphonse.

Anyhow, on the chance, I may as well add a word or two to dear old Quatermain's narrative.

He died at dawn on the day following that on which he wrote the last words of the last chapter. Nyleptha, Good and myself were present, and a most touching and yet in its way beautiful scene it was. An hour before the daybreak it became apparent to us that he was sinking, and our distress was very keen. Indeed, Good melted into tears at the idea—a fact that called forth a last gentle flicker of humour from our dying friend, for even at that hour he could be humorous. Good's emotion, by loosening the muscles, had naturally caused his eye-glass to fall from its accustomed place, and Quatermain, who always observed everything, observed this also.

'At last,' he gasped, with an attempt at a smile, 'I have seen Good without his eye-glass.'

After that he said no more till the day broke, when he asked to be lifted up to watch the rising of the sun for the last time.

'In a very few minutes,' he said, after gazing earnestly at it, 'I shall have passed through those golden gates.'

Ten minutes afterwards he raised himself and looked us fixedly in the face.

'I am going a stranger journey than any we have taken together. Think of me sometimes,' he murmured. 'God bless you all. I shall wait for you.' And with a sigh he fell back dead.

And so passed away a character that I consider went as near perfection as any it has ever been my lot to encounter.

Tender, constant, humorous, and possessing many of the qualities that go to make a poet, he was yet almost unrivalled as a man of action and a citizen of the world. I never knew any one so competent to form an accurate judgment of men and their motives. 'I have studied human nature all my life,' he would say, 'and I ought to know something about it,' and he certainly did. He had but two faults—one was his excessive modesty, and the other a slight tendency which he had to be jealous of anybody on whom he concentrated his affections. As regards the first of these points, anybody who reads what he has written will be able to form his own opinion; but I will add one last instance of it.

As the reader will doubtless remember, it is a favourite trick of his to talk of himself as a timid man, whereas really, though very cautious, he possessed a most intrepid spirit, and, what is more, never lost his head. Well, in the great battle of the Pass, where he got the wound that finally killed him, one would imagine from the account which he gives of the occurrence that it was a chance blow that fell on him in the scrimmage. As a matter of fact, however, he was wounded in a most gallant and successful attempt to save Good's life, at the risk and, as it ultimately turned out, at the cost of his own. Good was down on the ground, and one of Nasta's highlanders was about to dispatch him, when Quatermain threw himself upon his prostrate form and received the blow on his own body, and then, rising, killed the soldier.

As regards his jealousy, a single instance which I give in justice to myself and Nyleptha will suffice. The reader will, perhaps, recollect that in one or two places he speaks as though Nyleptha monopolised me, and he was left by both of us rather out in the cold. Now Nyleptha is not perfect, any more than any other woman is, and she may be a little *exigeante* at times, but as regards Quatermain the whole thing is pure imagination. Thus when he complains about my not coming to see him when he is ill, the fact was that, in spite of my entreaties, the doctors positively forbade it. Those little remarks of his pained me very much when I read them, for I loved Quatermain as dearly as though he were my own father, and should never have dreamed of allowing my marriage to interfere with that affection. But let it pass; it is, after all, but one little weakness, which makes no great show among so many and such lovable virtues.

Well, he died, and Good read the Burial Service over him in the presence of Nyleptha and myself, and then his remains, in deference to the popular clamour, were accorded a great public funeral, or rather cremation. I could not help thinking, however, as I marched in that long and splendid procession up to the Temple, how he would have hated the whole thing could he have been there to see it, for he had a horror of ostentation.

And so, a few minutes before sunset, on the third night after his death, they laid him on the brazen flooring before the altar, and waited for the last ray of the setting sun to fall upon his face. Presently it came, and struck him like a golden arrow, crowning the pale brows with glory, and then the trumpets blew, and the flooring revolved, and all that remained of our beloved friend fell into the furnace below.

We shall never see his like again if we live a hundred years. He was the ablest man, the truest gentleman, the firmest friend, the finest sportsman, and, I believe, the best shot in all Africa.

And so ended the very remarkable and adventurous life of Hunter Quatermain.

.   .   .   .

Since then things have gone very well with us. Good has been, and still is, busily employed in the construction of a navy on Lake Milosis and another of the large lakes, by means of which we hope to be able to increase trade and commerce, and also to overcome some very troublesome and warlike sections of the population who live upon their borders. Poor fellow! he is beginning to get over the sad death of that misguided but most attractive woman, Sorais, but it is a sad blow to him, for he was really deeply attached to her. I hope, however, that he will in time make a suitable marriage and get that unhappy business out of his head. Nyleptha has one or two young ladies in view, especially a daughter of Nasta's (who was a widower), a very fine imperial-looking girl, but with too much of her father's intriguing, and yet haughty, spirit to suit my taste.

As for myself, I should scarcely know where to begin if I set to work to describe my doings, so I had best leave them undescribed, and content myself with saying that, on the whole, I am getting on very well in my curious position of King-Consort—better, indeed, than I had any right to expect. But, of course, it is not all plain sailing, and I find the responsibilities very heavy. Still, I hope to be able to do some good in my time, and I intend to devote myself to two great ends—namely, to the consolidation of the various clans which together make up the Zu-Vendi people, under one strong central government, and to the sapping of the power of the priesthood. The first of these reforms, if it can be carried out, will put an end to the disastrous civil wars that have devastated this country for centuries; and the second, besides removing a source of political danger, will pave the road for the introduction of true religion in the place of this senseless Sun worship. I yet hope to see the shadow of the Cross of Christ lying on the golden dome of the Flower Temple; or, if I do not, that my successors may.

There is one more thing that I intend to devote myself to, and that is the total exclusion of all foreigners from Zu-Vendis. Not, indeed, that any more are ever likely to get here, but if they do, I warn them fairly that they will be shown the shortest way out of the country. I do not say this from any sense of inhospitality, but because I am convinced of the sacred duty that rests upon me of preserving to this, on the whole, upright and generous-hearted people the blessings of comparative barbarism. Where would all my brave army be if some enterprising rascal were to attack us with field-guns and Martini-Henrys? I cannot see that gunpowder, telegraphs, steam, daily newspapers, universal suffrage, &c., &c., have made mankind one whit the happier than they used to be, and I am certain that they have brought many evils in their train. I have no fancy for handing over this beautiful country to be torn and fought for by speculators, tourists, politicians and teachers, whose voice is as the voice of Babel, just as those horrible creatures in the valley of the underground river tore and fought for the body of the wild swan; nor will I endow it with the greed, drunkenness, new diseases, gunpowder, and general demoralisation which chiefly mark the progress of civilisation amongst unsophisticated peoples. If in due course it pleases Providence to throw Zu-Vendis open to the world, that is another matter; but of myself I will not take the responsibility, and I may add that Good entirely approves of my decision. Farewell.

Henry Curtis.

December 15, 18—.

P.S.—I quite forgot to say that about nine months ago Nyleptha (who is very well and, in my eyes at any rate, more beautiful than ever) presented me with a son and heir. He is a regular curly-haired, blue-eyed young Englishman in looks, and, though he is destined, if he lives, to inherit the throne of Zu-Vendis, I hope I may be able to bring him up to become what an English gentleman should be, and generally is—which is to my mind even a prouder and a finer thing than being born heir apparent to the great House of the Stairway, and, indeed, the highest rank that a man can reach upon this earth.

H. C.

NOTE BY GEORGE CURTIS, Esq.

The MS. of this history, addressed to me in the handwriting of my dear brother Henry Curtis, whom we had given up for dead, and bearing the Aden postmark, reached me in safety on December 20, 18—, or a little more than two years after it left his hands in the far centre of Africa, and I hasten to give the astonishing story it contains to the world. Speaking for myself,

I have read it with very mixed feelings; for though it is a great relief to know that he and Good are alive and strangely prosperous, I cannot but feel that for me and for all their friends they might as well be dead, since we can never hope to see them more.

They have cut themselves off from old England and from their homes and their relations for ever, and perhaps, under the circumstances, they were right and wise to do so.

How the MS. came to be sent I have been quite unable to discover; but I presume, from the fact of its being posted at all, that the little Frenchman, Alphonse, accomplished his hazardous journey in safety. I have, however, advertised for him and caused various inquiries to be made in Marseilles and elsewhere with a view of discovering his whereabouts, but so far without the slightest success. Possibly he is dead, and the packet was posted by another hand; or possibly he is now happily wedded to his Annette, but still fears the vengeance of the law, and prefers to remain *incognito*. I cannot say. I have not yet abandoned my hopes of finding him, but I am bound to say that they grow fainter day by day, and one great obstacle to my search is that nowhere in the whole history does Mr. Quatermain mention his surname. He is always spoken of as 'Alphonse,' and there are so many Alphonses. The letters which my brother Henry says he is sending with the packet of manuscript have never arrived, so I presume that they are lost or destroyed.

GEORGE CURTIS.

A CATALOGUE OF SELECTED DOVER BOOKS
IN ALL FIELDS OF INTEREST

A CATALOGUE OF SELECTED DOVER BOOKS
IN ALL FIELDS OF INTEREST

THE DEVIL'S DICTIONARY, Ambrose Bierce. Barbed, bitter, brilliant witticisms in the form of a dictionary. Best, most ferocious satire America has produced. 145pp. 20487-1 Pa. $1.75

ABSOLUTELY MAD INVENTIONS, A.E. Brown, H.A. Jeffcott. Hilarious, useless, or merely absurd inventions all granted patents by the U.S. Patent Office. Edible tie pin, mechanical hat tipper, etc. 57 illustrations. 125pp. 22596-8 Pa. $1.50

AMERICAN WILD FLOWERS COLORING BOOK, Paul Kennedy. Planned coverage of 48 most important wildflowers, from Rickett's collection; instructive as well as entertaining. Color versions on covers. 48pp. 8¼ x 11. 20095-7 Pa. $1.50

BIRDS OF AMERICA COLORING BOOK, John James Audubon. Rendered for coloring by Paul Kennedy. 46 of Audubon's noted illustrations: red-winged blackbird, cardinal, purple finch, towhee, etc. Original plates reproduced in full color on the covers. 48pp. 8¼ x 11. 23049-X Pa. $1.35

NORTH AMERICAN INDIAN DESIGN COLORING BOOK, Paul Kennedy. The finest examples from Indian masks, beadwork, pottery, etc. — selected and redrawn for coloring (with identifications) by well-known illustrator Paul Kennedy. 48pp. 8¼ x 11. 21125-8 Pa. $1.35

UNIFORMS OF THE AMERICAN REVOLUTION COLORING BOOK, Peter Copeland. 31 lively drawings reproduce whole panorama of military attire; each uniform has complete instructions for accurate coloring. (Not in the Pictorial Archives Series). 64pp. 8¼ x 11. 21850-3 Pa. $1.50

THE WONDERFUL WIZARD OF OZ COLORING BOOK, L. Frank Baum. Color the Yellow Brick Road and much more in 61 drawings adapted from W.W. Denslow's originals, accompanied by abridged version of text. Dorothy, Toto, Oz and the Emerald City. 61 illustrations. 64pp. 8¼ x 11. 20452-9 Pa. $1.50

CUT AND COLOR PAPER MASKS, Michael Grater. Clowns, animals, funny faces ... simply color them in, cut them out, and put them together, and you have 9 paper masks to play with and enjoy. Complete instructions. Assembled masks shown in full color on the covers. 32pp. 8¼ x 11. 23171-2 Pa. $1.50

STAINED GLASS CHRISTMAS ORNAMENT COLORING BOOK, Carol Belanger Grafton. Brighten your Christmas season with over 100 Christmas ornaments done in a stained glass effect on translucent paper. Color them in and then hang at windows, from lights, anywhere. 32pp. 8¼ x 11. 20707-2 Pa. $1.75

THE ART DECO STYLE, ed. by Theodore Menten. Furniture, jewelry, metalwork, ceramics, fabrics, lighting fixtures, interior decors, exteriors, graphics from pure French sources. Best sampling around. Over 400 photographs. 183pp. 8⅜ x 11¼.
22824-X Pa. $4.00

THE GENTLEMAN AND CABINET MAKER'S DIRECTOR, Thomas Chippendale. Full reprint, 1762 style book, most influential of all time; chairs, tables, sofas, mirrors, cabinets, etc. 200 plates, plus 24 photographs of surviving pieces. 249pp. 9⅞ x 12¾.
21601-2 Pa. $5.00

PINE FURNITURE OF EARLY NEW ENGLAND, Russell H. Kettell. Basic book. Thorough historical text, plus 200 illustrations of boxes, highboys, candlesticks, desks, etc. 477pp. 7⅞ x 10¾.
20145-7 Clothbd. $12.50

ORIENTAL RUGS, ANTIQUE AND MODERN, Walter A. Hawley. Persia, Turkey, Caucasus, Central Asia, China, other traditions. Best general survey of all aspects: styles and periods, manufacture, uses, symbols and their interpretation, and identification. 96 illustrations, 11 in color. 320pp. 6⅛ x 9¼.
22366-3 Pa. $5.00

DECORATIVE ANTIQUE IRONWORK, Henry R. d'Allemagne. Photographs of 4500 iron artifacts from world's finest collection, Rouen. Hinges, locks, candelabra, weapons, lighting devices, clocks, tools, from Roman times to mid-19th century. Nothing else comparable to it. 420pp. 9 x 12.
22082-6 Pa. $8.50

THE COMPLETE BOOK OF DOLL MAKING AND COLLECTING, Catherine Christopher. Instructions, patterns for dozens of dolls, from rag doll on up to elaborate, historically accurate figures. Mould faces, sew clothing, make doll houses, etc. Also collecting information. Many illustrations. 288pp. 6 x 9. 22066-4 Pa. $3.00

ANTIQUE PAPER DOLLS: 1915-1920, edited by Arnold Arnold. 7 antique cut-out dolls and 24 costumes from 1915-1920, selected by Arnold Arnold from his collection of rare children's books and entertainments, all in full color. 32pp. 9¼ x 12¼.
23176-3 Pa. $2.00

ANTIQUE PAPER DOLLS: THE EDWARDIAN ERA, Epinal. Full-color reproductions of two historic series of paper dolls that show clothing styles in 1908 and at the beginning of the First World War. 8 two-sided, stand-up dolls and 32 complete, two-sided costumes. Full instructions for assembling included. 32pp. 9¼ x 12¼.
23175-5 Pa. $2.00

A HISTORY OF COSTUME, Carl Köhler, Emma von Sichardt. Egypt, Babylon, Greece up through 19th century Europe; based on surviving pieces, art works, etc. Full text and 595 illustrations, including many clear, measured patterns for reproducing historic costume. Practical. 464pp.
21030-8 Pa. $4.00

EARLY AMERICAN LOCOMOTIVES, John H. White, Jr. Finest locomotive engravings from late 19th century: historical (1804-1874), main-line (after 1870), special, foreign, etc. 147 plates. 200pp. 11⅜ x 8¼.
22772-3 Pa. $3.50

VICTORIAN HOUSES: A TREASURY OF LESSER-KNOWN EXAMPLES, Edmund Gillon and Clay Lancaster. 116 photographs, excellent commentary illustrate distinct characteristics, many borrowings of local Victorian architecture. Octagonal houses, Americanized chalets, grand country estates, small cottages, etc. Rich heritage often overlooked. 116 plates. 11³/₈ x 10. 22966-1 Pa. $4.00

STICKS AND STONES, Lewis Mumford. Great classic of American cultural history; architecture from medieval-inspired earliest forms to 20th century; evolution of structure and style, influence of environment. 21 illustrations. 113pp. 20202-X Pa. $2.00

ON THE LAWS OF JAPANESE PAINTING, Henry P. Bowie. Best substitute for training with genius Oriental master, based on years of study in Kano school. Philosophy, brushes, inks, style, etc. 66 illustrations. 117pp. 6¹/₈ x 9¼. 20030-2 Pa. $4.00

A HANDBOOK OF ANATOMY FOR ART STUDENTS, Arthur Thomson. Virtually exhaustive. Skeletal structure, muscles, heads, special features. Full text, anatomical figures, undraped photos. Male and female. 337 illustrations. 459pp. 21163-0 Pa. $5.00

AN ATLAS OF ANATOMY FOR ARTISTS, Fritz Schider. Finest text, working book. Full text, plus anatomical illustrations; plates by great artists showing anatomy. 593 illustrations. 192pp. 7⁷/₈ x 10¾. 20241-0 Clothbd. $6.95

THE HUMAN FIGURE IN MOTION, Eadweard Muybridge. More than 4500 stopped-action photos, in action series, showing undraped men, women, children jumping, lying down, throwing, sitting, wrestling, carrying, etc. "Unparalleled dictionary for artists," American Artist. Taken by great 19th century photographer. 390pp. 7⁷/₈ x 10⁵/₈. 20204-6 Clothbd. $12.50

AN ATLAS OF ANIMAL ANATOMY FOR ARTISTS, W. Ellenberger et al. Horses, dogs, cats, lions, cattle, deer, etc. Muscles, skeleton, surface features. The basic work. Enlarged edition. 288 illustrations. 151pp. 9³/₈ x 12¼. 20082-5 Pa. $4.00

LETTER FORMS: 110 COMPLETE ALPHABETS, Frederick Lambert. 110 sets of capital letters; 16 lower case alphabets; 70 sets of numbers and other symbols. Edited and expanded by Theodore Menten. 110pp. 8¹/₈ x 11. 22872-X Pa. $2.50

THE METHODS OF CONSTRUCTION OF CELTIC ART, George Bain. Simple geometric techniques for making wonderful Celtic interlacements, spirals, Kells-type initials, animals, humans, etc. Unique for artists, craftsmen. Over 500 illustrations. 160pp. 9 x 12. USO 22923-8 Pa. $4.00

SCULPTURE, PRINCIPLES AND PRACTICE, Louis Slobodkin. Step by step approach to clay, plaster, metals, stone; classical and modern. 253 drawings, photos. 255pp. 8¹/₈ x 11. 22960-2 Pa. $4.50

THE ART OF ETCHING, E.S. Lumsden. Clear, detailed instructions for etching, drypoint, softground, aquatint; from 1st sketch to print. Very detailed, thorough. 200 illustrations. 376pp. 20049-3 Pa. $3.50

JEWISH GREETING CARDS, Ed Sibbett, Jr. 16 cards to cut and color. Three say "Happy Chanukah," one "Happy New Year," others have no message, show stars of David, Torahs, wine cups, other traditional themes. 16 envelopes. 8¼ x 11.
23225-5 Pa. $2.00

AUBREY BEARDSLEY GREETING CARD BOOK, Aubrey Beardsley. Edited by Theodore Menten. 16 elegant yet inexpensive greeting cards let you combine your own sentiments with subtle Art Nouveau lines. 16 different Aubrey Beardsley designs that you can color or not, as you wish. 16 envelopes. 64pp. 8¼ x 11.
23173-9 Pa. $2.00

RECREATIONS IN THE THEORY OF NUMBERS, Albert Beiler. Number theory, an inexhaustible source of puzzles, recreations, for beginners and advanced. Divisors, perfect numbers. scales of notation, etc. 349pp.   21096-0 Pa. $2.50

AMUSEMENTS IN MATHEMATICS, Henry E. Dudeney. One of largest puzzle collections, based on algebra, arithmetic, permutations, probability, plane figure dissection, properties of numbers, by one of world's foremost puzzlists. Solutions. 450 illustrations. 258pp.   20473-1 Pa. $2.75

MATHEMATICS, MAGIC AND MYSTERY, Martin Gardner. Puzzle editor for Scientific American explains math behind: card tricks, stage mind reading, coin and match tricks, counting out games, geometric dissections. Probability, sets, theory of numbers, clearly explained. Plus more than 400 tricks, guaranteed to work. 135 illustrations. 176pp.   20335-2 Pa. $2.00

BEST MATHEMATICAL PUZZLES OF SAM LOYD, edited by Martin Gardner. Bizarre, original, whimsical puzzles by America's greatest puzzler. From fabulously rare Cyclopedia, including famous 14-15 puzzles, the Horse of a Different Color, 115 more. Elementary math. 150 illustrations. 167pp.   20498-7 Pa. $2.00

MATHEMATICAL PUZZLES FOR BEGINNERS AND ENTHUSIASTS, Geoffrey Mott-Smith. 189 puzzles from easy to difficult involving arithmetic, logic, algebra, properties of digits, probability. Explanation of math behind puzzles. 135 illustrations. 248pp.   20198-8 Pa.$2.75 ·

BIG BOOK OF MAZES AND LABYRINTHS, Walter Shepherd. Classical, solid, and ripple mazes; short path and avoidance labyrinths; more —50 mazes and labyrinths in all. 12 other figures. Full solutions. 112pp. 8⅛ x 11.   22951-3 Pa. $2.00

COIN GAMES AND PUZZLES, Maxey Brooke. 60 puzzles, games and stunts —from Japan, Korea, Africa and the ancient world, by Dudeney and the other great puzzlers, as well as Maxey Brooke's own creations. Full solutions. 67 illustrations. 94pp.   22893-2 Pa. $1.25

HAND SHADOWS TO BE THROWN UPON THE WALL, Henry Bursill. Wonderful Victorian novelty tells how to make flying birds, dog, goose, deer, and 14 others. 32pp. 6½ x 9¼.   21779-5 Pa. $1.25

DECORATIVE ALPHABETS AND INITIALS, edited by Alexander Nesbitt. 91 complete alphabets (medieval to modern), 3924 decorative initials, including Victorian novelty and Art Nouveau. 192pp. 7¾ x 10¾. 20544-4 Pa. $3.50

CALLIGRAPHY, Arthur Baker. Over 100 original alphabets from the hand of our greatest living calligrapher: simple, bold, fine-line, richly ornamented, etc. — all strikingly original and different, a fusion of many influences and styles. 155pp. 11⅜ x 8¼. 22895-9 Pa. $4.00

MONOGRAMS AND ALPHABETIC DEVICES, edited by Hayward and Blanche Cirker. Over 2500 combinations, names, crests in very varied styles: script engraving, ornate Victorian, simple Roman, and many others. 226pp. 8⅛ x 11.

22330-2 Pa. $5.00

THE BOOK OF SIGNS, Rudolf Koch. Famed German type designer renders 493 symbols: religious, alchemical, imperial, runes, property marks, etc. Timeless. 104pp. 6⅛ x 9¼. 20162-7 Pa. $1.50

200 DECORATIVE TITLE PAGES, edited by Alexander Nesbitt. 1478 to late 1920's. Baskerville, Dürer, Beardsley, W. Morris, Pyle, many others in most varied techniques. For posters, programs, other uses. 222pp. 8⅜ x 11¼. 21264-5 Pa. $3.50

DICTIONARY OF AMERICAN PORTRAITS, edited by Hayward and Blanche Cirker. 4000 important Americans, earliest times to 1905, mostly in clear line. Politicians, writers, soldiers, scientists, inventors, industrialists, Indians, Blacks, women, outlaws, etc. Identificatory information. 756pp. 9¼ x 12¾. 21823-6 Clothbd. $30.00

ART FORMS IN NATURE, Ernst Haeckel. Multitude of strangely beautiful natural forms: Radiolaria, Foraminifera, jellyfishes, fungi, turtles, bats, etc. All 100 plates of the 19th century evolutionist's Kunstformen der Natur (1904). 100pp. 9⅜ x 12¼. 22987-4 Pa. $4.00

DECOUPAGE: THE BIG PICTURE SOURCEBOOK, Eleanor Rawlings. Make hundreds of beautiful objects, over 550 florals, animals, letters, shells, period costumes, frames, etc. selected by foremost practitioner. Printed on one side of page. 8 color plates. Instructions. 176pp. 9³/₁₆ x 12¼. 23182-8 Pa. $5.00

AMERICAN FOLK DECORATION, Jean Lipman, Eve Meulendyke. Thorough coverage of all aspects of wood, tin, leather, paper, cloth decoration — scapes, humans, trees, flowers, geometrics — and how to make them. Full instructions. 233 illustrations, 5 in color. 163pp. 8⅜ x 11¼. 22217-9 Pa. $3.95

WHITTLING AND WOODCARVING, E.J. Tangerman. Best book on market; clear, full. If you can cut a potato, you can carve toys, puzzles, chains, caricatures, masks, patterns, frames, decorate surfaces, etc. Also covers serious wood sculpture. Over 200 photos. 293pp. 20965-2 Pa. $2.50

THE JOURNAL OF HENRY D. THOREAU, edited by Bradford Torrey, F.H. Allen. Complete reprinting of 14 volumes, 1837-1861, over two million words; the source-books for Walden, etc. Definitive. All original sketches, plus 75 photographs. Introduction by Walter Harding. Total of 1804pp. 8½ x 12¼.
20312-3, 20313-1 Clothbd., Two vol. set $50.00

MASTERS OF THE DRAMA, John Gassner. Most comprehensive history of the drama, every tradition from Greeks to modern Europe and America, including Orient. Covers 800 dramatists, 2000 plays; biography, plot summaries, criticism, theatre history, etc. 77 illustrations. 890pp. 20100-7 Clothbd. $10.00

GHOST AND HORROR STORIES OF AMBROSE BIERCE, Ambrose Bierce. 23 modern horror stories: The Eyes of the Panther, The Damned Thing, etc., plus the dream-essay Visions of the Night. Edited by E.F. Bleiler. 199pp. 20767-6 Pa. $2.00

BEST GHOST STORIES, Algernon Blackwood. 13 great stories by foremost British 20th century supernaturalist. The Willows, The Wendigo, Ancient Sorceries, others. Edited by E.F. Bleiler. 366pp. USO 22977-7 Pa. $3.00

THE BEST TALES OF HOFFMANN, E.T.A. Hoffmann. 10 of Hoffmann's most important stories, in modern re-editings of standard translations: Nutcracker and the King of Mice, The Golden Flowerpot, etc. 7 illustrations by Hoffmann. Edited by E.F. Bleiler. 458pp. 21793-0 Pa. $3.95

BEST GHOST STORIES OF J.S. LEFANU, J. Sheridan LeFanu. 16 stories by greatest Victorian master: Green Tea, Carmilla, Haunted Baronet, The Familiar, etc. Mostly unavailable elsewhere. Edited by E.F. Bleiler. 8 illustrations. 467pp.
20415-4 Pa. $4.00

SUPERNATURAL HORROR IN LITERATURE, H.P. Lovecraft. Great modern American supernaturalist brilliantly surveys history of genre to 1930's, summarizing, evaluating scores of books. Necessary for every student, lover of form. Introduction by E.F. Bleiler. 111pp. 20105-8 Pa. $1.50

THREE GOTHIC NOVELS, ed. by E.F. Bleiler. Full texts Castle of Otranto, Walpole; Vathek, Beckford; The Vampyre, Polidori; Fragment of a Novel, Lord Byron. 331pp. 21232-7 Pa. $3.00

SEVEN SCIENCE FICTION NOVELS, H.G. Wells. Full novels. First Men in the Moon, Island of Dr. Moreau, War of the Worlds, Food of the Gods, Invisible Man, Time Machine, In the Days of the Comet. A basic science-fiction library. 1015pp.
USO 20264-X Clothbd. $6.00

LADY AUDLEY'S SECRET, Mary E. Braddon. Great Victorian mystery classic, beautifully plotted, suspenseful; praised by Thackeray, Boucher, Starrett, others. What happened to beautiful, vicious Lady Audley's husband? Introduction by Norman Donaldson. 286pp. 23011-2 Pa. $3.00

SLEEPING BEAUTY, illustrated by Arthur Rackham. Perhaps the fullest, most delightful version ever, told by C.S. Evans. Rackham's best work. 49 illustrations. 110pp. 7⅞ x 10¾. 22756-1 Pa. $2.00

THE WONDERFUL WIZARD OF OZ, L. Frank Baum. Facsimile in full color of America's finest children's classic. Introduction by Martin Gardner. 143 illustrations by W.W. Denslow. 267pp. 20691-2 Pa. $2.50

GOOPS AND HOW TO BE THEM, Gelett Burgess. Classic tongue-in-cheek masquerading as etiquette book. 87 verses, 170 cartoons as Goops demonstrate virtues of table manners, neatness, courtesy, more. 88pp. 6½ x 9¼.
  22233-0 Pa. $1.50

THE BROWNIES, THEIR BOOK, Palmer Cox. Small as mice, cunning as foxes, exuberant, mischievous, Brownies go to zoo, toy shop, seashore, circus, more. 24 verse adventures. 266 illustrations. 144pp. 6⅝ x 9¼. 21265-3 Pa. $1.75

BILLY WHISKERS: THE AUTOBIOGRAPHY OF A GOAT, Frances Trego Montgomery. Escapades of that rambunctious goat. Favorite from turn of the century America. 24 illustrations. 259pp. 22345-0 Pa. $2.75

THE ROCKET BOOK, Peter Newell. Fritz, janitor's kid, sets off rocket in basement of apartment house; an ingenious hole punched through every page traces course of rocket. 22 duotone drawings, verses. 48pp. 6⅞ x 8⅜. 22044-3 Pa. $1.50

PECK'S BAD BOY AND HIS PA, George W. Peck. Complete double-volume of great American childhood classic. Hennery's ingenious pranks against outraged pomposity of pa and the grocery man. 97 illustrations. Introduction by E.F. Bleiler. 347pp. 20497-9 Pa. $2.50

THE TALE OF PETER RABBIT, Beatrix Potter. The inimitable Peter's terrifying adventure in Mr. McGregor's garden, with all 27 wonderful, full-color Potter illustrations. 55pp. 4¼ x 5½. USO 22827-4 Pa. $1.00

THE TALE OF MRS. TIGGY-WINKLE, Beatrix Potter. Your child will love this story about a very special hedgehog and all 27 wonderful, full-color Potter illustrations. 57pp. 4¼ x 5½. USO 20546-0 Pa. $1.00

THE TALE OF BENJAMIN BUNNY, Beatrix Potter. Peter Rabbit's cousin coaxes him back into Mr. McGregor's garden for a whole new set of adventures. A favorite with children. All 27 full-color illustrations. 59pp. 4¼ x 5½.
  USO 21102-9 Pa. $1.00

THE MERRY ADVENTURES OF ROBIN HOOD, Howard Pyle. Facsimile of original (1883) edition, finest modern version of English outlaw's adventures. 23 illustrations by Pyle. 296pp. 6½ x 9¼. 22043-5 Pa. $2.75

TWO LITTLE SAVAGES, Ernest Thompson Seton. Adventures of two boys who lived as Indians; explaining Indian ways, woodlore, pioneer methods. 293 illustrations. 286pp. 20985-7 Pa. $3.00

THE MAGIC MOVING PICTURE BOOK, Bliss, Sands & Co. The pictures in this book move! Volcanoes erupt, a house burns, a serpentine dancer wiggles her way through a number. By using a specially ruled acetate screen provided, you can obtain these and 15 other startling effects. Originally "The Motograph Moving Picture Book." 32pp. 8¼ x 11.　　　　　　　　　　　　　23224-7 Pa. $1.75

STRING FIGURES AND HOW TO MAKE THEM, Caroline F. Jayne. Fullest, clearest instructions on string figures from around world: Eskimo, Navajo, Lapp, Europe, more. Cats cradle, moving spear, lightning, stars. Introduction by A.C. Haddon. 950 illustrations. 407pp.　　　　　　　　　　　　　　　　20152-X Pa. $3.00

PAPER FOLDING FOR BEGINNERS, William D. Murray and Francis J. Rigney. Clearest book on market for making origami sail boats, roosters, frogs that move legs, cups, bonbon boxes. 40 projects. More than 275 illustrations. Photographs. 94pp.　　　　　　　　　　　　　　　　　　　　　　　　20713-7 Pa. $1.25

INDIAN SIGN LANGUAGE, William Tomkins. Over 525 signs developed by Sioux, Blackfoot, Cheyenne, Arapahoe and other tribes. Written instructions and diagrams: how to make words, construct sentences. Also 290 pictographs of Sioux and Ojibway tribes. 111pp. 6⅛ x 9¼.　　　　　　　　　22029-X Pa. $1.50

BOOMERANGS: HOW TO MAKE AND THROW THEM, Bernard S. Mason. Easy to make and throw, dozens of designs: cross-stick, pinwheel, boomabird, tumblestick, Australian curved stick boomerang. Complete throwing instructions. All safe. 99pp.　　　　　　　　　　　　　　　　　　　　　　　23028-7 Pa. $1.50

25 KITES THAT FLY, Leslie Hunt. Full, easy to follow instructions for kites made from inexpensive materials. Many novelties. Reeling, raising, designing your own. 70 illustrations. 110pp.　　　　　　　　　　　　　　　22550-X Pa. $1.25

TRICKS AND GAMES ON THE POOL TABLE, Fred Herrmann. 79 tricks and games, some solitaires, some for 2 or more players, some competitive; mystifying shots and throws, unusual carom, tricks involving cork, coins, a hat, more. 77 figures. 95pp.　　　　　　　　　　　　　　　　　　　　　　　21814-7 Pa. $1.25

WOODCRAFT AND CAMPING, Bernard S. Mason. How to make a quick emergency shelter, select woods that will burn immediately, make do with limited supplies, etc. Also making many things out of wood, rawhide, bark, at camp. Formerly titled Woodcraft. 295 illustrations. 580pp.　　　　　21951-8 Pa. $4.00

AN INTRODUCTION TO CHESS MOVES AND TACTICS SIMPLY EXPLAINED, Leonard Barden. Informal intermediate introduction: reasons for moves, tactics, openings, traps, positional play, endgame. Isolates patterns. 102pp. USO 21210-6 Pa. $1.35

LASKER'S MANUAL OF CHESS, Dr. Emanuel Lasker. Great world champion offers very thorough coverage of all aspects of chess. Combinations, position play, openings, endgame, aesthetics of chess, philosophy of struggle, much more. Filled with analyzed games. 390pp.　　　　　　　　　　　　　　20640-8 Pa. $3.50

How to Solve Chess Problems, Kenneth S. Howard. Practical suggestions on problem solving for very beginners. 58 two-move problems, 46 3-movers, 8 4-movers for practice, plus hints. 171pp. 20748-X Pa. $2.00

.A Guide to Fairy Chess, Anthony Dickins. 3-D chess, 4-D chess, chess on a cylindrical board, reflecting pieces that bounce off edges, cooperative chess, retrograde chess, maximummers, much more. Most based on work of great Dawson. Full handbook, 100 problems. 66pp. 7⅞ x 10¾. 22687-5 Pa. $2.00

Win at Backgammon, Millard Hopper. Best opening moves, running game, blocking game, back game, tables of odds, etc. Hopper makes the game clear enough for anyone to play, and win. 43 diagrams. 111pp. 22894-0 Pa. $1.50

Bidding a Bridge Hand, Terence Reese. Master player "thinks out loud" the binding of 75 hands that defy point count systems. Organized by bidding problem—no-fit situations, overbidding, underbidding, cueing your defense, etc. 254pp. EBE 22830-4 Pa. $2.50

The Precision Bidding System in Bridge, C.C. Wei, edited by Alan Truscott. Inventor of precision bidding presents average hands and hands from actual play, including games from 1969 Bermuda Bowl where system emerged. 114 exercises. 116pp. 21171-1 Pa. $1.75

Learn Magic, Henry Hay. 20 simple, easy-to-follow lessons on magic for the new magician: illusions, card tricks, silks, sleights of hand, coin manipulations, escapes, and more —all with a minimum amount of equipment. Final chapter explains the great stage illusions. 92 illustrations. 285pp. 21238-6 Pa. $2.95

The New Magician's Manual, Walter B. Gibson. Step-by-step instructions and clear illustrations guide the novice in mastering 36 tricks; much equipment supplied on 16 pages of cut-out materials. 36 additional tricks. 64 illustrations. 159pp. 6⅝ x 10. 23113-5 Pa. $3.00

Professional Magic for Amateurs, Walter B. Gibson. 50 easy, effective tricks used by professionals —cards, string, tumblers, handkerchiefs, mental magic, etc. 63 illustrations. 223pp. 23012-0 Pa. $2.50

Card Manipulations, Jean Hugard. Very rich collection of manipulations; has taught thousands of fine magicians tricks that are really workable, eye-catching. Easily followed, serious work. Over 200 illustrations. 163pp. 20539-8 Pa. $2.00

Abbott's Encyclopedia of Rope Tricks for Magicians, Stewart James. Complete reference book for amateur and professional magicians containing more than 150 tricks involving knots, penetrations, cut and restored rope, etc. 510 illustrations. Reprint of 3rd edition. 400pp. 23206-9 Pa. $3.50

The Secrets of Houdini, J.C. Cannell. Classic study of Houdini's incredible magic, exposing closely-kept professional secrets and revealing, in general terms, the whole art of stage magic. 67 illustrations. 279pp. 22913-0 Pa. $2.50

DRIED FLOWERS, Sarah Whitlock and Martha Rankin. Concise, clear, practical guide to dehydration, glycerinizing, pressing plant material, and more. Covers use of silica gel. 12 drawings. Originally titled "New Techniques with Dried Flowers." 32pp. 21802-3 Pa. $1.00

ABC OF POULTRY RAISING, J.H. Florea. Poultry expert, editor tells how to raise chickens on home or small business basis. Breeds, feeding, housing, laying, etc. Very concrete, practical. 50 illustrations. 256pp. 23201-8 Pa. $3.00

HOW INDIANS USE WILD PLANTS FOR FOOD, MEDICINE & CRAFTS, Frances Densmore. Smithsonian, Bureau of American Ethnology report presents wealth of material on nearly 200 plants used by Chippewas of Minnesota and Wisconsin. 33 plates plus 122pp. of text. $6^{1}/8$ x $9^{1}/4$. 23019-8 Pa. $2.50

THE HERBAL OR GENERAL HISTORY OF PLANTS, John Gerard. The 1633 edition revised and enlarged by Thomas Johnson. Containing almost 2850 plant descriptions and 2705 superb illustrations, Gerard's Herbal is a monumental work, the book all modern English herbals are derived from, and the one herbal every serious enthusiast should have in its entirety. Original editions are worth perhaps $750. 1678pp. $8^{1}/2$ x $12^{1}/4$. 23147-X Clothbd. $50.00

A MODERN HERBAL, Margaret Grieve. Much the fullest, most exact, most useful compilation of herbal material. Gigantic alphabetical encyclopedia, from aconite to zedoary, gives botanical information, medical properties, folklore, economic uses, and much else. Indispensable to serious reader. 161 illustrations. 888pp. $6^{1}/2$ x $9^{1}/4$. USO 22798-7, 22799-5 Pa., Two vol. set $10.00

HOW TO KNOW THE FERNS, Frances T. Parsons. Delightful classic. Identification, fern lore, for Eastern and Central U.S.A. Has introduced thousands to interesting life form. 99 illustrations. 215pp. 20740-4 Pa. $2.50

THE MUSHROOM HANDBOOK, Louis C.C. Krieger. Still the best popular handbook. Full descriptions of 259 species, extremely thorough text, habitats, luminescence, poisons, folklore, etc. 32 color plates; 126 other illustrations. 560pp. 21861-9 Pa. $4.50

HOW TO KNOW THE WILD FRUITS, Maude G. Peterson. Classic guide covers nearly 200 trees, shrubs, smaller plants of the U.S. arranged by color of fruit and then by family. Full text provides names, descriptions, edibility, uses. 80 illustrations. 400pp. 22943-2 Pa. $3.00

COMMON WEEDS OF THE UNITED STATES, U.S. Department of Agriculture. Covers 220 important weeds with illustration, maps, botanical information, plant lore for each. Over 225 illustrations. 463pp. $6^{1}/8$ x $9^{1}/4$. 20504-5 Pa. $4.50

HOW TO KNOW THE WILD FLOWERS, Mrs. William S. Dana. Still best popular book for East and Central USA. Over 500 plants easily identified, with plant lore; arranged according to color and flowering time. 174 plates. 459pp. 20332-8 Pa. $3.50

AUSTRIAN COOKING AND BAKING, Gretel Beer. Authentic thick soups, wiener schnitzel, veal goulash, more, plus dumplings, puff pastries, nut cakes, sacher tortes, other great Austrian desserts. 224pp. USO 23220-4 Pa. $2.50

CHEESES OF THE WORLD, U.S.D.A. Dictionary of cheeses containing descriptions of over 400 varieties of cheese from common Cheddar to exotic Surati. Up to two pages are given to important cheeses like Camembert, Cottage, Edam, etc. 151pp. 22831-2 Pa. $1.50

TRITTON'S GUIDE TO BETTER WINE AND BEER MAKING FOR BEGINNERS, S.M. Tritton. All you need to know to make family-sized quantities of over 100 types of grape, fruit, herb, vegetable wines; plus beers, mead, cider, more. 11 illustrations. 157pp. USO 22528-3 Pa. $2.00

DECORATIVE LABELS FOR HOME CANNING, PRESERVING, AND OTHER HOUSEHOLD AND GIFT USES, Theodore Menten. 128 gummed, perforated labels, beautifully printed in 2 colors. 12 versions in traditional, Art Nouveau, Art Deco styles. Adhere to metal, glass, wood, most plastics. 24pp. 8¼ x 11. 23219-0 Pa. $2.00

FIVE ACRES AND INDEPENDENCE, Maurice G. Kains. Great back-to-the-land classic explains basics of self-sufficient farming: economics, plants, crops, animals, orchards, soils, land selection, host of other necessary things. Do not confuse with skimpy faddist literature; Kains was one of America's greatest agriculturalists. 95 illustrations. 397pp. 20974-1 Pa. $2.95

GROWING VEGETABLES IN THE HOME GARDEN, U.S. Dept. of Agriculture. Basic information on site, soil conditions, selection of vegetables, planting, cultivation, gathering. Up-to-date, concise, authoritative. Covers 60 vegetables. 30 illustrations. 123pp. 23167-4 Pa. $1.35

FRUITS FOR THE HOME GARDEN, Dr. U.P. Hedrick. A chapter covering each type of garden fruit, advice on plant care, soils, grafting, pruning, sprays, transplanting, and much more! Very full. 53 illustrations. 175pp. 22944-0 Pa. $2.50

GARDENING ON SANDY SOIL IN NORTH TEMPERATE AREAS, Christine Kelway. Is your soil too light, too sandy? Improve your soil, select plants that survive under such conditions. Both vegetables and flowers. 42 photos. 148pp.
USO 23199-2 Pa. $2.50

THE FRAGRANT GARDEN: A BOOK ABOUT SWEET SCENTED FLOWERS AND LEAVES, Louise Beebe Wilder. Fullest, best book on growing plants for their fragrances. Descriptions of hundreds of plants, both well-known and overlooked. 407pp.
23071-6 Pa. $3.50

EASY GARDENING WITH DROUGHT-RESISTANT PLANTS, Arno and Irene Nehrling. Authoritative guide to gardening with plants that require a minimum of water: seashore, desert, and rock gardens; house plants; annuals and perennials; much more. 190 illustrations. 320pp. 23230-1 Pa. $3.50

THE STYLE OF PALESTRINA AND THE DISSONANCE, Knud Jeppesen. Standard analysis of rhythm, line, harmony, accented and unaccented dissonances. Also pre-Palestrina dissonances. 306pp. 22386-8 Pa. $3.00

DOVER OPERA GUIDE AND LIBRETTO SERIES prepared by Ellen H. Bleiler. Each volume contains everything needed for background, complete enjoyment: complete libretto, new English translation with all repeats, biography of composer and librettist, early performance history, musical lore, much else. All volumes lavishly illustrated with performance photos, portraits, similar material. Do not confuse with skimpy performance booklets.

CARMEN, Georges Bizet. 66 illustrations. 222pp. 22111-3 Pa. $2.00

DON GIOVANNI, Wolfgang A. Mozart. 92 illustrations. 209pp. 21134-7 Pa. $2.50

LA BOHÈME, Giacomo Puccini. 73 illustrations. 124pp. USO 20404-9 Pa. $1.75

ÄIDA, Giuseppe Verdi. 76 illustrations. 181pp. 20405-7 Pa. $2.25

LUCIA DI LAMMERMOOR, Gaetano Donizetti. 44 illustrations. 186pp.
22110-5 Pa. $2.00

ANTONIO STRADIVARI: HIS LIFE AND WORK, W. H. Hill, et al. Great work of musicology. Construction methods, woods, varnishes, known instruments, types of instruments, life, special features. Introduction by Sydney Beck. 98 illustrations, plus 4 color plates. 315pp. 20425-1 Pa. $3.00

MUSIC FOR THE PIANO, James Friskin, Irwin Freundlich. Both famous, little-known compositions; 1500 to 1950's. Listing, description, classification, technical aspects for student, teacher, performer. Indispensable for enlarging repertory. 448pp.
22918-1 Pa. $4.00

PIANOS AND THEIR MAKERS, Alfred Dolge. Leading inventor offers full history of piano technology, earliest models to 1910. Types, makers, components, mechanisms, musical aspects. Very strong on offtrail models, inventions; also player pianos. 300 illustrations. 581pp. 22856-8 Pa. $5.00

KEYBOARD MUSIC, J.S. Bach. Bach-Gesellschaft edition. For harpsichord, piano, other keyboard instruments. English Suites, French Suites, Six Partitas, Goldberg Variations, Two-Part Inventions, Three-Part Sinfonias. 312pp. 8⅛ x 11.
22360-4 Pa. $5.00

COMPLETE STRING QUARTETS, Ludwig van Beethoven. Breitkopf and Härtel edition. 6 quartets of Opus 18; 3 quartets of Opus 59; Opera 74, 95, 127, 130, 131, 132, 135 and Grosse Fuge. Study score. 434pp. 9⅜ x 12¼. 22361-2 Pa. $7.95

COMPLETE PIANO SONATAS AND VARIATIONS FOR SOLO PIANO, Johannes Brahms. All sonatas, five variations on themes from Schumann, Paganini, Handel, etc. Vienna Gesellschaft der Musikfreunde edition. 178pp. 9 x 12. 22650-6 Pa. $4.00

PIANO MUSIC 1888-1905, Claude Debussy. Deux Arabesques, Suite Bergamesque, Masques, 1st series of Images, etc. 9 others, in corrected editions. 175pp. 9⅜ x 12¼. 22771-5 Pa. $4.00

INCIDENTS OF TRAVEL IN YUCATAN, John L. Stephens. Classic (1843) exploration of jungles of Yucatan, looking for evidences of Maya civilization. Travel adventures, Mexican and Indian culture, etc. Total of 669pp.
20926-1, 20927-X Pa., Two vol. set $5.50

LIVING MY LIFE, Emma Goldman. Candid, no holds barred account by foremost American anarchist: her own life, anarchist movement, famous contemporaries, ideas and their impact. Struggles and confrontations in America, plus deportation to U.S.S.R. Shocking inside account of persecution of anarchists under Lenin. 13 plates. Total of 944pp.
22543-7, 22544-5 Pa., Two vol. set $9.00

AMERICAN INDIANS, George Catlin. Classic account of life among Plains Indians: ceremonies, hunt, warfare, etc. Dover edition reproduces for first time all original paintings. 312 plates. 572pp. of text. 6⅛ x 9¼.
22118-0, 22119-9 Pa., Two vol. set $8.00
22140-7, 22144-X Clothbd., Two vol. set $16.00

THE INDIANS' BOOK, Natalie Curtis. Lore, music, narratives, drawings by Indians, collected from cultures of U.S.A. 149 songs in full notation. 45 illustrations. 583pp. 6⅝ x 9⅜.
21939-9 Pa. $5.00

INDIAN BLANKETS AND THEIR MAKERS, George Wharton James. History, old style wool blankets, changes brought about by traders, symbolism of design and color, a Navajo weaver at work, outline blanket, Kachina blankets, more. Emphasis on Navajo. 130 illustrations, 32 in color. 230pp. 6⅛ x 9¼.
22996-3 Pa. $5.00
23068-6 Clothbd. $10.00

AN INTRODUCTION TO THE STUDY OF THE MAYA HIEROGLYPHS, Sylvanus Griswold Morley. Classic study by one of the truly great figures in hieroglyph research. Still the best introduction for the student for reading Maya hieroglyphs. New introduction by J. Eric S. Thompson. 117 illustrations. 284pp.
23108-9 Pa. $4.00

THE ANALECTS OF CONFUCIUS, THE GREAT LEARNING, DOCTRINE OF THE MEAN, Confucius. Edited by James Legge. Full Chinese text, standard English translation on same page, Chinese commentators, editor's annotations; dictionary of characters at rear, plus grammatical comment. Finest edition anywhere of one of world's greatest thinkers. 503pp.
22746-4 Pa. $4.50

THE I CHING (THE BOOK OF CHANGES), translated by James Legge. Complete translation of basic text plus appendices by Confucius, and Chinese commentary of most penetrating divination manual ever prepared. Indispensable to study of early Oriental civilizations, to modern inquiring reader. 448pp.
21062-6 Pa. $3.50

THE EGYPTIAN BOOK OF THE DEAD, E.A. Wallis Budge. Complete reproduction of Ani's papyrus, finest ever found. Full hieroglyphic text, interlinear transliteration, word for word translation, smooth translation. Basic work, for Egyptology, for modern study of psychic matters. Total of 533pp. 6½ x 9¼.
EBE 21866-X Pa. $4.95

BUILD YOUR OWN LOW-COST HOME, L.O. Anderson, H.F. Zornig. U.S. Dept. of Agriculture sets of plans, full, detailed, for 11 houses: A-Frame, circular, conventional. Also construction manual. Save hundreds of dollars. 204pp. 11 x 16.
21525-3 Pa. $5.95

HOW TO BUILD A WOOD-FRAME HOUSE, L.O. Anderson. Comprehensive, easy to follow U.S. Government manual: placement, foundations, framing, sheathing, roof, insulation, plaster, finishing — almost everything else. 179 illustrations. 223pp. 7⅞ x 10¾.
22954-8 Pa. $3.50

CONCRETE, MASONRY AND BRICKWORK, U.S. Department of the Army. Practical handbook for the home owner and small builder, manual contains basic principles, techniques, and important background information on construction with concrete, concrete blocks, and brick. 177 figures, 37 tables. 200pp. 6½ x 9¼.
23203-4 Pa. $4.00

THE STANDARD BOOK OF QUILT MAKING AND COLLECTING, Marguerite Ickis. Full information, full-sized patterns for making 46 traditional quilts, also 150 other patterns. Quilted cloths, lamé, satin quilts, etc. 483 illustrations. 273pp. 6⅞ x 9⅝.
20582-7 Pa. $3.50

101 PATCHWORK PATTERNS, Ruby S. McKim. 101 beautiful, immediately useable patterns, full-size, modern and traditional. Also general information, estimating, quilt lore. 124pp. 7⅞ x 10¾.
20773-0 Pa. $2.50

KNIT YOUR OWN NORWEGIAN SWEATERS, Dale Yarn Company. Complete instructions for 50 authentic sweaters, hats, mittens, gloves, caps, etc. Thoroughly modern designs that command high prices in stores. 24 patterns, 24 color photographs. Nearly 100 charts and other illustrations. 58pp. 8⅜ x 11¼.
23031-7 Pa. $2.50

IRON-ON TRANSFER PATTERNS FOR CREWEL AND EMBROIDERY FROM EARLY AMERICAN SOURCES, edited by Rita Weiss. 75 designs, borders, alphabets, from traditional American sources printed on translucent paper in transfer ink. Reuseable. Instructions. Test patterns. 24pp. 8¼ x 11.
23162-3 Pa. $1.50

AMERICAN INDIAN NEEDLEPOINT DESIGNS FOR PILLOWS, BELTS, HANDBAGS AND OTHER PROJECTS, Roslyn Epstein. 37 authentic American Indian designs adapted for modern needlepoint projects. Grid backing makes designs easily transferable to canvas. 48pp. 8¼ x 11.
22973-4 Pa. $1.50

CHARTED FOLK DESIGNS FOR CROSS-STITCH EMBROIDERY, Maria Foris & Andreas Foris. 278 charted folk designs, most in 2 colors, from Danube region: florals, fantastic beasts, geometrics, traditional symbols, more. Border and central patterns. 77pp. 8¼ x 11.
USO 23191-7 Pa. $2.00

Prices subject to change without notice.
Available at your book dealer or write for free catalogue to Dept. GI, Dover Publications, Inc., 180 Varick St., N.Y., N.Y. 10014. Dover publishes more than 150 books each year on science, elementary and advanced mathematics, biology, music, art, literary history, social sciences and other areas.